Other DAW Novels by
KATE ELLIOTT

Crown of Stars

KING'S DRAGON
PRINCE OF DOGS
THE BURNING STONE
CHILD OF FLAME
THE GATHERING STORM
IN THE RUINS
CROWN OF STARS

The Novels of the Jaran

JARAN
AN EARTHLY CROWN
HIS CONQUERING SWORD
THE LAW OF BECOMING

&

with Melanie Rawn and Jennifer Roberson
THE GOLDEN KEY

Crown of Stars

VOLUME SEVEN

of

CROWN OF STARS

Kate Elliott

DAW BOOKS, INC.
DONALD A. WOLLHEIM, FOUNDER
375 Hudson Street, New York, NY 10014

ELIZABETH R. WOLLHEIM
SHEILA E. GILBERT
PUBLISHERS
www.dawbooks.com

First paperback printing, January 2007
4   5   6   7   8   9

ACKNOWLEDGMENTS

In other volumes I have thanked people whose research or comments have aided me in this endeavor. I would like to thank them all again, seven times over, and mention two I missed: Robert Glaub for the book on cataclysms that turned up unexpectedly in my mail one day and proved quite useful; and Maria, a graduate student in geology, for sitting at length in a coffee shop in State College, Pennsylvania, and discussing geologic cataclysm with me during the developmental stage of this series—I'm sorry I have forgotten your last name and didn't write it down in a safe place.

All deviations and errors are my own, managed either consciously or out of ignorance. I have tried at the least to remain internally consistent, although frankly I think next time I ought to hire a fact checker.

I would also like to thank the enthusiastic community at *The Official Kate Elliott Fan Page*. The staff's for you, guys. (that's the generic "guy", female and male God made them).

I must as always thank my wonderful extended family, especially my long-suffering husband (he knows why) and my reasonably patient children.

Finally, I want to thank my readers. As you know, you're the best.

AUTHOR'S NOTE

Although I did research the Middle Ages as part of the writing process, these novels do not attempt to re-create our own Western medieval period. Rather, I borrowed what seemed useful and incorporated this into a fantasy world with similarities to but also profound differences from our own. If you are looking to get a glimpse into the Western medieval period, there are a number of good historical and historical fantasy novels available by wonderful authors—but this isn't it.

What did I try to do? I tried to give a sense of a working economic system. I did my best with the military aspect, including what may seem to us astoundingly small numbers involved in the great battles of the day but which are consistent with the social organization of such a time. Some of the magic was "stolen" from medieval practices, although I've embellished and altered it. Most of the astronomical knowledge is consistent with what was known either in Christian Europe or in the Islamic world of our early Middle Ages. Certain quotes that may seem modern actually come from the writings of medieval churchmen, but I'll leave it to you to guess which they are.

The religion is, obviously, not Christianity, although the blessed Daisan and his sayings are in part adapted from *The Book of the Laws of the Countries* (translation by

H.J.W. Drijvers), by the 2nd century Bardaisan, whose popular interpretation of Christianity was later branded heretical. What I tried to do more than anything is get across the sense of how religion and magic are *alive* to the people who live within it.

I've posted a bibliography on www.kateelliott.com for those interested in such details.

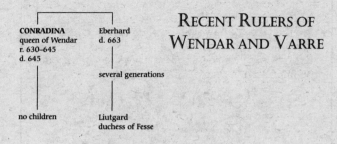

RECENT RULERS OF WENDAR AND VARRE

CONRADINA
queen of Wendar
r. 630–645
d. 645

no children

Eberhard
d. 663

several generations

Liutgard
duchess of Fesse

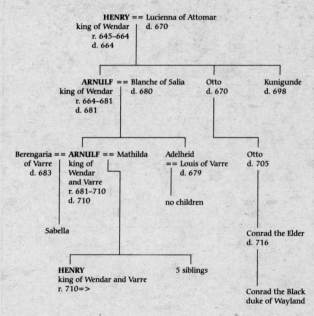

HENRY == Lucienna of Attomar
king of Wendar   d. 670
r. 645–664
d. 664

ARNULF == Blanche of Salia   Otto   Kunigunde
king of Wendar   d. 680   d. 670   d. 698
r. 664–681
d. 681

Berengaria == **ARNULF** == Mathilda   Adelheid   Otto
of Varre   king of   == Louis of Varre d. 705
d. 683   Wendar   d. 679
              and Varre
              r. 681–710   no children
              d. 710

Sabella   Conrad the Elder
                                                              d. 716

HENRY   5 siblings
king of Wendar and Varre
r. 710=>   Conrad the Black
                                                              duke of Wayland

== married
r. reigned
d. died

× Battlefields	7 Hersford	17 Hefenfelthe
III Crowns	8 Autun	18 Sliesby
	9 Kassel	19 Rikin Fjord
Towns or Places	10 Walburg	20 Kartiako
1 Osna	11 Machteburg	21 Qurtubah
2 Lavas	12 Handelburg	22 Verna
3 Heart's Rest	13 Medemelacha	23 Mountain of the
4 Gent	14 Novomo	World's Beginning
5 Osterburg	15 Arethousa (city)	24 City on the Lake
6 Quedlinhame	16 Darre	25 Queen's Grave

NOVARIA

THE WORLD AFTER THE CATACLYSM

(steppe)

POLENIE

⑫

㉕ III
Austra ×
Eastfall

UNGRIA

Dalmiaka
×
III
ASHIOI
㉓
㉔

⑮

ARETHOUSA

Heretic's
Sea

JINNA

Sea

N

(desert)

III

Ocean

0 40 80 120 160
LEAGUES
(3 miles = 1 league)

CONTENTS

Part Two

THE BLOOD-RED ROSE

PROLOGUE

BEYOND Gent, moving into the east toward the march-lands, the king's progress journeyed slowly because of the immense damage caused by the great winds of autumn. Along the roads and in every village they passed through the regnant heard the same desperate complaints: the farmers dared not plant because frost kept coming long past its accustomed time; there was no sun; too little rain fell despite the haze that covered the sky.

They ate on short rations and collected a meager tithe from the estates and villages they passed through, but none among the king's progress complained, because they ate every day. Each afternoon when they set camp and gathered wood for fires, folk approached the camp, materializing out of woodland, out of the dusk, out of the misty night air.

"I pray you," a ragged child might whisper, clutching the hand of an emaciated younger child, both barefoot although the ground had a sheen of frost. "Have you bread? Any crust?"

Haggard young women and youths beckoned from the twilight. "Anything you want, for a bite of food. Anything."

Peddlers made the rounds. "Rope. Cloth. Nice carved bowls. For a good price. Very cheap. I'll take food in trade."

Exhausted stewards and villagers begged to see the regnant. Noble lords and ladies grown lean with hardship asked for an audience.

"A plague of rats, Your Majesty. They ate all of our grain. Even that we had set aside for seed. Gnawed through half the leather we had tanned and worked. They came out of nowhere, a flood of them. Horrible!"

"It's this frost. We daren't plant because it will kill the seedlings. Yet if we wait, there'll not be enough season for the crops to ripen."

"Have you seen the sun on your travels, Your Majesty?"

"Wolves carried off a child, Your Majesty, and killed two of our mild cows. We hunted them, but they attacked us when we tracked them to their lair. They killed four men. I'm an old man. I've never seen them so bold as they are now."

"My husband and sons were killed, Your Majesty. They were only walking to market. I have no one to plow the field. My daughters are just now barely old enough to be married. My husband's cousins claim the land and wish to turn me and the girls out homeless, with nothing."

"Bandits, Your Majesty. No one is safe on the roads without an armed escort. I have but a dozen milites in my service. The rest were called to serve King Henry, may he rest in peace in the Chamber of Light. They never returned from Aosta."

Their desperation gave Liath a headache, but Sanglant would sit for hours and listen even and especially when there was nothing he could do for them except listen.

"I have been told," he might say, "that if you cover the fields with straw it protects seedlings from frost. There lies plenty of deadwood because of the tempest. Set bonfires at night to warm the air along the rows."

"Here is a deed to the land, signed by my schola. If you have no nephews or kinsmen who can help with the land, then here are a pair of crippled soldiers in my retinue who agree to marry into your house. They can't fight, but together they can manage the fieldwork."

"Speak to Lady Renate of Spelburg. She is also plagued by bandits, no doubt the same group. Her estate lies only two days' march east of here. You must pool your resources. If you have lost this much of your population, then for the time being you must consolidate in one place. Offer protection there for the common folk who rely on you. Combine your milites. If you do not cooperate, you will certainly drown."

"The sun will return. Be patient. Act prudently until the crisis has passed. Do not abandon those who will turn on you if they have no other way to save themselves."

These pronouncements his audience absorbed with an almost pitiable gratitude, but in only one case could he act immediately. A guide led them to the wolves' lair. Liath called fire down within the warren of caves where the wolf pack laired, and the soldiers killed over a dozen as the beasts tried to escape flames and smoke. The wolves were dangerous predators, but they were beautiful, too, in the way of dangerous things, and she hated to see them slaughtered like sheep. Yet afterward they found the much-gnawed bones of several children in the outer cave. The wolves had grown too bold. Such a pack could not be allowed to keep hunting.

"A small act in a desperate time," Sanglant said the next day, when they were riding again. His voice was hoarse with apprehension and the helpless anger of seeing so much trouble that could tear the realm asunder, but then, he always sounded like that. "I am ashamed to have them fall at my feet with such praises. If the weather does not improve, half of them will be dead by next spring."

"Eventually I must go to St. Valeria," she said. "What sorcery raised may possibly be dispelled by sorcery."

"Stay with me a while longer, into the marchlands, at least."

"I will. But eventually I must go."

He nodded, although his expression was grave. "Leaving me with the dogs biting and growling at my heels as I settle once and for all who is regnant in Wendar and Varre. Eventually you must go. But not yet."

PART ONE

DEATH AND LIFE

I

TRAVELERS

1

ALL morning Alain and the hounds walked east and
southeast as they had done for many days. Lavas Holding
lay far behind them. Their path this day cut along an up-
land forest, mostly beech although what seedlings had
thrust up through the field layer were fir. The view through
the woods was open but because of the clouds the vista had
a pearly sheen to it, as though he were staring into a lost
world just out of reach. Into the past, or into the future.

Yet the present had an inevitable way of intruding into
the finest-spun thoughts. Sorrow barked to alert him. A
massive beech had fallen over the path in such a way that
although Alain might climb with difficulty over its barrel of
a trunk, he could not hoist the hounds up and across. Nor
was there room for them to squeeze through the hand's-
width gap below. He beat out a track along the length of the
trunk upslope only to find that a score of other huge
trees—more beech together with silver fir—had fallen parallel so close that he was fenced in. Returning to the path
and the waiting hounds, he ventured the other way, skirting
the thicket of branches at the crown, and discovered that
here, too, more fallen trees barred his path.

All had fallen in a northwesterly direction, snapped by a
gale out of the southeast, the same tempest, no doubt, that

had swept Osna last autumn. That tempest had changed
the world, and created a vast trail of debris.

He pushed through the branches at the crown of the
tree—a difficult path to break but one on which, at any
rate, the hounds could follow. Dry leaves crackled under
his feet and dragged at his hair and skin. Twigs poked him
twice in the eye and prodded his limbs and torso. Sorrow
whined, ears flat and head down, and Rage picked her way
with surprising delicacy for such a huge creature, very
dainty as she set down each paw into dying wood rush and
the splintered remains of the tree.

The trunk was crowded with branches, a maze to confound the hounds, but the bole was negotiable at this point,
not as big around as the thicker trunk lower down. With his
help they scrambled their way through clumsily. Branches
rattled. They were as noisy as an army of blundering farmers lost in the woodsman's domain.

A sound caught him. A strange croaked cry made his
limbs go stiff with apprehension. He heaved Rage by the
scruff past the worst of the inner branches, and there the
hounds stood frozen within the shelter of the branches.
They did not bark. A large creature passed by, but they
could not see anything clearly through the screen of leaves
and brittle branches, only hear its heavy tread, a snorting
under-cough, the uncoiling disturbance as branches were
pressed back and either cracked, or sprang back with a
rattling roar. A smell like iron made him wince. Unbidden,
he recalled Iso, the crippled brother at Hersford Monastery. Had Iso survived the tempest? Did he work there
still as a lay brother under Father Ortulfus' strict but fair
rule?

The noise subsided. Sorrow's tail beat twice against
branches as he lifted his head, eager to get on, but neither
hound barked nor made the slightest noise. They struggled
out of the branches and Alain beat a way back to the path.
About a hundred strides ahead he found the ground disturbed as at the wake of a monster pressing through the
forest. He knelt beside a scar freshly cut into the ground by
claws as long as his forearm and traced the curve of the im-
print.

"A guivre," he said to the hounds. What they heard in his voice he did not know, but they whined and, flattening their ears, ducked their heads submissively.

Sorrow sniffed along the trail left by the creature and padded into the forest, back the way it had come. Rage followed. They vanished quickly, moving fast, and Alain went after them but soon fell behind. He found them several hundred paces off the path, nosing the carcass of a half eaten deer. Like him, they had eaten sparsely on their journey, dependent on what they could hunt in the woodland and beg in whatever villages and farmsteads they passed through. Now, they tore into the remains. He sat on a fallen tree and gnawed on the last of his bread and cheese. He trimmed mold from the cheese with his knife and contemplated the buds on the standing beech. Frost had coated every surface at dawn, and he still felt its sharp breath on his cheek although it was late spring and late afternoon. The cold chafed his hands. An ache wore at his throat, as if he were always about to succumb to a grippe but never quite managed to. The trees had not yet leafed out, although they ought to be bursting with green at this time of year. A spit of rain brushed over them and was gone. Its whisper moved away through the forest.

At first hidden by the rustling of branches and forest litter stirred by raindrops, another sound took shape within the trees. The hounds were so hungry that they cracked bones and gulped flesh and took no notice, but at the moment he realized he heard a group of men, they growled and lifted their massive heads to glare down the trail, back the way the monster had come from originally. He walked over to stand beside them with staff in hand, listening.

"Hush, you fool! What if it hears your nattering?"

"We thunder like a herd of cattle as it is. We'll never sneak up on anything."

"Ho! Watch that shovel. You almost stove in my head."

"You should go in the lead, Atto. You've got the good spear."

"Won't! I never wanted to come at all. This is a stupid idea! We'll all be devoured and to no purpose."

"Shut up."

He saw the men in the distance past fallen trees and shattered branches. They had not yet noticed him, so he whistled to get their attention and called out before they could react in a reckless way that might cause someone harm.

"I'm here," he said, "a traveler. The creature you seek passed by some time ago. I and my hounds heard it pass."

They hurried forward. They were what he expected: a nervous group of local men armed variously with spears, staves, shovels, and scythes and driven by one scowling big-boned man who walked at the back of the group holding the only sword.

"Who are you?" he demanded, pushing forward through the rest but halting when he saw the size of the hounds.

"I'm a traveler called Alain. I hope to find shelter for the night and continue my journey to Autun in the morning."

"You saw the beast, yet live to tell the tale?" He indicated the carcass and the bloody muzzles of the hounds. "Pray excuse me, friend, if I doubt your tale. None who see the beast live to tell of it."

"Has it killed human folk, then? What manner of beast is it that you stalk? Are you not feared to stalk a creature that will kill you once you see it?"

Several of them scratched their beards, considering these questions.

The one called Atto was young, with but a scrap of a beard and an anxious way of glancing from one side to the other. "That's right, Hanso. We just found the one dead man, and him stark naked and so thin he more likely starved to death."

"He'd been gnawed on."

Atto shrugged. "Anything might gnaw on a dead carcass. A bear. Wolves. Wild dogs. Rats and crows and vultures."

"What about the missing sheep and cows, then?" asked the leader belligerently. "How do you account for those? We must protect ourselves."

"And get killed in the bargain?" Atto shook his head. "This is a fool's errand. I'm not going any farther."

"Then you won't be marrying my daughter."

That arrow hit home. That the two men disliked each

other was apparent in their stiff posture and jutting chins, in the way the other seven men hung back as if fearing that a fistfight was about to erupt.

"Try and stop us!" said Atto with a smirk. "We'll walk to Autun. The lady is taking in men for soldiers. They say she'll feed any man willing to carry arms in her service. We'll manage, and you'll not be able to run after us and drag her back like you did last time. She's two years older now, old enough to choose for herself."

"And pregnant with your bastard!"

Feet shifted, scuffing the dirt as each changed position. Hanso drew a fist back.

Rage trotted forward and sat down showily between the two. Her growl drew such a hush down over the assembly that Alain clearly heard the tick of one of last autumn's dead leaves fluttering down through branches as it fell at long last to earth.

"It's settled between us," finished Atto, flicking an uneasy glance at the hound.

"It will never be settled," muttered Hanso. But he lowered his fist and turned his scowling glare on Alain. "What did you see?"

Alain described the encounter, and the men listened respectfully. "Have any of you seen the creature?" he asked.

Nay, they had not, but rumor grew like a weed. The corpse of an unknown man discovered by a holy spring. Missing ewes and cows since the autumn tempest that had blown down the trees and torn the roofs off a dozen sheds and houses in the hamlets hereabouts. Both strong ploughing oxen, owned in common by the villagers, gone and never recovered. The roof of their tiny church had cracked and fallen in, and the deacon had been killed. Then noises echoed out of the forest, dreadful cries and frightful coughs. The carcasses of deer, such as this one, had been found along animal trails disturbed by the passage of a huge beast: more than twenty such dead animals and all of them crawling with maggots and worms spat from the monster's mouth. Two months ago a party of refugees had staggered out of the forest along the path and told of four of their number turned to stone and lost.

"Yes, but later that night we found them counting the sceattas they'd stolen from their dead companions," noted Atto sarcastically, "so I'm wondering if they didn't just kill them and blame it on something else."

"You think there's no beast out there?" Hanso demanded.

"There's a beast," said Atto with that same cutting smirk, "but it's as likely found in men's hearts as stalking in the forest."

"You're a fool!" Hanso spat, but he kept an eye on Rage and did not attempt to brawl.

Some of the other men clearly agreed with this assessment of Atto's character, but Atto had the good spear and a sarcastic tongue, enough to keep even the furious Hanso at bay. He had the pride of youth and the reckless heart of a young man who is sure of himself, whether or not he is wrong. He had gotten a woman pregnant, and sometimes that is enough to make a man feel that nothing can defeat him.

"It's a guivre," said Alain, noting how their gazes all leaped to him as though they had forgotten he was there. "A guivre will do you no harm as long as you do not injure it. Leave it be, and it will hunt only in the forest. Attack it, and you'll find yourselves turned to stone."

"You're as crazy as he is!" Hanso spat again, his anger turned easily from the one he could not control to a new object. "Come!" he ordered his fellows. They were staring at Alain as though at the beast itself, and with grumbling and muttering they shouldered their tools and set off back the way they had come, kicking at debris, cursing the rain.

Atto lingered, studying the hounds. "Those things bite?"

"They do, if they're provoked. They'll defend themselves, that's all. Otherwise they're as mild as sheep."

He snorted. "A good tale! Who are you?"

"I'm called Alain. I'm a traveler."

"So you said. Where are you from?"

"Osna. That's west, at the coast. It's five or ten days' walk from Osna to Lavas Holding. I've been on the road ten or fifteen days since I left Lavas Holding."

"Never heard of it. What are you going to Autun for? To

join the militia, like me? If you'll wait until morning, me and Mara will walk with you. We know part of the way. Not that we've ever been there, you understand. Have you?"

"I've seen Autun, yes."

"They say it's got so many houses you can't count them all. And a big wall, to hold them in. And a cathedral tower so tall that up at the top you can rake your fingers through the clouds. They say it's a holy place, where the old emperor died, the Salian one. I can't remember his name."

"Taillefer."

"That's right! Are you a learned man? A frater, maybe?" He rubbed fingers through his own coarse stubble. "Nay, you've got a bit of a beard. You'd have to be clean shaven to be a churchman. Still." He shrugged. "Bandits travel in wolf packs, and thieves skulk. So maybe you're just what you say you are. A traveler. A pilgrim."

The hounds had settled down to demolish the dregs of the carcass. Alain had a bag woven of reeds slung over one shoulder, and into this he placed some bones, still messy with bits of flesh and tough tendon strings.

"Too bad you didn't get any of the meat," said Atto. "We could have roasted it. Deer are hard to come by this spring. We're all afeard to go into the forest, not knowing what we'll find there. Can't slaughter what livestock we have left, and even so we had a poor lambing season, no twins at all."

"This beast. Has it killed your cattle and sheep?"

"It hasn't come into our pasture and byre. Maybe it got those that wandered off. No one's brave enough to track it to its lair." He coughed out a laugh as he gestured toward the north. "And I won't be the one to find out! There's rough land that way. Deep forest. Wolves, they say. A lake, though I've not seen it, and a ravine. That's where it hides." He had thick lips, blue eyes, and a funny way of looking at other people, as if he didn't want to like them. "So they say. They don't really know. They just talk and talk and do nothing but complain about their bad fortune and how ill luck dogs the village and the frost still comes and the crops won't grow and how it'll be worse before it gets better."

"Perhaps they're right. Have you seen the sun since last autumn?"

The comment startled Atto. He glanced heavenward, but there was nothing to see except the canopy of branches and the leaden silver of the sky. "I'm not waiting around. I'm going to Autun, me and Mara. Things will be better there."

2

WHERE the road forked, an impressive barrier made up of downed trees and the detritus of shattered wagons lay across the northeasterly path. Hanna rode at the front of the cavalcade beside Lady Bertha. They pulled up to survey the barrier.

"That's been built, however much it might resemble storm fall," said Bertha.

"There's a village down that path," said Hanna. "I recall it. They welcomed me when I was riding for King Henry."

Bertha glanced at her, then at the barrier with branches sticking out at all angles and brittle leaves rattling in the spatter of rain.

"Seems they're less welcoming now." Her gaze ranged farther afield, past the tangle of dense thickets and an unexpected stand of yew that lined the roadside. Farther back one could tell that the field layer lightened where tall beech formed a canopy. Drizzle dripped on them. Everything dripped. Hanna wiped the tip of her nose.

"Ho! You there! In the tree!" Bertha had a strong high tenor, suitable for cutting through the din of battle.

Hanna was not more startled than the lad in the yew, who slipped, grabbed branches, and gave away his position where needles danced.

"We want shelter for the night. I am Bertha of Austra and Olsatia, daughter of Judith, margrave of Austra and Olsatia, may her memory live in peace. I'm sister of the current margrave, Gerberga. I have with me members of the king's schola. We've been months on the road. We've

traveled north out of Aosta, over the Brinne Pass, and
through Westfall. It's been a long road that brings us at
last to Avaria, and Wendar. We need shelter, a fire, and a
meal, if you will."

The tree was still again, then branches swayed and
pitched and a shrill horn call rose on the wind with a blat
like that of a frightened goat. The goats in their retinue
bawled in answer. Their three dogs barked madly, and
Sergeant Aronvald quieted them with sharp commands.

Bertha raised her eyebrows. She beckoned, and the sergeant—the captain was dead—trotted forward on the
skewbald gelding.

"Be alert," she said.

"Yes, my lady." He called out orders.

The rear guard moved up to set a shield wall behind the
three wagons. The men marching behind Bertha fell back
to protect their flanks as the clerics ducked under the bed
of the cargo wagon to hide themselves. It was an old routine, honed over months of travel.

Only a dozen horses remained plus the three stolid cart
horses who got the best of the feed because without them
they would have no way to pull those wagons. Three dogs
trotted alongside, having been adopted by the soldiers as
mascots and guardsmen. On the road, they had expanded
their herd of goats from three to eleven and acquired stray
chickens here and there whose bones and meat leavened
the wild onion stew they often ate. It was on stew and
goat's milk and cheese that they mostly subsisted. On their
long journey, the horses had fared worst, goats best, and
humankind somewhere in between.

"Beyond this village, what?" Bertha asked.

Hanna considered. "The village itself is at the end of that
path. There's a small river twenty or thirty leagues downstream, that feeds into the Veser. The village lies within a
bend of the river on higher ground, so water gives it protection on three sides. They have beehives. An orchard. A
bean field. Oats. Spelt. No church, but a good carpenter
and shop."

"And this way?" She gestured toward the other fork,
which led north-northwest.

Rain trickled into Hanna's mouth through her parted lips. "Another day's ride or more to the palace at Augensburg."

"Best to go on, then? A palace sounds more appealing than a village walled with storm wrack."

"It's burned down, my lady."

"What's burned down? The village?"

Hanna shuddered. "The palace, my lady. It burned down a few years back."

"There must be a settlement beside it, a town made prosperous by palace traffic?"

Hanna shut her eyes. She fought as memories surfaced. She was hot all at once, sweating, but it was only the drizzle hardening into rain. "I don't know, my lady. There might be."

"Did it burn in the conflagration, too? Eagle, what ails you? It's not like you to—" Bertha was a steady commander, but she had a temper. "Give me the information I need!"

Hanna discovered that her hands were shaking on the reins, and she had to tighten her knees to hold her horse in one place as it caught her mood. "I pray you, forgive me, my lady." She spoke in a rush. "That town fell into the path of the army of the Quman. I don't remember. I don't know if any survived."

A drum of footfalls and a scattering of shouts alerted them that someone lived still in the village beyond. Bertha raised a hand to ready her archers and spearmen.

Along the path came a trio of hardy men, each armed with the kind of weapons farmers make for themselves: one bore a staff sharpened to a point, one had a staff with a scythe bound securely to one end to make of it a halberd, and the third held an actual iron sword of the kind a lady's guardsman might wield. He also had a length of board cut into a teardrop shape and fixed to his left arm as a shield, crude but effective and unmarked by any heraldic sigil.

It was this man who climbed atop one of the logs and regarded them with no smile and no welcome.

"You can't come here. We've blocked the road."

"We need shelter," said Lady Bertha. "We are loyal subjects of the regnant, good Wendish folk all. I am escorting these holy men and women who served King Henry as part of his schola. We have been months on the road out of Aosta. We ride north to Saony."

"You can't come in," he said. "You might be carrying the plague. What's in those wagons?"

"Feed for the horses. Supplies. Most importantly, we carry with us a holy abbess, aged and weak. She needs shelter and a warm fire against the frost that afflicts us every night."

"A plague-ridden beggar, no doubt." He was a stocky man with the broad shoulders and thickset arms of a man who works every day with his hands. "Or men with animal's faces, hiding under the canvas. We can't chance it."

"You're the carpenter's son," said Hanna suddenly. "I recognize you. I am a King's Eagle. I sheltered one night in your village a few years back. Do you remember me?"

He sized her up. He had dark brown eyes, eastern eyes, they called it in these parts, a memory of raiders out of the east who had come and gone but left something of themselves behind in later generations. He shook his head, and seeing that he did not know her, she pushed back her hood.

"I was here with four Lions," she added. "We'd come from the east."

"Ah!" he said. "I recall that hair. You're out of the north, so you said."

"That's where I was born. I pray you, friend, do not forget what courtesy is due to clerics and Eagles. Let us bide just this one afternoon and night. We'll go on our way in the morning."

"No."

Lady Bertha pushed Hanna aside. "Give us shelter this one night, and porridge and ale, if that is all you have. In the name of Henry and his son, Prince Sanglant, I command it."

He gestured toward her with his sword as if to ward off an evil spirit. "We will not fall for that trick a second time!"

"What trick?" asked Hanna.

His gaze shifted past her face, and she turned in the saddle to see that Sister Rosvita and several of the young clerics had walked forward through the mud to see what was holding them up.

"These are only a few of the clerics we protect," Hanna added. "This is no trick. I pray you—"

"No!" He gestured. That horn call blatted again from deeper within the trees. Feet clattered on the earth. Branches rustled. "Go on! Go on!" He seemed furious, or near to tears. A scar blazed his forehead. One of his comrades was missing a finger on one hand, and the other was painted with a startling red rash across his cheek and down one side of his neck. "No one will come in. We can trust no one."

"I am a King's Eagle!" cried Hanna indignantly.

"Where is the king and the king's justice? It's vanished, that's what! You'll get no shelter from us. We'll fight if you try."

"I've never been treated so disrespectfully by Wendish folk! Can it be you are not Avarians after all but creatures of the Enemy come to inhabit the bodies of decent people?"

"You would know, would you not, who speak of Henry's bastard son! Spawn of devils!"

"Aronvald, make ready!" Bertha called.

The sergeant signaled. The archers raised their bows. The carpenter's son called back to unseen folk in the forest and out of sight down the track, but he did not move to take shelter from arrow's flight.

Sister Rosvita moved up to take hold of Bertha's reins.

"Let be, Bertha," she said in a pleasant voice.

"They owe us shelter!" said Bertha, but she looked down at the cleric, frowned, and lifted a hand. Archers lowered their bows, but did not otherwise shift.

"Look at his face," said Rosvita. "He means what he says. He is desperate, fearful, determined. Yes, your good soldiers will win the skirmish. We are armed in leather and mail and have good iron swords and spears and six fine archers. But what if we lose even one soldier, if even one of my faithful clerics is wounded or killed when we have come so far over such a treacherous road. If we lose this

Eagle, who guides us. For the sake of one night's shelter, I judge it not worthwhile."

Bertha grunted an answer, too angry to agree but too wise to object. Hanna fumed, but she, too, said nothing as the soldiers fell back into marching order and they moved on. The villagers gathered on top of the roadblock, staring, until the fork in the road was lost behind the trees and the contour of the road.

"How could you?" demanded Hanna at last. "They *owe* us shelter. . . ." She sputtered, too angry to continue.

Rosvita paced alongside them. The entire cavalcade moved slowly enough to accommodate the wagons, which seemed always to be half mired in muck, but in truth Rosvita had not weakened on this journey. She had grown wiry, strong enough to walk all day without flagging. She often commented, with surprise, how much better her aching back felt, although she slept on the ground most nights.

"I know that look in a man's eye, Eagle," she said now. "This is not a battle worth fighting."

"What can have made them so desperate?"

Bertha snorted, half laughing. "War between neighboring lords. The Quman barbarians. Plague. The great storm. What else may have afflicted them I cannot tell."

"I am puzzled," said Rosvita, "by what he meant by men with animal faces. Why he turned against us when Lady Bertha mentioned Prince Sanglant. It makes no sense."

"Any man may shake his fist at the regnant when he suffers, and love the king when he prospers," said Bertha dismissively. "Yet I wonder. We have seen few enough folk in these last weeks when we ought to have seen more. Seven abandoned villages. Children hiding in the woods without their parents. Freshly dug graves. Solitary corpses. This is not just famine at work."

"What, then?" asked Rosvita.

Bertha shrugged. Hanna, too, had no answers.

II

ARROWS IN THE DARK

1

IN the end they camped along the damp road. The next day when they rode into the ruins of Augensburg, Lady Bertha insisted they set up camp where they had at least some shelter against the unrelenting mizzle that Hanna could not quite bring herself to call rain.

In some ways, theirs was an impressive procession, with fifteen horses, three wagons, one noblewoman, eleven ragged clerics, fourteen stolid soldiers, one sequestered Kerayit shaman and her slave, the goats, the clucking chickens, and the steadfast dogs. Many had died after the battle with Holy Mother Anne's forces: all of the Kerayit guardsmen, Sorgatani's two slaves, and sixteen of Bertha's war band. But since that day in Arethousa when Hanna had joined them, they had, miraculously, lost no one else and had sustained only one permanent injury, to a soldier whose right foot had been crushed when the smaller wagon had slipped sideways down an incline at the side of a mountain path while he walked alongside.

Two men scouted for the water supply while Sergeant Aronvald set up a perimeter around the remains of the stone chapel attached to the palace. The wagon wheels were braced against rocks and the horses taken out to graze, water, and roll. Soldiers tossed tiles out of the ruins of the chapel to make room for sleeping while some of the clerics rigged up canvas to shelter the apse where the altar had once stood. Brother Breschius emerged from the Kerayit cart. Carrying two covered bronze buckets, one riding light and the other heavier, he walked toward the rear of the palace compound where kitchens once stood.

Lady Bertha paused beside her. "Will you come with me, Eagle? Sister Rosvita and I mean to look through the ruins of the town to see if there's anything we can scavenge." A trio of soldiers loitered behind her, chafing their hands to warm them.

"I'll walk through the palace ruins," said Hanna. "If I may."

"A good idea. No telling where the rats are hiding. Come!" The last was addressed to her retainers. They left.

After rubbing down her horse and turning it out with the others, Hanna walked through the ruins of the palace. Fallen pillars striped the ground. She traced corridors and rooms reduced to outlines on the ground. A strange feeling crawled along her skin, like fire that warmed but did not burn. She had walked here with Bulkezu and his brother Cherbu. In this place Cherbu had discovered the name of the woman whose sorcery had consumed the vast building.

"Liathano," she said softly. She shut her eyes and listened, but all she heard was the hiss of a light rain on the ruins and the grass and the rattle of wind in the distant trees. This was a dead place.

"What happened to the town?" asked Brother Fortunatus, coming up beside her.

She coughed and jumped.

"I beg your pardon!" he said, chuckling a little as he touched fingers to her elbow. "I did not mean to startle you." She offered him a false grin, but he narrowed his eyes. "What ails you, Hanna? Ghosts?"

From this vantage point they could see most of the town below, a skeletal presence rising in the midst of deserted fields and the outraged wreck of a substantial orchard. A number of trees had fallen, most likely torn down by the storm. Dusk-drawn mist drifted along the broken palisade.

"Not ghosts, but memories. Ghosts enough, I suppose, if memories haunt us." She swallowed and found even that trifling movement caught and choked her.

"Memories are the worst ghosts of all." His hand curled around her elbow, and the gesture gave her courage.

"Years ago. The Quman army rode through this place when I was their captive. There are no good memories for me here."

"I'm sorry. Did they burn the town?"

Meadow grass and fescue had swept over the ruins, grown everywhere they could take root. Hawthorn and twining canes of raspberry had found a foothold as well. Nettles thrust up where the last stains of ash mottled the earth. Soon The Fat One would overtake what the princes had built and cover it in flowers, although only a few dusky violets bloomed now.

"It's late in the season for violets," she said, pointing to a spray of delicate petals.

He cocked his head, considered her, then followed where she led. "It's the cloud cover. I fear we'll face a late growing season. And a short one."

"I forgot about the town," she added. "I don't know what happened to the town. After the palace burned, it was still standing. The flames never touched the town. We took shelter there that night, all of us in the king's progress. King Henry stayed in the hall of a prosperous merchant, slept in the man's own bed. How can that all be gone? Where did it go? Did Bulkezu burn it down? I don't re-member."

An odd spark of color caught her eye and she knelt and swept aside chaff and dirt and ash and the detritus of years of abandonment to uncover a brass belt buckle shaped in the form of a lion.

"Look here! I wonder if it belonged to one of the Lions who died in the fire." She looked up. Fortunatus was smil-ing sadly down at her. He had gotten leaner, cutting his face into sharper planes, but somehow more kind. If Bertha was the goad that drove them and Rosvita the sustenance that gave them heart to keep going, then Fortunatus was the arm that steadied Rosvita whenever she faltered.

"Liath burned down the palace," she said, although he asked nothing. "Hugh attacked her. He meant to rape her. She was so scared. She called fire. She never meant to. Her fear burned down the entire palace. She killed a dozen or more people."

"I know, Hanna," he said gently. "I was here when it happened."

"Ai, God, of course. Of course. I forgot. I came late. We came over the hill, the Lions and I. We saw the smoke. That was: Ingo, Folquin, Leo, and young Stephen, who wasn't a Lion yet but he wanted to become one. . . ." Once started, she could not stop herself, not even when the story wound into that terrible captivity among the Quman. She babbled on for a time while Fortunatus waited and nodded and listened and murmured the occasional meaningless word to show that it mattered to him that these memories overwhelmed her.

In time as the drizzle melted away to become a gauze of mist ghosting up from low-lying ground, the rain of words abated.

"I'm sorry," she said.

He smiled in a way that warmed her heart, offered her a hand, and helped her to rise. "We all must speak sometime. You endured much."

"Not as much as others. Not as much as those who died."

"No use comparing, unless you were the one who chose who lived and who died."

His hand touched her shoulder, but a ghost clutched her heart. She remembered Bulkezu's voice as clearly as if he stood beside her. *"Mercy is a waste of time. If I choose, I will leave ten behind for the crows."*

"It was always ten," she whispered. "For them, life. And for the rest, death."

"It was not truly your choice, Hanna. If you had not chosen, then ten more would have died. At least you saved ten where you could. You must forgive yourself. I pray you." He had tears on his cheeks.

"Thank you, Brother."

He kissed her on the forehead as a benediction. He was a cleric, after all, able to plead with God on behalf of those who have repented and those who suffer although they are innocent.

From here they could see the flickering light cast by the fire although not the fire itself, tucked away within the stone walls of the chapel. One of the soldiers laughed, another Stephen, an older man who had ridden for years with Lady Bertha. She knew all their laughs now, their favorite swear words and curses; she knew Ruoda's confident way with the dogs and Gerwita's fear of the big boarhound called Mercy, Jerome's shy way of stammering when he had to speak with more than two people paying attention to him and the dry sound of Jehan's constant nagging cough. She knew each silhouette, such as the one ambling along a fallen length of wall as aimlessly as a sheep.

"Strange," she said.

"What is strange?"

"I never think to count Princess Sapientia, although surely she must be counted before all others in our party. Even Lady Bertha forgot to mention her when those farmers refused to let us pass."

He turned to look where she looked. Sister Petra caught up with her charge and herded her back toward the safety of the chapel and the fire.

"What will become of her?" Hanna asked.

Fortunatus only shook his head, but she could not tell whether the gesture meant "I do not know" or "may God have mercy" or "all hope for her is lost."

A shout rang out of the twilight. They turned to see five shadowy figures and the three dogs striding along the road that led from the town. The tautness of those shoulders and the cant of those heads told of trouble.

Hanna ran to meet them, but Lady Bertha brushed past her and hurried on toward the camp with the three soldiers. Sister Rosvita halted, took hold of Fortunatus' arm, and bent to catch her breath.

"Whh!" She gripped her side as at a spasm, but when she saw Sister Petra shepherding Princess Sapientia within the walls of their makeshift fort, she frowned. "Best hurry. What of the men who went to the well?"

Without waiting for their answer she climbed on, and

Hanna and Fortunatus followed, looking at each other. There was nothing to say. As they picked their way through the fallen remains of the portico, they heard Lady Bertha speaking.

"Bring the horses up. We'll need a guard on them all night. I want those men sent to fetch water called in, and a double sentry all night."

"What's wrong?" asked Hanna.

From this angle the slope of the hill hid the town. It was by now too dark to see the fields as anything distinct, only alternating shades of gray in patches that ended abruptly in the darker line of trees.

"The orchard trees were chopped down, not blown down," Rosvita said, still wheezing. "Fresh sawdust from the chopping, scattered everywhere. The mist hid the pockets of smoke. This fire and destruction is recent. The town might have been attacked yesterday."

"God have mercy," murmured Fortunatus, drawing the circle at his chest.

"Were there corpses?" Hanna asked. "Any survivors?"

"We did not search closely. If an enemy waits in the forest, they know we're here. Morning will be soon enough."

A whistle carried on the breeze, a silky, twisting tune Hanna had never heard before. Soldiers came alert. Swords were drawn and arrows measured against bowstrings. A rank of spears lowered. Yet the dogs barked in greeting not in challenge. The figure who emerged out of the ruins carried two covered buckets, one sloshing with water and the other empty. Brother Breschius set his buckets down beside the painted cart and turned, seeking first one face then another.

"What is it?" he asked.

"You found the well?" asked Lady Bertha.

"I did. Set somewhat back where the hill is steep. I came through Augensburg many years ago. I recalled it because of a particular . . ." He shook his head. "What is it?"

"Laurent and Tomas went before you. Did you see them there?"

"No sign of them. Did they know where to look? They might be lost in the ruins."

"Did you hear anything?"

"What is it?" he asked again.

When they told him, he rubbed his clean-shaven chin with the stump of his right arm as if he had momentarily forgotten that he lacked the hand.

"Do we send out a search party?" asked Sergeant Aronvald.

By now night had swept in. Beyond the halo lent by the campfire it was impossible to see anything except the wall of darkness that marked the distant line of trees.

"They can see our campfire," said Lady Bertha. "They can shout, if they are injured."

She was a hard commander. Hanna had seen her drive her men over mountain paths more suitable to goats, had seen her set her own noble shoulder to pushing the wagons where the road became nothing more than a series of dry rills dug into earth by runoff. She had suffered an injury in the infamous battle against Anne's forces that no one would talk about in detail, and had lost most of the range of motion in her left arm, but if the injury pained her day in and day out she never complained. Yet she never smiled, and her frown dug deep as she faced her muttering retainers.

"If they have been ambushed, then sending out a search party will only offer our adversaries more swift kills. If they are lost, and in no danger, they can find us by the light of the campfire or at dawn."

"There's some rough ground back there," said Brother Breschius. "A defile, a few drops where the ground falls away. This palace was built to take advantage of the high ground. They might have fallen."

Her expression did not change. "They might have. If so, it is unlikely in this darkness we will find them. We'll search at dawn."

She looked at Sister Rosvita. After a moment, with genuine reluctance, Rosvita nodded to show she agreed. Hanna looked past the two women to the fire where Sister Petra had gotten her charge seated and was fussing to get her to drink broth out of the stewpot.

Princess Sapientia stared into the flickering fire. She did

not look as if she had lost her mind. She did not act as would
a madwoman, babbling and cursing and flailing her arms in
the manner of the moon-mad who had lost their wits, or
spitting and frothing at the mouth as might a soul possessed by a demon. She just did not speak and did not respond and seemed to have cut the thread that binds one
person's actions to those of her companions, which threads
are all that stitch the world of living things into a single
fabric of being. She acted as if she were already dead.

"Pull the two cargo wagons across the open side,"
Bertha was saying. "Fix shields to cover what they can. Set
men up where they can watch along the height of the wall
on the other sides. Yes, even up there, in those rafters that
can take their weight."

"Eagle." The sergeant addressed her. "First watch, if you
will, out at the second line of wall. Keep a particular eye
out for will-o-the-wisps, any strange glamour of light. Listen hard."

The other Stephen joined her about fifty paces out from
the opening of the chapel, where a low stone wall made a
protected vantage point. He was a good dozen or more
years older, pale-haired, blue-eyed, steady, smart, patient,
and tough.

They braced themselves a body's length apart to get the
broadest view of the slope of the fore hill and the lower
ground, all lost in night. In good weather they might have
marked the passing of time by the rise and fall of the stars,
but as it was they just sat, watching and listening. Now and
again a shimmer of rain passed over, but it always faded. It
was silent and cool. He shifted occasionally, feet scraping
on the ground. For some reason her hands ached, and twice
she inhaled a curious scent of charred wood melded with
the acrid flavor of juniper.

Stephen said, "did you hear that?"

"No."

Night noises, nothing more: a brief hiss of rain, the
crackle of branches where the wind stroked them. The
shifting and settling of the earth as it cooled. A cold breeze
poured out of the heavens, seeming to drop right down on
them from the height of the sky.

We are alone in the world, she thought.

And then: All things are alone, yet nothing is alone, it is all tangled together, woven as in a weir to create an obstacle or diversion or as in a tapestry to make out of its parts a vision of a greater whole.

She felt Stephen's presence, how he shifted to find a more comfortable position for his right knee, how he stifled a cough by turning it into a grunt. She felt the pool of air beyond where the land sloped away downward. She smelled the sparks and ash of the wood fire and the aroma of horsehair and horse piss and horse manure. A man coughed, back in the shelter of the chapel.

She yawned, swaying, and slipped into that semi-alert twilight state that is neither waking nor sleep.

The wind picked her up as if she were a downy feather, and she spun away across the ruins, across a river, across forest and distant hamlets and stretches of meadowland and woodland farther and farther still, uncounted leagues flashing beneath her until the landscape that fell away under her feet was grass and only grass, pale in the dawn twilight. There comes blindingly and amazingly a glimpse of the rising sun tinted blue behind a veil of dust as it shoulders up over a golden-green horizon of grass. A procession moves at a steady pace through this grass, strange folk with almond-shaped eyes and eastern complexions. Some are Quman, wearing feathered wings attached to their armored coats; some are women whose hips flow into and become the bodies of horses. One is a shaman stippled with the tattoos of his kind, the spirit companions whose magic he can call on at need. She follows them. They are taking her where she needs to go.

Where a silver river ribbons in long looping curves across the golden landscape, the land sinks into a marshland of tall reeds and shallow pools of standing water. Beyond, paler grass grows in clouds like mushrooms, but these are, after all, tents sighing in the wind. The camp wakens. Its inhabitants crowd onto the margins to mark the group that approaches them.

Far above, a shrill cry reverberates. A woman who is also a mare turns and sights and points, calling to her companions to warn them, then raises her bow and releases an arrow into the sky. It burns, and Hanna tumbles. Tumbling, she sees griffins spinning above her, one gold and one silver, flying east toward the dark spires of distant mountains. They pass over her, and she twists and finds herself wading in ankle-deep water, pressing through reeds, scratched by blades of grass as she pushes up out of the shallows onto dry land that at first sinks beneath each step and then dries and stiffens to dusty earth and a sheen of green-gold grass so fresh and new that it smells of spring.

"We return," says the centaur who leads the others. She stands in the center of camp, where the grass is flattened in a circle. "We have seen terrible things. Our ancient enemy has returned."

"Where is the child?" asks the Quman shaman.

"Gone, gone," the others sigh, shaking their heads. "Vanished from underneath the hill."

"Where has she gone?"

They do not know.

"Where is the Holy One?" asks the centaur woman who leads the newcomers. "I am charged with a message for her."

The Holy One walks slowly, favoring her hind legs in a manner that makes it obvious each step brings intense pain. She is not silver-white but rather so old that every hair has turned gray; she is so old that it is impossible she still lives. Magic has kept her alive all this time.

Her ears flick. "You have returned, Capi'ra, young one. What message? What news?"

The herd listens in intent silence as the story is told, and Hanna hears the news she has sought for so long: Liath is alive, traveling with Prince Sanglant. Except now he is king. Henry is dead.

She wipes her eyes, but the tears keep flowing. She touches to her lips the emerald ring he gave her, but even that gesture gives her no comfort.

King Henry is dead.

A great cataclysm has shaken the Earth.

"War is coming," says Li'at'dano. "The ancient paths along the burning stone are closed to me now. The aether is too weak to hold those paths open for more than glimpses. So this is the first I have heard of these events. This changes everything. We are too distant to aid those who would be our allies."

"I am here!" calls Hanna.

Li'at'dano's head raises in surprise. At first, seeking, she does not find Hanna among the herd, but at last, spying her hidden in the grass, she nods. Hanna steps into the open.

"Luck of Sorgatani," the centaur shaman says, but where she looks none of the others can see anything. Not even the Quman shaman can see her. He stares, he seeks. The others stare, they listen, but Hanna understands that only the Holy One can see and hear her because Hanna inhabits this land as a part of that dream known soley to the Kerayit sorceresses, who are bound to the Horse people by threads woven in the time long ago.

"What news?" Li'at'dano asks her.

Quickly, Hanna tells her what she knows: the battle between Anne and Liath fought by the standing stones and reported to her by Bertha and Sorgatani; the fiery tempest as seen by Bertha's party and by Hanna and the clerics within the Arethousan army; the destruction along the coast that wiped out the imperial city of Are-thousa; the little band that has trudged through mountains and forest across a vast distance to reach Wendar at last. She is an Eagle, trained to distill and to report.

"Why are you come to me? Where is my daughter, Sorgatani?"

"Sorgatani sleeps in her cart. I am on watch. We fear enemies may stalk us, robbers or outlaws. The wind carried me here. I don't know why."

"Hai!" The Quman shaman points to the heavens. "Beware!"

Smoke curls up into the heavens, dirty streamers against the white-blue sheen of the sky. Distant shouts ring. Horses trumpet in alarm.

"Raiders have set fire to the grass!"

"Where are they? What happened?"

"They wear the faces of animals!"

Li-at-dano staggers as if she has been shot. Horse people

and their Kerayit clansmen bolt into action. The swirl catches Hanna, spinning her away as on a rising plume of smoke.

"Beware!" the Quman shaman cries again.

A hiss burns her cheek.

"Aie! Unh!"

Stephen's shout yanked her back into the night shadows. In the camp, the dogs barked furiously, whining and growling. At first, she could make sense of nothing except that it was night. The air tasted of rain, but no drops struck her.

A second hiss teased her ear. The air trembled, displaced, and as if it had sprouted there, an arrow quivered in the ground a finger's width from her left knee.

That woke her.

"Unh! Unh! Ai, God! God!"

Stephen had fallen onto his back. She flung herself down alongside him. Blood coated his shoulder. A shaft protruded from his flesh. A third arrow whistled overhead.

"Attack! Attack!" She jumped to her feet, got her hands under his good arm, and dragged him backward. He was a big enough man that he ought to have been difficult to pull along, but he pushed with his legs and anyway she was racing in her heart, every limb on fire and her face flushed and her breath catching in her throat. Lady Bertha shouted commands, barely heard above the clamor of the dogs, and not soon enough Hanna stumbled into what shelter the half fallen walls of the chapel offered. Other hands grabbed Stephen and hauled him away. She sank down on her knees, bent over her thighs, and tried desperately to catch her breath. Little thunks peppered the other side of the wall as the enemy shot at them from the safety of the darkness.

By the light of red coals simmering in the fire pit, she measured their position. The dogs swarmed around Lady Bertha's feet, yapping and circling. A dozen soldiers were ranged around the chapel, a few fixed up on the wall, others braced behind the wagons or the shields. One man cut away at the arrow in Stephen's shoulder.

"You've suffered worse, old friend!" the surgeon joked. "You're just wanting a scar to impress new lovers—"

Stephen gagged, stiffened, and went into convulsions, twisting right out of the other man's grasp. Hanna stumbled forward, dropped beside him, and held him down, but when the fit passed, he stopped breathing and fell slack.

Dead.

The other soldier—it was Sergeant Aronvald—looked up at her, eyes wide with disbelief. "That shouldn't have killed him."

Hanna touched the shaft where it met the skin. She circled it with her finger, then sniffed. "Poison, perhaps. Or magic."

"Poison!"

She wiped her moist skin on the dead man's leggings, then for good measure in the dirt, rubbing it and rubbing it to make sure it all came off.

On the wall, a man cried out. "Uhng! Damn. Scraped me, but I'm still good." She saw him only as a shadow. He twisted the arrow in his hand and set it to the string.

"So far no sign of any but these damn arrows out of the dark," said Bertha from the corner where wagon met stone wall. She hushed the dogs.

"Best smother what remains of the fire," said Hanna, not realizing she had a voice.

The coals gave only enough light to distinguish one form from another. The horses had been moved back to the raised dais where the altar had stood. Their hooves rang on stone as they shifted nervously under the control of Bertha's groom Geralt, Sister Ruoda, and Brother Jerome, who calmed and comforted them. The skewbald kept his head, nipping younger horses who wanted to kick up a fuss. Canvas had been rigged to form a measure of shelter against rain.

Sorgatani's cart was set against the right-hand wall. Tracery gleamed on its painted walls, patterns that to Hanna's eyes seemed to slowly unravel and knit together. The goats had been tied up on a line behind it, and they protested with a constant chorus of bleats.

They had shoved Mother Obligatia's pallet under the Kerayit cart. Others huddled there with her, as many of the clerics as could fit: sobbing Gerwita, Petra and

Princess Sapientia, Hilaria, Diocletia, slight Jehan. Heriburg was wedged between cart wheel and stone wall stubbornly sharpening willow wands into pointed sticks which might be used as weapons in close quarters if all else failed. Hanna could not see Sister Rosvita or Brother Fortunatus.

"Let us pray they get bored and fade back into the woods," murmured the sergeant.

"Ai! Ai! What fire burns me!"

The man up on the wall who had been scraped by arrow shot roared in pain, thrashed, and tumbled. He did not fall more than ten feet, but he fell hard and wetly and lay dead still. His bow smacked into the dirt beside his body. The terrier trotted over to him, sniffed the glistening tip of the arrow that had felled him, and backed away growling.

The sergeant looked at her, and she looked at him. He scrambled for the fallen man, pressed his own head down over the other man's head. For a moment no arrows struck the stone; only the wind wept among the ruins.

He flung back his head. "My lady! Lady Bertha! I fear these points are poisoned. Any scrape, any strike, will kill us. Ai, God have mercy!"

An arrow clacked against the wall.

"I'm hit," said Jerome, from among the horses.

Every person startled, as if his words were a blow. For the longest time, no one moved or spoke as from the night came no fresh shower of arrows. Even the scrape of Heriburg's knife ceased. Rain clattered in the trees.

Or was that rain? Pebbles shaken in a gourd might make such a sound. Whining, the dogs slunk under the wagons.

A man's scream rose out of the night. No one moved. They were all afraid of exposing themselves to an arrow's poisoned barb. The cry cut off. The rainlike sound ceased.

"That was Wilhelm," said the sergeant. "At the first wall, twenty paces out."

The men stared into darkness. They were nothing but silhouettes, barely visible. Spears and swords and bows had no more substance than branches. When the next flight of arrows poured in, anyone might be scratched, and die.

Hanna stood. "Under the wagons. Under shields. Under

canvas, any cover at all. Cover your faces. No matter what you hear, don't look. Be blind."

"We can't fight if we're blind and hiding!" said the sergeant.

The enemy didn't have their range quite right. Half the next volley snapped on stone and a dozen arrows skittered along the canvas awning, but one buried its point into the dirt an arm's length from the sergeant and another skipped across Lady Bertha, but surely her mail had protected her.

"Ai, God!" cried the sergeant. "Are you hit, my lady?"

Bertha's face was pale, but Hanna could not tell if the arrow had drawn blood. She did not answer.

Above, another soldier shrieked. "Ai! Ai! I'm hit!"

Two dropped out of the wall. "Peter's touched! We're like trapped ducks there, strung up for market day!"

"It burns!" screamed Jerome, and Ruoda began sobbing and wailing, "No, no, Jerome! God! I pray you! Spare him!"

"Down!" cried Hanna, and Bertha answered her.

"Down! All of you! Take cover! Cover your faces! Do as the Eagle says!"

Hanna ran to the cart, not waiting to see if they obeyed her, although she heard them scrambling. The shaking rain began again.

They are advancing.

She pulled open the door and shoved past Brother Breschius, who was poised a hand's breadth from the threshold. Out of the darkness, cries rose from inhuman throats, but their battle cry was a name she recognized:

"Sanglant! Sanglant!"

"Sorgatani! We're lost if you do not come now! We have no defense against their weapons. I pray you! I do not know what enemies these are—"

"I know who they are."

The Kerayit shaman was bright in her golden robes, beautiful and terrible. Her expression was cold. In one hand she clutched an anklet of bells. She said nothing as Hanna stepped aside to let her pass.

"Hanna," said Breschius. "Don't ask this of her."

"She must go, or we'll all die."

Sorgatani crossed the threshold and descended the stairs, shaking the slave's bells like an amulet in front of herself. There was power in her. Her robes captured the fading light of the coals and shone with a dull gleam whose trail left a ghastly miasma along the ground, almost a living, breathing, crawling mist of shimmering copper intertwined with mottled patches of blood-red vapor.

"This is a terrible thing," murmured Breschius. "I cannot watch." He hid his eyes against a forearm.

Hanna went to the door. One of the horses had fallen, and in its screaming and thrashing had driven the other horses out beyond the aisle, where they milled about in the open chapel. Jerome's body lay trampled under their hooves. Of the groom and Sister Ruoda, Hanna saw no sign, nor of anyone, not one except a half dozen pairs of feet and two rumps peeping out from beneath the canvas awning, pulled down on top of them, and shapes huddled under the wagons and the shields. Sorgatani whistled softly, and every horse quieted. The dogs fell silent. Even the goats ceased their complaining.

Movement flashed by the narrow gap where the cargo wagon met wall. At first, Hanna thought it was their enemy, come to fight at close quarters. Then, horribly, she saw otherwise.

Lady Bertha staggered into view, leaning against the wall, struggling although there was no sign of a wound on her. Her grin was lopsided, as though half of her face had already lost mobility and feeling.

"Ah! Ah!" she said, in gasps of pain as she tried to speak words to the golden presence approaching her. "Too late for me. Too late. Blooded. But I had to see. I always wondered what you looked like. So beautiful!"

She sagged, slipped down onto her knees, and slumped against the wall, eyes still open but staring sightlessly.

Sorgatani walked past without faltering, through the gap. Hanna ran to the sheltering line of wagons. Sorgatani walked into the darkness. She was her own lantern. The mist boiled out from under her robes, streaming down the slopes in a flood that insinuated itself into every fold of ground, every crevice and gap of the ruins.

Their cries changed at first into those of unknown animals heard at a distance in a trackless forest: faint, clipped, despairing. A few arrows flew. None touched the Kerayit woman. Figures darted among the low walls, but they dropped in their tracks as Hanna watched in astonishment. They could not outrun the sorcery that stalked them. Where it touched them, they died, until that light washed the ruined palace and the slopes of its hill, everything Hanna could see, like the moonlight she had not seen for months but turned here into a curse not a blessing. The color was wrong, a haze of corruption.

Hanna stood at the breach. The wind had died. In all that world she heard each footstep as Sorgatani circled back and circumnavigated the chapel to flush out anyone hiding behind.

Even that noise failed, as if she had fallen deaf and the world gone mute.

She stumbled out, cautious of her feet, seeing shapes tangled on the ground where they had fallen, and sought through the weeds and stone until she found Sorgatani awash in a pool of pale light shrinking around her. She was kneeling. Retching. Braced on her hands, shoulders heaving as she coughed and spat.

Hanna crouched beside her but did not touch her. "Sorgatani?"

The light contracted, stealing back into her robes. Ribbons of angry brilliance twisted along the ground like brilliant snakes but these, too, faded. At last they waited together in night. A slight, copper gleam still shone from Sorgatani's palms but otherwise shadow covered them.

"The curse is real," Sorgatani said in a hoarse whisper. Hanna could make no sense of her expression. Was she resigned? Triumphant? Appalled? Detached?

"You saved us," Hanna said.

The shaman rose, staring at her shining palms. "I am a weapon the Cursed Ones do not know and cannot remember. My kind was not yet bound to the Horse people, our mothers. Do you think it is for this we Kerayit were made?"

"It is only a few of you who are so cursed."

"It needs only a few." She did not look at Hanna. All the Eagle saw was her troubled profile, eyes and brow tightened with disquiet, lips pressed firm, and the golden net of wire and beads that covered her black hair gleaming uneasily where the light gilded its webbing.

"Can the Horse people have been planning for so long?"

Sorgatani looked at her, half laughing, half grim. "Can they not have been? The Holy One is as old as the exile of the Cursed Ones is long. She must have wondered if they would return, if the spell might weave itself with its own pattern, unknown to us until it was too late."

"What will you do?" Hanna did not want to walk in the morning out among the dead. She did not want to make an accounting. Yet it would be done.

"Make sure ours are still hiding. I must go to my cart."

Back to her exile. Her prison.

For the first time, Hanna really understood what it meant. Even Sorgatani's slaves had more freedom than she did.

2

AT first light they crawled out from under the wagons and gathered their dead: the archers Peter and Rikard; Brother Jerome; Aurea, Rosvita's beloved servingwoman; Stephen and Wilhelm and Gund who had been out on sentry duty. It wasn't clear if Gund had been killed by the enemy or by the curse, because he was quite a ways away, caught in the midst of a group of warriors as though they had captured him and dragged him off still alive.

It scarcely mattered now. Lady Bertha was dead, and their enemy wiped out. They gave up counting enemy dead when they reached nineteen. There was some talk of burning the corpses, but no one wanted to touch them because these were creatures who appeared scarcely human. They had bronze-colored complexions and frightening animal masks and bronze body armor, molded to fit the slopes of their bodies as good masons built cunningly along the contours of hills. In truth, no one wanted to take their weapons or steal even such a trove of armor. No one wanted anything except to leave as quickly as possible. Sister Rosvita told them that the convent of Korvei lay ten or twelve days' journey from here, in the borderlands between the duchies of Avaria and southeastern Fesse. From Korvei they could head north toward Quedlinhame and Gent, or west to Autun.

Hanna helped dig two graves, one for the soldiers and Jerome and Aurea, and a separate pit for Lady Bertha. Sister Rosvita and the older nuns stripped her and wrapped her in her cloak; in this fur-lined shroud they buried her. Rosvita sang the blessings over the dead. Bertha's seven surviving soldiers wept. Everyone wept, all but Hanna, who had no tears, and Mother Obligatia, who had seen too much death to be scoured even by this.

"How comes it that those who attacked called the name of Prince Sanglant?" asked Sergeant Aronvald.

"I do not know," said Rosvita.

"They're like him in looks. His kinfolk."

"It's true," she agreed, looking troubled.

"Think you he has betrayed us?" asked the sergeant.

"You traveled with him last of all, Sergeant. What do you say?"

He stared at the mound of dirt. "My lady trusted him. Yet the creatures did call his name. How could they know it, if he was not in league with them? Yet my lady would not put her trust in one who meant to betray her." He glanced sidelong at Princess Sapientia, who remained mute and emotionless, like a puppet dangling from slack strings. "Better if this one had died, than our bold lady," muttered the sergeant, but he was careful to pitch his voice so only Hanna heard him.

Afterward, as they saddled and harnessed the horses, as they wedged their supplies into place and made ready to leave, Hanna saw how they looked at the painted cart in their midst.

They feared her, who had saved them.

"Eagle." Rosvita beckoned her over, and they walked

apart, shying away from a dead man masked behind a
lizard's snout. Fortunatus stood rear guard.

"What is it?" asked Hanna, although she already knew
by the way their eyes shifted toward the cart and away
again.

"I thought . . ." Rosvita sighed, frowned, touched her
forehead as if her fingertips might coax out words. "Lady
Bertha and I discussed, yesterday, that it might be time to
send you ahead as Eagles ride, to carry news of our coming."

"Where meant you to send me?"

She shook her head. "It no longer matters. Yesterday I
did not know. What she is."

"She is no Daisanite," said Fortunatus. "She does not believe in God."

Their expressions chilled Hanna. Anything might happen if Sorgatani were left alone among those who could
not speak to her, those who could never look into her face.

"Trust her," she said, hating the way her voice quavered,
the way it betrayed her desperation and sudden fear. "I
pray you. She saved us."

"What if she turns on us?" asked Rosvita, not with anger
or bitterness or suspicion but as a leader must ask, seeking
information. "She is not our kind."

"Trust her, and she will trust you. Distrust her, and she
will distrust you."

"Is that all of your advice, Eagle?"

"There is nothing else to say."

"She is a terrible weapon. A curse." The gray light of
morning softened the lines on Rosvita's face. The journey
had aged her, yet she was not bowed. She led them now
that Bertha was dead. She would hold firm.

"Terrible, yes," said Hanna, thinking of Bulkezu and his
Quman hordes, of lizard-snouted creatures shooting poisoned arrows at her out of the dark, of griffins and centaurs.
Thinking of Hugh. "But it is better we hold such a weapon,
is it not? Better that we do, than that our enemies do."

Fortunatus looked at Rosvita, and she at him. Perhaps
he raised an eyebrow so imperceptibly that Hanna could
not quite mark it. Perhaps it was a slight movement of his

lips. These two were intimate in the same manner as family fit hand in glove. Hanna knew they were communicating although she could not hear what it was they said.

"Yes," replied Rosvita to the words he had not spoken. "Mother Rothgard is famous for her knowledge of sorcery. It might be we should consult her. To protect ourselves."

"To protect *her*!" protested Hanna.

Fortunatus closed his eyes, looking pained and weary.

"So it might also be argued," agreed Rosvita. "Alas it has come to this, that it is good for us that we grasp such a poisoned arrow to our heart."

"She is what the Horse people and her own mothers made her. She is a good person!"

They looked at her. They doubted. They did not believe.

Maybe, in her heart, she did not believe either, but she remembered Sorgatani's tears.

"God ask us to remember compassion, do They not, Sister?"

"They do. Why do you say so?"

"Think of her, then, no older than I am. Think of her imprisoned in that cart for all of her life except when she might wander in woodland or grassland where no one unsuspecting can stumble across her. Think of her, and feel compassion. Then you will trust her."

Fortunatus batted a fly away from his face, his mouth twisted, his gaze fixed on the dirt.

"What of this other whisper?" Hanna demanded, sensing that to press forward might distract them from Sorgatani. "Some of the soldiers are saying that the raiders must have been in league with Prince Sanglant."

"As easy to say they were seeking Sanglant so they could kill him," said Rosvita. "These are fears speaking. I do not believe it. Do you?"

Do I? Hanna could not speak to refute it, or admit it. Rosvita smiled sadly and seemed ready to speak, but she paused, cocked her head, and listened.

There came an unspeakably faint rattle, like buckets clanging together. The dogs barked. Sergeant Aronvald shouted a warning. The men, made furious by exhaustion and grief, grabbed their weapons and cursed.

In silence, except for the dogs barking and wagging their tails, they waited.

Like a miracle, there came walking Laurent and Tomas up the road with buckets swinging They started as they came closer, seeing the wagons laden and ready to leave.

"Did you mean to leave us?" called Laurent cheerfully. "Can't get rid of us so easily!"

No one moved, only watched them stride closer, as if they might be possessed by ghouls.

"What happened to you?" demanded the sergeant.

"We got lost, turned around entirely. Figured it was too dangerous to try to get back at night. Likely break a leg! So we bedded down in the woods. Whew! Had one damp spell when the rains came over, and fool Tom got a nettle sting on his left hand, but otherwise we survived without being eaten by wolves or swallowed up by . . ."

Laurent was a dark-haired lad with a round, rosy face unaltered by their travails. He was younger than Hanna and pleased at having played a practical joke even if he hadn't meant to, but as he looked around at their faces, his own expression shifted, darkened, and fell, and he shut up.

Tomas saw a corpse. Whitening, he nudged Laurent and pointed. His left hand was, indeed, blistered with the fading red rash of a nettle sting.

"Ai, God!" Laurent exclaimed. "What's wrong? What have we missed?"

"Move along," said the sergeant, not answering him. "Move along."

III
OLD FRIENDS

1

THE king's progress came after many days to the Oder River and rode south to Walburg, reaching the fortress of the Villams in time to celebrate the Translatus at the holy cathedral begun by Helmut Villam and not yet complete. Here, in the east, his aunt, Biscop Alberada, left him to return to Handelburg in the easternmost marchlands. Here, three days later, Margrave Gerberga declared that it was her intention to take her leave of the progress and, together with her royal husband, ride southeast to her lands of Austra and Olsatia.

"There is trouble abroad," she said in her matter-of-fact way as Sanglant's intimate companions reclined at their ease in a large chamber set aside for their use by Margrave Waltharia. "I dare not remain away longer. I fear raids out of the wilderness. Anything might happen."

The shutters stood open, admitting a cold breeze. By morning, every puddle in the forecourt would be iced over, but within the tower chamber the heat of so many bodies kept them cozy. A carpet insulated them from hard planks. Besides the fire, a half dozen braziers stood on tripods around the room, radiating warmth. Sanglant sat in the chair that had belonged to his father, the regent's seat with its back carved to resemble a span of wings, its feet ending

in a lion's solid paws, and its dragon-faced arms. It had survived the tempest and firestorm on the shore of the Middle Sea. Each night his servants set it up and each morning,
when they set out to ride, took it apart again. It was cunningly made, easy to handle, and impressive to see. But it
was uncomfortable to sit in, even with a cushion placed on
the seat. He often wondered if Henry had wanted it that
way, to remind him of the dangers and difficulties of ruling
should he ever begin to relax too much.

The nobles of the realm rested more easily on couches
and well-cushioned chairs or on sturdy benches padded
with feather pillows. Sitting cross-legged on the carpet,
Prince Ekkehard played chess by the fire with Gerberga's
young sister, Theucinda. She was a pleasant enough girl,
old enough to marry but young enough to giggle, as she did
now when Ekkehard moved his Biscop to a vulnerable position and, too late, realized his mistake.

Theophanu was also playing chess. She sat at the table
across from one of the clerics from the schola, but hers was
a serious game, all maneuvering done in silence. Her gaze
did not once leave the board as her opponent assessed the
placement of red and white. Theophanu had left one of her
Castles in jeopardy, but Sister Elsebet had lost one of her
Eagles and looked ready to lose the second. Neither had
the advantage, but either could win in five moves.

Duchess Liutgard was writing a letter with her own
hand, supervised by a cleric of her household. Now and
again she addressed a comment to Waltharia, who was
seated beside her. Waltharia worked steadily with her needle as she embroidered the sleeve of a fine midnight-blue
tunic sized, Sanglant noted, to fit a man. Obviously
Waltharia was preparing to welcome the husband she expected to replace Lord Druthmar, the one she had asked
Sanglant to find for her.

He sighed.

"I did not drop it."

"You did!"

"No, you misplaced it. It wasn't my fault, it was yours."

"You're always blaming me!"

This from the corner, where Rotrudis' daughters, Sophie

and Imma, sat and whispered. Despite hating each other, they were rarely apart. Their brother Wichman snored on a couch, an empty cup just about to slide out of his right hand.

Clerics, stewards, servants: he marked each one. He knew them all. Those who were new to his retinue were revealing their quirks and temperaments to him, day by day. Naturally, the only one missing was his beloved wife. He frowned.

"Anything," Gerberga repeated. Her gaze dropped briefly onto her husband, and she flushed and waved a hand in the air as if to fan away a fly.

Ekkehard looked up. "Why must 'Cinda stay behind?"

That got their attention. Every head lifted. After a breath, or three breaths, most looked away but everyone continued to listen. Even Wichman stirred, opening his eyes. On a quiet night such as this, they had to enjoy whatever entertainment came their way.

"You are too attached to her, Ekkehard."

Theucinda looked up at her sister, trembled, and said nothing. She was the youngest of Judith's brood. Coming after the beautiful Hugh, the forthright and commanding Gerberga, and the blunt and combative Bertha, it was no wonder that she was a mouse.

"She is like a sister to me!" objected Ekkehard. "Aren't you?" he said, pressing Theucinda, although it was obvious the girl would have preferred to remain silent. "Aren't you?"

Something shifted in her expression. Perhaps, after all, she hid her stubborn Austran streak beneath that fragile, freckled complexion and rosy mouth. A pretty enough girl, but not at all to Sanglant's taste. Thank God he had escaped marriage to her!

The diminutive creature spoke in a soft voice. "I don't want to enter the church, Gerberga." The words came out as if she had learned them by rote. She looked at Ekkehard, then blushed.

"I said I'd marry her!" cried Wichman, rallying from his stupor. He scratched his crotch, burped, and stared with incomprehension into his empty cup.

Gerberga snorted. "Let your cousin Sanglant find a suitable husband for you, Theucinda, and you will not have to enter the church. He means to do as much for Waltharia, so why not for you?" She smiled at Sanglant.

A challenge! He lifted a hand off the arm of his chair to acknowledge her request.

Theophanu had, after all, been listening. Her hand, poised to move her Castle, froze in midair as she looked over. How cool her voice was, yet her words scorched. "If there are any suitable men to be found, a circumstance I doubt. Yet I pray you, Theucinda, do not despair. You may not have to wait long. Perhaps an institution could be founded for you, as it was for my dear brother Ekkehard. Then after you have said your vows, you will be sure to be called to marriage."

"That is the end of it," continued Gerberga, soundly irritated now. "Theucinda remains with the king's progress. We leave in the morning, Ekkehard."

"God, I have to pee," said Wichman.

Rotrudis' son had tactical flair. It was just possible that he rose and made a scene of departing in order to break up the gathering, to allow folk to retire to their beds without battle being joined. Or it might be that he simply had to pee after drinking five or ten cups of wine. He staggered out, and in twos and threes they followed him. Sanglant remained seated, waiting, and at last he was alone with Waltharia. She handed her embroidery to a servant and raised an eyebrow, waiting in her turn. Coals were brought. The servingwoman folded up the tunic and stored it in a chest. A man gathered up cups and took them away on a tray.

He found that solitude, with her, made him uncomfortable. Without meaning to, he touched the gold torque at his neck, the one she had persuaded him to wear, and he felt heat burn in his cheeks and knew he was blushing.

She smiled. She knew him that well.

"I know where Liath is," she said, rising.

"I thought she came up with us," he complained, "but she has not been here this past hour. How do you know where she is?"

She chuckled. "She asked me about a certain person living in retirement here."

The words stung him. They had secrets, Waltharia and Liath. They confided in each other. It was disconcerting and, in truth, a little irritating. But he said nothing, only stood and beckoned to Hathui, who was waiting by the door.

They came down the broad stone steps of the tower and passed through the dark hall where so recently the crowd of nobles had feasted. The lamp carried by a steward illuminated alcoves and benches in flashes. Here rumpled shapes slept, crowded together for warmth. A pair of dogs nosed along the floor, seeking scraps lost in the rushes. Sanglant could still smell the tantalizing odor of roasted meat, just as the dogs could. They barked, seeing a rival, but slunk away.

A door led onto the courtyard where the kitchen buildings stood far enough away from the hall to protect it from the ever present danger of fire. Waltharia led them past these to a tiny cottage set back by a well amidst a withered flower garden. She pushed the door open and they went inside. A pool of light created by a single lamp graced the room. Liath sat on a three-legged stool, bent forward to listen to an elderly woman who was propped up on pillows in her bed and dressed in a plain linen shift like an invalid. He recognized her lean, lined features, squared shoulders, and keen gaze at once, but the expression on her face as she spoke with Liath was not hostile, not as it had been when he had first met this old woman years before in Walburg. In those days, her hostility had been directed toward the old Eagle, Wolfhere.

She looked up first. As usual, Liath was so intent on what she was doing that it took her a moment to notice the arrivals. Not so with him; she could not enter any room he was in without him immediately being aware of her presence.

Ah, well.

"Sanglant," she said, beckoning. She nodded to Waltharia, not needing to greet her. Somehow, it made the relationship between the two women seem more intimate than the one she shared with him.

"Here is Hedwig," Liath added. "She was an Eagle."

The old woman stirred, groping for a cane and looking quite startled—but not, he thought, because of his presence.

"I pray you, Eagle," he said, "no need to rise. I recall your old injuries. I'll sit here."

There was a chair. He grabbed its back and swung it over.

"I thank you, Your Majesty," she said with a hint of sour humor as she cast an accusing glare at Liath. She released the cane to rest against her bedding.

He sat beside Liath, facing the old Eagle. Waltharia remained standing at the foot of the bed. Hathui circled around to warm her hands at the hearth fire. Smoke swirled in the lamplight. A servant hurried forward to place more wood on the fire. It was so cold in the cottage, despite the blaze, that Liath's breath steamed when she spoke.

"Repeat what you told me, I pray you, Hedwig."

The old woman frowned, first at Liath and afterward upward at the loft of darkness that hid the ceiling. She was measuring her words in her mind before she spoke them. He almost laughed, because the look of her made him feel so young. She was exactly the kind of old woman who had frightened him most as a boy because this sort were apt to scold a hapless child for stealing tarts from the kitchens when it was only hunger that drove him. This kind was merciless, even in the face of honest need. Even to a royal prince who in other hands might expect a little leniency.

"Wolfhere brought the Eagle's Sight to our order," she said.

"Did he?" The statement surprised him.

"I thought this knowledge was handed down from regnant to heir. Before that time, we rode, and we observed, but we could not see or speak through fire."

"No wonder King Arnulf made Wolfhere his favorite. Eagle's Sight granted him a powerful advantage."

"Yet Eagle's Sight is closed to me now. I can see only snatches, glimpses." She nodded at Liath. "This blindness affects all of us, so this one believes. The sight has been somehow damaged in the wake of the tempest that swept over us last autumn."

"That's what we were speaking of," said Liath to Sanglant, "just now."

"Explain it again, I pray you."

Liath had a way of frowning that wasn't actually a frown but more of a thoughtful grimace as she collected her thoughts, a task of undoubted complexity since she knew so many complicated things.

"I think that Eagle's Sight runs on the threads of aether. Aether resides in the heavens, beyond the mortal Earth. Normally it is rarefied and weak here in the lands below the moon. The crowns channel and intensify these threads of aether, which is how they can be woven into a gate. But Eagle's Sight touched the aether differently. It was drawn through a portal, which some of us saw as a standing stone burning with blue fire. That stone acted as a crossroads. The stone was itself the portal, between this world and the higher spheres. It was created by the spell woven in ancient days when the country of the Ashioi was torn from its roots and flung into the heavens. Through that portal aether filtered down to Earth in greater quantities than it normally would. So, once the portal between the aether and Earth was severed by the return of the Ashioi land, then the Eagle's Sight was diminished, so damaged that it is as if we cannot see at all. The crowns were raised long ago, before the portal was opened by the spell in ancient days. The crowns should still weave, but our Eagle's Sight is lost to us. Possibly forever. I don't know."

"My lady." The old woman's voice and demeanor had changed. She bent her head respectfully. "I thought you were an Eagle, one like me."

"So I am! Well. So I was."

"Now I see you are not who I thought you were. Else you would not address the king regnant with such familiarity. Who are you? Are you the one—?" She broke off.

"What one?" asked Liath.

Hedwig shook her head. "No need to ask. You are the one Wolfhere sought when he came back from his exile."

"His exile?" asked Sanglant.

"Yes, Your Majesty. You must know of this, surely. When Arnulf died, Henry exiled Wolfhere. Or perhaps it was later, after the prince was born. That would be you, Your Majesty." Her hands shook as she smoothed down the rumpled bedclothes. "Nay, nay. My memory weakens. You were a boy when King Arnulf died, Your Majesty. You had already been born and survived some years."

"I was five or six," he agreed. "I remember his passing and my father's grief. I recall, too, that Wolfhere vanished for some years."

"Yes, that was his exile, as soon as King Henry could compass it. But I knew Wolfhere was not dead. He's the kind that's hardest to kill—those who most deserve death! At intervals I glimpsed him through the fire, but I could not see where he was or what he was doing. Then—how easily we lose track of the time—he returned. The Eagles never cast any one of us out, you see."

"I'm surprised he came back," said Liath. "Or that King Henry allowed him to return."

She chuckled, then coughed. "So you may be, my lady. I convinced King Henry to take him back."

"*You* did?" asked Sanglant with a laugh.

"I did," she replied in the voice a woman of her kind used to remind a boy that he was not permitted to pilfer from the kitchen on such an important feast day. "Wolfhere was too valuable. He had done so much for the Eagles, and for Arnulf. King Arnulf trusted no one better than Wolfhere. The young prince—that would be you, Your Majesty—was old enough to be more easily protected. You were not at risk. But Wolfhere was indifferent to you in any case, perhaps because by then your sisters were born. He was seeking someone else."

Liath nodded. "Yes, he was."

"I pray you, Mistress Hedwig," said Waltharia, "I've heard this tale before but not, I see, all of it. If you are the one who argued for Wolfhere's return, then what made you and Wolfhere fall out later?"

It was difficult for the woman to lift her hands, but she managed to get one hand off the covers, indicating Liath. "This girl. Wolfhere felt no loyalty to Henry, to Arnulf's

son, not as he should have. He felt no loyalty to Wendar,
not as he should have. He returned only to discover what
news he might. Of this one. I soon realized that was the
only reason he came back. So I no longer trusted him."

She coughed again, and the steward found wine, and
Liath helped her drink.

"Where is Wolfhere now?" asked Waltharia.

"No one knows," said Sanglant. "He escaped me in Sordaia. Maybe he is dead."

"What does it matter what has become of Wolfhere?"
Waltharia asked.

Liath handed the cup back to the steward. For a while,
she sat with hands folded on her lap, gazing at Hedwig.

Sanglant listened to the old woman's labored breathing,
with its telltale sign of a consumption eating at her lungs.
She was ill. She was old. That she had survived so long with
her crippled legs and body and failing health was entirely
due to Waltharia's care of her. What did this old woman
mean to Waltharia? Why should the Villams give her shelter?

"This is what I understand of the matter," said Liath.
"Wolfhere sought me because my father stole me from the
Seven Sleepers. It was their intent to wield me as a weapon
against Sanglant, whom they considered to be a tool of the
Lost Ones in their plot to conquer humankind."

Waltharia eyed him sidelong. She seemed about to
laugh, but did not. "A strong spear," she said.

Liath snorted. Sanglant flushed.

"Wolfhere did not betray you, Liath," said Hathui suddenly. "He protected you. Was it Wolfhere who led you
back to the Seven Sleepers?"

Liath regarded Hathui with a curious smile. "He told
them where I was to be found. So it was that Anne found
me in Werlida and lured me to Verna. Do you think matters transpired otherwise, Hathui? Is there something you
know that we do not?"

They all looked at the Eagle, even Hedwig.

"No man can serve two masters," said Hathui. "I believe
that there were two people that Wolfhere loved above all
others: Anne, and Arnulf. In that way he is like the story of

the man who at the full moon turns into a wolf, loyal to both parts of himself and yet unable to be whole. Torn between two bodies."

"You speak truly enough," said Waltharia. "No man *may* serve two masters. How can a man torn between two masters serve either one faithfully? He must choose one, or the other, because in time they will come into conflict."

"What is his secret?" Liath asked. "He is the last of the Seven Sleepers who knew Anne well, who knew all or most of what she intended. If he still lives, I must find him, because I believe he has secrets yet to reveal."

"What if he does not?" asked Hathui. "What if he is exactly what he seems, and nothing more?"

"A traitor?" asked Waltharia with an acerbic laugh.

"A wolf among men?" asked Sanglant, "loyal to no one?"

"A servant meant to carry messages," retorted Hathui. "By all accounts, although I never saw him, King Arnulf was a kinder master than Anne."

"Weary," whispered Hedwig.

Liath leaned forward. "We have exhausted you. I pray you, pardon us."

"He was weary," Hedwig repeated, strengthened, it seemed, by a hint of annoyance that she was dismissed so easily when it was to her that Liath had come in the first place. "When I saw him here. The last time. Weary. Troubled. Sad. So might a man be who is at war within himself. Such a man can never be trusted. He can never trust himself."

Her breath whistled. The speech had winded her. They waited, listening to her labored breathing.

Finally, Liath shook herself and rose. "I thank you for what you have told me, Hedwig."

The old Eagle's fingers stirred but she could not, it seemed, lift them off the blanket. Nor could she speak. She wheezed a little.

"I will send Clara to attend you," said Waltharia.

They left, stepping out into the cold, dark night. The wind stung nostrils and eyes as they walked across the courtyard. At the entrance to the hall, servants were dispatched to take coals, a hot poultice, and an attendant to sit out the night with the old woman.

"Why do the Villams shelter her?" he asked. "Has she no family to take her in?"

Waltharia's smile made him uncomfortable, and she glanced first at Liath and only after that at him. "She was for a short time one of my father's many, many mistresses."

The Eagle was so old a woman that it was easy to forget that Villam, too, had lived a long life.

"My mother, before she died, made me swear to take her in if she needed shelter in her old age."

"Your *mother?* Why would she trouble herself in such a way?"

She glanced at Liath. They looked. They smiled, each a little. They did not look at him. "Because my father would not. My father was a good man and a strong and canny margrave, Sanglant, but thoughtless in other ways. Hedwig was one of my mother's young servants. She became an Eagle after—well, it was considered a disgrace in her family. They threw her out. Had my mother not made provision for her care, she would have died as a pauper."

"This history surprises me," said Liath. "I thought the Eagles took care of their own."

"So they do. Not many survive to such a respectable age. When they are too crippled or old or ill to ride, they are pensioned off, just as old Lions are—those who survive their service. The Villams accepted the pension for the care of her."

"It was a saying among the Dragons," remarked Sanglant with an unexpected swell of bitterness, "that all Dragons died young, guarding the honor of the regnant."

"Will you muster a flight of Dragons?" Waltharia asked him. "You must think of these things, you know. There are Eagles and Lions to be recruited, to strengthen your army, And Dragons, to fly swiftly to where the need is greatest."

He frowned. "Who to lead them?"

"Sapientia has a daughter, does she not?"

"Still a child, not more than six or eight at the most. Nay. Let me see what noble youths are cast up at my feet. Then I'll decide what to do."

Liath had stepped out from under the eaves and stood

staring up at the sky as if her gaze could pierce the clouds. He thought she wasn't paying attention, but she spoke. "I will have my own mustering, of scholars." She chuckled. "A nest of phoenix. That's what I'll call them."

"Phoenix?" Waltharia was startled, and showed it.

"I think not!" said Sanglant.

Liath turned to look at them. He could only see her shape, but he knew that her vision, in such darkness, was much keener than his. What she saw, seeking in their expressions, he did not know. "The phoenix flies, like the eagle. It is born out of fire, out of passion, and renews itself. Would the phoenix not be a fine beast for scholars?"

Sometimes she was so naive!

"I pray you, Liath," he said, then faltered, hearing how annoyed he sounded and knowing it was not her but his memories of Blessing that hurt him.

Hathui stepped forward. "Perhaps you are not aware that the phoenix has become spoken of in the same breath as the heresy, the Redemptio. A story circulated—"

"If Wichman can be believed, it was true enough," said Sanglant, "since he was among those who slaughtered the beast."

"Slaughtered a phoenix?" Liath breathed, horrified.

"The townsfolk said it preyed on their cattle. But there was talk of a miracle, a mute man healed, and so on, and now—nay, Liath, no nests of phoenixes for you unless you are determined to turn heretic yourself."

"I am not," she said thoughtfully, "but it interests me to hear this tale. I must speak to Wichman."

"When I am present!"

"If you wish. I do not fear him."

"Prince Ekkehard witnessed the whole as well," pointed out Hathui unhelpfully. "Although I admit most of those who were present in that party are now dead in the wars."

"Ekkehard and Wichman!" Liath said, in tones of astonishment.

"Not now," said Sanglant, "I pray you. Morning is soon enough."

"Soon enough," said Waltharia, backing him up, as was her duty as margrave. "My hands have turned to ice. Let us go in."

2

LIATH was up as soon as night grayed with the early twilight.

He groaned and said, closing his eyes, "Neither Wichman nor Ekkehard will have risen yet, my love. Wait but a moment. Come back under the covers with me."

"I can't stop thinking about it."

She dressed without servants to aid her, not calling anyone in, and he heard the door open, felt the draft of frosty air from the stairwell kiss his cheeks—better had she done it!—and the thud of its closing. A decent interval later the door opened and he heard the stealthy footfalls of four servingmen as they entered the chamber and busied themselves as quietly as they could with water, coals, clothing, and the rest of his gear and necessaries. He still thought of them as Den's brother, Malbert's cousin, Johannes' uncle, and Chustaffus' brother, although in fact their names were Johannes, Robert, Theodulf, and Ambrose. Warm air breathed along his skin as the one of them—that would be Johannes, who had an unevenness in his gait due to a deformity in his right foot—moved a brazier closer to the bed in preparation for his rising.

Outside, he heard voices raised to that pitch of intensity that betokens an upset bubbling into an emergency. He cracked an eye, but it was still dim in the chamber and would be until they had his leave to take down the shutters.

"No," came Hathui's voice from outside. "I'll go in *now.*"

The door opened. He sighed and sat up, giving in to the inevitable. When he had been captain of the King's Dragons there had been days when he'd had to move at first light, and swiftly, but there had also been days when he'd had no more pressing engagement at dawn than . . . well, never mind that now.

"What is it?" he asked.

She gestured toward the door, which meant that trouble was coming. "Margrave Gerberga."

Robert handed him his under-tunic, and he slipped it on and swung out of bed as Ambrose took down first one shutter, then the next. The chill exhalation of the outdoors sighed in, bringing with it the smell of smoke, dung, and freshly split wood. A carpet insulated him from the plank floor, and it was just as well since he was still barefoot but decently attired when Gerberga stormed in, face red and braided hair pinned back for her night's rest.

"He's gone!" she cried. "Vanished!"

Only the peers of the realm or his intimate servants dared storm in without announcing themselves. After Gerberga came Theophanu, expression so blank that he marveled, wondering if she were furious or joyful.

"This is not the first time Ekkehard has acted rashly," Theo said to Gerberga as if continuing a conversation begun earlier. "Do not forget that he stole Lord Baldwin from your mother."

"Damn him!"

"And that he then debauched himself in Gent while pretending to be an abbot in a monastery founded by his own father," added Theophanu with such a look of composure that Sanglant imagined her actually laughing inside—if Theophanu ever laughed. "And after that betrayed his own countryfolk and rode with the Quman monster."

"When I find him . . ." Gerberga glared at Sanglant as if he had spoken and, without addressing another word to him, departed in the same manner as a summer squall, leaving a moment of sparkling clarity behind.

"Hathui," he said, "go see that horses are saddled."

She nodded and left.

"When you find him, then what?" asked Theophanu coolly. "I am surprised you allowed the marriage to Gerberga to take place without making it clear to Ekkehard that he must respect your wishes. By this act, he challenges your authority."

"Theo," he said mildly, seeing how everyone else there had gone very quiet indeed, "I do not for a moment suppose that Ekkehard has anything in mind other than his own gratification, since he has never appeared to have more than one thought in his head at a time."

She watched him with an expression of calm consideration that made him stand to alert as though she had a knife she might pull.

"They love you," she said.

"Who loves me?"

"All of them. These servants. The Eagles. The soldiers. The common folk. It's you, the bastard, they look to, to save them, although I am the legitimately born child. There are a few who do love me, my dear retinue, but they are a trifle compared to the ones who love you."

Since there was no answer to this, he said nothing.

"They stare at you so, Sanglant. I suppose I do, too." Her smile sharpened her expression. "I know better, yet I can't help myself. I'm no different than they are. I believe you can save us, if anyone can."

"Perhaps. I am only first among equals. Without the strength of the duchies and the marchlands, Wendar will fall."

"As Varre has?" she challenged him. "Fallen to Sabella and Conrad's ambitions?"

"So we will see, when the king's progress marches west. You are steady, Theophanu. I need you at my back."

She had their father's height and the robust build common to their ancestors, yet a hint in her coloring and eyes and the unnatural opacity of her expression marked her half foreign blood. *Never trust Arethousans bearing gifts.*

"Always at the back." There came a spark of emotion into her face he could not interpret: resignation, amusement, envy, or anger, or some other, less simple, reaction. He knew her well enough, but in truth, he did not know her well.

Footsteps warned them of Hathui's return. She appeared in the door, looked from one to the other, and said, "The horses are saddled and ready, Your Majesty. Your Highness."

Theophanu indicated the door. "I follow where you lead. Let us make sure that Ekkehard does not escape *his* duty."

"So are we all what our father made of us," he said to her.

She cocked her head to one side, lips thinned, the mere quirk of a smile. "That's true enough." She was both amused and bitter. "Father always got what he wanted. Even when it killed him."

3

THE frosty air of early morning chilled skin and made strong men shudder. The horses bogged down in soggy ground that had never dried out because there was no sun to bake it dry. On the whole, the morning had a miserable air that weighed on everyone and made them ride in disgruntled silence. Why must Ekkehard act like such an idiot?

"Some questions cannot be answered, Your Majesty," said Hathui, and Sanglant realized he had spoken out loud.

The guards at the gate had pointed north. At a hamlet where the road forked, an old woman, who according to her testimony never could sleep well at night because of the particular ache in her hip that made lying down an agony, had heard a troop of horsemen turn down the northwest fork and rattle off in the twilight hours before dawn. A nervous peddler pushing his cart along that narrow way had seen and heard a dozen men pass his hidden campsite at dawn.

"We're getting closer," said Captain Fulk. "See, here. Hoofprints at the verge. Still fresh."

Liath had fallen to the back of the troop of two-score riders so she could talk to Lord Wichman. Sanglant glanced back, then turned a little to watch them. Liath talked. Wichman seemed to be answering in monosyllables. Hathui snorted.

"Nay, have no fear, Your Majesty," she said.

"Fear of Liath seeking comfort from Wichman? I think not!"

"Nay. Fear of him harming her. Look at his posture."

It seemed that Wichman rode a little off-balance, that he was in fact leaning somewhat *away* from his interlocutor, keeping his distance.

"That damned phoenix," said Sanglant. "She will gnaw at it."

"She is what she is, Your Majesty."

He sighed.

Ahead, a scout appeared at a canter. The man reined in

and waited, and when the king's party were in earshot, announced:

"Ahead! The lady's mount has gone lame and they're arguing over whether to leave it."

"There's the wrong battle to be fighting," muttered Fulk. Hathui chuckled.

"The better to fall into our hands," said Sanglant wearily. "I am relieved we have no great hunt to pursue."

The noise of their company reached Ekkehard's party before they came upon them in a clearing surrounded by hornbeam and oak. A few trees lay cracked and fallen, trunks stretched over hawthorn and dogweed and flowering stitchwort. The others towered like pillars, overseeing the hapless soldiers and frightened lady scrambling to mount horses made restive by their handlers' fear. Ekkehard was already in the saddle. He rode forward to confront his brother, placing himself between his pursuers and his retinue.

"What have you come for?" he demanded imperiously. "I won't go back to Gerberga!" He drew his sword.

Sanglant motioned the others to fall back and rode himself to meet the younger man on the path. He pitched his voice to carry. "I pray you, Ekkehard, come quietly. Lady Theucinda cannot marry a man who is already married. Or do you mean to bed her and then cast her off?"

The girl looked up, hearing Sanglant, but she was just a little too far off for him to study her expression.

"I do not!" objected Ekkehard. "That's not what I intend! I'll marry her!"

"Are you not already wed to Gerberga?" Sanglant asked as pleasantly as he could. "Did you not already consummate the marriage?"

Ekkehard's deep flush made him look furious and ridiculous. Sanglant felt a flash of sympathy for the rash fool, but it passed as soon as he remembered that Ekkehard had ridden with Bulkezu and his Quman invaders.

"For shame," Sanglant said in a voice only the two of them could hear. "For shame, Ekkehard. Take your punishment, which you have earned. Does Gerberga abuse you?"

"She does not," admitted Ekkehard sulkily. "But she doesn't respect me. She only respects my rank and title. She wouldn't have wanted me if I wasn't Henry's son."

He brandished his sword. Sanglant's men murmured with alarm, but Sanglant raised a hand to quiet them. Ekkehard was only expressing his frustration.

"Why can you have what you want?" added Ekkehard craftily. "Why can you, but not the rest of us? No one wants her as queen. She's born of no particular noble house, only a minor landholding family, she admits it herself, that she isn't really Taillefer's granddaughter. She's some kind of creature, a daimone. Maybe she has no soul. And she's a sorcerer. So why must I marry for the sake of alliance, to benefit my family, if you don't have to?"

There was no answer to this reasonable question.

Ekkehard grinned triumphantly. "It's just that you can, and I can't. Because you have the army, and I am a prisoner."

Was that ringing in his ears his blood and anger rising? Everyone listened and watched. In battle, he always knew how to counterstrike, but in the courtier's world he was not as adept.

A sharp tang as of iron made him sneeze. Had there been a chapel in that last village, where bells might be ringing?

Ekkehard lifted his chin, very much like the boy who has at last defeated his powerful rival. "You can't answer me!" he crowed.

"Sanglant!" Her voice cut through everything else.

He turned in the saddle to see Liath pressing her mount forward, to see her speaking as she rode in a manner that caught Hathui and Fulk's attention. His guardsmen scattered like chaff before wind.

"What?" he began.

Too late, he recognized the threat.

"Behind me!" she shouted, riding toward him. "I still have my bow and a dozen griffin feathers. Best if Ekkehard's men spread out. They must not clump together."

This he had seen for himself that awful night on the foothills of the Alfar Mountains.

"How many?" she asked. "I can't see them."

Galla.

He smelled them now. He heard their bell-like voices tolling, two of them, four of them, whispering his name and Liath's name: *Sanglant. Liathano.* But he could not see them through the trees.

"Four, I think."

"Who are they after?"

"Only you and me."

"Ai, God." She was furious, scared, and determined. "Who has sent them?"

"There!"

Branches swayed and snapped. Where their track led across the underbrush it left a barren trail in its wake.

"I see only three." Her bow was already strung. She drew an iron feather out of her quiver and set it to the string, heedless of the trickle of blood on her skin.

The galla approached from the south, two of them moving one behind the next and one about thirty paces off to one side. He hissed, then shut his eyes, seeking, listening, smelling, letting the touch of the wind on his cheek speak to him. He heard a fainter set of bells, but the ringing of the other three drowned it and he could not mark its direction.

Horses screamed. Men shouted, trying to control them. He heard a man fall, the thump of his impact on the ground, a shattered bone, a weeping curse at the injury.

"Fulk!" Sanglant shouted, not looking to see where Fulk was. He dared not look away from the advancing galla. "Scatter the men and keep them away from me and Liath! Do as I say!"

"Ride quickly!" said Ekkehard, behind them. "We'll get away."

Sanglant drew his sword, because he could not stand his ground without his sword in his hand, even knowing the sword was useless.

"Back up," said Liath to him. "I need a clear shot."

She drew but held it, lips parted, gaze drawn as tight as the bowstring. Her braid hung down her back. Her chin was lifted and her shoulders in perfect alignment. The mellow light gave her skin a rich gleam. Her eyes flared with blue. She was as beautiful as any creature he had ever seen, bright, poised, and deadly. No wonder he loved her so much.

The galla shuddered as they came out from under the trees, as if the pale light of this cloudy day hurt their essence. Light hurt them, because they were creatures formed out of shards of darkness. They were pillars of black smoke, roiling, faceless but not voiceless. He heard them speak.

"Sanglant. Liathano. Liathano." And, more faintly, *"Liathano."* One for him, but three for her. Why not twenty? Why not a hundred? He was sweating; he was cold.

They glided forward over the ground.

"Nay!" shouted Fulk. "Stay back! Stay back!" He sounded likely to weep, but he had seen galla before. No human weapon could defeat them.

Liath loosed her first arrow.

The leading galla vanished with a ringing wail, and a sizzle, and a snap. The smoky pillar simply flicked out of existence. He no longer heard his own name, only hers.

"Get away from me," she said to him as she pulled a second griffin feather from her quiver. He sheathed his sword and rode to her to pull a feather out of the quiver. The hard vanes cut right through his leather gloves and into the skin below, but the pain seemed trivial compared to the threat.

"Damn it." Her face was slick. A sick pallor made her skin gray, but her hands were steady. "Move off. I need a clean shot."

He reined Fest aside and saw how close those other two creatures had come, as if the death of the first one had caused them to leap forward without hesitation. Were they intelligent, or only mindless servants? She shot. A second winked away.

The wind gusted out of the east, and the third galla veered west as though blown off course by that wind. Liath set one more arrow to the string. He heard Ekkehard's troop clattering away up the road, the cowards. She swore as the arrow slipped crookedly in her bloody hands.

There came, from behind, a sudden horrible shriek of

pain and fear and a cacophony of terrified screams. He
shifted, and what he saw made his breath catch. Ekkehard's
troop had fallen back from the western path crying and
wailing, scrambling to get out of the way of the fourth galla
which emerged unexpectedly from the western trees.
Theucinda's horse bolted, so panicked by the demon sailing across the clearing that it headed straight for the galla
coming out of the woods.

Too far to shoot.

Liath had seen. She fixed her gaze on Theucinda. The
girl tugged hopelessly at the horse's reins. Ekkehard
screamed.

Fire exploded up from the grass, running in a line that
quickly separated Theucinda from the galla. The horse
veered sharply away from the blaze, stumbling. She tumbled down, landing hard, shouting out in pain. The horse
galloped out of the way. The galla passed through the fire
behind her, untouched by the flames, and kept on coming,
leaving Theucinda unharmed.

"You take that one," said Sanglant, "and for me, the other."

Without waiting to hear Liath's reply, he drove Fest forward toward the third galla, which had by now tracked back
to approach them. An overpowering stench of iron and
blood swamped him as he neared the galla. He could hear
nothing but that clamorous ringing and Liath's name, tolling
on and on. It seemed at this angle to reach as tall as the trees,
a vast horrible black tower. Singing *death*. Singing *give me
release*. He tugged Fest to the right and leaned left with the
griffin feather extended, and slashed right through it.

Fest charged toward the trees with nervous energy. He
fought the gelding back around to see the fourth galla dis-
appear between one gasp and the next. Smoke poured into
the sky as the fire spread. Men shouted in confusion, but he
heard, faintly, Fulk's commands as he rounded them up.
Sanglant could not catch his breath. He rested in the saddle for the longest time as his troops herded Ekkehard's
party into line and retrieved Theucinda's skittish mount.
The girl limped but seemed otherwise unhurt. One of
Fulk's soldiers had been dumped and had broken an arm.
All told, they had come off lightly.

Liath rode up beside him. She wiped sweat off her forehead and afterward clasped his wrist with her unbloodied hand. "You're clammy." Her voice shook, but she held steady.

"The griffins have left us," he said to her in a low voice, as if it were a secret. "We have only fifteen feathers left."

"Eleven, now."

"If the galla come upon us again . . ."

"Are sent against us again, you mean."

"They must kill to raise them, slaughter men like sheep." It made him sick to think of it.

"Then for the sake of the ones who will die, let us hope they give up." Her smile told a different story. She knew their enemies would never give up.

4

FROM Walburg, the king's progress rode west along a grassy track that dipped south through fertile countryside before swinging back north to Osterburg along the Veser River. At length they crossed the Veserling and rode through woodland along the broad track where three years ago Sanglant's soldiers had chased down and broken the Quman army. It was a gray day, so cold that the shallow puddles along the road were iced over. That hard skin of ice cracked and shattered where hoof, foot, and wagon wheel struck. Moisture dripped from branches. Some of the trees had budded, but there was little spring-green foliage in the forest.

In a clearing she saw a hillock that looked strangely familiar, although at first she could not place it. Only when she looked closer did she see scattered bones and the shattered remains of rotting Quman wings. Her chest pulled tight; she found herself short of breath.

"Here, in this meadow, we broke the Quman," he said in a queer voice. "That was a bad day, thinking Blessing was dead."

He could say nothing more. Nor could she. It hurt too much to think about Blessing, yet she did think. In silence, they passed through the clearing. She stared, but except for the tree at the crown of the hill and the unmistakable shape of that odd little hill, she could not relate this peaceful, isolated clearing with the carnage and chaos of a desperately fought battle, one she had seen only in a vision.

They came out of the forest close by a low, isolated hill which was surrounded by boggy ground, brackish puddles, and rotting reeds and bracken.

"There Bayan died," said Sanglant, pointing to the hill. Its crest lay bare of vegetation, as though recently burned. He indicated a patch of open ground in the western hills that rose beyond the Veser River. "There the Quman set their camp."

Liath felt a bite in the air, as at a cold snap of wind, but this was not wind. "A powerful spell was woven here. I can still taste it."

"Two spells, in truth. The first killed Bayan. The second was his mother's revenge on the sorcerer who killed both her son and her self."

"Killed her as well? How?"

"Bayan was her luck. She was a Kerayit shaman."

"Ah." She felt the same prickling discomfort along her skin that she might feel before a thunderstorm breaks. She thought of Hanna and Sorgatani, but they were lost, and she had no way to find them.

Horns called from the battlements and were answered. Sanglant's straggling troops fell into line as they approached the gates of Osterburg. The hymn surfaced deep in the ranks and, like a storm, swept over the entire army.

> *Open the gates of victory that I may enter,*
> *That I may praise God.*

It was a familiar psalm, and by the time they entered the streets of Osterburg much of the populace had taken up the hymn, repeating its verses in ragged, heartfelt voices. So many folk flooded onto the streets to watch the regnant and his noble companions ride that it was difficult to pass. Some were certainly refugees who had fled from outlying areas where they could no longer find food or safety. Five or ten thousand altogether, she supposed, a vast number, yet she could not help but reflect that Osterburg and all the Wendish cities were only towns compared to the great cities of the south along the shores of the Middle Sea and in the lands of the heathen Jinna. Even Darre, now only a humble shadow of its imperial self, dwarfed as important a town as Osterburg. Yet Wendish soldiers had defeated Aosta's best armies. The new often overruns the old as the old gets worn and tired. That was the way of the world, so her father had taught her.

Newest of all were the Ashioi, the refugees who had at long last come home.

5

AT dawn, the morning after the magnificent feast to celebrate both the feast day of St. Sormas and the investiture of the new duchess of Saony, Sanglant slept, but Liath woke. She had trouble sleeping past the break of day. As soon as she woke, she thought of Blessing, and as soon as she thought of Blessing, she could as easily go back to sleep as fly. Sanglant slept soundly, one arm splayed over his head and the other thrown across his torso. He was out cold. He'd had a lot to drink. She dressed and left the inner chamber of the royal suite. Although she stepped carefully, she woke Hathui, who lay on a pallet athwart the door that let into the inner room.

"What? Eh? Ah. Liath."

"No need to rise. I'm just going out to walk."

Hathui groaned, pressing the heel of a hand to her forehead. "You've the head for it. Mine aches."

"As it will, if you drink so much," said Liath with a laugh.

Hathui burped. "Ai, truly, it was a good feast."

"Well deserved," said Liath, sidling on, wanting solitude. "Princess Theophanu will rule Saony wisely and well."

Which was true, and scarcely needed to be said. Still, Theophanu was a puzzle to her. She respected Theophanu but felt no warmth and no camaraderie. Theophanu was nothing like Waltharia. She smiled a little, thinking of the margrave. Maybe a friend. Certainly an ally.

She was careful not to wake the other stewards and servants, rafts of them, it always appeared to her, floating on their pallets that, when the day properly began, would be stored out of the way together with the bedding. Yet half of them were already waking, stretching, rising. Nodding at her with murmured respectful greetings. She could never interpret their expressions in any way that satisfied her that she understood what they were thinking. She had not half the skill that Sanglant did. It always seemed to her that he could judge mood and tone to a nicety. She reached the outer door to find a pair of drowsy whippets huddled at the feet of a snoring servant. They sensed her coming and, whining, ears flat, slunk out of her way. She let herself out and hurried through the barracks room, lined with sleeping soldiers bivouacked along both walls. This room opened onto a landing, crowded with dozing men. Even on the stairs folk slept but so uncomfortably that she wondered they could sleep at all. So many retainers were crammed into Osterburg's ducal palace that it was only outdoors one could smell anything but the stink of unwashed bodies. When she emerged into the central courtyard of the square palace tower, she found folk stretched out on the raised and covered walkways that linked the old two-storied tower to the newer one-story wing. They huddled under eaves and under wagons, anywhere they might keep dry or off the ground. Her feet crushed the skin of ice that made the ground glitter. She slipped out through the inner gateway. Guards stared at her and backed up a step. Belatedly, they dipped their heads and said anxiously, "my lady."

In the outer courtyard, surrounded by the hilltop palisade, servants gathered by the well to draw up water and gossip about last night's feasting. Smoke steamed out of the kitchen. A score of soldiers were marching out of the main gate, heading down into town, but they did not call or speak or sing. Only the tramp of their feet gave them away.

She found one of the narrow stairs set into the wall alongside the oldest tower, a stone donjon built a hundred years
before by Saony's first duke. Here, by tradition, the duke
lived when she wasn't traveling her domain. Theophanu's
soldiers stood on guard, but they let her pass. She walked
out along the palisade walk to one of the corner brace-
ways. Mounting a ladder, she got up to a sentry post, planks
built out over the wall.

Someone was here before her, a slight figure leaning on
the rail and staring east toward distant hills and endless
forest.

"Lady Theucinda."

The girl had not even heard her coming. She yelped,
jerked, and flushed, turning to see her, but recovered
quickly. "My lady Liathano. Did you come looking for me?"

"No. I came to admire the view."

The view was remarkable. The town opened like a skirt
around the palace hill. The river flowed in a broad bend,
fading into the hazy distance south and north. Farmers
were already moving beyond the town wall, pushing carts
filled with night soil and herding livestock out to field and
pasture. The bell rang at the modest cathedral, which had
been built in the new part of town about thirty years ago in
the days of the younger Arnulf.

Theucinda seemed inclined to remain silent, so Liath
leaned on the railing and watched as the day unveiled. The
clouds seemed lighter today, but the sun did not break
through. It was still ungodly cold although last night they
had celebrated the Feast of St. Sormas, which marked the
thirteenth day of the month of Avril, about six weeks after
the spring equinox. In Heart's Rest, folk usually planted at
the end of the month of Yanu or, in a particularly cold year,
at the very beginning of Avril. Osterburg lay many days'
journey south of Heart's Rest. Seen at this distance, the
wide forest remained bare. Only the evergreens showed
signs of life.

"Liath?"

She turned. A redheaded man stepped off the ladder,
staring at her in surprise. He wore a Lion's tabard, much
mended, and the insignia of a captain.

"Captain Thiadbold!" She grinned, delighted to see him. "How come you here?"

"I've been here for a year or more—three years, now that I think on it. We've made some expeditions to the north coast and west of here to drive out bandits and rebels. And you?" He recalled himself, and offered a more respectful bow. "An Eagle no longer, my lady. I pray you, forgive my boldness."

"There is nothing to forgive. I would rather be treated as your comrade of old than—this other thing. You marched east, did you not? With Prince Bayan and Princess Sapientia? That happened after we parted ways."

He whistled. "A long road that was. You know the route as well as I after we put down the rebellion in Varre."

They chatted a little about that time, old comrades recounting shared adventures: Lady Svanhilde and her reckless son, Charles; the battle at Gent and the death of the Eika chieftain Bloodheart.

"We traveled on progress after that. Down to Thersa and afterward to Werlida." He looked a little embarrassed. "You'll recall that, I suppose."

"I do. And after that, where did you go? You've had a long, difficult journey, I think. In the king's service."

"That we have, and lost half my men, alas. It was quiet for a while, in Varre. We went to Autun and saw the holy chapel where the Emperor Taillefer sleeps. Now that was a fine sight!" He grinned, but an instant later he frowned. "After that, indeed. We were sent east with Princess Sapientia and Prince Bayan. He was a good man, Prince Bayan. A good commander. I suppose we reached too far. Wendish folk ought not to walk beyond the marchlands."

He went on for a while about the grassy eastern reaches, about a battle at a place he called "Queen's Grave" on account of an old burial mound with a ruined stone crown at its height. Their retreat, it seemed, had succeeded only on account of Prince Bayan's steady nerves and canny tactics. There had been trouble in Handelburg.

"And through no fault of her own, I will tell you," he said harshly, "that Eagle, Hanna, was sent out to her death.

For that I blame . . ." He faltered, looked right at Lady Theucinda, and with some effort made an obvious decision to be prudent rather than bold.

"She didn't die," said Liath, suddenly cold.

"Nay, so we discovered later. Her tale is no good one, though. We met up with Prince Sanglant—His Majesty, that is—at Machteburg. There we recovered a few of our men, a handful, nothing more. They'd turned heretic. Yet I tell you, I think in a time as troubled as now it should not matter if a man is a heretic but whether he can fight."

Theucinda looked at him and seemed about to say something. But she did not.

"You'll hear no argument from me," said Liath, "but the church mothers will say otherwise."

"I pray you, then, do not repeat what I have said."

"I will not. After Machteburg?"

"After Machteburg, we sought out the Quman. They had pressed far into Wendar. They burned and looted and killed as they went. It was a terrible thing, that brought us in the end to the battle at the Veser."

"You saved my daughter in that battle."

He shrugged. "It was a hard fight."

"I know."

He looked at her, puzzled by her words, and she fell silent. She could not tell him that, as she walked the spheres, she had glimpsed the fight on the knoll and stayed her hand. She had not loosed her one remaining arrow to save her own daughter. Even so, assailed with guilt, she knew she had made the right choice. The necessary choice.

Perhaps that was why she often felt like a monster.

"Yet we did win it in the end," he added. "We did win."

"Tell me."

Thiadbold was a good observer, and he had the knack for recounting the worst episodes with a kind of wry humor and the best with modesty. He described the battle quickly and with a remarkable sense for the movements of the various groups. "Just as we thought all was lost, that we'd be slaughtered to a man—and child, too, I'm sorry to say—the prince came. His Majesty, that is. A better sight I have never seen!" He laughed, but his laughter was leavened by sadness. "Good men I lost. Too many. Still, that's the way of it. We won, and they lost."

"You did not march east afterward with Sanglant."

"We did not. His Majesty took only mounted troops. We were sent west to escort an Eagle—well, Hanna, again."

"She did not ride east with Sanglant?"

"She was very ill. She'd been held captive by the Quman, by the beast himself." He hesitated. "I hear he's dead now."

"He's dead."

He paused, as if expecting her to say more, but she did not, so he went on.

"Well. We escorted the Eagle to Gent. Afterward, she was sent south to Aosta. That's the last I have heard of her. We were sent by order of the prince—His Majesty, that is— to serve Princess Theophanu while he was in the east. That we did. Here in Osterburg mostly, repairing the walls as well as those expeditions I mentioned before." He traced his Circle, which dangled at his chest. "Full circle, I suppose you would say. Now we will serve the regnant again."

"Is that what you hope for?"

He grinned. "What must I say to the woman who knows him best? Of course it is what I hope for!"

She laughed. It was easy to fall into the companionable banter she'd known before. It was easier to be an Eagle than a queen.

He sobered. "He's a fine commander. The best, after his father the king."

She wanted to talk about Hanna, but Theucinda still stood there. She had turned her back to them and was staring east into the haze.

"Why are you out here, Thiadbold? Is this your watch?"

He indicated Theucinda with his chin, then gestured toward the old tower where Theophanu had taken up residence. Sanglant had placed Theucinda in Theophanu's custody. The girl had a mouselike exterior, petite, fine-boned, with a delicate prettiness that could easily attract the notice of a stubborn, spoiled, and disaffected youth like Ekkehard. She had not wailed and wept when Sanglant's hunting party had caught up with her and Ekkehard outside Walburg. It was difficult to tell if she had wanted to be caught, or if she saw that weeping would do her no good and so did not indulge herself. In either case, her lack of tears made her interesting.

Thiadbold waited.

"I pray you, Lady Theucinda," said Liath. "Do you come here often, so early in the morning?"

The girl looked at her as if deciding whether she wanted to speak. At last she shrugged one shoulder. "At times. We have only been here seven days. They watch me." She glanced at Thiadbold, not meeting his gaze. "They think I'll run again," she said bitterly.

"Will you?"

"Where would I run? Gerberga won't have me back, and Ekkehard is gone with her. Even so, with no retinue I could never hope to ride all the way to Austra to find him. Therefore, why should I try?" She shrugged again.

"I would have done it," said Liath. "And farther yet."

"So you say! If all the stories I hear of you are correct, then you are nothing except a frater's by-blow, or else you are an emperor's lost heir. You are the king's concubine, or his queen. You are an excommunicated sorcerer, or else you were touched by the hand of a holy saint. You can cause the heavens to burn, or men's hearts to be swayed by lust for you. A simple Eagle, or a soulless daimone. How easily it comes to you to say such words! Why do you think it should be so simple for me?"

The bitter words took Liath aback. Thiadbold coughed and looked away, as if he wished he had not heard.

"Forgive me!" the girl whispered. Tears brimmed. Her mouth trembled, and she clutched the railing as if she expected to be blown off the ramparts in a gust of furious wind. "Don't burn me!"

Liath felt sick. That look of terror was its own judgment.

"Don't fear me," she said raggedly. "I do not mean to hurt any person."

"I'll go now, Captain," said the girl in a choked voice. She swept up her skirts in one hand and clambered down the ladder.

It took all Liath's courage to look Thiadbold in the eye. Would he reject her as well?

His gaze remained steady. He brushed a finger along the dimpled scar where he had lost part of an ear. "You fought with us. We Lions don't forget our friends."

"I thank you." It was difficult to get the words out without bursting into tears.

He nodded gravely, and left to follow Lady Theucinda.

Liath rested her elbows on the railing and studied the beauty of the land and the hazy pearllike glamour of the early morning light. Maybe the clouds had lightened. Maybe the sun would break through soon. But her pleasure in the day had vanished.

How could Sanglant ever hope to make her his queen when such rumors spun through his own retinue? Especially when many, even most, were true. And did she really care? She had no wish to be queen, to be saddled with the burdens, duties, obligations, and intrigues that any consort must shoulder. Yet to be his concubine, to share him with another woman—because the regnant must wed—was unbearable. To leave him was unthinkable.

What a fool Theucinda was! That girl could never understand that it *had* been easy to leave the Eagles and ride away with Sanglant, back when Sanglant had been nothing more than captain of the King's Dragons.

"I will not be defeated by this," she said, and she listened, hoping the wind had an answer for her, but naturally it did not.

IV
FOOL'S ERRAND

1

WHERE they first caught sight of the cathedral tower the road bent through the remains of an old oak wood, now eaten in from all sides by clearing and felling.

"God spare us!" Atto exclaimed. "Mara! Look!"

She stopped obediently and lifted her head. Midway through pregnancy, she was also weary and dirty. "Are we there yet?" she asked as she squinted into the distance.

"Look how tall!" exclaimed Atto. "How can a person build so high and not have it fall? All of stone!"

"Yes, truly," she said in a bright voice as her gaze tracked over the tops of trees and the wash of sky without stopping on the tower. Finally she looked at Atto, waiting for him to give the word to start walking.

The cathedral was easily seen in a gap between trees. Smoke drifted out of the cover of wood, but those streamers could not conceal the massive block of stone that marked the bell tower, fully three stories tall. The clouds lay in a high gray-white sheet across the heavens; maybe it was brighter today than it had been yesterday, although it was certainly no warmer.

"Can you see the tower, Mara?" Alain asked in a low voice that Atto, still exclaiming, would not notice.

She shrugged, but he had learned enough about her in

the past few days to understand that she never contradicted Atto and never said one word that might displease her betrothed. It was strange to Alain that Atto took no notice of the way she could not see things far away.

Atto sniffed. "What's that up ahead? I smell woodsmoke. And shit."

Alain smelled it, too, and more besides, a pall in the air that he had come to associate with despair. He started forward, but Mara did not walk until Atto told her to, and she hung between the two men, nervous of the hounds and shy of each footfall. She had brown hair pulled back away from her face and mostly covered by a scarf, and a pleasant face at its liveliest when she was exclaiming over the beauty of flowers, but her shoulders were hunched all the time. She was like a dog wondering if it is about to be scolded. Alain pitied her, caught between two strong-minded men, yet he also wondered what would happen if she ever spoke up for herself.

The hounds, ranging ahead, loped back with ears raised and noses testing the breeze. Where the path bent under the trees they came upon a haphazard ring of settlement, hovels built out of crooked branches and roofed with patched canvas or tightly woven saplings smeared with leaves mixed into mud, now dry. The woods had been hacked back around the shantytown, leaving gaping holes in the canopy. There must have been three-score people squatting here, huddled in threadbare cloaks, staring at the travelers with the numbed anger of folk leached of hope and weakened by hunger. It stank, and it seemed people had done little more than move a few steps away from their ragged shelters to relieve themselves, not even digging pits or designating one spot for refuse. What possessions they owned sat in baskets or chipped pots. In one cage, guarded by a young man with a sharpened stick, rested a scrawny hen. Children crouched in the dirt and did not scamper along the path as healthy, curious children do when travelers pass by. This lapse caused even Atto to look nervous. He slammed the butt of his spear showily on the ground with every other step so everyone would see they were armed. Mara covered her nose and mouth with a hand and was stifling either cries or retches.

The people watched as they passed. None spoke or moved to disturb the lonely crackle of fire in the single pit dug into the ground and fueled by smoking green wood. Their silence was its own voice, telling him that these ragged folk had given up hope. They did not stir until they heard a new sound.

It came first as a hollow rat-a-tat, as if a distant woodpecker drummed its spring call. Alain was so surprised to hear bird life that he halted and tilted his head, seeking the direction of the sound. All around the hush deepened. One woman gasped audibly. Goaded by that noise, people stumbled up, grabbing children and sacks and baskets. They bolted for the shelter of the woods. By the time the band of cavalry swept around the bend, shouting and laughing, the clearing was empty, the shelters and fire pits abandoned. One forgotten little child sat on its naked rump with hands balled into fists and face red as it bawled in terror.

"We should have run," whispered Mara, trembling as she clutched Atto's arm.

"Hush!" he scolded her. "We're nothing to do with them. Stand your ground!"

Alain whistled the hounds in close as four men challenged them. Other soldiers ranged through the camp cutting ropes and beating down roofs with spears and knives. There was no point to the destruction; they were just enjoying themselves. Two carried lanterns, and they set fire to the hovels, which burned quickly as the child continued to scream.

"Shut that thing up!" said the sergeant without looking toward it. His men wore leather jerkins, but he had a mail shirt and a real iron helm with a brass nasal and leather sides. He waited on his mount two horse lengths from Alain, eyeing the hounds with the squint-eyed interest of a bored fighting man who has at last seen something he considers dangerous.

One man dismounted and cuffed the little boy, but his shrieks doubled in their piercing shrillness.

"Eh!" cried the man, snorting and coughing in an exaggerated manner. "He *stinks!* Whew! This is no boy, but a sow's get!"

"Stay!" said Alain to the hounds.

"Hold! There! You!" said the sergeant, as Alain pushed past the outthrust spear and strode over to the terrified child.

The soldiers looked curiously at him and did not interfere as he knelt beside the child. The little boy did stink. He was a stick figure, skin and protruding bones, nose running, skin rimed with dirt and worse filth, and his face was covered with sores and the fading scars of cowpox. It amazed Alain that so frail a child had survived the contagion. He wondered where the boy had suffered the outbreak, and where the demons that spread the disease were traveling now.

"Hush," said Alain softly. "Hush, child. What is your name?"

The boy hiccuped. Where his gaze slid across Alain's regard he hesitated, stilled, calmed, and looked at him, as if transfixed by Alain's face.

"What is your name?"

"Dog," whispered the little boy.

"Your name is 'Dog'?"

"Dog." He lifted a whip-thin arm to point at the hounds.

"Yes, two dogs. Where are your father and mother? Your sisters and brothers? Where are your kinsmen, child?"

"Dog."

"Where is your mother?"

"Dog."

The soldiers had gathered to enjoy the spectacle. The sergeant grunted. "Certain it is! That child likely had a bitch for a mother!"

His men chortled at his wit.

The child's face pinched. His lips trembled, and he drew in breath for a cry.

"Hush," said Alain, although it was difficult not to speak in an angry tone that would frighten the child. Without standing, he turned to frown at the sergeant. "What sport is there, I pray you, in teasing a creature as helpless as this one is? Had you orders to drive off these poor folk?"

"These poor folk! You're not from hereabouts, are you? They say all manner of people have taken to the roads since last autumn. It's a sign of the end of times."

"Is it?"

"These poor folk! Swindlers and beggars and whores and thieves and murderers, each one of them. We had to drive them out of Autun because they made so much trouble. Now they camp here and trouble honest travelers on the road and honest farmers in the fields. That brat is the bastard of some bitch who sold herself to any man who would pay. No one will miss him. Look!"

The sergeant's gesture encompassed the entire squalid encampment, now burning. Beyond, Alain saw a flash of movement out among the trees. Someone was watching from a hiding place.

"Maybe he's got no mother. Maybe she died. No one wanted him. They just left him here. What will you do with a filthy creature like that who has no kinfolk to take care of him? He's better off dead. Can you say otherwise?"

"Do you mean to take God's place and judge the worth of the soul of another human creature? We are all equal in the sight of God."

"Are you a frater? With that beard? What matter, anyway? Who has bread for an orphan child? I don't."

"What of the lady who rules in Autun? Doesn't she feed the poor, as is her duty?"

The sergeant's amused expression soured. He beckoned to his men. "Let's go. We've driven them out."

"For today," said Alain. "Won't they come back? Where else have they to go?"

The sergeant turned his attention elsewhere. "What about you?" he said, indicating Atto. "Why didn't you run?"

"I'm nothing to do with the ones who were camping here," said Atto. Mara huddled beside him. "I come from my village to join the milites in Autun. I heard the lady seeks soldiers."

"Hoo! Ho!" Some of the soldiers jeered. "A country boy come to swing his spear in the town!"

Flames eating through a heaped mattress of dry leaf litter caught in a length of canvas and blazed. Elsewhere, fires ebbed down to glow as they lost hold of good fuel.

"We share and share alike," said the sergeant. "How about your girl? Or is she your sister?"

"My betrothed," Atto said, measuring the look in their eyes and, by the expression in his own, not liking it.

The sergeant marked the hounds, who sat, and Alain, who knelt beside the silent boy. He marked the shadows out in the far trees, but it was obvious from his expression that he had no intention of striking into the woods although it would be easy to do so.

"I like the way you stand up for yourself," he said to Atto. "Can you ride?"

"I've ridden donkeys. We have no horses in my village. I'll learn."

"Maybe." The sergeant examined Mara, who shrank closer to Atto's side. "You rode that girl, I see. Come on, then. If the captain will take you, maybe he'll set you up in the guard. They need men to police the streets and man the gates. Lots of beggars these days causing trouble when we don't have enough food for those who deserve it." He lifted his chin defiantly as he looked at Alain, as if daring him to contradict his judgment, but Alain only watched him, waiting to see what he would do next. He gestured, and his men fell into ranks for the ride back.

"Where do they come from?" Alain asked, rising. The hounds looked at him but did not move.

"My soldiers? Autun. Villages nearby. From the lady's estates, and elsewhere."

"I meant the beggars causing your lady so much trouble."

The sergeant raised a hand to command his men, and led them off at a walk. Atto and Mara abandoned Alain without a word, although Mara glanced back at him and seemed, perhaps, to be crying. But she made no protest.

He had not, in truth, come to like Atto as the three of them had walked the road together these past few days, and although he pitied Mara he could not manage to respect her, even if he was sorry to find himself so hardhearted toward a person as anxious as she was. So it was that, scolding another man for being judgmental, he had already succumbed to the same fault himself.

Once the patrol was out of sight, Alain rose slowly so as not to frighten the boy and with his knife cut into the bottom portion of his cloak and ripped off a length of fabric. He had just tied this garment around the boy's scrawny shoulders when the first figure ghosted back into the clearing, clutching a stout stick and a precious bronze bucket dented on one side as if by the kick of a horse. They came in pairs and trios and now and again as a single form clutching a precious bundle, or a cracked bowl, or a ragged handkerchief knotted around an unseen prize. They scavenged through the camp pretending to take no notice of Alain and the boy and the hounds, looking once and not again, as if by ignoring the stranger he would vanish. They took what they could carry. They looked like scarecrows, awkward, pale, ridiculous except for the desperation visible in their scuttling walks, their pinched shoulders and lowered heads, their sharp gestures and the way their gazes darted toward the road and the trees at each snap or thump or whisper of branches when the breeze gusted into a moment of real wind. The boy took no interest whatsoever in the people among whom he had been living. He kept staring at the hounds.

"Where are you from?" Alain asked finally, wondering if anyone would answer.

His voice, not loud, sounded as a crack of thunder might on a sultry day. Most of the refugees scattered into the woods. Where they meant to go he could not imagine.

There was one bolder than the rest, a man whose age was impossible to guess because he was missing most of his teeth and was so thin his face had sunken in like that of an ancient tottering elder. His skin was weathered. His hair was matted with dirt and therefore colorless, tied back with a supple green twig to keep it out of his eyes.

"Better not to go to Autun," the man said. "Honest folk lose their homes there. Beggars are beaten on the streets and tossed out the gates."

"Are you from Autun?"

"I am."

"Now you hide here in the woods. Why is that?"

"Driven out, when the milites needed places to barrack troops." He spoke in a level voice, as about the weather. Whatever outrage or grief he felt remained hidden. He looked too weary and weak to shout or cry. "We've nowhere else to go, so we camp here." He gestured, indicating the filthy campsite.

"Has the lady of Autun no barracks in her palace for troops?"

"Not for so many as serve her now."

"Why needs she so many soldiers?"

He flicked a fly off his arm and sank down into a squat. He was so thin that he looked likely to topple over if the wind came up. "How would I know?"

"You might guess. You might see things, and come to your own conclusions."

He blew his nose and wiped mucus away with a forearm already streaked with unnameable substances. "I might. She fears some will take from her the duchy as they did before. Her Wendish brother took it from her. I saw that, I did." He tapped himself on the chest. His ribs showed like bare twigs, his chest was sunken, yet he squared his shoulders a little, proud of what he remembered and what he had worked out, a common man never privy to the plotting and planning of his noble rulers. "Now she's gathering soldiers to fight, she and that one they call Conrad the Black. I've seen him, too. Him and his lady wife, the one they call our queen."

The one they call our queen.

There, in his heart, Alain felt the tremor, the pain of the affection and loyalty he had offered her which she had rejected. She had turned on him twice over. She had tried to kill him.

But the memory was only that. It no longer had purchase. It no longer dug deep. He was sorry for it, that was all, that folk caused pain because of their own fears. He was angry because folk did do so much damage to the innocent and guilty alike because of their own fears. On his own account, he was free of the burden of desiring revenge. That gave him a measure of strength.

"Lady Sabella. Conrad the Black. Tallia. Who do they mean to fight?"

The man shrugged. "How am I to know the comings and goings of the great nobles?"

"Why must they cast out the innocent folk who lived honestly in Autun, such as you and these others?"

The man said nothing. A rattle of illness sang in each of his exhaled breaths from a rot settled into his lungs. The child sat unmoving, fixated on the hounds, and that one word slipped again from him.

"Dog."

The hounds waited patiently, heads lifted as they sniffed the air. Out in the woods he heard the rustle and snap of movement, but no one joined them in the clearing. After a while Alain realized he would receive no answer.

"What of this child? Where are his kinfolk?"

The man picked at a scab below his lower lip. "Mother's dead. Has none else."

"None to take charge of him?"

A shake of the head gave him his reply.

"Who cared for him?"

"None cared. He ate what scraps he could reach. He'll be dead in a few days more."

"If none among you cared whether this child lived or died, then truly it's as if you have turned your back on humankind. We must be compassionate and look each after the other."

"There's not food enough for all." The man gestured with an elbow. "You've somewhat in your sack. Do you mean to share it or keep it to yourself?"

"I've bones for my hounds, nothing more. I've myself not eaten since this morning."

"I'd eat what I could gnaw off a bone. I'm that hungry. I beg you."

Over the last few days he had fed all but two of the bones from the dead deer to Sorrow and Rage. Alain rose and, crossing the clearing, gave one of these to the man. The strip of flesh and fat and tendon still attached gave off the odor of meat that is turning bad. The man grabbed it out of his hand, grunting and slobbering in his haste to choke down what he could. As he ate, half a dozen ragged souls crept out of the woods with gazes fixed on Alain as on a gold talisman held dangling before avaricious eyes.

"Please, please," they said.

The boy braced himself on his stick arms and, panting and snuffling, dragged himself toward Alain. His legs trailed after him, and now it was possible to see both had been broken and healed askew, so he couldn't use them. Alain scanned the clearing. A trio of men crept up behind him and a woman approached with a stout stick raised in one hand.

"Told you," said the man with the bone. "Best give us the rest of it and your cloak and clothes if you want to walk out alive."

Desperate men cannot be shamed.

Rage and Sorrow rose, growling. Alain hoisted his staff.

"You may choose now," he said clearly. "I do not want to fight you, but I will not be robbed."

"If you will be merciful, then give us all you own for we need it, I pray you, master!" called the woman with the stout stick. She was so thin and ill looking that at first glance a decent person would pity her, yet she crept forward with lips pulled back in a rictus grin that was no smile.

Best to move swiftly.

He whistled. The hounds loped toward him, and once they moved the folk scattered back, fearing those teeth. He grabbed the little boy and hoisted him up and over his back, and with Sorrow and Rage at either side strode into the forest. All the way through the woodland he heard them shadowing him to either side, waiting for an opening, but none came; the hounds were vigilant.

The child said, "Dog. Dog."

He reeked, the poor thing, and as they came out of the woods and to the open fields striping the land around the distant walls, he peed. Warm liquid trickled down Alain's side. There wasn't much urine in the child, but the scent of it stung. Rage barked, swinging his head around to sniff Alain's hip.

Out here farmers ploughed, although it was late in the season for such work. A pair of soldiers patrolled on horseback. They cantered over, looking him up and down while circling clear of the hounds. The younger was a freckled lad about sixteen and with a tentative grip on his spear. His companion looked tougher, twice his age, with darker hair and a scaly patch of skin on one cheek that had been scratched until it bled.

"Who are you?" the elder asked. "What's your business in Autun?" He indicated the child with the blade of his spear. "Beggars not allowed in Autun. Go elsewhere."

"I found this child abandoned in the woods. Has the biscop no foundling home? Is there no monastery nearby that takes in orphans?"

"I don't know," said the man, "but not likely, I'd say. Haven't grain enough to feed the lady's household and her army. Certain there isn't spare for a dirty crippled brat like that one. See you there, Jochim," he said to the lad, "see his twisted legs."

"He's crippled," said the lad brightly.

"So he is, but was he born with the twisted legs? Or did his mam or uncle gave it a twist so as folk would pity him and give bread and coin?"

"Nay." The lad shook his head. "Nay, no mam would do that. Would she?"

"Some might. Or a handsome uncle, like this one who carries him. Look at his decent clothes, who leaves a babe wrapped in only a bit of torn cloth. He found a babe forgot in the woods? I know what lurks in the woods. All those driven out of town by my lady's order. Thieves and whores and murderers. Nay, fellow." He lowered his spear to block the path. In the distance a pair of farmers looked their way. "We want none of your kind in our town."

"His cloak is shorn off," said the lad. "See? That's what the babe is wearing. Why would he tear his own cloak, if it's true he cares nothing for the babe but only his own comfort? He could buy a rag from a peddler for nothing and save the cloak."

"Dog," said the child.

"Unless he were kicked out of town and the babe's rag lost in the wood."

Alain sighed. "I'm no beggar. If you'll tell me where I can find a foundling home, I'll take this child there."

They shrugged. The youth seemed eager to depart. The elder lingered. "Don't matter whether I believe you or think you're lying. You can't enter the city with that beg-ging child. Everyone can see he's a beggar's child. No en-trance."

"Are there no poor sitting in the lady's hall, fed by her stewards?" asked Alain. "Can it be she has forgotten the ancient custom? Did not King Henry feed a dozen beggars every day off his very own table?"

The elder spat. "Get on. Speak not of Henry, the usurper. Well! He's gone now. Some say he's dead."

"Did he so?" asked the youth. "A dozen beggars, every day?"

"Or more, on feast days," said Alain, standing his ground.

"How do you know?" demanded the elder. "How could a man such as you know? How could you have stood in the hall where noble folk took their supper?"

"I was a Lion, once." And more besides, but he would not speak of those days to this man.

"A Lion!" The youth whistled appreciatively, with a look of respect. "A Lion! They take some tough fighting, it's said. Duke Conrad takes in any Lions that come this way. Strays, like."

The gaze of the older soldier had shifted in an intangible way. "Were you now? Seen any fighting? Ever kill a man?"

Weary, Alain met his gaze. "I have seen fighting. I killed a man." One who was already dying.

"Huh. I believe you. Huh." He glanced toward the town walls where twin banners curled limply at the height of the tower, concealing their sigils. The clouds moved sluggishly overhead, although it often seemed to Alain that they did not move at all, not anymore. "The lady needs soldiers. There's a bed and a meal every day if you join up with her. Interested?"

"What of the child?"

"Is he some kinsman of yours?"

"I found him abandoned in the woods, just as I said."

"Then why burden yourself with him? Look at him! That child's half dead, crippled, useless. Can it even speak?"

"Dog," said the babe.

"Dog!" snorted the youth. "A good name, don't you

think? We could clean him up and take him in the barracks as a mascot, Calos. Put him up on a chair by the door and teach him to say 'dog' every time one of Captain Alfonse's Salian braggarts comes past."

Calos choked down a laugh, but it was easy to see the notion amused him.

"The lady has Salian soldiers in her retinue?" Alain asked.

"Oh, plenty of them, the cursed snails!" said the youth with the good humor of a man who has suffered no real harm from disparaging his comrades. "Foul-tempered and gluttonous. They come with that Salian lord who is one of my lady's commanders but I don't recall his name. Lots of Salians. They've got no king now. All at each other's throats, so it's said. No wonder they come east, these ones. It's safer here."

"It wasn't for those driven out into the woods," said Alain, waving an arm back the way he had come.

"They brought their own trouble down on them," said Calos with a sneer. "What of the little lad? I'm liking this idea of Jochim's the more I think on it. Up their craw, and them not daring to hurt a tiny babe so crippled as this one is."

"Would you treat a dog so?" Alain asked, angered by their suggestion.

"We treat our dogs well!" retorted Calos indignantly. "What do you take us for? Any dog we take in, we treat well. Train it. Feed it."

"You'd treat this child as nothing more than that?"

Calos shook his head. "What are you thinking, friend?" he said, with a tilted smile and a narrowed gaze, as if he were scolding Alain or laughing at his naivety. "This poor child has never in his life been treated as well as us troopers under the command of Captain Lukas treat our good dogs. I'll swear to you he'll do as well. Better than he's done. We need a laugh in our barracks."

"What happens to the child when you go home to your villages?"

Both of them laughed, but the laughter concealed pain.

"I was born in town," said Calos. "The lady's service is

my life, friend. As for Jochim here, he's got no village to go back to. Flooded out, it was, when the river went running backward last autumn. His whole family died in them floods and most of the other folk in the place likewise. The rest had to beg in the lanes and I suppose most of them died over the winter and early spring. He's lucky to get a meal every day and a bed to sleep in. He's lucky we took him in, seeing him a likely soldier. So will you be—lucky if we take you in. Or haven't you heard? Times are hard. If these frosts don't lift, if the sun don't come, if the crops don't grow, they'll get worse. Much worse."

"I pray you," whispered young Jochim, wiping a tear from his eye. "Don't speak such ill words. The Enemy hears us."

"Are you coming?" asked Calos. "Can we adopt the little lad?"

He wasn't afraid to meet Alain's gaze, dead on, searching as much as he was searched. An honest man, of his kind, not compassionate but not cruel either; he meant what he said. He did his job, and was loyal to those he had pledged his loyalty to. Maybe he was right about the child. Maybe the most a beggar's crippled and abandoned orphan son could hope for in these days was to be treated as well as a well-kept dog.

2

CAPTAIN Lukas was a hard-living man who found the idea of a child mascot who could only say the word "dog" just as amusing as did his soldiers. That he hated the Salian interlopers need not be spoken out loud. The locals in Autun had always hated the Salians. It was in their blood. That the beloved Emperor Taillefer had been himself a Salian, had been emperor of Salia and Varre and much more land besides, and had built his famous chapel and palace in Autun and ruled from here as much as he ruled from any one place, was beside the point. That he had chosen to be buried here just went to show that Taillefer wasn't a Salian, not really. He'd been born on an estate in what was now Varingia, so the story went, so he was really of Varre and that meant that Varre had once conquered Salia, not the other way around.

"I like it," said the captain, laughing with his sergeants as Calos and Jochim looked on. He slapped his thigh. "Yes! Best keep him well fed, though, and get the dogs to guard him, so we can say he's just speaking to them. All innocent!"

Alain didn't like it, but he understood he had no viable alternative. The world could not be changed in one day or one year and it was possible it could not be changed at all. It was just possible that this trivial and even selfish act of kindness toward a crippled, illegitimate orphan outweighed a hundred more apparently momentous acts involving the great and powerful of the land. Dog, as they were all calling the boy now, was sitting in a corner slurping down porridge and had shown no fear in the barracks with men coming and going and talking in loud voices, jostling, coughing, laughing, and singing out crude jokes.

"Someone has got to wash him," added the captain. "Calos, you take care of it, as you brought him in."

"Jochim, you take care of it," said Calos. "What of this man, who says he was a Lion?" He gestured toward Alain, who stood quietly to one side.

"Let me see those dogs you say come with him," said Captain Lukas, and he strolled with exaggerated casualness over to the door and squinted along the porch. Sorrow and Rage regarded him with their dark eyes. When they saw Alain, they thumped their tails on the plank sidewalk but did not otherwise move.

The captain looked at those dogs for a long time. Then he looked at Alain. The captain recognized him. Alain saw it in the smile trapped on his lips, in the way he scratched at his forehead to give himself something to do while he considered, in the way he tapped a foot three times on the porch as he reached a conclusion.

"Best we go see the lady," he said to the air. He turned back to beckon his sergeants closer. "I'll need a dozen men. Sergeant Andros, you are in charge here while I'm gone."

"There's to be a sweep of the southwest quarter this afternoon, Captain."

"Proceed as usual."

"Yes, Captain."

"If you will." The captain indicated to Alain that they would walk together. "Surely you have come here in order to see Lady Sabella." Without allowing Alain a chance to answer, he began issuing orders to the dozen men hurrying out to accompany them.

They stood in the dusty forecourt of what had once been a merchant's warehouse complex but was now both barracks and stable. There were two long warehouses linked at their northern ends by a spacious hall. An open kitchen and small storage sheds fenced in the southern end of the compound. The men lived in one half of the hall, their horses in the other. There were three troops quartered here, one in each structure, about three hundred men in all if Alain's estimate of the size of Captain Lukas' troop was correct. Men lounged by the open doors of their living space keeping an eye on the comings and goings of the other soldiers, friends and rivals alike. Dogs slunk along at the base of each porch, looking for scraps of food or a friendly pat. They kept clear of Sorrow and Rage, but a rare bold bitch ventured up and sniffed them over. A cart laden with manure trundled past, pushed by a pair of soldiers headed out to the fields. The open dirt yard stank of sweat and shit and urine and dust and that peculiar intangible scent of men sizing each other up for weakness. A pair of men were joking in loud voices.

"Eh, those Varre boars! Look, there goes the ass-licking captain now!"

Alain glanced at the captain, but he took no mind of the words. In fact, Captain Lukas seemed not to have understood them at all. As if they were speaking in a language he could not understand, but one that Alain could. The swirl of movement, of men going about their business and dogs hanging back to allow the hounds to pass without challenging them and a horse backing nervously away from the entrance into the stables, so disoriented Alain that he felt the world spinning around him. He staggered and reached out to catch himself

they skate into Rikin Fjord across a skin of still water so clear that he dreams he can see fathoms into the deeps, down to the ancient seabed carved aeons ago out of glittering rock. But that is only an illusion. What he sees are the backs of a swarm of fish schooling around his hull.

One surfaces.

No fish, these, but an entire tribe of merfolk. He leans on the rail, studying them. On deck, soldiers exclaim. Always, as they crossed the northern sea, they sailed with an escort of merfolk off their bow and behind the stern. These here, he thinks, are more like a ravening pack of wolves descending on a slaughter ground.

"Beware!" calls Deacon Ursuline, among his counselors.

Papa Otto calls from the stern. "A swarm has gathered here. I don't like the look of these! I think they mean to do us harm!"

As if the words are sorcery, the boat heels starboard. His heels skid backward and he grabs the rail to stop himself from falling onto the deck, but just as he gets his feet up and under him, the ship heels again, seesawing to port side so abruptly that he cannot stop himself. He pitches forward, loses his hold on the railing, and plunges into the cold blue water of the fjord.

Icy water splashed his face as he caught himself on a hitching post, finding his balance although the ground still seemed to tilt and rock.

Captain Lukas swore. "Bitch of a weather! Feel that rain! You'd think it was still winter, by how cold it is!"

Alain blinked rain out of his eyes and shook his head to clear it. The shower had taken them all by surprise as it swept across the courtyard. Dogs and men ran for shelter. The captain laughed and shamed his men into moving more slowly.

"What? Are you running at the first cold drop? What, are you prissy snails?"

The vision, come so fast and unexpectedly, faded as the

sights and smells of the compound drowned him. They
passed between the kitchens, which smelled of porridge
and smoke, and a storehouse, whose door was propped
open. Inside, a score of folk huddled in the interior around
a cluster of beds, sitting, lying down, coughing: a sickroom,
perhaps. A child at the door watched them walk by with
wide eyes and a somber expression.

"You've been on the road too many days," said the captain.
"The lady does not like the smell of the road. Baths first."

"Can I take the plunge, Captain?" asked one of the escorts.

"Eh! I'd like a good washing, Captain!" said another.

"There's some new wash girls at the baths, I hear,"
laughed a third. "Not like in the old days, if you take my
meaning. More to our liking."

"Hush," Captain Lukas said, but he wasn't angry at his
men. If anything, the comments caused him to lapse into a
thoughtful silence.

These barracks lay near the southern gate and were not
particularly close to the palace complex, which sat on a hill.
The streets had little traffic considering the time of day.
Twice they passed warehouses, each one guarded by a
dozen soldiers.

"What do they guard?" Alain asked.

"Grain. As precious as gold."

A few folk tended garden spaces in empty lots. Autun
had not quite filled out the space between the walls built in
the days of Taillefer, or else old buildings had fallen down
and not been reconstructed, with the dirt around the foundations left to go to seed. A woman and man straightened
from poking at freshly dug troughs to watch the soldiers
pass. Like the child at the storehouse door, they called out
no greeting, nor did the captain nod at them to acknowledge their presence. Their silence troubled Alain, who had
an idea that relations between townsfolk and soldiers had
once been easier.

The baths lay at the base of the palatine hill. The origi-
nal structure was built by the old Dariyans, but it had been
refurbished a hundred years ago and had not deteriorated
overly much since then. Sorrow and Rage sat under a por-

tico with a pair of nervous minders to guard them. Within
the stone halls a pair of old women held sway, although it
was true they were assisted by a quintet of younger, fairer
lasses, banished to the back chambers as soon as the soldiers came in.

"This one," said Captain Lukas, pushing Alain forward.
"I'll be back to fetch him."

They took him to a room where he stripped. The attendants examined him with the look of women who have
seen every possible thing the world has to offer. They even
pinched his buttocks and measured the span of his arms
with cupped hands.

"Pleasing enough," the taller commented to the shorter
in a murmur he was not meant to hear. "Too thin."

"Aren't they all these days?"

His clothes were taken away and two buckets of water
brought by a gangling youth, who retreated as soon as he
set the buckets on the stone floor.

"Raise your arms!" said the old woman.

Obedient, he raised his arms.

"Shut your eyes!"

He shut his eyes.

*The water hits so hard he thinks his heart will seize. The
cold sluices down his face, his neck. He is wet through in an
instant and so cold he goes stiff, lips locked in a grimace,
limbs in a rictus.*

How can anything be so cold?

*Then he remembers that cold causes him no injury, not as
it does humankind. He is drowning in his vision. He must
open his eyes, and quickly. Why did the ship surge in the
waves so suddenly?*

*He opens his eyes as the water streams past, as a weight
nudges him, then pushes, hard, and he flails through the
water trying to get his bearings so he can reach the surface.*

He is surrounded by merfolk.

They are circling, as for a kill.

They mean to kill him.

"Why?" asked the taller crone sarcastically. "*Why?* You
don't think we're letting you get in the baths as filthy as
you are? You wash that dirt off first. Then you can soak."

"So cold!" he said between gritted teeth. Goose bumps had erupted all over his skin, but he could not tell if it were the cold water or the upwelling of fear that made him shiver uncontrollably.

"We should heat it up for you? Well, if you'd split the wood and paid for it before-times, maybe we'd consider it!"

"Don't curse your fortune, young man. You're one of the lucky ones!"

They were both old and spry, well enough fed by the evidence of their plump cheeks and ample hips, cheerful enough to be amused by him but nevertheless watchful, glancing at frequent intervals toward the door as if expecting someone to come charging in. They went on chattering, and the flood of words calmed his trembling.

"Getting a bath at all! Used to be under the rule of Biscop Constance that the common folk in town might pay a sceatta for use of the baths on Hefensdays, Secundays, and Jeddays, but not now. Reserved for the lady's noble entourage and her captains."

"Will you stop it?" said the other one in that same undertone. "If they throw us out of town for speaking sedition against the lady, my family will starve! You might speak, and I keep silence, and I'll be guilty same as you." She handed Alain a greasy lump of scouring soap. "Begging your pardon, my lord. We mean no harm by our whispering."

"I'm no lord," he said, taking the soap gratefully, "and I thank you for your trouble." He scrubbed. He was not as dirty as he might have been, not nearly as filthy as he had once been, but it felt good to feel the dirt loosen and come free.

They chortled, as if he had made a joke. The taller one left. The shorter swept water into the drain as he washed his hair.

"All done?"

He braced himself for the deluge. The water hit.

Ice. Gasping. The air leaves his lungs and bubbles to the surface. A shape looms out of the water, so close that those teeth seem about to close over his face. He finds his knife and draws it, but it catches in folds of his trousers.

"Too late," whispers the merman, and it is strange he can

speak underwater in words Stronghand can understand. "It is too late for you, Stronghand. Now I am the victor, although you won at Kjalmarsfjord."

It is strange that he speaks with the voice of Nokvi, Stronghand's last rival among the Eika.

Gasping, he flailed.

"Hey, now! Hey!" said the attendant. She poked him in the ribs with the end of her broom, and the jab got him coughing. "If you're going to be violent, I'm calling the guards!"

"No, I beg your pardon. I just—" There was nothing he could say.

Nokvi, Stronghand's last rival for the overlordship of the Eika, was dead. Stronghand had himself struck the killing blow and pushed Nokvi overboard into the grasp of the merfolk. That battle at Kjalmarsfjord Alain had fought in between breaths as he had himself fought on the hill with the doomed Lions by Queen's Grave, when he had at the last been cut down and killed by the Lady of Battles. How was it that Nokvi spoke out of the depths?

"Yes," said the crone, amused now that she saw Alain would not act rashly, "it strikes all the healthy young men so, bawling like babes when the cold water hits them. On you go, to the hot baths."

She prodded him with the broom, the straw bristles harsh on the tender skin of his buttocks, and he yelped—and she chuckled—as he hurried into the next chamber. This vaulted stone chamber was taken up with a tiled bath smelling of mineral salts. Steam rose from vents in the floor. He stepped in, sitting straight down onto a shelf resting a torso's height below the surface, but the intense heat took him by surprise. A wave of faintness swelled up into his head as might a surge in the sea, and he sank

water pouring over his face. This time will it be the end?

No.

Never.

Not this way.

He means to die peacefully in his bed, not taken by surprise in this ignominious manner by a vanquished enemy who is dead. Whom he killed.

It is only a merman, smarter than a dog and not as intel-

ligent as a man. Nevertheless, a furious merman bent on revenge while his enemy drowns in the water remains a formidable opponent.

As the creature dives in for the kill, Stronghand rolls in the water and kicks, connecting with the torso of the merman. The move is sluggish, the reaction oddly muted, because the water causes all movement to become slow and ungainly—for humankind. The merfolk have no such restriction. The sea is their element, just as rock and fire and air are his.

There are a dozen mermen, or a hundred. He cannot see into the depths. Hulls block the light. Another Eika flails in the water nearby, trying not to sink, but that brother remains untouched as the merfolk swarm around Stronghand. In another moment Stronghand will black out and inhale seawater, and he will sink and drown. They will devour him, as they devoured all the others thrown into the sea. That was the bargain, made long ago.

Why would they desire man flesh and Eika flesh when there are, after all, so many fish in the sea?

The knife has twisted free of his trousers. He kicks upward and plunges it into the side of the merman, using the flesh of the merman as leverage to launch himself to the surface while his victim thrashes and others close in to feast on blood and entrails.

A hand grips his ankle. Teeth sink into the flesh of his calf. He breaks the surface, coughs and splutters, sucks in air

Alain gulped in a mouthful of water. Thrashing, he found himself underwater

but too late. The water closes back over his face as he is dragged down by the leg. Harder than iron are the teeth of the merfolk, able to pierce easily the skin of the Rock-Children. He has lost his knife, but he has other weapons.

His claws, unsheathed, rake through the writhing hair of the creature that has fastened onto him. Like eels severed in half they squirm through water now clouded by sheets of blood rising off the one that spoke in the voice of Nokvi. His leg is released. He swims up and breaches the surface again just as a hand gropes in his hair, grips, yanks, and drags him onto the ship

The pain of being tugged up by his hair washed all other thoughts out of his head. He yelped and, all at once, heard the hounds barking madly and the sound of men swearing and shouting in alarm.

"What are you doing?" cried the crone. "Trying to drown yerself?"

A closer shriek startled her. She released his hair and turned, then yelled in fear. He was still gulping for air. He barely had time to register the clippity of nails on stone, the big shapes coming at a run, and they jumped and with a mighty splash shuddered the entire bath.

After that, the uproar erupted like battle with folk running in to stare, or roar, or laugh, or shriek complaints, each according to his or her nature. Alain could not help but laugh to see Sorrow and Rage swim to the lip of the bath, but they could not climb out and so he had to swim over to shove them, with great difficulty, out of the water. They sneezed, and shook themselves in a cascade of droplets, and sneezed again, disgusted with the taste and heat.

"Out! Out!" cried the taller crone, and the shorter one traded her broom for a many-tined rake to try to get dog hair out of the water. So much shed in so short a time!

Alain scraped his knee climbing out and was not even given a scrap of cloth to dry himself with before Captain Lukas yelled at him to hurry up, although the captain kept a safe distance. The hounds yawned hugely, displaying their teeth.

So they proceeded with Alain damp and dressed in a spare wool tunic furnished by an unknown donor; it smelled of dried cod. He wore his own worn sandals and, under the tunic, the loose linen shirt packed by Aunt Bel that he had so far kept clean. He walked without protest, climbing the steep stairs that led to the palace. A spitting rain started up, but a roof covered the stairs all the way up the hill; no sense in the emperor getting wet on his way to or from the baths. Stone pillars supported the timber roof. There were no walls. As they climbed, the town opened up before them, alleys and courtyards and cisterns coming into view below in an orderly layout whose bones reminded the educated man that Autun had begun its days centuries ago as a Dariyan fort. Square, orderly, explicable. His thoughts, in contrast, churned like the disturbed waters of Rikin Fjord, still flashing in remembered bursts of vision before his sight.

Gasping, he spits out seawater and turns to confront his rescuer. It is Papa Otto who has grabbed him and hauled him free, while his Eika brothers thrust with spears at the swarming mermen in the water. Now that he is clear of the waters, the attack breaks off. The Eika brother swims, unmolested, to the third ship and is hoisted aboard.

He passed pillars carved in the likenesses of magnificent beasts: a phoenix, a guivre, a dragon. A noble griffin, staring at him with painted sea-blue eyes. A wolf, an eagle, and a proud lion.

The blue waters roil as a second swarm of merfolk surge into the fjord in the wake of Stronghand's ships. They circle the tiny fleet before diving into the abyss. Are they warring, one faction against the other? It is impossible to pierce the depths, now clouded and hazy like the heavens but with a darker veil of streaming blood released by battle joined below.

Stronghand stands at the stem of the ship staring down in the waters, but he can see nothing and he has only questions. His leg bleeds, the pale blood dripping onto the deck and diluted by the skin of salt water slipping back and forth over the planks with each slight pitch of the ship as it glides into the sound.

He calls to Papa Otto. "You saved me," he says. "How can I reward you?"

The man shakes his head. "My lord." He says nothing more.

"What do you want? You were a slave once. Now you speak on my council. What do you want?"

"My lord," says the man, trembling now, and it is evident that some strong emotion has overcome him. He will not speak. He cannot.

"Well, then, Otto. When you know, you must tell me. You have earned a reward this day."

"Yes, my lord," the man says obediently, but he weeps, as humans do when their emotions overwhelm them. And de-

spite everything, Stronghand still does not truly understand them.

From ahead, he smells the fires of home. A faint hum raises the hair on the back of his neck. His dogs yip.

OldMother is waiting for him.

"She's at prayer," said a guardsman to Captain Lukas.

Alain shook himself to a halt just before he slammed into the captain's broad back. Lukas had stopped at the top of the stairs, below a gate carved with Dariyan rosettes. Beyond lay the remembered courtyard, lined on one side by a stone colonnade and on the other, just to their left, by a stone rampart that opened onto a spectacular view of the town below, although from this angle Alain saw only one corner of the cathedral tower. The graveled courtyard had recently been raked and tidied. Opposite stood the famous octagonal chapel with its proud stone buttresses. He heard hymnal singing and, from farther away and therefore harder to place by direction, male laughter.

"An odd time to be praying," commented the captain, "unless you're the queen."

The guardsman and Lukas were clearly old friends, and indeed the other man wore the badge of a captain as a clasp for his cloak. "True enough." He chuckled and said, with a smirk, "Praying in thanksgiving, the lady is. The queen gave birth at dawn."

"Is that so?" asked Captain Lukas, eyes widening as he leaned toward his comrade. "Girl or boy?"

"A lad, wouldn't you know it? It'll be proclaimed in three days if the mite survives that long. The other two didn't."

"Yes, I recall it, but the older girl seems likely to stick. Still." He glanced around to make sure none of the other guards could overhear, and leaned closer. "Still. How is the duke taking it?"

"Look there," said the other guard, pointing back down the stairs. "Here he comes. He went out hunting."

The stairs wound down the slope, switching back several times, and because they were sheltered under a roof, with no walls, it was difficult to see the procession the guardsman alluded to, but the lively clatter of their progress drifted on the breeze. The hounds had their ears up and were looking that way with interest.

"What are these great beasts?" added the guard, extending a hand toward Sorrow. "Here, boy. Are you the friendly one? You're a big one, aren't you?"

Sorrow gave a warning growl, ears flattening, and the guardsman withdrew his hand. "I've seen the like of these beasts before, but I can't recall where. You'd think a man would never forget such monsters!"

"Come on," said Captain Lukas, beckoning to his men who were, after all, waiting on the stairs in the path of the approaching company. "Move along to the chapel, but keep at the back, and make sure you're quiet." He nodded at Alain. "The lady won't mind it if the hounds rest just inside the door. She often brings her coursers with her, as does the duke. His alaunts and whippets are usually with him. Will they fight with other dogs?"

"Only if they're attacked."

The captain took him at his word. It was a rare man who did not know his dogs well enough to understand and predict their behavior, and such dogs would never have sat still for long stretches; they would have been off and sniffing and snuffling into every crook and cranny they could find no matter how furiously their master called them back. Most folk did not have time for ill-trained dogs, and certainly would not go to the trouble to feed them.

A number of soldiers loitered under the colonnade, watching with interest but without initiative.

"There are many soldiers here in Autun," remarked Alain.

"Truly," agreed Captain Lukas good-naturedly as they crossed the gravel, footsteps shifting and grinding on the rocks. "More soldiers than commoners, it's said."

"How are the soldiers all fed?"

"Taxes. Tithes." He shrugged. "The lady takes what she needs. It's to the benefit of all to be protected."

"What if there's a poor harvest this year? It seems likely, doesn't it? So cold as it is still that folk can't risk planting for fear a late frost will kill the seedlings."

"That's not my concern."

"It might become so, if the lady can't feed her soldiers."

"She'll not turn us out. War's coming. Perhaps you haven't heard."

"Coming from where?"

"They say the Wendish mean to drag us back though we've no wish to cower under the yoke of the Wendish regnant. Not anymore. Not now we have a queen of our own."

To think of Tallia no longer hurt him. They entered the chapel and took a place at the back, under the ambulatory where the other servants and hangers-on waited.

This was prayer, of a kind. Lady Sabella knelt on a thick pillow, her chin resting on a fist. She stared not at the altar where a cleric intoned psalms but at the stone effigy of Taillefer. After a moment she leaned to her right to murmur to an attendant, a youthful man with the burly shoulders of a fighter and hunter. A dozen noble companions surrounded her, and the buzzing murmur of their conversation provided an undertone to the pious prayers of the clerics.

Alain had stood inside the famous chapel before. There was something missing. Alternating blocks of light-and-dark stone gave a pattern to the eight vaults opening onto the central floor. Above, the dome swept into the heavens, ringed by a second and third tier of columns. So might the faithful rise toward heaven, the righteous yet higher above, painted onto the stony piers, until at last the bright and distant Chamber of Light far above could be touched by the angels.

The chapel had not changed. The tempest had not shaken it. But something really was missing, and he had to search the chapel a second time before he realized what it was.

The hands belonging to the stone effigy of Emperor Taillefer were empty. The crown of stars was gone. The stone figure clutched at air. The sight struck Alain so strangely that he smiled. So often we grasp at the very thing we cannot keep hold of, and even after we have lost it, our life is shaped by that wish and the action of grasping. So it is with those who, like stone, are carved into an unchanging form. We make ourselves into stone because we fear to change.

" 'How can I repay God for all that They have given me?' " sang the clerics. " 'I raise the cup of deliverance and speak my vows to God in the presence of all of Their people.' "

There came in a rush through the door a pack of hearty, laughing, chattering men still sweaty and dirt-stained from their ride. Sabella looked up. Even the clerics faltered, turning to see, but one nudged another while a third put pressure on a fourth's foot, and so the service lurched forward despite the unseemly interruption.

Conrad the Black knelt beside Sabella, pulled a dry stalk of grass out of his beard, and crumbled it into dust between his fingers.

"News from the borderlands." Perhaps he was trying to keep his voice low in deference to the prayers of thanksgiving, but the acoustics of the hall magnified his speech so every soul in the ambulatory could hear him although he was not, in fact, shouting. "We've got control of the mines again, but I need workers. That Eika raid last year cleaned out the countryside. They've got a throat hold all along the coast and some ways down three of the rivers."

"Haven't you workers in Wayland?"

"The roads are worse there than here, what with the landslides and fallen trees from last autumn. Easier to march from Autun to the mines than from Bederbor to the mines, although it's a longer road from Autun."

Her fist had opened. Her stern and rather bored expression had altered to one of intense interest. "Then Salian workers."

"Raid into the nest of hornets? That's a poor use of my soldiers. I might need them at any time."

"Nay, nay," she said irritably, "I meant you to take as many as you like from among the refugees. That will get them off the roads and stop them from making themselves a nuisance. Round them up and drive them in a herd. There are folk in Autun, too—some we've already driven out, but others you may take as you wish. More than we need. Consult with my captains. Plenty of labor here for the mines. It will save us bread later."

"Yes," Conrad mused, "that will work. But it will still take a long time to get benefit from those mines."

"Better we control them than the Salians do. Better we control stores of precious metals against the coming battle."

"Will it come to battle?" he asked her. "If Mother Scholastica means to support our cause, then it need not come to battle."

"Do you fear the bastard?"

He snorted. "I am no fool. He's a strong commander. Call that fear if you want, Cousin. I call it prudence."

"Are you a dog unwilling to fight? I call that submitting."

"These are cheap tricks meant to goad me. I'll fight if I must, but not if the odds are against us."

"Shall we just hand Varre over," she asked sweetly, "and pray for our Wendish cousins to place their feet atop our backs while we wallow in the dirt? We might have everything, Conrad. Everything!"

He laughed curtly. "Then you lead the charge! If you're so eager."

"Do not speak disrespectfully to me!"

He glowered. He was flushed, hot, irritated. The clerics drew in breath and began a new psalm.

> *"I praise God, and God have answered me.*
> *God's love is steadfast.*
> *God's faithfulness is eternal."*

Rage whined, ears flattening, and swung her head around to stare at the door.

"You're right to be cautious," said Sabella, "nor do I mean to mock you, Conrad. But I believe that my aunt is sincere in her communication with us. If we are bold, and clever, then we will rule Varre *and* Wendar. Just as I ought to have done all along, since I am eldest child of Arnulf."

Conrad's companions had settled themselves wherever they could find room, blocking many of the lines of sight beneath the vaults, although Alain could still see Sabella, Conrad, and Taillefer's carved visage. Conrad was a good-looking man, powerfully built, tall, broad, muscular. He had a dark face and a trim black beard and mustache around mobile lips.

"What's this?" He looked toward the doors. "Good God!"

His expression darkened. He rose, hands set on hips as he frowned.

The commotion spilled into the gathered worshipers as wind disturbs an autumn meadow, turning leaves and scattering branches. Folk exclaimed. One, unseen, cried out in fear. There came stewards in bold red tabards pushing open a path and behind them a litter borne by four servingmen. Behind these staggered a weeping nurse with a bundle swaddled in white linen nestled in her arms.

"Tallia!" said Conrad.

"What are you doing?" Sabella extended a hand, and two of her companions leaped forward to help her stand.

Yet, after all, to see her pained him. It was not an agony, only a pinprick, like a point of pressure that bit until, just piercing the skin, it drew a bead of blood. He had forgiven her. He had grown beyond her and had loved and been loved by a woman worthy of all these things. But the innocent love he had once offered Tallia was still a part of him, and that part, betrayed, could not help but remember.

Tallia reclined on the litter, propped up on pillows. She was pale, as if she had lost a great deal of blood, but her skin had a shining gleam, still swollen taut with pregnancy's aftermath. She moaned, shifting uncomfortably. By the curve of her limbs traced by the drape of the fabric pulled tight, he saw that all trace of her ascetic's starvation had been obliterated. Someone had made her eat, and eat well. Her beautiful wheat-colored hair was slick with sweat, all in a tangle across her torso. She lifted her head.

"Pray!" she said in a low, tortured voice. "Pray for the child. Ai! It is too late."

Conrad struck the heel of his hand to his chest once, twice, and three times. "Ai, God! So I feared!" He wept, as a bereaved father should, and his companions wept with him.

"Bring it here!" ordered Sabella.

The nurse came hesitantly, but when she offered the child to Sabella, the noblewoman waved her away. "I can see! No need to touch it! Where is the midwife?"

No one knew.

"Hunt her down." Sabella snapped fingers, looked around, and caught sight of Captain Lukas at the back of the crowd. His height made him easy to mark among the mob. "Your hunt, Captain. See that you find her."

"Stay here," he said to Alain. He gathered his men and hurried out, leaving two men, one on either side of Alain. The hounds whined, forced up against the back wall by the press of more folk crowding in to see what was going on. Tallia's procession had attracted notice outside. Everyone was whispering.

Her shriek cut through the rumbling. "Ai! Ai! God save us!"

Lady Sabella turned to stare at her daughter. Conrad lifted his head in surprise. Tallia had pushed herself up on one elbow. With her other hand she pointed, forefinger extended, arm trembling. Her face was white, and her eyes flared in horror.

"A ghost!" she cried hoarsely. "A spirit, sent by the Enemy to haunt me!" She pointed at Alain, where he stood in the crowd. "Begone! Begone! You have no power over me!"

Conrad wiped away tears with the back of a hand. "What are you babbling about?"

Lady Sabella had seen, and understood. "What is this?" she asked as she smiled. Alain didn't like that smile, but he did not fear it. "Come forward. I recognize you. Lavastine's by-blow who tried to steal the county from Lord Geoffrey."

With the hounds at his heels, Alain walked forward. Folk shoved each other to get out of the way.

He did not kneel. "My lady," he said. "My lord duke." And, last, although the words came harder than he thought they would: "My lady Tallia."

She screamed, covered her eyes with her arm, and collapsed onto the pillows as in a faint. The litter rocked, and the servingmen carrying it lurched a few steps to steady themselves. In all that crowd, no one spoke. Silence weighed over the mute effigy of Taillefer. Silence lofted into the dome as if to strike the heavens themselves dumb.

"Yet here you are," added Sabella, "and I admit I'm interested to know where you came from and why you are here."

This close to the nurse, he saw the bluish-white features of a baby peeping out from under the linen wrappings. So still, without expression or any least sign of animation. Sorrow barked, and the nurse shrieked and skittered back, slamming into the tomb. She lost her grip on the infant. It tumbled out of her arms.

He lunged forward and

On the shore of Rikin Fjord the good, strong folk of Rikin Tribe wait to greet him. Here are Eika warriors grown too slow to sail the seas and fight in foreign lands but strong enough, still, to build and labor and fight in defense of their home. Here are the home troops, doing their duty to protect the fjord until they are given a chance to sail. Here are Deacon Ursuline's flock looking healthy and eager, crowding forward as they would never have done in the days when they were kept penned and mute.

"What have you brought us, Mother?" they call when they see the deacon.

"What gifts will enrich us, Deacon?" they ask her. "You must see what we have built in your absence!"

"Ask your lord what he has brought with him to enrich the tribe," she tells them, and they see him and fall silent, heads bowed respectfully. They fear him, too, but fear is no longer the only spear that drives them.

"The riches of Alba belong to us," he tells them. "Silver brooches and spoons. Tin. Iron ingots. Shields. Swords. Glass beakers and jars and drinking horns. Wool cloth. Ivory arm rings. Amber and crystal beads. And more besides. Let the cargo be brought ashore and into the hall."

He looks out onto the waters, but the surface lies still. The fight that exploded so suddenly has vanished into the depths and he still cannot explain it. Truth to tell, he hesitates before he disembarks, recalling that moment when he saw Nokvi in the flat face of the merman who attacked him. Nokvi is dead, devoured by his allies—some of whom are not, after all, his allies any longer. Or perhaps some of the merfolk were never his allies at all.

He comes ashore. First Son bears his standard behind him. His counselors move in a group, whispering among themselves.

The SwiftDaughters stand in their ranks by OldMother's hall. They wait, so beautiful in their sharp metallic hues: copper, silver, gold, iron. Snow lines the valley, a white tracery among the fields and rocks. Small ones race down from the main hall, shouting and laughing, and they tumble into place before him, some of them on two legs and some on four, nipping and snapping and pinching and shoving. They are born with the instinct to struggle and compete. Yet he notices that there are fewer four legs and more two legs than is usual among the litters.

Sensing his interest, they fall together into their packs and become silent. Watching him.

They are half his size but growing fast. In another year they will be full grown and in a year or two after that they will be what humankind would call adults: as smart and fast and strong as they will ever be, the new generation of Eika warriors. He has himself, after all, only lived through ten or twelve winters since he hatched from the nests. Their life is short, but after all, a short life is all most creatures on Earth can expect.

"Answer me," he says to them sharply. "Brute strength and bright baubles will not give you victory."

At first they answer with silence. The old, fading warriors and younger home troops and the human tribe look on. This is the first time the sire has met the hatchlings.

One among them speaks up boldly. "Then what?"

"Who are you?" he asks.

"I am First Son of the Third Litter."

He nods.

"First," he says, "observe. After this, learn. And when this is done, think. These are the three legs on which we stand."

"We only have two legs," says First Son of the Third Litter. A different small one snickers.

"What is your name?" he asks the snickerer.

The small one flinches. Never a good sign. But after all, not all these will survive, nor should they. Some will never grow beyond a reliance on brute strength and swift running.

It is those who observe, learn, and think who will thrive. Who will rule.

"Third Son of the Sixth Litter," says the snickerer. "There are four legs also. Three is between two and four, but there is no creature with three legs."

"Is there not?" He frowns at the hatchlings, yet after all they are a handsome looking group, not the biggest he has ever seen, but he does not have girth and breadth to give them. He has given them something more valuable. "The third leg is your brother. Two legs only, if you stand by yourself. But if you stand with others, then you cannot easily be knocked down."

caught the corner of a linen band as the tiny body struck the floor. Cloth pooled around it in loops and heaps. He swooped down and grasped at it with a gasp of dismay.

It gurgled. Its lips smacked and pumped. It squawked out a feeble wail, then hiccuped.

Would it name itself? First Son? Fourth Child? Nay, it was a helpless human infant, doomed to many years of childhood, not ready to run and fight within a pair or three years after its birth. It was so tiny and feeble! No wonder the Eika thought that humankind were soft.

The nurse ripped the baby out of Alain's hands, pulled down the front of her bodice, and put the baby to her breast. It rooted for a moment, then got hold and sucked.

Such an uproar ensued that he had to grab the collars of the hounds and hold them to stop them from biting as folk swarmed, yelled, cried, gesticulated. The crowd surged in and out, right and left, until Sabella's ringing voice brought order and soldiers herded companions, attendants, and courtiers out.

"This way," said Captain Lukas, appearing at his side as if he had never left. "Come now, I pray you." He said the words urgently. His frown had a storm cloud's menace. Alain went along because it was easier to and because the sight of that infant's face troubled him. So quiescent. It had seemed to hit the ground so hard, but that was God's mercy, surely: some substance had clogged its breathing and the shock had jarred it loose. Newborns were such fragile creatures. Weiwara's twins—how could he forget

them? The smaller one had been born, likewise, too weak
to draw breath on its own. What had happened to that
baby? Had it survived the great weaving or been consumed by the tempest? Had Adica known the spell would
doom those she loved? Had she gone forward despite that
knowledge?

He would never know.

"Wait here," said the captain, opening a door. Alain went
gratefully into a dim room and sank down onto a bench.
The tears caught him by surprise. He missed Adica so
badly. The hounds licked him, leaned on him, pawed at
him, and at length lay down on his feet being too big to settle in his lap as they wished to do. At length he calmed,
lifted his head, and measured his surroundings.

This chamber housed a noble's luxurious furnishings: a
fine burnished table and benches; two silk-covered
couches for reclining and conversation; a backless chair
that could be folded up and easily carried; tapestries on the
walls; and a cold hearth. It was too dim to see the scenes
woven in the tapestries. A single candle burned, fastened
into a brass holder fixed onto the left of a sloped writing
desk. Someone had abandoned a sheet of parchment, half
inscribed with words he had lost the knack of reading.
There he saw *regnant*, a word he knew because it also appeared in the Holy Verses. Below that he recognized "a
strong driving wind" like to that mentioned in the story of
the Pentekoste, and then a series of sevens: seven towns,
seven days, seven portions of grain, seven nobles whose
names he laboriously puzzled out. They were all Salian or
western border lords, it seemed: Guy, Laurant, Amalfred,
Gaius, Mainer, Baldricus, Ernalda. The page bore no illumination. It was written in plain ink in the common script
used by Lavastine's clerics when they wrote up contracts
and cartularies. The inkwell had been stoppered.
Untrimmed quills lay in a box resting on the level top of
the desk beside a closed book. All the shutters were closed.
The chamber had the moldy smell of a room that hasn't
been aired out all winter.

With some effort he pulled his feet out from under the
hounds, which had the guile to rest heavily by not resisting

him. A side door opened when he turned the handle. He stepped out onto a walk along the battlement wall. It was raining, cold, and miserable, an unrelentingly gray day. The clouds hung lower than ever. The main part of the town could not be seen from here. The river ran at the base of the bluff. There seemed no obvious exit from this narrow stone court, only a pair of low doors in the wall that most likely concealed a necessarium.

He turned back to enter just as the hounds rose, stiff-legged and ears flat. First, two stewards entered and took down the two shutters. After them came a brace of guardsmen, then Captain Lukas, and finally Lady Sabella. She sat on one of the couches and examined Alain for a while without speaking. In this light, he saw that the tapestries depicted the famous battle of the Nysa River in which young King Louis, the last independent king of Varre, had met his death.

"They say," remarked Sabella into the silence, "that no one knew whose hand struck the blow that killed Louis the Fair. In Wendar it is said he was killed by an Eika prince. But in Varre, it is said he was killed by a traitor in thrall to the Wendish king, who wanted all for himself."

"I've heard that tale. I grew up by Osna Sound."

"Within the lands overseen by the count of Lavas."

"Yes."

Her stare was meant to intimidate, but he accepted it placidly. The hounds grumbled very soft growls whenever she looked their way. Outside, rain hissed on the stones.

"Why have you come here? What do you want?"

"I have promised to discover the true heir to the county of Lavas."

"Ah." She smiled without showing her teeth. "You have heard that Lord Geoffrey betrayed me."

Rage yipped as the door opened and half a dozen people flooded in, led by Conrad the Black. His presence filled the room. He was laughing.

"Squalling like a rooster!" he was saying to one of his companions. "Good God! What can she have been thinking, to believe the little lad was dead just like that?"

"I hope you slapped some sense into her," said Lady Sabella.

Conrad looked at her with disgust, perhaps with loathing, and flung himself onto the other couch. He noted Alain standing with his back to the cold hearth, and then the hounds in shadow to either side. "Look at you!" he said in the tone of a man who loves and understands dogs. "What handsome creatures you are!"

Sorrow's tail thumped once. Rage's ears lifted, but neither hound moved one paw.

"He is the one," said Sabella to Conrad as though Alain could not hear them. "Lavastine's bastard."

"Yes, yes," he said impatiently, still admiring the hounds. "What matter to us?"

"Lord Geoffrey matters to us."

"Ah! What benefit to us?"

"Geoffrey has betrayed us. He is sheltering Constance. There are rumors of unrest and discontent in his county in recent years. This one might provide the excuse we need."

"I see. We ride to Lavas to restore Lavastine's rightful heir, the man he himself proclaimed as his successor but whom Henry deposed. Tallia will protest. She was weeping and moaning and in a mad rant when I just left her."

Sabella shrugged. "That makes no difference. She is shed of the child now. You can put her back in Bederbor, the sooner the better for my peace of mind."

He grunted. "Your distaste for her does you no credit."

"You like her?"

He shrugged. "I accept what is necessary. But my children will not grow up to become like her! I hope you will treat the little lad better, or I will have to take him away."

"Do not insult me, Conrad." Her hand tightened on a pillow, but she kept her tone cordial. "Or threaten me. Where are your daughters?"

"Admiring their new brother, since they will soon be leaving him. I admit, I have set them to guard him. I do not trust Tallia's ravings. She says he is tainted, polluted." He jerked his chin up to indicate Alain. "This one—what is your name?"

"I am called Alain."

"He touched the little fellow, in the chapel. Didn't you see it?"

"I saw it," said Sabella. "Tallia is insane, Conrad."

"Certainly she is weak-minded. So." He nodded at Alain. "That child might have been yours." He seemed about to say more but did not. He had an easy presence, dominating the room without needing to intimidate, as Sabella did. He studied Alain a while longer, and Alain watched him calmly in return. At last he grunted under his breath and nodded.

"You want Lavas County back, do you?"

"I am not the heir."

"That need not trouble us. We can set you in the count's seat easily enough."

"Why would you do so? I have no retinue and no army to support you."

"I want a loyal man in Lavas County," said Sabella.

"Rumor is the strong driving wind that rattles the branches," added Conrad. "They say civil war has broken Salia into a dozen warring factions. They say Henry and his favored child Sanglant have returned from Aosta and even now march on Varre to reclaim us."

"Is it true you reject the Wendish regnant? Although you are both descendants of that line?"

"We are descendants of the Varren royal line," said Sabella sharply. "This is our land to rule."

"And rule wisely, I trust," said Alain. "The tempest still rages. The storm is not yet passed."

"What babbling is this?" demanded Conrad, laughing. "I feel I am in the presence of a wise and mysterious oracle!"

"Last autumn a great storm passed over the land. You may believe that you survived the worst, but the worst is yet to come. Have any planted, although the season is late? Or does frost still kill seedlings every night? Have you seen the sun? When will the cloud cover lift? What are you doing to prepare, if the weather does not change?"

"Why would the weather not change?" asked Sabella. "Summer will come soon. We have stores to last a while—and more to be gained if our current venture prospers."

Conrad whistled softly, trying to lure the hounds, and although they whined a little and thumped their tails, they looked at Alain and, without receiving permission, refused to move. The duke sat back, letting them be.

"These are not unreasonable concerns," Conrad said in the mildest voice Alain had heard from him. "As in battle, even the best laid plans may be overturned. One must expect a flanking attack, or disaster. And act so as to overcome it." He nodded at Alain. "That is why we need Lavas County. That is how you can help us."

"Geoffrey has not ruled in a manner pleasing to me," said Sabella. "Lavas needs a stronger hand."

"What do you say, Lord Alain?" asked Conrad genially. "Are you interested? We can help each other."

"It's not why I came here."

"Nor need it have been," replied Conrad with that same hearty camaraderie. "Let it be a windfall. You have acted boldly. Boldness can expect reward."

"He'll need a wife," said Sabella, shifting her pieces on the board. "We can find someone suitable. Duchess Yolanda has a daughter. You yourself, Conrad, have a daughter almost of marriageable age."

There was a great deal in this vein Alain could hear without comment or reaction, but the sight of Tallia had singed him. He winced, thinking of her, of the baby she had given Conrad but denied him and by so doing denied Lavastine. That was the one thing that was hardest to forgive. The one thing that he had tried to conceal with a lie. He had failed Lavastine.

Briefly, the idea teased and flattered him: he might marry again, be count again, and fulfill his promise to the man he had called "Father."

"Or my granddaughter," added Sabella, as if the thought had just that moment occurred to her. "Berengaria is—what? Four or five? She could be betrothed now, and married later, when she's older. In another ten years she'll be old enough to bear children. It would repay him for the loss of Tallia."

"Is it not incest to marry a man to the daughter of a woman he once had to wife?" asked Conrad.

"Tallia claimed an annulment. They did not consummate the marriage."

He had to shut his eyes, but if he breathed, if he thought of Adica, these words had no power to burn him.

"That's so! In that case, it doesn't count as a marriage. Yes, it might serve. Berry will need a good marriage. She'll need a consort strong enough to support her regnancy. One whose power and lands give him respect in his own right."

Marry Tallia's daughter. Rule Varre as her consort. And perhaps rule Wendar as well.

These were serious temptations, indeed.

"I pray you," Alain began, but the door opened and a steward hurried in, windblown and red in the face.

"The rider has returned," he said, making way for a messenger who staggered in and knelt before the two nobles. He smelled of leaves and rain and wind and dirt, and of smoke, as though he had sat by many campfires and never washed afterward. He peeled gloves off his hands and accepted a cup of wine gratefully.

"What news?" Sabella demanded.

"Ai, God!" said Conrad. "Let him finish his drink."

Before he could speak, a second steward appeared at the door.

"My lady. The soldier you wanted is here."

She beckoned.

Captain Lukas entered with Atto. The young man was sweating, as pale as if he were ready to faint. He dropped to his knees at once, caught sight of Alain, and started noticeably.

"You are the one who brought report of the guivre's trail?" Sabella had a way of looking over young men that made them squirm, but in this case she dismissed his physical charms.

"Y–yes, my lady. I come from a village along the West Way. We call it Helmbusch, for the ridge, you know. The rock juts up just above where the chapel sits. There are ten houses and three milk cows and we have our own pair of plowing oxen . . ." He trailed off, licked his lips, and swallowed.

"Can you lead us to it?"

"To Helmbusch, my lady? Oh, yes, certainly, but I had no intention of returning. Things aren't so good there, now, with the weather and the livestock wandering off and the refugees bothering us along the road. I came from there to seek employment—"

"To the guivre!"

"To the guivre?" He had long since undergone the change from a boy's voice to a man's, but his voice shot up an octave nevertheless.

"The creature's lair. If you've seen its trail, you can guide my soldiers to its lair."

"But I don't know about that," he said desperately. "I came to serve as a soldier."

"So you will. You'll guide us to the guivre." She examined him as he shifted his knees on the floor and pulled nervously at his sleeve. He kept his head bowed, but his torso, leaning away from her, spoke as clearly as words. "When I command," she added, "my soldiers serve."

He did not answer.

"There is a young woman who came with him," said Captain Lukas. "His betrothed. I put her in the kitchens."

Sabella's smile was slight but chilling as she examined young Atto. She did not suffer fools or cowards. She appeared to be the kind of woman who didn't like anybody very much. "Could she not serve us better in the brothels? We have enough servants in the palace."

Atto flung back his head, shifting forward onto one knee, with the other leg tucked up under as though he meant to push up to his feet. "She is my betrothed! She's pregnant! She can't—" Too late he recalled to whom he was speaking, and he broke off.

She nodded, satisfied that she had gotten the reaction she wanted. "If you serve me well, I will see she retains a protected position in the kitchens."

The threat had jarred Atto. He twisted, angry enough to be bold, and pointed at Alain. "He knows better. He saw the guivre. So he claimed."

"Did you?" asked Conrad with a jovial interest that barely masked his sudden intense attention. He set his elbows on his knees. "Saw it, and lived to tell the tale?"

"I heard it in the forest," said Alain, "although I did not see it. I was concealed within the branches of a fallen tree."

"He can guide you! Better than I could!"

"No, you'll guide us," said Sabella to Atto, who shuddered. She turned to Alain. "Perhaps you had best go also. I remember it was said of you when you were Lavastine's heir that you fought well in battle. In fact, I recall it said that you helped Brother Agius kill my last guivre. In recompense, you can help me capture another."

"It seems a dangerous venture for small gain." Conrad shook his head.

Sabella turned her gaze to the waiting messenger, who had by now caught his breath and drunk his fill. "What news?" Then she settled back as if she already knew what he was going to say.

"I am come from Quedlinhame, my lady. Prince Sanglant was crowned as regnant in the presence of Mother Scholastica and at least five or six biscops, and many noble lords and ladies."

None murmured in shock or alarm. No one exclaimed out loud in surprise or indignation. This news was expected.

"You rode as quickly as you could to bring us this news?" she asked him.

"I did, my lady."

"Must we expect an attack soon?"

"We have yet some time. He turned east, to ride his king's progress through Saony and into the marchlands. So that the populace could see him and the nobles acclaim him. He will ride west once he has made himself king throughout Wendar by displaying his crown and his sword. Afterward, he will march west, into Varre."

"We must be ready," said Sabella. "Captain Lukas!" She gestured, and he came forward. "It is time to make ready our attack."

"Past time," muttered Conrad. "As I've been telling you. We need Kassel's grain stores."

"There is one other thing, my lady," the messenger added, hesitant to continue. "Difficult to believe, yet I saw with my own eyes."

"Go on."

"Griffins, my lady."

"Griffins?" asked Conrad, sitting up. "What do you mean?"

"The prince marches with a pair of griffins, my lord duke. He captured them in the east. They follow him like . . . like dogs."

Courtiers glanced at Sabella to see if she would believe this outrageous tale.

She merely nodded. "Now you see, Conrad, why we need a guivre to counter this threat. A guivre will allow us to strike first, before Sanglant expects battle."

"We are already striking first, by allying with one he trusts."

"Perhaps. But a guivre will guarantee victory." She smiled bitterly as she shifted her attention. "Do you not think so, Lord Alain? Would this not be a wise strategy?"

Alain nodded. A sense of peace settled over him. He had done the right thing by coming here. He saw now what he had to do. "Yes," he said, "a guivre will grant victory."

3

ONCE the necessary formal greetings were fulfilled at the shore, once folk began to unload the cargo of Alban goods, Stronghand climbed the slope of the valley. He walked into the shadow cast by the heights and across the skin of soft green grass that surrounded OldMother's hall. Late-blooming snowdrops speckled the ground. SwiftDaughters eyed him from where they stood by the mouths of their cave. Their hair swayed like a glamour, and he paused by the threshold, distracted by their beauty. Wind trembled against his back in an unexpected gust, and he shook himself and walked forward.

He crossed into a gulf of darkness too large to be confined in any finite space, much less the eaves and timbers visible as the outside dimensions of the hall. A tremor teased the ground. He heard as at a great distance a breathy piping like a wheezing breath. No stars shone; blackness veiled the heavens. It was as still as if wind had never been known in the world, utterly silent and cold as the skin of stone in the dark of winter.

She said, "Stronghand."

"I am here."

She said, "Go to the fjall. The WiseMothers await you."

The air twisted around him, spinning the staff he held in his right hand, and he staggered backward and found himself tossed out the doorway, surprised by the light. The SwiftDaughters had vanished. Below, the ships rode high, or had been pulled up onto the strand, lightened of their load.

How had time passed so swiftly? Around the hall and the farther village, seen through a fence of pine and spruce, folk were busy sorting and accounting. Most had gone back to work now that the excitement of his arrival had faded.

They had not forgotten him. He walked among them to reach the trail that led up into the highest reaches of the valley, and as he bent his path in that direction he found himself with an escort, mostly children, none daring to ask what venture he'd set himself this late in the day.

The children loped alongside like a pack of overgrown puppies, all in a tangle that sorts itself out into pairs and triads before melding together again. Human children ran with the hatchlings he had sired. They jostled each other like littermates, and the softer, weaker human kin whacked at the four-legs with stout sticks to keep their sharp teeth at bay when the nipping and tussling got out of hand. The sight of this extended pack caused a stab of foreboding. What strengthened the human children would surely weaken the children of rock, who did not leap to the kill as they would have done in the old days in such a crowd. They ran as one great many-limbed beast, so that he could scarcely tell one limb from another as they tumbled and shouted and galloped and giggled around him.

Perhaps it was too easy to condemn, he thought as he strode on tireless legs, as he inhaled the sweet scent of home flavored with burning charcoal, pine sap, and the cold bite of northern air. The old days, by the reckoning of his kind with their short lives, were easily swallowed by the longer span of years in which humankind revel and which they did not fully appreciate. To live seventy years, as some of them did! Even Deacon Ursuline, who claimed to have survived forty or fifty seasons, could boast of a life span unknown even to the sorcerers of the Eika tribes, the ones who schemed and stole hearts and souls and magics in order to extend their lives.

No matter. A flame may still burn brightly, though its wick is short.

Rikin Fjord prospered because it was now a many-limbed beast. Sheep grazed where meadows found purchase on level ground, although he noted few twin lambs among the ewes: harbinger of a hard year ahead. Goats scrambled nimbly along the steep slopes of the valley. Pens held pampered cattle, who needed a cozy byre to outlast the winter. It was winter still, with frost crackling under each step and snow heaped where shadows lingered longest. A late sowing might prove too short for a decent crop.

Still, the Eika could rely on raiding to fill their larders. Long had they honed their skills as the wolves of the sea. Now, it seemed, they must learn and change, so learn and change they would. There was no going back.

The ground grew rockier as the path cut steeply toward the fjall. The children quieted. Many turned back although a few dogged his heels, too curious to stop. No adult followed him this far, although down the path he saw a dozen or more looking up after him. The trees became withered and stunted, and fell away altogether, leaving boulders and skirts of moss and a patchy carpet of lichen. He looked in vain for the youngest of the WiseMothers, climbing this path, but she had gone.

He crossed over the rim and onto the undulating plain that was the fjall. Snow dusted the open reaches, where the wind battered at all things. In the sheltered lee of boulders and along the uneven rise and fall of the earth, old snow had hardened. It was so cold that his footfalls resounded as his weight cut through the remains of last winter's snowfall.

In the distance, where the land dipped into a hollow, the WiseMothers congregated. One more stood among them:

she had reached her destination who was most recently
OldMother, the one who spawned him and his brothers.
He crossed the plain, slipping once where the snow concealed loose rock debris along a slight incline. The wind's
howl muted to a moan, and as he reached the edge of the
circle the wind ceased altogether. The clouds cast a gray
pallor over the day. Every object seemed muted and lessened. Even the WiseMothers looked, for an instant, like
nothing more than big, unshapely stones fixed in an irregular oval around a sandy basin, whose smooth surface was
untouched by snow or stick or even a wrinkled scrap of
torn lichen. The hummock that marked the center had altered. Once, its curve had borne a pearlescent gleam. Now
it sat with a kind of menace he could not describe. Corruption had infested it, turning it as black as charcoal, as
though it had rotted from the inside out.

He shuddered, afraid, but of nothing he could touch or
smell or hear or see. It seemed stupid to make his way
across the sands in order to stand on a place that looked as
likely to hold his weight as the deck of a ship eaten away
by fire. The smell of sulfur made his eyes water and his skin
itch. The stench actually seemed to ripple off the ground.
He began to think he could *see* the stink rising in waves.
That smell made him reel, gulping air and expelling it as
quickly as he coughed and gagged and, at last, calmed his
breathing.

Of the ice wyrms, he saw no sign, not even a tracery
under the glitter of sand.

He stood for a long time, trying to decide what to do, and
after a while he heard the whisper of the wind among the
stones and after a longer while he realized that the wind
remained becalmed and that these were voices tugging at
him, faint and far off, receding as a traveler recedes as he
sails away from shore.

"Your. Brother. You. Owe. Him. A. Debt. Is. It. Repaid."

A life for a life. He knew what they spoke of.

"Go. To. Him. Now. Repay. This. Debt. Now."

Now.

A sound cracked, as explosive as a heated rock splitting
asunder. Not meaning to, he ducked. The air had changed,

thickened, hardened until he could scarcely draw in breath. Wave upon wave of heated air rippled out of the hollow.

Their voices were as faint as the hiss of a feather falling.

"Our. Task. Is. Ended. You. Are. Now. Alone. Our. Children. Our. Children. Born. Of. Mute. Rock. Human. Flesh. Dragon's. Blood. You. Must. Make. Your. Own. Way. Without. Us."

A temblor eased through the earth. Its groan sighed like longing. The surface of the hollow shifted. In branching lines no wider than his claws, the sands poured away as though, underneath, tunnels were caving in. The black hummock snapped fiercely, so loud that the sound echoed off the far mountainsides. He heard it as through a vast chamber, down along a far-reaching path, multiplied over and over as if he heard not one sound but a hundred cracks each one of which sent him plummeting into the ancient past:

Screaming rage and pain, the dragons plunge. Before they reach the shelter of earth their hearts burst from the pressure of the great weaving. Their blood rains down on the humans who shelter against the stones. The hail of scalding blood burns flesh into stone, melding them into one being, born out of humankind, dragon's blood, and mute stone.

A crack shivered across the surface of the hummock, widened, and without warning the slick black curve shattered into pieces. The hollow sagged and collapsed inward as a dark shape uncoiled out of the spilling sands.

Stronghand scrambled back from the brim, tripped over a rock, and fell to his rump as the hatchling reared up. It raised its golden head on a golden neck and with an effort unfurled moist wings, shaking them in the wind. It was as big as a warhorse, bigger, if more slender and equally graceful. Its eyes were like coals, black and fathomless. It swept its gaze over him without appearing to mark him as anything different than the stone and the sand and the tufts of lichen. It shook its wings, which spanned what was now a sinkhole. Flecks of an acidic spray spattered him, burning him, but he gulped down a cry of pain.

A call chased along the horizon.

The hatchling twisted its neck to stare toward the north.

Somewhere, out there, another has been born.

As soon as the thought took form, he understood how foolish it was. Not one, but a hundred and more, one for every tribe, for every circle of WiseMothers, who for this span of time had incubated the eggs of the FirstMothers, the ones who in ancient days bred with the living spirits of earth and gave birth to his kind.

So the story was told among the Eika.

It leaped. The pressure of its fledgling wingbeats battered him supine against the ground. It caught an updraft, and yet it beat those flashing wings as though to churn the still day into a gale. The clouds tore apart as it vanished into them. Lying stunned on the ground, he saw revealed the hard blue pan of the sky and felt—so briefly!—the melting warmth of an early summer sun.

The wind whirlpooled around him as though trying to suck him up into the heavens. Pebbles scooped up by the gale pummeled him. Lichen and moss writhed in strips through the air. The wind poured into him, blowing right through his skin and into every part of him, enveloping him, drowning him.

Alain stands at the wall staring toward the north, although he isn't sure how he has come to be out here with the evening settling in and the wind pouring through him. He burns as if the wind is fire on his skin.

He hears their calls, even though they rise so far away that he should not be able to hear them. They raise a clangor, deeper than bells, that resonates in his body until he weeps without knowing why. The hounds whine, licking his hands, but he cannot stop the tears.

A puny, cold, fragile creature moves up beside him, only it is after all the servant assigned to make him comfortable in the palace. "My lord? I pray you, my lord, is there something the matter? How can I help you?"

It hurts, but he doesn't know why. He listens for the last echoes whispering out of the north.

Their voices came to him, a thousand, a myriad, but all familiar to him and beloved in their way.

"Good. That. You. Are. Strong. Of. Hand. Son. Fare. Well. Be. Wise."

The tempest quieted. A ragged wisp of lichen settled out of the air and onto his face. He brushed it aside, shook himself, and jumped to his feet. Above, the clouds were knitting themselves together again. The wind had failed utterly, and the day became silent and colored with the pearl-gray filter of a clouded sun. The fjall lay empty. Nothing moved, nothing spoke, nothing breathed, except him. He might have been the last creature alive in the entire land.

Certainly he stood alone here.

Altogether alone.

He sensed it at once, greater than emptiness: an abyss where once earth had lain firm beneath the feet of his people. A strange dullness afflicted the ache of the wind and the whisper of sand where grains rolled down the steep sides of the new sinkhole into a shallow chamber half filled with the birth sands that had once covered it. A few tiny ice-white forms lay tumbled in the collapse: the ice wyrms that had long protected the treasure that the WiseMothers had incubated. They, too, lay as still as death.

He was surrounded by death, although life had sprung from it.

He stepped forward and pressed a palm against the nearest WiseMother. It felt only of stone. No consciousness animated its core. They were absent. Gone.

Dead.

"Can you hear me? Can you answer me?" he called to them, who were the life of their children. They had for so long guided them with the foresight of the ancient, who saw farther than their short-lived children could ever do.

He waited, and he listened.

But all he heard was the wind.

V

OLD GHOSTS

1

AS they rode west along the Osterwaldweg, an Eagle met the king's progress where dappled shadow met open road at the edge of a wide forest wilderness.

"Rufus," said Sanglant.

The redhead had been with King Henry in Aosta and lately left behind in Saony together with a few other Eagles when the king had ridden east into the marchlands.

"Your Majesty. I am sent ahead by Mother Scholastica to let you know she intends to meet with you in Osterburg. I did not expect to meet you on the road."

Once, a well trained Eagle could have looked through fire to discover the king's whereabouts by means of observing landmarks glimpsed through the flames. No longer.

"We shall meet my aunt in Quedlinhame, before she expects us." He liked the thought of surprising her, anything to put her at a disadvantage.

"She has already left. I rode ahead to alert the stewards in Osterburg. You'll meet her on this road, Your Majesty."

Outflanked. Still, two could play that game. "Take drink and food, Rufus. You'll get new mounts, and return to her. Tell her to await us at . . ." He paused, considering the route.

For once, Liath was paying attention. "Goslar has a small palace."

"At Goslar. Is there more, Eagle? Sent she a message? What does she intend?"

"Nothing more, Your Majesty. Nothing she told to me, anyway." He was a good rider with an easy seat, but very serious, pacing alongside the king. If he meant his remark wryly, Sanglant saw no sign of it.

Liath fell out of line to ride with the young man back along the cavalcade to the supply wagons. Sanglant listened as they moved away. It was always easy for him to catch her voice out of the multitude.

"When was it again that you first met Hanna? At Darre? Not earlier, then? You never met her before—did you ride east with Princess Sapientia? Oh, I see."

Her words faded into the creaks and clops and chatter of the procession.

Liutgard, at his right hand, glanced back, and he did as well. Although scouts, and a vanguard, rode in front, most of the progress rode behind him, a line of four riders abreast twisting back into a landscape of woodland, open ground, and the occasional farmstead. Half of these small estates and humble holdings were recently abandoned. One had been burned and looted. He and Liutgard had ridden somewhat forward of his other companions, who were bogged down by the incessant palaver of Sophie and Imma. The Saony twins always rode more slowly when they started in on one of their long harangues. They were, as always, being egged on by their bored brother. Their voices had a shrill tone that carried easily above the clatter of the army.

"Did you see Gerberga's face when Sanglant brought Ekkehard back to her? She was red. Red! To think of it!"

"How humiliating to find your husband has run off with your sister."

"At least," remarked Wichman, "neither of you need worry about that! No man would possibly run to either of you."

"How dare you! As if you could hope for better—!"

"You'll be murdered by the brother or husband of some poor woman you've raped, Wichman."

"Before or after I am installed as margrave of Westfall?"

"An insult to us, Sophie!"

"It is! It is! To offer him a margraviate, and us—nothing! Not even respectable husbands but only second and third sons of minor lords!"

"I had hoped," Sanglant said to Liutgard in a low voice, "that they would run to Conrad, but I fear they mean to stick." He grinned.

She did not. "I pray you, Cousin, forgive me for speaking bluntly."

He sighed.

"Henry was right after all. He intended to marry you to Queen Adelheid. That would have been a good match. All this would have been avoided."

"Not all of it." He indicated Rotrudis' squabbling progeny.

"Well." She smiled crookedly. "Not all of it."

"What do you mean to say, Liutgard? You have supported me faithfully. I know your worth."

"You must marry. Soon."

He waved away her question.

"Nay, do not dismiss me! You know I am right."

"I will not yield on this matter. I am already married."

She had endured much and complained not at all. She had not seen her own lands in more than four years. Her daughters grown apace while she was gone, her stewards in charge of Fesse, all this she had left behind because of her loyalty to Henry. She had lost half her men, and she had not complained. She had lost her heir, and she had not complained.

"There is a line even I will not cross, Sanglant. I have suffered too much to allow my lands to be laid under a ban because you have fixed on such a creature as that one."

"A *creature*—do not insult her!"

"Do not misunderstand me. I do not dislike her. But they whisper about her. They fear her."

"In Gent they placed flowers at her feet."

"So they did," she admitted. "Let the biscops and abbesses be content with her. Let the excommunication be lifted and the holy women offer their blessing. Then we shall see."

"Will you support me, in that case? In Autun, when the ban is lifted from her?"

"We shall see."

It was all she would promise. Her words worried at him as a dog worries at a much chewed bone.

"What have you heard?" he said at last. "What whispers?"

She was a cool one, educated, strong, fertile, and confident, his peer, equal to him in rank. Legitimately born, she needed no justification to hold her position and title as duchess of Fesse, the last descendant of Queen Conradina through the queen's younger brother Eberhard, who had been Liutgard's great grandfather.

"Do you listen to what you do not want to hear?" she asked him. "You ought to."

2

THE palace at Goslar was one hundred years old, built in the days of the last queen regnant, Conradina. It boasted a sturdy hall, a stable, and a motley collection of outbuildings including a kitchen and a smithy. A shoulder-high palisade surrounded the palace. Beyond it lay gardens, orchards, fields, and the estate whose inhabitants tended the grounds year round. Goslar belonged to the Wendish regnant, but, as Liath recalled, the steward who administered it was appointed by the abbess at nearby Quedlinhame.

Thus they arrived to find Mother Scholastica entrenched with her retinue. Although outriders rode ahead to alert her to the king's arrival, she did not emerge to offer Sanglant greeting but waited inside to receive him.

"She means me to appear as the supplicant," he said to Theophanu and Liutgard, who rode on either side.

Liath sat, mounted, away from the rest of the noble companions, examining the scene thoughtfully. She appeared more interested in the layout of the buildings than in the architecture of court politics. For some reason she looked particularly beautiful today with her hair drawn back into a braid, her dusky face filled out and healthy, her blue eyes bright; that uncanny way they had of seeming now and again to spark with laughter or anger still startled him. She was no longer too thin, as she had been before: when he first met her; in their days at Verna; when she had returned to him after the cataclysm. Despite their constant travel and the occasional dearth of food on the trip north, she had gained flesh in all the right places. As he knew, and yet wanted to rediscover again and again and again.

Liutgard tapped his arm. "If you do not stop staring at her like a lackwit, then every soul in this army will continue to believe she has used her sorcerer's power to bewitch you."

Her sharp comment caught him off guard. He looked at her, then at Theophanu. Theophanu shrugged.

"Do you believe it?" he demanded.

"I do," said Liutgard. "It's said she ensorcelled Henry in the same manner."

"That wasn't her fault! Or her intent! She never had any interest in Henry. She'd already chosen me."

"A wise decision, since Henry would never have married her," observed Liutgard.

"What do you say, Theophanu?" he said, really irritated now.

She smiled as a cat might be said to smile, having the cream set before it. "I think you are famous for your weakness for women, Brother. It is remarkable that one contents you. Some might call that a form of magic."

"Do you?"

She raised a tidy eyebrow. "I do not. She is handsome in a way that attracts men. The question might better be, why does she care for you above all other men when, it seems, she might have had any of them?"

Liutgard laughed for the first time in weeks. "Are you become a wit, Theophanu? Look at him! So brawny and handsome as he is. Women fall at his feet, and into his bed."

"This is not amusing."

"True enough," replied Theophanu to Liutgard. "But he is not so beautiful as Hugh of Austra. Hugh never cared one whit for any woman except his mother, or excepting if a woman could give him something he wanted. But he wanted that one."

"As for what Hugh wanted, I can't answer, although it's true enough that Hugh is quite the most beautiful man I have ever seen. May my poor Frederic rest at peace in the Chamber of Light, for I mean no insult to him. Yet if Hugh of Austra wanted her as well, does it not suggest sorcery to you, Theo?"

"Let her be," said Theophanu abruptly. "Leave her at peace, I pray you, Liutgard."

"She has certainly found a champion in you! Is there something you know that I ought to know, to put my mind at ease?"

"I pray you, Liutgard, let it rest." A shadow of anger darkened Theophanu's placid face, and she gestured toward the palace and its phalanx of milites dressed in the tabard of the ancient Quedlinhame County: crossed swords on a green field. "What will you do, Sanglant? Set up a siege as you did at Quedlinhame when you first returned to Wendar this spring?"

"If you will be patient, I ask you to await me here. I'll go in alone, as a humble nephew asking for my holy aunt's blessing. That may content her."

He gave Fulk the order to set camp. Dismounting, he offered the reins to Sibold, then sought Liath, but she had wandered off. A few moments searching discovered her: she was chatting amiably and easily with a pride of Lions.

"Who is that?" he said to Hathui, who had come up as soon as Fulk departed.

"That is—I think—yes—Captain Thiadbold's troop."

"Yes. Yes. I see him now. His helm covers his red hair." He chewed his lower lip, then said, "She seems to know them well."

Hathui looked at him strangely. "I can't say, Your Majesty. An Eagle meets many folk upon the road. Eagles and Lions often depend on each other in a tight spot."

He frowned, but shook himself. "Attend me, if you will."

They crossed the grassy forecourt and walked up onto the porch. The guards opened the doors to let them through. Inside, clerics scribbled at tables set up along the length of the hall. Scholastica presided from the dais, although she was not seated in the ducal chair but rather in a handsome seat with a cloth back and pillows. She was making a show of reading, but it was obvious she was expecting him. A nun whispered into her ear. She handed her the book and raised a hand, to give Sanglant permission to come forward.

"I pray you," he said to Hathui, "hurry to Theophanu and Liutgard and tell them I have mistaken the matter. If they will come at once, I will be grateful for their help. We'll need my throne as well as their chairs. Make haste."

She left.

From down the length of the hall, Scholastica regarded him with patience, or interest, or puzzlement. She said nothing. He said nothing. Theirs was a standoff. The guards had closed the doors, but elsewhere all the shutters had been taken down. As he waited, he heard the noise of the army settling down for the day, goats complaining, men laughing, sergeants shouting, a hostler cursing, dogs barking as they would. Quills scratched indoors; outdoors, wind skimmed the branches of Goslar's orchard.

He heard them approach the porch and walk up the stairs. The door opened, and they entered, just the two of them, with Hathui at their back. Without speaking, he beckoned them forward and with one on either side approached his aunt. She looked stern and unbending, not even amused.

"I come with the Dragon of Saony and the Eagle of Fesse beside me," he said to her.

"What of Rotrudis' children?" she asked, dispensing with pleasantries.

Yes, she was annoyed.

Servants came forward to unfold the traveling chairs. Theophanu and Liutgard waited until he sat; then they sat. Now all four made a cozy little group, but three of them were young and one was getting old. She was holding on to

the past when, in fact, the past had been demolished in one
night last autumn.

"Rotrudis' children are not capable of ruling, Aunt.
Theophanu is, as you know."

"If Theophanu is capable of ruling, then she should by
right be regnant," said Scholastica. "Yet she is not. I have a
proposition for you, Sanglant."

He nodded, but she was not waiting for his permission,
only pausing to collect her thoughts.

"Theophanu is not the only candidate. There are others.
If you accept retirement, you can retain your place as captain of the King's Dragons. The realm will need your
strength. You can serve best where you are most suited."

"I am already crowned and anointed. At your hand. To
what purpose do you raise these objections now?"

"I wish to prevent war, Sanglant."

"How will my stepping down prevent war? Who then
would rule as regnant?"

"Conrad and Tallia."

"No!" cried Theophanu, standing up. She was furious.

"Conrad?" Liutgard's laugh had a mean heart. "Tallia?
Do you mean Sabella's daughter? That whey-faced creature who wept blood and moaned and cried?"

"She professed a heresy," said Theophanu. "You yourself
threw her out of Quedlinhame, did you not?"

"I did not," said Scholastica coolly. "Henry took her to
marry Lavastine's heir, the one who was a thief and a liar
and a bastard."

"Conrad?" murmured Sanglant, but as hard as he could
think this through, he could not figure how his aunt would
be willing to throw the regnancy out of Henry's line. Her
own line.

"Conrad has a *claim*." Liutgard was white with anger.
"And I have a claim, Mother Scholastica. What of me? I
am the last descendant of Queen Conradina. She, after all,
did not give the crown to her younger brother but to her
rival and ally, the elder Henry, who was then duke of
Saony. Her words are famous. In truth, we learn them
early in Fesse so as not to forget the stain upon our family's honor. 'For it is true, Brother, that our family has

everything which the dignity of the regnant demands, except good luck.' Sanglant has brought us this far out of disaster. Who else could have done so? It was Henry's last wish that Sanglant become king after him. I witnessed Henry's last words."

Sanglant tapped one foot, waiting. The plank flooring of the hall was swept clean. No carpets covered the long boards. The scritching of quills continued unabated. Clerics bent their heads over tables, writing and writing and writing. He wondered that their hands did not begin to ache.

"Then a proper marriage," Mother Scholastica said.

"We settled this at Gent," he retorted.

"A subtle player made that move. Her kinfolk out of Bodfeld are not even counts, nothing more than minor lords. Her father was dedicated to the church and should never have fathered a child. It can't even be proved that she is legitimate rather than a bastard. It can't even be proved she has a soul. Without your support, Sanglant, she is nothing more than an excommunicated practitioner of forbidden sorcery. Subject to execution, if the church so desires."

"With such plain speaking, you can scarcely expect me to withdraw my 'protection,'" he answered. "I weary of this game."

"The throne, or the woman."

"It is a false choice. Why are you so stubborn?"

"Why are you so stubborn?" She was mightily displeased. Her anger made him uneasy, but he would not back down. "You are a fool, Sanglant. It would have been better if Henry had married you to Villam's heir, as Villam wanted."

"You were against the match at the time, as I recall."

"So I was. Then. Villam had already too much power in Henry's council."

"Waltharia is unmarried, at this moment. Would you object to her now?"

Scholastica hesitated. Liutgard looked surprised, but Theophanu smiled in that elegant, enigmatic way she had, giving away nothing.

"I would object," said Liutgard finally.

Scholastica still gave no answer.

"Had you someone in mind?" he asked his aunt.

"An alliance might be sealed," she said slowly, "with a princess out of Salia or Alba. Even, in these times, with the Polenie, although I account them rather small. A worthy match, bringing with it a worthwhile alliance. Something that will aid us."

"As Liath did. She saved us. *All* of us."

Scholastica's frown was hard and her tone bitter. "No one knows what she did. Not even you. No one witnessed. She might have done or said anything. You do not know."

"I know what she told me. I know what happened. I know Anne is dead and her cabal of sorcerers scattered."

"How do you know that the great tempest was not brought about by that creature's magic? By her doing? Or with her as accomplice who then murdered her master? You do not know anything, Sanglant. You cannot prove anything. Those who accompanied her are lost. They cannot tell us what they saw. She is a sorcerer. A daimone's get. Soulless. Dangerous."

"Visited by a saint in Gent."

"An illusion!"

"An illusion—if you say so—believed by half the population and most importantly by those who witnessed. Those whose lives she saved!"

"They are fools, easily led! She could have said anything to convince them to follow her."

He rose slowly, hands loose, shoulders tight.

"Sanglant," whispered Theophanu, warning him.

"I was there!" he said, really angry now. "She saved lives at the risk of her own. She could have run, but did not. Don't tell me it was an illusion! All my Dragons died, and half the city besides!"

His anger did not sway her, nor did his height and his strength as he towered over her.

"You did not die." Her lined face showed no fear and no apprehension, only her stubborn will, not to be cowed by the likes of him. "Although it seems to me that you should have. It is said that your mother bound a spell into your flesh. It is said you cannot die. At times I have wondered if your courage in battle is due to honor and duty and loyalty, or to the knowledge that no matter how many of your men die, you will not suffer their fate."

Almost, he growled at her. She was his enemy, and he had not seen it before. She had lulled him when he stood before her with his army and his griffins and his father's blessed remains. But he had discipline. He remained silent.

"What if your concubine was in league with the sorcerers all along?" Scholastica continued, tight and controlled. "Now she is in a significant position of power. In your bed! The histories tell us that other women have ruled in such a way, although it grants them no dignity to do so."

He was too angry to speak.

Liutgard looked troubled. "It's true. All this talk of a secret cabal, these Seven Sleepers. It would make sense they would have a deeper plan."

"Aunt," said Theophanu in her cool voice, "I pray you, if that is true, then why would Liathano deny that she is Taillefer's heir? There is no one to say otherwise, except her. We all believed it. Why would she throw away a claim to power if she sought power?"

"Are you defending her?" asked Scholastica.

"You have not answered Theo's question." Sanglant nodded at Theophanu, and he could not keep a smirk from his face. He liked seeing his aunt discomfited. She deserved it.

"She is subtle," said the abbess finally.

"She is not subtle," said Theophanu with a shake of her head. "She is a cub among wolves, here at court. She is awkward and as likely to say the wrong thing as to keep silence. Begging your pardon, Sanglant."

He shrugged. "It's true enough."

"Were she subtler," said Liutgard, "there would be less disquiet. But it's true, she's no courtier. She has not the least idea of the duties and obligations that bind the consort. Folk fear her, for they have heard many strange stories about her. Yet it seems there are those among the progress who champion her." She smiled a little. Maybe it, too, was a smirk, to answer his. "Eagles and Lions. Common-born folk."

"A common-born woman cannot become queen, not in

Wendar," said Scholastica. "In Salia of old, as it says in the histories, a slave might become a queen if she caught a king's fancy and aroused his lust—"

Naturally, having said it, she stopped. She thought. She looked at Sanglant, and, God Above, he felt himself blushing.

"So it seems not only in Salia of old," she remarked, her voice tainted with an ugly tone. "I had forgotten that in her history, so it is said, she was for some time a slave because of her father's debts. It was said she was Hugh of Austra's mistress—and he a fine and upstanding frater!"

Sanglant kicked away his chair and strode to the back of the hall, unable to stand still.

"Does this not trouble you, Nephew?" she said to his back.

He turned to make a retort, but paused.

Theophanu leaned forward to clasp her aunt's hands. Scholastica winced as Theophanu tightened her grip. "Never believe that she went to Hugh of Austra's bed willingly. If I say anything, Aunt, if you believe me at all, believe that."

"What do you know of the matter?"

"I know enough. She saved my life many years ago, when she was only an Eagle and I was—foolish and blind."

"What do you mean? Say more!"

Theophanu would not be drawn.

"Thus is the spider's web of deceit woven," said Scholastica as she pulled her hands out of Theophanu's grasp.

"You are being stubborn," said Sanglant, pacing back to stand with his hands on the wings of his chair.

"I am? You are the one being stubborn, Sanglant. You, a bastard, born of a foreign woman. King Arnulf said all along that Henry was indecently obsessed with that woman. That Henry had made rash promises to bring her to his bed. I am only a few years younger than Henry. I recall it well!" She smiled mockingly. "An obedient son. Our father's favorite. Yet for a woman he defied the king. How like Henry you are!"

"I can think of no greater compliment than to be compared to my beloved father," he said grimly.

She cut him off. "Yet when I look at you, when any person looks at you, they see your mother's face. They see the face of a people already at war with us."

There, she struck the blow that stopped him. "At war with us? What do you mean?"

"You have not heard? Ah." Her eyes tightened. Her mouth became a flat line as she regarded him.

Liutgard shifted.

Theophanu sat back.

"I pray you, Nephew, account for me the disposition of your forces. Who rides with you, and who remains behind? Then I will tell you the reports I have heard. I hope they will surprise you."

"I am already surprised." He sat, but he was too restless to stay still. He tapped a foot a dozen or more times against the floor before switching to the other one. "What do you mean?"

"I mean villages and estates in the lands west of Quedlinhame have been attacked most viciously by the Lost Ones made flesh. Our enemies look like you." She surveyed the hall. Her silent clerics, her noble kinsmen, the distant guards: all had a similar Wendish robustness, light hair, big builds. His coloring and his features alone were markedly different. He alone was the bastard, with an outland mother.

Theophanu touched him on the knee as if to remind him that she, too, had an outland mother, a foreigner who had never quite been trusted by good honest Wendish folk. Still, Theophanu resembled her father more than her Arethousan mother.

"There are some who murmur that *you* have brought this down on us," said Scholastica. "There are many who wonder how you have come to be regnant. If it is all part of a larger plot to conquer Wendar from without and rule over us. You see, the survivors of these recent assaults have told us that when the Lost Ones attack, they call out your name."

3

SHE made ready to leave for the convent of St. Valeria in that twilight passage before dawn when all things stand betwixt and between.

"Can you not bide here?" she asked him, troubled because all yesterday evening he had gone about his business in such an unusual silence. "Until I return from St. Valeria?"

"To what purpose?" He turned as Ambrose set a covered pitcher of heated water down on the table beside the washbasin. Sanglant thanked the man. He was attentive to his servants. He knew their names and their histories and their skills and, it sometimes seemed, their sins. Ambrose poured. Sanglant washed his hands and face and accepted a cloth to dry himself. "Best march to Varre early in the season, before they expect me."

"If your aunt has spoken in their favor, might she not already have sent word of your intentions to them?"

"She may have. Hesitation still does not serve me well. Conrad and Sabella gain the longer I wait."

"Do they want Wendar, or only Varre?"

"Does it matter?" His expression dismayed her. He was Henry's son. She must not forget that. Henry had ruled Wendar and Varre as had his father and grandfather before him. His heir must not lose what Henry had held so dear.

"What if there is a battle?" she asked.

He shook his head as Robert and Theodulf brought his under-tunic, leggings, and fine wool outer tunic. The dazzling blue seemed to shine in the dim room, which was lightened only by one burning lamp and the misty gray light, seen through the single open window, that heralded the coming day.

"Conrad does not want to fight me. His position remains strong as duke of Wayland. It is only Sabella who goads him on, if I am any judge of the matter. She eats at her bitterness. That is all that sustains her."

"Fierce words. Are you sure?"

He lifted both hands. "I cannot answer so many ques-

tions for which there is no good answer. You know that. Do
what you must, and catch up to me quickly." He caught her
shoulders, kissed her, and released her. "Go, before I
change my mind. I have not forgotten about the galla we
met upon the road. I also have in mind these stories of Lost
Ones attacking helpless folk out in isolated villages and
farmsteads."

"Do not forget bandits," she said, piqued by his strange
mood. Anyway, she was scared, not for herself but for him.
Yet this one thing she could not bring herself to say to him:
Do not die, my love. Only do not die, and I will be content.

"Bandits are the least of it. Yet you are armed and
shielded by a power I cannot match. Do not fear to use it,
if you must." He touched her on the arm, frowned at her,
brushed a lock of black hair out of his eyes, and let her go.
She blinked back tears, picked up her saddlebags, sword
belt, and quiver, and left him.

Sickness dwelt in the pit of her stomach, a fear that made
her heavy and weary and nauseated. This tangle had grown
into an impossible maze.

He would be regnant because his father had asked it of
him. Some supported him because they loved him. Others
supported him because he rode with an army at his back.
His own relatives played a deep game on the chessboard,
offering him a pawn on the one hand while they lent their
strength to his rivals with the other. Had he been Henry's
eldest legitimate child, there would have been no question,
but he was not, and she was no fool. Her presence aided
him not at all. What Theucinda said aloud snaked through
the company like poison. It was Sanglant's weakness that
he would hear no word spoken against her, and hers that
she could not sacrifice herself on the hearth of duty. *Me for
the sake of the kingdom.* She could cast herself on the
mercy of the unknown Mother Rothgard, pledge herself as
a nun, and leave him free to marry as a man of his rank and
position must, to save the kingdom in its darkest hour.

Ai, God! She laughed weakly, seeing her escort waiting.
What a miserable nun or deacon she would make! Her life
with Da had spoiled her. Like the twilight morning, she
stood betwixt and between, not quite suited for anything

and not quite willing to be content with that which it was reasonable and responsible to aspire to.

No doubt God frowned at her selfishness, but surely it were God who poured love into the world. Surely to turn away from love was to turn away from God.

Unanswerable.

Or else she had only posed the question in such a way that she could hear the answer she wanted.

4

SHE brooded all that day as her party traveled a little worn path, but still took time to remark on the cool late spring landscape. They followed a trail through hilly country. The great estates and farming lands of Saony lay several days' ride west and east, anchored by Osterburg and Quedlinhame. Goslar was a hunting lodge built in uninhabited countryside where lords and regnants could find a profusion of game wandering the hills and dense forest.

None among the Eagles currently traveling with Sanglant had ever ridden this way, but Hathui had heard the directions from Wolfhere some years ago and had described them in detail to Liath. By late afternoon of the second day they would come to a small outpost, a free holding established by settlers given the imprimatur of King Arnulf the Elder. Beyond that a river crossing and another two days' journey would bring them to the convent, sequestered in a tiny valley among rugged hills.

Liath walked in the van beside Captain Thiadbold, setting the pace along the soggy track. Her horse, saddled, was led by a groom. Ernst and Rufus rode behind her. Fore and back came the rest of the company, two-score Lions under the command of Thiadbold. Not as swift as horsemen, but, Sanglant had noted, a seasoned captain with disciplined infantrymen in his command would serve best for a journey through the wild forest hills. Common knowledge told that

St. Valeria lay hidden in the hills so that the holy nuns who used scholarship to battle evil might make their study in peace. Or be cut off so none of them, tempted by the hope of power wielded through the black arts, could easily escape into the wider world.

"Although it seems to me," she said to Thiadbold, with whom she was having this conversation, "there are folk aplenty who dabble in the black arts hoping to make their crops prosper or their heir fertile, or their rival barren. Would it not be better to train folk to combat it in its turn?"

"That may be. But some such folk will be tempted to use their power for ill, against the neighbors they're supposed to help."

"They do that anyway."

"That's true enough. The miller in my village was a prosperous man. He got a lust for a girl—a cousin of mine as it happens—and put out his old wife and made it plain to my aunt and uncle that he'd grind no grain until they gave the girl to him. They went to the deacon, who refused to help them because the miller tithed generously and she did not wish to offend him."

"So you see, my point is made."

His answering smile held a touch of irony. "The story's not done. He beat her and treated her cruelly, so at length her parents went to the lord to beg him to intercede. And when he saw the girl, he took her away to become his concubine."

"Beauty gave her no advantage."

"Maybe so. When her parents complained again to the deacon, the holy woman said only what we all know: That it is God's will that some are set high and others low."

"Is it? So say the noble clerics and ladies and lords who stand atop the tower."

"Not only them. So said my cousin, too, after she gave birth to a child who was given, as birthright, title to an estate."

"It's easy to say, if the advantage is yours. Yet every person stands equal in the Chamber of Light."

"Do you believe that?" he asked her, genuinely curious.

He was not, she thought, a man *tempted* to philosophical speculation, but he had a keen eye and a good mind.

"I have to believe it. Else my sense of what is just would suffer grievous harm. I have met too many nobles who are fools to believe otherwise."

He chuckled, then looked around nervously before recalling, she thought, that there was no one to hear them except his own men. "Perhaps so. The church would not approve your words."

"Look!" She pointed. A lumbering shadow moving away into the forest and vanishing in the brush.

"An aurochs! Mayhap we'll have game tonight for our supper."

They did. In the rear guard a scout hauled in a deer. At the fore, a pair of men ranging in the woods to seek out trouble shot an aurochs that had stopped to graze in a clearing a spear's toss off the road.

"It might do for a campsite," said one of the scouts, coming to report the kill to the captain. "There's an old stone circle, and cleared ground."

"Let me see," said Liath.

She went with an escort of a dozen soldiers while the rest waited on the road. At the clearing, the other man had already begun butchering the aurochs, and the sharp smell of its blood hit her first. As she pushed aside the low-hanging branches, she saw what manner of place they had come to.

She shook her head, scanning the wide span of ground where a low field layer of feather grass and flowering honeysuckle grew. No trees had encroached despite the passage of time. The stones stood upright.

"Some power has raised this crown recently," she said. "See the pattern of growth around them. You can see where the stones once lay on the ground."

"Who could raise such big blocks of stone without leaving a track of their labor?" asked the scout.

Sorcery could raise the crowns, but she could not imagine anyone having so much power. After all, how many were left in the world who could even weave the crowns?

Me.

And Hugh of Austra.

She looked at Thiadbold.

He nodded. "We'll march on and hope to find a better spot."

"No," she said, because she did not like to surrender to fear. "Easier to rest here and eat that good aurochs. My mouth is already watering."

He shrugged. "If you don't like it, we'll move on. I've seen my fair measure of strange places. I know to respect their power."

She smelled nothing but vegetation, moist soil, and the innards of the dead animal spilling free as the scout cut a slit in its belly. "If bandits come upon us, we'll have a better view for our archers if we bide here with the stones as cover. What do you think, Captain?"

He took his time considering. He paced the circumference of the clearing, and walked through the stones, but there were no holes, tunnels, or hiding places. It was a dead place, all five stones standing, their faces unnaturally smooth and unmarked with moss or lichen. Although she had seen many a fallen stone cracked and hollowed by centuries of rain and ice, none of these stones showed any such wear.

"It seems dry," he said, and sent a man to fetch the rest of the company. "We'll set fires as our perimeter."

She laughed, liking his pragmatism. "Fair enough, Captain."

They ate well around six fires set at points around the clearing just beyond the crown's circle. Deadwood came easily to hand. It caught and burned with relish, and the meat tasted good, better than any meal she'd had in days because she sat easily with her companions and chatted about nothing and everything.

Eventually she discovered that some among these men had known Hanna rather better than the others.

"Yes, it's true, lady," said the one called Ingo, a broad-shouldered, good-looking man with a scar and a wicked smile. "We knew her from before, from the march east with Prince Bayan, may he rest at peace in the Chamber of Light. We're them who found her at the Veserling. We ripped her from the hands of the monster. We marched with her west and got her settled at Gent, although she was deathly ill there. It's a miracle she survived, but survive she did. And she did come with us, then, to Osterburg. After that she was sent south to Aosta. As you've already heard."

"She spoke of you," said the youngest of them, shyly.

"She is a good friend to me," said Liath. "I'd be pleased to know she has survived this tempest."

She found it easy to chat with these men. They acted, at moments, in awe of her knowledge and education, but Thiadbold and the cheerful scamp called Folquin had no fear of questioning her about what they did not understand. The older men could not be intimidated; they had seen too much. She had saved the life of one of their own. That was enough for them to accept her as a comrade. The endless battles waged on the royal progress had no claws here.

Later, when the sentry changed, those few men still awake lay down to sleep, but Liath was restless, as if the night's insomnia that often afflicted Sanglant had passed into her. You would think that afflictions might be rubbed from skin to skin or breathed from mouth to mouth. Anyone who studied medicine knew that sick people often left illness in their wake. Why not other afflictions as well?

She paced around the sentry circle, pausing between each bonfire to stare up at the heavens. Clouds veiled the stars, yet it seemed to her that she could *almost* see the faint threads of their light trailing down into the waiting crown. Would it be possible to weave the crowns if the heavens weren't clear? Any good mathematicus armed with an astrolabe and a table and a knowledge of the date and approximate hour could predict which star was rising and which setting. Could point near enough to the place in the sky where this constellation, or that one, rode and turned as the hours passed.

She had none of these things, only her memory, and even her capacious memory could not *quite* hold as much information as an astrolabe. That, after all, was why the Jinna astronomers had devised them.

"Hey!"

The shout turned her around to stare at the bonfire burning at her back, beyond the crown, about forty strides away. A sentry staggered back, a hand clapped to his right shoulder.

" 'Ware! 'Ware! I've been shot!"

Sentries called out. A pair of men grabbed sticks and lit them out of the fires to create swift-burning torches. She ran to the cursing sentry. By the time she got there, the captain and Sergeant Ingo were standing beside him, examining the arrow. It was a shallow wound. The arrow danced up and down each time the man winced and swore.

"Where?" she asked him.

"Don't know," he said through gritted teeth. "Aih! Either pull it free or stop touching it!"

"Back here so I can see if the point is barbed," said Ingo, and hauled him away.

"Silence!" she said, as the camp roused around them, men calling to each other, swords thudding against shields and mail giving its distinctive slinky rattle as men armed themselves.

"Silence!" roared Thiadbold.

In that silence, quickly fallen, she heard a twig snap, straight ahead, in the trees. She needed no bow. She bent her will to the crown of the trees and called fire.

The forest flashed into a ghastly bright false day as treetops caught fire, revealing a dozen raggedly dressed men armed with spears and sticks and bows. They ranged just out of the halo of light given by the bonfires, under the shadow of the trees, but with sparks and ash raining down over them and the flames blazing above, they fled into the darkness. Arrows skittered after them, until Thiadbold called the cease. The Lions cheered and hooted to see their foe routed.

"That's a neat trick," said Thiadbold somberly, studying the flames, "that might turn a battle or two. Yet I wouldn't try it in dry lands. Will it spread?"

"I hope not."

This was no white-hot anger, no blast of fear, to create a wildfire. It was a bigger fire than she had intended, scorching six trees altogether, but with some effort she managed to pinch off its edges so it would burn itself out. The sentry had taken only a slight wound, quickly bandaged. The men settled down as the captain set out a double guard for the rest of the night.

Even so, Liath could not sleep. Only when the fire had died completely did she lie down, and even then whenever she closed her eyes she saw burning men, their flesh melting off their bodies.

Is this why Da had sealed her off from her own magic? Had he only been trying to protect her from herself? But this question struck her as impossibly naive. Da's motives could not be so easily divined, nor were they simple. Da was not stupid, even if he hadn't had the strength of will necessary to combat Anne.

Without the stars to mark the passing of time, the night dragged on as if forever, but at length the air lightened and a bird chirped. The sound made her jump. A bird! She rose, unsteady on weary legs, and listened hard and peered into the surrounding foliage, but she did not see it or hear that call again.

5

THE outpost had a name, Freeburg, and a population of some four-score wary persons housed in an impressive walled holding consisting of five thatched longhouses, a dozen or so smaller buildings and, remarkably, the blunt spire of a tiny chapel. One lonely cottager lived outside the walls, just where the path emerged from the forest, but it wasn't clear if this spry old fellow had chosen his exile or lived close by the protecting palisade on sufferance. He watched their company march past without saying a word and turned back to clearing his garden. Six beehives lay within his fence.

The gates lay open. Folk worked in the fields and women

washed clothes in the sparkling river. Meat dried under fenced-in shelters, ready to be brought in and cured. The ring of a blacksmith's hammer surprised them; smiths, like gold, were usually found in more exalted settlements.

Folk paused to watch them. A dozen young men stood along the palisade rampart armed with bows.

"They're not trusting," murmured Liath to Thiadbold, but he only nodded thoughtfully and led the Lions right into what might be a trap, crossing over the ditch and through the open gate. The Lions halted inside the gate, in an open area with enough space for arms practice, or a market, or foot races. Soon they were surrounded. The council of elders met them.

"We heard news of you along the road," said their spokesman, a genial man with silver hair, silver beard, and a twisted smile from a palsy afflicting the left side of his face. He looked otherwise hale. "I'm called Master Helmand."

"I'm called Captain Thiadbold. We're on the regnant's business—my Lions and these three Eagles—on our way to St. Valeria's. If we might bide one night within your walls, we'd be grateful. We were attacked by bandits last night. One of our men got hurt, but we drove them off."

"Where was that?" asked Master Helmand as the folk around him whispered and nodded.

"There's a stone circle. That's where we camped last night."

"Old ghosts walk there. No one goes willingly to that place."

It was clear to Liath that the man thought them fools for having camped on haunted ground, but the confession seemed to peel off a layer of suspicion from his scrutiny. After all, how badly can fools threaten an armed village?

"You know the convent?" she asked him. "We had hoped to ask for a guide to show us the way."

"Oh, yes. They come twice a year to trade with us and sing a mass and read the prayers for the dead."

Liath gestured toward the chapel, seen now to be so small that no more than twenty folk could crowd into its nave. "You have a chapel, I see."

"Yet no deacon." He hesitated, glanced at the other elders, and went on as they fluttered their hands and nodded their heads eagerly. "Perhaps you'd take a request to the regnant, Eagle. We'll host you gladly, though we haven't much in our stores after this long winter and no good spring. We're beholden to the regnant here, as you know. Freeholders. We have a charter!"

"Have you?" Liath asked with interest. "When was it written?"

He cleared his throat. Everyone looked embarrassed. "Well, then, in the time of the old Henry, father to the first Arnulf, long since. We only hear it read aloud but twice the year at spring and fall, and this year at springtide none came from the convent to us."

"Did they not?" Liath looked at Thiadbold. He shrugged. "Have any gone to see if there is trouble there?"

"The river flooded. The ford hasn't been passable for months. There's no other way through."

"Is there no hope of us winning through?"

He beckoned to a man standing up on the walls. This one came down, and it appeared he was a hunter and tracker for the holding, one who ranged wide.

"I'm called Wulf," the man said by way of introduction after Helmand had explained the situation. He looked to be about Thiadbold's age, somewhere between late twenties and middle thirties, dark-featured, wiry, tough, with handsome eyes and a warp to his chin from an old injury. "I was up that way ten days ago. It might be better now. We can try."

"We must try," said Liath to him before turning to the elders. "We'll be grateful for your hospitality. I can read that charter for you, if you've a wish to hear it."

Oh, they did.

An entire ceremony had collected around the twice-yearly reading of their charter in the same way flotsam collects around a boulder rising from the sandy seashore. A table and chair were carried out into the open air and a cloth thrown over the table. Every household brought cups and drink and set them on the common table. Last, a pale horn was produced from a locked chest. Its call rang four times, once at each corner of the stockade, before they put it away. Lanterns were lit as the inhabitants gathered, stationing themselves in a tidy semicircle, children at the front, adults behind. All remained standing as Master Helmand emerged from the largest longhouse with a small cedar chest in his hands. He set it on the table, opened it reverently, and uncovered folded parchment. This he opened on the table, one hand pinning down the top and the other the bottom. Lanterns were set on either side, although there was still enough light for Liath, at least, to read the bold letters.

The text was succinctly written and began on the paler, flesh side of the vellum. The cream-colored grain side was blank and the corners showed a tendency to curl in that way. The parchment had a hole in it, and the scribe had drawn her ruled lines and written in her text around the flaw. The script had an old-fashioned look to it. For one thing, it used all uncials, as they had done in those days. The scribe's hand had no beauty; Liath could have done a better job. But she could read it.

" 'I, Henry, by the Grace of God in Unity, Regnant over Wendar, do grant to the inhabitants of Freeburg the customs and privileges written below . . .' " Reading, she was reminded of that day years ago in the forest holding west of Gent, when she had read aloud a charter very like to this one. "Whoever shall acquire property by clearing wastelands shall hold it for the same price as her house. . . . No one, not the regnant nor anyone else, shall demand of the householders of Freeburg any requisition or aid. . . . They shall pay neither tariff nor tax upon their food or the wine they have grown in their own vineyards. . . . Whoever lives in the holding a year and a day shall afterward remain undisturbed.' "

The formula had a parallel construction to that diploma given to the freeholders in the Bretwald by the younger Henry, although the details differed. The villagers listened as intently as scholars as she read slowly and in a clear voice.

" 'This privilege was confirmed by Henry, by faith and oath approved and accepted by the following persons . . . in the year 660 since the Proclamation of the Holy Word, on

the 11th day of Sormas, on the feast day of the Visitation.' "
She looked up in surprise. "That's today!"

Having no deacon to count the calendar for them, they,
too, were shocked and delighted. They set to drinking with a
cheer. First the children—who would lay claim to these
lands when they inherited—drank. After them, the elders,
who had husbanded the land, and last of all the householders who now worked the fields. There was enough for all, a
rare enough thing, Liath thought as she sipped at the sour
cider, which was starting to go to vinegar but had not quite
turned.

On such an auspicious occasion all lingering suspicion
vanished. Lions and Eagles were fed, and housed at random, some in the longhouses and some in byres or stock
sheds on beds of heaped straw. Liath asked for no place
greater for herself than any other, and the captain, seeing
this without commenting on it, offered her no primacy. For
the first time in many days she slept soundly, half buried in
a heap of scratchy straw with only a blanket beneath and
one thrown over herself where she had wrapped herself in
her wool cloak. In old days, long ago, she had often slept so
on the road, traveling with Da and later as an Eagle. Slipping into sleep, she could imagine Da near at hand, murmuring under his breath, talking to himself, as he often did
when there was no learned adult with whom to converse.
How he loved to chat. For all his lonely isolated ways, Da
had loved people and loved talking and discussion and argument for argument's sake. He had had a restless, roving
mind, unsettled, dissatisfied, and most likely unsatisfiable.
She tucked her saddlebags against her chest. The book was
a comforting presence, for all the trouble it had caused her.
It was, in a way, Da's conversation with himself all those
years. She wept a little, thinking of him, and fell asleep, and
dreamed of Blessing as a tiny baby sleeping at peace in her
arms.

"Liath? Ai, God! It is her!"

That Hanna's voice should so trouble her dreams did not
surprise her, not after marching for two days with the
Lions. They were in the dream, too.

"Well, I *told* you it was her," said one, sounding aggrieved.

"Since when should anyone believe your wild tales, Folquin?"

"Since I learned better from following your example, Ingo!"

"Liath!"

That a hand should touch her shoulder in such a familiar way, jostling her out of sleep, did surprise her. She opened her eyes.

She was still dreaming.

For five long breaths she stared at the apparition, the dream figure floating before her but in fact not floating at all. The figure crouched in a manner very like that of any creature that has weight and heft. Her leggings creased and bunched around the knees. Her white-blonde braid of hair had pooled on her shoulder, and as the woman shook her head with a smile, it tumbled free down her torso.

"Hanna?" Liath sat up.

Then, after all, came the hugging and the weeping.

VI

NO GOING BACK

1

THEIR company set out at once for the convent.

"I rode from St. Valeria with a request for some laborers to come and rebuild the damaged wall," explained Hanna. "We thought to let our party rest there a few days in peace while I rode here to ask for aid."

"You managed the river crossing," said the one called Wulf. He hadn't been able to take his gaze off Hanna since she and Liath walked out of the byre. "Had you no guide? How high was the water running?"

As Hanna described her journey between convent and village—she had spent the night sleeping outdoors—Liath stared at her. It seemed she had walked into a dream, something hoped for so long that she could not believe it to be true. Had Sanglant stared at her in this manner when she had returned from the aether? Yet she felt less awkwardness with Hanna than she had at first with Sanglant. She felt, more than anything, relief, as though she had discovered that the hand she thought missing was, after all, still attached.

As Hanna finished talking, she glanced at Liath, grinned, and shook her head. "I still can't believe it. I've thought of you so often over the years. I must still be dreaming. Sorgatani will be eager to see you!"

These astounding tidings must all be explained. As the two women chattered back and forth without pause the day seemed, as the poets said, to fly past. They marched along a grassy track barely more than a cow path footed in mud. The river still ran high—Hanna had managed the crossing because of the weight of her horse—and they strung a rope across for the Lions to grip so they would not get swept away in the current. After this, the way wound in rugged leaps and switchbacks up into steep, forested hills troubled by ancient ravines and fresh gullies. Now and again the woodsman exclaimed over a landslide that had obliterated a portion of the path, or a new waterfall pouring down through a cleft in a rocky outcropping. Trees had snapped and tumbled. It was, in truth, a miracle that Hanna had managed to get through at all, let alone with a horse.

"This is no ordinary steed," she said, "but Lady Bertha's own palfrey, a noble steed, impossibly brave and strong-hearted. She's Wicked."

"Then why are you riding her?"

Hanna chuckled. "That's her name. The story goes that when Lady Bertha acquired her, the mare bit her. I don't know if it's true. She can jump, though, and she isn't afraid of anything."

"I pray you, Hanna, tell me again of what has transpired since the tempest last autumn. I cannot believe—Lady Bertha survived with some few others of those that accompanied me—and yet so close to home she is killed! Are you sure of what you saw?"

"I'll tell you again," said Hanna, soberly, not taking offense at the question as Liath had known she would not. "Ask me what questions you will. Maybe I'll remember something I've forgot. It was a horrible night. Those arrows flying out of the darkness!" She shuddered. "Should another have spoken to me of it, I would not have believed him."

She repeated the story. Hanna's testimony was well observed and, as far as it was in her power given her place within the night's events, related without too much emotion clouding her comments.

"Ashioi, then," Liath agreed. "They have attacked in other places as well. How can they have come so far north?"

"On their own two feet, I suppose."

"Well, then. Why?"

"To kill Wendish folk, I must guess. Or to kill Prince Sanglant. They called his name."

"Some think they are allied with him, now that he is regnant. That he means to conquer Wendar and Varre and hand the kingdom over to his mother's people."

"You do not think so."

Liath gave her a sidelong look and wondered if Hanna distrusted Sanglant. If Hanna distrusted *her* because of Sanglant. "I don't believe it."

When Hanna frowned, she looked years older. "I don't know what to think. I fear those warriors with their poisoned darts more than I ever feared Bulkezu and his Quman."

"Maybe so, but that doesn't make Sanglant their ally. He would never betray his father's memory."

A stream had changed course in the last months and cut a gully across the path. They had to dismount. The Lions scrambled down and cut enough of a ramp into the sides with shovels that the horses could negotiate the obstacle. Pine whispered above. The forest cover made the path dim as they moved forward along higher ground.

Hanna lengthened her stride. Hurrying to catch up to her, Liath found they were walking out in front of the others, beyond earshot.

"What troubles you, Hanna? I see it in your face."

Hanna looked back, looked ahead, even looked up at the canopy of green above them. The heady aroma of pitch caught in Liath's throat; for such a long time she had smelled only mildewed leaf litter and the icy breath of unseasonable wintry winds.

"I admit, I'm still angry at Prince Sanglant for letting Bulkezu live when he should have executed him. I'm sorry to say so. It's the truth. Whether it speaks good or ill of me, I don't know."

"It's honest of you. None of us are saints."

"That's truth!" She smiled wryly, then frowned in a way that made Liath want to touch her, but she held back. "I should know better. If you trust him, so should I."

"Thank you."

"It's thinking of Sorgatani just now that made me realize. The others fear her, because of what she did at Augensburg."

"They knew the curse laid on her by her power. She never said otherwise, did she? Was she not honest with them?"

"Honesty is not the same as trust. It was worse than the poisoned arrows. They died only from looking at her." She made a kind of hiccup, like a laugh or a cough. "Sorgatani told me you are like sisters, that you alone are not bound to her but are powerful enough to see her without dying. Did it not scare you the first time, knowing the nature of her curse?"

"I don't remember thinking of it at all."

Hanna halted and faced her, looking awful.

"I spoke too lightly," said Liath. "Forgive me. Of course it would terrify them. As much as it must frighten folk to be around me."

"Around *you?* Why so?"

Liath felt how crooked the smile must look on her face. "Because I can kill people, too."

"So can we all, with a sword or a spear thrust. With our own hands, if we're strong enough."

"I can burn them alive. People fear me, and they should."

"But you would *never*—!"

"Sorgatani would never, would she?"

"She cried, afterward."

"Yet folk will look at her and see a foreigner. A demon."

"Yes, truly, so they will." With a sad smile, Hanna lifted her hand to touch Liath's dusky cheek. "I am so glad we have found each other again, at last."

Liath's throat was choked, and her voice trembled. "At last," she agreed. It was all she could manage to say without bursting into tears.

2

THE convent hid in a ravine whose entrance was so cleverly concealed that Liath would have walked right past it and kept moving southeast on the trail, on into the wilderness. Hanna turned aside where honeysuckle concealed a path. They made their way down a rocky track between high cliff walls of streaked stone. Two men could not walk abreast; it was barely wide enough for the packhorses to squeeze through. A bird whistled, and Hanna responded with a shout to identify herself. The clop of hooves and stamp of feet threw weird echoes into the air. These ceased when the ravine opened into a neat jewel of a valley. A stream crossed their path, straining its banks. Beyond, a substantial stone wall blocked the valley's mouth, but it had crumbled in three places where floodwaters had eaten away its foundation. Fence segments woven of branches patched the gaps.

Beyond, a low stockade surrounded a whitewashed long hall and a collection of outbuildings. Chickens clucked. Goats bawled. Fruit and nut trees stood in tidy rows. Freshly turned earth marked a substantial garden.

Everyone turned out to greet them: lean soldiers armed with spears and swords, clerics in ragged robes, and a dozen nuns of varying ages dressed in sober wool robes and holding rakes and shovels and scythes in their hands. A party of Ashioi could have devastated their ranks in moments, had they only known where to find them.

Hanna was so excited that she raced forward, leaving her horse behind with one of the Lions. She was still very much the girl Liath remembered from Heart's Rest—her first true friend—and yet the years had tempered and molded her to become something different as well: the good nature, the pragmatic eye, and the true heart remained unaltered, but when she wasn't talking, she pinched her lips together in way that made Liath want to hug her, as if hugging could erase pain. What had she suffered that she did not speak of? Those gathered here might know.

Their joy at seeing Hanna could not be misinterpreted: they trusted and liked her.

Liath dismounted and approached with more caution as Sister Rosvita came forward to greet her. The journey had turned the cleric's hair to silver, and she was as lean as a scarecrow, but she had a ruddy gleam to her face and vigor in her stride.

"Eagle! Or must I call you otherwise? We are hopelessly behind in our news. How do you fare?"

Liath greeted her in the formal manner, clasping arms in the way of courtiers who do not quite trust each other but hope to by reason of their mutual love for the regnant. "It is a long tale. I have business here with Mother Rothgard. Is she here?"

Rosvita shook her head. "She is gone."

Disappointment did jab. She felt it under her ribs. "Gone where?"

"Dead." Liath heard no grief in Rosvita's voice, only weariness. "So we discover, arriving here ourselves only two days ago. Here is Sister Acella, who stands as mother to those nuns who remain."

It took time to sort things out. First, Liath greeted those few of Bertha's retinue who had survived—the sergeant and a dozen or so men. She felt sick at heart seeing so few of them, and yet they greeted her respectfully and with every evidence that they were relieved to be reunited with the woman who had marched them to their doom. Each member of Rosvita's schola made a pretty introduction; the only one she recalled from before was Brother Fortunatus, gone as lean as he once was chubby. The nuns of St. Valeria watched from afar as Sister Acella led her into the hall and sat her at a table, bringing a pitcher of ale.

"The Lions and the other Eagles will be thirsty, too," said Liath, noting how only Rosvita and Acella sat with her. Hanna had not come inside. A pair of nuns watched her with uncomfortably intent interest from the shadows at the far end of the hall, but they did not approach.

"They will be taken care of," said Acella. "Tell me what you have come for."

"I'll do so, gladly, if you'll tell me what became of Mother Rothgard and how she died."

The tale was quickly told. Autumn's tempest had torn part of the roof off the long hall. Mother Rothgard had died after falling from a ladder while repairing the thatch. Floods had uprooted the wall, and wolves, growing bold, had killed four nuns over the course of the winter. Weaker souls would have abandoned the site, but few chose the isolated, difficult life at St. Valeria's in any event and those left had voted to bide in the hall and rebuild rather than flee the onslaught of so many troubles.

"Otherwise we would have to burn the books," said Sister Acella in her dour voice. She seemed a kind of cheerful cynic.

"Burn the books!"

"So it commands us in our charter. Such books as have been collected here must never leave this library or be copied and taken away. Otherwise they might fall into the wrong hands."

"Not even if the regnant commands it?"

Acella had a cordial laugh. Like all of her sister nuns, she was as thin as a reed but with real muscle in those arms, a woman who labored as hard as she prayed. "Especially if the regnant commands it. Our charter comes from the skopos, not the regnant. Many years ago, of course. We were founded in the last year of the reign of the Emperor Taillefer, back when this was wilderness for ten days' walk in every direction, beyond the frontier."

"A strange place to collect such dangerous and rare texts," said Liath, "when any raider might sweep down and carry them off."

"We are well hidden. And better guarded than you might think." She indicated the door, left open to admit a hazy midday light that did not, quite, penetrate to the rafters or under the eaves. "The labor of those Lions would be a great aid to us, if you can spare the time."

"A bargain, perhaps," said Liath, "as I come at the regnant's urging to seek knowledge. These clouds must be lifted so that crops can grow, else many will starve in the months to come."

Acella looked at Sister Rosvita, then back at Liath. She had a feather-light mustache, barely noticeable, the mark of a strong woman who has survived into middle age. "What knowledge is it that you seek? We have heard of you, the Eagle called Liathano. Princess Theophanu was healed here, some years ago. She said that you saved her life. We've heard you were excommunicated at a council in Autun. Has that been lifted?"

"I am here," said Liath, wishing that she did not have to dance this merry round again. "I pray you, if you mean to refuse me, do so at once. I do not have the courtier's gift of persuasion. I seek the secrets of the tempestari in the hope that sorcery can ease the cloud-ridden weather." She laughed, looked at her companions, realizing she had seen no sign of the Kerayit wagon, and sobered quickly. "Where is Sorgatani? She is a weather worker. She learned from the eldest of all, the ancient one."

"This is holy ground," said Sister Acella, smiling easily. "No heathen is allowed to set foot within the walls."

"You said yourself you've been attacked by wolves at least four times over the winter and spring." Liath stared at them indignantly. "What if there is another Ashioi raiding party? You can't have left her alone out in the forest!"

They did not answer, although her voice rose passionately. Their silence dismayed her.

"Do you know what she is?" Sister Rosvita asked at last. "No one may look on her and live, only except those who are her slaves and her servants."

"Hanna is not her slave! Nor am I!"

"You? What are you saying?"

"That I have 'looked on her and lived.' "

It was the wrong thing to say. Sister Acella said nothing but Rosvita exhaled sharply, and then looked sorry she had done so.

Liath rose. "I pray you, show me, or tell me, where her wagon lies, and I'll go to her myself. As for the rest, let the Lions labor as long as I may consult your library."

"It seems we have no choice," said Acella dryly. "If we deny you?"

"If crops will not grow, folk will starve."

"Waters unleashed may irrigate one field while flooding the rest."

"Are these riddles, Sister Acella, that I am meant to answer?"

"They are cautions. Sorcery lies under ban, for good reasons. I have labored in these 'fields' all my life. We here in St. Valeria know that knowledge can be more dangerous than arms, that magic can do more harm than steel."

"The storm that swept us last autumn was no natural storm, but one raised long ago by sorcery. How else to combat it except with sorcery of our own?"

"That path is a treacherous one."

"I prefer not to see folk starve when I might have done something to prevent it."

"Even if you will be damned for it?"

"The church may damn me, if they must. I do not believe God will."

Rosvita stood and pressed a hand to the shoulder of Acella to stop her from leaping to her feet.

The anger in Acella's face, however, could not be kept still. Her words were clipped and furious. "That was ill spoken, Eagle. Do you claim to know God's mind?"

Liath raised a hand, then swept it back down to her side. "Do you?" She was too angry to speak further.

"I pray you, Sister Acella," said Rosvita placatingly. "Let us see the diploma this Eagle has brought from King Henry. She carries the regnant's seal and the regnant's authority."

"Henry is dead," said Liath. "Did you not know?"

"Dead?"

The cleric staggered. She paled. She swayed. Brother Fortunatus, who had stood all this time by the door watching them without trying to overhear, ran to help her sit down on the bench.

"Is this true?" The look on her face broke Liath's heart.

"It's true. He died in Aosta."

Rosvita hid her face in her hands.

Fortunatus looked at Liath. He was pale but not as shaken as Rosvita. "In Aosta? If this is true, then . . ."
Strangely, he glanced toward the shadowed end of the hall

where those two watchful nuns stood as straight and alert as soldiers on guard. "Can it be that after all . . . ?"

Rosvita lowered her hands. Through tears, she looked at Liath. "Who stands as regnant? Who granted you the power to ride to St. Valeria? Who rules these Lions? Who rules Wendar?"

"Sanglant."

She might have said "the Enemy" and seen them less shocked.

Sister Acella got to her feet. "Enough! I cannot allow her in the library, Sister Rosvita. We have no way of knowing if her tale is true. How can a bastard rule in Wendar? Not by right, but by the sword."

"Wait, Honored Mother," said Fortunatus placatingly. "Surely there is an explanation that comes with this news. Lady Bertha and her soldiers were sent into Dalmiaka as an escort to this one, Liathano. To battle against King Henry's enemies."

"To battle the skopos, so you say," hissed Sister Acella. "How can we know this tale is true? How do we know that Prince Sanglant did not march into Aosta and *kill* his own father to gain the throne?"

Liath could barely force civil words out, but she knew she had to. She felt like slapping the bitch, with her smug expression and stony words. "Ask the other Eagles, then, or the Lions."

Except the Lions had not witnessed the events in Aosta. Stupidly, she had not asked for anyone to march with her who had actually been with Sanglant on the field that night last Octumbre. She had no one with her who had witnessed Henry passing the crown of Wendar into the hands of his beloved son. She had not brought anyone with her who would be believed.

"If only Hathui had come!" She turned to leave, sick of them and of this turmoil in her heart.

"Hathui?" Fortunatus reached to catch her sleeve, but withdrew his hand before touching her.

"Hathui lives?" Rosvita asked. Grief hoarsened her voice.

"She is with Sanglant. She *serves* Sanglant."

"You may say anything you wish," retorted Sister Acella.

"So I may. In this case, it happens to be true."

"I pray you." Fortunatus placed a hand on Acella's elbow. "I pray you, Honored Mother. Sit down. Calm down." He was staring at Liath. They all were.

"God Above," whispered Acella, in the tone a woman might use when a minion of the Enemy has appeared on her doorstep. "She *shines*."

Liath took a step back, as if struck. She saw how they looked at her with fear and with doubt. It was the same expression she had seen when they spoke of Sorgatani, who was to them a kind of horror that might rise in the night to devour them. She had no words, no argument, to convince them. She retreated, wanting to flee.

"I pray you, Liathano." The voice came from the shadows, a woman's alto beckoning her with clarity and composure. "If you will, the Holy Mother wishes to speak with you, lady."

"Let her be gone from this house!" cried Acella.

It pleased Liath to flout her, so she crossed the hall into the shadows where that pair of nuns waited. They were older women, wiry, strong, determined. Their robes had worn so thin that in patches, about the knee and shoulder, they were almost translucent, just waiting to rip. This she saw because she had salamander eyes, able to spy where light failed, and that was no doubt another argument against her.

"I thought Mother Rothgard was dead," she said. "What means this?"

"We serve another one," said the elder, stepping to one side to reveal a pair of beds built in under the eaves.

In the right-hand bed two woman sat, staring at her. With a shock, she recognized Princess Sapientia—but so changed! The princess gazed at her without reaction. The princess' companion, a nondescript woman in nun's robes, watched Liath with brows furrowed and lips turned down in an uneasy frown. The nun held the princess' hand as one holds the hand of a restless child, but Sapientia did not move or speak, only stared and stared as if her stare were her weapon. Or as if she did not know who Liath was.

No wonder Sister Rosvita was surprised to hear that Sanglant had taken the throne, when she had his legitimate sister riding with her.

"My lady?" she said, not sure what to say or how to approach this delicate matter. Ai, God. Sapientia had vanished as a prisoner of the Pechanek Quman. She had no reason to love her brother and every reason to hate him, and here she sat. Her brooding stare was beginning to frighten Liath, who had long since lost her fear of most threats from knowing how easily she could destroy them. The desire for revenge was beyond her power, and it scared her.

How would Sanglant react when the sister he'd led to her doom reappeared on the scene?

"There, there, lady," said the seated attendant, chafing Sapientia's hand between her own. "Best if you lie down again."

"She doesn't speak," said the elder nun in a practical tone, "and has not for many weeks, not since the cataclysm. Poor creature. We fear she lost her wits."

"Let her sit, if she will," said a new voice, one rich with age and oddly familiar. "How bright she is! I see Bernard in her. The resemblance is remarkable. Dear child! Dear child! Let me hold your hand."

A person lay in the shadows of the second bed, a frail figure propped up on pillows. She was perhaps the oldest person Liath had ever seen, older even than Eldest Uncle. As if drawn by that voice, by an emotion in the words she could not name or resist, she moved a step closer and halted at the rim of the bed, staring into a seamed face that crowded her memory and made her sway, dizzy with bewilderment.

"I know you. I have seen you before."

"Yes, yes, dear child. You are she. Bernard's child."

"I am Bernard's daughter."

"Sit. Take my hand. I will touch you."

One did not say "no" to a woman of such advanced years, a woman, moreover, who was wearing the ring of an abbess.

Liath sat obediently and reached out hesitantly. That

wrinkled, pale, withered hand gripped hers with a fierce strength. The eyes that examined her had a startling heavenly blue color, not unlike her own.

"Bring the candle closer," said the old woman. Her attendants knelt on the bed with the illuminating flame.

"The galla!" said Liath, recognizing her. "You are the ones the galla stalked."

"It was your arrow that saved us," said the old woman. "We would have been dead had you not come."

Liath found no words, although she searched. She had held on to that arrow through storm and battle and she knew now that she had done the right thing and saved the right person, only she did not know why.

"The brightness is fading," said the old woman.

She blushed. "It only comes on me when I'm very angry. When any passion takes hold, it fans the flame."

"So I see. 'Liathano.' This is the name Bernard gave you."

"You speak of him as if you know—knew—him."

"Why, dear child," she said with a chuckle, "I am grown absentminded in my last days. I have waited so long for this that I have supposed you already to know what I have so long dreamt on." She had tears in her eyes and an expression of ineluctable joy on her face, a radiance that took Liath's breath away. Those fingers stroked hers weakly. The contrast between the light touch of her frail hands and the strength of her voice was striking.

"I am Bernard's mother. Your grandmother. We are met at long last. My prayers are answered."

Surely this was how the ox chosen for Novarian's slaughter felt when the first hammer blow slammed into its head to stun it before its throat was cut. Once chosen, there was no going back.

The old woman had expanded to take up Liath's entire consciousness, the entire cosmos, only her, this delicate crone who claimed so astonishingly to be her *grandmother*. That the universe should be both vast enough and narrow enough to encompass such a being could not be explained.

No one spoke to trouble her marveling. There came in due time trailing into her consciousness a faint aroma of mildew rising out of the darkest corners of the bed and blending with it the fragrance of olive oil and sweet rose oil. She began to hear sounds: the rustle of the mattress as someone shifted position nearby; whispering voices as far away as daylight; the strain in her thigh because of the way she had twisted her knee under herself; the scrape of a bench being dragged over the plank floor; Thiadbold's hearty laugh, from outside.

His laugh brought her back to earth. The world recovered its normal proportions only it was forever altered by its possession of so simple a thing as a grandmother. Da's mother.

"Impossible," she said.

"Certainly unexpected," said the old woman with amusement. "I am called Mother Obligatia. I am abbess—or was, for we are refugees now. I was abbess of the convent of St. Ekatarina's. We bided there in our rock tower in Aosta for many years in peace. All that is gone. I have much to tell you, dear child, and many questions to ask."

"How can it be?"

"Will you hear the tale?" It was difficult to tell if a sudden diffidence had overtaken her or if she was out of breath.

"I will hear this tale," said Liath, who found she could herself scarcely catch breath to form words. She leaned closer. "Rest when you must. I pray you, speak softly. Do not strain yourself."

How strange that it should seem that the old woman was comforting *her,* stroking her hands as she spoke in a voice that did not penetrate farther than the tiny audience drawn in tightly around her: Liath, and the two nuns who held light aloft. They, too, seemed to be weeping, in silence, as if their bodies resonated with whatever emotion thrummed in the soul of their abbess. The ridges and shadowed valleys of the rumpled blankets were the only landscape in this scene. Rain pattered over the roof and faded.

"I am Bernard's mother, but before that, I gave birth to another child."

The tapestry of Liath's life and lineage had always concealed more than it revealed, but Obligatia's story wove in many of the gaping holes. So it became clear as Liath asked questions where she must and answered those she could. An hour passed as the story unfolded. She drank a cup of ale, shared with the old woman. The grandmother. It was still unthinkable to use that word, but she must use it because although it might all be a fabrication or a mistake, she knew in her gut that this piece of the story made all the rest explicable.

Bernard and Anne were half siblings. Obligatia herself had been used as a pawn in the dynastic schemes woven by the Seven Sleepers. It was hard to know what Biscop Tallia and Sister Clothilde had hoped for when they had shoved the fourteen-year-old-girl into the path of the fifty-year-old monk, except that they needed a compliant, kinless female to breed with the last direct legitimate son born to Taillefer. No one would ever know the whole, now that Anne was dead, and even Anne could not have comprehended everything because in many ways she had also been their pawn, their creation.

"Some part of the tale I learned from Sister Rosvita," Obligatia finished. "The rest I know of my own experience."

"Are you tired? If you must rest, I will wait."

The hand squeezed her; strength lived there still! "No, I will go on. I have lived past my rightful measure of years. I dare wait no longer, dear child. I held on only for this, to see you and to touch you. I can see in your face that my beloved boy Bernard was your father, but how comes it that Anne claimed to be your mother? Is it true?"

"It is not. My mother was a fire daimone enticed to Earth and trapped here by a net of sorcery. Bernard loved *her*. Not Anne. The daimone was my mother. This I know because I have walked the spheres . . ."

What walking the spheres entailed, and how she had come to do so, she explained to Obligatia, who showed no sign of distaste, distress, or fear at discovering—or at any rate having confirmed—that her granddaughter was not wholly human. She was kind and generous and affectionate and wise and calm and amusing and indeed she possessed every quality that Liath had ever dreamed she might find in a grandmother, the one she had long since resigned herself to never having and never knowing.

"There is one thing, though," Liath added. "Brother Fidelis was the son of Taillefer and Radegundis. My father was born to you and a lord born into the line of Bodfeld."

"I always called him Maus, to tease him. His name was Mansuetus, fitting enough, for he was quiet and small and gentle." She chuckled. The memory was so old that it no longer seemed to cause her pain. "And nervous of his aunts and uncle, though he defied them to marry me."

"That quality runs true, then," said Liath with a laugh. "But who were *your* parents?"

Obligatia smiled sadly. "No one knows. I was a foundling. I was raised at the convent of St. Thierry. I had a different name, then. Left behind like so much else."

"Where is St. Thierry?"

"In Varre. In the duchy of Arconia."

Liath lifted the old woman's hands and kissed each one and set them back on her blankets. "You lost two husbands and two children—all taken from you. How can it be you have lived so long without falling prey to grief and anger?"

She lifted trembling hands toward Liath's face, and Liath grasped them. "I suppose," she said, her voice as shaky as her arms, fading as exhaustion overwhelmed her, "that in some part of me I was always waiting, I was always hoping."

"For what?" Liath asked her, and bent close to listen.

"For you."

3

"MOTHER Obligatia is a powerful ally," said Hanna to Liath much later. They had shared a bowl of porridge—so strongly flavored with leeks that Liath could still taste them after two cups of ale—while Hanna told of her adventures in Aosta and farther east. Now, as Hanna finished her tale, they paused at the wall. Lions labored in what remained of the day's light, lifting stones back into place.

Thiadbold left off working to come speak to them. Like most of the other Lions, he had stripped down to his undershift and was nevertheless sweating despite the cooling temperature. He had dirt streaked on his face and his hands were caked with earth. He had tied a kerchief around his hair to keep it clean; red strands curled around his ears, and he used a wrist to wipe a strand out of his left eye.

"No stonemason would admire it," he said, gesturing toward the hasty work and the laboring men, "but it will hold for a season or two until better work can be done."

Folquin, down the line, waved at them, then yelped and leaped when Leo dropped a rock a hand's breadth from his foot.

"How long will it take to fill it all in?" Liath asked.

He shrugged. "A day or two, not more with this company." He smiled at Hanna. "You've seen them in action."

"So I have," she said, and Liath saw how she reddened, just a little, and how her smile turned crooked, just a little. "The best soldiers in the regnant's army."

He laughed. "Fair spoken, and even true. These Lions have served faithfully through hard trials and hard losses." He indicated the forest. "We've heard there's a witch and a wagon out in the trees. Need you an escort?"

"It's close by," said Hanna, "and there is some danger involved to your men, which I suppose you will have heard as well."

"That a look from the witch's eyes brings death? We've heard such a rumor."

"To look on her will kill you, yes, and it's no rumor. It's a curse set on her, no sorcery that she sought of her own will."

"A terrible fate for any person, to be always alone," he said, and Liath saw how he looked searchingly at Hanna and how she colored, and spoke to cover her discomposure.

"Send a pair of archers out to that stump, there. If we have any trouble, or see any wolves, they'll hear us shout."

Thiadbold wiped his forehead again as he looked at Liath. "You'll not be having any trouble with wolves, I doubt."

"I hope not." Liath brushed a hand over her bow. She had obtained a quiver and arrows and sword and sheath to replace those lost. The griffin-fletched arrows had a metallic smell. "We're armed well."

"So you are," he agreed cryptically.

As soon as they crossed the ditch Liath said in a low voice, "He's taken a fancy to you, Hanna. How well do you know him?"

"Not *that* well!"

"You're blushing. He's a good man, good looking, level-headed, and has the regnant's trust. Have you given no thought—"

"Leave it, I pray you. I've walked no easy road these past few years." But she relented, smiling with what looked like regret. "I admit all that you say of him is true. At another time, in another place—they're good men, those Lions. They're the company that rescued me from Bulkezu. I suppose when I see them I'm reminded of the monster."

"Bulkezu? He's dead."

"Dead." She halted and looked at Liath. "Sorgatani told me he was dead. How did it happen?"

Liath reached over her own left shoulder and, again, touched the curve of her bow, which was strung, ready for battle. "I killed him."

Hanna covered her eyes and Liath took two steps before realizing that her friend was weeping. She turned back, hugged her, and they stood under the forest cover until Hanna was done.

"There. I promised I wouldn't do that."

"How badly did he hurt you?" whispered Liath.

Hanna pressed a hand to her own forehead. "I saw horrible things, but I was never touched. Ai, God. I will never forget what I saw."

"No, of course you won't. Nor should you."

"I wish I could. Is it bad of me to wish I could?"

Liath took her hand. "No. Come, let's go see Sorgatani."

A path frequented by sheep and littered with their droppings took them across a burbling stream into a meadow rimmed on three sides with an old earth berm, the remains of an ancient habitation. Along the fourth side the

nuns, or their servants, had built a fence so they could corral livestock here. The painted wagon sat in the middle of
the green, violets blooming around it. Four horses grazed
peaceably. Brother Breschius crouched beside a fire, which
was spanned by an iron tripod. He was crumbling herbs
into an iron pot hung from the tripod's upper supports
when he heard their voices.

"Lady!" he cried, striding to her with an expression of
delight. "Ai, God! We thought you lost!"

He would have knelt and kissed her hand, but she
would not let him. He laughed when he saw she was determined in this, winkled his hand out of hers, unhooked a
small bell from his belt, and slipped the tiny hood off its
clapper. The overtones of its resonant ring echoed back
from the forest.

The door at the back of the wagon opened, and Sorgatani looked out. She saw him, and saw Hanna—and
Liath. Her mouth dropped open.

"Liath!"

"It's safe for you to come out," said Hanna. "We're
alone."

Overtones still teased at the edge of Liath's hearing.
"Does the convent have a bell? Do you hear it?"

"Hear what?" asked Hanna.

Sorgatani paused on the steps.

Breschius surveyed the clearing and the surrounding
woods anxiously. "I hope you told them to keep well away.
I only ring the bell when it's safe for her to come out."

The breath of that sound floated on the breeze, lighter
than the kiss of a butterfly's wings on waiting lips.
Liathano.

"That's no bell." Liath got her bow out and an arrow
free. "Get in the wagon. I'll run into the trees to draw it
away."

"Galla," said Hanna. "I've heard them before."

"It's after me. Get in the wagon. I can kill it easily
enough with a griffin feather, but if you are in the way, it
will devour you."

Breschius watched them, nervous but uncomprehend-
ing. "It's getting dark. An archer is blinded by night."

"Not dark yet for me. Go, Hanna!"

Hanna grabbed Breschius' wrist and tugged him after. "Get inside, Sorgatani!"

Liath ran out of the enclosure, then ducked into the trees, seeking open ground. Better to have met it in the clearing, but she could not control its movements there, where the wagon lay. As she jogged along, leggings rattling against underbrush, she felt its presence veer after her, heard the change of direction in its bell voice as it shifted its course. There was only one.

Twilight turned to gray. The last of the day's cloudy light sifted down through the canopy, which here consisted mostly of bare branches and the occasional pine or lonely spruce, densely and darkly green. She saw a lightening beyond the trees, ahead of her, and dashed into a meadow cut by a trickling creek. She splashed through the water—it was no more than ankle-deep—and waded through knee-high grass until she reached a central place in the clearing. After turning, she listened; seeking, she examined the forest. The wind shifted, hiding the galla's iron tang and muting its deep voice.

From the trees behind her a warbler droned its chiff-chaff call, answered by the chatter of a magpie. She squinted, wondering, marveling. There was hope still, if the birds had returned to build their nests.

She heard the sound more as a breath released, too late. She spun. An arrow bit into her thigh. Stumbling backward, she grabbed the haft of the arrow and to her amazement it came free, slipped right out of her flesh all bloody. Blood spilled down her leggings and around the curve of her knee.

Ai, God, it stung, worse than the arrow that had pinned her to the corpse of a horse. She staggered, fell, but caught herself on a hand.

Liathano. The galla's voice rang in her heart like the pulse of her blood; it breathed with her as it closed in.

She fumbled for her bow, dropped in the grass, but the pain spreading from the wound in her thigh boiled so hot that it burned her flesh from the inside out.

This is what it feels like to be eaten alive by fire.

Still kneeling, she fought to keep herself braced up on that hand. If she fell, she died. Grass tickled her face as she swayed. Her entire leg had gone to fire, and the fire sped into her chest until she could not breathe, only burn.

When the shadows slid free of the forest and came running up to her, she understood at last. They were men with the faces of animals. The Ashioi had come. She had been poisoned.

Liathano.

To her right, the towering blackness that marked the galla's mortal body swept out of the trees. The smell of the forge washed over her, blinding her. She fumbled with her right hand—the left was ash—and found the cutting feathers of the griffin-fletched arrow. Pain cut her fingers. She felt her balance going, her body toppling sidelong as the toxin roared into her mind, searing everything before it, even that lingering sour-leek taste from the porridge.

She tried to speak but had no voice.

Cat Mask leaned over her. "What creature have you called down on us?"

Shifting the arrow a finger's length got him to look down at it. "Kill it," she whispered. "With—griffin—feather."

A fox face loomed over her. "This is the one we seek! You've killed her!"

"Stand back! Let me aim!"

Liathano.

Dead anyway, she thought bitterly as her vision clouded, hazed over by a veil of darkness. The galla will devour me. Ai, God, Sanglant. The baby, the precious blessing. The flames devoured her, and she fell.

I couldn't even warn Hanna.

A spark flew. In a shower of light, the galla snapped out of existence. And so did she.

4

HAVING once tasted the air roiling around a swarm of galla, Hanna now felt her flesh attuned to their presence. Although Liath had vanished into the forest, Hanna knew, at once, when the creature vanished, as she would know the instant a great weight pressing down on her body was lifted.

"Come!" She opened the door of Sorgatani's wagon and clattered down the steps. She grabbed her staff, which she had left outside, leaning against high wheels. She stared around the clearing, hoping to see Liath reappear.

"What think you?" Breschius blocked the door. The Kerayit shaman stood behind him, rubbing her forehead.

"My face hurts," she said. "So it hurts, before a storm front breaks. Something has happened."

"The galla is gone."

"Best you not go hunting her," said Breschius, "with the night coming down. You'll be stumbling through the dark all lost. There's no telling what you might meet out there, wolves, darts, bandits."

It had grown too dark to see more than shapes and shadows, no detail, and only the starless sky above, nothing to mark direction or the passing of time.

"I curse them for fools," said Hanna fiercely.

"Who?" asked Breschius.

"The nuns, all of them, even Sister Rosvita, for leaving you out here."

"No." A lamp burned behind Sorgatani; the golden net that capped her black hair glittered in its illumination. "They are safe without me. I am safe alone."

Hanna had learned not to argue with Sorgatani, who had become morose since the attack in Avaria. "Very well. You wait here for Liath. I'll warn the nuns and Lions about the galla. Where one comes, another may follow."

"Is there anything they can do if a galla comes?"

"No. That's what they must know."

She drew her sword. She didn't much like the feel of it in her hand. She had no real confidence that she could kill with it, but like so many other things, it was necessary. She was lucky to have a sword—this one had belonged to one of Lady Bertha's soldiers, now deceased.

A warbler trilled from the woodland, and she frowned. "I'll come back at dawn. Stay inside."

"I don't like this," said Breschius suddenly. "Best if you stay, Hanna. You'll be safer if you bide by us."

She ran as much to escape his pleading as to return to the convent. Something was wrong. She knew it, but she could not explain it. Liath should have returned—unless the galla had caught her. Devoured her.

She must not think like that.

Twilight ate at her vision, but she had walked this path a dozen times in the last few days. A breath—a pale arrow—whistled past her.

"Oh, God." She ducked down, running with short, rapid steps, heart racing, utterly alert. She plunged out of the trees into the open ground surrounding the convent.

"Attack! Attack!" she cried, and heard her own voice choke on fear, and tried again. "To arms! To arms! Aronvald! Thiadbold!"

A shaft sprouted out of the ground a body's length from her. She zigged and zagged, stumbled once, kept going although she had scraped her hand raw. Blood trickled off her palm. A torch bloomed at the wall, then a second and third and fourth, so much light she could see their figures scrambling to take up defensive positions where the wall protected them. The work they had done this afternoon would not be enough.

"Get cover! Get cover!" The light exposed them. She sprinted, making for the ditch. Arrows thunked into the dirt.

A horn lifted to sound the alert. *Alarm! Alarm!* it seemed to cry. *Awake! Stand ready!*

"Archers! Hold your fire!" That was Thiadbold, taking command of his men from the shelter of the wall. Voice carrying from the far side of the compound, Sergeant Aronvald called for his three remaining archers: "Stand where you're covered! The rest of you, get down! Keep your heads down, dammit!"

She ran under the gate, dropped the sword, and fell panting to her knees as Ingo, Folquin, Leo, and Stephen ran to her. She'd had no trouble breathing while she'd been running but now couldn't get any air in.

"Hanna!"

"Got . . . to . . . warn . . . Arrows are poison. Dead . . . if you're hit, you'll be dead. *Dead*."

She searched their expressions for some sign that they understood how serious the situation was. On the ride here from the village, she had told the story of the attack at Augensburg, but who could believe that a man might sustain the merest scratch on his arm and yet die in convulsions?

Thiadbold knelt beside her. "Here, now, Hanna."

She grasped his arm so hard that he gasped. "You must take cover. If . . . any arrow cuts the skin . . . they have poisoned arrows. It will kill at once. Even a scratch. Believe me!"

"I believe you!" he cried with a glance over his shoulder toward the gate, being shouldered closed by a pair of brawny Lions. Barely visible as the night swept over them, Lions clustered in shield walls where the wall gapped. The wall had minimal defensive capability; no inner wall walk offered a vantage for sentries and archers. The nuns clearly had never used swords and bows and spears to defend themselves.

"Still," he added, "they'll be cautious about attacking against walls when it's dark."

"They'll shoot arrows." She coughed, and he helped her stand. Her sides heaved as she struggled to catch her breath. "They need only scratch . . ."

A trio of arrows spat down out of the night, sticking in the dirt.

"Take cover!" shouted Thiadbold as men scattered, startled and dismayed. He looked at Hanna, frowning. Because he had his helm on, she could only see his eyes and the lower part of his face, but he looked as steady as ever. "They can't afford to waste arrows uselessly. If that's but a raiding party, they'll hoard their arrows and their poison."

"Maybe so, but we are no more than sixty or seventy people all told. If there are only ten raiders and each one has ten arrows, even that could kill every one of us."

"You fear them." He had his hand on her arm in the manner of a man comforting a loved one.

"I fear their poison. I saw my companions fall. Ai, God."

He nodded. "Have you a bow?"

"I do, but I'm only a middling shot. Sergeant Aronvald will have more weapons, for he kept with us the weapons of the soldiers we lost. He has only three good archers left but another half dozen strong bows. We've been making arrows as we go."

He released her and called to Ingo. "Sergeant, you're in charge while I go to the other side. Keep their heads down and their bodies under cover. Do not shoot unless you have a target. Let no man be exposed by the light of torches."

"Shall we douse the torches, Captain?"

He worried at his lower lip. "If only we had lit a ring of torches out beyond the wall we might see them coming, if they choose to storm our position." He shook his head impatiently. "But we have not. Leave the torches be for now. Let no man stand where the light will give him away. Come, Hanna. Tell me the story again." He began walking and she sheathed her sword and jogged up alongside him, still puffing.

"Aronvald!" he called, and was answered from the shadows by the weaving shed, where a strong section of wall separated the shed and the orchard from the darkness of the forest.

"A good place to creep up close," he muttered.

She stumbled on a rock, an old building stone half buried in earth and grown over with moss—what in God's names was that doing here? Once a structure had stood here, but in the darkness she couldn't guess what it might have been. Wincing, she got to her feet and dusted off her gloved hands. Seeing her unhurt, Thiadbold hurried to consult with Lady Bertha's sergeant. The two men stood close together under the eaves of the weaving shed. Hanna looked around, getting her bearings. Her eyes had adjusted—as much as they ever would—to the dark; she hadn't seen this portion of the compound closely during daylight.

Sergeant Aronvald had lit no torches. His men waited in the shadows, four of them up on ladders to get aim over the wall. They were all in mail and helmets, some inherited from the dead. The half dozen Lions waiting below beside the narrow orchard gate wore brigandines and decent helmets. All had boiled leather greaves, gloves protected across the back of the hand with chain mail, and good boots—a soldier's stout friend on the march. This she had noted when she'd first met them at the village; after so long on the road she had learned to assess quickly what manner of armor her friends, and her foes, kept on them.

A moaning cry rose out of the forest, more wail than sob, an awful racket that made her cringe and then hate herself for her fear.

"What was that?" whispered one of the men as the sound died. Wind rattled branches. The orchard swayed as if each tree were trying to come unstuck, to move its roots, to flee that noise, which rose a second time, hung in the air, and faded.

"I don't like this," said another Lion.

She encountered no more obstacles as she came up beside Thiadbold and Aronvald, who were talking with the intensity of men who know a decision must be made swiftly and decisively.

"... fire," Thiadbold was saying. "So we can see them. We might see if we can shoot flaming arrows into the trees."

"It's not likely to work," replied Aronvald, " as it is so damp, but I tell you, Captain, it's better than no idea at all, and no idea is what I'm having, for we lost half our company and our good lady to these creatures."

"If that's what's out there. It might be bandits. We came across some the night before we reached Freeburg, but Liath chased them off. With fire, that is. Which is how I came to think of it."

"There's a trick to getting the flame to hold as the arrow flies."

"I'll put my men to work on it. Mayhap the good nuns have some pitch—here! Hanna!"

"I'll go and ask them at once, and take the message to Ingo, of what to expect," she said.

"Folquin and Leo can be in charge of fixing the arrows. They've done something like in the past, and are clever. Go."

This time she knew enough to skirt the stone that had tripped her before, and as she swung wide around it a golden light flared above her, hissing as it spit sparks. Had one of Aronvald's archers gotten fire fixed so quickly?

The bright missile pierced the thatched roof of the main hall and at once streamers of flame blazed down the slanted roof. A second arrow skittered along the incline and tumbled to the ground. Two more lit the sky, arcing in over the wall, but they missed the hall and skipped over the tiles of the small chapel, the only building not roofed in thatch.

" 'Ware! 'Ware!" shouted Aronvald. "Laurant! Tomas! Get to the horses! Go!"

She turned just as an arrow buried its burning head in the thatch that roofed the weaving shed. The roof of the hall smoldered but did not catch, but when a second arrow slammed into the weaving shed's roof, flames caught and leaped and danced. The light threw twisting shadows all around, and cast yellow into men's complexions as they backed away. Their enemy had settled on the same plan of attack: burn them out.

"Water! Water!" cried Thiadbold.

Horses neighed from the corral where they had been confined. If they panicked—

Sister Rosvita and Sister Acella appeared on the porch of the hall. Smoke leaked out of the door, wrapping them in a writhing gray aura that dissipated an instant later in the wind.

Must go, she thought, knowing herself vulnerable out in the open, but she could not make her feet move as a fire broke out in the thatch of a storage hut. A clamor began out by the main gate, men shouting an alert, men running. A man screamed.

"Hit! Hit!"

"Pull him back!" That was Ingo calling out commands. Ai, God. "Where's that cart? Faster, boys! Get it in place! Keep your heads down!"

"It burns! Ai! Ai!"

"Hold him down! Get him to the hall!"

"Hanna!" The cry came from Thiadbold.

She turned toward him, and saw a streak, a shadow. "Thiadbold!"

Too late. The arrow cut through his glove and stuck, bobbing as he cursed and yanked it free. Aronvald, behind him, sprang forward, shoved the captain to the ground so hard that Thiadbold collapsed straight down on his back, arms flung out. The sergeant swung with all his strength and with precise aim. He severed Thiadbold's left arm midway along the forearm, cut it clean off.

Thiadbold seemed in shock, perhaps from hitting his head on the ground, as the sergeant dropped his own sword and fell to his knees, unbuckling his belt. There was blood, but Hanna was too far to see it gush from the wound, only trails of it rushing past Aronvald's kneeling figure. The flow slowed to a trickle.

Aronvald twisted. "Hanna!"

An arrow thudded into the ground a body's length from her. Another shivered in the earth behind the sergeant, who grabbed his sword and rose.

"Ai, God!" said a calm voice from the wall. "Sergeant, I'm hit. In the shoulder."

"Come down," said the sergeant in a voice just as calm. Dead men walk because they have no need to run, already knowing their fate. Thiadbold stared heavenward, his left hand lying at an impossible angle to his body.

Hanna got a foot to move at last, followed by the other. As in a dream, she saw an arrow circling spinning streaking out of the darkness from over the wall, lit by the hellish yellow of the flames as it found its target: it scraped hard across Thiadbold's remaining arm just above the elbow.

Aronvald, mute, raised his sword a second time.

"I would rather die than lose the other one, too," said the captain, his voice as even as if he were discussing the weather. "Get to cover, I pray you. Hanna, if you'll help me up."

He had, after all, been watching her this whole time; in

this dim writhing light it had been impossible to tell. The roof of the weaving shed roared as the flames rushed skyward. The harsh smoke burned in her nostrils as—at last—she found her legs and dashed forward. Her eyes stung from the smoke pouring off the roof and along the beams and posts of the building. She grabbed Thiadbold under her arms and heaved him up as Aronvald ran to the wall and got there in time to catch a man collapsing down a ladder in convulsions.

That eerie cry wailed out of the forest as Hanna lugged Thiadbold along. His remaining hand clutched her shoulder. He could move his feet; he was still in shock. Blood pumped lazily from the stump of his arm. She got him up onto the porch. There was a pallet inside, one of several. She laid him down, and he grunted—with pain, perhaps, or with fear, or simply with relief. She didn't know and couldn't tell.

Sister Acella knelt beside him. "Sister! A length of stout cord, quickly! This belt hasn't stemmed the flow of blood. Get the coals hotter. I want a lotion of betony—"

"We've none left, Sister."

"Then dead nettle. Bay, if we have it. Best yet, feverwort. I know there is a small stock remaining." She did not look up as she spoke. The younger nun hurried to do her bidding.

Smoke streamed down from the roof. Hanna coughed. She was weeping from the stink of it.

"Go, Hanna," said Sister Rosvita, coming up beside her. "If there's aught else you can do."

Out into the terrible rain of arrows.

Hanna shuddered, and yet how was she safer here if more burning arrows lit the thatch of this hall? She hadn't delivered her message to Ingo about flaming arrows and Thiadbold's plan. From outside, she heard another bout of screaming, echoed by a second drawn-out wail, that hideous cry emanating from the forest. Under the eaves, clerics huddled in silence, their faces pale as they stared at her. She hated them for hiding here, but only for an instant. There was nothing they could do. They didn't wield weapons; they wielded pens and prayers, and, by the murmuring, she guessed they were praying as fiercely as they could.

Thiadbold had his eyes closed. Perhaps he had passed out. Convulsions would begin in moments, and in truth she just could not bear to see him die although she hated herself for her cowardice.

"Let me watch him." Rosvita crouched beside Thiadbold as Sister Acella got the cord she wanted and set to tying a better tourniquet.

Hanna retreated like the coward she was. She went onto the porch to see fire consuming the weaving shed and flames spurting along one corner of a hut, not quite catching, not quite dying. A ladder had been thrown up against the eaves at the far end of the hall and there stood Ruoda handing a bucket of water to Fortunatus, to throw atop the smoldering roof. They were just as exposed as she was, except they had nothing with which to defend themselves.

Ashamed, she ran for the front gate. No arrows struck around her. She came to the shelter of the wall, those stones shaped and settled one atop the other higher than a tall man could reach. The wall had a slight inward incline, being broader at the base than at its top.

"Hanna!" Ingo gestured to three bodies lying on the ground. "As you said. Only a scratch and they died."

His whisper sounded to her like a shout. It had gone so silent around them that she did not even hear wind rattling in the branches, only the hiss and crackle of the fire. The heat of the blazing weaving shed pressed against them. Suddenly, thunder cracked the silence. Rain pattered, turning between one breath and the next into a downpour that took them so by surprise that no one moved, only got drenched until the deluge ceased as abruptly as it had started.

They waited, braced for the worst, but no attack resumed. It was as if the world had died beyond the walls' barrier, as if every living thing had died and maybe even the forest and the land vanished into the pit so they were surrounded only by an infinite black yawning nothingness.

"Hanna?"

"Eh! What?"

"You were whimpering, Hanna." That was Folquin's familiar, pleasant voice. She recognized it now.

"My head hurts."

He grunted his assent. He was crouched behind her, with Leo and Stephen close behind him.

"Think they're still waiting out there, Ingo?" Folquin asked.

"I'm not betting otherwise. Are you?"

"Well, I'd not volunteer to be the first to walk out past those torches, if that's what you're asking. But Leo will gladly take that stroll, will you not, Leo?"

"After I piss on your grave," said Leo amiably.

"Who's dead?" asked Hanna.

"No one you knew," said Ingo. "But anyway, there is one we called Corvus for his black hair." He pointed to the closest body. It was too dark to see the corpse's face; he was only the anonymous dead, unknown and now unknowable except as a name and a few anecdotes. "There's poor Ermo who had a girl he wished to marry back home. There, his cousin Arno, who was not quick in his wits but could split a cord of wood faster than any man I've seen."

The old, sick choking swelled in her throat, and she knew she was about to weep. She rose, instead. "I'd best see to the captain."

"Hurt?" asked Ingo, voice dropping into a register of dread.

"Is the captain dead?" whispered Folquin, laying a hand on her shoulder more for his own comfort than hers, she guessed.

"Let me go see," she said, "though I fear it."

Leo cursed under his breath. Stephen caught in his breath in a sucking sound, between clenched teeth. Folquin released her. Ingo rose with her.

"Let me know," he said quietly. "I'm next to be captain, as I'm most senior of those left. Better if he lives, to my way of thinking."

"And for the rest of us, not wanting to dance to Ingo's tune," said Folquin, trying a joke, but it fell flat.

She loped back to the hall, pausing at the steps that led to the raised porch. Beyond the wall she heard the wind sough through the trees, picking up again. The flavor of the night with its taste of dying smoke and scent of lush damp green growing things had shifted imperceptibly to something familiar and seemingly safe, almost like an ordinary night.

From inside, a man screamed in raw agony. She cringed away, then caught herself before she bolted. She stood there, gasping, as the cry cut off—as sharp as a sword's cut. Voices murmured. She smelled a horrible stench. Caught there, she wept freely until Sergeant Aronvald emerged from the hall, found her, and clapped her roughly on the shoulder.

"There, now, Eagle! Stop that! You're yet living. I lost another man."

Four in all.

"Is the captain—?"

He shrugged. "That nun is not one I'd want to cross. Whew! She burned the stump to stop the bleeding." He swayed a little. "Thought I would faint, but she never wavered." Abruptly, he stumbled sideways and vomited and, in between heaves, waved a hand at Hanna as if he wanted her to go.

Cautiously, she went inside to discover a dead man, a living one who had been wounded in the leg but not yet convulsed into death, and an unconscious Thiadbold with Acella kneeling beside him. Acello held the stump, which was all raw and singed and stinking, but was lecturing to a pair of younger nuns, one of whom looked interested and the other of whom looked like she was ready to follow Aronvald's example. All of Rosvita's young clerics except Gerwita had fled into the shadows. Hilaria sat at Thiadbold's head, holding his shoulders in case he moved. She had, evidently, helped Aronvald hold him down.

"It is the minions of the Enemy who kill," Sister Acella was explaining to her charges. "They can't be seen by mortal eyes. They inflame the humors that balance the body. Fire chases them out and will staunch the flow of blood, which would also kill him. We'll need salves to further staunch the bleeding, to ease the burn, and to lessen the inflammation. If we can hold the Enemy at bay, the captain may yet survive. I'll need dead nettle. Sister Hilaria, will you help me?"

All at once, the four nuns rose and walked away to the other end of the hall, where a single lamp burned. Above, noise thumped along the roof beam; someone had gotten up on the roof and was probing for hot spots. There was a leak down where Mother Obligatia lay. Hanna saw someone moving there, pacing back and forth. After a moment she recognized Sapientia's posture and form.

"Sister Acella knows a great deal about healing," said Gerwita in a small voice. "Do you think, when it is safe, that I might come study with her, Sister Rosvita?"

Rosvita smiled at the young woman, patting her hand gently. "Surely you may, child, when it is safe."

Hanna knelt beside Thiadbold and took his hand in hers. He still lived. His hand was warm. His fingers twitched, and she looked up to see his eyes open and fixed on her.

"Attack?" he said.

"Quiet for now," she answered.

Rosvita got up and, holding Gerwita's hand, moved away.

"You'd best sleep . . . while have chance."

She smiled at him. "I can't sleep now. You're the one must sleep."

He made a kind of grin although it was more a grimace. "Can't. Hurts too much. God!" His eyes hooded as he gathered strength, then opened again, so fixed on her that at once she knew what was coming and what Rosvita had seen that had caused her to slip away. Dying men said things they might otherwise keep secret.

"Have you given any thought . . . to what you will do . . . when you leave the Eagles?" He had a hard time talking, but he was determined. "Thought . . . of marriage?"

She pitied him and hated herself, and pitied herself and hated him, all in the space of a breath. She could not lie, yet dared not sadden him, not if he had a chance of living. Mostly, she expected he would die, yet even so she could not lie to him in his last moments, and anyway, what if Sister Acella had certain magical healing arts and he lived and she was faced with a promise she could not honor? Best to speak what was true, even if it was only part of the truth.

"I am already promised. If I were not, I would be thinking about you a great deal, Thiadbold. You're a good man."

He smiled, although he was in so much pain that his jaw was clenched and his neck as tight as rope pulled to the breaking point.

She bent and kissed him on the lips. To her surprise, she found it true as she tasted the sweat and sweetness of his mouth; she did find him attractive. On another day, in another place, she might have chosen him.

He slipped away into sleep, of a kind. She waited for a long while, and after a longer while she wondered if he had died from the poison.

Sister Acella eased down beside her. "If he lives out the week it is likely he'll survive the wound. As for the others—six were struck, and four died at once. Some poison, it is agreed."

"Deadly," murmured Hanna, who was still holding onto Thiadbold's grimy hand. "Yet why did he and that other one not die?"

"Surely the arrows that struck them were not poisoned."

"Then did he lose that hand for nothing?"

"Ah." The nun had a way of smiling that suggested an old and deep conspiracy. "By cutting the first wound away from the rest of the body, Sergeant Aronvald saved his life—if that arrow was poisoned. So, you see, we will never know. Are they gone?"

Hanna startled, lost in contemplating Thiadbold's curly beard, neatly trimmed and rather handsome and noble looking, now that she thought on it. "Are who gone?"

"Those who attacked us with poisoned arrows," replied the nun dryly.

She laid her hand on his chest, to feel his breathing, then rose. "Best to see, although I've heard no alarms." Ill at ease, she left.

Outside, the night remained silent but for the wind and the occasional restless whicker from one of the horses, under the control of half a dozen men. Those horses were precious, having survived a terrible journey. She saw Wicked standing among them, recognizing the mare's sleek contours.

Ingo stood at the gate with Folquin, Leo, and Stephen on watch to either side. Half the men were down, trying to sleep right up against the shelter of the wall. The weaving shed still smoked, but all the fires had gone out. It had stopped raining but still smelled of rain. The three dead men were gone.

"The captain still lives," she said to Ingo. "The nun says if he survives the week then he'll likely survive."

He sighed.

She said, "Let me stand a turn on watch, I pray you. I can't sleep. Better I look, in case there is something to be seen of the Kerayit shaman. Or had you heard that tale?"

He had. "Down," he said sharply to the others. "Hanna will stand sentry for a while."

The wall had a ledge built into it two thirds of the way up, alongside the gate, where a watcher could sit almost at her ease and keep an eye on the valley and on the cleft where the ravine gave way to open ground. From here also she could see the forested eastern stretch of the valley to which Sorgatani had been exiled. Hanna settled herself on slickly wet stone and surveyed the dark vista.

Of the four torches burning earlier three had gone out. The fourth burned fitfully atop a post. She saw the curve of a helmet at the edge of its aura, but after looking again that way, and a third time, realized that no man inhabited that helm. It had been propped there to draw arrow shot.

Was it a lie to tell half a truth? Was it right to spare a dying man another sorrow? Or had she only spoken that way to Thiadbold to spare herself the awkwardness?

I am already promised—to the Eagles.

Yet after all, alone on this wall, she knew she had not lied. What she had said, discounting the Eagles, was true enough, only she had not known it or had not admitted it to herself. Tears dried on her cheeks and still a few more slid from her eyes, a ceaseless trickling waterfall fed by sorrow and loss. Was this what it meant to have a broken heart? After all, her heart had promised itself what it would never have. Thiadbold would be a good man for a husband, but it would never be fair to him.

Yet why not? She could come to love him well enough.

Love wasn't everything. In a marriage, it counted less than so many other qualities: respect, liking, trustworthiness, hard work, steadfastness, honor, alliance between families. Or she could stay in the Eagles, like Hathui, always and forever, because she loved being an Eagle even after all this, even after everything. Here she felt at home, standing watch in the middle of the wilderness with enemies all around and a few stout friends at her back, all in service to the regnant. Here she felt a measure of peace, perched on the wall with the damp air and the spattering of rain and the night wind breathing on her. Not knowing what the next day would bring and aching with the misery of wondering what has happened to the ones she loves.

Her family, mother and father, brothers, selfish sister.

Sorgatani. Liath.

Ivar.

With a groan, the weaving shed collapsed. Ash and smoke cast a pale cloud into the air, visible against the darker night. She followed its thread up, and up, and caught her breath as she craned back to stare at the heavens.

For the first time in months, stars shone where that brief storm had torn the clouds into rags. So it remained all night, just a few stars shifting as they passed across the zenith. At dawn, the red rim of the sun rose over the trees so bright and glaring that everyone came running outside to stare and rejoice despite their losses, and laughed and cried as the haze bled back over the heavens, covering the rift.

She saw no sign of anyone out in the trees.

"I must go look," she said to Ingo, who had remained below her, watchful but silent, all that time.

"I think it's a bad idea."

"I can't abandon Sorgatani."

"If all that's said is true, then she's in no danger. And can protect the frater who bides with her, as well. Say." He slanted a look at her, speculating. "A few have said he's her lover."

"He is not. For many years he served Prince Bayan, who was later Princess Sapientia's husband."

"Here, now." He reached up to help her clamber down, and Stephen climbed up past her to take her place, but Ingo kept his big hand on her upper arm and bent close, drawing her away to speak privately with her. He smelled of smoke—no doubt they all did—but he had a slight minty smell to him, as though he'd been chewing leaves.

"What?" she asked him, taken aback by his size and strength.

"Is it true? None of us have seen, but all speak of it. That Princess Sapientia lives?"

"She does."

"You've traveled with her all this time? Tell me the tale, Hanna, I pray you. We must know."

She hesitated, and he frowned.

"Sanglant is a strong ruler," he said, more quietly still, so close that he could have kissed her, but his interest in her had always been that of an older brother. "When he came to Osterburg, we were heartened for the first time since King Henry departed for Aosta. I pray you, Hanna, what does the princess intend? Will she challenge him?"

"I don't know."

He sighed, shoulders sagging, glancing away and making a face.

"She is ill, Ingo. Listen closely. In the days I have traveled with her—months now—I have not heard her speak. She suffers some disease of the mind. She's little better than a simpleton, although I have no right to say such a thing of a royal princess."

"Best to say it if it is true! Sanglant is regnant, and the army loves him, and we'll follow him, but there are those who mutter he is not the rightful heir. What will those noble folk do when Sapientia returns?"

"How can we know?"

"Who will you serve, Hanna, if you must choose?"

"Are you saying there may be civil war between them? The princess cannot feed herself, much less lead an army."

"An army can be led in her name."

"Who would do so? Her sister?"

"Nay, not Princess Theophanu, unless she plays a deeper game than we ever glimpsed. We bided in Osterburg for some two years or more, building walls and chasing down bandits. She's a faithful steward. King Sanglant named her duke of Saony, and she accepted."

"Then who?"

He shrugged. "Only wondering, that's all."

"Best I go and find Liath, if you wish to keep Prince Sanglant happy."

He considered this, still frowning.

"What are you thinking?" she asked.

"It would be easier for him were he to marry a proper queen, which he will not. Still, the captain knows her of old and speaks no ill of her, although some say she is a sorcerer and has used ill-starred magic to bind the regnant to her."

She shook off his hand. "I know her of old, too. I'll hear no ill words spoken of her. She is not what you say she is. Who has whispered these things? Who?"

He held up both hands as a shield against her anger. "Here, now. I'm only repeating whispers. She's good to look on, as any man will tell you."

Hanna snorted. "There is more to her than whether men think her attractive!"

"Thiadbold swears she can hold her own in a fight. That she saved the life of a Lion, in his old cohort, a few year back. We saw it ourselves, just a few days back." He would not look at her. Somehow, the words embarrassed him. "She called flame right out from the treetops. It's said she can burn a man alive, if she wishes."

Hanna said nothing.

"Doesn't that scare you?" He still would not look at her, and the sight of this big, strong man with a queasy look made her want for nothing more than to get away from him.

"I am not afraid of Liath," she retorted. "Nor should you be."

"Burned alive," he repeated. "What matter my weapons and armor then?"

"Best, in that case, that the regnant keep her tied to his bed," she said sarcastically, but he nodded in all seriousness.

"Perhaps so. Good strategy on the part of King Sanglant."

In his eyes, evidently, Sanglant could do no wrong. Strange that he never mentioned that Sanglant had used his own sister as a hostage and later abandoned her with his enemies. That Sanglant had kept Bulkezu alive. That Sanglant had marched against his own father.

Yet what choice had the prince had? Henry had been possessed by a daimone. Sanglant had saved his father, or come as close as anyone could. The Lions had told her the tale of the battle under the wings of the storm, which had been told to them by the soldiers who had survived, those who had witnessed, those who had returned from Aosta and the death of their emperor and their hopes for empire.

All this she could now put together, the last story she needed to understand the events of those days when she and the others had been prisoners of the Arethousans.

"Well, then," said Ingo uneasily, "I'll get the lads started on that wall again. How many do you want to come with you?"

"None. If the enemy waits, it's best if only I die."

"Nay," he said irritably, "I can't send you out alone—"

"Hey!" Stephen shouted from the wall and a moment later a second sentry, posted farther down, called out as well. "It's a man—he seems unarmed, coming out of the trees—he's got only one hand . . ."

"Let me see." Ingo laced his fingers under her boots to give her a boost up. "That's Brother Breschius. Open the gate."

She met him just beyond the ditch. He grasped her hand as she came up beside him. He had tears in his eyes.

"I feared for you," he said, "when we heard the Lost Ones."

"Sorgatani?"

"Unharmed. As am I, as you see." He looked toward the walled convent. A score of heads had appeared along the wall, watching them, but no one ventured out. "She walked, last night, for we knew they would attack you."

"Did she scatter them? We heard an ungodly wailing."

"I know not what that was. Will you come? Liath did not return. Best we look for her."

"Ai, God," she whispered, sick at heart, with a dull grinding pain in her belly. Well, no doubt the worst would please Ingo, she thought furiously, hating him.

"We'll search more quickly with more scouts," he continued, "but if the Lost Ones bide in the woods, then they'll kill them."

"They did not kill you, walking here."

"I am no threat to them. They may fear Sorgatani, as they should."

She nodded. "I'll come alone, and Sorgatani will search with us." She ran back to the gate and told Ingo what she meant to do, and when he began to protest, she cut him off. "Let no man walk beyond these walls lest he see what will kill him. Believe what I say, and if you will not believe me, then believe Aronvald or Sister Rosvita. Stay close."

The path lay quiet. Nothing disturbed them, although water dripped now and again from branches. She stopped once to drink from a brutally cold stream. She had forgotten how thirsty she was, and she gulped down the water and felt her head ache as if the iciness of the water were trying to freeze it.

Sorgatani waited by her painted wagon, anxious as she scanned the forest. "They are gone," she said to Hanna without turning to see who it was.

"Are you sure?"

She pointed. "Liathano went in that direction. Come."

They made of themselves a line with Sorgatani in the middle and Breschius and Hanna to either flank. Moving into the trees, they found no bodies. If Sorgatani had killed any, then some had survived to carry away the dead. The light trailing through the trees had a brighter edge today, although haze again covered the sky. Was it thinner? Was there hope that the weather would change?

"Here!" called Breschius.

Hanna beat a path to him with her staff, cutting through thickets and slogging through a patch of mud that slimed her boots. He stood in a clearing staring down at an object hidden by grass. Sorgatani stood beside him; she hid her eyes behind her hand, as if she did not want to see but knew she had to look. Hanna came up to them.

Liath's bow could never be mistaken for any other. It

lay, strung, in the grass, carelessly dropped. Beside it her quiver rested untouched, still full of arrows. A polished black beetle crawled across the clustered shafts of arrows, then balked as it tested the cruel ledge made by a griffin feather.

"Do you think . . ." whispered Breschius, as if the words actually hurt ". . . that the galla caught her?"

The beetle vanished down the shaft of one of the ordinary arrows, hidden by the stirring of grass as the wind gusted and died. A weight settled on Hanna's chest and she could not shake it loose. But she must observe. She must report. Such was her duty. She released a clenched hand and bent to pick up the bow.

"There would be bones. That's all the galla leave of their victims."

"Where is she gone?" Sorgatani scanned the forest. Only the wind cried in the trees.

Hanna steadied herself. The bow *hummed* in her grip, as though trying to communicate. Its touch prickled her skin rather like the wasp sting that bound her to Sorgatani. *Magic lives here,* she thought, setting down the bow. She hoisted the quiver, and strained because of its unexpected weight. Tucked in with the arrows, wrapped in oilcloth, rested another object whose dimensions were familiar to her. She unwrapped it to glimpse the cover, but she already knew what it was. How had *The Book of Secrets* come back into Liath's possession?

No matter. Seeing it, she despaired.

She looked at her companions. "Liath would never have left these things behind of her own choice. Never."

"Is she dead?" cried Sorgatani.

"The simplest answer is usually the best one," said Hanna. "Though it makes me sick at heart to think of it. Because it would also explain why the raiders disappeared."

"Ah," said Breschius.

She nodded. "They captured her, and ran with their prize."

"How could they have captured her?" demanded Sorgatani. "She is too powerful for them to bring down."

Breschius knelt, reached, and brushed his hand over the grass where, having some time ago been flattened, it was slowly springing back. "Blood." He sniffed it, but did not taste it, turned his hand up so the two women could see the red stain on his fingers.

Sorgatani tilted her head back and without warning trilled a high, long, keening wail that made Hanna shudder to her bones. Folk might cry so over the grave of one lost.

"She is always vulnerable to arrow shot," said Breschius pointlessly, since they could all see for themselves, "if she is taken unawares."

"Oh, God." Hanna collapsed to her knees. She thought she would faint, but she did not. She held on. "A poisoned arrow would kill her!"

"Stay, now." Breschius steadied her. "Why, then, would they take the body?"

"To prove they killed her," said Sorgatani. "Such is the custom among my people. A trophy. A prize."

How had it come to this, that she had found Liath only to lose her?

"This is not news that I look forward to bringing to Prince Sanglant," Breschius added.

She shook her head and rose. After all, she would go on. It's what she had done before. It's what Eagles must do, even if their hearts were broken. "You don't have to, because I will do so, as is my duty as the King's Eagle."

5

THE king's progress arrived in Quedlinhame late of an afternoon to find an Eagle waiting in the audience hall of the old ducal palace, dozing by a warm hearth. She had been wounded in the left shoulder, and although she wore clean, mended clothing and a linen bandage over the wound, it was clear she'd been lucky to survive an arduous road.

"What news?" he asked her, before tasting the drink offered him, before taking off his armor. His courtiers crowded into the hall, a smoke-stained structure about half the length and breadth of any of the newer palaces built by either of the Arnulfs. It dated from a time when the lords of Quedlinhame had more modest ambitions. "When did you arrive?"

"Four days ago, Your Majesty," she answered, overawed by him. If she wondered what had happened to King Henry, she knew better than to ask *him*. He had a vague memory that he had seen her years ago, younger, less weathered, but he did not clearly recall her name or her origin. Elsa, maybe, something common. "Ill news, I fear. I barely escaped with my life, as you can see. Kassel is fallen to treachery."

"Kassel!" Liutgard grasped Theophanu's arm to steady herself. "What news?"

"An unexpected attack by Lady Sabella's troops, out of Arconia. They arrived asking for guest rights. Lady Ermengard offered them respite for the night. There was talk that the company had been attacked. They said creatures lurking along the forest road assaulted them with poisoned arrows. Maybe that happened, or maybe it was a lie. At night, they rose up and killed most of the palace guard and took your daughter prisoner. The steward—that is, not her, but her son Landrik—got me out, with a horse, but he was shot down defending me so I could escape. I was wounded." She touched her bandaged shoulder, but it was obvious that the injury pained her far less than did the memory. "I knew some little-used paths, so I evaded them who pursued me. My lady, your daughter was alive last I saw her."

Having spoken, she wept.

"Let her sit down," said Sanglant. "What is your name, Eagle? You've done well."

"Elsa, Your Majesty," she said through tears. "Of Kassel, years past, before I became an Eagle." Ambrose led her to a bench.

Liutgard let go of Theophanu and gripped Sanglant's elbow so hard he winced. "This I paid for following your father to Aosta on his fool's errand," she said, her voice hoarse and her expression grim. "One daughter lost, and the other in the hands of a woman who has proclaimed herself my enemy through her actions!"

"Sit down, Liutgard," said Theophanu in her calm voice.

She allowed Theophanu to lead her to a bench, where she sat staring accusingly at Sanglant.

He nodded, acknowledging her anger. "We ride on in the morning, Cousin. I will not fail you."

By the door, Mother Scholastica watched them. She looked stern and annoyed and superior—and not one whit surprised.

He woke at dawn out of a restless sleep filled with the noise of horses being saddled and men making ready to ride. The bed he lay in had seen a hundred years of restless sleepers, no doubt. Boxed in and placed under the eaves at the midpoint of the hall, it had recently been furnished with a new featherbed and feather quilt, which kept him as warm as anything could, although he never really felt warm unless Liath lay beside him.

He sat up and drew one curtain aside to see that someone had already thrown the doors open. Cold air blasted in as folk rose from their bedrolls and prepared to travel. Many still slept. All those up and moving wore Fesse's sigil.

Hathui walked in from outside. Seeing him awake, she hurried over. She smelled of the stables.

"Your Majesty."

"What news?" he asked her. "Any news of Liath?"

"None, Your Majesty. You can't expect to hear from her for many days."

He shut his eyes. He had abandoned his own daughter, as God witnessed. He had himself made, after all, choices no different than those Liath had made years ago, the same choices he had been so angry at her for making. So be it. At this stage of the journey, there was no going back.

"She will be well," he said hoarsely. "She is more powerful than any of us."

Hathui nodded, although she seemed pale. "Yes, Your Majesty. What is your wish?"

He beckoned to his servants, who came forward bearing his clothing and armor. "We can't wait here. Liath must follow us, as she'll know to do. We ride west, to Kassel."

VII

A CHANGE OF DIRECTION

1

SHE burned.

As she twisted in the flames, she saw the face of Cat Mask hovering above her. First he was a cat, sleek and bold, and then he was a man, proud and handsome, with that beautiful reddish-bronze complexion she adored so much in Sanglant and the broad cheekbones and broad shoulders of a man who is not a hunting cat but only looks like one sometimes, as he did now. He had changed again.

He did not speak, but she heard him or she heard others speaking as she floated in a bed of fire. The words came to her as through a muting veil. The hiss of their voices reminded her of the sound of water ebbing along a sandy shore.

"The poison should have killed her."

"She has sorcery in her blood. She walked the spheres."

"Walked the spheres? She was sacrificed? What can you mean?"

"When we lived in exile, some who studied magic walked the spheres. They walked up into the heavens. I don't understand it, but it happened. Most who tried it died, but Feather Cloak survived. That is how she grew so powerful."

"This one did such a thing? I don't believe it. Walking up into the heavens! She was only lucky. Not all of the arrows are poisoned."

Cat Mask's voice was the only one she recognized. "All *mine* were poisoned! Why would a shallow arrow wound plunge her into this delirium? It is sorcery that spares her from the poison."

"She fell so fast. How could she have had time or opportunity to twist sorcery to save herself?"

"Maybe not sorcery but something deeper saved her. Secha—who was Feather Cloak before—banished this one when she walked in our country. Secha said this one had more than one seeming. More than one aspect."

"Abomination!"

"She said this one was heir to the shana-ret'zeri."

"Let her die!" murmured the other voices. "The blood knives can take her, and her blood will feed the gods."

"We can't give her to the blood knives," said a woman's voice, spiking over the others. "This is the prize *he* wanted."

Cat Mask's scorn was unmistakable. "You care for what that Pale Hair wants?"

"His knowledge is a weapon. It has already aided us. We sealed an alliance. Go to the stones and wait for him. When he comes, tell him what we have."

Cat Mask snorted in the manner of a proud man who has turned stubborn. "I will not act as his procurer. You do it yourself."

"Better yet, better yet," said a new voice. "Let Feather Cloak decide."

"Yes. Yes. Let Feather Cloak decide." Their voices caught her as on a breaking wave and drove her under.

2

THEY called him "count" and "my lord," and he rode at the head of the procession beside Lady Sabella and Duke Conrad and their noble companions, all of whom were eager to take part in the sport of capturing a guivre. The dirty and dangerous work would be done, of course, by the men-at-arms marching behind them, but this hunt had attracted an unusual crowd, several hundred folk at least. Duke Conrad ordered fourscore eager soldiers to remain with the force garrisoning Autun, and they went with frowns and sighs of displeasure but did not disobey.

For several days the cavalcade rumbled northwest—back the way Alain had come—along the main road. Of riders at the front there ambled two dozen noble folk on fine horses and behind them mounted soldiers. The wagons carrying hooks, nets, grapples, and the cage rattled along afterward, followed at the rear by the twoscore men-at-arms who would hunt on foot and three packs of hunting dogs with their handlers. The dogs barked incessantly, but no one minded, being accustomed to a clamor.

The first night they slept in comfort at an estate belonging to a royal monastery, the second at a lord's outlying manor house. They camped a pair of nights, but on the fifth night they spread their company around a village, and in the morning carried supplies out of the village storehouse although folk wept to see their stores depleted, for Sabella demanded all of the sacks of grain.

"This is our seed corn," said the man who set himself forward as their spokesman. He twisted his hands, fearful as he knelt before Sabella. He could not look her in the eye. "I pray you, lady. This is what we saved aside from last year, and not even all of it, for we've ourselves of necessity nibbled at it. With this weather! It's almost Quadrii, but the frosts still hit us every night." He gestured toward puddles rimed with ice. His hands were red from the cold. "We dare not plant."

"Soon it will be too late to plant!" called a woman from the crowd.

"I pray the weather turns soon." Sabella was already mounted, and impatient to depart. Her stewards would finish their provisioning and follow after the forward party. "I have need of these stores for the sake of the duchy."

The man grimaced anxiously and spoke again, gaze fixed on the ground. "If we've nothing to plant, we'll have no harvest. We'll starve."

"If we lose this war, if Wendish and Salians and bandits and Eika invade our shores and there is none to defend you, then your corpses will be rotting in your fields before you starve! Do not trouble me further!"

"I pray you," said Alain, for all the company remained silent and the villagers knelt in the dust, "let them keep half of their stores. There is truth in what they say."

She glared at him—she was a woman who did not expect or appreciate being questioned—but he did not cower.

At length he said, more softly, "Their sweat and toil makes you rich."

Her expression tightened. Her courtiers hunched their shoulders, waiting for the blast, but it did not come.

Unexpectedly, she chuckled, not so much because he had amused her but because she was unused to being challenged. "Spoken like a frater. Very well. Let them keep half the stores. The rest we take."

3

LIATH woke into darkness. Her thigh throbbed. When she rolled to shift position and ease the pressure, her stomach spasmed and she retched, although she had nothing to throw up. Not even bile.

She hurt all the way down to the bone. Her lungs felt as ragged as if she had been breathing smoke, and perhaps in some way she had. She was burned clean, made weak and thirsty, but she was still alive—or so it seemed to her, because she could feel the rise and fall of her chest with each inhalation, because she could feel the gritty rock under the palms of her hands, because there was dried blood on her cheek where she had scraped her face. She possessed nothing except her clothes and her life. Her bow, quiver, book, knife, sword—all this was gone.

She rested until her stomach quieted and risked sitting up. For a while after that, she had to swallow convulsively and repeatedly as she struggled to control the nausea. She was so exhausted that the simple act of sitting seemed impossible, but she braced herself on her arms and hung on until she could think. Even with her salamander eyes she could not penetrate the darkness. She must listen, and seek with her mind's eye, but all she sensed was air and rock.

I am buried alive in a vast cavern.

She had not the strength to grasp the tendrils of fire that slept within the rock, so she lay back down and rested. She probed the rent in her leggings and touched dried blood. Tracing the contours of the blood led her inward to the wound itself: a shallow, ragged hole that hurt to press anywhere near it.

She grunted and withdrew her hand, thinking of those who waited for her: Sanglant. Blessing. Hanna and Sorgatani. *A grandmother!*

She slept.

Woke, hearing a noise, a stealthy murmur, a foot sliding along the ground. She sat up. She was still weak, but the nausea had lessened. She heard the sound again, although now it sounded more like someone sweeping, two scrapes, a silence, and a rapid series of scrapes.

Was it better to remain silent and hope to escape notice, or to assume that whatever creature made the noise already knew she was here? She chose prudence, and therefore silence.

Once more she heard the scraping but this time, after the second scrape, it did not resume.

Cautiously, she probed the wound, and while it remained tender and painful, it was already drying out and knitting. She rolled carefully onto hands and knees and found she could crawl without pain overwhelming her. She felt her way forward. The rock floor proved unnaturally level. No abyss gapped. No loose stones impeded her path. She counted each hand fall so she could gauge the distance, and at two hundred and eight the feel of the air changed markedly and in ten more hand paces she reached a wall. It rose sheer out of the floor, almost perpendicular. Its relatively smooth face and the curve where wall joined floor suggested that man-made effort had helped form it. Her thigh ached and her knees hurt and her hands stung, but the darkness made her too nervous to stand and walk. After a rest she felt around for anything to mark her place but could not find even enough loose pebbles to construct a marker. Finally, she eased down her drawers and peed, like a dog. She hadn't much; she desperately needed water, but waiting in the middle of the pit was no way to go about getting it.

She crawled. She was too weak to crawl quickly, so it was possible to taste the air and run her right hand up the rock face as high as she could go to search for an opening. She forced herself to pace a hundred hand falls before resting, and to rest no more than a hundred slow breaths before going on. Her knees became bruises and one of her palms bled, but the wound in her thigh did not reopen, so she kept going.

It was hopeless. She found four shards of rock, which she tied up in her sleeve. One was sharp enough to use as a weapon, if it came to that, and the others could mark her starting point if she ever got back there in such time that her mark was still moist. She found no trace of water and no hint of any kind of opening that might lead her out.

After one thousand three hundred and sixty-nine hand falls, she found a smear of liquid smelling of urine: her own mark. She had come full circle. If there was a tunnel leading out of this cavern it was either high up in the wall or somewhere out on the cavern floor, drowned in darkness and easy to miss no matter if she crossed and crisscrossed the floor a hundred times as she weakened, thirsted, and failed.

She was trapped.

There it was again: two scrapes, a silence, and two scrapes. But she listened for a long time after, and heard nothing more.

4

ROSVITA sat in the hall of the convent of St. Valeria with *The Book of Secrets* open on a table before her. She had stolen this book years ago, and lost it again soon after, so she had never had leisure to examine it page by page. A monstrous document, absolutely fascinating. The book contained three books. One was written on paper, in the infidel manner, and with the curling script used by the Jinna. It was impossible to decipher. The middle book was written on ancient, yellowed papyrus, the alien letters glossed here and there in Arethousan. "Hide this" read the first words of the gloss, and so Bernard had hidden it. Most of the text was not translated, but what was written in Arethousan allowed her to guess that this scroll preached the most dangerous heresy known to the church, that of the Redemption.

She hadn't the strength to consider it now. She turned to the first portion of the book.

The man called Bernard, Liath's father, had compiled a priceless florilegia. For years he had written down every reference he had found to the arts of the mathematici. She was familiar with the methods of timekeeping according to the rising of stars and constellations, but much of what was recorded here she found difficult and technical: quadrant, angle, equant point, trine, and opposition. There was a catalog of several hundred stars, including the latitude, longitude, and apparent brightness of each one, written in such a tiny hand that it was almost impossible to read. But other selections she could skim as she paused on each page to marvel at its secrets, many of them contradictory.

The whole universe is composed of nine spheres. The celestial sphere is outermost, embracing all the rest ... In it are fixed the eternally revolving movements of the stars. Beneath it are the seven underlying spheres, which revolve in an opposite direction.

Below the moon all is mortal and transitory. Above the moon, all is eternal. In the center is the Earth, never moving.

Her hypotheses are that the fixed stars and the Sun are stationary, and that the Earth is borne in a circular orbit about the Sun.

It is easily demonstrated to anyone that the immutable aether is distributed over and penetrates all the wholly changeable substance around the Earth.

The most chance events of great importance clearly display their cause as coming from the heavens.

The stars weave the fate of humankind.

Maybe so, but God had created the stars and every part of the universe, as the blessed Daisan taught, and she recalled the blessed Daisan's words as well:

The sun and the moon and the fixed and wandering stars are subject to law, that they only do what they are ordered to do and nothing else. However, it is given to humankind to lead life according to free will.

"Sister Rosvita!"

The voice startled her out of her book. "I pray you, Sister Acella! I did not see you come in."

Sister Acella had the pouched mouth and narrowed eyes of an angry woman, and she did not hesitate to speak her mind. "What rumor is this I hear? You send the Eagle to call me, yet already I hear the soldiers saying that you mean to abandon the convent and force us to leave!"

"You must."

"We will not go."

With a sigh, Rosvita closed the book. She had lingered over it for too long since Hanna had dropped it in her lap together with the news that Liath was gone, possibly dead, and almost certainly in the hands of the Ashioi.

"Sister Acella, you must go. In the name of the regnant, I command it."

"Henry is dead! So they say. If the bastard Sanglant is king, you have no status in his progress."

"I maintain my position in the regnant's schola, having not heard otherwise."

"You cannot command me!"

"I can, and I will, because I must." She rose, sorry that it had come to this. "It is no longer safe here. Do you think, Sister Acella, that I wish your treasure-house of books to fall into the hands of the Ashioi? Into any hands, except that of the church?"

Acella remained silent, but she nodded, to show she would listen. Already, Rosvita saw in her expression the first bitter acceptance of the unfortunate truth.

"If one raid can come, so can another. I ask myself, how can the Ashioi raid in so many places so far apart in place and so close together in time? We ourselves suffered an attack in Avaria, and the one last night. We hear reports from these Lions of raids to the north and west. Everywhere, it seems. Although it took our party weeks—months!—to journey over the Brinne Pass out of the south."

Acella looked at the book, and Rosvita opened it to display the closely written pages of the star catalog.

"The Ashioi are using sorcery. They are walking the crowns. Some among them can weave the crowns. We cannot take the chance that they do not know of this library. We must protect it at all costs. You will pack up your books and take provisions and any animals and seed corn and cuttings from your best trees. All else, abandon. If we are fortunate, you may lead your sisters back here one day."

"We must burn the books, as it is written in our charter."

"I cannot allow it." She did not say, but she knew it was understood: I have a cohort of Lions to carry out my will.

"Do not be tempted by sorcery! That one, called Liathano—she cannot understand what we have studied for generations here at St. Valeria. Tempestari can change the weather, call in winds, or a storm, but this passes briefly. They can bring no great change."

"A spell woven thousands of years ago brought a cataclysm to us all. There must be a way to counteract its effects."

"Beware of tampering with what you do not understand, for if this tale is true of a spell woven long ago that brought about this cataclysm, then who knows what meddling will bring! This is why the church condemned these arts. They are too dangerous. No person can control them, not truly. So Mother Rothgard taught."

"I believe you," Rosvita said, "but we must not turn

aside onto the path of deliberate ignorance if there is any possibility that we might save ourselves by walking a more treacherous road."

For a long time Sister Acella said nothing, but the subtle play of feeling on her face spoke as in words.

"It must be done," repeated Rosvita, "and the entire library given into the hands of Mother Scholastica at Quedlinhame, if you will not have it given to the custody of the king's schola."

"We dare not trust the king," said Acella, "who, if the rumor we hear is true, beds the very woman whose hands are black with sorcery."

She walked out, passing Hanna, who walked in.

Hanna looked at Acella's tense back, at Rosvita's expression, and whistled softly. "Did she protest?"

"She did. Never mind it, Hanna. What news?"

"Aronvald says that we can leave in the morning. All will be ready. There are a pair of wagons in one of the sheds that can be repaired easily." She paused, and Rosvita listened with her to the telltale sound of hammers pounding.

She still had a hand on the book. "Frater Bernard traveled in the east, and there he found strange things," she murmured.

"I beg your pardon, Sister?"

"Nay, nothing. If you will, Hanna, find Fortunatus and ask him to oversee the packing of the library. Him alone, none other. Let Heriburg and Ruoda aid him."

"You think Sister Acella will try to hide books from you?"

"Impossible to know. There must be a record in the library of every codex and scroll that is here. Ask him to find that, and match each book as it is packed away. Nothing can be left behind or forgotten."

"Yes, Sister." She hesitated.

"Is there something you wished to say, Hanna?"

"It's just—what did you think of Liath's plan, Sister? That she wanted to learn the arts of the weather workers, in order to banish the clouds and cold weather. Do you think the church would allow it?"

"I don't know."

"Do you condemn her for thinking so?"

"For thinking like a mathematici, which she is?"

"I suppose."

"Well, it is difficult to know if the ends justify the means in a case such as this one, after we have seen the terrible cataclysm wrought by sorcery. Had the ancient ones not troubled the orderly working of the universe with their spell, we would not suffer now. You must understand, Hanna, that I am skeptical at this notion that sorcery can save us when it is sorcery that harmed us in the first place."

"You saved us with sorcery, when you wove the crown and we escaped Lord Hugh."

"I cannot believe otherwise. I am alive because of it."

Rosvita smiled. "I thank you, Eagle. I am not always sure that my path is a righteous one."

"That is why we trust you, Sister, because you lead us with honesty."

Unexpectedly, the words brought tears to Rosvita's eyes. Hanna saw it, and she leaned forward as if to touch Rosvita's hands but pulled back at the last moment with a wry smile, and hurried off on her errand. Eagles did not comfort noble clerics. It was not their place.

Yet the gesture reminded Rosvita of Hathui, whose dignity was unimpeachable. *The Lord and Lady love us all equally in their hearts,* Hathui had said. *We are equal, before God.*

Rosvita stepped outside, onto the porch, and watched the Lions and guardsmen at work, hammering, packing, hauling. There were sealed jars of oil and a basket of last year's apples hauled up from a cellar. There were precious iron and bronze tools, copper-lined buckets, and baskets filled with iron nails and tallow candles. Skeins of spun wool, wool cloth, a churn, a cream pot and paddle, strickles, parchments still stretched on frames, an ox yoke but no ox, and the convent bell with its clapper sheathed. The library was an annex built off the chapel and sharing its tile roof, and here Fortunatus directed half a dozen nuns as they wrapped and stowed books in baskets and in crates being nailed together on the spot by a pair of Lions. Sister Acella emerged from the infirmary, carrying bundles of dried herbs.

"Sister Rosvita, how may we aid you?" asked Sister Hilaria, coming out onto the porch with Diocletia beside her. "If you will sit with the Holy Mother, we will do what we can."

"Diocletia, if you will take an accounting of the bedding and household items in the hall, and pack what is necessary for the journey or too valuable to discard. Hilaria, I pray you, attend Sister Acella."

Hilaria smiled sharply. Nothing escaped her. "I'll see that no stray items are left behind."

It was a relief to return into the hall and seat herself under the eaves beside Mother Obligatia. Princess Sapientia bided in the bed next to them, singing a nonsense song:

> *tru la tru lee tru lo tru lye*
> *where the river flows, did the crow fly*

"Books are a precious treasure," said Mother Obligatia, when Rosvita had poured out her concerns to the old woman.

"Even books as dangerous as the ones hidden here?"

"Even so. In ancient days folk recalled all things in their heads and in this way passed down knowledge from mother to son and father to daughter. What is written in books is more easily lost."

"Do you think so?"

"Think of the library at St. Ekatarina's. I still weep to think of it abandoned, perhaps forever lost."

"We have a copy of your chronicle. My history. The *Vita* of St. Radegundis."

"So few! What if they were the only books which escaped this cataclysm? All of St. Marcia, lost!"

"There are other copies."

"A few, and those scattered. Eustacia's *Commentary* on her dream. St. Alisia's *Memoria*, and the holy writings of the Holy Mother, St. Gregoria. St. Augustina's wise words—although now that I think on it, she was a bit of a prig, running wild in her youth and then scolding others ever after. What of St. Peter the Geometer and his *Eternal Geometry*?"

"Which I do not fully understand."

The abbess chuckled. "You are not the first to make that admission. What of the *Catechetical Orations* of St. Macrina? What of Biscop Ariana's *Banquet*?"

"That's a heretical text. By an Arethousan!"

"So it is, but so entertaining. Have you never read it?"

"I have not!"

"Ah! She had a wicked eye and a wickeder tongue, that one, rather like our dear Brother Fortunatus. I cannot believe it is better that even *her* heretical writings be thrown out. Best they be remembered, so we remember how to argue against them. They are chronicles in their own way. Like Eusebē's *History*."

"Like the *Chronicle* of Vitalia," agreed Rosvita, recalling the books she and her novices had read in Darre, "and the *Annals of Autun*."

"Just so. Memory is our armor, and our weapon, Rosvita. Otherwise we are vulnerable again and again."

"So we are." Rosvita squeezed Obligatia's cold hands as gently as she would handle a newborn pup. "We must soldier on and do the best we can."

"Where do we go?"

"To the regnant."

"Ah. Then I shall meet my grandson-in-law." She smiled. "I look forward to it. A fine, brawny, handsome man, so they say."

"So he is. More than what he seems."

"Cleverer than he looks?" the old abbess chuckled.

"So it appears from the news we have heard of the battle in Dalmiaka and these new tidings from Wendar, if it is all true."

> *tru lo tru lye tru la tru lee*
> *where the river flows, did the deer flee*

"What will happen," Obligatia asked in a low voice, "when we are come with Sapientia?"

"I don't know. She does not seem capable of ruling."

"Our chronicles tell us that fitness was no barrier to the kings of Salia and Aosta. There are here and there stories of feebleminded children raised up to the throne, and ruled by those who held their leading strings."

"It is not true of the Wendish, for we Wendish have always demanded that our regnants be worthy of the name."

"Is Prince Sanglant that one? Worthy of the name?"

"Laws are silent in the presence of arms, so it is said. Sanglant possesses the loyalty of the army. And, if the story is true, Henry's blessing, and the luck of the king, without which no regnant can prosper. The rest of his claim is not as strong. According to the Lions, there is debate and dissension on the matter of his queen, who was excommunicated and is known to be a sorcerer. That cannot help him."

Mother Obligatia considered these words, and at length touched the book Rosvita held on her lap. "Will we see her again? Do you think her lost?"

"Like the books?" Rosvita had forgotten *The Book of Secrets*, clutched against her. She was afraid to let it go, as if it would vanish once no part of her body grounded it to the Earth. "She is lost to us. We must leave, quickly, before we are attacked again. We must pray we reach Quedlinhame and the king's progress safely. As for the rest, I cannot know. It is taught that the daimones of the upper air can see into both past and future. But we are mortal, you and I, bound to the present."

"Mere clay," agreed Obligatia, and the thought made her smile as she patted Rosvita on the hands in the same manner she would pat a child's head to comfort it. Her gaze strayed toward the nuns busy at their packing and came to rest on Sister Diocletia, who was peering into a chest and counting something on her fingers: *eleven*. At the far end of the hall, a young nun hung shutters and locked them into place against the coming departure. It was a sturdy hall, meant to weather storms and years. When all this trouble passed, it would still be standing.

"I would be at peace, having met her at long last," said Mother Obligatia, "but I have a few questions I must still ask her. Therefore, I am selfishly sure that she must still be alive and that she will return to us."

Rosvita nodded sadly. "That is hope enough for me, then. Let us pray you are right."

5

"LI-AT-DANO."

She woke disoriented and still blind. She hadn't meant to doze off, knowing that something moved in the darkness with her, but the lingering effect of the poison had swallowed her.

"Li-at-dano."

The voice was female, caustic, and familiar. It came from out of the darkness but from no particular direction.

"Why am I here?" she asked. It was difficult to speak. She was desperately thirsty.

"Accident, perhaps. The favor of the gods, perhaps. Do you know who I am?"

"I know who you are. Let me go free. Let me return to your son."

"The rock that cages you is more powerful than the sorcery that runs in your veins."

"Where am I?"

"You lie at the Heart-of-the-Mountain-of-the-World's-Beginning. You can burn stone, I suppose, but not quickly. It will tire you. You will not work your way free of this place easily."

"I will be dead of thirst and hunger before then. If that's your aim."

"It might be more effective than the snake's poison, now that I think on it. You will find water and food against the wall."

"Why keep me alive at all?"

"I have a use for you."

"Show yourself."

"I will not."

"I could burn you!"

"If you did, you would still be trapped. You do not know the way out. Only I do."

Liath rose, but she hadn't the strength to keep to her feet. She left one rock shard to mark her old position and moved as quickly as she could, hoping to creep up on her enemy. She had to crawl, despite knees and hands already abused and scraped raw. It hurt to crawl, and the ache in her thigh was worse than before.

Five hundred hand paces from her starting point, she found a cache of leather vessels where there had been none before. The water was cool, and there was enough for several days, if rationed carefully. She drank first, almost weeping as she savored the touch of liquid in her parched mouth. She felt, then tasted, wedges of salty, dried fish, nibbled to test tough rounds of flatbread, and explored the oblong shape and smooth skin of a dozen sweet fruits. The softest proved easy to peel open with the edge of her rock scraper; its moist sweetness had a flavor she had never tasted before, like ambrosia, surely—the food of the gods in ancient Arethousa. She ate and drank cautiously, not sure if she would feel nauseated again, but the worst effects of the toxin had passed.

Food and drink then, enough for a hand or so of days.

Of Kansi-a-lari, whose voice had mocked her, she heard and felt no sign.

6

IVAR had been left behind with a dozen outriders to guard the horses in case the bandits slipped away from Captain Ulric and the strike force. They waited in a clearing ringed with beech trees. Faint trails of mist spun away through the forest. He gazed downslope, where oak trees encroached and bramble flourished. Beyond, at the base of the long hill, lay a fen populated by low-growing wet birch, stands of alder, and every manner of sedge and meadow grass. The captain knew better than to ride into such ground; the soldiers had gone in at dawn on foot.

Ivar and the others listened. Because of the lay of the ground, they heard the attack as if it were the peal of distant chimes: the ring of weapons clashing; a shout; a dog barking; a silence as the wind turned; and scattered shouts and noises as the wind shifted back. He blew on his hands. Sentries prowled at the edge of his sight. Two dogs snoozed on the damp ground. Above, clouds lingered, but it seemed to him that the mist was white and the heavens whiter still, as though the sun were trying to burn through.

"You'd think it'd be warmer, or that summer would come," muttered one of the grooms, stamping his feet.

"Hey!" shouted a sentry. "It's Erkanwulf!"

Ivar stayed aloof as the others crowded to meet the returning hero, who had blood on his cheek and a frown on his face.

"Well, it's over." He caught Ivar's gaze, and nodded. "Dedi got slashed on the thigh, and Guy got knocked cold, and a couple of lads have scrapes and bruises, but we're all safe. We took them by surprise. We got a dozen prisoners for the biscop. The rest are dead."

"For Lord Geoffrey," objected the man who had complained about summer. He was a Lavas retainer.

"For the biscop," repeated Erkanwulf. "For justice."

The smell of smoke cut the air, wafting up from the fen.

"What about those murdered girls?" asked Ivar.

Erkanwulf made a face. "Yeah, we found them. Dragged off to one side like rubbish. Seems to me they treat their soil better, burying it, like, so it doesn't attract flies. Animals had gotten into them. I didn't stay, but I know the captain meant to bury them there instead of hauling their bones back, which we couldn't do anyway seeing as how what was left was all scattered." He had gotten red as he talked, and he wiped his forehead with the back of a hand, although it wasn't at all warm.

"Bad?" asked Ivar, and Erkanwulf looked right at him and nodded. They had traveled far enough together that they no longer needed long explanations to be understood. "I could have said a prayer over them."

"Captain's orders," said Erkanwulf. "He wanted you to command the rear guard."

"He didn't want me to come along at all, as I recall."

"You're a cleric, Ivar. You're not meant to be soldiering."

But Ivar was restless. Since Biscop Constance had established herself at Lavas Holding, he felt himself betwixt and between. He had few clerical skills to bring to her schola, but likewise he was no soldier to serve her in that guise. In truth, as hard as that journey with Erkanwulf had been, he had liked it best of all the things he had experienced and suffered in the last few years. It made him think of Hanna, riding as an Eagle. On the road, he had felt that he was at least going somewhere, and the rescue of Baldwin had brought him a measure of peace even if Baldwin was no longer what he had been.

So are we all changed, he thought.

He wished Hanna was there, so he could tell her his thoughts as he had used to do, but no doubt she would only laugh at him. If she was even alive to do so. Fear pinched him, and he ducked his head, rubbing his eyes.

"Good land there at Ravnholt Manor," continued Erkanwulf, oblivious to these signs. "Shame to see it gone fallow, like, with no one left to farm it."

"There they come!" called a sentry.

Captain Ulric led the company out of the mist. Among that number walked Gerulf and Dedi, the two Lions Ivar and his friends had rescued at Queen's Grave. They saw Ivar and nodded to acknowledge him. Dedi was limping.

The victors had bound the bandits with rope at the ankles and wrists. The prisoners shuffled with heads down, broken in spirit, wounded, sniveling, and groaning. One man with a bloodied nose staunched the flow with a fist pressed against his blistered lips. A younger lad cradled a bleeding hand in the other arm. Lord Geoffrey walked at the end of the line, but everyone knew that Captain Ulric had plotted the raid and commanded it in all but name.

"They'll be shown more mercy than those girls they murdered," said Erkanwulf.

"How so?" asked Ivar, who was wondering how any folk could fall so low as these. They looked worse than he felt! They were the filthiest people he had ever seen, coated in dirt and worse things, besides their sins.

"They'll receive a trial, and their death'll come quick. Lucky for them." He spat.

"There was a woman, the one that man Heric said goaded them to murder the girls."

Erkanwulf looked away and wiped his mouth. "She was dead. I don't know who killed her."

The lad with the injured hand wept. To Ivar, the day seemed dark; the clouds would never lift. Ravnholt Manor was avenged, but no one seemed likely to rejoice.

In Lavas Holding, the prisoners were locked into the kennels once reserved for Count Lavastine's famous pack of hounds. Ivar paused to speak to Sergeant Gerulf, who had been assigned to the first shift of guards.

"How is Dedi?"

"He'll do, as long as the wound doesn't get infected, but Biscop Constance knows a bit about healing and anyway that one, Brother Baldwin, can heal him, surely, if it comes to that."

"Maybe so."

"You doubt it?" asked Gerulf, with a hint of a smile. "They say he's a saint, that one."

Ivar sighed, but he and Gerulf had a bond sewn up out of grim circumstances survived together. "It's difficult for me to see Baldwin as—what you say."

"It might explain his handsome face, since some say that's a sign of God's favor." Gerulf chuckled. "There now, my lord, I'm just joking. Dedi will do well enough. It was a shallow cut."

"Are you satisfied, still, with your service with Captain Ulric?"

"Duke Conrad assigned us to the captain, and I hold no grudge against the duke, since he treated us fairly considering the lady wished us all dead. It must have been for a reason that Dedi and I came to Ulric's troop. My loyalty remains to King Henry, my lord, and I serve Henry by serving his sister, don't you think?"

"If Henry still lives."

"Then Henry's heir. That's not all. There's a widow in Ulric's following I've a mind to marry. That lad Erkanwulf got to talking about taking a small company of men to settle Ravnholt Manor, now that it's abandoned. It's something to think about, especially for a man of my age. I'm content, my lord Ivar. Are you?"

Ivar shrugged, and Gerulf smiled crookedly, as if to say he knew what words Ivar would speak, if he dared—which he did not. Restlessness ate at him, a mortal disease. Somewhere, surely, events of great importance transpired and as usual he was stuck here waiting in the backwaters while the battle moved on and left him behind.

In the hall, Constance was seated beside the blazing hearth with her schola and young Lady Lavrentia in attendance, listening to testimony from a pair of woodsmen.

"That was a few years back, Your Holiness. We got a good look at these refugees, and we knew they was likely to be dead come winter. But the next year we swung back that way on the trail of a boar and they were still living. They said it was the cloak, that they had been blessed by God or some such. It were a little hard to understand them being as they did not speak quite right, coming up from the south as they did."

Baldwin and Sigfrid were writing, and Ermanrich was cutting quills on the opposite side of the table. Lavrentia was seated awkwardly on a chair beside Constance, with her hands folded in her lap and her twin canes resting against her knees. She uttered no word and made no sign, and Ivar could not tell what she might be feeling except that when, on occasion, Constance smiled at her, the girl smiled back.

On the other side of a hall a trio of wounded soldiers lay on the floor. Hathumod knelt beside one of them, smearing a white salve on the cut that had opened his thigh. That was Dedi, grimacing at the pain, but then he gave a snort of a laugh as Hathumod said something that amused him.

The woodsmen left. A man twisting a soft cap in his hands walked forward hesitantly.

"Do not fear," said Constance gently. "Are you the one who came all the way up from the southern borders of Lavas County? Lady Hildegard holds the land in that part of the county. I hear it was a long walk—five days!"

He dropped to his knees as if she had shot him. "Six,

Your Holiness. I was sent by our village to bring our request to the count." He glanced around the hall apprehensively, looked at Lady Lavrentia, rubbed his cap against his chin, and coughed. "I wasn't sure who to speak to, Your Holiness."

Constance touched the girl on the arm, and she piped up in a clear, soft voice. "Where are you from?"

"We call it Shaden, my lady. Begging your pardon, Your Holiness, but is it true there's a new count? We heard some folk say so, which is why we folk at Shaden thought to send one of us to speak, but it seems from what I hear at the holding they were talking nonsense."

"Lord Geoffrey still stands as regent for his young daughter, Lavrentia," Constance said, indicating Lavrentia. "Is that who you meant?"

He ducked his head, too flabbergasted to speak. The girl stared at him but said nothing, and finally looked at Constance.

Before her injuries, Constance might simply have overawed him, being a noble woman so grand and mighty that a simple farmer would be too tongue-tied to utter a word in her presence, but what she had suffered had made her less formidable in appearance, although Ivar knew that she had not changed.

"Lord Geoffrey is resting, and I am here with Count Lavrentia, as you see. We will write down your statement, here," she gestured to Sigfrid, "if you will tell us to what purpose your village sent you."

A man might frown so, Ivar thought, making ready for a charge against an armed and powerful enemy. But the man swallowed, braced himself by letting out a sharp exhalation, and began in a firm if slightly rushed tone.

"We lost our deacon last summer to the black rot, and most of our seed corn, as well as a dozen or more good folk in our village. We were hoping the count might see fit to send another deacon our way so that we can live properly and pray when it is fitting and hear the stories of the Holy Verses told out to us. We were promised a few year back that we'd have the use of this new plough we heard tell of, to break up some bottomland, but we've heard no more of it. It would aid us this year especially with the weather bad as it is. We've had a score settlers come to our valley, driven out of a pair of villages that were torn right down in the great storm last autumn. We can't feed all without this new land put to the plough. And with them, we're asking we be allowed to pay a lower tithe this year, to hold back more of what we grow so as to feed the many more mouths we have and will have next winter. My lady. And if I may be bold, Your Holiness."

"Go on."

Sigfrid's quill scratched as he wrote. Baldwin was staring dreamily at the fire.

"We have a tax we pay to Lady Hildegard, but she died when the roof of her hall fell in the storm."

"Yes, it's been recorded," said Constance. "She left no immediate heirs. I've been told there is a cousin from farther east who will inherit, but there's been some trouble finding her."

"Yes, Your Holiness. So we pray, Your Holiness, for the lady's steward has dealt poorly with us in the past and now is threatening to come with men-at-arms and rob us to pay our back taxes. If the lady doesn't come soon, we are come to ask if another steward might be set over us who will govern more justly."

"You are bold," said the girl.

"Begging your pardon, my lady. We are desperate, Your Holiness. We thought all was lost last year, and then—" He faltered, twisting the cap.

Baldwin smiled in that way that calmed because it dazzled.

"Go on," said Constance kindly.

"There were signs and portents, Your Holiness. A scythe I had borrowed—I lost its iron blade in the pond, and yet it was returned to me although it was hopelessly lost in the water and weeds. My niece, a good girl, was killed when a wall fell in on her, I swear to you in God's name that she stopped breathing, but she lived, and lives still, a sharp-tongued brat but one we all love. These were portents of change. Don't you think?"

"Miracles," said Constance sternly.

He bowed his head.

"Tell us again, and in more detail," she said, "for I have a wish that my clerics will record all these stories. I have heard many tales these days, here in Lavas, and others on the road. Strange tidings."

Lavrentia looked at her hands.

Constance looked at Ivar and nodded, but he was of no use to her. He could barely scratch out his letters in the crudest fashion imaginable, and unlike some clerics he had no trained memory to recall the Holy Verses in their entirety or recite the genealogy of regnants and nobles back to the tenth generation.

The farmer began telling a confused story about a madman dressed only in dirt and moss. As Baldwin began writing, Ivar went outside where he kicked pebbles across the courtyard and all the way to the gate and farther yet to the fosse and walked aimlessly before coming to the little church where the peculiar and unsettling stone effigy of the last count rested.

He set foot on the porch but saw that another person knelt, praying and weeping, in the dim interior: Lord Geoffrey.

I am not the only troubled soul. And were his troubles so very desperate? Discontent was not the same as desperation. Watching the shadowed figure from the porch of the little church, Ivar sensed that, outside, he waited under the skies of a far finer day than the one that, inside, plagued Geoffrey with rain and tempest. Lord Geoffrey had lost his wife, and his cousin—if he had held much affection for the deceased Count Lavastine, which Ivar had no way of determining. His now-crippled daughter had only a tenuous hold on the county claimed in her name, and his two young sons were being held in Autun in the tender care of Lady Sabella. The local folk muttered against him, and some said openly that Geoffrey had usurped the place of the rightful heir in order to get the lands and title for his daughter and thus—because she was still a child—himself.

No wonder he wept.

Back by the gate, the watch bell rang. A pair of banners fluttered in the distance as a party of riders approached the holding.

"What news?" demanded Geoffrey, emerging from the church.

"I don't know," said Ivar, taken aback by that brusque tone.

"Didn't Biscop Constance send you? Who are those riders?"

"I know no more than you do."

"Then you know that this life is only tears and suffering! Or do you clerics have some psalm for that, to tell us otherwise?"

Ivar couldn't think of any. The psalms all ran together in his mind, praising God, smiting foes, rejoicing at deliverance, and punishing those who did not act as they should, although the blessed Daisan had taught that to act against what is right was, in a way, its own punishment since humankind knew that it were better and easier to do what is good than what is evil.

"The actions of humankind are a mystery," he said at last, "since many do evil things who ought to know better, and some do good when they mean to do ill."

Geoffrey grunted as if irritated and set out for the gate to greet the newcomers. Ivar hastened after him, and came to the hall in time to hear a haughty young man, with the bearing of a youth raised in a noble house, speak to Geoffrey and Constance while a crowd gathered to listen.

"Lady Sabella sends this message to Lord Geoffrey of Lavas, regent for Lavrentia, count of Lavas. 'Tidings have reached me that you are sheltering Biscop Constance, who has fomented rebellion against me. Turn her over into my custody, in Autun, or your sons will be forfeit, executed for your treason.' "

"Treason!" Geoffrey raged. The messenger held his ground, unmoved by the lord's anger. "They are children! The younger hasn't seen four summers." He pressed the heels of his hands against his forehead and muttered curses while his daughter sat small and quiet behind him. "It would have been better if they had died with their mother!"

Lavrentia's face crumpled as she fought to restrain tears.

"Despair is a sin, Geoffrey," said Constance, taking hold of his arm and drawing his hands down.

"Am I to rejoice instead?"

She caught his gaze and held it, and after a moment his wild look subsided to something more like shame. Ivar squeezed forward through the ranks to his friends, who were waiting beside the hearth. The messenger glanced their way, attracted by Ivar's movement through the assembly, and dismissed them with a smirk.

"I would not have burdened you with my presence if I had known Sabella would threaten you in this particular way," said Constance.

"She's listening to Salian advisers!" Geoffrey seemed ready to laugh. "Salians are always murdering their children to clear their own path to the throne or to riches."

"So the chronicles suggest," agreed Constance in a mild tone that was meant to warn him, but Geoffrey was not able to listen.

"They might be dead already. Then nothing will be served by giving you up to her as well. Better stick with what we know is true. Or Sabella may be bluffing. She may not have the heart to kill two innocent children."

"Do you think so?" asked Constance.

He swayed, jerking side to side as though tugged this way and that by a sharp pull on a rope. "I don't know what to think! How can it have all gone wrong? I must go! I'll exchange myself for them! Let her kill me if she wishes! I would welcome death!"

"Lord Geoffrey! For shame!"

He hid his face. His daughter sobbed into her hands, echoing her father. The company of retainers and servants stood in awful silence, and a few crept away like beaten dogs hoping not to be noticed. The messenger watched carefully, absorbing the scene into his memory so that, Ivar suppose, he might report Geoffrey's weakness to Sabella.

"You must stay here in Lavas and guard your daughter and these lands, Geoffrey. Captain Ulric and his company will remain behind. Consider that this may be a feint to draw you out."

"Why? Lavas County is nothing to Sabella, surely. She wants you because you represent Henry's claim to sovereignty in Varre. Because you are the rightful duke of Arco-

nia, after Sabella forfeited the title by her own rebellion.
She is the traitor! I am not. I am not! Anyway, if you go to
her, she will have no reason to give up my sons. Then she'll
have you back, to do with as she please—even to kill—and
she'll still hold my sons."

"No child of Arnulf would dare kill her own sibling,"
said Constance. "We are not Salians!"

"I must go, or I'll be dishonored!"

"You must stay, and guard Lavas together with Captain
Ulric. I'll leave you a hostage in your turn—this messenger."

The young man started and took a step back, looking
around as for an escape route, but Ulric had already
moved his men into position to block his retreat.

"I will take my trusted retainers." She gestured toward
her clerics.

"Then it is all for nothing," moaned Geoffrey, "freeing
you from Queen's Grave. All this! It has all rotted in my
hands!"

"We are not dead and defeated yet, Geoffrey!" She got
hold of her walking stick and pushed to her feet, and her
smile might have come because of the pain of rising or her
annoyance at Geoffrey, or because Sabella's messenger
looked so flummoxed at being outflanked as he realized he
was now a prisoner. "Trust in God. I do."

"Truth rises with the phoenix," muttered a voice in the
crowd.

"So I have come to believe."

Ulric met her by the door into the inner apartments.

"Your Grace. We know that bandits haunt the roads, and
worse things, perhaps. Wolves. Shadows. I trust God, but I
wish you will take armed men on the road to protect you."

"Sabella has kindly sent an escort. I'll return with them,
all except for the messenger, who will remain here. Most of
my schola are too frail to travel, and I trust you will see
them well cared for here, Captain. But I think a few of my
faithful clerics can accompany me!" She smiled at Ivar,
Sigfrid, Ermanrich, and Hathumod. Her gaze lingered
longest on Baldwin, whom she examined with a slight
frown.

"They may even be able to bear weapons," said Ulric

with a look of disapproval, "although I don't know how much good they'll do you in a fight, Your Grace."

"We've fought!" said Ivar. "We've ridden into battle with Prince Ekkehard."

Ulric began to roll his eyes, but stopped himself with an inhalation and a sharp cough.

"My bold clerics!" she said, and somehow, from her lips, the statement did not sound mocking.

7

WHAT woke her? She lay still, listening, but heard nothing and saw nothing. A sour scent teased her; it was as pungent as rotten eggs but fading fast.

At length she decided that nothing unusual had woken her. She shifted, sitting up, and in that moment a puff of sulfurous air gusted against her cheek. She heard two scrapes as of a weight dragged across gritty rock, a sigh like those of a bellows, and again two scrapes. The stink of the air made her eyes water, but it had direction, wafting at her from the north-northwest if she deemed her back against the rock wall to measure due south. Out there, some movement made the air shift. Where there was a breeze, there was a breach to the outside.

She tested her thigh. The old blood was flaking off, and there was only a smear of moistness at one end of the wound where it had ripped a little. A long scab was beginning to form. She still ached throughout her body, but food and drink and rest had eased these hurts and her mind had regained its clarity.

I can win free, if I can only be patient and clever.

She sat for a long while and listened. The weight of rock oppressed her, but power lived here, too, felt as a hum deep in the earth. Kansi-a-lari had called this place "the Heart-of-the-Mountain-of-the-World's Beginning."

The Ashioi cities she had seen looked different than the

towns and habitations erected by humankind, which rose
haphazardly although any one might be built around a central building grounded with sacred power—a cathedral or
church or, in older days, a fort. The crowns held power;
weaving threads into a stone crown brought to Earth the
melody of the spheres.

She breathed into her belly, into the stone, and it seemed
to her that the deeper she breathed the deeper she fell. The
Ashioi understood the power that lies in the landscape,
and they built to encourage and enhance it. This heart was
a kernel around which the city had risen. So deep, and so
high, and pulsing with a force whose heat and contours, almost too faint for her to perceive, had the taste of the
aether, funneled into this place as canals channel rainwater
into a central pond.

She stood, and called her wings.

They flared golden, and she lifted a hand's breadth off
the ground. A vast ceiling vaulted so high that its peaks lay
in shadow. Above, frozen spears of lightning glistened, rock
formations hanging from the ceiling like so many points.
The cavern was immense, its far walls lost in dimness. The
floor stretched smooth and unbroken.

Except *there*.

A narrow, black spire, somewhat taller than a man, rose
out of the floor, so far from her that it was barely visible in
the gloom. Blue fire flickered along its length where the
aetherical glamour cast by her wings brushed it. Like a
shadow, a second, insubstantial pillar blossomed into existence beside it, a burning stone through which she could see

*"Liat'dano! Where are you?" The shaman speaks to her
from beyond that gateway. The centaur woman is insubstantial but nevertheless present. She shades her eyes as
against a harsh light and peers through the gateway toward
Liath.*

*"I am here, at the Heart-of-the-Mountain-of-the-World's
Beginning!" Liath cries.*

*"I have been looking for you, Daughter, but the aether is
thin and the gateway closes. Come to me! Quickly!"*

The pulse of the aether was too feeble, even here, to sustain her wings. They withered, and she dropped the hand's

span to Earth and stumbled as too much weight came down on her injured leg. The glowing illumination faded and the burning stone dissolved into a pale nimbus, rapidly dissipating.

Caught in the last lambent twilight, a figure hunched out of the shadows and scuttled to the spire. It turned, and she saw that it was not human. It had luminous bulges where eyes ought to have been. Its skin had the look of granite.

Blackness swallowed her, and it. She heard two scrapes, that bellows sigh followed by two scrapes, and then nothing.

She dug deep, and fought to call her wings again, but the first effort had taken its toll on her and they only flickered, like the spark of a wick catching for an instant before snapping out. She could not get illumination enough to make her way to the black spire.

She had not hallucinated that creature. Indeed, she had a good idea of what it must be, because Mother Obligatia had told her of the inhuman creatures deep in the rock beneath the convent of St. Ekatarina's whose charity had sustained the sisters for many months. In legend, humankind had many names for them: goblins and "Old Ones" and more besides.

Creatures who lived in the earth must have some means of moving around, just as moles shifted through tunnels. Where they could crawl, so could she. It was only a matter of having provisions and steady light.

Ai, God, if only the gateway of the burning stone had not collapsed so suddenly. If she could step through— reach Li'at'dano—she could gain her freedom *and* be reunited with Blessing, if her girl lived.

She must live.

"I will it so," she murmured, knowing that words are not magic in themselves but only because we weave them in a way that, like sorcery, creates a spell around our listeners.

She sat for a long while, breathing to quiet her heart and mind but also fighting against the exhaustion that washed at her and between one breath and the next swept over her. Pain from the wound in her thigh stabbed every time she twitched, and she braced herself against the wall to

stop her legs from moving. Could she reach Li'at'dano?
Thoughts wound down lazily, and she dozed off.

What had woken her?
Liathano.
Was that the shaman's voice? It nagged at her. She must
have heard the shaman calling her name in the dream she
had just been having, which had already faded, leaving a
slow trembling ringing in her ears as if she had dreamed in
sounds and not images.
Liathano.
One voice, tolling like a bell.
A sick dread infested her, shuddering her body inside
and out.
Ai, God. A galla.
Kansi had captured her and meant to kill her. No, that
was fear talking. She had no reason to believe that Kansi
knew the galla or had ever used them.
Liathano.
The galla came from a plane outside of this world, and
therefore they did not fully inhabit this world. Air and
water meant nothing to them. Heat and cold could claw no
purchase into the forms that passed for their bodies. Rock
did not halt them.
It was coming for her, and she had no weapon with
which to kill it.
Liathano.
She was cold, and determined, and flush with the heat
that comes of a racing heart and bitter knowledge. *I am
dead, but I will not go down without fighting.*
She rose, fixed her feet and, ignoring the pain of her
wound, sought by taste and smell and hearing for the direction of the galla.
Where is it coming from? There!
There! The cavern was pitch-black, without light enough
even to see her own hand held right in front of her nose.
But the galla was blacker still. Seen in such darkness, she
perceived it as a void cut through onto another place, a
worse place, a plane of existence racked with torment that,
to the galla, seemed a blessed mercy compared to the tor-

ments of Earth. It was not like humankind, not meant to
dwell in this world even for the space of a breath, her own,
one in and one out, as she stood her ground and sought
deep into the rock for the scattered grains of fire embedded within the structure of stone.

So faint they were, but she was desperate, and it rang
closer and closer, floating across the vast black expanse of
the cavern.

Liathano!

It knew her. It only wanted to go home, and she was its
gateway.

The thought gave rise to ugly hope. She swept her
awareness past the grains of fire and sought those attenu-
ated veins of aether. Through the gateway she could find
griffins. She might escape through the gateway.

She called her wings. As they flared, the towering black
pillar that was the galla fluttered as in a strong wind.

She sought: At the heart of the aether lies the burning
stone, the gateway—so far off, so faint . . .

It bloomed, frangible but present, a man's height and
breadth in size, shimmering with the pulsing blue aether.

The shaman stood there still—or had come again to seek
her. The pale figure of the Horse woman wavered, limned
in blue as she reached out her arms in a gesture of welcome.

"Liath!" called the shaman.

"I'm coming! There is a galla—" she cried out as she
lunged forward, but her leg collapsed under her. Already
the gateway was collapsing from man height to child height
to knee height. Too late! Too weak! There was not enough
aether to sustain it. Her wings shredded into sparks. The
galla swept down upon her.

The shaman's voice rang clear through the last hand's
span of the opening. "I am Li'at'dano. Come quickly, to
me!"

It was the same name, blurred by the centuries into a
word that breathed more softly from the lips but which in
its essence had not changed.

It was the same name, and she had carried it for far
longer than Liath had.

The stinging presence of the galla scorched her, but it passed her by and twisted through the vanishing gateway on the trail of the one called Li'at'dano. Liathano.

There came a cry of pain, and a dazzling blaze that flared as the galla engulfed and consumed its prey.

The last light of aetherical fire curled in on itself, and winked out as the gateway collapsed.

Dead.

Devoured.

Into silence, into darkness, Liath fell. Her ears rang and her pulse throbbed, beating wildly as she knelt on the cold stone and sobbed so raggedly that it seemed she could never stop.

8

THE weather held fine. It did not rain, or even feel like rain. They luxuriated in a string of pleasant early summer days that might have run warm had it not been for the constant veil that concealed the sun and cooled the land. All the noble lords and ladies watched Sabella day by day to gauge her mood; it was Conrad's heartiness that warmed the party.

"So I said to her, 'then, pray tell, if a woman as lovely as you has held to your vows these four years and had no congress with any man or his member, why does this toddling sprout cling to your leg and call you Mother?' She looked me dead in the eye, and she spoke coldly, I will tell you! 'Because I am abbess of this poor institution, my lord duke, not the serving maid you take me for. I am Mother to those who rest under my care.' "

His listeners laughed, and he went on. "It is a shame, truly, that God should steal such treasures and lock them in the church. I have rarely seen a finer looking woman, as ripe as Aogoste berries. But I had no fortune that day! Her scornful look was enough to wither any man! Still, I wondered about that little child. He had a dusky complexion, you know."

One of the courtiers chortled. "Mayhap you came to her in the night, like an incubus, Conrad, eh! A year or two previous? She all unwitting? They say holy women have moist dreams!"

Conrad raised a hand to stop the chatter and laughter. "Not me! I would have recalled it! Mayhap, back in those days, the Dragons of those times might have ridden by. In truth, now I think on it, I recall there was talk of them sheltering a night or more in the convent's guesthouse two years before I came calling. Where such men shelter, one at least might have found a more inviting hall to rest himself. For you know, this was at St. Genovefa's Convent, and she the saintly patron of dogs."

That brought a new round of laughter.

"Are you only prattling, Conrad?" asked Sabella, "or do you honestly believe it to be true? Did Sanglant get some bastard child on a holy abbess back when he was captain of Henry's Dragons? Where is this supposed to have taken place? How can the child's existence give us an advantage? Otherwise, do not waste my time."

Her glare cowed the courtiers, but Conrad laughed. He had a remarkable smile, one that invited all folk to smile with him, and he was not afraid to poke fun at himself, although it seemed to Alain that he had made sure that the knife thrust more deeply into his unwitting rival's flesh. "I will tell tales to please myself and my companions while we ride this dreary road. If not, then you must listen to me sing."

Even Sabella must chuckle, although the softening lasted only a moment. "Best tell your tales, for I will have none of your singing without my good clerics to make it sweet."

"And your sweetest singer is fled," remarked Conrad with an innocent expression. "Fled to the angels from which he arose."

Her eyes flared, and her horse minced as she jerked the reins. Off along the verge, where the hounds padded, Rage barked, a rumble that startled the nearest horse and set off a chain of missteps among the riders and then the stewards and mounted soldiers behind. "Enough, Conrad!"

"She did not sing for me, that lovely creature," said Conrad, continuing as if he had not noticed the rogue current he had stirred into life. "Mother Armentaria, I think her name was. I do wonder about my cousin and that dark little creature who held the holy woman's skirts and stared at me with eyes so rich a brown. A taking thing. I don't know if it was girl or boy, but it was pretty enough to be either even if scarcely old enough to walk. It might have been a beggar's child, or a prince's. How can we know when the mother will not or cannot speak?"

He glanced at Alain before turning his attention back to his courtiers.

"It's said Prince Sanglant sowed a hundred bastards, being a bastard himself," said one of the younger courtiers, "but is it true?"

"He's a handsome man," said Conrad. "Were I born a woman, instead of a man, I suppose I might try a kiss from him. As it is, I can only envy him, for he has a fair beauty for a wife, a fine creature as bright as fire."

"Of uncertain lineage," said Sabella. "Both bastards, most likely. She is excommunicated and accused of being a sorcerer."

"Yes, truly," said Conrad with a crooked smile, "it is as well you and I, Sabella, make our way to save our grandfather's precious kingdom from such usurpers."

"Your great grandfather," she said curtly. "Tallia is your very distant cousin."

"Yes, indeed, distant enough that we might be married with the sanction of the church," he agreed cordially. He had an expression that might have been amused or annoyed. "Yet when I pressed my suit elsewhere, my dear cousin Henry deemed my cousin Theophanu too close to agree to the alliance."

"Don't speak to me of Henry!"

Her look was meant to quell, but Conrad smiled. "We are among allies, Sabella. No one in our retinues will cry to the church that I have married consanguineously. What is it? Seven degrees? Eight? Six? Far enough except for

Henry's taste, since he wanted no such connection between his children and mine."

"He feared you."

"Perhaps. I think all along Henry was only waiting."

"For what?" she asked him, and all the courtiers, heads turning side to side as they looked first at Sabella and then at Conrad and then back again, fixed their attention on Conrad.

"Waiting to find a way to raise Sanglant as heir above Sophia's children. He found it. We battle not Sanglant, but Henry's sentimental attachment to the child who could not have the thing Henry most wished to give him. He has gotten it anyway. Sanglant always did seem to get his own way, though he was never gloating or crude about it. The best of men!"

Sabella smiled harshly. "Say you so, Conrad? Will you be turning your milites east to join up with him? The best of men?"

Conrad had such an infectious way of laughing that everyone joined in. When the fit of hilarity had passed, he spoke in a voice whose easy charm did nothing to affect its sincerity. "I am sure of what I want, what I deserve, and what I intend to claim."

"Horses ahead, my lord duke. My lady." A sergeant called from the foremost line of riders, and a ripple—men checking swords, easing spears free—passed backward through the company. "Nay, it's only the scouts."

Atto returned with the trio of men sent ahead to help him seek out their way, and to make sure he did not bolt. Certainly the lad looked nervous enough, sweating and pale and hair a rat's nest since he couldn't stop running his hands through it. He consulted with Sabella's captain, and in time they came to a fork in the road. Instead of continuing on the main road, they cut into broken woodland along a rutted track where they had to ride two abreast. Their line of march stretched back a good ways. The other nobles competed for position, but Alain hung back and let the main part of the company pass before swinging into line with the wagons. He nodded at the soldier who was riding beside the great cage meant for the guivre.

"My lord," said Captain Tammus reluctantly, dropping his gaze while his hands clenched on the reins.

Sorrow growled, low in her throat, but Alain let the captain and these foremost wagons pass as well and came up behind the supply wagons with their barrels of ale and sacks of grain or flour and small woven sapling cages filled with squawking chickens and a furious goose. A trio of steers paced at the end of ropes. Two dozen sheep followed, pursued by a pair of shepherds and their clever dog. Behind the last wagon walked a half dozen men, each one pushing a flat-bedded cart on which lay the trussed carcass of a deer.

"Where have these come from?" he asked one of the stewards.

The woman rode a stocky pony and was young and weary, hair covered by a pale yellow scarf. She wore a glove on her right hand and her left bare, revealing a rash prickling across her three middle fingers.

"You know the way of it, my lord," she said cautiously, recognizing him, as any good steward must recognize by sight every noble who rode with the lady. "Three our hunters brought down yesterday and the day before. We hung them all night, though they'll still be tough. The others came from the manor. Folk are hunting deer in numbers early this year. The sheep we took as part of the tithe, together with the grain. Out in the forest we'll not find much provender, for few folk live in the wilderness. We must feed all with what we gain here."

He nodded, and to her evident relief he fell back to ride alongside the rear guard. Farther behind might be found the rear scouts, but he held his position the rest of that day. The land changed its character, and they entered a region of precipitous hills, rugged rocky outcrops, and low spines of rock protruding from otherwise unexceptional earth. Streamlets flowed in plenty, and there was no sign of human habitation. Folk whispered that they were nearing the lair of the guivre, who hid within a maze of stony dikes. Even the animals grew nervous. A faint odor of rotting carcasses laced the breeze at intervals, but faded as quickly as he caught its touch.

9

KANSI'S voice came sooner than she expected, echoing out of the darkness. "What creature stalked our land? What was it?"

"Set me free, and I'll tell you," said Liath, hoarse from weeping and exhausted with rage.

"Tell me!"

Although Kansi-a-lari cursed her and commanded her, Liath did not speak.

After that came silence for a long while during which she slept, drank, ate, and slept again. Although she had taken no physical harm, she felt battered and she felt bruised, and the right side of her face where the galla had swept closest was as tender as if she had scraped it against rock. Strangely, the wound in her thigh did not hurt as much.

When the exhaustion passed, the rage remained, but now she knew better than to curse impotently at Kansi-a-lari, who had her own schemes and hopes but who had not, after all, called the galla. She hoarded her strength, and made her plans.

"Li'at'dano!"

It hurt to hear her name spoken in the antique manner, but although she wanted to scream in fury for everything she was guilty of and quite a bit she was not, she answered in as calm a voice as she could muster.

"Here I am. What do you want?"

"The answer to my question. That creature murdered a child, four adults, and many precious goats in its passage through our land. Flensed them to the bone. Is this your way of doing battle against us?"

"Lower down more food and drink. Then I'll tell you."

"I know how much you have. There is enough, if it's rationed."

"I want more. And a knife."

She laughed. "No knife. Knives you will have enough of, if I decide to give you to the priests."

After that came silence, but later, listening, Liath heard a faint scraping and a fainter thump.

Out of the darkness, Kansi spoke. "Answer my question. I have done as you asked."

She is above me.

"I will," said Liath, "once I am sure I have what I want."

Since Kansi-a-lari was speaking from above, surely the provisions should have hit the floor in the same place she had found them the first time. Since it had not, there must therefore be other openings, hidden to her salamander eyes. Kansi-a-lari could not be speaking from a place where daylight gleamed, or Liath would have discerned any least particle of light's being. A cave above a cave? Rock sheltered Kansi. Liath could get no sense of her position, her scent, or even her presence except for her voice.

She walked the circuit of the wall, sweeping her feet and finding her leg aching, but sturdy. After 435 footfalls she struck riches: a dozen bulbous fruits; a dozen flat circles of bread; three big leather pouches swollen with a sweet-tasting nectar; a cheese that tasted better than it smelled; eggs cushioned in greasy uncombed wool.

No knife.

"I am satisfied," she said, pitching her voice to carry upward, "that you have dealt fairly with me in this particular matter. Set me free."

"I will not."

"Then listen. The creature is called a galla. It comes from another plane of existence."

"From the aether?"

"I think not. Step sideways through a crack in a wall and you may come to a lost garden. Step sideways through the spheres, and there may be other worlds."

"A curious notion," said Kansi. "Go on."

"The galla are called, with blood, to this world. The one who calls them grants them their freedom in a name. This person they must hunt down and devour. When they have devoured the one they sought, the crack in the wall opens, and they can return to their home."

"Why did you call it?"

"I did not call it. I have been attacked by such creatures before. That is how I know what they are."

"How did you rid yourself of it? Is there a spell?"

She choked, but eventually found her voice, because she had to speak. "Griffin feathers dispel the galla. It is the only way to banish them, that I know of."

"You came to us naked except for your clothes. How did you banish this one?"

"You may believe I came to you with nothing, but I banished it nevertheless." She had to push on, before she thought too hard and burst into tears. She burned with anger, and she must remember the right person to blame. "I have no griffin feathers now. If another galla comes for me, I am helpless." She could not swallow; she could not speak lest her voice tremble. Yet, why not? Let Kansi believe her terrified. It was the truth.

"If you want me alive, understand that I am helpless *now* against the galla. And understand this: The galla are after your son as well."

"Zuangua says Sanglant has griffins. He is well protected. Wise boy!"

"He *had* griffins. They are flown back into the east to breed. He has seven feathers left him. For each galla that comes, he has one less. Do you mean to let him die once he runs out of griffin feathers?"

"I cannot fight these galla without griffin feathers? Then tell me, Liathano, if you care for my son: what sorcerer calls the galla to pursue you?"

Liath smiled, and her lips formed a silent prayer as she weighed her words and spoke. "I cannot know for sure, I admit. There is only one person who in the past had the knowledge and the skill and the desire to call galla. Her name is Sister Venia, although she was also once called Biscop Antonia of Mainni. I don't know where she is."

There came silence for such a long time that Liath finally decided that Kansi must have left. She peeled open one of the fruits and savored the sweet, sloppy mess inside. She tasted bitter to herself, wiping her chin with her fingers and licking off the trails of juice.

Kansi's voice slipped out of the darkness, surprising her.

Her tone was cool, but it made Liath shiver. "My people will find her, and I will deal with her."

"Why do you keep me here?"

"That is a foolish question. You are—what would they call it at the court of Wendar, this game of carved pieces moved across a board? You are a pawn, in my keeping. With you in my hand, I have power over those who desire to take you for themselves."

"Who would that be?" Liath demanded, for it seemed strange and ominous that Kansi used the plural.

"The blood knives, and of course—" She broke off, then finished. "—my son."

"Sanglant wants peace. He needs peace, to rebuild after the cataclysm. Why do you wish to fight him?"

"I wish to protect my people. We cannot trust humankind."

"You let Henry raise him."

"That was all along the intention of the council of elders. A poor plan, which failed. We will do better, I promise you."

"Those days are long past. We must trust each other in order to survive."

"These are tiresome words. Do you even believe them yourself?"

"Sanglant is not your enemy."

There was no answer, and in time Liath had to accept that Kansi had gone.

So be it. She rested a while longer and ate and drank a little more, starting with the raw eggs, which were sure to get broken. Afterward she chipped away at one of the blunt rocks to get more of an edge on it. She took off her wool outer-tunic and stripped off the lighter linen under-tunic before putting the over-tunic back on. The wool itched, but it was better to save the sturdier, warmer tunic. With the scraper she severed threads and managed with real effort to separate the tunic so that with knots and curls she could hang all of her provisions safely around her hips. She finished the eggs, rose, and walked and jumped a little to test the security of her knots.

They held.

Facing the center of the cavern, she called her wings.

They flared and faded so quickly that it left afterimages against her eyes. She tried again, but it was no use. The undercurrents of aether still thrummed through this heart, but something was missing: Li'at'dano's power calling to her from the far side of the gateway.

Had it always taken two to open the gateway of the burning stone? Was there a thread woven between one and the other? Did she need more of a focus, or was the burning stone fading surely and slowly from the compass of the world?

She wiped away stinging tears and scratched her itching shoulders and allowed herself one burst of frustrated overpowering thwarted despairing fury, not a scream but a wash of emotion like the tidal surge that had obliterated the shore.

"Liath."

Just like that, she snapped alert. In like manner, a hound comes to point, sensing an enemy. Any creature does. She was clear and empty and as sharp as steel.

"Liath," he said again.

It was like an hallucination, because there was no possible way that Hugh of Austra should be speaking to her in this place at this time when she was imprisoned at the very heart of the land belonging to the Ashioi.

But it was his voice, and it was obvious from his tone that he knew she was there.

When she did not reply, he went on.

"I am a prisoner of the Ashioi."

This comment bestirred her, because for some reason she found it amusing. "Not so deep in prison as I am, it appears, since you are there, and I am here. How came they to capture you?"

"They caught me on the road as I was fleeing Queen Adelheid."

He paused again, and she played along. "What cause had you to flee Adelheid? Before, as I recall the story, you were her ally."

"No longer. Adelheid blames me for Henry's death."

"Can you possibly believe that I might believe you innocent of any share in Henry's death?"

"Believe what you will. Adelheid desired to kill me."

Liath forbore to comment, and in any case she was having a difficult time parsing his tone into its component emotions without the text of expression and his body's language to study.

"I took Blessing away from Adelheid," he added.

Blessing! The name felled her. She sank, found herself sprawled on the ground. Her hands had gone numb. Hugh's smooth words flowed over her as though she were stone.

"I freed her from captivity. Adelheid would have murdered her in revenge for the death of Berengaria."

She tried words on her tongue and found that she could speak. "Who is Berengaria?"

"The younger child. She had two by Henry, Mathilda and Berengaria."

Two children, Henry's youngest offspring. Of course she remembered them. They held a claim to the Wendish throne that many would consider more legitimate than Sanglant's, even if their mother was Aostan.

"I stole Blessing away to save her from Adelheid. The Ashioi captured us. We are prisoners here, as you are."

This story made no sense, but no matter. She wiped sweat from her forehead, although it wasn't hot.

"How did Blessing come into Adelheid's custody?"

"I don't know. She and her party were discovered by Adelheid's soldiers on the road near Novomo. How did the child's father come to carelessly leave her behind in Aosta? I would not have done so."

She hesitated, knowing she must phrase both questions and answers precisely in order to get the information she needed without giving away too much. "She was too ill to be moved," she said as evenly as she could.

He laughed. "She has recovered. Her uncle Zuangua is training her to be a warrior. You and I, however, have common cause. We desire to escape. I will help you."

She found herself trembling between one breath and the next, only there was nothing within arm's reach to strangle. At last, she sorted past laughter and weeping and found pragmatism. "In exchange for what?"

"Nothing. I seek only to aid Wendar."

The first shock survived, this made her smile cruelly. Surely Hugh was too subtle to believe that she would believe this!

"It is strange to me that small parties of Ashioi mask warriors strike in Wendar. They come unheralded and without any trace of how they have arrived and where they go after. Yet if a mathematicus had allied with the Ashioi, he might weave gateways through the crowns for such raiding parties. How would that be aiding Wendar?"

"My plan is deeper than it seems. I will destroy Feather Cloak."

"So you say. Many innocent souls have lost their lives."

"But the rest will live in peace because of it." He fell silent, awaiting her response.

What flowered within her was an astonishing sense of peace.

Hugh had no power of his own except what he could wreak against others, a man armed with a sword who must stand on the field against disciplined ranks of archers and cavalry. This made him no less dangerous. A man with a sword can still kill anyone who comes within arm's reach. As long as Hugh could twist others to do his will, he could, and would, harm his enemies and every innocent soul who got in his way.

He was the bastard child of a powerful noble who had used him poorly, giving him education and desire without any way to wield it or the strength of will to rein it in. Margrave Judith had put him in the church, where he could rise to be presbyter, as he had done by a circuitous route. But becoming presbyter was not enough for Hugh. He wanted a different sort of power, and he had no way to obtain it except through sorcery. He had wielded power through Adelheid's agency, by ensorcelling Henry, because he had no power in his own heart.

Any person with the will to do what is right has power of a kind, however frail a reed that may seem when it comes time to stand tall against the storm. But in the end, in God's heart, it is the only power that matters.

He had seen, before anyone but Da and those who knew

what she was, that she had power he wanted to possess. But it was the fire at the heart of her that he desired, not her. Never her, that person whom Sanglant was perfectly willing to argue with, cajole, irritate, and love.

She had what Hugh wanted. She was what Hugh wanted to be.

"What is your plan?" she asked him.

"I have a rope. I'll throw it down to you, and haul you up. We can escape through the crown that stands near here."

"Where is it?"

"A few days' walk, beyond the White Road."

"Very well. Throw down the rope."

She heard it uncoil with a scraping slither. Its final lengths thumped lightly on the cavern's floor. She fished for and found the greasy wool, tossed it high into the air, and called fire into this cloud. It blazed.

There! Alongside the smooth cavern wall dangled the rope, with no more than a single coil remaining on the ground. She reached it before the wool burned itself into nothing.

She jerked hard on the rope, but it held.

"I've made it fast. You must hurry. Tie it around your waist, and I'll haul you up."

"How did you come to find me?"

"You're imprisoned in a secret place in the midst of their great city."

"I know. How did *you* find me?"

"The priests are in a rage, claiming they are owed a sacrifice. A raiding party had taken a powerful captive, rumor said, but the members of that raiding party would not speak of it. The Feather Cloak need answer no questions."

"Feather Cloak?" She recalled Feather Cloak, that stern and pregnant leader who had banished her from Ashioi country.

"Sanglant's mother is Feather Cloak."

She caught a surprised laugh, making a kind of a snort. Sanglant's mother had grasped the reins of power among the Ashioi. What had happened to the other Feather Cloak?

"It was Feather Cloak who told you I was here?"

"It was not. I am her prisoner, but I have other sources of information."

No doubt a woman—some flint-eyed warrior girl who spilled the truth to him in the hope of gaining his smile and, perhaps, a kiss. Women could be stupid, that was certainly true. Liath did not hope to be one of those women today. Hugh was certainly lying, she just wasn't sure what part of his story was false, and which truth.

Blessing is recovered. Alive. Living.

"I want a knife before I'll come up," she said, "to defend myself with. I have no reason to trust you."

"If you don't trust me, you'll remain their prisoner. At their mercy. Do you know what the priests do to their sacrifices? Why they are called the blood knives?"

"I want a knife. Or I won't come up."

"If I drop it, it might hit you."

She slid backward along the wall ten paces, and called. "A knife, or I won't come up."

"I pray you, Liath. If we wait too long, we may be discovered."

"A knife."

He wanted her so badly that he betrayed himself. An object rasped along rock. Silence swallowed its fall, then it rattled on stone.

What manner of fool gave a knife to a prisoner?

How had Hugh of Austra come to be allied with the Ashioi?

She moved forward in darkness, knelt, and patted the ground until its cool blade came under her hand. Good iron, this. The hilt bore an embossed crest which she read by touch: the letter 'A' surrounded by a circle.

"Liath, you must hurry," he said.

She rose, gripped the rope, and looked up. The rock clouded her vision, and the vision that lay beyond those things seen with the open eye. Rock was heavy and slow moving, but there was something there, a presence. It was as if she could *smell* the edge of Hugh, like smelling a perfume: lavender for beauty, wolfsbane for deadliness, and something less tangible, twisted and rotten.

She could not quite grasp him, but she forged with her

awareness as high as she could reach up the rope to a place
where it tightened against a curve in the ceiling, perhaps a
narrow vertical tunnel. There, where the rope receded into
oblivion, she kissed the sleeping fire within it, and told it to
burn.

His shout woke fire. The rope burned hard, far above her,
just out of her sight. The red glow spit flakes of ash, and she
yanked. The rope tumbled down around and on top of her,
the fraying end smoldering and blackening at the tip.

"Ai, God! Liath!"

No need to answer. She had what she wanted. The glow
gave just enough light for her salamander eyes. She coiled
the rope over and under around shoulder and torso like a
bulky sash, holding the slowly burning end out away from
her, and tested the knots of the complicated arrangement
of food and drink tied up against her body. It would hold.

She pushed into the darkness. When she approached the
black spire, she found what she had prayed for: a stairway
into the depths.

10

IN the late afternoon he rode into a clearing ringed by
stately beech trees just coming into leaf. Beyond lay a tangle of mixed woodland with many massive trees listing
sideways or fallen to the ground and slender saplings and
a thick layer of shrubs grown up in a profusion that
blocked all lines of sight. An ancient wall formed a crumbling pattern within the clearing. No place along the wall
was more than knee-high, but it provided a barrier of sorts
where otherwise they must lie open to whatever the forest
might bring them. Within this ruin he found canvas tents
being erected and fires burning and the deer being skinned
and butchered and prepared for spit roasting over the remains of stone hearths. The offal was thrown to the hunting dogs, to keep them strong, although in any village such

fare would have been served up as a stew. Alain had put
aside some bones saved out from yesterday's dinner, and
these Rage and Sorrow gnawed on while he walked
through the camp speaking here and there to servants and
soldiers.

He came at length to the cloth screens set up on poles
that divided the main portion of the camp from the smaller
camp where the nobles would eat and sleep. No guards patrolled this gate, situated where a second inner ruin lay
within the first.

Servants and soldiers moved about freely, but none lingered where the nobles sat on stools at their leisure while
waiting for their roasting supper. The lords and ladies
laughed and chatted, at their ease. He went to pee, leaving
camp behind and stepping under the trees for a little privacy. The dogs lifted their heads and beat their tails one
two, growling to warn him that he was being followed. Finished, he greeted Duke Conrad, who came accompanied
by a swarm of nobles, servants, and faithful soldiers. Half of
them followed the duke's lead in taking a piss, a social activity on any noble's progress, but when the duke was finished, he waved his retainers away and gestured toward a
mossy stretch of thigh-high wall thrust up from the dirt and
grown about with honeysuckle and crocus.

"A pleasant bench," Conrad said amiably, but in his
smile Alain saw the expectation of obedience.

They sat, and considered the woods around them, oak
and hornbeam with a scattering of ash and this one proud
circle of beech, obviously planted decades ago for an unknown purpose. Ivy had worked its way along the shadowed folds. Sorrow and Rage settled at Alain's feet, staring
fixedly at Conrad.

"You're a quiet one," said the duke, "most of the time."
A servant approached, Conrad dipped his head slightly,
and the man retreated. The swarm had spread out of
earshot, leaving them a measure of peace. "What do you
think of, Lord Alain? What goad whips your mount? Do
you envy me my wife?"

"Do you believe I must?"

He smiled as he glanced away from Alain, then back

again. "It would be natural to envy the man who holds the treasure you once possessed yourself."

Alain waited. Conrad, by all appearances a restless and energetic man, had the unusual ability to sit without the least appearance of becoming impatient. Men walked out in the woods, and over by the unseen fires singing broke out, a lewd song relating the amorous adventures of a young man peculiarly afflicted with a member whose size varied depending on the weather. "But when the sun came out, oh! When the sun came out!"

Conrad smiled slightly, but did not stir as the impromptu verses ground on.

Realizing that neither Conrad's silence nor the song was likely to end soon, Alain felt obliged to answer. "I was sorry to disappoint Count Lavastine, who hoped for an heir."

Conrad bent to pluck a plant out of the dirt. "Bastard balm." He crumbled the leaves in his big hand and tested the scent its oils left. "Not to my taste, the flavor of this plant. Did Lavastine believe you to be his baseborn son? Or was that only a lie? Not that it matters to me, mind you. I'm content with matters as they stand between you and me. But I'm curious." He indicated the hounds. "These give you a powerful claim. The tale was well known, that the black hounds answer to none but the rightful heir of Lavas County. That they would kill any other person who sought to claim them."

He whistled softly, extending his hand palm up. Both Rage and Sorrow whined piteously and thumped their tails on the ground as they looked at Alain for permission.

"Go on," Alain said, and the hounds crept closer to Conrad, snuffled at his knees, and groaned a little, not quite a growl, allowing him to rub their huge heads and fuss a bit over them.

"I like dogs," Conrad said. "They are more faithful than men—with the natural exception of my good retainers." His grin charmed effortlessly. "I trust my dogs not to turn on me. What about you?"

"Am I your dog?"

Conrad laughed. "A hard question. Yet again I must say,

I don't know. You came to Autun with some purpose. We offered you Lavas, and you have not precisely turned us down. We spoke of your marriage to my daughter Berengaria, which might bring you to rule Varre at her side. Yet I see in you no grasping servility, seeking our favor in this scheme. I see no testing of bonds with the other lesser lords, whom you may one day hope to command. No clawing and biting and growling for precedence."

"I am sorry," said Alain. "I am not what you think I am."

"So it would seem," said Conrad as the hounds moved away from him to flank Alain. "Yet these hounds puzzle me. You puzzle me. What do you want?"

"Healing."

"Healing for the scar in your heart? From the marriage gone wrong? The lady torn from you and given to another? The loss of your father? The loss of Lavas County, and its riches?"

"I am but one man. Observe the world, Duke Conrad, and you will see what I mean."

"I have taken the measure of the world, Lord Alain. It is a cruel abode, containing many pits for the unwary. So do I act."

"So must we all."

Conrad looked closely at him. "You do not speak of Lavas County, or the woman who was once your wife and is now mine. You do not speak of my sweet daughter, Berengaria, who might possibly become your wife. You do not speak of a consort's chair."

"I do not."

Conrad folded his arms across his chest. Alain was tall, but Conrad had bulk in addition to height, arms made thick by many years riding to war and wielding the reaper's scythe. Alain had met few men more formidable than the duke of Wayland. He had a sword, and Alain only his crude staff, and his hounds.

Conrad made no move, although his frown suggested his displeasure. "A spy might speak so, sent into my ranks to learn my secrets. Yet it's also said that wise men speak in riddles. Seek you revenge for the wrong done to you when Henry took Lavas County out of your hands?"

"Was it wrong to cast me out as the count of Lavas?"

"I cannot answer that question! Lord Geoffrey has a legitimate claim in the name of his daughter. In his own name, truth to tell, since he is the great grandson of the last countess, Lavastina, and the grandnephew of Lavastine's grandfather, Charles Lavastine. Still, Geoffrey preferred to push his daughter forward instead of himself, since she is a girl and the old countess ruled by the ancient law."

"The ancient law?"

"Still held to in Alba, I might add, and in much of Varre. The identity of a woman's children is always known, since they have sprung from her womb. That of a man's offspring—well, no matter what anyone says, in the end it is always a matter of faith. Therefore, by that custom, a daughter will always hold precedence over a son because her heirs are assuredly the descendants of her foremothers. Geoffrey chose to ally himself with the old custom, while Lavastine chose you, a boy of uncertain parentage. No doubt that influenced Henry's decision. Yet, for Geoffrey, the rule of Lavas County comes to the same thing, as his daughter is still a child and he must therefore be her regent for many years."

"She is an invalid now. Lamed in a fall from her pony."

Conrad had a ready sympathy for daughters. "Poor creature! What incompetent taught her to ride? Or gave her the wrong mount?"

"Perhaps it was only an accident."

"Or justice served on her because of the sins of her father."

"An innocent child? I do not believe so."

"Do you know God's mind, then?" Conrad chuckled. "I ask my clerics every day, and they remain blind. Only my wife insists that she speaks with God's wishes brimful on her tongue, and in truth, Lord Alain, I despise her. She is a sniveling, lying, whining weakling, no better than a ... a ... God know there is no creature I despise as much!"

"She deserves respect from the man who married her."

"So the church prattles, but they are not wed to her—although they were once, and cast her out because of all her puling and moaning! She brought me only one good thing, and that is Berry. Tallia is like to ruin the child if she got her way, which I will not let her do."

"Tallia brought you an alliance with Lady Sabella and a claim to the throne of Varre for your daughter."

"Yes, it's true. I am hasty in condemning her. A duchy for Ælf and a throne for Berry. Ai, God. My poor Elene."

"Who is that?"

"Never mind," he said so curtly that both hounds stiffened, coming to stand, and growled, ears going flat. "Something I gave away, because I am an obedient son."

Amazingly, he wept. Alain was too surprised to speak because the duke's grief was so stark and expansive that it seemed the heavens themselves must weep in sympathy, although no rain fell and only the wind's rattle through late blooming leaves and the distant clatter of the company about its twilight business accompanied Conrad's tears.

He sighed but did not wipe away the remaining tears. He was a man who need never apologize for any strong emotion.

"I pray that which you cherish be restored to you," said Alain, unexpectedly moved by the display.

"Do you so? She is dead. I was warned it would be so, and I feel it in my heart. How, then, can she be restored to me? Even a miracle cannot bring her home."

"Who is she?" he asked again.

Conrad rose. He wore a light cloak against the cool evening. Its hem slid down to lap at his hips, and he moved away, answering only when he had gone several paces out, and even then casting the words over his shoulder as though they were a dart meant to wound. "My eldest child. My own beloved daughter. My chosen heir, who will not now sit in my place when the time comes. Henry had that advantage over me, did he not? I feel inclined to spoil his wishes."

"Who could have taken this beloved child from you?"

"My mother. To whom I owe my life."

Alain bowed his head.

Sorrow growled, and Rage lifted her ears. A familiar figure walked toward them, accompanied by a trio of young men whose handsome faces were illuminated by the lit lamps they carried.

"Here you are, Conrad." Despite her age, Sabella moved as easily as a much younger woman. She marked Alain, seated, and Conrad, standing, and the hounds with their alert if not quite threatening posture on either side of Alain. "I wondered where you had gone. Is there anything I should know?"

A suspicious woman will see intrigue flowing on all sides. No doubt the duchess of Arconia drank deeply at that river.

"You know everything I know," said Conrad, wiping his face before turning to face her.

She snorted. "I doubt it. Had you kept no secrets from me, I would not respect you."

Conrad gestured toward Alain. "As for this one, you know what I know. He makes no claims, no demands, no refusals."

"None, but for grain. What do you make of that?"

"I judge him too subtle to measure."

"A common man pretending to an eminence he does not deserve?"

"Think you so?"

"He does not appear so to me," she admitted. "No common-born man speaks to Arnulf's heir with such words and such boldness. What have you to say to this, Lord Alain?"

"Nothing."

She had a twisted kind of grimace that posed as a smile. If she had ever known happiness, it was by now buried under a mountain of worldly cynicism that must make her dangerous because of the weight on her heart. "It is my experience that people do want things, and want them more the closer they are to grasping them. Are you a spy, sent to ferret out our secrets?"

"I am not."

"Yet here you are. Well. Lavas may be yours again, and more besides. Men are all the same. Easily teased to attention by a glimpse of treasure. Is that not so, Conrad?"

"So the church teaches," he said without looking at her, as if the shadows of the forest hid something he needed to see. "There's something out there," he said in a changed voice.

A sentry called out a challenge just as he spoke. A second call alerted the camp, but as the soldiers jumped to their feet and servants hustled to the safety of the wagons, pale figures wandered out of woods with hands extended, murmuring the familiar refrain.

"I pray you, noble one. Have you food?"

"Just a corner of bread for my child, I pray you."

"God's mercy, help us. Any that you can spare."

"Beggars!" said Sabella, retreating. "Captain! Chase them off."

Alain walked after her. "Surely you can spare your leavings for these poor creatures. They are harmless, and suffering."

"Chase them off!" she ordered.

Conrad fell back into the circle made by his retainers, all of whom had drawn their swords. "Be on alert," he called. "They may be a distraction, I'm thinking."

The beggars faltered before they entered the camp, seeing the weapons. Children sniveled, held tight against their mothers' hips, and all weeping, adults and small ones alike. They were afraid, and yet again and many times one of the half-naked, starving beggars would look behind toward the deeper darkness of the forest as if wolves were driving them into the light. From back in the camp Alain heard Atto cry out, and the sound of a scuffle.

"Stand ready!" Conrad's voice carried easily; he meant unseen others to hear him. "We'll slaughter them, my good fellows, and let the maggots clean their corpses."

"Nay! nay! I know these folk!" Atto's voice was a wail. "How comes it my kinfolk beg here in the wilderness? They live but a day's walk from Helmsbuch, cousins to us. I beg you! I beg you! Do not harm them! They are innocent!"

Soldiers clattered into position. Shields fell into line to protect the ranks if arrows flew from the woods. A horn called twice. Horses whinnied nervously.

"Step back!" called Conrad to Alain.

But it was Conrad and Sabella's soldiers, standing with their backs close to the fires, who were easiest to see. In the darkening twilight, Alain knew he appeared as no more

than a shadow. The undyed linen-and-wool clothing of the
beggars and their exposed limbs made them conspicuous,
but he was cloaked by the fine dark colors of his clothing,
by his gloves and boots, and by his dark hair and darker
hounds. He was not at risk, not as the beggars were, caught
between the noble company and whatever pushed at them
from deeper in the woods.

He stood in silence, hearing the scrape of feet, the muttered comments of the soldiers, the nervous laughter of
one of the lordlings, the *tick* of a branch clacking against
another, the snuffling of horses, and the thump of a spear
haft against the ground. A child whimpered. In the distance, an owl hooted, and he threw back his head, surprised, and listened as hard as he could. As he breathed, he
caught the inhalation of the world and the slow trembling
and settling of air as the earth cooled with the onset of
night. Under the trees waited the wolves who hunted in
this night, concealed by underbrush and broad tree trunks
and the uneven carpet of the ground with its low rock
dikes and knee-deep hollows. The outlaws were a sturdy,
cautious band, and he listened carefully, counting each
man's breath: thirty-eight in all—no, there was the thirty-
ninth, behind the bole of an ash. Not enough to attack a
company some three times greater and better armed unless a cunning intelligence led them, but he smelled and
sensed no such mind among their number, not unless it was
hidden from him.

"Stay," he said to the hounds. He walked into the trees, as
silent as death, and came up behind each crouching man
out of the darkness and lay a hand atop each head, each one
so unsuspecting that the touch made him freeze in terror.

Alain said only, in a whisper, each time, "Go. Do not
prey on the weak and helpless any longer."

They ran, a scattering of footsteps as the first he
touched fled, and then the second. The sound turned
briefly into a tumult, like a shower of hard rain, and pattered away into the depths as the last of them bolted. He
waited, but all he heard were cautious shouts and answers
coming from the camp as Conrad and Sabella shifted their
sentries farther out to probe the darkness, and the quiet

misery of the score of beggars abandoned betwixt the company and the wild.

He walked back to the hounds, and said, "Duke Conrad, I pray you. If you'll spare me a dozen loaves of waybread, I'll give them as alms to these poor beggars."

"Come into the light," said Conrad, and Alain did so, coming right up to the wall of shields set on the ruin of the outer wall. After a moment a soldier arrived with his arms basketing half a dozen loaves of the flatbread commonly baked by travelers on the coals overnight. These were several days' old.

"What has happened?" Conrad pushed past the shields to stand beside Alain, alert to the noises out of the woods.

Back in the camp, Atto sobbed.

"I believe they have fled, seeing a superior force. May I now feed these poor beggars?"

Conrad laughed. "A godly man is a good ally, so the church mothers tell us. I'll walk with you."

"I pray to God this shall be enough to strengthen these unfortunates," said Alain as they came among them. Conrad walked boldly, but it was clear he marked each one, looking closely at their rags and their emaciated limbs for sign of disease before he handed them a hank of bread out of his own hands. Filth and hunger and desperation did not make him flinch. Any person saw such things every day. But even a strong soul might quail at the mark of plague or leprosy.

These were only poor, landless, and starving, nothing out of the ordinary except that they had retreated so far into the wild lands and so near to the guivre's lair. When Alain and Conrad returned to camp, Sabella scolded them.

"Now the creatures will plague us," she said, "hoping for another morsel. You have only encouraged them. I hope they did not hear that lad shouting. I'll not be burdened with a train of beggars."

"Where, then, should they go?" Alain asked her.

"What concern is that of mine?"

"You are duchess here in Arconia, I believe," he answered. "Are these people not your concern?"

"Why should they be? What if those thieves creep back and try to surprise us a second time?"

"God have given you these lands to administer, have They not? It is your duty and obligation to be a just steward of these lands. Even beggars and outlaws are among your subjects."

"As inside, so outside, my clerics tell me. These beggars must have sinned grievously to be punished in such a manner."

"Do you believe it is only their own sins that have brought them so low? That they deserve whatever suffering they endure?"

"Each of us faces justice in the end. I do not mean to interfere with the punishment God has ordained for them."

"Justice must be tempered with mercy. What mercy should God show to you if you will show none in your turn?"

Conrad clucked, while the courtiers muttered their shocked outrage that their lady should be spoken to in such a manner by a man who had only the expectation of rank but no actual lands and title in his grasp.

"Do you speak so, to me?" she demanded. "Let them perish, if they have not the strength to survive. I cannot aid them, and why should I, if it will harm my cause and weaken my rule? Food given to these wretches will not go to feed my soldiers and retainers, who aid me. What matters it, anyway? These creatures are the least of God's creation, far beneath us."

He shook his head. "Do not say so. In birth and death we are alike. Their bodies will turn to dust, just as mine will. Just as yours will."

Her aspect grew cold and she clenched her jaw tight before finding her voice. "This I will not endure! Captain! Bind him and cast him in the cage. He who insults me with such insolence will be first to feed the guivre."

"Feed the guivre?" cried Conrad. "You cannot mean to feed the beast on human flesh!"

"The monster must be strong so it can defeat Sanglant. Human flesh and human blood strengthens beasts as no other nourishment can. Take him!"

Her captain waited with a dozen men, eyeing the hounds and the man, and as they hesitated Alain met each guard's gaze in turn, looked each one right in the eye.

None ventured forward.

"Take him!" repeated Sabella furiously. "Why do you wait?"

All at once every dog in camp began barking. Only Sorrow and Rage remained silent as soldiers hoisted their shields and held their weapons ready. It was too dark to see anything in the forest, but a wind picked up, whipping the treetops into a frenzy. The beggars erupted, like the dogs, into a clamor, and crying and weeping they fled into the forest.

"It is not the bandits they fear," said Conrad. He stepped back toward the safety of the line with his sword drawn and his head cast back to scan the night sky. There was nothing to see except the darker toss and tumble of tree-tops as they danced in the wind. Unseen, but heard, a branch snapped explosively and crashed to earth.

"What is this?" demanded Sabella, and it wasn't clear if she spoke of Alain or the inconvenient storm.

An ungodly screech tore through the air, causing every man there to start and turn his eyes upward.

"Light! Light!" called the captain.

Men lit sticks and held them up as flaming torches, and perhaps half those kindling flames were whipped right out by the wind.

Overhead it flew, vast wings beating as it skimmed over the camp. It was far bigger than the first guivre Sabella had captured and maimed years ago. The flames cast glimmers along the scales of its underbelly, like golden waters rippling. From the company below there came no sound, not even gasps of surprise. There they all stood, rooted to the ground like stone and staring at the creature they meant to track down and make captive.

This was all the chance Alain needed. He had already made his decision. He had caught the scent. He saw its tail flick out of sight as it vanished into the night, flown into the northeast where the rough ground reached its worst. He whistled softly to alert Sorrow and Rage and, while the rest of the company stood frozen with shock and fear, he and the hounds walked away into the dark forest.

PART TWO

THE BLOOD-RED ROSE

VIII

ON A DARK ROAD

1

SECHA sat cross-legged on a reed mat, holding her elder daughter in her left arm as the baby nursed while, with her right, she turned the wheels within wheels of the astrolabe. The astrolabe was a strange and cunning tool that gave power and precision to the one who understood how to use it. This particular one had been hammered and shaped and incised in the forges of the land once called Abundance-Is-Ours-If-The-Gods-Do-Not-Change-Their-Minds but now commonly named Where-We-Are-Come-Home or Feet-Dug-In-This-Earth. The smiths had copied it from the one possessed by the Pale Sun Dog, and it had been delivered to her three days ago by the latest band of eager young warriors off to try their skill in raiding, burning, and killing.

She sighed as the alidade rotated smoothly through the scales inscribed into the disk. The cruder instrument she had used for the last two months had a tendency to stick. This was a well-made, handsome tool, a testament to the skill of her people's artisans now that they were freed from the limbo of the shadows to again ply their metalworking. In the old days, so it was said, they had worked in bronze long before such knowledge had spread to the primitive Pale Ones. Now, of course, humankind bore weapons of hard iron, and it was the Ashioi who must scramble to forge stronger weapons and tools to combat their ancient enemy.

"Secha!" Sparrow Mask called from the watchtower. "Dust on the road! Looks like a good-sized band! Maybe more!"

"I hear you!" she called back, but she did not move. No wise woman dislodged a suckling infant from the nipple except for fire or blood.

From her seat on the mat, unrolled on a plank walkway out under the cloudy sky, she surveyed the settlement built by humankind and taken over by her own people. The high palisade blocked her view of the landscape. The houses and hovels had heft and weight, constructed out of blocks of stone with tile or thatch roofs, but she could never live easily in this place. It was too dark and heavy. The humans lived without a temple raised up on an earthen platform; there was not even an altar. There was no market corner, no community salt pit or meeting ground. They did not decorate the exterior of their houses, and within the deserted eaves she had found tools and cloth and tables and benches and crude beds but little she found beautiful. She could find no house of youth where the children would be instructed. Altogether, she found their life poor even compared to the hardship she had endured in exile. They might possess the secret of iron, and various cunning tools that made work easier, but in all other ways they lived little better than savages.

The baby loosed the breast, gurgled, burped, and dozed off. Secha called to White Feather, who came and took the child. The other infant slept as well; she always fed them one after the next—otherwise she would be feeding all day!

Zuchia the weaver waved to her as she walked to the watchtower. From the building that had once housed the humans' animals she heard the voices of the children reciting in unison.

> *"These are the names of the days:*
> *Darkness*
> *Cave*

> *Stone*
> *Flint*
> *Jade*
> *House*
> *Reed*
> *Grass*
> *Flower*
> *Deer*
> *Buzzard*
> *River*
> *Sea*
> *Wind*
> *Lightning. . ."*

Their voices faded as she moved past, but she filled in the rest in her own mind: *Rain. Storm. Hill. Mountain. Sky.*

She climbed the ladder and greeted Sparrow Mask, then looked southeast to the telltale dust.

"Yes, larger than usual," she said. "I wonder who is coming."

From this vantage point, she surveyed the place humankind had once called Siliga-Eleven-Stones but which the Ashioi had named Seven-Days-Walk-Beyond-The-White-Road. Moctua, who was also called Big-Eating, was cooking lizard at the charcoal pit beside the bread oven, seasoning the good meat with salt and herbs. Some of the young warriors who protected the outpost were digging irrigation canals through the desiccated fields. A square field of beans and precious *mahiz* had been planted, nursed with water hauled from the stream. A pair of women were half hidden within the orchard of oil trees, but she wasn't sure what they were up to.

There came the water haulers: a trio of emaciated adolescent humans who had shown up at the outpost two waxings of the moon ago and made it clear they would work in exchange for being fed. So they worked, and were fed the same gruel and honey as everyone else, and although they had at first refused lizard meat, soon they came to eat it.

Over at the western limit of her sight, at a slant to the road, lay the heaped soil of the grave site where the corpses of the human villagers—long dead before the Ash-ioi arrived here—had been buried and ringed with stones to keep unquiet spirits from roaming. It was an old superstition which the old ones had insisted on, but she had grown up in a different time, where death could not be sealed away even within a ring of stones dedicated to She-Who-Creates.

"Death and life are warp and weft," she said to Sparrow Mask, who still stared at the dust cloud. "I think those stones are unnecessary."

"It is the customary way." He was a young man in appearance although centuries older than her, caught in the shadows for a time whose duration had little meaning to him—or to her. "We cannot cast away the old ways between one moon dark and the next. Look! Is that Feather Cloak's wheel?"

It was.

Feather Cloak strode at the head of a substantial army. Sparrow Mask called down, and a pair of warriors opened the palisade gate. The water carriers paused in the middle of the fields to stare at the huge procession, and scuttled away toward the people working the fields, those they knew.

"Where will they camp?" asked Sparrow Mask. "The southern quarter is the best camping ground, but it hasn't been cleansed yet by the blood knives."

"Maybe they are not staying long."

Secha climbed down and walked back through the village, past the chanting voices.

"Eighteen Bundles of days make one Year.
Thirteen years make One Long Year.
Four Long Years make one Great Year.
When the Great Years run their full count,
and the Six-Women-Who-Live-Upriver walk overhead,
We are come back to where we began."

She walked out the gate and met Feather Cloak beyond the ditch, at the fork in the road. Here a path snaked up toward the stone crown, which was hidden from this vantage point by the irregular slope of the hill. She had heard tales of the great armies of the old days, marching on campaign, so numerous that it would take an entire day for the procession to pass any given spot, but these tales were legends to her, having little meaning in exile. The dust of their halting choked her. They were so many, wearing eager faces and bold bright clothing that made her chest squeeze tight with apprehension.

"What is this, Feather Cloak?" she asked. Counting on her fingers by bundles, she estimated there were twelve hundred as far back as she could see, and more beyond, whom she could not see. "Surely you have left our home lightly defended."

"Even after our exile, we can field several strong armies. In these days, there are none close by us who can attack us. What is your report? We passed no war bands on our journey here."

"All is quiet," said Secha. "Since the dark of the moon I have sent two bands into the north, and received word from one that their hunt goes well. Of the rest, there are five bands of whom we have no word and sign. Perhaps they are lost."

Feather Cloak nodded. If she worried about those who might be lost, Secha saw no more sign of it than her scouts had of the missing warriors. No doubt this was why Kansi-a-lari must lead in war. Secha hadn't the stomach for it.

In the third rank walked Zuangua, fist tight on his spear. Its feather ornaments swayed as he walked. A tall girl dressed in warrior's garb stood beside him, clutching a feathered shield and a quiver of arrows. She wore no mask—that had to be earned—and only a long woven shirt and knee-length breech clout without cape or ornamentation. Even so, Secha had to look twice to recognize the youth with her hair pulled back and trimmed to display the offering marks where her ears had been cut to draw the sacrificial blood.

"Isn't that your granddaughter?" she said to Feather Cloak. "She is too young to begin weapons training!"

"She has earned the right of an apprentice, to carry the shield and arrows of a veteran."

The girl did not even look at Secha. She stood perfectly still and straight, gaze bent on something behind Secha's back which she watched as does a hawk, sighting prey.

"Your own son has also chosen the path of the warrior's shield carrier, I think," added Feather Cloak. "Would you wish otherwise?"

"He is older! Of proper age!" Secha scanned the line of march but could not see his familiar, beloved face. "Is he with you?"

"He is with the garrison at Flower Garden. There is still much work to do to cleanse the city so people can live there properly."

Secha was not sure if she was pleased, or disappointed, that he had been chosen to remain behind.

"The Flower Garden garrison plans to conduct raids into the north," added Feather Cloak, smiling in her sharp way. "We hope to capture more of the eastern ironworkers to teach our smiths the secret of iron. There is plenty of chance for your son to fight."

"All of the young ones will fight, now that you are Feather Cloak."

"Humankind must have no chance to rest."

"So it seems." Secha knew better than to open this argument again. After all, she was the one who had lost. "Where do you mean to go?"

"We are marching to war," said Feather Cloak in her usual blunt, careless style. "The Pale Sun Dog is come to help you weave a new path."

She indicated the man riding in the fifth rank. His hands were bound, and he was trussed up on the horse in the most demeaning manner possible. The blood knives taught that real people walked on their own feet, and did not rely on the strength of the Horse people's mute brothers to carry them. Naturally, everyone but the most stubbornly traditional could see the advantage of horses, so they had begun to capture and breed their own.

The Pale Sun Dog had a red flush on his face, as though someone had slapped him, although it did not fade. Skin singed by flame might sheen in such a manner, but who was foolish enough to play with fire?

"You have bound his hands," remarked Secha.

"We found him beneath the Mountain-of-the-World's-Beginning. We think he was trying to help the Bright One to escape, but we stopped him before he could cause any trouble."

Secha smiled. "How long do you think you can hold the Bright One as your prisoner, in the heart of the world?"

"There is no entrance or exit except the hidden way that the blood knives guard. It opens in the ceiling above the cavern floor. Anyone coming out of the heart of the world must be lifted by rope."

"So you mean to kill her."

Feather Cloak said softly, "I need her alive until I am done with the Pale Sun Dog. She will be hard to kill, but she is trapped. If the blood knives cannot control her for their ritual, then we can always let her die of thirst. The gods will be pleased to be offered any manner of sacrifice in the Heart-of-the-Mountain-of-the-World's-Beginning, even if her blood is not spilled."

"How came the Pale Sun Dog to know of the Bright One's presence there?"

Feather Cloak did not look at him as she smirked. "The same story. A weak-minded woman sought his favor by telling tales."

"What became of her?"

"The blood knives took her. Her crime will be measured by the gods, and she will receive a sentence."

Secha shuddered. "According to the stories, that is how the blood knives acted in ancient days."

Feather Cloak shrugged. The matter, out of her hands, no longer interested her.

The Pale Sun Dog lifted his bound hands to brush at a fly that had landed on his chin. When his fingers brushed the reddened skin, he winced as at a sting. He saw them talking, but his gaze wandered. He looked away, into the distance, and seemed to be dreaming, distracted, lost.

"Why should he help you, now that you have bound him?"

"He still wants that woman, and he knows I have her." She looked along the path that led over the rise to the crown. "Best we make ready."

"Where are you going?"

"We are going to kill a sorcerer, at the habitation the Pale Ones call *Novomo*."

The Ashioi had found the crown complete, except for one stone fallen where the ground had broken away in the hillside beneath. Over the last months, and with great effort, this stone had been raised. Ridges of earth marked the remains of a ramp used to lift it. Charred logs had been rolled away from post holes; plain wood could not sustain weaving because the threads of starlight set it smoldering.

The Pale Sun Dog sat cross-legged on a blanket on the ground just behind and to one side of the weaving ground. An open book was laid over his thighs, and his astrolabe dangled from his left hand, but he did not look at it. Secha knew he watched her as she sprinkled the weaving ground with a dusting of chalk. Her apprentices—she had three—crouched a body's length from her, studying her movements. Four mask warriors stood farther back holding ceramic bowls filled with oil, their wicks as yet unlit. Lined up on the road in ranks of four, the army waited with growling cat masks—panthers, ocelots, lynx—in the lead and, ten ranks back, Feather Cloak's bright wheel. There was no wind. Each feather in the wheel glimmered as if sunlight caught there, but that was only a quality of light inherent in the feathers themselves, an ancient magic that lingered in the holy wheel, the symbol of turning, of fortune, of change as the world shifted onward.

> *"What is alive will become dead,*
> *and what is dead will become alive."*

We are come home at last.

Secha paused to breathe in the dusty air not quite settled from the tramping of so many feet. It was good air, a little coarse in her throat because it was dry and gritty, but she smelled on that air the breadth of the wide world which, so the blood knives claimed, ran in a circle until it came back to itself.

*"The world has no end,
although it, too, has a birth and a death,
ever turning into the dawn of a new sun."*

Thus runs the song of She-Who-Creates.

She smiled.

"This night you weave a new gate," said the Pale Sun Dog.

He sounded weary. He looked away from her and sighed as he examined the book. Its pages were filled with a script she could not read. In truth, none among the Ashioi could make sense of the human script, not even Feather Cloak. Not even the girl, Blessing, who could recognize a few *letters* but could not string them into a necklace of meaning. Not even the servingwoman, Anna, had knowledge of script; it had become clear to Secha that the humans built no house of youth in every village in order to teach the rudiments of learning to every child. They kept this knowledge a secret, reserved for the few. As if the blood knives did not reserve enough power for themselves!

So be it. Naturally, the Pale Sun Dog refused to teach his apprentices to read the script for fear of losing his secret. Instead, he had learned to speak the language of the Ashioi, thereby hoarding his treasure to himself in the hope it would buy him what he wanted or feared to lose.

In his situation, Secha thought, *I might do the same. He must suspect Kansi meant to kill him when she was done with him.*

"It lies west and this much north. I am thinking many days how it is possible to hold open the gate for long enough to march a large army through the gate. It must happen in stages." He toyed with the astrolabe as he spoke. For the first time she heard real passion in his voice. The puzzle fired him. "We begin with the Houses of Night. Early in the evening they set in the west-northwest. At dusk we hook the bright hair of the Sisters. The threads hold only a short time. Then we close them and we hook the Lion's Claw. Because it sets this much more westerly, we add a thread to pull north off the Ladle. It keeps our passage west-northwest. After this, the Houses of Night shift to set at a point in the west-southwest. So we hook the

Scout's Torch and then later the Queen's Bow and then later the Queen. This way we open and close the gate at intervals, so we can march a hundred men—or more men— through the arch each time it is open. If we hold our threads tight, we deliver each group at an equal interval to the crown at Novomo. I predict a week in passage, perhaps less. Hold you the correct climate on the astrolabe?"

"The same one we always use." Surely he should know that she was not such a fool! But he only looked at her, noting the pitch of her voice, then back at the book.

"See!" cried one of the apprentices, pointing overhead.

Sharp Edge, called Looks Good by the young men who courted her favor, was a lithe young woman with a gift for noticing things. She had left the priests in order to become Secha's apprentice, and had never quite lost the habit of superiority that every blood knife wore like a second skin.

The haze had thinned, and again—this was the eighth night running—they saw the deepening cast of the true sky as twilight overtook them. A vivid orange star blazed near zenith. Humankind called it the Scout's Torch; the Ashioi named it the Shepherd's Satchel. Secha had never seen it at all until two nights before. All this was new to her, who had grown up without sun and moon. Its incandescent beauty transfixed her.

"No delay!" said the Pale Sun Dog impatiently.

She raised her shuttle, which was long and thin and well worn, easy to grip. She fixed her feet in the chalk and measured her angles, which were also traced out in lines of chalk laid down around the stone circle. The astrolabe and his catalog of stars allowed him to weave even if he could not see the heavens unveiled by clouds because the stars did not change their places, but the chalk lines marked around the circle helped her measure and weave correctly. Hook the wrong star, and you would end up in the wrong crown, many days or weeks of walking away from your chosen destination. It was a cunning puzzle, a genuine pleasure, and if she envied anything, she envied the Pale Sun Dog his knowledge of how to weave these looms that was far greater than hers. She was dependent on what he told her, on his directions. She wanted to do it all by herself. She was not accustomed to being any man's servant.

Sharp Edge moved to crouch beside the Pale Sun Dog, watching as he rose with a sigh and sighted along the observing bar of the astrolabe. He adjusted the rete slightly, showed it to Sharp Edge, and she stepped over to make a similar tiny adjustment to the astrolabe held by Secha. He measured the Scout's Torch, its altitude and azimuth, and although she had turned to watch, and although Sharp Edge watched avidly as well, he moved swiftly, rotating the rete.

"Here," he said. "Here are your angles for the gate to Novomo's crown. Thirty-one degrees altitude. Seventy-five degrees azimuth. There you catch the head of the golden-haired Sister."

She sighted to the clouds. She reached with her shuttle, and caught the thread and wove it into the angles as he had taught her and as he coached her, standing behind. The gateway of light budded and blossomed. As soon as that brilliant archway shone before her, the forward ranks sprang into step at a brisk jog. They vanished through the gateway, rank after rank, until the Pale Sun Dog called a warning. Then the march ceased, and she closed the archway. She was panting, sweaty, and tired, yet the night's work had only begun.

"The Lion's Claw," he said, taking his measurements.

She wove, and the army moved, each rank of four running tight up against the one before it. They ran silently, only the drum of their feet to accompany the faint music running down the threads from out of the heavens.

"The Ladle," he said.

Much later, the Scout's Torch plunged to the horizon.

She closed this gateway as the heavens continued on their inexorable turn. She swayed on her feet, and Sharp Edge stepped onto the weaving ground and steadied her.

"I can weave," said the young woman.

It was true, although Secha hated to give up the tools, the power, the way the music coursed through the net within the stones and hummed in her body. But she would drop if she kept on, and the gate would crash down on those who traveled through it. She stepped out of the weaving ground, and Sharp Edge took her place, fitting her feet into the imprints left by Secha. Astrolabe and shuttle changed hands. Secha stumbled back several paces and would have fallen, but one of the other apprentices got a hand under her arms and eased her down.

The Pale Sun Dog spoke. "The Queen's Bow, where the jewel shines."

A cup was thrust into Secha's hands. She sipped without thinking and sagged, almost dropping the cup as the fermented sting of mahiz liquor hit her throat. Drops spilled. Hands removed the cup, and she slumped sideways, blinking as the gateway opened before her, blinding her. It was so bright. She shut her eyes.

When she woke, she lay curled on the ground with a shawl draped over her shoulders and torso. Her feet were bare, and cold, and it was early in the day with a light haze covering the heavens. In another breath, it would all burn off.

Laughter startled her. With a grimace, she sat. Every muscle hurt, although she had not exerted herself physically. She should not be this tired.

Looking around, she saw only a handful of people standing where pale grass covered the hillside. Three bored warriors were squatting farther down the road, just where it curved over the hill and out of sight; they were rolling bones, counting the marks, and calling out wagers. Sharp Edge was the one laughing, telling a tale to a semicircle of four admirers. She had a hand on one hip, and the hip jutted out provocatively. That girl would cause some trouble!

The trail that led into the crown was scumbled by the passage of many feet. The crown itself, and the rolling landscape, lay empty but for the eight Ashioi she saw now.

Sharp Edge turned. "You are awake!" She grinned fiercely, pleased with herself, trotted over at once, and solicitously helped Secha to her feet as if the older woman were a crone so crippled by age that she could not walk by herself. "Let's go down. I didn't want to wake you. Maybe we can leave these barking dogs in the fields and talk about what we learned! I have some ideas! That Pale Dog shouldn't be allowed to clutch all he knows to himself! This weaving could be done even without the astrolabe. We would have to have clear weather, of course, but the stones and the notches in the hill—do you see how they align with the stones?—could act as a cruder tool to remind the weaver where the stars will rise and where they will set, which is north and which is south."

Secha rubbed her neck and turned in a slow, complete circle that took in the lightening sky, the massive stones, and the irregular slope of the surrounding hill covered with calf-high grass and a sprinkling of yellow-and-white flowers. To the south the bramble had been cleared away; the land ran in a gentle incline down a long, long slope, and a distant glint marked where shore met sea a morning's walk away. To the west, a goat ambled into view right at a pronounced notch in the sheltering hillside. It spotted them and dipped its head truculently before vanishing back the way it had come.

It was so quiet that she heard a distant ring of hammer on stone, from the village.

"All gone?" Secha asked, but except for the trampled path she saw no sign of the army.

Sharp Edge nodded, still grinning. "All gone."

2

THE duke's banner did not fly from the tower in Autun. The party escorting Biscop Constance rode through empty streets in a town lying quiet beneath dreary skies. At the stairs leading up to the palace on the hill, they waited while a sturdy chair with arms was found. Fixing poles beneath the seat, soldiers braced the poles over their shoulders and carried Constance up the steps, walking sidewise to negotiate switchbacks and pausing at landings to catch their breath.

"Lady Sabella is gone, Your Holiness," said the steward who came out into the courtyard to meet them. A few servants paused to stare at Baldwin. Otherwise, the place appeared almost deserted. The dust of the courtyard was darkened by the drizzle, which slackened and ceased as a wind blew up from the south.

The sergeant said, "Still out hunting the guivre?"

"No, she and Duke Conrad returned days ago from that expedition. She and Autun's milites have marched east in the company of Duke Conrad and his army. There's talk that Varre is to be invaded by the usurper and his army, out of Kassel."

"I came about the matter of two young boys," said Constance, "the sons of Geoffrey of Lavas."

The steward eyed Constance uneasily. "Lady Sabella has left Autun," she repeated. The leader of the escort—a phlegmatic sergeant—rubbed his forehead. The soldiers who had carried the chair panted like dogs hoping for a drink. "Best take her on after the lady, Sergeant. I was given no instructions."

And do not want the responsibility if I make the wrong choice, thought Ivar, looking at Sigfrid and Ermanrich, who raised their eyebrows and twisted their lips into little grimaces of speculation.

The steward looked at Baldwin, flushed, and hurriedly returned her attention to Biscop Constance. "It would be best," she added, without conviction. "Your Holiness."

"What of the boys?" said Constance, with a kind smile.

"I received no instructions."

"Lady Sabella sent these men to Lavas, to find me, and yet left you no instructions as to my care should they succeed in their efforts? Considering, I might add, that I was told that the lives of two innocent boys were at stake?"

The steward stepped next to Constance's chair and bent her head to speak softly. Ivar sidled closer. "The lady sent the party to seek you the same day she departed with Duke Conrad and others to hunt the guivre."

Constance shook her head. Carefully, she took hold of the steward's wrist in a light but firm grasp. "What mean you by this mention of a guivre?"

As the sergeant turned away to order his men off to get drink, the steward bent until her lips were within a hand's breadth of Constance's ear. "There came reports that a guivre had been sighted in the forest lands west of here. It was killing people and livestock. The lady and the duke went riding, hoping to capture it. They came back mightily displeased, for they found no trace of it despite all their tramping and hunting. Then the news of the usurper came from Kassel. They left so quickly, the lady had no instructions except to bid me hold Autun safely against her return."

Constance glanced at Ivar. "Do you suppose she forgot me in the heat of the moment?"

"Surely not!" cried the steward, and the sergeant looked back as she hastily straightened up and continued in a normal tone. "I must ask that you be conveyed to the lady straight away, Your Holiness! You cannot return to Lavas Holding!"

"What news from Kassel?" asked Constance, but with the sergeant listening, the steward only shrugged.

"It was all so confused, Your Grace. Queen Tallia was sent to Bederbor to recover her health. A determined band of rogues are causing trouble along the border to the southwest where Arconia meets the lands of both Varingia and Salia. We hear rumors of reavers with poisoned arrows harrying travelers along the roads leading east into Fesse. The usurper was anointed and crowned in Quedlinhame, Osterburg, and Gent, and parades around with an adventus as though he were not merely a bastard. Then there came this news of some manner of skirmish at Kassel. A captain loyal to Sabella sent word he was attacked by the usurper's forces. So the lady and the duke rode out to bring him aid."

"Lord Geoffrey's boys?" Constance pressed.

The steward spoke in a forcibly cheerful voice. "In good health, together with Conrad's newborn, the little lad we all thought would perish but is marvelous robust and thriving, God be praised. It was a miracle."

"A miracle?" asked Constance sharply. "Why do you say so?"

"Him all blue and not breathing when he was born? The midwife fled, she was so fearful of being punished, because that one—Queen Tallia, that is, God bless her—throws weak whelps. Only the eldest girl lived out of the other three she bore. Yet I don't think the midwife was at fault."

"It's rare that a child born blue and not breathing can be described as robust," remarked Constance. "What happened to make you say it was a miracle?"

"His still body was dropped right in front of the altar. Accidentally, I mean. That man caught him, the bastard born—"

"Sanglant?"

"Nay, Your Grace. The one from Lavas."

"Ah!" Constance nodded. "Go on."

"Everyone said that any child dropped before the altar must be destined for the church, so God must have spared him for Her service and Her greater glory."

"Truth rises with the phoenix," said Baldwin.

The steward startled, like a rabbit spotting a hawk, and she began to weep.

"Best we ride on," said the sergeant. "No use waiting here. Lady Sabella was very strong with her direction: Bring the biscop to me."

He called to his soldiers, and they finished their mugs of drink and wiped their mouths and hurried back to pick up the chair. They hauled Constance away to a chamber in the palace where she was sequestered. Her clerics followed her, and by the time they had settled themselves for the night, they discovered that they had only closemouthed soldiers as their keepers and no servants to ask for the local gossip.

They rode out of Autun the next morning. Many folk waited along the streets to watch as they rode past, and many of these made a sign with their hands, thumb curled around bent middle and little fingers with the other two fingers outstretched like horns on the head of an animal.

"Truth rises with the phoenix," they called. Some strewed flowers in front of Baldwin's horse, while others wept and prostrated themselves as the wagon in which Constance rode rumbled past.

Beyond Autun their party rode to the ferry, where they waited half the morning as they were borne across in stages. The clouds were high today and the light almost made Ivar squint.

"Look there," he said, nudging Ermanrich. "Downstream. Is that smoke?"

The second cart arrived on the eastern shore with the last of the escort. The sergeant had also seen the smoke, which rose several leagues away beyond woodland and fields. He got his men moving eastward along the road but lingered with the rear guard as Constance's wagon trundled out. Ivar hung back as the other clerics rode off in attendance on the wagon. The smoke had a chary black undercoating to it, and it boiled.

"I don't like the look of that," said the sergeant to his trio of scouts. "Someone's good stable is burning down, that's what I think."

"Bandits?" Ivar asked, and the sergeant looked at him in surprise.

"Weren't you up riding with the others?"

"I like to keep my eye out, too."

This sergeant was a homely fellow, thick-shouldered, thick-necked, and with a habit of speaking slowly and simply that might make a person think him thick-witted. He nodded, squinching his eyes as he studied Ivar with a frown. "Fair enough. I don't like the look of that. Let's move on."

The scouts fell into position, two at the rear and one ranging, and the sergeant urged his horse forward to catch up with the main group. It hadn't rained recently, so the road had a good firm snap under the horses' hooves. Clouds scudded on a wind blowing out of the northwest. The road curled around stubborn coppices tended by woodsmen and the occasional ash swale, but at length they mounted to higher ground. A meadow lying upslope of a well-worked coppice of hornbeam and oak opened with an unexpected vista of the Rhowne River Valley and its rich holdings, the ferry crossing, and the distant walls and cathedral tower of Autun.

The ferryman's compound was burning. Flames leaped, and smoke streamed into the heavens.

The sergeant stared, face white. "Look!" he said hoarsely, pointing toward the river.

Skimming low, dragons flew over the water, their eyes high and black in gleaming gold-and-orange heads and their teeth white and sharp, close to the water.

"God save us!" said Constance. "What manner of ship are those?"

The dragons dissolved as Ivar saw what she saw: sleek ships with painted sails and snarling stem-posts, riding high in the water though laden with bristling spears and glowering shields held by a hundred warriors in each vessel. Beyond, the fields and city seemed to lie quiet in the afternoon stillness, but he imagined horns blowing and folk bellowing out the alarm.

"God be merciful!" cried the sergeant. "Those are the Eika, the dragon-kind. They laid waste the northern coast, but that was years ago! I thought they'd all . . ." His voice faded as his mouth worked, open and shut. No sound came out. He choked, coughed, and his next words cracked their paralysis.

"Move! Move out!"

"What about the townspeople of Autun?" Constance asked.

"Do you think we can fight so many, Your Grace?" he said, more with despair than anger. "Better if we get the word to those who can. Here, Johannes!" He pointed at one of his youthful soldiers. "Take a spare horse. You'll ride, and walk at night, until you reach the lady. She must learn of this."

"Ivar," said Constance. "Go with Johannes."

Hooves drummed from below. The rear scout galloped into view around the screen made by the trees. He was hanging over his mount's neck, barely holding on, and as he saw them, his mouth worked but no sound came out. He slipped sideways and tumbled to the ground. An arrow angled out of the meat of his shoulder.

"Move!" bellowed the sergeant.

The soldiers driving the wagons whipped the cart horses forward. The sergeant rode down to the scout, grabbed the man by the arm, and tugged him over the back of his saddle. The riderless horse trotted along behind as the sergeant turned to follow the party. Even the pair of mules, ridden by Hathumod and Sister Eligia, caught the scent and kicked up their pace. They toiled upward, but everyone kept staring behind, seeking, listening, knowing that the enemy would race into sight at the next moment. Wind rippled in branches. Leaves flashed. The horses put on a burst of speed, anxious to move ahead.

The sergeant caught up to the main group and thrust the reins of the loose horse into Ivar's hands. "Go!" he said. "You and Johannes. Go! At least if the rest of us are caught, you may get the message to Lady Sabella."

The soldier lying over the horse groaned. Without slacking his pace the sergeant pushed him off the horse and into the second wagon. The wounded man shrieked. The road struck into woods, and as they passed under the trees, Ivar shivered. He looked back one more time.

A pair of tall men appeared on the road far below. They did not seem to be wearing armor, but their skin gleamed. They pointed after the retreating group with their spears and shook their shields, then turned and waved their arms as though gesturing to companions still out of sight.

"Brother Ivar!" Constance's voice pulled him to attention. "You must ride quickly! Go!"

The rumps of Johannes' horses receded into shade and vanished around a bend in the road. Ivar urged his horse forward, and the spare followed eagerly. For a bit he rode alone on the shadowed path, seeing no one before or behind.

Then a voice called him.

"Ivar!" He looked back to see Baldwin galloping after him, holding the wounded man's sword and scabbard. Catching up, Baldwin gave him the weapon. "Go! Go!"

A terrible scream ripped out of the trees ahead. Both of Ivar's horses shied, sidestepping and flattening ears. They wanted to go forward no more than they wanted to go back.

Caught betwixt and between.

He and Baldwin pushed on to find Johannes stalled in the middle of the road, staring at a man's fly-ridden corpse sprawled on the road. Baldwin dismounted and bent over the body. The flesh had been gnawed, the abdomen torn open and innards devoured. The archway of ribs flashed white. The eye sockets were empty, sucked clean, and maggots and flies crawled in and out of the gaping mouth. One arm below the elbow was missing. The dead man had a dart lodged in his neck. When Baldwin jiggled the shaft, the slender arrow fell free and rolled along the dirt.

"That's a shade's arrow," said Ivar. His throat was dry, and his heart pounded.

"What do we do?" whispered Baldwin. "Those others—the Eika—coming up from behind. This—in front."

"That's days old," said Johannes. "See how the body is torn up."

The rumble of wheels became audible. Ivar swung down, grabbed the dead man by the ankles, and dragged him off the road. No time to bury him. No possibility of hauling the extra weight. He shoved the limp corpse out of the way and, as he straightened, the little cavalcade came into view: two wagons, a dozen guardsmen, Biscop Constance, the wounded man, Sigfrid, Ermanrich, Hathumod, and Sister Eligia. The scouts had moved up, leaving only the sergeant trailing behind.

A paltry, doomed retinue.

Two soldiers had dismounted to walk at the heads of the cart horses. Hathumod stared white-faced at him.

"Brother Ivar!" said Constance reprovingly, but then she saw the dead man tumbled in the undergrowth, and she turned her gaze away. Her face was pale, and her expression grim.

Baldwin did not move.

"I told you to ride!" shouted the sergeant. "Move!"

Ivar mounted and slapped Johannes' horse on the rump with his reins. "Let's go!"

The two riders pushed on, leaving the rest of the party behind. After a while, as the wind and their path twisted up a hillside, they heard shouting far behind. The sound faded at once; maybe he had only imagined it. Around them, there was nothing to see but trees, a tangled prospect of holm and oak most likely cut back a generation ago and now grown thick with young trees and vigorous under-growth. He halted, turning in the saddle to listen, as Johannes kept riding toward a half seen switchback. Hooves drummed behind. Someone was coming up fast.

"Come on! Come on, my lord!" cried the lad. He was so scared that he sounded indignant.

And why not? Why shouldn't the poor young soldier be aggrieved at fate? Why must it always be so difficult?

"Ai, God!" Johannes squeaked with fear, slapping a hand against his throat as at a wasp. "Ayee! Ayee! It burns!"

Ivar's mount startled, kicking, and turned a complete circle as Ivar fought to keep his seat and get hold of the trailing lead to his spare. All this passed in an instant. He lifted his gaze to see Johannes, about thirty paces ahead now, topple from his saddle and tumble gracelessly onto the hard path.

Above, a creature stepped out from the shadows onto the road. It had a shapely woman's body but the head of a snarling dog. Ivar was shaking so hard he could not calm his horses, and Johannes' pair bolted, one downslope too fast for him to grab, and the other only four steps when it stopped short as Johannes' weight dragged it to a halt. One leg had caught in the reins, but the young soldier lay there so limp it was apparent he was unconscious, or dead.

Below, a rider with an extra horse burst into view. A gust of wind wailed along the slope, bringing the distant taint of smoke up from along the river. The dog-woman cast back her head—he could see the curve of her smooth, human-like throat—and sniffed, then yelped words that meant nothing to him and leaped back into the cover of the trees.

Below, the rider snagged the loose mare that had gotten away.

"Ai, God!" Baldwin cried, pounding up. "What was that?"

"Shades!" Ivar croaked. "Shadows. Evil things! What are you doing here?"

Baldwin gulped but could not answer. Ivar swung off his horse and handed the reins of his pair to Baldwin before dashing up the path to kneel beside Johannes. With an effort, he got the leg free, but shook his head.

"Dead. Broke his neck, I suppose." He lifted a dart off the path. "Just a scratch." He tossed it aside and dragged the corpse into a thicket of lush honeysuckle.

Out of the empty woods a horn call rose, shrill and insistent. He grabbed Johannes' horse, mounted, and started riding. Baldwin pressed up behind him and, as they came to the switchback, they halted in order to tie the spare mounts one behind the next.

"There's a break just there," said Ivar. They tied the horses to a tree and pushed through the underbrush to a rocky outcropping that rode above the treetops. The wind roared off an escarpment, which plunged the height of five or six men, the face giving a vista of forest into the south, but they stared west, back the way they had come. They saw a haze on the horizon, and obscuring trees. Below, it was possible to see the last clearing through which they had passed, with its pair of lichen-stained boulders and its open space grown with green grass. Here came a score of Eika jogging in tight formation, pushing up from the lowlands. Light winked above them: a shower of arrows raining out of the woods. These fell among the Eika, and perhaps some struck, but the dragon-men did not slacken their pace at all, and none fell to the attack. Animal-headed creatures darted out into the clearing and threw flashing javelins and darted away again into the shelter of the trees.

"Best go," said Baldwin, tugging on Ivar's arm.

"God have mercy," he said.

They traveled that day at a bruising pace, speaking little. One of the spare mounts threw a shoe and began to limp, so they let it go. When it seemed they would blow the horses if they did not stop, they rested near a stream where there was also some grazing, but they pushed on soon after until it grew too dark to travel without light.

Ivar led them off the track until he felt sure no one could see them from the road.

"We could lash twigs together, make torches to walk by," suggested Baldwin as they rubbed down the horses.

"Light will give away our position. If they catch us, we're dead." They got the horses settled. Ivar threw down his cloak, and sat on it. "Why did you come after us?"

Baldwin smiled placidly. Somehow, miraculously, the dregs of twilight filtering through the trees managed to illuminate his perfect face and solemn expression, as serious as an angel. "Biscop Constance told me to hurry after and catch up with you."

"What of Ermanrich and Sigfrid and Hathumod?"

"She ordered me to go."

"Why?"

Baldwin sat beside Ivar. After a moment, he touched Ivar's knuckles, a fleeting brush that made Ivar shiver and remember old times. He bent his head, as though he was ashamed.

"Ivar." He hesitated.

There was so much they had never spoken of, one to the other: the affection they had once shared, the changes that time had carved in them, the sacrifice Baldwin had made because of his love for Ivar and the others. Ivar's rescue of Baldwin that Baldwin had, by his unexpected cleverness, turned into a successful rescue of Constance. Only, of course, it had all fallen apart in the end.

As usual.

"I'm sorry, Ivar," Baldwin whispered at last. "I love you best of all, I truly do, If . . . well . . . if there was something else you . . . I mean, peace is all I've ever really sought to be left alone. I hate being pestered all the time."

"Never mind it," said Ivar hastily, surprised to find himself both relieved and disappointed by this confession. "Peace you shall have, if I can get it for you. Although I doubt I can."

"But you're so brave! You always know just what to do!"

These words made Ivar smile bitterly, although Baldwin wasn't looking at him. "You never answered me. Why did Biscop Constance send you after me?"

Baldwin sighed, and slumped to sit back to back with Ivar, shoulders and heads touching like comrades who, having no secrets, are entirely easy and trusting each with the other. "She told me that I, at least, must not be captured."

"Captured! Are they going to be captured? *Killed?*"

Dreamily, Baldwin went on. "She thinks I am something

I am not. That's why she wanted to save me. I don't know how to say 'no.' "

Ivar wiped his eyes. Certainly it was true that, with Baldwin as his traveling companion, he did not have the luxury for panic or indecision.

"Never mind it, Baldwin. You did your best. We'll stay quiet here, and hope for a little sleep. Do you want to take first watch?"

They were, after all, both too tired to watch and too wound up to do more than doze. They huddled in darkness, with no fire, off the road under the canopy of trees. Late at night a wind roared up out of the southeast, rattling branches and brush. Later still they heard voices and the clopping of horses and saw a torch bobbing in time to a man's swinging walk. Too afraid to move, they held their breaths and prayed that the horses would stay quiet. The party passed by, moving east along the road, away from Autun. The night wind sighed and the forest creaked and muttered around them.

Of Biscop Constance and the others there was no sign.

3

HANNA dreamed.

Liath walks in darkness, her path illuminated by the merest dull red spark glowing from her fingers. The void that surrounds her is a pit of darkness so black that Liath herself can be seen glowing with a faint aura that seems like breath moving around her form. Out in the darkness, eyes gleam, and she calls to them, but they wink out, and no one answers.

She calls, and she listens, and where she hears the scattering of footsteps and sees the shadow of distant movement, she follows, although she does not know where she is going.

"Liath!"

Hanna bolted upright, heart hammering and a hand

caught at her own throat. She turned to see Sorgatani weeping on her bed. Hanna sat on the carpets, wrapped in her cloak. Brother Breschius snored softly beside the threshold, his body blocking the entrance.

"What is it?" Hanna untangled the blankets and shuffled on her knees to the bed.

"She is lost," said Sorgatani into her hands. "I dreamed her."

"Liath? I saw her, too. Wandering in darkness."

Sorgatani raised her head to stare at Hanna. The dark line that rimmed her eyes was smudged and runny from the tears. Her shift was twisted around her hips. "You dreamed it, too?" she whispered. Hanna nodded. "Then it is a true dream! What you and I dream, together, is a true dream. Did you see my teacher?"

"Li'at'dano? The centaur shaman? I did not."

Sorgatani's shoulders shook as she fought off another convulsion of grief. "Neither did I. I sense in my heart that she is gone."

"Gone?"

"Dead. Devoured. Gone utterly."

Hanna choked, finding no words. She pressed her hands into the thick carpet to steady herself. The air lay cold within the chamber. A curl of smoke from the altar fire spun upward and out the smoke hole into the hazy gray sameness of the Other Side, a place Hanna could never walk but which all Kerayit shamans had visited in their spirit trance—or so Breschius had told her. Sorgatani never spoke of it.

"I am cold," said Sorgatani.

Hanna sat beside her on the bed and held her. Although they sat this way for a long time, and night passed, Sorgatani did not sleep.

In the morning, stepping outside, Hanna covered her eyes against the brightness. The clouds seemed higher and thinner and whiter than before.

"I believe the sun will break through," said Rosvita, coming up beside her. They watched as horses and wagons were made ready in the courtyard of Goslar. The nuns of St. Valeria mustered under the cold eye of Sister Acella, who had laid a vow of silence on every sister under her command in protest of their removal from the convent. Lions waited patiently in marching order. Sergeant Ingo signaled to Rosvita that his troops were ready to go.

Servants loaded provisions, and the steward handed a cache of medicinal herbs to Sister Diocletia. The wagon holding Mother Obligatia had been repaired and refitted. It now held two pallets stretched lengthwise, one for the old abbess and the other for Captain Thiadbold, who was feverish and weak, sometimes delirious, but still among the living.

Rosvita sighed as the horses were led out of the stables. "In another time, we would send you ahead with the news of our coming. But any traveler alone on the road is not safe."

"It was never safe for Eagles," said Hanna.

"Less so now. It is those darts I fear. As you must, Eagle."

"As I do," murmured Hanna, looking toward Thiadbold. His eyes were shut. Sister Diocletia had shaved off his red hair to reduce lice and fleas whose presence might pester him to distraction as he healed. If he healed.

"Be patient," said Rosvita.

"I'm a coward, Sister," said Hanna. "I fear to be the one who must tell Prince Sanglant this news."

"Do not fear." Rosvita's smile had a hard edge. "I will tell him what has passed on our journey. It is my duty and my right. There is a great deal he must know. I have a good many questions as well." Like Liath before her, like Hugh of Austra, Rosvita carried *The Book of Secrets* everywhere she went. She held it now in a leather case slung across her back.

"The steward here says that Mother Scholastica anointed and crowned him, but now regrets that she acted."

"It is difficult to know what to think," agreed Rosvita. "Yet we have such treasures in our possession! This book compiled by Bernard of Bodfeld. The *Vita* of St. Rade-gundis. A copy of the chronicle of St. Ekatarina's Convent. Annals from St. Valeria's."

"Books of sorcery!"

"Those, too."

"And your history, that the others speak of."

"A small thing, compared to the rest, although naturally I am pleased it survived the storm. There is truth to be found in these books. I know it in my heart. Yet what if the truth is a truth we do not want to hear?" Her expression darkened as she glanced up at the sky. When she looked back at Hanna, her gaze was so stern that Hanna took a step back.

"What could be wrong with the truth?"

Rosvita shook her head and, without replying, touched Hanna on the elbow and went to find her mount.

4

IN the Heart-of-the-World's-Beginning coils a labyrinth as intricate and bewildering as the configuration of the human heart. Down deep, and deeper yet, the stairs descend. To find answers, or release from its prison, the questing soul must plunge into what seems all that is darkest but which is in fact a world of its own far below the outer world of light and air.

It was not her world, the land she knew well, nor yet was it the world of the upper spheres, where she had briefly journeyed and glimpsed her soul's true home. Here beneath the weight of the earth lay a fastness whose existence she had never truly suspected.

At the base of the stairs she found herself in a circular chamber whose polished walls bore a strange manner of ornamentation: they were carved and jabbed with tiny ridges and holes detectable most easily by touch. Eight corridors opened off at even angles; one looked the same as another, all of them smoothly paved and wide enough that four horsemen might ride abreast in procession and still have room to clear their heads and have a groom walk alongside. These were the spokes of a wheel. She chose a direction at random, and walked into a maze, where she soon became lost. She sensed as much as heard that creatures were following her at a distance.

At first, pausing, she listened; then at length called; then, receiving no answer, walked down a corridor whose walls reflected back the ruddy glow of the smoldering rope she carried. In the next chamber, which was also the next branching, she waited, but no one and nothing came into view.

Yet she did feel them. She knew they were there. She knew what they were, because her grandmother had told her the tale.

For a while she stood, motionless, and felt the weight of the earth, the weight of family, resting as on her entire body. To think of having a living grandmother still stunned her. She could not quite grasp that even knowing it was true.

The whispers—not of voices but of muted, skittering movement—ceased. They were waiting, as she was waiting.

Because she could not go back, she walked on.

The chief thing she learned after some hours of wandering: The knife edge of the spell woven in ancient days had severed this hidden world into two. On one side of that cut stretched tunnels and branching corridors whose walls were planed as by an adze; she emerged into spacious chambers, each proportioned with geometric precision, or happened upon narrow waterfalls pouring over sheer walls into fathomless pools.

Yet the other side, crossed into with a single step, had sustained immense damage: here a rockfall, there a ceiling collapsed that blocked the passage, and in another place a chasm where the ground had actually split apart to leave a gash far wider than she dared leap.

Pausing on this lip, she dropped a fragment of rock into the darkness and listened, but she could not hear the splinter strike bottom. A distant burning odor welling up from the deeps, a sour taste on the palate.

Up to now, the creatures had continued to track her at a distance, heard but never seen. They had kept a strict and precise distance from her except in this one case. They had not followed her down this particular branch, even though the corridor split by the chasm was large—a thoroughfare like the regnant's road—and must surely once have seen heavy traffic.

She had made the detour because of that strange taste in the air wafting from one of the tunnel openings. Back-tracking to the last chamber she had paused in, she halted to lick dust off her lips and consider her choices.

Mother Obligatia had called the creatures living in the tunnels beneath St. Ekatarina's Convent "the Ancient Ones." Liath had heard other tales as well, speaking of goblins, small people, who lived in caverns deep underground, who mined the mother lodes, and who, perhaps, nourished themselves on human flesh. Diggers and hewers of stone, the folk who scuttled in the earth and in the rock, where darkness reigned.

Ancient Ones had spoken to her before, when she lay entombed in rock beneath the central crown, waiting for the night when the Crown of Stars crowned the heavens. But these did not feel the same as those slow voices. These felt restless, skittish, sharp, metallic.

She blew hard on the glowing end of the rope, and put it out. Now she saw them—not their bodies, but a faint gleam, as though their recent presence left its trace as a phosphorescent glow. Any true human would not have been able to distinguish them at all, but of course, Liath herself had more than once been told that she emanated a breath like light off her own body.

Was there some aetherical connection between her and these earth people? It was hard to imagine there might be.

Of the six corridors that branched off this chamber, only one had in its dark mouth that scantling blush, the luminous trace of their retreating presence. Of course, they were leading her; they had been all along, and she had missed it because of her dependence on the lamp she had made of her coil of rope.

It was, really, the only choice left to her. She would never find her way back to the cavern in which Kansi had imprisoned her, nor did she want to return there.

On she went, walking, trudging as she tired, on down a broad tunnel that shot straight—with perhaps the slightest curve to its trajectory—as though an arrow had bored this passage. On and on, until even the trace glow faded and she had perforce to call fire to the rope. She had learned to finesse the fiber, burning it at such an ebb that the smoldering ends gave her just enough light to see the ground, so that she might not step unwittingly into a chasm.

But walking with no break, no light, no known destination, and in solitude, demanded its cost in the end. Just ahead, the tunnel branched like a forked stick, splitting into two corridors each one the same as the other. Nothing to choose between them. No hint of where to go next. No light but her own.

Her guides had vanished.

Exhaustion overwhelmed her. She sank down and sat against the wall, snuffed out the red sparks on the fraying end of the rope. In complete darkness she rested, and ate, and considered her situation. If she kept her mind busy, she would not panic.

A labyrinth lay beneath the Heart-of-the-World's-Beginning, as complex a network of pathways as the ones woken within any woven crown. It was, she supposed, like the earth's equivalent to the network that existed in some manner in the aether, to which she had had access when she had walked through the burning stone, which was both crossroads and gateway. Somehow, when it existed in exile in the aether, the Ashioi land had become intertwined within these aetherical pathways; that was why, when she had wandered in the mist of the borderlands with Eldest Uncle's rope tied around her, she had emerged on distant hills and in unknown marshlands in the far regions of Ashioi country, places she might otherwise only reach by many days or weeks travel on foot.

Yet this world below the world was not simply a trap of closed tunnels. The air she breathed was not stale, although it was a little dusty and sometimes flavored with a tang. There was nothing here she could recognize, nothing familiar, nothing to grasp, not even grandmothers. The sides of the tunnels ran slick beneath her hand; she could not imagine what kind of stone this was, or how these roads had been carved out of the rock. Where the knife's edge had cut off the land in ancient days she found debris. That was the old side, the lands that had remained on Earth after the first cataclysm. Where the creatures led her, beneath Ashioi country, the labyrinth was revealed as a sterile place seemingly untouched by the passage of time.

Rapping sounded behind her, a warning or a welcome. She scooted up, breathed fire onto the end of the rope, and turned as the air around her lightened from an unseen source. She waited; she even held her breath, not meaning to.

A creature shuffled into view. Its skin shone with the glamour of pewter, mottled here and there by crusty growths very like the stunted stalagmites she had seen years ago in a cave in Andalla where she had plumbed the depths with a careless guide and her inquisitive father. Had they descended farther, in that Andallan cave, would they have found a long-forgotten entrance to the great labyrinth? Did the maze weave its interlace below the entire land of Novaria?

Bulges marked the creature's face where eyes should be. Movement shifted within those bulges like the gathering and shredding of clouds. It wore a necklace of metal scraps that rang lightly when it halted. Wound around one arm, a copper armband gleamed brightly.

"I am called Liath," she said. "I pray you, friend, help me find my way out of here. I intend no harm to you and your people."

It shuffled past as if it had not seen or heard her, but as she turned to follow, she realized her mistake: it had avoided her, shifting sideways.

She followed it down the right-hand branching, which proved no easy task. Despite its awkward gait it covered the ground efficiently. She walked briskly to keep up. Fortunately, the floor remained so level that even in blackness she would not have fallen. The ceiling was too high for her to touch, but Sanglant might have been able to brush it with the tips of his fingers. Four or five women could walk abreast. Any wagon master would adore such a road, plain and wide and only gently curved where it did not push straight on.

Stairs opened beneath her feet, spanning half the corridor while the other half continued a level course onward. Following Pewter Skin, she descended. The creature took a turning and came into a triangular chamber that three corridors opened off. She paused to lay a marker of rock slivers so she could, if necessary, find her way back to that second set of stairs. Although she hurried to catch up, this new tunnel branched at sudden and awkward intervals, without benefit of geometric chambers, and by the seventh or eighth branching she lost track of her guide except for the fading nimbus trailing behind it.

Then even the memory of that light dissolved.

She was alone, trapped, lost. Abandoned.

She padded forward with a sick feeling in her stomach and cold fear along her skin. Deep in the earth, with no way out, no recourse. She could never find a way home.

Maybe the only way out is through.

The tunnel jinked three times within a short stretch. She blinked in surprise as she emerged into a broad, oval cave with an uncomfortably low ceiling, not quite so low that she had to stoop but low enough that she kept ducking anyway.

The walls of the chamber were pricked with holes that had a diameter as thick as her leg and, between collections of holes, were riddled with alcoves stuck off at odd angles. The floor extended, on the level and on all sides, about ten steps inward before sinking steeply into a large, central hollow. A still pool marked the center of the hollow. This basin was filled with what might have been water but which seemed to her eye too brilliant and too hard, for it cast outward a blue incandescence as if a strong light burned in its depths.

A dozen of the creatures inhabited this chamber, crouched on their haunches, arms moving side to side as though they were obsessively polishing the floor.

She circled the chamber, keeping well back from the rim. She blew on her rope's end, causing flame to rise, and lifted her torch to see what was inside one of the holes.

The flame reflected back at her, revealing a metallic object, like a sheet of bronze or iron, curled up exactly in the manner of a scroll.

The creatures ignored her. One squatted nearby and, cautiously, she moved close enough to get a good look at what it was doing. It had unrolled one of those sheets and was running its fingers up and down gashes and gouges torn into the fabric. The sheets were as long as her arm span and a third as wide, yet as thin as Jinna paper. How could such an object lie flat after it had been rolled up so tightly? What magic—or smithcraft—was at work here?

It took no notice of her scrutiny. None of them did. They did not lift their heads and sight, not as creatures did in the world above, the world of light and air. If the pool's glow was visible to them, she saw no sign of it.

But she recognized immediately what they were doing. Their task was like breath to her. She would have known that action anywhere, the way their fingers flowed along the lines. In the deeps, such creatures needed no light. They did not exist in light, not as she did. Their way was not so different from the mechanism she used, although she relied as well on her eyes for tracking and her lips for speaking each word as it crossed above the pointing finger.

They were reading, and this was a library.

5

FOR five days Ivar and Baldwin pushed the horses as hard as they dared. They expected with each step to be set upon, but on that fifth day they were still alive and trudging along a dark and lonely path through forest land flowering with green. All morning they enjoyed open vistas beneath a high canopy, but in time they reached an area where humankind had gone about its business managing the woods by felling mature trees. Here, young beech and opportunistic ash grew in abundance among clouds of flowering honeysuckle and swathes of sweet-smelling woodruff. It smelled like glorious spring, although it was early summer.

"There," said Baldwin, pointing to a gap in the tangle. "A clearing."

They stumbled out of the woodland and into a hamlet, a good-sized holding with several sturdy houses, a byre, a roofed storage pit dug into the earth, a chicken coop, and a lean-to with a shattered roof. Not even a dog barked, and if there had once been chickens, they were fled. It was as silent as the grave.

"Someone's buried here." Baldwin had a habit of stating the obvious, and after five days Ivar would just as soon that he kept his mouth shut.

A dozen mounds of dirt lined the roadway, so fresh that no weeds had yet sprouted.

"What do you think killed them?" Baldwin added, then went on nervously. "We'd better keep moving."

"You stay with the horses," said Ivar. "Find water, and check that shoe again. I hope to God she doesn't throw it before we reach a holding with a smith. I'll do a quick search. There might be aught of food or drink we can take."

"I don't like it. It's too quiet. It creeps me, to see it all silent. Look! That trough is half full of water. I'll water the horses there."

For the hundredth time, and with an overwhelming weight of guilt, Ivar wished that Baldwin was Erkanwulf, but he wasn't. He handed over his reins, then made a quick reconnaissance to make sure no creature was hiding in obvious places. After that, he explored the houses. They had been deserted for many days. In one, a loom sat abandoned, a strip of blue cloth half finished but covered in dust. Another, left with the door open, had been ransacked by animals. A bowl had fallen from a table and lay upended on the packed earth floor. An animal had dug a hole trying to get into one of the chests, but the lock was fastened, and Ivar hadn't the patience to try to pry it open.

The third house had been shuttered and closed up, although deep scratches marked the door, as if wolves had been trying to get in. He shoved open the door, which stuck twice before yielding. The smell hit hard. One bed built into a corner stank. A fetid mess had congealed and dried in the tumble of furs and blankets. He approached cautiously, a hand over his nose and mouth, and pulled back the topmost blanket.

The stench of rotting flesh boiled up at him. A half formed babe—not even as fully fleshed as a newborn—had been entombed in the blankets amid the leavings of birth: blood; feces; awful.

He gagged and turned away. Falling to his knees, he could not stop himself from heaving and retching onto the floor. When the worst had passed, he crawled away, then stumbled out, not even searching for foodstuffs. The stink was fastened into his nostrils. Every time he took a breath he sucked it in again, and he coughed and gasped and gagged, trying desperately not to heave again.

"Ivar! Ai, God, Ivar!" Baldwin ran over, having abandoned the horses at the trough. "What happened?"

"Let's go," he said in a choked voice, staggering up. Each step made his throat seize up again, and by the time he reached the horses he had retched a dozen more times. Fumbling for the reins, he flung his body up and over, as clumsy as a rag doll. Good horse. She waited for him to get into the saddle while Baldwin fussed. "Get. Now. Go."

He couldn't speak for forever. Baldwin stewed and fretted and his mount shied at every leaf fluttering on the road, until Ivar found his voice.

"Dead thing," he said. "We just go on. Dibenvanger Cloister is close along this way. I recall coming past here. They'll have news."

When the cloister's orchards appeared, he knew at once that they would find nothing different here. Death marched before and behind them.

"It's those creatures, the ones with animal faces," said Baldwin in a low voice. "They've come before us. They're the Lost Ones, only they've come back to get their revenge."

"We're doomed," muttered Ivar, and was ashamed to hear himself speak the words.

"For shame! Ivar! Do you not believe in the phoenix?"

"Of course," said Ivar, and he added, "I have to."

"Don't despair," said Baldwin affectionately, and his smile was so kind and so heartening and so beautiful that Ivar found his own dark mood cracked by a sliver of hope.

The cloister had housed a score of monks, novices, and lay brothers within a compound made of a tiny church, a miniature cloister with a separate novice's house, a workshop, a byre, and a cunningly designed mill now at rest. The gardens had been turned over and planted. The millrace burbled. But no one was home. Because it was getting on toward evening, they loosed the horses into the byre, brushed them, and fed them from the store of grain. While there was still light, Ivar sent Baldwin to find what he could from the storehouse and herb garden while Ivar walked through the cloister. The slap of his feet made the only sound. The wind had died. Not even the earth seemed to breathe. Beyond the cloister lay the cemetery, budding with twenty-six fresh graves. Where had the others gone? He checked in every cell, but he found no bodies.

"Must we sleep here?" Baldwin asked him when they met at the byre. "There must be better beds in the cloister."

"Yes, here by the horses. What did you find?"

"These turnips, although they're half rotten. Lavender. This oil, but I think it's turned."

"Eh! Phew! Throw that out."

"Peas. How I hate porridge!" He set down bunches of herbs, neatly bundled, and displayed a pair of loaves so hard that the knife wouldn't cut into them. "Plenty of grain, though."

Ivar nodded. "We can lade the spares, and walk as much as ride so they won't founder. We'll ride out at dawn."

They bedded down in the straw, back to back for warmth. That night they heard birds calling in the woods, as if a flock swept past from south to north.

"Are those geese?" Baldwin whispered.

"Hush! Those are no geese I've ever heard!"

He did not sleep after that, but the next day he nodded off twice in the saddle. They pushed the horses on a fine edge. A knife seemed held to Ivar's throat, ready to cut, but no one met them on the road coming or going. Over the next many days they traveled through a dozen more hamlets, all deserted. All ornamented with fresh graves. They might have been wandering alone in the world after Death had scoured the land. At length even Baldwin fell silent though, after all, it would have been preferable to hear his inane chatter.

What had become of Biscop Constance and the others?

Increasingly, Ivar's thoughts drifted, unmoored by the solitude and the constant expectation of some worse surprise lurking around the next bend in the road.

Life had been so easy in Heart's Rest with Liath and Hanna. Bright and brilliant Liath; all of the old anger at her was wrung out of him, and he thought of her now with a nostalgic fondness. He could never have resisted her, and it was idiocy to think she would ever have looked twice at him. She had never been faithless. She had befriended him, and Hanna, and they had been friends to her in return. It was unselfish, in its way, a bond that came not from family ties but from outside them.

Everyone said Liath was still alive. Rumor called her queen to Sanglant, but also a heretic and a maleficus. Excommunicated.

Except that, if she were a heretic, that meant she believed in the True Faith, in the rising of the phoenix and the glorious Redemption.

The road was overgrown where no summer work crews had hacked back weeds and brambles, but in other places they saw signs that a large company had recently passed this way: a broad clearing ringed with charred fire pits; swathes of grass grazed low and not yet recovered; remnants of leather and rivets and the shards of a broken pot. Shallow ditches where folk had relieved themselves and covered the leavings over. These, in turn, disturbed by creatures enticed by the odor.

It was muggy. The cloud cover had burned so thin that he saw traces of shadow rippling along the furrows made by wagon wheels. Baldwin had pushed ahead. The tail of his spare mount flicked and vanished as the road rounded away in a bend.

Everyone spoke of Liath. But what had happened to Hanna?

Dear Hanna.

All at once, he was weeping. Sobbing.

Ahead, branches crackled out in the wood.

Something is coming.

He sucked in his breath and unsheathed the sword the sergeant had given him.

A huge aurochs stepped onto the road. It bent a surly eye upon him before pacing majestically into the trees on the other side. Through his tears, he watched in awe as its broad back receded into the forest.

"Ivar! *Ivar!*"

The aurochs broke into a run and bolted into the trees. Why did that damn fool keep shouting, where their enemies might hear?

He urged the mare forward and passed out from heavy cover into broken woodland, blinking, startled. Baldwin waved cheerfully, and Ivar squinted. A procession of no more than twoscore folk had halted on the road ahead of them, all turned back to see what was coming up from behind. A pair of dogs barked. These were villagers with handcarts and children, their hoes and shovels and scythes raised to do battle, and men in the brown robes of the faithful.

"Monks!" called Baldwin. "Maybe these are the survivors from Dibenvanger Cloister."

As they trotted forward, the procession shifted as the children were thrust into the center and the monks and adult villagers fell shoulder to shoulder to meet the foe. But the closer Ivar and Baldwin came, the faster folk relaxed, staring and pointing.

"I pray you!" called Ivar. "We're out of Autun, riding east on the trail of Duke Conrad and Lady Sabella. What has happened here?"

A man stepped out of the crowd. He held a spear as if he were a warrior, although he wore an abbot's fine, if travel-stained, robe. He was young, vigorous, and handsome, ready to do battle with the worst the Enemy could throw at him. As he recognized them, his fierce, proud expression transmuted into one lit by a certain sarcastic gleam.

"The dazzling Brother Baldwin, beloved of the angels!

And Brother Ivar of the North Mark! You are returned to us! Be welcome!"

"The angels?" said Baldwin, scratching at the light growth of beard that was coming in on his chin. "What do you mean, beloved of the angels? What angels?"

"Is he an angel, Mama?" one of the little tykes cried, and some folk laughed nervously while others drew their hands in close against their chests.

"Father Ortulfus." Ivar dismounted and threw his reins over the mare's head. He brushed the front of his tunic compulsively, for no good reason except that he wore a layman's clothing instead of garb fit for a religious man.

The abbot smiled with a sharp amusement.

"How are you come here?" Ivar asked him.

"I may ask the same." He gestured at a burly monk whom Ivar recognized. "Prior Ratbold! The company must continue. We must reach Hersford before night falls."

Like the others, the prior was staring at Baldwin, only he was shaking his head. He raised both hands in the manner of a man warding off an attack, then turned and snapped a command at the stunned assembly. His words were echoed by the barking of the startled dogs, come to life, and the villagers shouldered their burdens and marched on with anxious faces and muttered comments. Children bent their heads and shuffled forward, but they glanced back at Baldwin so often that a couple of them stumbled and had to be hauled up by their ears.

Father Ortulfus waited until the group was out of earshot. "What news?" he asked wearily. "Be quick, if there is anything I should know. The rest must wait until we come to Hersford."

"Is it safe there?"

"Nowhere is safe, Brother Ivar. Have you not seen? Every habitation along this road has been attacked by raiders bearing poisoned arrows that kill with only a prick. Creatures with the bodies of men and the faces of animals. As well, many folk have starved because the spring gleaning came late, and they had already lost so many livestock and stores to the storms of last autumn that they hadn't enough stores to last out the season of want. What of Conrad and Sabella?"

"Did they not come this way?"

"I have not seen them at Hersford. There is another route they might have taken. If they were riding to Kassel, they would turn toward the Hellweg at the crossroads at die Eiche. That's a better road, the main route through this region."

"Where is that? Did we miss it?" demanded Baldwin.

Ortulfus smiled almost mockingly. "Fear not, friends. It lies a short way ahead. You may leave us there and go on your way. Yet tell me all before you go."

Ivar rubbed his face. He was so tired, and none of it ever made any difference. "We were come to Autun with Biscop Constance, whom you know."

"She lives?" The abbot's expression changed. For a moment it seemed the sun had come out to illuminate him.

"She lives, Father. She is burdened with troubles and injuries, but she is alive—or was when we saw her." Quickly he sketched the scene.

Ortulfus groaned aloud. "I have heard stories of these Eika raiders. I thought they were no longer a threat. And never a threat so far inland. If the biscop's party moves so slowly, and they race up behind . . ." He looked away, too stricken to finish the sentence.

"There's nothing we can do," Ivar said. "She escaped them, or she is dead. We must reach Lady Sabella and Duke Conrad, so they can turn back to save Autun."

"They are not the only ones who can save Autun."

"Who else can you mean?"

"Only this." Father Ortulfus wore a Circle of Unity hammered out of finest silver, but his hand briefly folded to form the hand sign depicting the phoenix. "King Henry's heir rides abroad in these lands. He defeated the invaders at Osterburg. He shattered their army and drove their remnants into the east. It is said he saved Henry from a terrible malefic spell set on him by an evil man. That he brought Henry's army out of Aosta when no other man could have done so. He could save Autun."

"You are speaking of Prince Sanglant. Lady Sabella and Duke Conrad are riding to Kassel to fight him."

"Best we get moving." Ortulfus set out, striding easily.

Ivar swung into the saddle and moved up alongside. "Will you ride, Father?"

He glanced up. "Nay, Brother. I must walk beside those we have salvaged from the ruins."

"Is that why you are come here, to find the survivors?"

"Yes. Ten or more days ago a woman staggered into Hersford. She brought with her a terrible story that none among us wished to believe. Who would believe the shadows that once roamed the deep forest would become flesh, and walk in daylight? We thought she was a lunatic, although we should have known better. Another came, crying the same tale, and more yet. So we set out to gather up what remained of the flock. You see them, there."

The party struggled at a staggeringly slow pace, but the monks chivvied them patiently, herding up straying toddlers and hungry goats, giving an arm to a stumbling man with an injured leg, taking turns pushing the pair of handcarts that held two elderly women too weak, it seemed, to move along on their own power. If the Eika were hunting behind them, these people had no chance to survive the encounter. If slender dog-women ghosted out of the forest with bows and knives, these people would all die.

"Hersford is close," said Ortulfus. "We boast a crossroads as well, a path leading east and a road that runs south and west. It joins up with the main road farther southeast from the crossroads at die Eiche."

"Did you not see Sabella's and Conrad's armies? No sign of them?"

"We did not. As I said, the main road bypasses Hersford. But if you look at the road closely, you can see the signs that reveal they passed this way recently. Grass cropped. Manure and waste. Scraps of cast-off leather. Splinters of wood, and abandoned campfires. Back in Dibenvanger this army camped out the night on the green court within the cloister, some of them."

"I didn't notice," said Baldwin.

"Perhaps the wind blew the signs away. Sabella and Conrad ride ahead of us. Thank the Mother they did not disturb Hersford in their haste to march on Kassel."

Ivar spoke. "What of these villagers? Did they see the armies?"

"I have not yet asked, but most of these have been hiding in the woods. Camping under the trees. They fear to return to the villages where they once lived."

"It's easier to hide among the trees," said Baldwin confidingly. "That's what we did."

Ortulfus' sharp smile was softened by this confession. "I'm sure it's true, Brother Baldwin, but you would be well served to spend the night within Hersford's walls before you ride on."

"How high are your walls, Father?" Ivar asked with a laugh, although he didn't mean his comment to sound so cutting.

"Faith keeps them strong," said Ortulfus without the least sign of irony. He frowned at his refugees. Their tight group was spreading out into a straggle, the faster like a rope tugging on those who lagged behind. "Faith is all we have."

6

OF course it made perfect sense to Liath that, at the heart of the world, she would find a library, a repository of knowledge.

Of course she settled by the entrance, in a quiet spot, and sat and watched them, trying to make sense of their purpose and their manner of language. After all, if there was a book, she would some day wish to read it!

Typically, a goblin would tap along the wall beside one of the holes and, after completing a set of tests at various compass points around the hole, would withdraw the scroll and carefully unroll it into a flat sheet. The copper armband, pressed into the unrolled fabric, caused the writing to unveil by means of a magic she did not understand. It seemed the language was read by touch; she simply saw no evidence that they read through their eyes or by speaking words aloud.

At length, after napping and eating, she wandered again among them—or among a different group, perhaps, as she could only tell them apart with difficulty. The tone of their skins, like those of the Eika, had substantial variation; in addition, each had a distinctive pattern of growths crusting its skin. Whether male or female she could not tell.

What riches did they peruse?

Theology? Mathematics? Physics? It seemed unlikely that the science of astronomy concerned those who dwelled under the ground, but geometry surely held their interest, for she had seen the proportioned chambers through which their maze of tunnels ran. They seemed savage in appearance, clothed only in barbaric ornaments, but they had devised the secret of writing, so surely the mechanical sciences engaged them. All sciences are matters of use before they become matters of art. How far they had come in matters of art she could not know, because she had no way to communicate. Did they possess the art of logic? Ethics? Physics? Did they search out and consider the causes of things as found in their effects? Had they recorded somewhere the reason for the tremblings and shakings that afflict the Earth? Was it true that the collapse of buried mountains deep within the Earth caused tremors? Or that the pressure of gusting winds in subterranean caverns tilted the ground and caused it to swing briefly this way and then that? What of the rivers of fire that flowed in the bowels of the Earth? Surely, living underground, they had wondered why gold is soft and iron is hard. Out of what arises the color of a gemstone? Was it true that death did not put an end to things through annihilation, but only broke up their constituent components into new combinations?

So many questions!

Of what essence were the goblins formed? Was there metal mixed within them? Had they any kinship to the Eika? All this remained a mystery. That these creatures existed at all astounded her. Of course she had heard the stories, tales told by grandmothers and old uncles at the hearthside in the cold of winter when folk must huddle indoors to protect themselves against the bitter cold. Back in those days, she had dismissed the stories.

But just as things cannot be created out of nothing nor, once born, be summoned back to nothing, tales do not spring from empty vessels. So the philosopher wrote.

Here walked the ancient ones, the crawlers in the deep, fabled miners, known also as goblins.

They moved in a pattern, some shuffling out while others shuffled in, all seen by her within that faint pulsing glow emanating from the pool. The substance in the pool was not air, not liquid, not flame, and certainly not earth.

Cautiously, she slipped down into the hollow and crept up to the lip of the pool. She knelt. A cool, sweet current flowed upward out of the pool's depths, pouring over her. She felt it through her clothes, through her skin, all the way into her heart.

Reaching, she brushed a hand down and touched the surface.

Like lightning, it struck, and she fell.

The river that is aether links the farthest reach of heaven to the deepest pit within the Earth. It runs shallow, denuded by the great cataclysm, but it runs nevertheless. She flows with it through the tributaries of Earth. It runs upward and outward, thin as a thread, and she rises with it, on it, seeing as with Eagle's Sight.

There are Ashioi, marching along a road. They are fitted out in bronze armor and feathered shields. None of them have human faces; they all wear warrior masks. Behind them lies a stone crown and before them lies a walled city, with its gates closed and guards patrolling the walls.

There is Ivar, riding alongside a raggle-taggle company of men and women and children who look like nothing so much as refugees.

There is Hanna, ascending the road that leads to the gate of Quedlinhame. Behind her rolls the wagon carrying Mother Obligatia, who is propped up so that she can take it all in. After all this, her grandmother still lives!

And there is Sanglant! He rides with an army behind him, moving through forested country on a well-traveled road that she suddenly recognizes as the eastern reach of the Hell-weg.

There flutters a daimone, but it is caught as in a haze; she shifts her gaze upward, toward the moon, and between one breath and the next, one step and the next, she vaults up the ladder and passes like lightning through the gate guarded by a daimone armed with a glittering spear as pale as ice. The sphere of the Moon gleams with a pearl's luster, but she crosses beyond it as with swift and unerring steps she mounts the ladder—for the ladder itself holds the structure of the aether within it. Through the blinding sea of whiteness that is the sphere of Erekes. Beyond the horned gate of Somorhas and its rosy glamour. Through the blazing furnace of the Sun, and crossing the vast charnel house that is Jedu's angry lair. The daimones who live in the upper spheres watch her pass, but lifted on the current of aether, she is too fast for them to catch or to threaten, even if they wanted to. They have seen her before, or will see her again—it is difficult to tell. They recognize her; they know who her kinfolk are. That is enough.

The feasting hall of Mok lies drowned in incense. Its heavy scent drags at her, but she pushes on, she pushes up, as the soul must, seeking release. The storm winds of Aturna buffet her, but she climbs past their darkness and into the dazzling realm of light toward the golden wheels that thrum and turn ceaselessly. Higher and higher, until she comes to the realm of the fixed stars, the white hot firestorm, as terrible as it is beautiful. Her mother's home, permeated by the elements of white fire and blue aether. A welcoming place. She need only choose, and she can leave her mortal body behind and return to her kinfolk.

And yet even so beyond this there is more.

The burning stone still flares, although its fire has been weakened by the cataclysm that tore through Earth and heaven alike. The river of aether runs in a trickle, like a stream late in summer when the water has almost gone. With winter rains, it will refill—but in the span of the heavens, who knows how many earthly years or centuries that will take?

Beyond this crossroads the aether spills outward. For there is no end to it. Does the aether filter from the heavens down onto the Earth, or does it well up also from the heart of the Earth into the heavens? What if there is an infinite circle of aether, a strip made of only one side whose reach, ever cycling, must be never ending?

Beyond the realm of the fixed stars lies an infinite span. Clots of black dust tangle in shifting clouds. A nautilus of light churns around a dark center. Nests of blue-white stars glow hotly, the birthplace of angels. A spiral wheel composed of unnumbered stars whirls in a silence so vast that it has weight, so deep that it is fathomless.

This is the Chamber of Light, the end and beginning of all things.

Not all change comes upon things from without. All this lies within us as well. We just have to find it.

Then she was yanked free, gasping and choking.

A fluttering against her wrist, like the brush of moth's wings, pulled her back to Earth, a very light touch to cause such a rude awakening.

One of the creatures squatted an arm's length away. It made no immediate move, now that it had her attention. She stared at it, but she could not tell if it stared back. It was impossible to determine if the bulges had a fixed point they focused on, and she supposed it was possible that it did not "see" in the same manner she did. How so, then?

She had no way to ask the question.

It tapped a rapid pattern onto the floor. All around, barely seen above the slope of the hollow, the others paused in their study. Like her, they waited. It tapped again. Wondering, she rapped her forefinger one, then twice, then three times on the floor. Was this a form of communication?

Her companion made no reply. It wore no facial expression she could comprehend. She thought she recognized it as the one with pewterlike skin, which had passed her in the tunnel and, she believed, guided her here. It had worn the glowing armband, although a different one carried that armband now.

Pewter Skin rose, shuffled up out of the hollow, and halted by the mouth of the tunnel. There, for a while, it subsisted as might a statue, moving not at all. When she did not move, it vanished into the darkness beyond.

After a moment, it reappeared, tapped again, turned and vanished; reappeared, tapped, vanished; reappeared.

She rose. "I see what you are trying to communicate," she said aloud. "I am no harm to you. I would like to understand your books."

It tapped, vanished. She scrambled up out of the hollow and picked up all her gear. After breathing a smoldering fire into the end of the rope, she followed it into the labyrinth.

The creature moved at a brisk pace. She often had to lope to keep up; there came no chance for her to mark her route. That was bad enough, but after they mounted the nearest set of stairs they soon looped into places she had no memory of, not that these corridors didn't all look more or less alike. No landmarks measured her journey. Bewilderment led to confusion. Was it taking her back to the cavern at the Heart-of-the-World's-Beginning, where she would become, again, Feather Cloak's prisoner, a sacrifice for the Ashioi priests?

They will not touch me.

And anyway, she thought not. This was new ground, untouched. Probably she was the only human—such as she was—to ever walk this way.

"Where are we going?" she asked it, but it did not answer.

"What is your name?" she asked it, but it did not answer.

Twice she tried to get its attention by rapping on the walls, but it did not answer.

They climbed in long, slow inclines that at intervals cut back upon themselves at acute angles or twisted in half circles, but by the aching in her legs she knew that they moved steadily upward. Once she stopped and tried to get its attention, to let it know she needed to rest, but it kept climbing and did not glance back. It was difficult to keep going, but she dared not fall behind.

They came to a strange intersection, a narrow cleft. It squeezed through, and she after it, careful of her pouched

tunic and coiled rope. They came into a low cave ragged
with spears of stone fallen from the ceilings to litter the uneven floor. A dangerous place, made more so by the
change in darkness and shot through with a tight smell of
smothering earth and mildewed leaves. Pewter Skin trundled forward, deftly avoiding the debris or kicking it aside,
and took the left turning where the narrow tunnel
branched into two routes. Away down the other branch,
water dripped.

The way grew steep. She toiled. Only imperceptibly did
she recognize a change in light like the kiss of gray. Ahead
lay daylight. Between one of her breaths and the next, the
creature turned right around, brushed past her, and trundled away into the depths, soon lost to sight although for
moments more she heard the scrape and whisper of its
passing.

So much for fellowship!

She burned, thinking of those books, lost to her now.
How had they captured aether in a form that could be contained in a pool? What manner of sorcery did they harness?

What did they know?

So much on and under and above Earth remains a mystery because so much remains unknown. The ceiling lowered until she could no longer stand upright. Crawling the
last length, she mused as she placed hands and knees carefully among the dusty, slippery scree of rock that lined the
tunnel's floor.

So much to discover!

Smiling, relieved, weary, and triumphant, she pushed
past a curtain of pale grass and scrambled onto a narrow
lip of rock hung on a steep hillside. The ledge was no wider
than the length of her leg from hipbone to knee and no
longer than the span of her arms, fingertip to fingertip. A
scraggly bush shrouded half of it. Grass hanging from the
slope veiled the cave mouth.

She blinked, shading her eyes, and for a while had to
cover her face with a hand as she adjusted to the strange,
bright light. She knew what it was; it sprawled over her, and
she basked, leaning back with grass crackling as the sparse

vegetation was crushed between her body and the rocky hillside. Light. Warmth. Fire.

Sun.

After a bit she could see without her eyes tearing or black spots dancing in her vision. Ai, Lady, that sun felt so good! She marked it, and the lay of the shadows, and judged that it was late afternoon here, wherever she was. The sun was setting over distant, pale hills. North lay wasteland, cut off from the hillside by a road that glinted with chalk white. Blinking, she stared.

She knew this place.

She braced herself on the ledge and twisted to look up the steep hillside—it was at its steepest here where the cave mouth opened—to see what lay above her.

After all, this was not a place she knew. A tower rose along the crest of the hill, neatly fitted, freshly mortared, with walls reaching to either side and vanishing into pine forest. There was no telling how far such a wall extended, only that it seemed to mark the border of someone's land.

Yet the sense of dislocation lasted only a moment. She shifted. Her right knee scraped against a sharp rock. Her left foot jammed up against the side of the hill. A stem of grass tickled her nose, and she sneezed, and everything transformed.

"Ai, Lady!" she said, and sat back on her heels, not knowing whether to laugh or cry.

She had certainly come back to where she started, to the very place in the land of the Ashioi where she had once dwelled. That tower had stood in ruins at the crest of a hillside which, in exile, had dropped precipitously into a vale of mist. Now the tower had been repaired, together with the wall. Fresh chalk brightened the White Road, as the Ashioi called it: the border of their land. The knife edge along which the ancient spell had cut the land of the Ashioi away from Earth.

She slid backward, careful with her gear, to let the hanging grass conceal her. If the Ashioi captured her, she would have to escape, and therefore she would have to fight. If they shot her with poisoned arrows, she might not survive a second brush with the toxin.

She would not go back.

She held out her hand, middle fingers curled in and thumb and little finger extended, and measured the horizon in the way that Da had taught her long ago. The sun stood one span above the rosy horizon. Above, much of the sky remained clear. Soon it would become night, and she could measure the stars and judge the season and, possibly, her latitude, comparing the angle and azimuth with what was stored in her city of memory. The catalog of stars written into Da's *Book of Secrets* and the cunning astrolabe were lost to her, but Da had taught her well enough that she was not dependent on them; they only made things easier, and more accurate. She must walk west and north. It would be a long journey to Wendar, but she had made that journey before. She could do it again.

She sighed and closed her eyes, and perhaps because of the lazy glamour of sunlight against her face or perhaps because she was really just that exhausted, she slipped into a doze.

Woke.

Day melted into night. The sun's rim winked gold at the horizon, caught in a notch in the distant hills and visible only because of that last spasm of light.

A person was sitting next to her, perfectly still and quiet.

She choked down a cry of surprise, and reached for the sword she no longer carried.

"It's just me," Eldest Uncle said.

She shrieked, and laughed as her heart pounded and her hands shook.

"Shhh!" he whispered. "We must get you out of here, Bright One."

"How did you find me?"

He smiled. "Despite your attempt to conceal yourself, you are visible from the road. I took a walk to seek out a particularly good meadow of earth-apple that lies a morning's walk from here. Its oil eases the ache in my joints, and the long walk does me good. Coming back, I saw you. I diverted the twilight patrol. Best we move quickly."

She grimaced, rubbing her thighs. "Yes. What do you suggest?"

"Only the patrols walk the outer roads these days. The great armies have run west and east to combat our enemies."

"Have the Ashioi gone to war?"

"There is much news to tell you."

"I have my own news. What I have seen—!"

He nodded. "In time, we can discuss all this. Meanwhile, there is also a person you can help, if you wish to. As soon as it is full night, we will walk in the shroud of darkness."

She looked up at the heavens. A high haze obscured the zenith. All that she had seen, climbing the thread of aether, was hidden to her. She could not see the fixed stars, the wandering stars, or even the moon. Only in the west did she glimpse the flash of a star in that gash along the far hills where the haze had not yet settled.

"Very well."

That easily she trusted him, as she would trust a beloved grandfather, or a grandmother. He was related to her, after all, by the bonds of marriage. But it was not the civil contract that allowed her to sling her coiled rope over her shoulders and slide down the steep slope in his wake, to begin walking westward with him along the White Road. It was a different contract, one she could not easily explain.

She trusted him.

That was all that was necessary.

IX
ALLIES AND TRAITORS

1

AFTER Zuangua took Blessing away, Anna wept. She wept out of fear for the girl but mostly because she had failed in her duty. She had not protected Blessing from the girl's own impulsive and immature nature.

Now the princess was gone away with the Ashioi army. It made Anna sick to think of it. What kind of barbarians allowed children to march to war? It made her cry, and cry she did. No one paid the least attention to her, who was a prisoner in the midst of prisoners. Lord Hugh's soldiers also remained behind, corralled like cattle in a structure ringed by a strong stone palisade and a garrison of bored guards, but their situation looked very different from her own. Anna sat on a shaded porch whose roof was woven out of saplings and, as time passed, watched her companions go about their business throughout the hot and dusty days.

Scarred John and Captain Frigo had set up a carpenter's shop with their iron adze and axes. Over the weeks they had developed an astonishing parade of customers. The iron tools and swords fascinated the Ashioi. Liudbold had once spent a pair of years apprenticing in a smithy, and he was soon carted away to the toils of their captor's furnaces. At first, Anna supposed they had slaughtered him or tortured him, but at intervals he returned to visit, each time looking sleeker and fatter. Most recently, he arrived for his visit accompanied by a sly-faced young Ashioi woman, who was pregnant.

Theodore the archer also had discovered an easy camaraderie with the locals. They admired his skill with the bow; he, like the other men, admired the easy manners of the women.

They were all deserting her, seduced by the flesh, but Anna could not blame them. She had made that same mistake herself, and anyway she did not regret it. Why should they? They could never go back to Darre, because they had betrayed their queen.

She cried again, just a little, thinking of Thiemo and Matto.

No use regretting the dead. Nothing she could do would bring them back, and nothing she had done had halted Blessing in her headlong rush to impress her powerful great uncle, the bold and handsome warrior Zuangua.

This day, scarred John was sitting out in the courtyard, on a stump under a shade roof, dressing wood. Captain Frigo was grinding down wood nails. One of the soldiers trotted over to him, leaned to speak, and in reply the captain nodded, got up, and ambled over toward the gate. Another man braided rope, while in the garden a pair of soldiers fussed among their green plants.

Anna regarded the basket at her feet with irritation. The rushes the Ashioi used for baskets cut her fingers and were too stiff to plait easily. Sometimes she saw the Ashioi guards snickering as they looked at her licking her bleeding fingers, and she had a terrible feeling that she was missing something about the task. She had tried soaking them in water but that only made them fray, while drying them made them crumble. No one helped her. Hugh's soldiers ignored her, and, in truth, no young Ashioi men looked twice at her, preferring their own half naked women. She was no use at all, not here and not anywhere. In Gent they had long since forgotten her, no doubt. Who missed her? Who thought of her at all?

Tears burned again, hot and angry. It was getting tiresome, crying all the time, but she worried about Blessing and she worried about herself, lost and drifting in a place that would never be her home. She had a body but she felt as if her soul had come unmoored and left her trapped in a husk. The constant dusty haze kicked up by men going about their lives ground into her skin, wearing her away until eventually she would dissolve into nothing.

If only there would come a miracle.

"Whsst! Anna!" Scarred John sauntered up. "There's an old man come to the gate, asking after you. Says he needs a servant to help him draw water and fetch wood and plait baskets." He grinned easily as he eyed her half made and utterly useless basket. The handsome, cunning baskets plaited by the Ashioi hung from the rafters of their huts, both beautiful and useful as she could never be. "Captain says you might as well go. You're no use to us now the lady princess has scampered off. Even if she comes back, she's gone to live among her noble relatives." He snorted derisively. "Likes them better than her own kind! Not that she's really like us."

He wore much-mended clothing, but he'd abandoned his worn boots in favor of the sandals favored by the Ashioi. He shaved like a churchman, as all the soldiers did now, because the women liked it better. Ashioi men did not have beards.

"I don't want to go," she said.

"Even an old man would be better than none, unless you have a sweetheart at home waiting for you." He grinned, to make the words twist more deeply, before turning and walking off. He would not protect her. None of them would.

Captain Frigo came to fetch her. She thought about fighting them, but she knew it was hopeless. She possessed a leather pack with a spare tunic and belt and her boots tucked away together with a comb and a precious silver spoon, now tarnished, but hers. These and other oddments were all that belonged to her, all that weighted her to the world from which otherwise she might just float away into the air without an anchor. She slung it over her back and plodded—in Ashioi sandals, because to wear closed boots in this climate made feet itch and rash and crack and bleed—to the gate. She was a husk, nothing more. She might be torn up and discarded, but she could no longer be hurt.

At first she did not see him, because he stood so unobtrusively beside four stately young mask warriors, Dog Spotted Leopard and Buzzard and Falcon. He produced, from a small basket, a number of stones and tokens, the kind the Ashioi used when they exchanged goods. Ashioi guards as well as Captain Frigo took a share, and then they all turned their backs in the way of folk refusing further responsibility.

Anna saw the old man's face. Her mouth dropped open. He caught her gaze and shook his head in a warning. She closed her mouth, and for an instant she was dizzy, wondering whether it was God, or the Enemy, who had answered her.

After all, it was God's work.

She knew better than to ask questions, but that night they sat beside a campfire, just seven of them, munching on freshly roasted rabbit and a stringy haunch of very old and unidentifiable meat, and she could hold in her questions no longer.

"Where are we going?" she asked. "My lady."

"West," said the one who was married to Prince Sanglant. The lady, Liathano, was a sorcerer, no more human than her Ashioi companions, only Anna found the Ashioi far less terrifying than she found this woman, although she did not know why.

Ai, Lady and Son! This woman had a soft fire about her, visible only at night and no more solid than the flash of steaming air visible on a cold night when breath is exhaled.

"I know what happened to Princess Blessing, my lady," Anna ventured, although the woman had not asked. She was neither kind nor cruel; in truth, she seemed indifferently tolerant of Anna's presence.

The lady glanced at her, and fixed on her face a false and chilling smile. "I know where she has gone. But that she lives was beyond my knowledge, before I came here. To know that she survived must sustain me."

No one had told Anna how the lady had come to Ashioi country, or why she had left the prince, her husband. She dared not ask. She ate, and she drank a little, and she even slept, although the dusty ground made her wake sneezing a dozen times before dawn lit the east.

They trudged all morning along the road, faces set to the west. It was a clear day, a faint haze lightening the sky to a blue-white pallor. The earth baked around them. Thorny bushes and swathes of dry grass rattled when the wind gusted. Off to their left, the sea shone like polished crystal, a dense lapis field cut off by the southern horizon.

In the heat of the day they rested under the shade of an awning tied up between stunted juniper trees. The mask warriors talked among themselves and occasionally with the old man, and the two young men flirted with the lady in that way men have when they're not being quite serious while the two young women made jokes with the lady as they teased the young men. No one took any notice of Anna because she was nothing. Only, that being so, why had they bothered to bring her along, to rescue her from her prison among Lord Hugh's soldiers?

As they broke camp in midafternoon she stood beside the lady, and spoke.

"Are we going to Aosta, my lady? To follow the army? All the others, the soldiers, they said the Ashioi army was marching to Novomo."

The lady smiled bitterly but did not answer. When they began walking, Anna tried asking the old man, but he could not understand Wendish and, because no one spoke to her, she had learned almost nothing of the Ashioi language in the months she had been their captive.

They walked through the remainder of the hot afternoon. On occasion, they sipped a nasty brew that made her whole face pucker but which quenched her thirst each time for another league or so of walking. The sun set among streamers of rich red cloud. In the east, a full-faced moon slipped heavenward, cloaked at intervals by stripes of haze and other times shining brightly down upon them. Still they walked, because where the moon shone the White Road gleamed as if it caught and reflected that light.

When the moon had walked a third of the way up into the sky, they paused to rest where an arrangement of flat rocks made pleasant benches. Anna drank, and chewed on one of the tasteless, tough flatbreads they carried for journey bread.

The lady lay on her back on one of the rocks, with an arm outstretched. She raised it and lowered it and raised it again, measuring those stars she could see. She spoke under her breath; Anna saw her lips moving, but she couldn't quite hear what the lady was saying. Eldest Uncle crouched beside the lady on the ground with his head tilted back. A tiny lizard scuttled within a crack in the stone. Anna shuddered, remembering that when she was young a boy had told her that such creatures were beloved of the Enemy.

Eldest Uncle rose and came to her, unrolled a blanket, and draped it over her shoulders. She smiled, because she didn't know how to tell him that she wasn't cold.

The old man padded to the warriors, and they began the familiar routine of leavetaking: taking a last sip of mahiz, tucking away leaf-wrapped journey bread, tightening the ropes on the baskets they carried before slinging them over their backs.

Anna got to her feet. The lady stood. In the moonlight, Anna saw tears on the other woman's cheeks.

"What are you looking at?" Anna whispered.

The lady's voice was slightly hoarse. "The stars. See, there. That is the Scout's Torch, almost overhead. It's faint because of the moon's light and the haze. To the west, there, the Lion's Claw is almost gone, and to the southwest—do you see it?—the blue star marking the Dragon's Eye. In the east—well—hard to see. It's hazy, and the moon outshines everything. The three jewels are barely visible because of the light. And to the south, the Serpent. There, that one— do you see it?—that is the Serpent's dreadful red eye."

"That's a lot of stars."

"Only the brightest are visible. But to see them at all!" She faltered, wiped her eyes, and with her head still canted back, staring into the heavens, she spoke in a low voice. "They're so beautiful. It's been so long since I have seen them. Or held my daughter in my arms."

They walked for several days and nights, their journey punctuated by long rests during the heat of the day and by an ongoing and protracted argument between the lady and Eldest Uncle in which Blessing's name was spoken many times. This much Anna understood. Of the rest, nothing.

At intervals, watchtowers guarded the approaches. They stopped at these places for supplies. The lady walked among them without fear, and they stared at her and spoke to her; Anna, they stared at but ignored.

They came at length to a place where the White Road bent southward to intersect with the sea where the shoreline was cut by a pair of chasms opening deep into the rocky wasteland. A fort spanned the road. No guardsman seemed inclined to question Eldest Uncle. They deferred to him as to a noble lord, and let the party pass without question, although it seemed every Ashioi guardsman felt obliged to comment at length and with much laughter as the little group set out into wilderness.

After this, they marched along a dusty road for five days— or six or seven; Anna lost count. Her feet were caked in grit. When she moved her hands, dirt ground softly between the skin of her fingers. Her face was masked with dust. Her hair itched all the time although she kept it pulled back in a tight braid and covered by a linen cloth knotted at the back of her neck.

One time they saw a party of about a dozen mask warriors walking east, some limping and one bundled up in a fetal position and carried on the back of one of his companions. The lady pulled a hood over her face and melted away into the scrub brush grown along the side of the road, and so it was that they met the group and spoke at length with them while the lady hid. There was some discussion of Anna. She could tell by the way the newcomers indicated her by lifting their chins as they looked at her. Eldest Uncle's authority carried them. Soon enough, the other party made their farewells and set on their way, east toward home. When all was clear, the lady emerged from the brush. They continued their journey, stopping for a long rest in the midday and for increasingly long rests at night as the moon dwindled and faded to nothing but a sliver at dawn.

The next morning, they came to a substantial village garrisoned by a contingent of Ashioi mask warriors, Ashioi farmers and craftsmen, and a few human workers who stared at Anna from the fields as she passed them on the road. Many gathered at the gate to ask questions as they came in, but Eldest Uncle fended them off with his usual good nature and greeted a woman carrying a chubby baby on each hip. She greeted him warmly, and spoke to the lady with more reserve but with evident interest. Anna thought she had seen this woman before, but she wasn't sure. It was difficult for her to distinguish one face from another because they looked so different from the people she had grown up with or even from the swarthy soldiers devoted to Lord Hugh. Others crowded around, so many faces that she had to look away for fear of drowning.

Pushed to the edge of the group and ignored but avoided by all, she followed as they settled into a council held out on the open common ground, where a post stood. Mats were rolled out. The lady and Eldest Uncle and the other woman sat facing each other. Many clustered behind, crouching or standing to listen. Drink and food passed around the circle as the three in the center began to speak. The lady had a habit of accompanying her words with spacious gestures, as though her hands talked. Eldest Uncle spoke with his hands resting on his bare thighs. The other woman mostly listened, asking a question now and again and occasionally responding to a comment from one of the three persons kneeling behind her, two men and a woman who hovered like servants or children. At last she turned to one of these attendants—a noticeably attractive young woman who wielded a fierce gaze—and an object changed hands. She held it out. It was round, formed out of polished metal, like the sun.

The lady stared, rendered speechless by this apparition. At length, she reached for it, and it was given into her hands. She turned it and spun it and held it at arm's length and laughed and cried and at length gave it back. And spoke an Ashioi word that Anna knew.

"Yes."

After this, as the council broke up and the lady walked away with the other woman, deep in conversation, Anna found herself in a backwater, unwanted and forgotten. When she wandered to the gate, no one stopped her or called after her. She walked through the gate and crossed the plank bridge fixed over the ditch. A square guard's tower rose at the northeastern corner of the palisade. There, a mask warrior with his mask pushed up onto his hair spotted her but looked away as quickly, uninterested.

She could run. She could escape.

She laughed, because it was better than crying. Would she never be able to go home?

A trio of young people—two boys and a girl—came walking up the road carrying buckets half full with water over their shoulders. They were born of humankind, as she was, with sweetly familiar features although they were dark-haired and with complexions neither as pale as Wendish nor as reddish bronze as Ashioi, but with a dusky olive cast. Southerners. Aostans.

Seeing her, they halted, set down their buckets, and stared. Whispers passed between them. One of the lads had a scarred chin and hollow cheeks; his companion was bow-legged, with a gimpy foot. The girl had scarcely hips or breasts to speak of because she was so skinny, but her gaze measured Anna without fear, and it seemed to Anna that she was the leader of this little clan. When the girl spoke, it was in a language Anna did not know, and when she could not answer them in a language they knew, they shrugged, picked up their buckets, and went in through the gate.

For a long while she stood in the middle of the road, going nowhere. At last, as her head began to throb from the midday heat, she turned around and went back inside.

She had nowhere else to go.

* * *

"Come, Anna! It's time to go!"

The words yanked her out of a doze. They had offered her a place to rest her tired feet within the cool and dark confines of a pit house.

Beyond the brightness of the low doorway—there was no door, only strings of wooden beads knocking together—the lady stood, her outline softened by the yellowing light of late afternoon.

"We're going, Anna. Come."

"Where are we going?" she asked before thinking, and then winced, because she ought not to ask. She ought only to obey.

But the lady took no notice. She answered the question tolerantly. "We are going to Novomo. It's a dilemma, whether to wait here for the army to return or to go after them, knowing that the tides within the crowns might bring us to cross without meeting. Yet I just don't know. I must act. I must find Blessing, now that I know she is alive. And you'll take care of her when we've found her."

"We're going to Novomo?" She felt wooly-headed. "But that's where the army went. They'll capture us."

"Maybe not, Anna. I have allies now, among the Ashioi."

"How can you have allies, my lady? Do they mean to join Prince Sanglant's army, if he is king now in Wendar, as I heard? Yet, if they do so, won't they be traitors to their own kind?"

The lady had already turned her head to look toward a sight Anna could not see. She replied, but her thoughts seemed already half a league away. "Not that kind of ally. We do not deal in land and gold but in something more precious to us. Something I have that they want, and that I am willing to share."

"What is that, my lady?"

Seen in profile, she grinned fiercely, and the dim room seemed suddenly brighter. "The secrets of the mathematici."

2

DIE EICHE was a huge oak tree with a massive trunk and a canopy of branches so wide and thick that grass did not grow beneath it. The crossroads was not precisely a village except for the straggle of houses built here because of a decent strip of arable land and the chance to house travelers in exchange for coin or goods. This hamlet, too, had been abandoned, but a large company had camped here recently. The interiors had been ransacked, and boards pried out of walls to throw onto campfires. Several animals had been killed, skinned, and eaten; their remains were scattered. Ortulfus weighed a scapula in his hands. With a finger, he traced the marks of a knife where it had scraped the bone. A single fresh grave stood in the shadow of the surrounding forest, beside a crop of young oak sprouting where there was no shade to kill them.

The company rested, exhausted more by fear than by the slow pace. Father Ortulfus sent monks with buckets to the nearby stream. A pair of lads offered to lead the horses to drink as Ivar and Baldwin examined the roads from this safe distance. The broader path, most traveled, struck southeast along the route made by the stream, while a grassier way pushed straight east into the trees.

"We must ride the fastest route," said Baldwin. "Don't you think that's what Biscop Constance would want us to do?"

Ivar studied Father Ortulfus, who was still examining the scapula. "Have you horses at Hersford, Father? Ours are spent, although rest will improve them. If we could give you ours in exchange for fresh mounts, we could make better time."

"Some horse met a sorry fate in the stewpot," said Ortulfus, tossing the charred scapula back into a fire pit. Its impact sent up a sputter of ash and soot. "We have donkeys, oxen, a pair of mules, but no riding mounts. I'm sorry."

"Have you a smith, then? It would help them to be reshod."

"That we do. Brother Adso came to us from Alba two years ago, fleeing the Eika invasion. He has a touch of the old magic in him when it comes to farriery."

A child coughed wetly. An old woman crooned to a restless baby. A trio of girls ventured as close to the three men as they dared, staring longingly at the handsome cleric, who seemed oblivious to their presence. The brothers came back with buckets three quarters full and began ladling out water to the parched company.

Baldwin leaned against Ivar and bent his mouth to his friend's ear. "I'll just go to the horses now. They're staring at me."

Without looking back, he crossed the road and walked over to the stream to supervise the lads, who seemed to know what they were about and needed no actual supervision.

It came without warning, except perhaps for a catching of breath within the woodland, as though all creeping and crawling ceased among the creatures who lived and died there. Of birds, he heard no sound. Nothing, and then the slap of feet, *pat put pat put*, someone loping in an easy rhythm.

Both of the dogs, lying on the ground, came to their feet and barked, as startled as everyone else.

It burst out of the forest and jolted to a halt, surveying their ragged company from a safe distance. It had a round shield painted with yellow-and-red dragons twined and twisting each around the others. It had ice-white hair pulled back in a ruthless braid, no strand left free, and its skin gleamed as though molten gold had coated its figure. It wore no tunic or jerkin, only a painted cloth tied around its hips. It held a spear in its right hand, and this weapon thumped once, twice, thrice, four times onto the ground, like the abbreviated knock of a woodpecker.

Then it turned and ran back the way it had come.

The villagers erupted, leaping up, shouting, crying, some running into the forest and others pressing children toward the grassy path that led through the trees to the monastery, still a half day's walk away according to the abbot.

"God have mercy," said Father Ortulfus, staring after

the vanished creature. He was pale and, in truth, he was angry. "After all this, can we not be spared? These poor suffering innocents?" He turned on Ivar. "They have followed *you!*"

Ivar choked. His gaze was caught by Baldwin at the stream, turning to look at them because he was puzzled at the commotion. From across the road and a little upstream, Baldwin had not seen the Eika scout but only the turmoil that spun out from its appearance. He lifted a hand to query Ivar.

"Forgive me," said Ortulfus, grasping Ivar's wrist. "I spoke in anger. This calamity is not your doing."

"I pray you, Father, there is nothing to forgive. Do what you must. We'll hide in the forest and hope they do not see us. I would offer to draw them off, but we must reach Lady Sabella and Duke Conrad before they do."

Ortulfus sketched a strange pattern at his chest. "In the name of the Mother and Son," he murmured, "be blessed as you go on your way."

Ivar stared at him, hearing the phrase, but shook himself. "Truth rises with the phoenix," he responded.

Ortulfus nodded sharply. "So we have ourselves seen," he said cryptically. He strode after his flock, scooped up a bawling child who was reaching after something left on the ground, and shouted at his monks to scatter with their charges through the forest. "Each one of you take some into your keeping and go by diverse routes toward home. Hurry!"

They fled. Ivar ran to the stream and sent the two confused lads on their way after the others.

"What do we do?" asked Baldwin.

"Hide, and fall behind." They splashed across the stream and led the horses into the woods. "I don't know how big a force is coming. We can't outrun them. If it's a scouting expedition, we can travel along whichever road they do not take."

Baldwin scratched at his beard again. "I hate this hair. I wish we had time to shave."

"If they have Autun to ransack, why march this way?" When Baldwin did not reply, Ivar muttered on to himself, furious that their luck just could not change for the better. "Why send scouts so far? It's days and days of walking ... and for what? Can't they just leave us alone? They don't want us reaching the lady! That's it! They know we're ahead of them, and they're after us!"

"Do you really think that's likely?" Baldwin asked in a calm voice that, like cold water, doused Ivar's fit of anger. "You and I are nothing. Not really."

Not really.

They kicked through a thicket of bramble and plunged into a tangle of saplings. Beech woods with their open vistas were a bad place to hide; the great oak in the clearing seemed out of place, an ancient survivor from an earlier time.

"There's a good thick coppice," said Ivar, pointing up the gentle slope to a wall of flourishing ash and hawthorn. "Thank God for the woodsmen! That's what my father always used to say. I wonder if he's still alive. Ai, God. Gero would be count in his place." The thought struck him to silence and, it seemed, dried up his tears as well. Or maybe it was the rumbling of thunder out of the west. "We must stop, or they'll see us moving."

They hid as best they could, hoping that leaves and distance and stillness would conceal them. That first scout loped again out into the clearing and halted, like a stone statue, to examine the deserted landscape. Or perhaps it was a different Eika, one carrying a similar shield. Ivar could not tell the difference between them, except that maybe this one's skin was more bronze than gold. More came, a pair, a foursome, a dozen. This advance group trotted past the oak tree and took the wide road that led to the southeast, the main way to Kassel and the duchy of Fesse. Yet the rumble grew louder.

Out of the trees a child came running with frantic steps. Father Ortulfus burst out of cover, chasing it. It stooped to grab a scrap of cloth, a doll, most likely, and as it turned to run back to the forest, it cast a glance westward down the road, took a pair of steps, looked back again, and went rigid.

Ortulfus reached it, clapped a hand over its mouth, and

swung the child over his shoulder as he shifted course to run back into the safety of the wood.

Baldwin took a step after them, but Ivar grabbed his arm. "No!" he whispered.

Baldwin shook him off, and seemed ready to run after the abbot, but then the horses shied at nothing and he had to turn back. Together they calmed the restive animals.

Together, they looked up as the steady rumble turned into an identifiable thunder of a mass of people marching. The first ranks trotted into the clearing. They jogged five abreast, each one armed with some kind of girdle about the hips—leather or shimmering metal—and a shield and weapon, spears, axes, bows, and a few swords. Dogs accompanied them, monstrous iron-gray beasts with saliva dribbling down their muzzles. Seeing Ortulfus and the child, they broke forward ravenously.

The ten Eika soldiers who ran in the lead broke into a sprint and raced out to encircle to abbot and his tiny charge, beating back the dogs. One stabbed a dog clean through, and where it twitched and howled on the ground, the other dogs converged, snarling and ripping.

"I can't look!" moaned Baldwin. "I should have gone after them!"

"Hush! You want those dogs to hear us?" Thank God the wind was blowing into their faces. At least their scent would not give them away. "They won't stop for your pretty face!"

The second ranks kept coming along the road, and more and yet more, too many to count unless he numbered each rank—two rows of soldiers—as a pair of hands.

"Ten pairs of hands make a hundred," Ivar muttered. "Of hundreds: One. . . . Two. . . . Three. . . . Four. . . . Five."

The army went on forever, and the horses didn't like it. Something about the smell or sound unnerved them. Baldwin kept up a steady, gentling murmur to keep them quiet and in one place as Ivar counted. The Eika pace seemed to swallow the ground; they moved without faltering along the road to Kassel, a new rank marching into view as the forward groups moved out of sight. With their horses pushed to the limit, Ivar and Baldwin could not possibly hope to overtake this army, even by ruining their mounts.

All this time, Father Ortulfus stood within a ring of Eika, held the silent child, and waited. The soldiers around him had also ceased moving. They also were waiting.

Banners streamed. Rippling strips of cloth in bright yellows and stark reds and heavenly blues marked the core of the army. A column of wagons rolled into view, pulled not by horses but by Eika and other creatures, ones who were like the Eika in walking on two feet and having hands and familiar-seeming faces but with blond and brown and black hair.

"Look!" whispered Baldwin, nudging Ivar. "Prisoners! Slaves!"

Humankind.

But they weren't slaves. They wore no chains. They carried arms and armor. They wore leather jerkins or mail coats. Those who were not taking their turn at pulling the wagons marched freely within the ranks. He'd seen a few of them scattered in the forward portion of the army but only now realized what they were: human men marching with the Eika. Allies, not enemies. Traitors.

Baldwin grabbed his arm. "God help us! They have her!"

Most of the wagons carried supplies, and Ivar would have missed the person Baldwin indicated because she was surrounded by a heavy guard of brawny Eika crowded together so tightly that they obscured the people seated in the bed of that wagon. He saw their faces in flashes, living faces drawn taut with fear and exhaustion: frail Sigfrid, steadfast Ermanrich, the glowering Sister Eligia, and brave Hathumod, who was seated, strangely enough, beside the driver. She seemed to be chatting amiably with the tall youth, who was clad in a boiled leather jerkin and no helm and who, despite having no horses to drive, was somehow in charge of this wagon. Biscop Constance sat beside Sister Eligia, in the bed of the wagon. She gripped the side and stared intently into the clearing. She had caught sight of Father Ortulfus amid his captors.

A commotion stirred within the ranks of soldiers encircling the abbot. The child squirted out between the legs of one of the soldiers and, grasping its rag doll, sprinted for the trees. A pair of dogs scrambled after it, but their masters whistled sharply and both, wisely, turned back as the Eika soldiers laughed as the child stumbled, fell, and scrabbled forward in a panic. They let it go, but Father Ortulfus was tugged forward and slung unceremoniously into the wagon without the army slackening its pace. He fell on top of Ermanrich, and Sigfrid went down as well as limbs thrashed and bodies righted themselves. Hathumod turned to stare, mouth agape. Father Ortulfus managed to get to his knees. He bowed over the biscop's hand and kissed her ring. Ivar was too far away to hear speech or see their faces closely, but the reunion of the biscop and the young man who had once served in her schola in Autun made him cry. As Ivar wiped away tears, Baldwin muttered under his breath.

"What of the sergeant and the others? Are they all dead?"

The army plunged onward. Of the sergeant and his company, they saw no sign.

"I thought the Eika took no person as prisoner," added Baldwin, "but only killed every soul they met."

"Even the Eika might think twice before killing a holy biscop. Hush, now. Until they're gone."

It seemed forever until the main force marched past and vanished down the road. No horses accompanied this army, only the dogs. They waited longer afterward as several parties of outliers trotted past. Ivar held his breath as dogs swarmed this way and that in the clearing, following the many scents, but in the end they were brought up short by the stream and by the command of their masters, who moved fast in the wake of the main army.

For a long while it was silent. At length, a crow landed on the ground beyond the oak, scratched at the ground, and abruptly took wing and fluttered away.

"Let's go!" said Baldwin.

Ivar put a finger to his lips just as a pair of loping scouts came into view, sniffed the air exactly as dogs would, and moved on.

They waited. Again the crow returned and this time, as it searched in the grass, a second and third joined it.

Ivar said, "we'll go to Hersford. There must be a woods-man's path out of Hersford that will take us cross-country."

Baldwin, like the horses, was eager to move. He got the reins in hand and coaxed the horses out of the coppice. They crossed the clearing quickly. The crows cawed at them and flapped a short distance away, but did not consider these two weary travelers a threat. The grassy path led them into the forest. Ivar recalled no landmarks. He and the others had been marched quickly along this route those few years back; he'd even forgotten the oak at the crossroads, although such a majestic tree must surely be memorable.

They had not walked for long before folk crept out of the forest to follow them, who were armed and who traveled with purpose. In time, a pair of monks emerged with more of the ragged party, and one of them was the very Prior Ratbold who had escorted Ivar and his friends as prisoners to Autun. When Ivar told him of the fate of Father Ortulfus, he met the news with a strange equanimity.

"He'll be safe," the prior said, making the sign of the phoenix. "So was it promised to us."

Baldwin nodded.

Ivar wished he possessed such faith, but he did not. He was relieved to see the palisade surrounding Hersford Monastery, rather more formidable a structure than it had been when he was led away from the institution. He tried to recall how long ago it had been, but the march into the east, the lost years beneath the crown, and the captivity in Queen's Grave wove into a confounding tapestry. Two years? Four years? It all blurred together.

So much had changed, except the pleasant collection of buildings that met his eye once he passed through the gate: the cloister and chapel ringed by the inner fence, the lay-man's barracks, a byre for the milk cow, the henhouse and beehives, the lush ranks of the orchard and the orderly gardens fenced with wire to keep out rabbits. Folk had set up tents around the fruit trees. A dozen men and women were digging up new ground to expand the gardens. A herd of sheep grazed beyond the vegetable garden, tended by a score of children. It was an eerie sight to observe those somber shepherds, so quiet they were, unlike lively children who might be expected to romp a little and play. A dog roamed at the edge of the herd, and it gazed at the newcomers for a measure and, apparently recognizing the monks, went back to its guard.

Ivar grabbed the prior's sleeve.

"Prior Ratbold, I beg you. We need the services of your smith. Provisions, if you have them. We must leave at dawn tomorrow. Is there a path through the woods that might allow us to reach Kassel before that army does?"

Ratbold looked at him and, most oddly, smiled. Ivar moved a half step away because the expression made him so uneasy. This was not the scolding, irritable man who had herded them to Autun and made sure to express his disgust with their heresy every league of the way.

"We were wrong about the lion," Ratbold said.

Ivar shook his head. "I don't understand."

"I told you there was a lion!" said Baldwin.

"Oh. Ah." Ivar knew his face was red. He could feel the heat. "Yes, the lion."

"Up there where the holy man lived," said Prior Ratbold. "Brother Fidelis. We were wrong about the lion, and about so much else. Will you forgive us? It was wrong to send you to Autun. After all, perhaps it was the right thing, since you brought the blessings of the phoenix to Varre. Surely God had a hand, through you, in setting Biscop Constance free."

"She's a prisoner of the Eika!"

"But she is free of Lady Sabella's treachery! If those Eika meant to kill her, they would already have done so."

"They might plan to roast her alive and eat her!"

Ivar's voice had risen. The villagers following in their wake looked at him with alarm and began to mutter among themselves. Children wept, and the dogs set to barking, which got the sheep restless. The herd dog broke into action. In the distance, unseen goats blatted, and a chorus of chickens serenaded them as monks rushed out of cloister and workshops to greet them.

"You shouldn't say such things, Ivar," said Baldwin in such a reproving tone that Ivar blushed.

Ratbold called over a young lay brother and told him to lead the horses to the smith's workshop. No sooner had he stopped to speak to one man but a dozen more swarmed around him, asking advice and offering grievances and problems. In this babble and flood Ivar got washed away from the prior and found himself in an eddy as the newcomers met and mingled with those who had stayed behind. Baldwin tugged on his arm, and he followed him unresisting past the inner fence where they, as noble churchmen, needed no permission to enter.

On the steps of the church a young nobleman dressed in layman's clothing watched the commotion. Ivar squinted and, with a shock, recognized that face. Impossible. He walked over. As soon as he moved in that direction, the youth's gaze transferred smoothly to examine him with the kind of caution kept by a traveler who must size up every encounter for its degree of risk. He held his ground, moving only to say something Ivar could not hear, and as Ivar reached the steps a pair of young men came from the church to join him. One, like the youth, was a lord similar in station to Ivar himself: the younger son of a minor house. He knew his measure as he knew himself. But the look of the other man made him stop in his tracks and stare as a deep chill knifed into the pit of his stomach.

This grim fellow was a Quman, one of the killers who had almost murdered him and his friends. A godless heathen.

Yet this young man stood as easily behind the noble youth as would a trusted retainer. The Quman was half a head shorter than his companions, and he was broader across the shoulders and chest without being stout. He scrutinized Ivar, exchanged a glance with the second Wendish lord, and made no more threatening move than flexing his fingers. His knuckles cracked.

"Who are you?" asked the noble youth with the barest twist of arrogance. He, too, was measuring.

"You're Lord Berthold, son of Villam," said Ivar.

"So I am. I don't know you."

"No reason you should. Last time I saw you, you were lying asleep under the hill on heaps of treasure."

Lord Berthold lifted his chin as if he'd been rocked back by a blow. "How came you to see this?" he demanded imperiously. "Tell me!"

"Just up here, by the crown up on the hill here. But the monks, and Father Ortulfus, did not believe our story and sent us as prisoners to Autun. It's a long story. I could as well ask you, how came you here, and at this time?"

"Who are you?"

"Ivar, son of Count Harl of the North Mark."

"God save us! Sister Rosvita's young half brother! Can it be?"

"You know Rosvita?"

"I was one of the noble youths on the king's progress. She taught me letters." Berthold's gaze turned intent as he stared at Ivar. His voice trembled. "What news of her? Everything is all gone tumbling. All the months have fallen like so many sticks scattering. I scarcely know where I am or what has befallen us. So many are lost, and only the remnants found." Ivar had a difficult time following this chatter, and anyway, Lord Berthold had already switched streams, turning to the Quman youth. "Where is Brother Heribert?"

"Still at the well, he looks, my lord," said the man in accented but comprehensible Wendish. "The old wolf, at the fire-worker's hearth, he waits. At the *smith*." He considered the word and said it again. "The *smith*. Of horses, the holy men keep none."

"Maybe we should go on, on foot," said the second lord, and the other two looked at him as if he had suggested they walk on their hands to get where they were going. Then they all laughed. Such a bond grew out of shared adversity. It could not be woven on any other loom.

"Where have you come from? Where are you going?"

"Strangely," said Berthold lightly, "we ride north from Aosta, which is where we found ourselves." His expression darkened, and he clenched his jaw and, with an effort, made himself smile, although it gave him a bitter edge. "We're going to Kassel. We hear that all the dukes and ladies and princes become king ride that way. We have news, and edicts, and many things to tell, and we have come to much trouble to get here in order to tell them."

Ivar felt silenced by this passionate, angry speech. As the son of a count, he was this man's peer, certainly, although of course Villam's son must outrank the child of a border-land count who rarely attended court to bolster his posi-tion. He knew himself an outsider, judged and found wanting.

"Tell me again," said Berthold after a pause, but his stare was fierce and his tone threatening. "Tell me again how you came to see us sleeping under the hill. How many of us were there? Just me and Jonas, or more?"

Ivar glanced back. Baldwin was gone, and a quick survey of the area revealed no perfect blond head.

"The tale may have to wait until another day. My com-panion and I are riding to Kassel also. Our message is ur-gent. There's an Eika army just passed this way. They're taking the Hellweg, marching east. They've taken both Bis-cop Constance and Father Ortulfus prisoner. Lady Sabella and Duke Conrad left Autun before the Eika attack came, so they don't know the Eika are moving up behind them."

"With Prince Sanglant ahead and the Eika behind, they will be crushed," mused Berthold, but Ivar could not tell if the prospect pleased or displeased him. "Jonas, I have a fancy to walk up the hill to the stone crown, and see for ourselves."

"Must we, my lord?" Jonas had a pleasant face a little hollowed from privation. He was slender in the way of people who are working hard without eating quite enough, yet he had the height common to noble lords. "Let us not, I beg you."

"Are you afraid?"

"I am just so weary." He looked away. "Why take the chance?" he said in a low voice. "Best let them rest."

"They might sleep there still! They might!"

"Seven in all," said Ivar.

Berthold jumped down the steps and grabbed Ivar's wrist. "Seven? Is that how many you saw?"

"Seven sleepers." He shook his arm free. "You are two. Where are the other five?"

"Lost!" groaned Jonas.

Berthold said nothing. His grimace told a tale that Ivar wasn't sure he cared to hear spoken out loud.

Behind, the monks and lay brothers scurried here and there within the grounds enclosed by the palisade, trying to get all the refugees settled for the night. Ivar smelled rain, but he didn't hear its patter in the nearby trees. The wind skated gently past them, still blowing out of the east-northeast. It was getting dark. They had reached Hersford Monastery just in time.

Like a flash of lightning, Baldwin's pale hair showed up within the crowd. Ivar raised a hand to hail him.

Jonas said, "Who's that?"

Baldwin strode up, rubbing at his beard. "They just won't listen to me! There's another man at the smithy with a dozen horses needing shoeing. I told him we were in haste, that we ride with an urgent message, but he said—" He took a second look at the men waiting on the steps, and choked, indicating the Quman. "That's a Quman, Ivar! I thought we'd escaped them!"

Even the Quman savage was staring at Baldwin with the look of a young bull stunned by a sledge blow between the eyes. Lord Berthold's eyes had gone quite round.

"He's not our enemy, Baldwin. In what direction have you come from, Lord Berthold?"

"From the west, and the southwest, before that. We have traveled all the way north from Aosta, through St. Barnaria's Pass. We only arrived here at Hersford this morning."

"Then have you been all this time before us? Did you not see the Eika massing before Autun?"

"We came up a woodsman's path east of the Rhowne. It's an Eagle's path, known to our guide. We did not see Autun at all, nor any Eika." These matters were of little interest to him. Impatiently, he turned to Jonas. "We should go up to the crown. Maybe we can still find them."

Jonas took a step back, shaking his head. "They're dead, Berthold. Don't believe otherwise."

"Who is dead?" asked Baldwin.

A file of monks appeared. Ivar moved aside. Even the

margrave's son shifted to let them pass into the church for Vespers and Compline. In their wake, Prior Ratbold hurried up.

"I pray you, my lords," he said. "Pray with us. It would do us honor."

Berthold ran a hand nervously through his hair, still staring toward the half hidden swell of hill and forest rising to the west-northwest. Jonas tugged on his sleeve, and he retreated backward and through the door, looking over his shoulder at the darkening sky. The Quman sank to his haunches in the posture of a man prepared to wait all night. The prior frowned at him without specifically inviting him inside, then turned his accusing gaze on Ivar and Baldwin.

"Will you come inside, Brother Ivar? Brother Baldwin?" The question was as much challenge as request.

"Perhaps it would be better if we rode on tonight," said Ivar.

"Of course we'll pray!" Baldwin mounted the steps and went inside.

Ivar hesitated, glancing toward the distant smithy, where smoke poured heavenward in a steady, thin stream that faded quickly from sight as the twilight deepened.

"It would be safer for you to leave at daybreak," said the prior. "Strange creatures walk abroad in the night, half man and half animal. You would be hard-pressed to see Eika scouts approaching you. Or their dogs."

Ivar shuddered. Ratbold was a hard but basically decent man with a sharp temper and a carefully hidden mean streak; he didn't mind seeing others squirm.

"Let the monks and the good folk see that you do not fear to bide here," the prior continued. "Their hearts tremble, for they know that Father Ortulfus is lost to the Eika."

"Not dead," said Ivar. "He wasn't killed, but only taken prisoner."

"Just so! I beg you, stand and speak this word before the assembly. They will believe you, for you have seen it with your own eyes. Let us pray together to God, and plead with God to restore him to us. Is that too much to ask of you?"

Ivar could not refuse. Before the service began, he raised his voice and told the assembly of monks what he had seen. Afterward, he knelt with the others when it was appropriate to kneel, and stood when one must stand to sing. The stone floor ground into his knees. His feet hurt, and his eyes stung from the fumes seeping off torches bound from wood not yet thoroughly dry, mark of a wet winter and wetter spring. With each breath he sucked smoke in, and a slow, throbbing headache flowered into life behind his eyes as the liturgy sang around him.

"Blessed is the Country born out of the Mother of Life. Blessed is Her Son. Blessed is the Holy Word revealed, now and ever and unto ages of ages."

One of the holy men paced out the stations of the blessed Daisan's life and ministry, the seven miracles, and the final redemption, but it all seemed so hazy and so unfamiliar. Baldwin was happy, speaking the responses with enthusiasm.

"Kyrie eleison. Lady have mercy. For healthful seasons, for the abundance of the fruits of the earth, and for peaceful times, let us pray."

Beneath the impassioned voices, beneath the pattern traced by the monk's feet, another, more shadowy form walked in the old manner, the words Ivar had grown up with, but he could no longer see those patterns clearly. He could no longer hear those old words as they were drowned in the new.

"For Thou art our sanctification, and unto Thee we ascribe glory, to the Mother, to the Son, and to the Holy Word spoken in the heavens, now, and ever, and unto ages of ages. Have mercy upon us."

"Have mercy upon us," he murmured, thinking his head would burst because of the pressure. The monks fell silent as they waited for leave to depart, but Ivar thought he would choke. He staggered out to the porch and there, blinking and wheezing, he found he had curled his hand into the sign of the phoenix.

Everything has changed. A cataclysm had shaken the church, and it would never be the same.

Pinwheels of light spun low along the dark horizon of

hill, white and golden and hazy. He rubbed his streaming eyes.

"Look!" cried Lord Berthold, arriving beside him as if out of a hidden door. "Look, Jonas!"

"What is that?" Ivar asked. "Is that from the Eika army? Are they burning . . . ?"

A man ran out of the darkness and up onto the porch, where monks now crowded up behind the lord and whispered and pointed and stared.

"My lord!" The stranger had silver-white hair and humble clothing. "Someone is walking the crowns. Do you see?" He turned, revealing his profile to Ivar.

"You're the Eagle!" Ivar said in a voice still hoarse from smoke, but the man ignored him, speaking with a frowning intensity to the equally grim Berthold.

"We can't know who it is from this distance. Who is left who knows the secret of the crowns? Hugh of Austra, as we know. Antonia of Karrone—that traitor! Each bearing as false a heart as any body can nurture without turning to dust."

"What do you mean?" Ivar took hold of the old man's arm and shook him. "Don't you know me?"

The Eagle looked first at the hand and second at Ivar's face. "I don't know you, my lord," he said in a toneless voice.

"Leave off!" said Berthold, with a curse. "Let him go!"

"What does he mean?" demanded Ivar as he released the old man's arm.

"I mean a mathematicus is coming. We must flee."

"Without the horses?" Jonas asked.

"My lord." The Eagle addressed Lord Berthold. "We must take with us everything that will reveal we were here lest we endanger these good and holy men. We must go at once."

"Liath is a mathematicus," said Ivar boldly, trying to get the man's attention. The smoke had clouded his brain; he could not remember the old Eagle's name.

"Very well," said Berthold. "At once. Odei. Jonas. Get our things." They raced off. "We need Brother Heribert, and Berda," he added to the Eagle.

"I'll fetch the good brother," said the old man.

"I'll meet you by the orchard gate, then," said Berthold. "I'll go at once to the lady's garden." The Eagle smiled, and the lord chuckled. "Yes, I beg you. One last glimpse at what is forbidden." His brief laugh sank into a scowl. "Yet it will make me think of Elene again." He rubbed his fingers together compulsively. "I will never be rid of her blood, Wolfhere. Never!"

"You did not kill her."

"I should have been stronger!"

"I pray you, my lord, remember that even she, an adept, was helpless. You are not to blame."

Berthold was younger than Ivar, with a way of shaking his head that made him appear passionate and headstrong, eager and bold; he shook himself all over, a young stallion champing at the bit, and plunged down the stairs. Wolfhere watched him stride away before walking back into the night. A monk hurried out of the chapel at the head of the procession and ran after Wolfhere. They consulted with heads bent together, although Ivar heard nothing except the rustle of robes and the shuffle of footsteps as Hersford's monks moved past him. Then the Eagle trotted away into the dark, and the monk flowed away in the stream of his brethren.

Ivar could not decide what to do.

Baldwin clattered down the steps and grabbed him by the arm. "Did you hear? The Holy Word of truth has reached this far! Even in this monastery they speak the righteous words of the Mother and Son. Truth rises with the phoenix!" He wiped away tears. He beamed, as the poets would say, and the last worshipers, leaving the hall, stared at him as they passed.

"Like an angel," they whispered as they scurried away.

"Some sorcerer has walked through the stone crown," said Ivar, waving toward the hill, now difficult to see against the blackening night. "It might be best if we don't wait around to see who it is."

"What do you mean?"

"An enemy, someone who will try to stop us. Come, let's see if Lord Berthold will let us travel with their party."

"Very well," said Baldwin compliantly.

They hurried after Lord Berthold and found the young lord standing beside the gate that opened into the enclosed garden where Father Ortulfus' pretty young cousin presided over that gaggle of noble ladies who had washed to shore at the monastery. The gate creaked open, and a young woman, hiding a smile behind a hand, let Baldwin in. Ivar squeezed in behind him. In the graveled courtyard, a table was set out under an awning and ringed by half a dozen tall tripods, each one supporting a burning lamp. Plain wooden bowls were set on the table beside several loaves of bread, still steaming from the oven, and a big pot that smelled very like dill-garnished porridge, nothing more elaborate. The cottages gleamed with a fresh coat of whitewash. The herb garden, glimpsed within the shadows, lay in trim boxes and rows.

"Oh!" said the serving girl, seeing Baldwin in the lamplight. With an effort, she looked past him toward the gate, which was opening again. "Here they come."

Ivar and Berthold turned to see a little procession enter through the gate, led by Ortulfus' cousin, the Lady Beatrix. There were five other persons with her, four in linen gowns like to hers and the last a stocky woman in foreign clothing and with features more like those of the Quman than of real people. As Ivar stared at this creature, Lady Beatrix approached with hands extended.

"Lord Berthold! Are you come to feast with us? We have been out among the refugees, giving what aid we can. Poor souls! We will pray for their safety, and for the safety of my cousin, Father Ortulfus. Did you hear? He has been taken prisoner by the Eika!"

This news she imparted with no sign of fear or grief, but more as if it were a reward granted to him.

"No meal, although I thank you, Lady," said Berthold with a rather shy smile. "We must depart in haste, I fear. I am come to take Berda away from you. We must ride out immediately."

"It is night!" she exclaimed prettily. "You may lose your footing and stumble . . ." She looked at Ivar, and it was obvious she had thought he was someone else—Jonas, perhaps—because she stumbled over a word, gaped at him, while around her, her ladies began to whisper each to the other with the fierce blast of intrigue.

"Oh!" she said, seeing Baldwin. She pressed a hand to her cheek. "Still among the living!"

Baldwin smiled prettily, but his interest had fixed on the untouched bread set on the table. Berthold had already collected the stocky woman, and they vanished out the gate.

"We have to leave," said Ivar, tugging on Baldwin's elbow.

"Oh!" cried the young ladies, circling in for the kill.

"Will you take bread, at least?" cried Lady Beatrix. She hastened toward the table, and before Ivar had quite pulled Baldwin out of the garden, she offered them each a loaf with her own hands.

"Thank you!" said Baldwin, grabbing both.

Ivar slammed the gate shut. "We must hurry!"

Baldwin tucked one loaf under an arm and tore off a hank of the other. The bread's insides had a cloudy, delicate look and a heavenly smell.

"This is good!" he said, and between mouthfuls, "horses might go lame . . . if keep riding . . . without new shoes."

"If we're captured here, we'll have no chance to alert Lady Sabella, or even Prince Sanglant."

Baldwin shrugged. "Aren't you going to have some?"

"Come on!"

Berthold and his companion had already crossed the green. Ivar ran after him and into the orchard, ducking under branches and twice detouring around encampments of refugees. He did not catch up to the others until they reached the orchard gate, where Berthold had halted to wait for the rest of his party to gather.

"It might be best, Lord Berthold, if my companion and I travel with you. We both wish to avoid the Eika."

"We seek the regnant," said Berthold curtly. "I have no wish to be captured by Lady Sabella, who once raised that evil woman to be biscop."

"Constance?"

"No! Antonia of Mainni."

"I don't know who you are talking about."

"Skopos now, or so she claims. She rules over a nest of vipers! Sabella can't be trusted if she once honored that awful woman! Ally to Hugh of Austra! A murderer! A foul maleficus!" Lord Berthold let loose such a tirade of filthy imprecations that Ivar blushed and looked away, and found himself staring at the stocky companion. She had the look of the Quman, but there was something indefinably different about her that Ivar could not identify. She wore a glittering headpiece, beads and gold sewn into a stiff, black fabric, and she had a strong jaw and broad cheekbones, big hands, and a stolid expression. She said nothing. It was not clear if she understand the flood of lurid curses, which did not cease until the rest of Berthold's group came up to meet them.

Besides Lord Jonas and the Quman man, a slender cleric attended patiently, almost absently, pausing under the canopy of a walnut tree. All carried saddlebags slung awkwardly over their shoulders. The Quman soldier handed two saddlebags to the silent woman. Wolfhere strode up with Prior Ratbold, heads bent together as they talked, and both looked up to count the people waiting beside the gate.

"We'll close all the gates after you've left," said Ratbold, repeating instructions, "and let no man in."

"Nor woman either," said Wolfhere.

"Who will carry the lamps?" asked Berthold. "Where are the horses?"

"No light," said Wolfhere. "And no horses."

"We must *walk?*" asked Jonas disbelievingly.

"How will we see?" asked Berthold.

"I know this path. My lord, the horses are nearly spent. Prior Ratbold has none to offer us. We'll go faster on foot because we can march night and day. We must move swiftly. The Eika will."

"The Eika have no horses," said Ivar. When everyone looked curiously at him, he added, "We saw their army. We were hidden in the trees, upwind. They didn't know we were there."

"My lord," said Wolfhere to Berthold. Berthold nodded, and, that quickly, their party left through the open gate.

Ivar's feet had grown roots; the wind played around him as branches rattled above and Prior Ratbold watched into the night beyond the gate.

"He never answered me," muttered Ivar.

"I beg your pardon?" Ratbold asked, without turning.

"I thought," said Ivar irritably, "that we might join together. Walk southeast together, for safety. Better if Baldwin and I wait for our horses to be reshod. . . . yet if what the Eagle says is true . . ."

"Go, or stay," said Ratbold. "I am about to close this gate, Brother Ivar. Then the choice will be made."

"We don't know the path," said Baldwin.

The others were already out of sight, because of the darkness, but Ivar heard their soft footfalls and a comment from Wolfhere.

"If you would go ahead, Brother Heribert. The night seems no hindrance to your eyes."

Ivar had a light kit slung over his back, a leather bottle half full of stream water, his sheathed knife, and the injured soldier's borrowed sword. The night was cool and dark and it smelled of greening, the first rush of spring, although it was summer by the calendar of feast days.

"What must we do?" asked Baldwin.

"I hate to leave the horses."

"I have a pouch of ale, the bread, and my knife," said Baldwin brightly.

"Choose," said Ratbold.

"What do you advise?" asked Ivar desperately.

Ratbold glanced in the direction where, years ago, Ivar and his companions had stumbled down off a hillside crowned with a stone circle. All lay dark along the horizon and in the high heavens. A campfire beyond the orchard had burned down to red coals. A distant lamp glimmered beside the main gate, and another lamp bobbed out on the green where someone walked.

"Best you go," said Ratbold. "We are better protected if you who are messengers for the noble folk who contest these lands do not sleep within our walls. Then we can claim honestly that we do not take sides in earthly contests."

"You changed your liturgy," said Baldwin suddenly.

"You pray to the Lady and Her Son. You have accepted the truth."

"We could not ignore the sign God sent us," said Ratbold.

The words troubled Ivar. He felt poked as with the butt of a spear. Be alert! His head told him one thing, but his gut told him another.

"Let's go," he said, knowing he had to take the leap or he would never move. "Before they're too far for us to catch up to them."

"But our supplies—!" objected Baldwin.

"Almost gone. The horses need a rest. It isn't far. We'll be safer with an Eagle to guide us and stout arms to fight by our side."

He crossed through the gate and, outside, turned back to see that Baldwin remained inside. "Are you coming or staying?"

"What if Hersford is attacked and we're not here to help them? We can't just abandon these poor folk, now that their abbot is stolen away from them!" He rubbed at the beard again, which fretted him. "I don't like traveling."

He was like a dog that has become accustomed to the leash.

"Then stay and do what you can for these brothers and refugees. I'll come back for you when all this is over."

"Ivar . . ."

"I'm not angry with you, Baldwin. But if I mean to go with those others, I must hurry, or I'll lose them."

"It might be best," muttered Ratbold.

Baldwin shoved both half and whole loaf into Ivar's arms, then wrestled with a hand and twisted off his lapis lazuli ring, the one he had claimed from the barrow. Shaking, he clutched Ivar's hand across the open gate and closed Ivar's fingers over the ring.

"Haven't we given this back and forth enough times?" Ivar asked, half laughing because he wanted also to cry.

"It will keep you safe."

"I'm closing the gate," said Ratbold. And then, "Hush! Do you hear?" The honking of geese swelled out of the night. "This is the wrong season for geese."

Baldwin jumped back, and the prior scraped the gate closed in Ivar's face. But he was poised now, ready to fly, and he found the path and walked as swiftly as he could, stumbling twice but able to see the path because it had a slightly lighter color than the ground to either side. He heard a cough, and where the path branched he heard a branch snap and a hissed complaint down along the right fork, and in this way he was able to follow them, although it seemed they were moving fast despite the dark night. Of the unseasonable geese, he heard no further sign. As he gained confidence in his footing, he increased his pace, and a dozen or more paces later he tripped over a foot and found himself facedown with a blade laid against his back.

He gasped into the dirt and choked out his name.

"Ivar? That one who just came, with the refugees?" That was a Wendish voice, thank God. "Let him up. What means this?"

"I pray you, let me travel with you."

The pressure of the blade eased. He rose to hands and knees, spitting dirt out of his mouth.

"Send him back," said Lord Berthold.

The Eagle knelt beside him as if examining his face or his weapons. "Nay, best let him come this way, with us."

"He's in league with Lady Sabella!" whispered Lord Berthold furiously.

"So can he be there in Hersford, or here with us, and if the latter, we can better keep an eye on him when he is with us."

"Ah, I see," said Berthold. "We'll take him to Prince Sanglant instead."

The Eagle rose and tapped Ivar on the shoulder. "Come, then, Brother. We're moving fast. Best you keep up with us, for if you're lost or stumble behind, we'll not wait."

3

"I offer you and your company sanctuary here at Quedlinhame for as long as necessary," said Mother Scholastica.

Rosvita was standing.

The abbess was sitting with her hands spread on the table, her posture rigid, and her mouth fixed in a flat line. "Do not follow my nephew. This is my command, Sister."

Rosvita nodded humbly. "I hear your words, Mother Scholastica. But I cannot obey. We will continue our journey in the morning, with or without your permission."

They were alone in the room, although the doors leading into the garden stood open. A nun weeded along a row of lavender not yet in bloom. Although the sky was entirely overcast, the light was bright enough to cast shadows stretching longer and longer as the afternoon crept by. Footsteps grated on a graveled path, and Sister Petra came into view, leading Sapientia as a shepherdess would lead a lamb.

"Is this rebellion?"

"I have always served Henry faithfully, Mother Scholastica."

Her mouth pinched. One hand balled into a fist. "Your reputation has been spotless, Sister Rosvita. Until now."

Rosvita remained silent.

"It is a disease, spread among you who rode south into Aosta. Among those who pledge loyalty to Sanglant. I begin to think it is sorcery."

"I pray you, Mother Scholastica. I respect and honor you. But I will not be insulted. Henry is—was—my regnant, and I served him faithfully. Now I will serve the one he named as heir."

"Sapientia?" the abbess asked wickedly as she turned to look out the open door into the summer garden. The walkers had vanished, but their step could still be heard, crunching softly and accompanied by the singsong of Petra's constant soothing chatter. "Henry named Sapientia as heir."

"He changed his mind. You have seen her and spoken to her. You can see as well as I can that she is not fit to rule."

"Perhaps. She may yet recover, if given time to rest. The story you have told me, about her ordeal, suggests that her brother left her in the wilderness to die. How does that make him fit to rule? We Wendish do not murder our kinfolk. We have enough trouble here without civil war."

"That being so, why did you then anoint and robe and crown Prince Sanglant and name him king?"

"I had no choice, at that time. 'Laws are silent in the presence of arms.' Witnesses claimed that Henry favored Sanglant—that he named him heir in Aosta. But it appears that Henry believed Sapientia to be dead, at that time. As did I. As did we all, until you brought her here, Sister Rosvita."

"Henry knew that Theophanu lived. He might have named her as his heir, but it appears he did not."

Mother Scholastica was a formidable woman, and her glare was that of an eagle ready to strike. Rosvita stood her ground; she did not fear her, although it might be more prudent to do so.

"I will not have this conversation again. I have taken steps to do what is best for the realm. You are well advised to choose carefully, at this time. Do not follow Sanglant, Sister Rosvita."

"I crave your pardon, Mother Scholastica. My road is set."

Like opposing armies battling to a standstill on a bridge, they had reached an impasse. Outside, the gardener began raking.

"So be it," said Scholastica in a cold voice. "Let the nuns from St. Valeria and their treasure of books remain here."

Rosvita wished fleetingly for a pen or a book, something to shift with her hands to bleed off the disquiet that made her fingers twitch and her ears burn. "What will become of the books?"

Scholastica's gaze flickered toward a letter folded and sealed with—strangely—the skopos' gold stamp, signifying the crown of holy stewardship. Underneath the letter rested a single book, wrapped in cloth, which Rosvita recognized as one taken from the chests brought from St. Valeria's. That yellowed cover with a torn corner had

belonged to *The Zephyr and the Tempest*, a book record-
ing the proscribed arts of the tempestari, the weather
workers.

The abbess shook her head, offering no answer. This was
to be an armed truce. Outside, the raking ceased, and water
splashed.

"The nuns and their treasure will remain here," the
abbess repeated, "and the old abbess. You can't expect her
to continue traveling. She is so frail."

"It's true it would be better for Mother Obligatia to rest,
but she will insist on accompanying me. You may speak to
her yourself."

"I will do so. You have forced my hand, Sister Rosvita. I
am displeased and angered. Because you insist on continuing on this road, I must travel with you to escort Princess
Sapientia. To see that she is not put at risk."

"What risk do you fear? That we intend to murder her?"
These impolitic words slipped out of her mouth before she
realized she intended to say them. She flushed.

"Is this my answer?" Scholastica asked, with cold irony.

"I am made weary by the long road we have traveled,
Mother Scholastica. Forgive my harsh words. She has survived much, these past months. So have we all. Had we
wished to see her come to harm, we could have disposed of
her at any place along our journey. We could have left her
to die in Dalmiaka. But we did not. We have cared for her
as well as we could. Many good servants have died on this
road—some of my own personal attendants among them—
seeing her brought to safety."

"We shall see." Scholastica touched the letter and flicked
one corner, as if making ready to open it, before pointedly
looking at Rosvita. "If you will leave me now, Sister."

Rosvita had suffered too much to go quietly. Her voice still
trembled, and she was still angry. "I pray you, Mother
Scholastica, let us be honest together. Do you escort Sapientia because you do not trust me?"

"You will deliver her to Sanglant."

"You cannot possibly believe that Sanglant would harm
her?"

Scholastica gestured toward the garden where, propitiously, the slack-faced Sapientia had come back into view as Petra coaxed her along. "He already has."

4

"HOLY MOTHER! I pray you! Wake up!"

The twilight had barely begun its transition toward day, so the servant held a lamp to lighten the gloom. Antonia did not scold her. Over the months she had bided in Novomo after the fall of Darre, she had purged her retinue of any servants who displeased her. Felicita would never disturb her without cause. They feared her, as all people must fear God and, thus, God's holy representative on Earth.

"What news?" She had the knack of coming instantly alert, without confusion.

Felicita was holding the lamp close to her own face, and her startled, wide eyes and parted lips betrayed her anxiety.

"An ill wind," added Antonia.

Felicita began to weep while struggling to speak. "I pray you, Holy Mother. I am so frightened!"

Too frightened to speak sensibly, the woman babbled of creatures with human bodies and animal heads, of a flashing wheel of gold, and of folk falling into a writhing, spitting death from the merest prick of a dart. Other servants, newly woken, brought robes and a belt and slippers and helped Antonia dress.

"Hush! Take me to the queen and her consort!"

Captain Falco appeared at the door to her suite and escorted her to Novomo's proud gate, a legacy of ancient days when the old Dariyans had founded the city as, so the story went, an outpost along the road that led north over the mountains into barbarian country. The captain said nothing, and she asked no questions, preferring to see for herself. Felicita trailed after, coughing out sobs and heaving great sighs as she fought to control her fear.

The weak always panicked. They were chaff, fated to be cast to the winds.

Folk walked abroad, calling and crying in the half light. Soldiers marched toward the walls, fastening on thick leather coats as they hurried. One dropped his spear and got kicked for his pains as he stumbled back to pick it up.

"Move! Move!"

Goats bawled from a courtyard. A horse neighed, and was answered by other nags. All over the town, dogs set up a wild clamor, howling and barking and yipping as though their ears hurt them.

Stairs set into the wall had to be climbed, and her feet ached and her back complained, but she mounted them step by step without uttering a word. Falco walked two steps behind. On the wall walk the queen leaned out, staring south. Her cloak billowed in the dawn breeze lifting out of the southeast. She was alone, but as Antonia reached the walk, she saw Lord Alexandros pacing back from the corner tower; he was too far away for her to see his face. The queen was drawn and anguished, and she clutched Antonia's hand as soon as the skopos drew near.

"What are we to do? What are we to do?"

"Hush, Your Majesty. You are overwrought."

"Look!"

Look!

In ancient days the Enemy whispered in the hearts of men, and men listened to these lies and found themselves so swollen with vile cravings that they bred with animals. This congress engendered monsters so grotesque in form and hideous in spirit that God flensed the Earth with a vast and terrible storm to drive the beasts forever out of the mortal world. So was it written in the Holy Verses.

How the world had fallen! What was once banished by God's pure and righteous power walked abroad again at the behest of the Enemy. The gates of the Pit had opened and disgorged foul creatures. No doubt they had crawled north out of the stinking wasteland that had once been the lush and bountiful plain of Dar.

"There are so many," said Adelheid.

The monsters waited in silence. They wore armor and

carried spears and swords and shields. Like animals, they strayed side to side, unable to hold firm ranks, but they walked on two feet in a mockery of humankind.

Alexandros swept up beside them. "I have a count obtained from a circuit of the walls. Fifteen centuries, more or less. In the old days I would call that a small force, easily beaten. If we arm every man in Novomo, we will outnumber them. They have miscalculated. They are too few."

"What are they?" Adelheid asked.

"Monsters," said Antonia. "Creatures of the Enemy. Abominations."

"They're human, wearing animal masks," said Alexandros, squinting his eye as he surveyed the besieging force. "They don't have numbers enough to hold a siege, so we should be able to send for help."

"Who will help us?" Adelheid asked.

"Folk must rally to support their skopos," said Antonia. The sight of so many warped faces—even if they were masks—nauseated her. Her throat burned.

In front of the walls sprawled the corpses of folk who had tried to flee the onslaught but had not reached the gates in time.

"If Novomo falls, they'll go on to attack others," said Alexandros, as if he had not heard her. "You must appeal to self-interest. Those who aid us, aid themselves. If they do not aid us, they are themselves fated to fall to this army."

"It's true." Adelheid's hunched shoulders straightened a little as she took heart from his considered words. "We must appoint messengers to ride as swiftly as they can."

"Immediately," said the general. He called Captain Falco, and the order was given and men sent running. "We'll send a second batch at nightfall. Meanwhile, your stewards must take control of all grain stores within the walls, and every well or cistern. A strict ration will be applied. Any who violate the law will be killed."

"Cast out," said Adelheid. "To the mercy of our enemy."

He nodded approvingly. "Yes, that is better." He gestured toward the corpses tumbled here and there in the fields around Novomo. A man lay on his back on the road.

A woman had fallen on her side, trying to protect a child, who was also dead. "They seem not to be taking prisoners or slaves."

Antonia watched this interplay, knowing herself ignored and dismissed. She fumed, but the general had captured Adelheid's attention and, increasingly, the queen ignored her, who ought to be first in her thoughts. Even the child liked him!

"From what direction did they come?" she asked.

"What do the guards on the wall say?" Adelheid asked the general, not looking at Antonia.

"From the southern road, out of the twilight before dawn. The watch say they saw sparks rise on the hill, a weaving of light, for half the night."

"Impossible!" cried Antonia so forcibly that both turned to regard her with surprise. "Clouds still conceal the sky. No one can weave the crowns if they cannot see the stars."

"Why do the guards tell me this tale, then?" he asked her.

"At night any manner of wisp may be seen, sometimes illusion drawn by the eye and sometimes a phantom called up by the Enemy to lure weak-minded folk to their doom."

"Yet here they are." Alexandros waved toward the massed army still shifting and moving as ranks filed away from the road to encircle the walls. "They will mass the main part of the force here before the gates. A thinner line will be deployed to watch, and to defend against skirmishes around the rest of the town. That is what I would do."

"If none come to our aid," said Adelheid, "what can we do to defeat them?"

"I will think," he said, and the queen smiled at him, hearing confidence in his words. Even Antonia was swayed. He had seen many years of war, and although he was an Arethousan and therefore untrustworthy, he was also trapped and might be expected to fight as a cornered lion.

In the east, a strange light rose along the hills, a color like that of blood diluted until it runs pink. Guards along the wall pointed, and a murmur swept the men standing nearby as they—as all of them—stared at a thing they had

not seen for months and had come to believe might never
appear again.

"That is the sun!" cried Adelheid. "An omen, surely!"

The clouds had thinned to nothing at the eastern horizon, and the sun flashed as its rim breached the horizon.
South, a haze veiled the lowlands. North, the rising hills
turned from black to gray as light swept the heavens.
Above, it was still cloudy, but all around, folk wept to see
the sun.

Antonia blinked, reminded of the day she had walked
free at long last from the prison beneath the rock of Ekatarina's Convent, where she had been held. As she grimaced,
shading her eyes, it seemed her vision sharpened. It
seemed she saw a golden wheel moving off the road and
into place along a low rise where grapevines were trained
along rail fences. It seemed a man with a human mask for
a face rode alongside the turning wheel. She knew him, although in truth he was too distant for her to make out his
features.

"That is Hugh of Austra," she said, finding that her voice
was cold and her heart hot. "He has betrayed us."

The name was only an abstraction to Lord General
Alexandros, but Adelheid wept fiercely and then, as the
storm passed, set her fists on the wall and stared as if her
gaze were killing arrows. No one in that army fell, but
movement rippled within the distant ranks surrounding
the golden wheel and a person came running out of their
ranks toward the gate.

"Hold! Let them approach!" called Alexandros.

The call was repeated along the wall.

A bedraggled, frightened man stumbled up to the gates.
His tunic was ripped and dirty. He had blood on his cheeks
and he cradled his right arm in his left hand.

"Let me in, I pray you!" he shrieked. He was obviously
a local farmer, scared out of his wits and in pain. "I beg
you! They spared me only so I could bring a message."

"It's a trick," said Adelheid. "They want us to open the
gates. They believe we will be merciful. Kill him."

Alexandros signaled with a hand, and a dozen archers
raised their bows and sighted.

"What message?" called the captain of the watch.

"Just this." The man sobbed hoarsely, and for a moment Antonia thought he would be unable to talk, but fear goaded him. He croaked out a muddled speech. "The ones . . . the Lost Ones they call themselves, come home, they say. Ai, God! God have mercy! Let me in, I pray you!"

"The message!" called the captain.

"Just this. Ai, God!" A glance over his shoulder proved him terrified. He huddled on his knees and stretched his hands toward the soldiers half seen on the wall. "That one, they call her who wears the feathered cloak, she is the leader among them. She is mother to a field of blood. So we see! So we see! All my kinfolk slaughtered . . ." He choked on his weeping. He collapsed forward onto his hands. To the south, past the hill on which stood the stone crown, smoke rose from a dozen conflagrations as the enemy moved out across the countryside.

"Sanglant!" muttered Adelheid. "These are his allies! His kinfolk!"

"Blood calls to blood," said Antonia. "Evil begats evil. He could never be trusted, after all."

The farmer struggled up to his knees, looking back again as though he expected the minions of the Enemy to ride down upon him. And were they not there, in truth? The Lost Ones had been banished from Earth because they were the creatures of the Enemy, and now the allies of the Enemy had collaborated in their return.

"Let me speak!" he gasped. "Let me in, I pray you. Help me!"

"Your message," repeated the captain. The archers had not shifted position. They were ready to loose.

"The feathered cloak sends this message. She wants peace between your kind and hers."

A few guardsmen snickered, but most held to silence.

"She wants peace, but she comes with a demand. Peace, between you, in exchange for one person." He trembled and coughed. He could, it seemed, barely scrounge up enough courage to go on. "The Holy Mother! She says, peace in exchange for the Holy Mother, who is a foul sorcerer and must be laid into death." He bawled and pounded fists on the ground. "Forgive me! I pray you! I am only sent to speak the words. Help me!"

"She fears the galla," said Adelheid. "But how comes she to know of them?" She turned to Antonia, and her frown was fearful and her bright eyes stricken with a kind of wildness. "How is Hugh of Austra still alive? You told me that he must be dead!"

"He can still be killed," said Antonia. "Give me a prisoner, some man who deserves death. Let me raise a galla! He is so close. He cannot avoid the Abyss, not now. Not here."

"Is this wise?" asked Alexandros. "A fearful thing, to kill a helpless man in front of the soldiers."

Adelheid nodded. "A fearful thing, indeed. The enemy will see what we are capable of. That will make them fear us!"

Below, the farmer at the gates wept and pleaded, creeping forward to pound at the closed gates. Adelheid called one of her sergeants, and he was sent to roust a prisoner out of the dungeon. As they waited, the sun rose and slipped behind the skin of clouds running along the horizon. The light changed to a high sheen like the reflection of lamplight off pearls, something higher than the dull gray of a cloudy day but less than direct sunlight. Still, it heartened Antonia that they had been dazzled even for so short a time. Wind and time and tide must wear away the veil of clouds, just as in the end evil is ground down by the weight of God's justice.

"What would you have us do with the messenger, Your Majesty?" asked the sergeant of the watch, sent by the captain to inquire.

"Do not open the gates," Adelheid said.

Alexandros said, "Leave him below. Then we can see what these Lost Ones do. If they kill him. If they spare him. If they ignore him. By their action, they speak to us of their nature and their plan."

The Lost Ones only waited, arrayed in ranks as they watched the walls and waited for a response.

The sergeant returned leading a wary, filthy prisoner, the worst sort of scum, a man with an unkempt beard and a rotten smell to him, unwashed, toothless, and pestered by flies and fleas. He'd scratched his arms raw in patches, and he could barely shuffle on bandy legs. With the butt of his spear, the sergeant forced him to his knees, and he whimpered, too weak to fight and too stupid to beg for mercy. But he was still living, and the living possessed the blood of life.

She always carried a knife on her. She never went anywhere without it. "Step back, and avert your gaze. All of you!"

"Yes, Holy Mother." The soldiers spoke with gratifying respect, and they moved away obediently.

Adelheid turned her back, but Alexandros only took a pair of steps to one side without looking away. No doubt he had seen worse things in the east, since the Arethousans were known to have a wicked lust for tormenting their captured enemies.

A knife is a fine and beautiful tool that can grant life or deal death with a single thrust. She knelt beside the man, whose fetid stink almost overwhelmed her until she closed her mind to it. She turned her face away and took in a deep breath of cleaner air and, turning back, shoved the blade up between his ribs.

He made a gurgling sound, and sagged, but her arms were strong enough to hold him and she had breath with which to speak.

"*Ahala shin ah rish amurru galla ashir ah luhish.* Let this blood draw forth the creature out of the other world. Come out, *galla*, for I bind you with unbreakable fetters. This blood which you must taste that I have spilled, makes you mine to command. I adjure you, in the name of the holy angels whose hearts dwell in righteousness, come out, and do as I bid you."

A shadow spilled into the light as a galla shuddered into being, called away from the other side. She twisted the blade. The man bled furiously as he slumped forward, bleating in a way that grated on her nerves. She dropped him and stepped away. Behind her, a soldier retched, and another began to cry in terror. The galla's darkness took on substance as it drank from the gushing stream of blood.

"I adjure you, *galla*, you will do as I command. Kill the man called Hugh of Austra."

A ripple ran through that towering darkness as her will took hold. It slipped through the stone battlements as through air. The air around it stank of the forge, and its voice rang like the blacksmith's hammer on steel.

Hugh of Austra.

It descended through the air in the manner of a feather floating free, coming to earth on the road only a few paces from the gate. The farmer panicked. Bolting, he scrambling to the right to escape it, yet the wind on which it scudded pushed it straight into his path. It glided over him, through him. The voice of bells swallowed his scream. Where it passed, bones clattered to the ground. A clamor rose from the enemy, howls of alarm, the beating of drums as against an evil curse, the blast of moaning horns that died away. There was Hugh, who did not move and who could not escape.

Glory to God on highest, who brings punishment down on those who simmer evil in their hearts!

"No one is safe from such sorcery," said Alexandros.

"No one," she agreed. "The galla cannot be harmed, only banished. They are implacable."

"You are the only sorcerer who knows how to raise them," he added.

She did not answer. Out from the ranks stepped a creature with the body of a woman, the head of a fox, and a bow that reached from head to knee. Even the Enemy desires beauty, and this creature had beauty in her form and her stance as she sighted and loosed. The arrow gleamed as it sped toward its target. Antonia cursed under her breath.

The galla did not veer to avoid the missile. Indeed, it seemed to shift to meet it. Where the arrow pierced, a void of pure black snapped open, and the galla sizzled and vanished, popped right out of existence, as if it had never touched this world.

"Fletched with the feather of a griffin," said Adelheid angrily. "He has outwitted you, Holy Mother."

"Griffin feathers are not easily come by. In time, he will use up his entire store, or become careless and wait too long to let his arrow fly. It is only a matter of time."

"So am I thinking," agreed General Lord Alexandros,

looking at her and her bloody knife. "Only a matter of time."

5

WITH Liutgard and five centuries of cavalry, their best men, Sanglant pressed at speed toward Kassel, leaving the rest of the army and the baggage train to travel as swiftly as they could. At midday one day midway through the month of Quadrii, they met scouts, a band of men loyal to the duchess who had fled the town and were camping in the woods and spying on the eastern road.

Their leader, called Adalbert, boasted a pair of gruesome scars on his face, and his left arm hung uselessly at his side. He wept, seeing Duchess Liutgard appear before him, and kissed her ducal ring as he swore fealty.

"Here is your regnant, come to drive the usurpers out of Fesse," Liutgard said, stepping aside to reveal Wendar's banner and Sanglant, who was still mounted.

They knelt and bowed their heads.

"You have served your lady well," said Sanglant, nodding to her to go on. He could see that she wanted no lengthy obeisance but rather swift news.

"What can you tell us?" she asked them.

"The usurpers hold the town, but no more territory than that. Even so, my lady, they only have troops enough to garrison the palace tower, although they keep a watch along the town wall and a guard at the gates. Many townsfolk have fled. Those who remain inside send news to us by way of peddlers and whores."

"What do these tell you?"

"The usurpers expect Duke Conrad and his army to relieve them. I don't know if it's true, but I do know they sent messengers west. We killed one man ourselves a fortnight ago."

"What of my daughter?"

"You know of the sad fate of your heir."

"So I have heard," she said grimly. "She stands within the comfort of the Chamber of Light, beyond our reach. What of Ermengard?"

He wiped away tears. "Still held hostage, my lady duchess. Many with her, who refused to run when they saw she was taken."

"Why does Conrad want Kassel?" Liutgard asked.

"He's casting a deeper net," said Sanglant. "Tallia is granddaughter of the Younger Arnulf. She also has claim to Varre twice over. Sabella seeks the throne so long denied her. If necessary, she'll take it through her daughter's body—and her daughter is now wed to Conrad."

"Henry should have killed Sabella after the first revolt!" said Liutgard. "He was too lenient!"

"Wendish do not murder their kinfolk, not even in the pursuit of power," said Sanglant mildly. "We are not Salians, Liutgard. Thank God."

Her smile was tight. "I will not hesitate to kill Sabella— or any who plotted the downfall of my house. If Ermengard is harmed—!"

"We must pray she is not." He turned to the waiting soldiers. "Is it best if we continue on this road, or is there a better vantage from which to spy out the land around Kassel?"

"We'll guide you, Your Majesty. My lady duchess. Best if you see what they've done, meaning to starve us out."

A trail branched off the main road. On this hunter's path they pressed through woodland single file. They were tremendously vulnerable, strung out in such a line and with the open vistas of beech forest offering little concealment, but Sanglant trusted to his instincts, and his instincts told him that the old and cunning Sergeant Adalbert could be trusted. At length the sergeant asked king and duchess to dismount and led them via a footpath to a clearing that opened up on a steep hillside where rain and wind had caused a massive slide. Broken trees had tumbled to the base of the steep hill, caught there all in heaps and splintered piles like so much wrack. The hillside had a slick, unstable look beyond the last rank of standing trees.

"Careful, not down there, past this line. That's where the ground gave way. But from here, if you hold fast to these trees as an anchor, you'll be safe."

"God have mercy." Liutgard had a hand hooked around the bole of a young ash and her feet fixed in the dirt. At the base of the slide, trees of every age and size had smashed into each other, some splintering and the biggest ones crushing the smaller beneath.

"See here, now," said the sergeant. "There is Kassel. Even from this distance, you can see what damage the autumn storm did her."

The town of Kassel lay at the foot of the low, isolated hill—more a bulge in the landscape—on which the palace and tower had been erected. The town was laid out in a square with two avenues set perpendicular to each other, dividing the habitation into four even quarters. An old wall, reasonably kept up, surrounded it, but it was obvious from this height that the town had long ago been larger and more densely populated. There was room within those old walls for vegetable gardens and an orchard as well as some pasture for cows, and although in the main part of the town houses clustered one up against the next near the inner gate that admitted folk to the palace hill, along the outer spaces many houses boasted a big fenced-in garden. Old paths and house foundations marked abandoned homes. Middens grew where once folk had lived up against the town wall. There were signs—hard to discern from this distance—that many halls and houses had lost roofs or had their walls smashed by falling timber. The only sign of scaffolding and repair lay along the town wall and up on the tower rise, where a steeply-pitched roof gaped, half covered by canvas.

"Did the damage from the autumn storm spread so far?" Liutgard demanded. "Did they not plant the fields this spring?"

The fields beyond Kassel's walls should have been green with early summer crops, but they had the reddish-brown stain of highland clay exposed to rain and wind.

"They did, my lady, rye and barley, as is customary. Even a few oats. But those men from Varre did trample the fields. See, there." He waved a hand but he could have been waving at anything. "We heard that they confiscated the grain stores and even burned some, but that last I just can't believe."

Sanglant's gaze had drifted back to the palace and tower on the hill. From this height, he could discern the footprints of more ancient structures where the newer buildings of the wooden palace and stone donjon overlapped the mark of ancient walls. Long ago a Dariyan outpost had stood here and before that a yet more ancient holding constructed with huge stones set in place, so the legend told, by daimones of the upper air. The Dariyans had worked with dressed stone blocks, so Heribert had instructed him, and it was easy to imagine a workforce of men hauling such manageable material up an incline. But massive stones could as easily have flown as been hauled, even on rollers; the story of the daimones building them with magic made as much sense as any other.

"Hoping for a miracle, some folk hung out the feast day streamers when first day of summer dawned," said the old sergeant.

"I can't make them out from here," said Liutgard. She looked at Sanglant. "How do we win back my city?"

He surveyed the valley of Kassel. On the east the steep rise of hills made a natural barrier, which had been breached in Dariyan times with a massive ramp constructed of rubble and faced with stone. "There the Hellweg emerges from the forest," he said, pointing to a scar in the forest cover where the ridge edge dipped lowest. "We'll be easily visible as we descend the ramp. There is no other reasonable route down into the valley. So if we ride straight in, they will certainly know in advance that we are coming. Sergeant, how many men hold the palace?"

"Perhaps a hundred."

"Even with the men we have, we'll be hard put to take the tower in a frontal attack," said Liutgard. "It's built to withstand a siege."

"Yet if we wait for the rest of the Varren army to come up, we'll find ourselves caught between the enemy at the heart of the town and that which surrounds us from without. I do not like to think of setting a siege only to be besieged myself. Is there some other way into the tower, Sergeant? A river gate? A crawling space where a small group of men can creep in to surprise the defenders?"

"Nay, Your Majesty. Not even a servant's gate."

Liutgard smiled thinly. "There is no traitor's gate, Cousin. My great-uncle Eberhard—the very one who gave up his claim to the throne in favor of the first Henry—had that tower built. He didn't trust his enemies."

"Or his allies, no doubt, who might wonder if he would take up arms against the new king. Well, then, we cannot sneak a contingent inside and open up the gates to let the rest of us through. Sergeant, have you any signals by which you communicate with your allies inside? Could any person be persuaded to open up the tower gates at a prearranged signal?"

The sergeant considered. "Folk in the town we can have some speech with, but there's a heavy guard at the town gate. As for those in the tower, there's none go in and out except the enemy."

Sanglant frowned. "If only we had Eagle's Sight, we could arrange our attack as we did at Walburg. Well, never mind it now. That avenue is closed to us. Can you smuggle in a score of men to assault the town gate and open it to us?"

"One or two at a time. It would take several days to manage it without being caught. But if we're caught, the enemy will know aught is afoot."

"And we haven't several days. So be it. I'm of a mind to try a parley."

"What of Ermengard?" asked the duchess. "I would gladly ransom myself for her."

"They'll not take you. If I hold Ermengard, I can sacrifice you and set your daughter in place with a regent. If they hold Ermengard, they hold your heir. I think they would rather have her than you, Liutgard. Still, it might be worth offering, to see what manner of men hold the tower."

They returned to the troop and continued down the trail, returning at length to the main route of the Hellweg lower down. When at length the road broke free of the forest, they had a breathtaking view of the valley and the immense ramp down which they must ride. A sentry standing watch on the high tower walk would easily spot the banners of Fesse, Wendar, and the black dragon on the height. He nodded at Fulk, and the captain commanded the soldiers forward, down into the valley. The ramp was amazingly solid, although its slopes had, over the years, grown a carpet of low ground cover and fragile grasses.

"We'll need to protect our flanks and rear so we aren't surprised by Conrad's army," said the king, and once they reached the base, Sergeant Adalbert guided them south toward the banks of the river where a tangle of scrub brush and coppices of ash grew alongside the watercourse. They rode over a trampled field dusty from lack of rain. Red dirt coated the legs of the horses.

From the town, a horn sounded three times. Sanglant sent scouts back to get a closer look. Their route dipped into a hollow, and they turned and rode west in this cover until one of the men appeared on the rise, waving one arm frantically but not riding down to them. Sanglant spurred his mount forward, with Captain Fulk, Hathui, and a brace of soldiers behind him.

"What news?" he called.

But as soon as he surmounted the rise, he saw what the scout had seen. He turned, gesturing toward Liutgard, and Captain Fulk raised the horn to his lips and sounded the advance.

A party of about a hundred riders exploded from Kassel's lower gate and galloped away across fields until they reached the west-wending road. They vanished, riding toward Varre. It was too far to catch them without the risk of falling into an ambush or meeting Conrad on the road where numbers would give the Varren army the advantage.

Liutgard rode up beside Sanglant. Her face was flushed and her expression fierce. "Kassel is ours!" she cried. "Taken without a fight!"

Sanglant frowned. "Hathui! Find Rufus—he's with us, is he not? Send him—send two Eagles, by different routes, and Sergeant Adalbert will provide guides for each one, in case they must take to the forest trails. Give them each a spare horse. They'll ride back to the main army. Tell them this: that we are settled into the tower of Kassel and will guard the town against imminent attack. They must proceed in haste, and with provisions sufficient for a siege, gathering anything they can along the route. It may also be that they will interrupt a siege laid in upon us by Conrad and Sabella. Go!"

"Your Majesty!" She rode away, calling for her Eagles.

"Fetch Lord Wichman," he said to Benedict.

"What are you thinking, Your Majesty?" asked Fulk.

Liutgard stared at the city, straining like a hound against the leash, eager to ride in to her home.

"We'll send Wichman and fifty riders north into the forest. It's fairly open beech wood there, is it not?" The sergeant nodded. "Well enough. He's accustomed to harassing the enemy. Let him wait in reserve. He can prowl the western road to ambush small parties and messengers. We'll give him some signal if we need him to attack in force once Conrad and Sabella arrive."

"Yes, Your Majesty."

"Can we not go, Sanglant!" demanded Liutgard. "I want to see my daughter."

Yet, after all, when they rode into a town ravaged by storm and parched by the enemy's raid, with a grateful population swarming onto the streets to greet them with hosannas and hallelujas, they found the tower deserted and Lady Ermengard gone. The enemy had taken her. She was Conrad's hostage now.

6

AT dusk, Captain Falco came to the chapel where, for most of the day, the skopos had led prayers to soothe the terrified schola. He accompanied her through the palace to the queen's chambers. Folk labored like ants anxious to put in their stores of food. Barrels brought up out of the town were being rolled into the lady's storehouse. Old men sharpened stakes in a courtyard, and a constant din floated up from the distant blacksmith's quarter. A pair of guards kept watch beside the cisterns while a trio of youths spilled water from full buckets into the waiting reservoir and, empty buckets dangling, trudged away to get more.

"This way, Holy Mother," said the captain.

In the outer chamber reserved for Adelheid's use, Lady Lavinia was speaking to a pair of stewards. Seeing Antonia, she bent and kissed the hand offered to her.

"Forgive me, Holy Mother," she said. "I must depart in haste. Certain matters have come up, as we prepare for this siege. They could attack at any moment."

"Is there news?" Antonia asked her. "Did the man we sent to offer a parley, did he return?"

Without answering, Lavinia nodded toward the closed doors that, when open, offered passage into the queen's innermost chamber. She excused herself again and hurried away. In the corner, Mathilda sat alone on a couch clutching a doll. She had her eyes closed, although she was not asleep. Her lips moved as she murmured under her breath, but Antonia could not hear her words.

Almost Antonia went to her, to soothe her and offer a prayer to strengthen her. Captain Falco opened the door and stood aside to allow her to enter. He closed the door behind her without following her inside.

In the inner chamber, Antonia found herself alone with Adelheid and Alexandros. A barred window looked over a garden of cypress hedges and sleepy lavender. Alexandros stood in profile, staring into the deepening twilight as Adelheid paced. He seemed preoccupied; indeed, he did not even acknowledge Antonia's entrance.

"You are come, Holy Mother," the queen said, her voice dull.

"Has the messenger returned?" Antonia asked. "What news of our offer for parley?"

Adelheid glanced at Alexandros, but his gaze did not shift from whatever he was staring at out in that garden. A

faint whiff of burning incense caught at her before trailing
away, lost in a sharper scent of anxiety and fear.

"Refused," she said in a low voice. "They sent the man
back with an arrow in his heart, dumped him outside our
gates. They will not negotiate."

"They are shrewd, these Ashioi." Alexandros spoke
without looking toward either woman. He mused in the
manner of a man speaking to himself, hoping that a passing angel might overhear him and stop to give him advice.
"They know the woods and the land. I believe that the
messengers we sent out at dawn may not have made it past
their guard. We cannot expect relief to come quickly, if at
all."

"They haven't the strength to sustain an attack on us,
surely," said Antonia. "I saw no siege engines. We are well
set up with provisions and water."

"It remains in our interest to end this with parley, not
blows." His fingers were hooked into his belt, perfectly
still, all of him still.

Only Adelheid paced, and her restlessness began to irritate Antonia, who walked over to the side table and picked
up an apple, the last one resting in a polished bowl. The
fruit was withered, out of last harvest's store, but when she
bit into it, the flavor remained sweet.

"Their demands are unconscionable in the eyes of God.
What do you suggest, Alexandros? Since they will not negotiate?"

Five paces brought him to the side table, next to her. She
had forgotten how fast a determined man moved. She did
not like that bulky presence next to her, so she slid around
the corner of the narrow table and shielded herself with
her back to the wall.

"It is only a matter of time," he said, following her.

His right hand snapped forward, and his fingers closed
around her throat. "Understand this, Holy Mother. I trust
swords, and I have good reason not to trust the women
who bind sorcery. I will not allow my life to hang from this
thread of your goodwill. You may take my life with any
change of the wind."

His fingers tightened. She released the apple, and heard its soft flesh splatter on the floor. With her left hand she grasped his forearm and pushed her nails into his flesh, but his grip did not waver. With her right, she groped for her eating knife and wiggled it out of its sheath, and struck for his side.

He twisted, caught her hand, and bent it back until the bones cracked in her wrist. The knife fell, ringing like a high bell where it hit cold floor. The pain blinded her, white hot and as sharp as steel, and at first she could not react, but she could hear with uncanny keenness as Adelheid began to murmur a prayer under her breath.

> *"God, make us strong.*
> *God, be a swift sword.*
> *Let justice fall heavily upon the wicked."*

He let her wrist fall and she heard the hiss of steel leaving its scabbard. Her sight flashed back. His long hunting dagger poised above her. Lamplight burnished its dark blade.

"In God's name, I command you—!" she gasped. "I am Holy Mother. This is—!"

"This is prudence," he remarked.

The dagger fell. It punctured the flesh between her breasts and rasped along bone until the point scraped against the stone wall behind her. Blood spilled along her skin. So much pain! She tried to tighten her grip on his arm, but it was too much effort. She was so weary, and wished only to lie down.

Adelheid's pretty voice caressed her with prayers.

> *"We will not turn away from You.*
> *Grant us Your help. Preserve our life."*

How had Alexandros corrupted her?

In the same manner the other men had, first Henry, then Hugh, and now this one-eyed, goat-footed, bristly monstrosity who called himself a lord although he was no more than a peasant's brat who had pulled himself to the top of a heap of dead men.

Brave words and brilliant eyes cozen a weak-willed woman. Adelheid had always been susceptible!

A pounding at the door shattered the prayer into a thousand shards. A voice shouted, loud enough to be heard through the thick door. "Your Majesty! My lord general! They attack!"

"Adelheid," he said.

"Oh, God," the queen said.

"She might have turned on us at any time."

"She is more powerful than we are. This is the only way to protect ourselves. There is much in the world we do not like that we must suffer because it is the only way to achieve the ends we seek."

Blood warmed Antonia. Her hearing remained keen and focused. These were Hugh's words, pouring from Adelheid's treacherous mouth. She tried to speak, to chastise the queen, but nothing came out.

"We give them her body," agreed Alexandros, "and they leave."

Antonia still had eyes. Adelheid glided away toward the door, but too quickly her form receded into a darkening distance, out of sight although she was almost close enough to spit on.

"Tell Captain Falco," he said to Adelheid, "to send this message. We meet their demand. Hurry! Of this act, speak to no person."

"She will betray you!" Antonia croaked, her voice nothing more than a whisper, but he heard her. He flinched. "She holds power over you, knowing you murder me. This she will use when she finds a new man to support her."

He grinned, the hateful creature. His breath stank of onions, sweetened by a touch of mint. "You are dead, old woman. What passes in the land of the living is out of your hands."

But he was wrong. He was so wrong.

He turned half away from her, not paying attention to her as he listened and looked toward Adelheid at the door.

She was failing fast, but she found her voice.

"Ahala shin ah rish amurru galla ashir ah luhish."

Her voice gurgled, and blood sputtered from her lips.

Her voice was almost without sound, too broken for him to hear, but the galla did not hear with ears of flesh.

"Let my blood draw forth the creature . . . out of the other world. Come out, *galla,* for I bind you with unbreakable fetters. This blood which you must taste . . . makes you mine to command. I adjure you, in the name of the holy angels whose hearts dwell in righteousness, come out, and do as I bid you."

He thought her already dead. He twisted the blade free with a casual turn and released her, stepping away. Her body slid to the marble floor, a restful place but cold.

I adjure you. No words passed her lips, but the galla heard. *Avenge me.*

A shadow loomed over her. Adelheid screamed, and Alexandros swore furiously and scrambled away from the killing touch of its black form. In the far distance, a door slammed open and shouts and the clatter of footsteps fell away.

As the tendrils of that darkness snaked forward, she felt these limbs seize on her blood. She felt its suck, draining her life as it filled the emptiness within. It had neither personality nor substance as she understood them; not fish or fowl, not male or female, not thinking and yet neither was it a dumb beast. It desired to fill itself with her because it had no real existence in this world, which to it was nothing but agony. Its wordless, soundless howl of pain consumed her.

Its killing caress also sharpened her mind and her heart.

The desire for revenge is a mortal failing. She must do God's work, here at the end. Adelheid is weak, but her child will rule after her; neither is a worthy target. Alexandros acts out of fear, because he is a treacherous Arethousan, corrupted by the false church and thereby willing to strike at the most holy skopos. The worst sort of criminal.

But he is still human.

Now that she has seen them, she knows that the abominations threaten God's order more than any other. Anne was right, after all. They were banished from Earth once. God cannot want them here, because they are a perversion. It is the Ashioi who must be harmed. They must be stopped, before anything else.

Hugh has joined them, but even Hugh is no more than a parasite, like the galla, sucking away the power that resides in others. The leader in the "feathered cloak" has no name that she knows. But there is one who does. One she tried to harm before, who might yet possess griffin arrows.

She must try.

God's work comes before all else, even before trifling thoughts of revenge. She herself is nothing compared to God's glory and God's justice.

"I adjure you."

She reached deep into the gash that opened into the other world, a place of terrible winds and unrelenting darkness. More came, a dozen, a score, crowding, eager for the blood. Her own blood—the most righteous—was sweetest to them.

I adjure you. Kill the man. The one. Who is called.

Sanglant.

X

A WELL-LAID TRAP

1

THEY used an old ruse, but it worked. With rope loosely bound around her hands, Liath walked with the young Ashioi woman called Sharp Edge in front and the four guards—Dog, Spotted Leopard, Buzzard, and Falcon—behind.

Secha wove the gate; she and Eldest Uncle would remain behind. The other seven crossed through sparks and the bright blue light of the aetherical gateway to another place. As her feet found earth again and the blue aether surrounding them faded to air, Liath glanced immediately toward the sky, but a dawn haze hid the heavens.

"What's this?" A dozen mask warriors approached. The perimeter was held by double ranks of bold soldiers.

"Two prisoners for Feather Cloak," said Sharp Edge tartly. She sauntered past with a sly smile. Every male there watched her go, amazed by the sway of her hips and the ripple of braid falling in a line down her half-naked back to brush the low-slung band of her skirt. She had a shocking amount of skin exposed, but the Ashioi were not, on the whole, a modest people.

Liath followed, head bowed but eyes lifted, and Anna walked behind her, frightened enough that Liath heard her panting. When they came safely past the outer line of the guard and started down the path that led to the base of the hill, Liath raised her head to survey the landscape. A town, ringed with a stone wall, nestled where the higher foothills broke into a rolling plain. All seemed quiet, but the gates were closed and there was no traffic in and out. A wide road, no doubt paved in the time of the Dariyan Empire, cut northward into the hills toward distant peaks, most shrouded in cloud. North beyond the reaches of Karrone and Wayland lay Wendar and Varre, closer now. She breathed in, wondering if she could discern any least change in the air, some hint of northern spice. They had in one "stride" crossed a vast region of land, all of Dalmiaka and much of eastern Aosta. Except for highland trees, the landscape was brown and gold, little different than the sere countryside of Ashioi country. It smelled of dust more than anything.

The Ashioi walked in Aosta, a land their half-breed descendants had once ruled. The Ashioi army led by Feather Cloak had laid in a siege around Novomo. They did not have quite enough soldiers to encircle the town, and no doubt the paths leading northward remained poorly guarded. But they were here, and Blessing was with them.

The small company tramped down to the main road and turned toward the town. A sparse woodland covered the slopes of nearby hills. Vineyards and olive trees ringed the town, among them small hamlets and long fields striped by sprouting grain. No one moved in field or village.

Anna moaned. "They've burned all those houses." She wept with fear. "Do you think they've killed everyone? They hate us."

"Maybe so," said Liath, "but 'they' do not all think alike, Anna. Some will help us. Some will wish to kill us. Do not despair. Consider Blessing, who will need your help."

"She won't come with us, my lady. She's training to be a soldier."

Sharp Edge, hearing their speech, dropped back to walk beside Liath. "Bright One, do you think your daughter will follow us? It's said that Zuangua, who is a bold leader and a very handsome man, I might add, has taken her under his wing."

"So I hear."

"She may not want to leave him. Then it will all be for nothing, if Feather Cloak takes you and kills you. I do not want to lose you. Without you, I will never have a chance to learn properly. The Pale Sun Dog hoards his knowledge. He'll never teach us everything he knows. He'll never trust us."

"It is a risk," Liath admitted. "But if I allow my daughter to remain with your people, then she will always be at war with her father's kin. She must not be allowed to be brought up by those who will always counsel war with humankind. If Secha were Feather Cloak, I might think differently."

"It is hard to imagine there can be peace with the Impatient One sitting on the Eagle Seat and Zuangua the Handsome—her own uncle!—as her chief councillor and war leader among the masks," admitted Sharp Edge. "But I am willing to try to get your daughter back. I will help you, and you will teach me. I don't see how I can get what I want any other way!"

Liath chuckled, although her mood was grim. "In this way, we are alike."

"Hush now!" said Dog Mask, who with Falcon Mask led the way. "See, there are human guardsmen standing along the walls of the town. But our own camp does not stir. I see sentries, but no flights of warriors ready to strike."

"There!" said Sharp Edge. "The war party is holding a convocation, there on that hill. Do you see their banners? Nay, stop here!"

They halted where the curve and height of the road gave them a good vantage. The camp spread across lower ground. Individual folk were easily visible among tents slung low along the earth. A procession led by Feather Cloak's spinning gold wheel broke free of the assembly and marched toward the gate, halting just beyond bowshot of the walls.

"There is Blessing," whispered Anna.

Liath scanned the folk in that procession. It was difficult for her to distinguish individuals at this distance, although Feather Cloak's vivid costume was remarkable from any distance. With a jolt that made her shudder, she saw Hugh's golden head. He was tallest, surrounded by a dozen tense mask warriors. He turned, staring back her way as if he knew she was there. A pair of masks broke away from his escort and trotted to Feather Cloak. They gave her a message, it seemed, and after a brief exchange they retreated at a run toward the main camp.

Where was Blessing? Belatedly, Liath saw a slender girl standing beside the proud warrior Zuangua. Yes, indeed, it would be difficult to drag Blessing from her place beside such an impressive uncle, there at the front of the lines. Blessing was old enough in body to be allowed conditional entry into the adult world, and young enough in mind to have no true understanding of its dangers and consequences.

"Above the gate!" said Dog Mask. "Look!"

Within Novomo, many people had gathered along the parapets and in the watchtowers set on either side of the gate, but there was no hostile movement, no shouting or cursing, only a sense of anticipation as they stared at the waiting Ashioi. A large sack was lifted onto the battlements. Wrapped in rope, it was lowered to the ground outside the gates. When the sack reached earth, the rope was released and tossed after it.

A trio of mask warriors dashed forward, grasped the sack, and hauled it back to the procession, whose ranks opened to receive it. Liath and the others could see nothing of what transpired, only that Hugh's golden head disappeared as if he had dropped down to examine the contents of the sack.

After a bit he reappeared.

"What would the Pale Dogs be throwing out of the city," asked Sharp Edge, "that Feather Cloak would be willing to receive?"

"It's hard to imagine."

The golden wheel, lifted by the standard-bearer, spun lazily as the procession split asunder, re-formed, and retired back toward camp. A conch shell blew a five-note pattern, repeated twice. At this signal, first a single tent, and then four, and then a score sagged and sank and were folded and rolled as the army began the business of lifting the siege.

"It's a body," said Sharp Edge, staring at the crumpled heap revealed on the ground by the retreat of the procession. They had abandoned the corpse. "The Pale Dogs gave a body to Feather Cloak. She must have gotten what she came for."

"The body of the sorcerer who sent the galla," said Liath softly. "Is there any person left who knows that secret?"

"You do not know how to call these creatures?"

"I do not. Perhaps Hugh of Austra knows."

"It would be good to kill such a man," remarked Sharp Edge. "I would do it myself." She grinned.

Liath laughed, not meaning to. The young woman was close to her in age, stubborn, fixed, blunt, and an unrepentant tease, comfortable in making males uncomfortable. As their gazes met, she felt an intense feeling of kinship similar to that she felt for Sorgatani.

"What must we do?" asked Sharp Edge. "My people are leaving. Should we follow them back to our country?"

"No. I must journey north, and I mean to take my daughter with me."

"What is your plan?"

"I'm not sure."

"We'll want shelter soon," said Dog Mask, always alert, his dark gaze sweeping in all directions. "Look how those clouds are coming down from the north."

"Storm clouds." Liath noted how swiftly the front was moving in, and how black its face was, and how high the dark clouds had piled one upon the next over the hills.

"Too late," said Sharp Edge. "A bundle of masks comes to intercept us."

A score of masks, mostly birds and cats, charged her group at a full run, ready to cut her off if she tried to escape.

"Now what will you do?" Sharp Edge asked. The four mask warriors looked expectantly at her.

"I will negotiate. And hope they possess no poisoned arrows."

*   *   *

They met beside the golden wheel, which spun in the brisk wind blowing down off the foothills. The clouds had not quite broken over the hills, but they would at any moment like a flood let loose. The air was charged; the hair on her arms tingled, and her eyes smarted.

There were many witnesses, but the only ones who mattered were Feather Cloak, Hugh, Zuangua, and Blessing. Her own attendants stood back ten paces, waiting for the signal they had agreed on.

"I did not send for you," Feather Cloak said, eyes narrowed with displeasure. "How and why are you come?"

"She escaped," said Hugh in a low voice.

"Impossible. No one can escape the Heart-of-the-World's-Beginning. Who freed you?"

"I freed myself. Give me my daughter and safe passage, and I will tell you how I did it."

"I won't go," said Blessing. "I don't want to go. I'm training to be a warrior!"

"Hush!" said Zuangua.

She snapped her mouth shut.

Feather Cloak shrugged mockingly. "I cannot force the child to go with you. You have fallen into a trap of your own making, Bright One." She glanced at Sharp Edge and the four mask warriors who accompanied Liath. "Those who aided you will be punished."

"Liathano is mine," said Hugh. "So you promised."

"Mine to give you when I am ready," retorted Feather Cloak, "and I am not ready." She beckoned. Two-score mask warriors closed in to trap them within the ring made by their bodies. "Guard these."

"This was not our agreement," said Hugh in an even lower voice, almost a whisper. He had hidden his hands in the folds of his robe, and the cloth shifted and rippled over them.

"The sorcerer who raised the galla is dead."

"So she is," he agreed, glancing toward Novomo's walls. Wind raced through the air and whipped his hair back. "She is no longer a threat."

"You are right to say so," said Feather Cloak. "I have been too cautious, too kind. No more. I will tolerate no more human sorcerers who can threaten me. Enough!" She raised both arms, tilted her palms to face the heavens. "Masks! Kill them!"

A shock passed through those mask warriors close enough to hear, like an intake of breath. Even Liath was too surprised to react immediately.

"Too late," said Hugh into this pause. "My trap is already sprung."

The storm front crashed down like waves breaking. The wind hit. Within the encampment, the gale uprooted stakes and sent the cloth of the shelters into a frenzy, blowing, curling, or torn loose to ripple away south. Thunder boomed, although Liath saw no flash of lightning. This was no natural storm.

"Get down!" she cried.

Her companions dropped flat.

She leaped toward Blessing. Lightning blinded her, striking so close that her skin seemed to rip off her body. She flew away from the strike, blasted sideways by its power, and smacked hard onto the earth. She blacked out.

Startled back into consciousness, her scalp buzzed.

Thunder roared. Without meaning to, she clapped her arms over her head, shut her eyes, and prayed. Even with her eyes shut, a second lightning strike flashed through her eyelids to leave streaks in her vision. The crack and boom that came after deafened her. When she wiped her running nose, she opened her eyes to see blood on her hand.

"Oh, God." She pushed up to hands and knees and with a curse struggled to her feet because she had to find Blessing. She had no idea how long she had been unconscious.

The Ashioi camp had dissolved into chaos as mask warriors raced to capture tents and gear blown to pieces by the wind, as others staggered for help because they were injured. She blinked rapidly to clear her vision of the jagged streaks etched into her sight. Her gaze tracked aimlessly over hillside and distant wall and jumbled field until with an effort she focused on what lay immediately around her.

The golden wheel burned. Smoke poured heavenward. All around her, the ground was scorched. A dozen bodies—two score—more—sprawled on the ground. They were charred husks, twisted and gnarled in grotesque figures, so blackened that their clothing and even their features had been burned off. The stench made her retch.

"Bright One!" Sharp Edge called at her ear, her voice like a whisper although it seemed clear from the stretch of her lips and the tightening of her eyes that she was shouting.

A shadow approached out of the north. A cloudburst raced toward them across the open ground, hammering into the dirt.

The rain struck.

Her companions pressed up beside her and spoke words, but she could not hear them over the pounding rain and the echo of thunder in her ears. She pushed into the ranks of the stunned onlookers.

Amazingly, Zuangua had survived. He was kneeling. Rain streamed down his body. Leaning on a spear, he cradled his left hand against his chest. His fingers were curled into a claw; streaks of weeping skin scored that arm. His neck was red and raw.

Seeing her movement, he looked up. As calmly as if he were greeting a long-expected friend, he shouted in a strong voice that penetrated her deafness. "So it happened in ancient days, when the Horse witch called lightning and struck down her captors, the blood knives. I saw it happen that day, as it happened this day. Is this your work, Li'at'-dano?"

"It is not." She would have grabbed him to shake him, but she could see any touch would overset his tenuous balance. "I am no weather worker. Are you all such fools to let a man like Hugh of Austra walk as your ally?"

"She was."

The body lying at his feet was blackened and distorted, the feathered cloak reduced to wisps of bright green and gold mixing into the sodden earth. Her throat burned, and her stomach rose, and she turned away, catching a hand against her stomach. Behind her, she heard one of her companions retching. Anna bawled.

"Where is my daughter?"

"Not among the dead. The Pale Sun Dog has taken her."

The rain lashed them. She sucked in air, but it tasted of ash and roasted flesh. She spat, but the flavor coated her tongue. She tried to catch rain in her mouth, but that only made the taste run down her throat, and she could not bear to swallow the ashes of the dead. There were at least a dozen dead and twice as many wounded. More, a hundred at least, stumbling, vomiting, mouths opening and closing with no sound she could hear, and one screaming in pain like a wounded rabbit, but the sound existed a hundred leagues from her, audible only because it was so high and so ghastly.

It was strange to discover that nothing could surprise her, not after that bolt called from the sky. She had always known Hugh capable of anything, limited only by the scope of his knowledge. While she walked the spheres, many years had passed on Earth; he had possessed Bernard's book, and other resources besides. He had studied with Anne and the Seven Sleepers. The laws of inheritance and custom had denied him power in the world of regnant and noble. Yet it wasn't true he had no power. He had reached for, and grasped, the only power available to him.

She touched the astrolabe tied to her belt. It was protected by a leather cover, slick beneath her fingers. Even clouds—even daylight—would not stop him from weaving the crown.

"Hai!" She turned her back on Zuangua. Buzzard Mask was vomiting, but hearing her voice he sat back, wiping his mouth although he still gagged and shuddered. She shouted. "Sharp Edge! All of you! We've been outmaneuvered. We'll run for the crown and catch him there."

"Wait!" Zuangua called.

She turned back. "Speak quickly."

His niece's twisted corpse held his gaze. "So briefly she came into her power. Now it is stripped from her and she returns to the earth which births us. Who will walk as Feather Cloak?" His smile was a challenge. "Will you, Bright One?"

"Don't mock me! Go to Secha, who led your people in exile. She is not a fool."

His expression and his smile were twisted because of the way his left side had been singed. Blisters were already forming along his arm and his cheek. "Secha has aided you. So has my brother. Some still listen to their words, but not many."

"Nay, better yet, send an envoy to Sanglant. Let there be peace between Ashioi and humankind."

He flicked his fingers in a sign of dismissal, as though casting away the evil eye. "I have had enough of humankind! Sanglant has made his bed among his father's people. We know where his heart lies. This one, the Pale Dog, he will betray you as he has betrayed all others."

"Yes."

"He wishes to be the last sorcerer known among humankind."

"Of course."

"He wants you to follow him. That's why he took your daughter."

"I know."

"Don't you fear him?"

"Not anymore. Enough! I am leaving. There is nothing more you can say to me."

"Let me go with you to avenge my niece." He stood and took a wavering step, followed by a stronger second and third. "A hundred mask warriors, scouts, trackers. He'll not expect you to come with a war party."

She had no time to argue. Sharp Edge and the others were ready to go. "Agreed. But if you cannot keep up, we'll leave you. And know this, your enemy is only Hugh of Austra. My countryfolk—Wendish and Varren—are not to be harmed."

"A truce only. Not an alliance."

"A truce only." She turned to her companions. "Quickly!"

She and her retinue broke into a run. Every step hurt, jarring up through her feet. Her entire body ached and burned, but she ran. Behind, his warriors fell in at the heels of her party, footsteps rumbling along the earth. They raced up the road, and with Zuangua behind them the Ashioi army fell away and did not challenge their passage.

The rain slackened, fading to a gentler, steadier shower. The storm had outpaced them. Lightning crackled above the hilltop among the stones, a half dozen furious strikes. While they were still too far away to interfere, she saw the archway of blue light blossom above the stones, threads pulling north. They ran panting up the long slope of the hill toward the crown, feet slipping along the chalk track. Mask warriors lay stunned or dead as rain washed along their bodies, red with blood and black with ash. Here, too, he had used lightning to clear his path. The smell of their dying was awful.

Even so, they came too late. As she sprinted out ahead of her companions to reach the weaving ground, the archway collapsed into a shower of sparks that not even the hissing rain could douse.

She stood there, panting, soaked through and furious, as the rest gathered around her. The smothering cloak cast over her hearing had begun to ease.

"He has escaped us!" cried Zuangua.

Sharp Edge said, "I watched, Bright One. I marked the angles, as well as I could."

Liath looked at her, and together—recklessly—they grinned. "I, too." She unhooked and lifted the astrolabe. "Like Hugh, we don't need clear skies, or night. Who is with me? I mean to leap now, or risk losing him."

Zuangua laughed through gritted teeth. How he kept his feet with those injuries she could not imagine. He was a very stubborn man. "We'll follow into the maw of death's grinning skull, if need be."

With her shuttle, Sharp Edge traced a pattern onto the sodden ground. The others stepped back, forming into disciplined ranks, as Liath began to weave.

2

IVAR had fallen asleep leaning against a fallen log when a boot prodded him awake. A second kick jolted him. The damp had soaked through to his rump. As he stood, cloth stuck to his skin, slowly peeling. Groaning, he brushed dirt off his calves and shook chaff off his fingers.

"Get on!" said Jonas, who possessed the boot. "We're moving. You walk ahead of me."

He trudged after the others, although the silent Quman guardsman—that horror!—brought up the rear, an implacable barrier. Even the Eagle seemed more fit than Ivar; the old man strode at the front, wary yet confident, as they pushed along a hunter's trail that unwound parallel to a merry brook tumbling over rocks and decaying branches drenched in moss. They kept to the brushy verge, since they walked through a predominantly beech forest and therefore had little enough cover should any soul spot them from afar. Birds chittered. A roly-poly brown animal scuttled away through leaves, and a moment later a splash sounded from the water.

Ai, God, he was so weary, but he kept one foot moving and then the next. The healer walked right in front of him. She carried a number of charms hung here and there, at her neck, her wrists, and sewn into the ankle of the weird leggings she wore which seemed woven and fitted all from a single piece of cloth. Some were beads and some polished wood, but others had a ghastly off-white color like beads carved from bone, and these cackled softly in time to her footsteps. He shuddered. Ahead of her went the cleric, so thin it was amazing he had the strength to walk, and before him Lord Berthold crowded up behind the Eagle. The green wood spread on all sides, a lacework of trees, shadows, and delicate light woven among the sedges hugging the ground.

"Are we near to Kassel yet?" asked Berthold.

"By nightfall we'll walk in through the gates, if they're open to us," said the Eagle.

"Think you we outpaced the Eika army?"

"I don't know. The road swings in a broad curve south around the deep forest and across a ford. Our route was shorter. We've kept up a strong pace. Perhaps. If Lady Fortune, and God, smile upon us."

"I have sores on my feet," said Jonas. Ivar glanced back at him, and in truth he was limping—favoring first one foot and then the other, like a man dancing on coals. "We should have kept the horses."

"Hush!" said Wolfhere.

They were all nervous and they were all tired, so when the *crack* exploded out in the far wood, they dropped like stones. It could have been a branch snapping off a tree, or a staff striking wood. A man's voice carried over an unknown distance. A horse blew, closer by.

"Into the bushes," said Wolfhere.

All rolled and scrambled into the tangle beside the stream. Twigs scraped across Ivar's face, and his right hand sank up to the wrist in a sink of mud. The rustling of their movement ceased, and they hid in silence. Leaves brushing at his face made his skin itch. Pray God, let these not be stinging nettles!

He heard a sneeze, but it did not come from any one of their party. Hoofbeats sounded, the creaks and coughs and jangle of a troop of horsemen passing near by, coming up from behind but not, it seemed, on the trail they were following. He dared not move his head. His hood had slipped, and the flash of red might draw the attention of any observant scout. Water seeped in around his sunken hand. A bird chirruped beside the flowing water. They did not move, and at length the noise of the troop faded.

Wolfhere shifted out of the brush, rose, and spoke. "We'll have to change direction. We can't risk running into them."

"Who were they?" asked Berthold. "My view was blocked by these damned branches."

"I did not have a good view, but in any case I saw no banner. Given that they're riding from the west, I must assume they are Conrad's men."

"Should we cross the stream and head south?" asked Berthold.

"That will bring us closer to the main road. We might be

caught between their main force and this scouting group. I think we must press north and see if we can swing around in a circle and avoid them that way."

The mud sucked and slurped as Ivar pulled his hand free. He crawled backward, stood, and wiped his hand on his tunic, which was already so caked with dust and dried mud that he shed it in flakes as he walked. He itched, but no blisters had broken out, so God had shown him this small mercy at least, that he had not hidden among the nettles.

They cut north off the path and trudged through the sparse field layer, spacing themselves a body's length apart so they might hide more easily behind the boles of trees should they spot armed men. It was a warm afternoon, with no wind, but not hot. Ivar had forgotten what it meant to be hot, just as he had begun to forget the nature of the sun in its glory, bright and fierce and blinding, like the angels. The servants of God—sun and moon and stars—were steadfast, never failing in their duty; he must serve likewise. He walked, and because he was tired, he fixed his gaze on his feet so he could keep from tripping over some small obstacle, a crumbling branch, a splintered stump, or a growth of sedge, now in flower. Everything was blooming late. It was hard to remember what he meant to do. Warn the noble commanders about the Eika attack, save Constance, find Hanna. He no longer particularly cared to what woman or man he gave his message. He just wanted a wash to ease the ache in his feet.

"Hush! Halt!" The Eagle raised a hand.

They staggered to a halt in their broken line. The old man looked east, and so did they all, hearing what he heard: the clash of arms, a man's high shout, and a great deal of crashing and cracking as men fought through the underbrush in the distance. Despite the open vista of beech forest, the rise and fall of the land hid the skirmish, but its ring and clamor sang clearly enough.

"Follow me!"

Wolfhere set off at a brisk walk north by northwest, heading away from the skirmish. They pushed through the low field layer easily, moving at a steady jog, and although

Ivar thought he would probably die as his thighs ached and trembled and his lungs burned, he refused to fall behind and be seen as less of a man than the others. Even the foreign woman loped as easily as a panther, never tiring.

Jonas tripped, and the Quman soldier—the others called him Odei, but Ivar could not bear to think of him as a human being with a name—swung down to help him up. All heads turned back to watch. Shapes moved in the distance as one flank of the melee whipped into view: A trio of mounted riders lashed their horses as half a dozen others pursued them.

Wolfhere swore. Ivar dropped to the ground and scrambled on hands and knees toward Wolfhere as the others hid in whatever cover they could find. Only the cleric stood, staring not at the fighting but at the treetops as though he were gazing toward an angel hidden within the trembling flash of leaves.

"Heribert!" Wolfhere grappled the cleric's legs, and they tumbled down together, but it was too late. The blow hit from an unexpected direction.

From the west came the pounding of footsteps and men panting as they closed in. "There! There!" they called. "Grab them! Give it up! Lay down your arms, and you'll be given quarter."

The riders had vanished into the wood, but as Ivar pushed up to kneel he found their party surrounded by a score of infantry, men whose tabards were blazoned with the stallion of Wayland and whose faces were streaked with dirt, as though they had tried to hide themselves in the forest cover by appearing as shadows and light. Each one carried a spear. All had bows and short swords. They were impressively armed.

"Move! Move!" said their leader. "We've been on your trail since yesterday. My lord duke wants a word with you."

"Damn," said Wolfhere as he rose. He looked around once as if he had a notion to cast magic into the air and confound their captors so that he and Berthold and the rest could escape. But he couldn't possibly do that.

"I've twisted my ankle," said Jonas sourly.

Wolfhere sighed, shoulders sagging. He glanced at

Berthold, and the young lord shook his head slightly. The other two—Odei and Berda—looked at Berthold, and the young lord lifted both hands, palms out and open, to show that it was, alas, time to surrender.

Conrad and Sabella had reached Kassel before them, but there was no sign of the Eika. The Varren tents circled two thirds of the valley, which was anchored to the north on a wide slope so steep that a recent avalanche had torn through the trees. In the broad valley, men chopped and hauled and hammered and dug siege works. Work was particularly busy along the eastern edge.

Ivar tried to estimate the number of Varren troops but could not. Beside him, Wolfhere spoke in a low voice to Berthold.

"More than ten centuries, my lord, but less than twenty. Yet see what banners rise above the citadel!" Behind Kassel's walls flew the Wendish banner, with eagle, lion, and dragon, and the Eagle of Fesse, together with a black dragon banner Ivar had never seen before. "Duchess Liutgard has returned. It must be true. Prince Sanglant has declared himself king."

"It was always Henry's wish, or at least so my father told me," said Berthold. "Although it was never to be spoken of. I think that's why Father wanted Waltharia to marry Sanglant. He had a good idea that she had a chance to become queen, and make his grandchildren royal."

"He meant her to rule both Wendar and Varre and the marchland?" Wolfhere asked.

"Nay. I think my father meant the margrave's ring to pass to me." When Berthold grinned at the old Eagle, Ivar sulked, wishing the youth liked him better. His cheerful nature and bold determination gave him the charisma usually only found in an older man. Yet Berthold ought to have passed as many years on Earth as Ivar had; it was only magic that had stolen so much time from both of them.

"Here, now," said the sergeant in charge of the men who had captured them. "Be quiet. Begging your pardon, my lord."

Men turned to stare as their bedraggled company

crossed fields and were herded into the outer reaches of the encampment. Two tents rose above the rest. One was striped red and gold and flew the banner of Arconia's guivre, while the other boasted pure gold cloth blazoned all around its sides with the stallion of Wayland, bold and strong. To the ground before these tents they were brought, and made to wait in the lengthening shadows while the sergeant went inside and came out again.

"My lord duke is out hunting," he said. In the distance they heard a chorus of cheers, and he looked up and in that instant his face opened to reveal all the loyalty and love he gave to his duke. "Well, here he comes. Get down now."

Berthold did not kneel, and so none of the others did, not even Ivar.

The procession arrived, two-score men in mail and helmets, with swords and spears tucked and ready.

"We gave that bastard a scare!" said the dark man Ivar recognized as the duke. He was laughing until he saw the prisoners, shorn of their weapons and strange to look on.

"Good God!" He tossed his helm to one of his attendants, swung down, and crossed to stand before the prisoners, surveying them with a sly smile. A trio of whippets loped up to lick his hands. "Good lord! You are Villam's son, the one that was lost. Can it be? What sorcery has restored you to the land of the living?"

"I was never dead," said Berthold stoutly. "In truth, Cousin, I think I might have slept under a stone crown for many years. What sorcery bound me I cannot say. This man, Lord Jonas, is the only one who survived of the six who accompanied me. I pray you, do you mean to make me your prisoner in this rough way? Surely we are kinsman!"

Conrad laughed. "Come inside, then, Cousin! I'll have drink and food brought. If you've been asleep for years, you must have developed a powerful thirst! Yet these others . . ." He stared for the longest time at Berda, shook his head, squinted at Odei, noted Brother Heribert, nodded at Wolfhere with the casual mark of a man acknowledging a servant he recognizes, and finally settled on Ivar. "Pull off that hood."

Grimly, Ivar obeyed.

"Ah, indeed, the rufus boy from the North Mark. You keep flitting in and out of my path. What is your name again?"

"Ivar, son of Count Harl of the North Mark and Countess Herlinda."

"Yes. Lord Berthold, you travel with a strange and puzzling retinue. A banished Eagle, a Quman barbarian, this . . . female person, whose origins I cannot account for, a cleric, and Lord Ivar who was last known to be dead. I am wondering how so many people who might long have been thought to be dead are walking on Earth like so many spirits roaming restlessly abroad at the Hallowing Tide."

"We are not dead, my lord," said Wolfhere. "I have news of your daughter, Lady Elene."

Like a hound catching a scent, Conrad went rigid. He dismounted, cast his reins to a groom, and trod right up to the Eagle until his height and breadth and stature overwhelmed the old man. The Eagle did not back down.

"She is dead," said Conrad. "So my mother promised me. Damn her."

"She is dead," agreed Wolfhere in a calm voice. He stood in the most relaxed posture imaginable, although Conrad loomed over him. "But not through your mother's agency. Duchess Meriam sheltered her from the backlash of the great weaving, and sent her home in my company. You may ask Lord Berthold, who will vouch that Elene came safely as far as Novomo, in Aosta. There, it is true, I failed her. It was Hugh of Austra who murdered her, when she was sleeping and helpless, and for no better reason than that he wanted no apprentice of Meriam's to challenge his knowledge of the magical arts."

Conrad was silent and still for so long that Ivar began to think he had gone into a trance, lost to the world, as grieving folk sometimes did. One of the dogs whined, tail arching down and ears flat as it caught its master's mood. Nearby, a man sawed at wood; a hammer pounded. Dirt cast from a shovel spattered on earth. A voice cursed, and a pair of men led a quartet of milk goats past on leashes, serenaded by goatish complaints. On their heels came another group of riders, who gave way as a silver-haired woman dismounted and strode over to Conrad.

"What is this I hear? Prisoners? Who are these?" She saw the old Eagle, recognized him, and laughed. "My father's faithful wolf, come back to bite—yet who means he to snap at? Is this Villam's brat? I thought him dead and lost!" She looked at the others, but when she examined Ivar, he saw her frown and, with a shrug, dismiss him. Thank God she hadn't recognized him!

"Come inside." Without further speech, Conrad plunged into his tent.

Ivar was herded inside with the others but forced to stand to one side along the canvas wall with a line of armed men so close behind him that the hilt of a sword pressed into one buttock. Conrad's tent was furnished with a pair of couches—difficult to transport—and a dozen chairs set on the ground scuffed to dirt. A girl sat on the single carpet, and its blue colors were far more brilliant than her scruffy clothing, which looked very like a servant's calf-length linen smock covered by a milite's well-worn tabard, belted but nevertheless so big on her that it hung in great awkward folds about her shoulders and hips. Seeing Lady Sabella, she rose and scuttled sideways to the chair where Conrad sat down. He noted her and put out an arm, and she melted into its shelter. From this fatherly refuge she stood as bravely as she could.

"She is a weapon," said Sabella.

"So have you said a dozen times since she fell into our hands," said Conrad easily, without shifting.

"Liutgard will want her back. This is now her heir, since it appears that the elder girl really is dead."

Conrad's right eye shuttered slightly, his mouth winced, and then he recovered. "I'll not use Lady Ermengard as a pawn. I'll assign men to escort her back to Autun for the time being. She can be fostered with Berry."

"You're sentimental and a fool, Conrad. Once this girl is dead, Liutgard has no living heirs. Queen Conradina's line will vanish once and for all time if Liutgard does not hereafter remarry and reproduce. Then Fesse is thrown into disorder."

That his tone remained calm made the duke seem suddenly quite dangerous. "I won't allow this girl to be murdered. If I must, I'll send her to Bederbor."

"Best not," said Ivar, prodded by a sudden sympathy for the frightened girl. She could not be more than thirteen or fifteen. "The road west is no longer safe."

That got their attention, although he hadn't meant to do so quite so dramatically.

Sabella swung round to glare at him. He squirmed, but he dared not move. "What do you mean?" she demanded. Then she peered at him as if she were shortsighted. "Don't I know you? You look familiar."

He saw by her expression that she could not place him. Conrad laughed.

"Don't you know this rufus bird? He flocked with that prettily plumaged creature you kept in your cage but which escaped you."

"Have done, Conrad! Do not mock me!"

He grinned.

A horn blared outside, and men shouted. Conrad jumped to his feet and set the girl aside as the entry was swept open and a captain strode in accompanied by a travel-worn scout. The man's left arm was bandaged, and the bandage stained with dried blood.

"My lord duke. My lady." The scout knelt. "Riders coming out of the east. They fly the banner of Saony."

"Rotrudis is dead," said Sabella.

Conrad nodded. "These must be her daughters, riding in support of Sanglant."

The scout continued. "They are a half day—if not less—from Kassel. If they camp at dusk on the road, then they'll reach here by midday tomorrow."

"What numbers?" asked Conrad.

"I could gain no good estimate, my lord. I had no opportunity to get around their flank. The woodland road restricted my view. But a good number."

" 'A good number' can signify a score, or two thousand," said Sabella with a sneer. "Can you give no better idea than that?"

"I beg your pardon, my lady. I sent other men into the

woods to spy out their numbers, but none of them have returned. Lady Theophanu will have her own scouts."

"An unknown number bide inside Kassel," said Conrad. "Our army caught between. Do we break the siege and retreat?"

"No," said Sabella, "we make our stand. We have good defenses. The north is impassable. The eastern hills are steep, and we control the ramp and, thus, the Hellweg. The south and west are ours. Our position is stronger than his."

He nodded. "It's true, especially now that we've received word from Mother Scholastica that she will put no impediment in our path."

"Should we defeat Sanglant," returned Sabella scornfully. "My aunt risks nothing."

"Perhaps not." He laughed. "The well-being of the souls of every person living in Wendar and Varre must be her first concern. In this manner, the displeasure of the church aids our cause."

"Why does that amuse you, Conrad?"

"Because my blessed mother began her life as an infidel."

"And departed it as a God-fearing woman of unimpeachable reputation."

"Well," he said tightly, "let's not speak of my mother. Our position is strong, and despite everything I must suppose we may even outnumber him."

"Think you so?"

"If Sanglant does not trust Mother Scholastica, and I doubt he does, he will have left behind a contingent to support his claim where rivals may hope to discredit him at her court."

"Think you so?" asked Sabella.

"I am sure of it. She is a strategist, just as I am. She'll have made sure to let him know she can't be trusted. In any case, he can't have ridden so far and so quickly with a large army. And if he has marched all the way north from Aosta, and with soldiers who spent three years in the south with Henry, he'll have lost many of his veterans—not just those who died, but those milites who demand to return home at once to care for their farms and estates."

"Then it seems our victory is assured."

"Perhaps not. Here, in Kassel, we will be forced to protect ourselves against a double siege. Because once this new force arrives, they will strike us behind while the others attack from the front. Despite superior numbers, we'll be hard-pressed to hold them off."

"Now you seem to be arguing that we cannot win."

"Not at all. Sanglant cannot hold forever. Once the nobles see him impotent in the face of opposition, their support will waver. They want no bastard to rule them. He'll have to give up."

"Yes, that will work," agreed Sabella. "Sanglant cannot defeat us once church and nobles both come over to our side."

"That's right. In the end, he will lose." Conrad nodded, then looked at Ivar. "What did you mean, that the road west is no longer safe? Do you mean Lord Wichman's men, out harrying us in the north? We skirmished with them today, the bastards."

Wolfhere said nothing. Lord Berthold glanced at each of his attendants; no other words passed between them. It was a conspiracy of silence, an unspoken agreement to support Sanglant over the Varren usurpers.

Ivar thought abruptly of Hanna. She would follow King Henry's wishes, wouldn't she?

"That's right," he said. "That's how we were caught, falling into the flanks of the melee."

"Three-score men will not harm us. I'm more worried about Sanglant's reserve coming out of the east in unknown numbers. Here, now. Captain! Take these men away and place them under guard. Give them drink and food. Keep them safe."

Their guards escorted them past men busy hauling dirt and sawing wood and raising a hasty palisade along the encampment. Not one said a word more until they were prodded into an old byre standing in a farmstead now abandoned and in disrepair. They kicked aside the remains of filthy straw to find the good honest dirt beneath and, tucked away in one corner, a desiccated nest that was the last resting place of a family of dead mice, seven of them exactly, like their own sorry company. Bread, cheese, and ale were brought to the gate. Guardsmen paced outside, talking in low voices about what was known and what was only rumored. A man sang a hymn, joined by a second voice. It was getting dark, the light melting into the long summer twilight.

"Here, Brother Heribert, you must eat." Wolfhere guided the cleric through his meal patiently. A bite, chew, swallow. A sip of ale. A bite, chew, swallow. "You must keep up your strength."

"We are close now," said the cleric. "Why do we not go on?"

"We are prisoners, Brother. We are set in a cage, here."

"A cage," the cleric repeated thoughtfully, or stupidly. Ivar could not tell which.

He leaned to speak to Berthold. "What is wrong with him?"

"Brother Heribert? He's never been the same—well, so the others said who knew him—after we came out of the earth up in the Alfar Mountains. He was buried in a slide of earth, but we dug him out. He vanished from Novomo after Hugh of Austra murdered Lady Elene. I thought perhaps he had run off with Hugh the Bastard, but we found him much later, at St. Barnaria's rest house, up on the pass as we crossed north. He was starving, for he never knew to eat, so I suppose some evil humor has disordered his mind. I wish I knew how he escaped, the night Hugh of Austra murdered Elene, and kidnapped the brat. But he won't—or can't—tell us."

Wolfhere squatted beside them, nodding toward the oblivious Heribert, who was now counting and recounting the dead mice. Jonas grabbed the nest out of his hands and tossed it into another corner. Heribert made no protest but merely turned his gaze to stare at the weathered and cracking boards, as if he could see the wind itself as it brushed through the gaps in the byre's walls.

"Poor creature," the Eagle said. "He was a loyal companion to Sanglant."

"So are we, are we not?" Ivar hesitated and glanced around but none of their guards stood within earshot.

"None of us said anything. Now Conrad and Sabella will not know until too late that the Eika are coming."

"They have scouts and spies and outriders, all on alert," said Berthold. "Listen, Wolfhere. How can we get news of the Eika to Sanglant? Or to his reserve army? They will be walking into the Eika trap as well."

"If I had not lost my Eagle's Sight . . . well, that is gone."

"There is one other thing." Berthold pressed an open hand over his tunic, patted his chest. "The writ of excommunication I carry here. If it's true that Mother Scholastica no longer supports Sanglant, then this will bolster Conrad and Sabella's claim."

"By their words, it seems if they may already know."

"Yet if they don't? What must we do, Wolfhere? Once they know, once the news gets out . . . maybe, after all, I should burn it!"

"Rash words!"

"Do you think that woman is the rightful skopos? That God have anointed her? I do not!"

"I pray you, Lord Berthold! Do not imperil your soul!"

"I don't care! I know what she is, and I don't care. I don't fear her. I hate her! I hate all of them, all the Aostans who imprisoned us and let Elene die! Let them all rot! Let them all fall into the Pit!"

"My lord Berthold! I pray you!"

His attendants gathered around him to soothe him as he raved, speaking of the one called Elene, letting his grief and anger fall as tears. The cleric watched with an expression of dumb curiosity. The Eagle sighed. But Ivar rose, and paced, and halted at last before the Eagle.

"You carry a writ of excommunication? From the skopos in Darre?"

"A new skopos. The elder—Anne—she who came before—" A speck of dirt had gotten into Wolfhere's eye and he had to cry a few tears and rub with a finger to pry it out. "Holy Mother Anne is dead. This new one was biscop of Mainni in the days before, called Antonia. She was sent south to stand trial before the skopos—that would be Holy Mother Clementia, in those days—on the charge of malefic sorcery."

"What does the writ say?"

"All of Wendar and Varre will be placed under anathema if Sanglant is anointed and crowned as regnant."

"Why?"

"Because he is a bastard," said Wolfhere in a calm voice, "and because his mother's people are heathens and savages, their blood not fit to rule a godly people like the Wendish. Because some say he killed Henry—that he is a patricide."

"Surely if Conrad and Sabella had this writ, they would want word of it to reach Sanglant? You heard what they said about Mother Scholastica. She has turned against the prince. If one of us was able to convince them to let us carry it there, then we could warn Sanglant about the Eika. Otherwise, you might as well burn it. Then no one will know."

"No use," said Berthold wearily. "Other messengers will have been sent. Clerics. Presbyters. Soon the news will reach Mother Scholastica and all the biscops and church elders. Maybe you're right, and it already has. It still seems to me that it's best that Sanglant find out sooner rather than later. Even if it means he must give up the throne to Lady Sabella or Duke Conrad."

"He'll have to give up the throne," said Ivar. "He can't be so stubborn as to cast the entire country into—"

Wolfhere laughed in a way that made Ivar flinch. "A stubborner man I have never met."

"Either way," persisted Ivar, "if he knows now, he'll be able to offer Conrad and Sabella a truce, so together they can fight the Eika."

"Fairly spoken words," agreed Wolfhere. "Let me scout, see what weaknesses this camp has."

"Do you mean to speak to Conrad and Sabella?" asked Berthold.

"No. The rest of you stay here until I return. Be ready to move at the least signal. Fly east or north, if you must run. Do not let Conrad or Sabella intimidate you, should they happen to call for you before I am come back. If the Eika attack, seek Kassel's walls and pray that friendly hands let you in."

Berthold nodded, but Ivar rose in protest.

"At least one of us must come with you."

"None of you can walk out of here without being captured. Not as I can. Lord Berthold, I pray you. Let me take the writ. It is possible I will break through. I can deliver it to Sanglant."

"That will make him love you more!" said Berthold with a laugh as he drew a length of carefully wrapped cloth out of his tunic and gave it to Wolfhere.

"Go to the gate and make some noise. Draw the attention of the guards, but not so much that they come inside. Sing, or joke with them. Ask for more ale."

"Jonas, with me," said Berthold. "Odei, finish off the rest of that wine sack."

Odei grinned, and guzzled.

They crowded up to the gate, hanging over the rail as Berthold called in a cheerful voice. "I beg you, friends! A little more wine, if you will! We've been walking days with nothing but stream water to drink, and you know what that does to a man! My companions are perishing of thirst. And if you have an accommodating woman in camp, we wouldn't mind a taste of that sweet wine as well."

"Oh, God," murmured Ivar, and just then he realized that Wolfhere was gone.

"Are we all going now?" asked Brother Heribert, rising to his knees.

Ivar dove forward and grasped the man before he could ruin their plan. "Nay, nay, Brother. Hold tight. We're to hold tight here. That's our work."

"Got a redheaded woman?" Jonas was asking, loud enough that any man within a hundred paces could hear him. "I hear they spit fire, hot in the bed, but I admit I've never tried one myself."

An older man's voice answered, close at hand. "Look at your face, lad! I'd wager you've never bedded a lass in your short life!" He and his fellows chortled with laughter as Jonas protested heatedly.

"But he is close. I must go with the other man, with the wolf. Why did he not wait for me?"

Ivar tightened his hands over the cleric's slender wrists. They were as small as a child's. The man was so thin it was a miracle he could walk, and that weird, intense gaze gave Ivar the shudders. In the dusk, the cleric's blue eyes seemed almost to burn on a wick flaring deep within.

"If we go, we'll be captured and put in a worse cage. We must wait here until it is our time to act. Lady Sabella is holding us prisoner."

"Who is Lady Sabella?"

"She is the lady who spoke to us, and to Duke Conrad. The noblewoman. Henry's half sister. She is Prince Sanglant's enemy."

"I must find the one I love. I must find the one called Sanglant. How can I reach him? He is close! The other one, the wolf, he is going there, to him."

"Only Lady Sabella can release us."

"Ah!" Heribert's mouth opened as though he were surprised.

A cold breeze snaked through Ivar's hair. Heribert's weight collapsed in his arms, and he fell backward.

"God! God!" he cried, half caught and panicking before he twisted the man in his grasp and laid him down on the earth.

"Ivar! We'll pray in a moment!" That was Berthold, who turned back to the guards. "Nay, never mind him. He's a frater, you know, a novice monk, and the fight today made him piss his pants. Any little thing sets him to shrieking!"

They all laughed, but Ivar still held Brother Heribert's cooling wrist in his own warm hand. Something was very wrong. His heart hammered, and he could not catch his breath, but after all, that pounding was only the sound of men still at work in the twilight as they readied their siege works.

Unexpectedly, the steppe woman knelt beside him and bent over the limp body. She pressed her face up against that pale mouth; she sniffed at his eyes, his throat, and his loins. She placed one hand on his abdomen and another at his breastbone and for a while sat in perfect stillness and with eyes closed as the jawing of Lord Berthold and his new friends went on and on. So close, Ivar noticed her musky scent, which was not the complicated spice he associated with women.

She opened her eyes and sat back. "He is dead."

Ivar choked. "Dead? Just like that?"

"No breath. The spirit—what word, it was taught me by the old shaman of the wolf clan—no spirit *animates* this body. The spirit run away. Heri-bert is dead."

That wind came up again, curling around Ivar's neck. The frater jerked, shuddered, and sat upright so quickly that his head slammed into Ivar's chin.

Ivar screamed. By the gate, Berthold and Jonas broke into loud gales of laughter, slapping each other on the back.

Heribert shook his head, as a man shakes water out of his ears after swimming. "He said to wait here until he returns."

Berda scooted away and made signs, as against the evil eye. "Bad magic," she breathed in her heavy voice. "This is very bad."

Ivar tasted blood on his tongue where he had bit himself. The cleric looked at him as if he smelled the iron tang of that blood, but turned away to search, in the corner, for the nest of dead mice.

3

THE road from Quedlinhame to Kassel was broad and smooth and in normal times it was heavily traveled. Hanna had ridden it several times, and she recognized any number of landmarks over the next days as they marched. What she did not see was any traffic on the road. In the summer, merchants and pilgrims at the least should have been traveling the Hellweg.

So it was with some surprise that in the middle of one morning, after many days of travel through empty or abandoned lands, they spotted outriders down a long straight stretch, waiting for them.

"Those are Saony scouts, Theophanu's soldiers," said Brother Fortunatus, who had eyesight as keen as an archer's.

The captain of their armed troop, riding beside him, agreed. "That's Saony's mark, all right. They've seen us."

He called out an alert to his men, and they slowed to a cautious walk as swords and spears were readied.

The outriders proved equally cautious. Two turned and rode away at a gallop, vanishing into the forest shadow, while a single man rode toward them at a trot. He halted just out of arrow shot and under the overarching spread of an old oak whose stout branches sheltered half the road. A wise position, shielding him somewhat from loosed arrow or cast spear. Here, to the east of Kassel, the forest boasted ancient oak and holm amid thick underbrush, with only a few of the slender beech which dominated farther west.

"To which regnant do you hold allegiance?" he called across the gap.

Hanna looked at the cleric and the abbess who led them, and beyond them to Princess Sapientia, who was holding a green leaf in her hand and staring at its flicker as the wind tried to tug it out of her grasp. The Lions marched as the rear guard, protecting the wagons and Mother Obligatia; she couldn't see them over the riders who formed the abbess' guard and the dozen monastics who followed on mules.

"Let me go," she said. Before either woman could answer —indeed, in the last several days, they had barely spoken to each other—she rode away from her company and over to the scout, who waited for her with a look of relief.

"I'm an Eagle," she said, and he said, "So you are," marking her badge and cloak.

"I'm called Hanna."

"Peter, after the disciple," he said as if it were all one name and commonly spoken that way.

"Well met, then, Peter. You're out of Saony."

"With Theophanu, duke of Saony," he said. "Marching west."

"We are come from Quedlinhame, and from farther away yet than that, but it's a complicated story."

"Those are the best kind, told in winter around the hearth fire."

"With all the wild beasts held at bay by stout doors."

A grin flickered. He nodded toward the distant company. "Those are church folk."

"Yes, all come to join King Sanglant at Kassel."

He nodded. "You'll be meeting him with some difficulty, then. We are stuck here, just at the edge of the valley. Lady Sabella and Duke Conrad have set a siege around Kassel, and we must siege them in our turn and hope to coordinate our attack with those holed up inside the town."

"Where is the king? Wasn't Duchess Liutgard with him?"

"They are inside Kassel. With five hundred men."

"Ah."

"I've sent my scouts back to let our lady know your troop is coming, so we wouldn't be surprised. You've a score or more fighting men there."

"And twoscore Lions, marching in the rear guard."

He gave her a heartfelt grin. "Well met, indeed, Eagle. I'll lead your party in."

"Let me follow the other scouts," she said, "and you return with our company."

He began to object, but she rode off quickly so she could not be stopped. She had to get to Theophanu first, before Mother Scholastica could drop this sword—called Sapientia—into Theophanu's lap without warning. Hanna did not understand how the currents swirled in this river, but like all the rest of the old company come so far out of the south, she placed her faith in Sister Rosvita. It was obvious that Rosvita and Scholastica were at odds.

The other riders had bolted so fast that she saw only their hoofprints, but no other sign. She rode through quiet forest, noises fading away around her, and wondered how far she had to go and where Duke Conrad and Lady Sabella's scouts might roam. A few birds chirped; it was a relief to hear them. If there was game abroad, it was drowsing in the early afternoon warmth, such as it was. She had yet to be warm enough to take off her cloak, and she had begun to think she never would be. But it was warm enough that she pushed down her hood and let the cool breeze brush along her hair.

She shivered, but not because of the wind. Something was watching. She felt the pressure of other eyes. Scanning the foliage, she saw nothing. But with a second look, she saw a flash of white. And there it was.

A creature stared at her from the cover of a screen of high bushes. It had hair as pale white as her own, skin the color of iron and eyes as black as those of a crow, slick and sharp as it waited to scavenge.

It saw her, seeing it. They shared that look, and she went cold and then hot. Fear choked her, and yet for some reason she kept to that steady walk as if to change pace would be to jolt her held breath into a scream.

The road curved. She lost sight of the veil of leaves behind which it hid.

Why did it not kill me?

Losing her courage, she urged her mount into a gallop, easy to do, since the horse caught her fear and ran. After a bit, when she still hadn't caught up to the scouts, she thought of how the breeze was blowing out of the north, allowing it to smell her while she—and her horse—could not smell it. She knew what it was. She had seen its kind in her dreams.

She rode another league at least through the empty forest, knowing that she neared the valley of Kassel because of the husbanding of trees, the coppices, and the clearings hewn where stands of big trees had been taken down. A pair of crab apple trees grew to either side of an old cottage, long since abandoned and with its roof fallen in. Noble white bloomed in patches where a meadow cut a furrow through the trees. Bluebells carpeted the forest off into the shadows.

"Hey!"

She rode up to a roadblock constructed out of lumber and the remains of a shattered wagon and a few extra broken wheels. A dozen stout milites stood on guard.

"I'm an Eagle, riding in the regnant's service," she announced breathlessly, wondering if she had sucked in any air at all over the last part of the journey. She was dizzy. The soldiers guarding the road looked at her with surprise.

"Where's Peter and the rest of them?" they asked.

"Peter's escorting my company on the road. The others came before me. Didn't they reach here?"

They had not.

"Oh, God." The burning hit her stomach. Her hands shook. "There's another scout out there, in the woods."

"What do you mean?" asked their spokesman, a husky blond fellow. "One of Conrad's people, got around us to spy?"

"Does Duke Conrad hire Eika among his army now?"

"What are you talking about? Eika? You mean those ones we heard stories of, raiding along the northern coast?"

"I saw one, as clear as I see you," she said, seeing that he and his compatriots were skeptical, "about a league back."

The others grinned, thinking she was pulling their leg.

"She saw it 'bright as day,' " said one, "so that means she saw no thing."

But their leader frowned. He was young to be in charge, but he had a clever face and a suspicious gaze. "Either you mean it, or you're having a game with us. Either way, I don't like what I'm hearing."

"Take me to see Princess Theophanu, I pray you. You may have my weapons as surety. I am an Eagle riding in the regnant's service. I have news for Princess Theophanu and King Sanglant that they must hear, and hear soon."

"You'll not be riding through to Kassel today," remarked the wit.

His leader elbowed him. "Shut up! Well, then, give your weapons to me, and I'll escort you back. Listen, you slow-witted hounds. I'd tell you to keep your wits about you, but I think you've none to gather. Be ready for anything. Expect the worst. Come on, Eagle."

The others hunkered down, glancing nervously along the road and into the forest; its vistas were wider here, as beech took hold. She led her horse around the barrier, handed sword and staff and bow to her escort, mounted, and followed him west along the road.

"I'm called Johan," he said after a while.

"I'm Hanna," she said and, without meaning to, she giggled.

"What's so funny?"

"I joined the Eagles to get out of marrying a man named Johan, that's all."

He considered her a moment, and offered her weapons back. "If I didn't before, I believe you now," he said cryptically.

She nodded, and almost giggled again, strung so tight she knew she was about to laugh madly or burst into tears.

Soon they reached a second barrier. She smelled smoke ahead and heard the thunk of ax blows and the ring of hammers. A short distance after, the camp came into view. Theophanu had taken the high ground just before the hills sloped abruptly down into the valley surrounding Kassel. There had once been a hamlet here, a dozen buildings strung along the road. Men dug ditches to break up gentle slopes where riders might strike. Fences made of sharpened poles snaked along the contours of the ground to create a barrier between storehouses. At the high point in the village, a group of people clustered by a narrow break in the trees that offered a view of the besieged town.

Guards paced before the old longhouse that would once have housed the most well-to-do family. When Johan brought her to the door, these guards indicated the distant gathering. She dismounted and walked out to the promontory, with four soldiers as escort. Johan rode back to his post.

Eagles rarely waited. When the nobles and captains saw her, they moved aside to let her approach Princess Theophanu. The princess wore over her tunic a tabard marked with the red eagle of Saony. Her hair was braided tightly and pinned up, and the cloak she wore, whipped by the wind up on this height, fluttered against her knees. Hanna had forgotten how tall Theophanu was, almost as tall as many of the men; she was her father's daughter, well built and handsome.

"An Eagle," she said, looking Hanna over with narrowed eyes. "Who has sent you?"

"Sister Rosvita, Your Highness."

Around her, folk murmured to hear the cleric named, but if Theophanu was surprised, she concealed her emotion. "She rode south with Henry long since, and was lost. It was said that she died in the city of Darre. Yet I see you reached the south, as I commanded you. How long ago was that? Two years? Three? Yet now you have returned to us."

"Would you have me speak to all those assembled here, or with more privacy, Your Highness?" Hanna asked.

Theophanu smiled thinly. "Your news must be shocking. Best you speak before all assembled here. Have you a message for me?"

"No, Your Highness. I must tell you what I know, and what I have seen, and what and who Rosvita brings with her, for that company rides several leagues behind me. It is a long tale to tell. First, I must tell you that not two leagues from this camp I glimpsed an Eika scout in the forest."

"Triple the guard," said Theophanu to one of her captains. "Command all to arm. Get these trees down, as we spoke of. Send two hundred men to escort Sister Rosvita's party in to safety. As for the rest, let this company retire to the hall. It seems you have traveled a long way to reach us, and I expect you will welcome a place to sit and a flask of ale to drink."

The hall was crowded with crudely-built benches, by which means it had been turned into a meeting house and chapel. It was not long abandoned, or not abandoned at all; possibly the large family living here had simply been told to leave.

Hanna was given a stool to sit on and wine to drink. Only after Hanna had slaked her thirst did the princess ask for silence. From outside, Hanna heard axes thwacking into wood.

"Tell me first, and in a few words, what is most important. Then I'll hear your tale at length."

"This, then, Your Highness. Sister Rosvita was taken prisoner in Darre because she witnessed the murder of Helmut Villam at the hand of Hugh of Austra."

"Ah!" Theophanu sighed, with a grimace, but waved her hand to show Hanna must go on.

"I have heard the Eagle, Hathui, survived her journey and joined the company of Prince Sanglant."

"She did. So it happens that all she reported is true?"

"Hathui would never lie." But as she said the words, she remembered how she had doubted, and she was ashamed.

"Henry trusted her above all others. Her, and Villam, and Sister Rosvita. Go on."

"When I reached Darre, I found King Henry altered. He was captive to his queen and to Hugh of Austra. Those among the schola loyal to Rosvita joined with me in fellowship. In the aftermath of a terrible earthquake, we helped Rosvita escape the dungeon. We fled north. Reaching the convent of St. Ekatarina, we took refuge, but we were pursued there by Lord Hugh. Then—" Long had they discussed this, but Rosvita had insisted on the truth. "Sister Rosvita and Mother Obligatia—she is the abbess who presided over St. Ekatarina—together they wove a crown. By this means we escaped. We came into the east, and found ourselves pursued by soldiers from the army of the skopos."

"Holy Mother Anne?"

"Yes. These we fled, fearing for our lives—"

Many around her broke into speech, hearing the skopos maligned in such a manner, but Theophanu hushed them sternly. "Nay, let the Eagle speak. These accusations we have heard before, from my brother Sanglant, from the Eagle Hathui, and from Duchess Liutgard and Duke Burchard. Holy Mother Anne was party to the plot by which King Henry was infested with a daimone, made into a puppet so those who controlled him could speak words through his mouth." She said it so coolly—as if it were only an interesting story she related to entertain the crowd— that it was only as Hanna looked around at the people crowded into the hall and saw how their posture and their gestures and their expressions turned angry, that the Eagle knew Henry's death was truly mourned. She dared hope that the indignity thrust on him would be avenged.

"Go on, Hanna." It was the first time the princess had used her name.

"Yes, Your Highness. We fled the army of the skopos, because she had come into the east in order to weave a spell into the crowns, to set herself against the coming cataclysm. We escaped her, but were captured by Arethousans. For many months we lived as their prisoners. In time we were brought to the camp of certain Arethousan lords,

Lady Eudokia and Lord Alexandros. They were marching in rebellion against their emperor. It was there, my lady, that we found your sister Sapientia."

"Alive?" The word was little more than a whisper.

"Married to King Geza of Ungria, who was now their ally."

Theophanu laughed, then recovered so quickly that the lapse might never have happened. Around her, her company chattered, and the lady lifted a hand to ask them to quiet. "She has gone over to the enemy."

Hanna let them chew on this statement for a while, all talking at once. Such an interpretation discredited Sapientia. Best not to protest, or make excuses. Or remind them that Sanglant had abandoned his sister in the camp of a worse enemy, the Pechanek Quman. Even if he had not meant her to come to grief, his actions had ruined her. It would be best for Sanglant if his court did not know the entire truth.

Instead, thinking of how much she had hated Bulkezu and how furious she had been to see Sanglant keep him alive because it was expedient, she sipped at a second cup of wine until all the amazed speculation ceased and they waited for her to go on.

"King Geza had pledged to take the throne of Wendar and Varre in Sapientia's name, Your Highness," Hanna said.

Theophanu nodded. "Of course. And his child by her on the throne after she was dead. Go on."

"After the great tempest destroyed their camp, both armies fled. King Geza abandoned Sapientia, divorced her, and left her in the ruins of the camp."

"Did he so?" the lady said without any trace of spite or glee. She might have been wood, untested by fire or flood, her face polished clean of emotion. Yet her court had fallen into a horrible, fascinated silence, hanging on every word. "What then?"

"We found her, for we had been abandoned as well." She paused, and decided to skip her own ordeal, her second captivity among the Arethousans, although the memory of the ruins of that great city haunted her. "We walked north, and stumbled in our turn upon a company under the command of Lady Bertha of Austra."

"So she lived!"

"You know the tale?"

"We heard it. It was thought she was dead."

"She is dead now, alas, murdered by a poisoned arrow loosed out of the night. But that comes later in the tale, my lady. Bertha died in Avaria, not in the south where we all thought we would die."

"Go on."

"We joined together—clerics and soldiers—and traveled north as well as we could. We did well, gathering goats and chickens to feed us and a few dogs to keep watch. We thought we had come home safely, but after we reached Wendar, we were set upon twice by masked warriors, creatures like nothing we have seen before. Liath said they are Ashioi."

Now Theophanu was piqued, but Hanna could not tell if she were overjoyed, or furious. "Liath? You have seen Liathano? She is with you?"

"The king will reward you well for returning her to him," said a captain among the company, and there was nervous laughter.

She could not get the words out. Better to change the subject. "Princess Sapientia rides with us, but she is much changed."

Theophanu shifted ground easily. " 'Changed?' I pray you, speak bluntly."

"It's as if she does not even know her own name."

"She's lost her wits," said her sister. "Is that what you mean?"

Hanna nodded, so uncomfortable that she downed the remainder of the cup of wine, just to do something.

Theophanu looked neither pleased nor sorrowing. She merely nodded, as if hearing that the laundry had been taken down because it was dry. "What of Liathano?"

"Lost," said Hanna, and choked.

There was a dead, awful silence, and a voice came out of the crowd and said, in the manner of a man who is hard of hearing and must have each comment repeated, "Is she *dead?*"

"Lost," Hanna repeated, more strongly. "Mother

Scholastica comes on the road with us, riding with Princess Sapientia."

"Henry's sister, supporting Henry's eldest legitimate child." Theophanu nodded. "Well, that does not surprise me, that my aunt would choose to champion her long after the rest of us have accepted that she is unfit to rule. Is that all?"

"Not by any measure is that all. It is not sure which faction Mother Scholastica supports."

"Are you suggesting that my aunt supports *Conrad*?"

Hanna found herself hoarse, and coughing did not ease her.

"Bring the Eagle more wine," said Theophanu, but her voice was as cold as the winter wind, not warm and sympathetic. Not as Prince Sanglant would have been, treating each least servant under his rule as though that individual was, for a moment, the most important person in the world. Theophanu was all business. In that, she reminded Hanna of Lady Eudokia.

"I will sit here until you have told it all, Eagle. Conrad and Sabella stand before us, and my aunt creeps up behind. What other knives wait to stab us, I cannot yet see. I must know what to expect before my Aunt Scholastica rides in with God—and Sapientia—to wield over us as a whip. I must hear it all. From the beginning. Take your time."

Hanna had not gotten further than recounting the earthquake in Darre when the door opened and a messenger ran in, a young man with cheeks flushed and eyes flared in genuine fear. A captain strode at his heels. Seeing them, Theophanu stood as the lad dropped to his knees before her.

"What news?" she demanded.

For a moment Hanna thought she sounded alarmed.

The messenger began to cough, and the captain laid a comforting hand on the lad's shoulder and spoke instead.

"Grave news, Your Highness. This young fellow was sent to ride to Mother Scholastica's company, as you ordered."

"Yet here he is."

The lad found his voice. "The road is blocked," he said faintly. He shuddered, bit a lip, and steadied himself. "Your

Highness," he said more clearly. The captain stepped back. "I pray you, I bring ill news. We can't reach the company you speak of because the road is blocked."

"Blocked by what?" she asked.

He groaned and covered his eyes.

"Go on," said the captain. "You must speak, because you were the one who saw it."

"An army, Your Highness."

A murmur of alarm passed through the court, but Theophanu called for quiet. "Have Conrad and Sabella flanked us? We've seen no movement in their encampment."

"This army isn't human, Your Highness. They're the northlanders, what were once used to raid the northern coast years back. It's an army of Eika, Your Highness."

"We saw no sign of Eika on the road."

He shook his head. "I know not where they came from, my lady. We are cut off utterly from the east."

Theophanu looked at her captains and her companions, who had fallen into stunned silence. "They have come out of the west, or out of the north, and if that is so, then they have circled most of the valley of Kassel. We are caught between them, and Conrad. Captain, to arms. See to our eastern defenses—if we have any. We must find some way to alert Sanglant, so he is ready when we sound our advance."

4

AFTER the rider named Peter joined them, they marched for about a league through quiet forestlands before a horn called the alarm from the rear guard. Rosvita heard shouts as a soldier galloped up along the road.

"Holy Mother! Sister! I pray you, fall back to the line of wagons at once!"

Rosvita swung her mount around immediately, but Mother Scholastica stared stubbornly at the flushed and frightened messenger. "What news? Why this alert?"

"Armed men, trailing us on the road!"

"Have they identified themselves?"

"I think they mean to do so." Trembling, Brother Fortunatus pointed west.

A score of beasts stepped out of the trees and onto the shaded road. In form they bore a remarkable resemblance to humankind, with bone-white hair, two arms and two legs and a human-shaped torso, and facial features that from a distance might be mistaken for those of a man, but they were not men. Many bared their teeth, which had a sharp splendor like to that of dogs. They made no other threatening move, although their silence seemed threatening enough.

"Ai, God!" cried their escort, Peter.

"This can't be Conrad's army," said Mother Scholastica indignantly.

"Pull back to the wagons," said Sister Rosvita in a quiet voice to the riders surrounding her, who were mostly clerics of her own party or those church folk attending the royal abbess.

"Look in the trees!" exclaimed Fortunatus.

The pallor of their hair gave them away, ranks and ranks of them ranged in the forest, all standing as still as if they were statues—and so they might have been, sheeted in tin or copper or gold.

"I believe we are surrounded." In the face of disaster, Rosvita found that she felt perfectly calm. "I pray you, Mother Scholastica, fall back to the wagons. I will remain here. Fortunatus, please find Sergeant Ingo or Sergeant Aronvald. We'd best discuss our options while we still have time to talk."

They waited in a chilling silence, Rosvita out in front with Peter remaining bravely beside her while Mother Scholastica led the others back to the wagons.

"If your wagons are all strung out along the road," remarked Peter with the even voice of a man who sees he can't escape death, "they'll offer little safety."

"We must rely on God to protect us," said Rosvita. "Why do you suppose they have not yet attacked?"

"What are they?" he asked her. "I've never seen men like them, if they're men."

"They are called Eika."

"I've heard tales of such beasts. But you never know whether to believe them."

"They're real enough. King Henry fought a battle against them at Gent and drove them out of the city. For a few years, the north coast was peaceful."

"Licking their wounds and making ready to invade again."

"So it appears."

Wind conversed in the leaves and branches, but the Eika did not speak or move. Fortunatus came up from the wagons with Sergeant Ingo.

"Lord have mercy." The sergeant surveyed the blocked road, then spat.

"So we must pray," said Rosvita. "Have they attacked the rear guard or the wagons?"

"Nay, they stand as if stone, on all sides," said Ingo. "Some among us Lions fought Eika in earlier years, Sister. I will tell you that we never saw the like of this behavior. They were always silent, but their terrible dogs would yammer and attack, and they themselves would leap straight into battle like starving wolves. I wonder."

"You wonder what?"

"I wonder what intelligence controls them."

On the road ahead the Eika soldiers stepped aside. Two individuals came forward. One was an Eika warrior, noticeably more slender and shorter than many of his fellows. Around his hips was slung a girdle of surpassing beauty, gold-wire lacework studded with pearls and gems. Loops and spirals, a garish display, were painted on his chest. He bared his teeth, seeing the four who waited in the van; jewels winked, drilled into the incisors. He carried a gruesome standard, like a crossed spar on which hung streamers of bone and frayed ribbon and the same sort of trophies chosen by a flash-eyed crow to decorate its gaudy nest.

The individual holding a parley flag stepped forward to address them. He was a young man, born of humankind, with black hair, swarthy skin, and dressed in the manner of a foreigner.

"I come before you as an envoy," he said in serviceable

Wendish and in the most polite and respectful of tones, "to ask if there are any mothers among you, deacons of your holy church. If there are, the emperor Stronghand invites them to speak before him. He gives safe passage to all holy women sworn to walk within the Circle of Unity. You will wish to confer with your party to choose a suitable envoy."

"That's one of the Hessi," murmured Fortunatus. "I saw them in Autun. They had a merchant house there, a daughter branch out of Medemelacha."

"Aren't they some manner of heretic?" asked Ingo in a low voice.

"Nay," whispered Rosvita, "they are unbelievers but not truly heathens. They pray to God, so it's said, but they don't recognize the Translatus of the blessed Daisan."

"Sounds like an infidel to me," muttered Ingo.

"They write in a cipher," said Fortunatus, "a secret language that no one outside their tribe is allowed to learn."

"Did you try?" she asked him with a smile as the envoys waited.

His grin was swift, if brief. "So I did, but nothing came of it. What will you tell these two?"

"I'll get more information. Yet we'll have little choice. We can't fight them."

"So we can!" declared Ingo stoutly, before making a scene of coughing, as he realized that he had spoken in a loud voice.

Peter rubbed his naked throat.

"Stay here." Rosvita took three steps forward. "Are your people slaves to the Eika now?" she asked boldly.

The youth's grin was as swift and subtle as Fortunatus'. "I am not a slave to any man, or any Eika master. Nor are my people ruled by one regnant, as yours are. What my mothers choose for my house may not necessarily be chosen by another house."

"How comes it you speak of an emperor? Taillefer is dead, and King Henry's imperial crown lost in the south after the cataclysm."

"If you wish to know, come and see," said the youth with that same charming, reckless grin, daring her.

He reminded her of the best of her clerics. Those she

loved best she had liked most quickly, knowing it a flaw to
make a judgment in haste but succumbing nevertheless to
that impulse. She liked him, and that would only make
worse the choice she knew she had to make. Maybe it was
a sin—surely it was—but in war you use the weapons you
have. These Eika would slaughter Henry's faithful Lions,
and Sanglant's hope to restore Henry's kingdom to peace.

She stepped back. "Ingo," she murmured, "go swiftly
with Peter. Let every person in our company know they
must drop to the ground and cover their face at once."

He blanched, but he nodded.

Fortunatus touched her sleeve. "I will stay with you, Sister."

"It will be dangerous," she said without looking at him,
seeking instead to be sure that Ingo understood her meaning. The Lion nodded. She offered him her ring. He kissed
it, then walked rapidly toward the wagons and his soldiers.
Peter followed him.

She turned back to the interpreter.

"I pray you, a moment of patience." She regretted the
lie, because he was a quicksilver lad with a bright expression and clever eyes. "I have sent the soldiers to summon
the most holy abbess who commands our company."

The envoy glanced at the standard-bearer. They exchanged a look, and it seemed to her a subtle request for
permission from the Eika. So much for not having a master. That gesture decided her. He might be a fine and graceful young man, but he was the enemy.

God enjoined mercy, but her heart must be hard.

There whispered through the ranks of the Eika a lazy
wind that she perceived as she saw their bone-white hair
lifted by that breeze, as she heard their handsome ornaments tinkling where the wind shifted through. That chime
provided a most peculiar and delicate counterpoint to their
forbidding silence and closed countenances.

The Hessi youth examined her with interest. He had a
light gaze that leaped here and there as though he could
not keep his attention on any one thing, and yet she mis-
trusted it; where he looked, he looked hard.

The wind sighed a second time, and changed direction to

blow up behind their backs. The hair on the back of her neck grew stiff. Her skin tingled.

"Keep your eyes forward," she whispered to Fortunatus.

He was pale. His hand touched hers, and a spark bit them where skin brushed. He winced. She heard a sound like a re-signed murmur, the whisper of doubt, people falling, dropping as they shielded their eyes.

So also do the dead fall, when struck in the heart.

She kept her gaze fixed on the young envoy. If she called death, then she must face what she wrought.

Behind, from the company, she heard a shout as bright as ecstasy, cut short. A shriek answered that interrupted cry, a sob—then it, too, died abruptly. A cart's wheels ground along the road as it rolled closer.

In a moment, the Eika would begin to fall.

The envoy's eyes widened, and his expression underwent a remarkable change. He had seen something on the road, behind Rosvita. He cocked his head sideways, as if this shift in angle might answer a question.

In the dead silence, the standard-bearer laughed, a strange, and strangely frightening because very human, sound.

He spoke, in perfect Wendish.

"My shamans sensed a locus of magic in your train, so I came myself to see what it might be. It is not what I expected."

She heard the feather brush of footsteps beneath the sound made by the passage of the cart. Fortunatus gulped audibly. He was sweating and trembling—she could smell his fear—but he kept his gaze focused forward.

Not one Eika or man allied with the Eika had fallen.

The cart scraped to a halt behind them.

Rosvita had heard Sorgatani's voice before—Hanna had taught the shaman Wendish—but she had heard it only through the veil of shutters. To hear it in the open air made it seem entirely different, more ominous because it sounded all the more pure and innocent, although such a creature could never be innocent.

"I come at your command, Sister Rosvita," said Sorgatani. "Breschius drives the wagon. But it is gone wrong.

A pair of people in our ranks falls because they forget to hide their eyes. But the enemy—they stand untouched."

The standard-bearer walked forward. "What manner of sorcery invests you?" he asked with genuine curiosity.

"How are you protected?" demanded Rosvita.

"That is my secret. What is it you expect to happen to my army?"

"Who are you?" she asked him, angered that she had imperiled her soul and to no purpose! How had they failed?

Behind her, Sorgatani began to weep.

"What do you fear, Holy One?" he asked.

Only when Sorgatani answered did Rosvita realize he had not addressed the question to *her*.

The Kerayit shaman spoke with a trembling voice. "Among your people, I am free. All others, they die, to see me. Even here, when they forget to hide their eyes."

"Ah. If that bothers you, then join me, Holy One. You cannot hurt anyone in my army. And I do believe that you are a powerful weapon, one I would be happy to wield."

Almost, Rosvita turned to see Sorgatani's expression, to see if this offer tempted, to see if this foreign woman would leap to shift alliances. Fortunatus clamped a hand over her wrist, reminding her—God help her—that to look was to die.

As someone had already died!

"We should have treated her better," whispered Fortunatus with the merest breath of ironic bitterness.

"I have already pledged my aid to the Wendish," said Sorgatani.

He nodded, a very human gesture of acknowledgment. Strange that he could look on the shaman, as they could not. "No man can serve two masters. This, I respect. You will be my prisoner, and honorably treated. I do not war upon the mothers in any case. Those who guard them will be spared if they lay down their arms."

"Sister Rosvita commands us," said Sorgatani. "It must be her decision."

Shamed, Rosvita replied more sharply than she intended. "I pray you, Sorgatani, go inside."

Slippers squeezed dirt as the young woman turned away. The door scraped open, and clapped shut.

"She is hidden." A halt in Breschius' tone made her look, and she had a fancy that he brushed a tear away from his cheek.

The one holding the banner, who had watched all this without comment, spoke lightly. "She could kill all of you, yet she obeys you. That interests me. Who holds her allegiance?"

Fortunatus let go of her wrist.

"We ride to support King Sanglant."

He nodded. "You are surrounded and your soldiers outnumbered. We can kill them and take you prisoner in any case, but I am curious about this shaman woman. That is why I offer mercy."

"How can we know you will keep your word?"

He bared his teeth in a grimace that imitated a grin but was more like a hound warning that it is prepared to bite. "You are in no position to refuse, but I understand that you remain suspicious. I speak in good faith, remembering your Circle."

With his free hand, he lifted one of the loops away from the pattern decorating his chest, and she realized that he wore a simple wood Circle of Unity around his neck, tied on a leather cord.

Fortunatus sucked in his breath.

She rocked back on her heels, seized with hope. "Do you stand in the Light?"

"I respect the mothers who guide you. On their honor, the honor of your church of Unity, on the honor of the one you know as Constance of Wendar and the holy deacon Ursuline who guards her charges at Rikin Fjord, I swear this oath, that I will not raise arms against those who do not raise arms against me."

"Who are you?" Rosvita demanded.

He shrugged, a casual, too-human gesture, so much so that she was beginning to see him as scarcely different than the young Hessi man standing so trustingly beside him, than the score of human men scattered back through the ranks. He and his brothers had a human cast of face; they had a human form except for the claws, and the metallic tone of their skin, and the bone-white hair. The old legends told that the Eika were born when the blood of humankind and dragons mixed in ancient days.

Maybe the old legends were true.

"I am who I say I am: Stronghand, emperor of my Eika brothers and of the lands of Alba and certain territories along the western coast of Salia and Varre."

Spoken with such an assurance of might and power!

She must speak to protect those she was responsible for. "You must see, Lord Stronghand, that I cannot ask the brave and faithful soldiers who march with me to lay down their arms and leave themselves defenseless."

"They are too few to harm me. Let them set a camp, a perimeter, here in the forest. My soldiers will set a guard over them but not come near. That will content me."

"What of the rest of us?"

"Naturally I must take a few as hostages to ensure that my guards will not be molested. The rest of your party can remain with your Lions. They are good soldiers, those Lions. I have seen them in action."

On this road in the forest with trees all around and no sign of bird life, with only a trace of wind in the branches, Rosvita wondered briefly if she had wandered into a dream as vivid as those she had on occasion suffered when traveling between the crowns. In a moment, no more, she would hear Brother Fortunatus' voice saying "I pray you, Sister, wake up."

But Fortunatus remained silent.

The Eika lord shifted from one foot to the other as he tilted his head, seeming to hear a sound hidden from her.

The hand grasping the pole of his standard uncurled. The pole began to roll off his opening fingers, and he unaware of its movement.

Almost, she called out to warn him, but she remained silent.

The hills just north of Kassel are rugged, their heights shorn by the tempest of last autumn that cut through the wealth of pine and beech. Dead trees scatter the ground like sticks. Low-lying shrubs grow in these clearings now that they have more light. Sometimes vistas open where forest once blocked the view.

This long ridgeline slopes sharply to both west and east away into rolling ground, polite hills easy to travel through, where the forest thrives. To the south it dips into the broad valley beyond the El River, the place where the town of Kassel rose a century ago on the ruins of a Dariyan outpost. The town's main gates face the south because it is protected to the north by that rough country where Alain walks on a deer trail.

He is alone in the forest, all but his faithful companions, the two hounds and the guivre, which follows him rather like a dog but a great deal more noisily. The creature's wingspan has made a tent over him at night, to shelter him from drizzle, and its vicious beak has torn into the only pack of wolves that dared attack them in the wild woods where animals roam.

That was days ago. Now he has almost reached his destination.

The first drops of rain spatter through leaves like a shower of pebbles. Above, the sky grows dark, and the forest floor grows dim. The few birds—he is always thankful to hear birds call—fall silent.

Ahead, the track opens into a meadow where a stream winds through tall grass and purple and blue flowers. He halts at the verge. Wind whips the grass, but he is untouched. Rage whines. Sorrow gives a single bark. Both sit, made uneasy by the weather.

Mist pours heavenward out of the stream. Rain lances through the meadow, so cold and hard that it stings his cheek like slivers of ice blown on a gale. It rains sideways as the rising wind howls. He cannot see the trees on the far side of the clearing.

This is no natural storm.

Even as he thinks this, light pierces the wall of mist. The rain ceases between one breath and the next. Above, clouds part as easily as if they have been sliced in two to reveal a sun so brilliant that he shades his eyes from its glare. Raindrops glisten on petals. Grass sparkles. The stream burbles. Out of the mist rising off those waters emerges a rider.

The horse is as white as untouched snow, almost blinding. The woman has seen many battles. Scars mar her face and hands. Her boots drip mud, as though she has only recently slogged through a rain-swept battlefield. The rings of her mail shirt are coated with rust except for those places where irregular patches of new rings have been linked and hammered closed to fill ragged gaps.

She reins in her warhorse beside him. Her long sword, sheathed in leather, sways in front of his eyes. A battered round shield hangs by her knee.

Her gaze is at once distant and utterly piercing. But he is no longer afraid to look her in the eye.

"What must I pay you, to ride to war?" she asks him.

He cannot tell if she recognizes him.

"I have dealt death and suffered death," he tells her. "I am no longer your servant."

As the clouds part, the light of the sun shifts until it strikes her, and her armor gleams as though new-made, shining and glorious as she is shining and glorious. She draws her sword. Its length blazes as though forged by sorcery. He weeps, because she is beautiful.

"All serve me," she says. "The trumpets of war are sounding. Arms will be joined soon. Friends and foes will perish. Do you abandon them to their fate? Hear!"

Out of the heavens a ringing sound floats, almost too faint to identify except that he knows it as the clash of sword and shield. On the wind drifts a rumble like thunder, quickly lost.

"Ride with me, Alain, son of Rose. Choose, and your choice shall win the day. You may make Sanglant emperor by the might of your arm. Stronghand is your brother by blood. Will you answer his prayer? What of the husband of the woman you loved once? Give him victory, and raise her to glory—or ruin him to ruin her. What of the offer made to you, to become consort in your own right? Choose, and you can be king, consort of a queen regnant. You are nothing, a whore's son raised by a humble family. I offer you glory. Come with me now, and your likeness, the memory of your exploits, will be painted on the walls of churches so that humble folk will sing of your victories and clerics will praise your deeds. You will be one of the great princes ever after."

The ground shakes with an undulating ripple. The guivre drags itself up beside him, and it stretches its wings to their full span, hissing at the lady.

"I no longer belong to you," he says.

"You march toward war. Even if it is peace that you seek, you must use the sword to achieve it. Fail me, and you fail those you wish to save."

"So you believe." He whistles. Rage and Sorrow come to attention behind him, ready to move.

She laughs, a bright sound that rings up into the heavens to join that clamor heard from afar. "Challenge me, if you will. Now you will see my power."

The fog takes her. Between one breath and the next, it swallows her, leaving him on the narrow deer trail hemmed in by scraping branches and damp leaves. The meadow has vanished, the rain has stopped, but the black clouds and the rising wind remain.

Almost, Stronghand dropped his battle standard, woven by the shamans of the Eika tribes so its magic shields from the touch of sorcery all who walk under the shield of his power. Its limits had been tested today, and it had protected them from a terrible threat. The thought roused him. His chin jerked sideways as he started like an animal waking from a doze and grabbed the tumbling standard before it could strike the ground.

"She is coming!" His voice cracked. His attendants shifted from watchful alertness to coiled readiness as a man standing casually rolls to the balls of his feet, preparing to sprint. "Swiftly! Now we move!"

His gaze caught on the cleric. "Stand by your agreement, and I will stand by mine. Yeshu, see that the shaman and her attendant come with us. Bring also this holy mother who speaks for the company."

He strode into the ranks of his army, which swallowed him. As quickly as water washes off rocks on an outgoing wave, his soldiers dispersed west down the Hellweg or into the forest. The plan was long since set into motion. The noise of their passage crackled, and as if by sorcery a wind rose out of the north to trouble the woodland. Branches cracked and fell. The clouds—what he could see of them above the treetops—had turned a sullen gray color, presaging rain.

Battle was coming, and so was Alain. Yet another scent teased his nostrils, a touch of the forge. It puzzled him, because although a lingering taste of sorcery shifted on the wind, that distant presence was not in itself magical.

A scout jogged into view from the west and fell into step beside him. "Lord Stronghand. All is ready as you have commanded on the western flank. A report has come in that a patrol to the north has fallen into a skirmish with a party of outriders, and retreated. Sharptongue of Moels Tribe has sent up another troop to push into that region, to make sure our eastern flank is not attacked unawares."

"Good. What of Duke Conrad and Lady Sabella's army?"

"Taking up arms. There is movement in Kassel. It seems the battle is about to start between the besieged and their enemy. It seems the princess on the eastern slope has been alerted to our presence."

"Good."

"Further orders, Lord Stronghand?"

He considered his troops in their thousands, a mixed Eika and human force raised from the northern tribes and the eager Alban recruits, the largest army to march through these lands since the armies of the Dariyan Empire. He considered his lines of communication and supply, stretched thin, and his imperfect knowledge of the disputes that had destabilized the Wendish and Varren realms. He considered Alain, and the last words of the WiseMothers, now forever lost to their children.

Repay this debt.

He nodded, a human gesture, but in these days he sensed in himself a fine balance between the cold ruthlessness of dragons, the hidden strength of stone, and the quicksilver emotion that rules humankind. Once, long ago, the part of him that derived from human ancestry had lain quiescent, barely acknowledged, but his chance encounter with Alain Henrisson had changed him and, in the long run, altered him utterly.

"No," he said to the waiting scout who, like all the Eika, had the patience of stone. "All is going as I have planned."

"Up on the cart, most honored one," said the Hessi youth sweetly as he walked up to Rosvita and Fortunatus without the least sign of nervousness. Of course, he had a hundred silent Eika soldiers guarding his back. He had no need to feel anxious. "There is room for you to ride with the driver, I think, holy one."

The color of the sky was changing, in accordance with her mood. The once light haze of clouds was darkening quickly as a storm blew in.

"Brother Fortunatus! You must go back to the main party and tell them what happened. Let the Lions remain watchful, but on no account unless they hear word from me or from King Sanglant himself are they to attack a superior force."

He grasped her hands. "I would not leave you, Sister!"

"Haste," said the Hessi interpreter kindly, but he smiled wryly to show he must enforce his orders. "I will go with the good brother, back to your company. I have a message to give them."

With a flash of his old smile, Fortunatus released Rosvita's hands. He had tears in his eyes, but he faced the youth with a cheerful expression that did not blind Rosvita to his true feeling. "Will you teach me the letters of your secret cipher?"

The lad laughed outright, the most pleasing sound Rosvita had heard all day, something to make the heavens a little brighter, although the storm boiled ever closer, sweeping down from the north. "It is forbidden, yet there is one letter I might teach you. That which came first of all sounds on the day of Creation."

He drew Fortunatus away, walking toward the rest of the company. From deep in the ranks, back by the wagons, a wailing rose toward the heavens, shouts of dismay and grief.

"What happened?" asked Rosvita in a low voice. "Did someone die?"

Breschius shrugged. "It's possible. But I was walking in front of Princess Sorgatani. I saw nothing of what might have happened behind me."

She took a step in the direction of the cries, but the Eika soldiers closed in around her and the wagon. The horses shied, fearful of that faint dry smell like stone baking under a hot sun. Breschius spoke softly to them, and they laid back their ears and began to walk with heads tossing anxiously.

Ai, God. She had called forth Sorgatani to vanquish the Eika, but instead some of her own people had died—and for nothing. They had accomplished nothing except to become prisoners of an invading army.

"Sister!"

Breschius tossed her a pair of old apples, quite wrinkled.

Busy hands keep the mind from straying to unproductive thoughts. What she had done could not be undone. She must keep her wits sharp for the road ahead. She caught up to the horses and walked alongside to coax the pair through the front ranks and onward along the Hellweg as they walked into the unknown heart of the Eika army.

5

"SOMETHING, but I don't know what." It was midday. Sanglant paced on Archer's Tower, the highest on the walls of Kassel, and surveyed the valley. Conrad and Sabella had used their ground wisely, not bothering with a complete encirclement, since the steep slopes to the northeast of the town were too unstable for anyone to negotiate even on foot.

"What manner of something?" Liutgard brushed hair out of her eyes with a forearm. She had stood up here most of the day and the wind had torn all that time at her tightly braided hair, culling wisps that fluttered with each gust in greater numbers. She glanced to the north. "A storm coming?"

"A whisper like the ranks of the dead approaching," he said, and she looked at him, puzzled, and only then did he realize he had spoken his thought aloud. "A taste like the eve of battle."

"Is that what makes you restless as a prowling dog? Not just those dark clouds? Will we fight Conrad today?"

"He's sent no herald, made no attempt to parley."

"Sent no word of my daughter," said Liutgard bitterly.

"It makes me wonder what his intentions are. But, in truth, there is another scent on the wind, and I'm not sure what it is."

"Where is Theophanu?"

"Close. See, there." He pointed to the southeast. "That color on the ridgeline. There."

She squinted, then shrugged. "I don't see it. Only the trees along the hills."

"My archer Lewenhardt caught sight of it yesterday. I wouldn't have noticed it myself, but his eyes are sharp. I believe that is her banner, set up to alert us."

"Too far for us to see." She stared and stared, shook herself with a measure of impatience and frustration, and shifted her gaze back to the encampment draped in a semi-circle about the valley of Kassel, one which girdled all roads and tracks.

"That's as close as she can come, with Conrad and Sabella in her path. If we could coordinate our attack, we could strike from two sides. At this juncture, neither army has an advantage. If I judge correctly, Conrad and Sabella have numbers about equal to our own."

"The margraves should have marched with us."

"Yes, I suppose they should have. Gerberga will wait it out in Austra and come to claim what she can from whichever is left standing."

"Gerberga can go rot! It was Waltharia I was thinking about."

"She sent three centuries of men, all she could spare. Think how many she lost—her own husband—when she sent a troop south with me."

Liutgard did not appear so much aged by the long campaign but hardened, made mirthless. She had laughed more, once upon a time, and she had been wont to cast quotes into her banter—she could read—lively lines from the poets or homilies out of the mouths of the church mothers. "I, too, lost many milites in Henry's wars, Cousin! Yet I stand beside you. Even Burchard went home."

"To die."

She snorted. "I've come to think that dying is the coward's choice."

He shook his head. "I have been sorely wounded many times. Perhaps it's true that being dead brings peace, but the dying itself is not so easy. I pray you, Liutgard, remember that I value your loyalty."

"Surely you do!"

"You have never faltered."

"Only in my heart."

"Well, then, listen to me. When the time comes to strike, you must remain behind the walls. Until your daughter is recovered, you must remain safe—"

"In case I am killed, and she is dead after all, and the inheritance thereby left in confusion? No. I will ride, just as you will. I want revenge."

"I need a strong captain to hold these walls!"

She gestured toward Fulk. "There he is."

"Hai!" A sentry shouted. "See there, Your Majesty."

Guards clattered to attention along Kassel's wall walk.

"There!" cried Liutgard, pointing.

The clouds split as suddenly as if they had been sliced asunder. Sunlight lanced over the valley, sharpening every detail of Conrad's camp. That light illuminated the southeastern ridgeline. A gash in the wall of trees opened as first one, then a pair, and then a dozen trees toppled. Banners made tiny by distance flowed like water as they rippled back and forth.

"That's her signal!" cried Sanglant. He turned to Captain Fulk. "Set Lewenhardt here to watch and listen. We arm. Spread the word by mouth alone. Let no trumpet or bell sound the alarm until the gates are opened."

"What of Wichman?" Liutgard asked. "Do you think he and his company are lost?"

"Always." He grinned. "We shall not count on them. But I will expect them, nevertheless."

As they moved to the stair to descend the tower and prepare for battle, a tingling in the middle of his back gave him pause, like the misgivings of a man new to war who imagines the ax blow that will bring his death. Stopping in mid-stride, he canted his head, lifted his chin, and tasted the air. "That is the smell of Eika."

"Eika?" cried Fulk.

"Can Sabella have made an alliance with those creatures?" demanded Liutgard. "Better to hold within our walls than ride into such an ambush."

"Conrad would not risk the entire kingdom with such a reckless alliance. This is only more reason to ride, and ride soon. At worst, we can guide Theophanu and her army into the safety of the walls. Be on alert." He shook his head. "Theirs is not the only scent that rides the wind today."

Before the gate they readied their arms. Horses were watered and barding was strapped tight. Sibold handed him his dragon helm. When he fixed it over his head, a murmur rose from the watching crowd. He adjusted his mail so it lapped over his belt, loosened his sword in its scabbard, then twisted his lance, checking for any warp or crack. It seemed only moments since the whispered "to arms" had summoned the battle-ready force to the gate, yet after all an interminable time dragged past as they waited for Theophanu's signal.

What if he was wrong? Perhaps her army was already overwhelmed, or she had changed her mind, choosing not to support him. The outcome of this day turned on the fealty of his sister.

The sound rose faintly, but clear, a long low horn call resounding across the valley, followed by three rising notes. Men strained at the ropes as they opened the gates. Within the walls, a horn lifted its voice in alarm, three blats. The city's dogs barked a rousing reply. In the citadel, a bell took up the call, mingling with shouts and the high-pitched wails of the lesser horns.

Sanglant put spur to Fest. The gelding pressed eagerly onto the field. The sun stood high over all, barricaded on all sides by a glowering wall of dark clouds. The valley lay in brightness, and the forest beyond, in shadow.

Answering trumpets came from the siege works, which were well constructed against a charge. Pickets of stout, sharpened poles and half-dug trenches guarded the bulwarks, with Sabella's and Conrad's banners stationed deep within. There were but two flaws. They had anchored their right flank upon the steep northern slopes but had not yet set defenses there, perhaps thinking the slope itself sufficient to reject a charge. Some trenches were partially excavated to their rear, but nothing was complete. The other flaw in Conrad's defense was, of course, that he had to defend from both front and behind.

A hundred strides off, Sanglant wheeled his force to the left and made for the slope. Some archers loosed arrows in vain. Others crawled through their own defenses so they might close the range against the riders that charged across their front. Even as they did so, infantry advanced at double time out of the gates of Kassel, shields held high and their own archers behind, letting fly as they closed the range. The Varren archers who had come out before the lines scrambled back to their defenses. A few fell.

Where the Varren line gave way to hill, Sanglant leaped the farthest and most shallow trench. A pair of archers rose to meet him. He thrust the first through the right eye even as that man tried to nock a new arrow. The other man stumbled as he staggered back. As Sanglant passed, lifting his arm and twisting up to free the lance, he kicked the second archer in the throat. He reset his lance, but it was hard work. The chase, the thunder of hooves around him as his troop smashed into the Varren flank, the first screams, that sharp stone scent that gave him flashes of vision of Bloodheart's hall in Gent, all these roused the fury that drove him in battle. He sucked it down. He was regnant. He was captain. The one who led. He pushed on as his riders scythed the ground behind him. They must push forward, no respite for those in front and no time to slay those left behind. To his right, he glimpsed Liutgard's cavalry press-

ing the line on either side of Kassel's milites as they pushed
and pushed. They had to cut through the lines and reach
the Hellweg at the base of the ramp so that any of Theophanu's troops who were riding in from the Hellweg would
have a clear descent into the fray.

Wind churned the heavens. A battlement of black clouds
rose in a ring around them. Waiting outside the hall, Hanna
shuddered as a cold rain drove over her, but a moment
later the shower ceased and only the towering thunder-
heads warned of the looming storm. The sun shone above
the valley of Kassel, yet nowhere else.

"Sorcery!" the Saony guards whispered.

She wiped rain from her eyes. Theophanu's army was in
tumult, units trotting out in all directions. The main force
of infantry moved toward the ridge slope where, moments
before, ax-men had toppled a dozen trees. Six men waved
cloth banners where the view opened, trying to alert those
trapped with Kassel. Their faces were caught in the sun, but
their backs were still in shadow.

"Eagle!" Theophanu emerged from the hall, armed and
fit for battle. A captain walked beside her, carrying her helmet. "Eagle, make ready. Kinship demands we warn Conrad and Sabella of the Eika. We must join to negotiate
against a greater threat. You'll be brought a fresh horse."

"And ride into the battle, Your Highness?"

"If need be. You will ride along the Hellweg and gain
herald's entry into Conrad's camp where they've set a barrier across the road, at the top of the ramp. If you cannot
reach Conrad or Sabella, then ride to Kassel's gates. I will
rally my forces at the gates of the town if they refuse to listen to reason."

Hanna could scarcely breathe, thinking of the Eika scout
she had seen in the forest. Why had he let her pass? Would the
Varren troops recognize and respect her Eagle's badge and
cloak? But she nodded, shucking her doubts and fears aside
because that was what an Eagle had to do. "I am ready."

A horse was led up and the reins given to her. She

mounted. It was a short ride to the Hellweg, and the descent of the road along a shallower rise briefly gave her a clear view back the way she had come.

From the top of the hill, where the banner flapped in the morning air, the trumpeter called and Theophanu's advance began. Lines of infantry descended the hillsides, breaking and re-forming around trees and outcrops of rock. Most of the cavalry led their horses down the slope, though Theophanu and her commanders rode, standing above the rest.

Hanna heard, from the direction of Kassel, an answering shout of horns, followed by the blare and call out of the Varren camp. She pressed her mount—a calm mare, thank God—and raced down the road and into the forest with braids flying and her heart galloping in time to the staccato of hooves. A bronze face stared at her from the trees, but she did not look closely into the dense foliage. Better not to know. At any instant she expected a cold arrow to pierce her flesh, but none came.

The feeling that swelled in his heart was the one that humankind called "amusement." For how many winters had he gathered his forces, forged alliances, destroyed his enemies the tree priests, and studied the ways of the enemies of the Eika? Never had it occurred to him that they would be so dedicated to their own destruction, their own petty quest for power, that they would burn their own great hall even as he battered upon their door. Their scouts knew of his army, yet still they commenced their civil war, clan brother against clan brother.

His troops had marched down along and beside the road called by its builders the Clear Way, for its width and straightness. He had learned that it was built upon an ancient road engineered by the Dariyans, and it was therefore. the quickest and easiest route from Autun to Quedlinhame. Hearing the start of the battle, he had backed his forces into the trees. Cavalry was always at a disadvantage within the forest.

"Last Son," he called. "We will advance to the rise where the road emerges out of the forest. There, it ramps down into the valley. In that place they have set a barrier across the road. We'll take that ground, and from the height we will watch. Do not throw down the banner that flies in that entrenchment. Let them believe their own people still control the barricade."

"Lord Stronghand! A rider approaches along the road, out of the camp of the Wendish army!"

He saw her, and he knew her, because he had dreamed her once—the only person in all of humankind whose dream he had ever shared besides Alain. She was one of the messengers called Eagles, but in all other ways a mystery to him, except for her pale hair so white that it might have belonged on any good Eika brother.

"Let her pass," he said.

He smelled the sweat of her fear, and he admired the stoic courage that had propelled her onto a road she must know was overrun by her enemy. She galloped past. The sound of her passage faded. He lifted his banner and tapped it three times on the earth, that infinitesimal tremor enough to alert his brothers, whose rock-born heritage gave them a keen sensitivity to any whisper in the earth.

His force was mixed with various groups of human allies, most of them former slaves and poor folk out of Alba and the coastal reaches of Salia. Well trained and finely honed, eager for glory and the fruits of victory, they moved out. Scouts ran up in stages to report that there was minimal defense at the barricade because the soldiers stationed there were peeling back to meet the double-pronged attack of the Wendish host.

He looked back to see the wagon of the shaman come into view, rattling along the stone of a road meant for foot and horse traffic, not for wheels. The horses were skittish. The one-handed servant had dismounted to lead them, leaving the cleric to cling to the driver's seat. Strange that it should all fall into his hands so easily.

As this wing of his army surged forward, he called Last Son to his side and gave the standard into his keeping. Together, they advanced.

The barricade had been thrown across the road where it came out of the forest. Just beyond the barricade, the ridgeline sloped sharply down, and here the famous Dariyan ramp descended into the valley.

Thanking the Lady and Lord with each panting breath, Hanna pounded up to the wagons braced across the roadway and shouted at the only pair of faces she could see within.

"Let me pass! I am an Eagle in the service of Princess Theophanu! I carry a message for Lady Sabella and Duke Conrad!"

She got no answer.

From this vantage, she had a wide view of the valley. The wind was strong up here. Behind her, she heard the drumming of rain, yet the sun shone over the valley. Riders had plunged out of the city and were now punching deep into the northeastern edge of the Varren line, where the entrenchments were weakest and the surrounding hill face very steep. Turning, she saw the flash of color as Theophanu's army worked free of the eastern hills. As the princess' soldiers closed with the rear entrenchments, her infantry tightened their ranks, and archers, working in the gaps in groups of twenty or thirty, directed their fire into the wood picket and at the heads peeking above the half finished earthen berm. The shields closed on the picket, and great axes reached out to hew or pull down what obstacles they could. Few had fallen as far as Hanna could see from this distance, but pikes, axes, and arrows responded from the other side of the berm.

The battle had begun in earnest.

"Ai, God! Ai, God! Run!" screamed the soldiers manning the barricade. They were only a dozen, but they scattered like rabbits as a hawk dives, some down the ramp and some stumbling over the side into brush and trees.

She turned.

On the road behind her, coming up through the trees, marched the van of the Eika army, shield upon shield, approaching in silence except for the tramp of their feet. But even this sight and sound did not make her freeze with dread. Not this, but another thing.

Above the fray drifted a resonant whisper, so faint she only registered it because she had heard it before and knew what it was: the tolling of bell voices, each of them calling.

Sanglant.

Horns shrilled the alarm. The Varren camp—what Ivar could see of it—erupted into movement.

Lord Berthold called to their guards, who were staring nervously toward the royal tents. "What news, friends?"

But the guards gaped at the heavens as abruptly the sun broke through the clouds. They shaded their eyes with their hands, squinting under the bright glare, paralyzed.

A captain ran past, and shouted at them. "To arms! To arms! Get to your unit!"

"What of the prisoners?" they called after him.

"Leave them! We're under attack!"

They bolted.

Berthold dropped into a crouch, Odei, Jonas, and Berda gathered around him, kneeling. Ivar stood off to one side, but Brother Heribert was still picking through the mouse nest, dangling the dead creatures by their tails and swinging them gently back and forth as if this movement might restore them to life.

"Listen," said Berthold. "We have to stay here. Await Wolfhere."

"Shouldn't we make a run for it?" asked Jonas.

"No. The Varrens might kill us for trying to escape, and the Wendish attacking might mistake us for Varrens and we'd still be dead. Just stay put."

"Oh, God." Jonas pulled a hand through his curly hair and tugged on it nervously, grimacing when he yanked too hard. "I hate staying put."

Heribert looked up, a tiny corpse hanging by its tail from his fingers. "He comes." He dropped the mouse on the ground and, when he rose, stepped on it without seeming to see it. Bones crackled, but it had no juice left in it.

Jonas winced. Berda scrambled away as Heribert took a pair of steps closer. Berthold stood.

Shouts and cries clamored from the direction of the town. The rumble of charging horses shook the air. They dashed to the boards and tried to peer through the gaps, where they had a chance of seeing the field of battle. Working two of the boards to get the crack to open wider, Ivar caught a splinter in the stump of his missing little finger. Cursing, he squeezed it out, together with a tiny pinch of blood.

"Do you see?"

"It's too bright!"

"Could you move? It's my turn!"

A crash sounded behind them. All turned, except Heribert. Just beyond the byre gate, a wagon had broken its axle and tipped, spilling barrels and weapons onto the ground. One barrel rolled out of sight. Another had broken open, and ale soaked into the dirt. Men swarmed over the wreck, cursing. An arrow whistled out of the sky and slapped harmlessly into earth. Berda lifted her head and sniffed at the air.

"Come quickly."

Ivar yelped. Jonas shrieked. Berthold jumped and stumbled. Even Odei, usually stolid and passive, skipped back to slam into the wall. Berda was already turning to acknowledge Wolfhere, who stood by the back wall. A cloud—like flour floating around a baker—of white mist evaporated as he beckoned. Light shone through a gap in the boards, illuminating his legs.

"Stay behind me. We'll run east. If we can make it up the ramp, we can hope to lose ourselves in the hills."

"Like we did before?" asked Ivar with a sneer.

"Better than staying here," said Berthold. "Caught in the middle."

"Put on these." Wolfhere placed on the ground six amulets, crudely woven out of grass and herbs. He shoved a board to one side, ducked down, and slipped through the opening. Heribert was gone after him before anyone else could react, and then Berthold dashed forward with his attendants behind. Only Ivar hesitated, but he hadn't the courage to stay behind.

He knelt to pick up the last amulet with his mutilated hand. It was as crudely and hastily woven as a child's daisy necklace, and when he lifted it to his nose, wondering what plants had been woven into it, he sneezed hard. Fern interlaced with wolfsbane; a few pale flowers he did not recognize were crushed in the tangle.

At the wagon's wreck, a sergeant showed up, shouting orders. Ivar pushed through the loose boards, then huddled there aghast, blinking in the sunlight, as he realized that the others were gone. Around him, groups of soldiers sprinted toward the entrenchments, but of Wolfhere and the others he saw no sign at all among the farmstead's buildings, the pitched tents, and the many wagons. Maybe it was only the light that blinded him.

"Hey! You, there!" cried a sergeant, coming around the corner of the byre. "We need help here!"

Ivar settled the amulet around his neck. The sergeant pulled up short, whipped his head from side to side with a comical air, and scratched his head; giving up, he trotted away.

But now Ivar could see a faint cloudy trail twisting and turning away past the farmstead cottage, around and under wagons, and cutting across open ground where it zigged and zagged in the manner of a drunken man weaving to avoid obstacles. He ran after them, praying under his breath. His hand hurt. Blisters rose on his palm, as though he had burned himself, and the scars on the stumps of his fingers began to ooze blood.

He jogged between tents, stumbled on a guide rope, jinked sideways to avoid a line of men marching double-time who did not see him, and paused midway toward the lines to catch his breath, hand pressed to his side. The pain bit deep in his hand. His neck was beginning to itch where the amulet brushed bare skin. He tugged it down, but that pressure broke it, and it unraveled to spill like water onto the ground. Steam hissed over him and dissipated in a cloud of stinging gnats that buzzed around him in two swift circles before roaring heavenward and transmuting into a blaze of falling embers.

"Hey! You there!" A brawny man armed in mail but no tabard strode toward him, brandishing an ax in each hand.

Ivar drew his sword.

"No, you fool! Take these axes and get east to Captain Sigulf's line there just north of the ramp. Can you take a pair of spears as well?"

"Best run with these and send another man after me," said Ivar as he sheathed his sword and grabbed the axes. He took off. Without the amulet, he could not find their trail. He reached the road and ran toward the ramp visible in the distance because of its immense size. Afer a while, he had to stop to get his breath and to measure the lay of the land.

The sun's heat made him sweat. On all sides, dark clouds built as for a storm. Wind creaked and groaned in the far forest.

The valley of Kassel was like an uneven bowl, with its steeper, higher rim to the north and east and a lower rim to the south and west. Most of the western ground was striped with fields, a long stretch of land that terminated where the slopes rolled up a shallow rise and sprouted trees. A line of unevenly spaced fruit trees ran through the middle of the fields, parallel to a narrow waterway. The Varren camp had been planted where the more rugged eastern and northern slopes gave them some protection, and also to straddle the Hellweg where it cut diagonally from northeast to southwest through the valley. Here, because of the contours of the earth, Ivar could sight easily both downslope and up, southwest and northeast.

On the northeastern flank, the siege works were under assault by cavalry smashing through the lines. He watched, in awe of the power of the warhorses. Infantry advanced out of the town gates, pushing straight for the middle trenches and pickets. To the east and southeast, troops wearing the red and gold of Saony poured down off the hillside to press the outer works. The banner of Arconia flew above this line, moving up and back as troops needed reinforcement.

The famous road, the Hellweg, was easily visible from here where the massive ramp lifted off the valley floor in a smooth incline that reached the low ridgeline and struck thereafter straight into the forest. Some idiot had thrown a barricade of wagons across the top of the ramp. He saw small figures poised there among the wagons. A rider—a tiny, toylike figure—galloped out of the forest along the road and pulled up before the barricade.

"Hai! Hai! For Conrad!"

The ground trembled beneath him. Several hundred horse trotted past, with Duke Conrad at their head. They moved twenty abreast, spilling to either side and splitting around Ivar where he stood on the road. He shut his eyes and held his ground and prayed, but they were past him before he finished the psalm. They thundered toward the northeastern flank.

Only a fool would run to the east now. The fighting was fierce all along the line of the valley from north to east to east-southeast. How Wolfhere expected to get up that ramp, even with sorcery, he could not imagine.

"God help me." He threw down the axes and ran for the west. If he could escape into the woods, then he might hide and crawl and get to Hersford Monastery safely. It was better than dying here.

The western siege works were lightly guarded as men peeled off in twos and threes when called to reinforce the entrenchments under attack. Ivar scrambled under a wagon whose wheels were wedged tight against blocks of wood. He skidded down the loose soil of a ditch and up the other side.

"Hey! You!" A soldier called to him from the pickets.

Ivar got up onto the level ground of fields, put his head down, and ran, expecting an arrow to slug him in the back, but no arrow came. Finally, he was winded and hurting and so ragged with pain that he dropped to his knees. He was well away, out of range, surrounded by shootlings of wheat or oats, he wasn't sure which because he was breathing hard and his eyes were watering and because anyway these fields had been trampled recently so there wasn't really much growing here, not as there should be.

His hand throbbed as if he had been stabbed. A shower of cold rain raked him and passed on, blurring the fields

and rattling through the fruit lines standing a stone's toss
west of him. A shallow irrigation canal cut away the
ground just in front of his knees. He stared at the streaming water until he thought he would drown.

Must go on.

He struggled to his feet. With one long dash, he could
reach the forest. Thank God the Eika had not come up
along the southwest road yet.

Directly ahead, several score riders emerged from the
cover of the woods and swept over the fields toward
Varre's now mostly-unprotected western flank. Horns
blared an alert. He turned to look behind. Arconia's banner swung neatly away from the battle along the southeastern entrenchment and, with several hundred horse,
raced to cut off this new threat.

He was trapped between. There was no chance he could
outrun them. With a shout, he flung himself into the canal.

After working the flank, Sanglant's cavalry cleared the
entire first line of defense. The Varrens retreated, or cow-
ered in the dirt, or died, while the infantry advanced to the
second line of defense built hard up against the base of the
road where it ramped up the eastern slope. Here, trenches
and barricades met them. Sanglant led the charge through
gaps carved by the milites in the stockades. His lance was
long since shivered in the corpus of some nameless Varren
soldier, but he worked mayhem to either side with his
sword. To his right, Liutgard's cavalry leaped shallow
trenches and low pickets but were at once caught in a
maelstrom of fighting and could not advance.

A rumble swelled as many hundreds of horsemen rolled
down on them from the center of the Varren camp. A red
stallion banner waved above the lead rank. Conrad was
riding to meet him.

A single line of pickets separated Sanglant's line from
the road, but the Varrens had massed here and were fighting fiercely as Kassel's milites struggled, numbers thinning.

The milites had taken the brunt of the assault, and had been outnumbered to begin with.

Dust rose from the hooves of Conrad's approaching troops, obscuring the battle joined to the southeast, where Theophanu was trying to break through. Best she hurry. He could no longer see Liutgard's white tabard among the hundred riders stalled before a low berm off to the right. She— or her captain—was trying to get through to the road some hundreds of strides west, in order to come up behind.

"Give me one more breach!" His hoarse voice rose over the tide of battle. "One more, and the day is ours!"

But a quick survey showed he had only two-score horse still up, and at best several hundred infantry, some joined by riders who had lost their mounts but could still fight.

A shout rose as the milites forced the barricade in three places, throwing down the pickets and fighting in the trench. Sanglant swung around. Fest jumped a trench and got up the berm to the roadbed, where they stood alone with the road open before and behind, fighting clashing all along behind him, and a shallow slope leading south to the open ground before. Many hundreds of riders galloped out of the Varren camp toward Sanglant's breach.

Hooves rang on the road as the foremost rank of Conrad's heavy horse, four abreast, gathered their charge. With spear held overhand, in blackened mail and black tabard and riding a fine black gelding, Conrad closed, pushing out to the front of his company.

A score of Sanglant's own good cavalry got up on the road behind him. He urged Fest to a trot, a canter, and the gelding broke into a full charge with Sanglant having nothing but sword and shield to fend off that long spear.

For once, Sanglant was taken by surprise.

As they closed, Conrad released his spear and veered so short that, although he pulled toward the shallow slope, his horse stumbled to its knees but rose with rider still on its back.

The spear struck true, piercing Fest through the meat of the neck and coming to rest against Sanglant's mail along the curve of his hip and thigh. The gelding crumpled,

spilling Sanglant forward. The shaft of the spear splintered
as Sanglant tumbled in a complete roll before pushing off
his shield onto his feet.

The ranks hit each other, passed through—as cavalry
sometimes did—with a few men going down and the rest
reining hard to get their horses turned around to strike
again.

As Conrad approached, high above, he drew his sword
and whistled sharply. His men circled, but did not move in
on Sanglant's unprotected back.

"I would not kill you, Cousin," Conrad cried. "Surrender, and I'll give you a grant of land, a wife of your choosing, and peace to live out your days. Once, I think, that was
all you asked for."

These words struck him as might a sword's blow. They
mocked him.

I don't want to be king, he had told his father at Werlida,
many years ago now. *I want a grant of land, Liath as my
wife, and peace.*

What had changed? Was it only his oath to his father,
sworn as Henry lay dying? Or had his heart changed? Did
he now covet the very things he had long ago scorned?

All this passed in a heartbeat as he raised his sword and
made ready to reply. It was strange how bright the sun was,
and how high the dust bloomed where the horses rode, and
how the music of war seemed muted once a man had fixed
his will on the one who opposed him.

"Your son, or daughter, to marry my daughter, or son,"
added Conrad, "and in this way your line and mine shall
rule jointly in the years to come. I am legitimately born,
you are a bastard. The army loves you, but the church does
not. I have Tallia and my own royal claim. It's the best offer
you'll get. What do you say, beloved Cousin?"

Ai, God.

The wind spun a whirlpool of bright air up onto the
roadbed. It swirled around him, making him blink, and
then flinch. A chilling touch bit at his mouth. An icy breeze
stung his nostrils. He staggered.

It poured into him like the breath of winter, and when it
grabbed his throat he could not speak and when it swal-

lowed his eyes he could not see and when it filled his limbs he could not move.

In the empty darkness that closed over him, all he heard was an echoing, inhuman voice.

"Where is he, the one I love? Where is Heribert hiding? Is he not in here? Where has he gone?"

6

HANNA abandoned her horse. She scrambled under the barricade and ran down the ramped road into the valley on the trail of the fleeing Varren guards. How stupid this was she considered only fleetingly, knowing what was behind her. The battle raged to her right, and horsemen flying Conrad's stallion banner galloped up from the left. To the east, Theophanu's army brawled in the entrenchments. It was impossible to tell who was holding firm and who falling back. Ranks of cavalry danced through the western fields, too distant to make out clearly.

The fighting along the northeastern pickets and trenches had the look of men tiring, pacing their strikes, parrying more than charging, just trying to hold their position, but who was winning and who losing she could not tell. It was all a churning mass of men and horses running, crawling, limping among the ditches and dead men and scattered stakes and broken stockades.

She had gotten about halfway down the ramp and, miraculously, no arrow had stuck her when, just beyond the base of the ramp on level ground, a lone horseman wearing a magnificent dragon helm broke up out of the entrenchments and gained the road. Riders struggled after him. She bent to grab a spear fallen onto the road. Lifted her gaze. Stunned at what she saw, she dropped to her knees.

Conrad was charging, out in front of his men. The rest of his cavalry thundered in from the south. Even if his remaining troops reached him, King Sanglant was hopelessly outnumbered.

"Tsst! *Sorgatani ahn na i-u-taggar.*"

A cloudy swirl of air spun up the side of the ramp. A stout woman appeared on the road in a showering mist of white powder, out of nowhere. A moment before *she had not been there.*

She was not Wendish; she had a flat, reddish-brown complexion and wore stiff skirts and heavy boots very like those of Kerayit women. A scrap of dried vegetation fell from her neck. It hissed where it struck the stones.

"Berda!" A young male voice called out of empty air. Hanna heard scratching sounds, like squirrels scrabbling on rocks, but she saw no one nearby.

Below, Wendish riders pushed their horses up to the road, following their king. Above, the woman who had appeared out of nowhere dashed up the ramp.

Hanna shouted after her. "Come back! There are Eika—"

A pair of Eika strode into view at the top of the ramp. They paused to observe the battle with the kind of leisurely posture that a man might wear in contemplation of a pleasant run of hunting in a field overrun with grouse. One held a spear and the other a banner pole fixed with a crosspiece and hung with strips and strands that waved in the wind tearing along the heights. Storm clouds rose like a wall behind them, black towers piled high in the heavens. The woman ran straight up the broad ramp toward the invaders.

"Hanna!"

She recognized that voice.

She turned.

Wolfhere stood behind her.

She shrieked and jumped backward, ramming into another body. They both fell in a tangle. Now that she was touching him, she saw a young man dressed in lordly manner in a fine linen tunic dyed green and trimmed with handsome embroidery, leggings, and handsome calfskin boots well worn from walking. Laid flat on the slope just below the rim of the road were two other young men, one Wendish and the other—she could never mistake those looks—born to the Quman tribes.

"Where did you come from?" she demanded of Wolfhere.

"G–g–got to get out of here!" the youth said raggedly. He was out of breath. Blisters had blossomed around his neck, which was curbed by a crudely woven necklace of dried leaves and fern fronds. "But where do we go now, Berthold?"

She pulled away from him and pushed to her feet. Eika above, battle on all sides, and below a tableau that fixed Hanna's gaze as though she looked down a tunnel. A man wearing blackened armor and riding a black horse charged solo against the dragon-helmed king, the two closing along the road, weapons raised.

In one breath, they would collide.

"It is time to go, friend," said Wolfhere as though talking to himself. "Go find him."

One breath caught in a gasp of exhalation as, beside Wolfhere, a cleric fell to his knees with gaze lifted heavenward and mouth open. Light spun in the air, like the flash of a mirror catching the sunlight, but when she blinked to protect her eyes, it winked and vanished. The cleric crumpled to the ground.

The crash of men meeting resounded. One horse stumbled, but came up with rider still on its back, while the other horse staggered and fell, tumbling its rider onto the ground. Men cried out in fear, while others shouted "huzzah!" or called frantic commands.

The young lord crawled whimpering back to his fellows, off the road. "For God's sake, let's get out of here. We're right in the middle of the worst of it, and we have no weapons! We'd be better hiding in the byre!"

Wolfhere knelt beside the fallen cleric and shook what appeared to be little more than skin and bones wrapped in tattered robes.

"What's happened to him?" Hanna knelt beside him.

"He's dead." Wolfhere grabbed the body by the ankles and dragged him off the road.

"What are you doing?" cried Hanna. She was stuck there, standing and staring first at Wolfhere, whose behavior made no sense and then at the appalling sight of

Sanglant alone on the road, unhorsed, with only a shield
and sword and no more than a score of riders to protect
him against hundreds of mounted riders armed with spears
and lances under the command of Conrad the Black.

Maybe if she could reach the duke before he struck the
killing blow.

She took a step, and a second. A hand closed on her
ankle and tugged her so hard she felt flat and barely caught
herself on her hands before her face smacked into stone.
The impact jarred up through her wrists and arms.

She shouted in pain. "What are you doing? Let me go
help him."

"I cannot," Wolfhere said, his grip like iron chains. "I swore
an oath long ago. Now, at last, I must pray it is fulfilled."

Stronghand's men cut a path through the barricade wide
enough to allow the Eika army to pass through four
abreast, and wide enough to admit the little wagon that
bore the Kerayit shaman in whose body was woven a spell
that killed. Stronghand pressed through the van and, together with Last Son, paused where level road hit the impressive ramp that carried the road down into the valley.

"Easy pickings," said Last Son. "Look there!"

A person dressed in stiff skirts bounded onto the road
and ran right toward them. Halfway down the long ramp,
the white-haired Eagle, who had been allowed to pass by
his troops unharmed only a short while ago, hesitated out
in plain sight where she was a target for every arrow and
anxious spear. Five other men scrambled up the rim where
the ramped road gave way into a sloping side.

But Last Son was pointing to the far west, not at the people below. "I see the signals, from the forest's edge."

Light flashed where his troops caught sunlight on the
faces of obsidian mirrors.

"Do you see her?" Stronghand had not looked west. He
surveyed the sprawling battle, spreading in the valley as
some units retreated and others advanced but in no order
whatsoever. Here, the Wendish flourished; there, they col-

lapsed. Among them, fighting in one place at the hand of the Wendish and in another place appearing on the side of the Varren levies, rode a woman who wore no distinguishing tabard, only plain mail, a battered shield, and a serviceable sword. He knew who she was all the same. No man could stand before her, who dealt death on all sides: the Lady of Battles, beloved of humankind.

"What are you looking at?" asked Last Son.

"Never mind," said Stronghand. "Our work will be done for us, as they slaughter their own kind. Hold the men back on all flanks. I'll hold to my word, that we will raise arms only against those who raise arms against us. Bring the Kerayit wagon forward."

Last Son gave him the standard before trotting off through the vanguard. Other Eika moved up alongside Stronghand, some silent, some laughing to see the carnage, some bored because they weren't fighting, and one sniffing at the air and rubbing at an ear as at a change in weather.

There was a change, a cold wind blowing out of the east and a hard hot iron scent, mingled with a dull boom that shuddered away and rose again and again. Rain pattered in the trees. Wind moaned and rattled as the storm strained against the unnatural leash holding it in: The power of his staff battled the storm, keeping it at bay.

There! Difficult to distinguish because of the shouts and screams and clangor of arms rising out of the valley, a shriek lifted from deep in the rear ranks of his army only to sigh away, buried under the din.

The human creature running up the ramp reached him. Showing no fear, it halted before him and spoke in the Wendish tongue.

"She is here. The holy one is with you. I am of her tribe. Let me join her."

He laughed. "What manner of animal are you?" he asked, because this one was like no other human he had met. It was dressed in the clothing and gold and bead baubles and headdress customarily worn by women and it moved with a woman's mannerisms, as he had learned to recognize them, but it smelled like a man.

"I am called Berda. Let me go to the holy one, lord."

Its lack of fear intrigued him. And he found loyalty commendable.

He signaled safe passage with a lift of his hand. The creature called Berda darted into the Eika army.

A duel between chiefs had broken out on the road below, where it leveled out, but its outcome did not interest him. His nose stung. An itch tickled his eyes. He shrugged uneasily, not liking the taste of the air.

He lifted his standard, testing the wind. An old magic licked his skin, quickly evaporating. This was not sorcery, then, but something natural. Perhaps after all it was only the tension of the storm that, lowering over them, could not break. No, they were safe from magic, as they had been since the day he bound the old sorcerer's magic into his staff.

He held his position, as still as stone, waiting for the tide.

The thumping feet of the Eika deafened Rosvita as the wagon rolled along, nestled within their ranks. They were like the ocean, stretching in every direction as far as she could see: a pair of them ducking past the bole of an ancient oak; a line of twenty to either side on the road; heads dipping in and out of sight in the woods; a sea of backs moving in disciplined order ahead of her.

How strange it was to see human soldiers marching with them, most with the golden-blond hair common to the Alban race. Conrad the Black's first wife had been a woman as fair as she was haughty, but her vexatious tongue had charmed Conrad and her milky-white skin, next to his dusky complexion, had caused a stir at court when she first arrived. They were a handsome couple, admired by all even though he had angered the Alban queen by stealing the princess away from her motherland.

Strange how the mind wandered, when it was trapped. A powerful wind raged at their back, heard as fury in the forest reaches. Rain sprayed them, but just when she expected to get hit by a squall, it faded off most uncannily. She shivered, although she wasn't cold. The horses felt it, too, or perhaps it was only the presence of the Eika—that unnatural smell like the flavor of stones baking in the sun—that unnerved them.

Through the door set into the cabin of the wagon, Sorgatani spoke, and although Rosvita tried to pity the Kerayit shaman, she feared her pitiless sorcery far more. *I am not so openhearted.*

"Hear you what comes?" piped the high voice. The accent rasped on the syllables. "Beware! We must run! Speak to Breschius."

All Rosvita heard was the tramp of a thousand and more marching feet, some slapping the roadbed and others trampling in the forest growth where branches scraped and leaf litter squeaked moistly underfoot.

Ahead, a vista opened where the hills gave way. The troops parted to let them through as they rolled past a crude barricade of old wagons meant to block the road but now shoved aside or chopped to pieces. Ahead, she saw the Eika standard, held by the one who called himself Stronghand. He seemed almost lost among the hulking bodies of his soldiers, who had crowded up to survey whatever scene unfolded in the valley below. What she heard—the clash of shield, the ring of sword and spear, the hissing of arrows, the cries of men and horses as they were cut down—told her the story of a battle raging beyond.

But after all, Rosvita did also hear a faint sound that rang eerily like the tolling of sonorous bells. Something moved in the forest off to the right. A rabbit shrieked in death.

Or was that a rabbit?

The smell of the forge swelled around them. Pitiful screams trembled in the air, each cut short. Breschius tripped, caught himself by the reins, and swung around to stare, with mouth agape and eyes squinted, back down along the road where they had come. The cart horses flicked their ears and jolted unevenly forward.

"Ai, God!" he cried, stumbling alongside. "Do you hear them, Sister?"

The tolling of bells had a voice. The voice spoke a name. *Sanglant.*

"What is that?" Rosvita demanded.

"We must run! Those are galla!"

"Lord and Lady bless us!" She clutched the seat. A stinging wind blew up from behind. Now, too late, she heard the screams of men dying close at hand. Fear prickled her neck. She broke into a sweat.

Breschius wailed. "Ancient and most terrible!" he cried. "We have no weapon that can harm them!"

The horses kicked in their traces and tried to bolt, but the harness held them. Around them, Eika turned to face the threat coming up from behind. At first she saw nothing, as they saw nothing from which one should run, nothing that one could fight.

Pillars of blackness swayed within the trees, swarmed along the road. They were towers of darkness moving in daylight, ribbons torn from the darkest storm and ripping through the ranks of the living. Most of the human soldiers panicked, dropping to the ground or pushing to get out of the ranks so they could run, but the Eika met the threat with a steadfast courage she had to admire. They held their ground as the galla engulfed first this man, and then another. Some leaped against the foe only to vanish within. Others danced at the edge, only to find themselves taken from behind by another of the creatures. None fled as any sane man would. Soldiers were flayed to the bone, although the remnant left of each Eika so consumed was not white bone at all but the color and texture of stone. A few cried out warnings to their brothers. Most died in silence.

"Rosvita!" cried Breschius. "Run! I cannot leave the princess, but you can save yourself."

The galla sailed through the forest and skimmed the roadbed. The throbbing of bells deafened her. She was too frightened and bewildered to move except to clap her hands over her ears. The gesture made no difference. This sound was not carried on the air but through the bones of the earth.

Sanglant.

The wagon rolled to the highest point of the road, just where it turned into the long incline down a massive manmade ramp. Here Lord Stronghand stood, staring with a most human expression on his face as the galla swept down on them: he was purely astonished, gripping his standard and shaking it at them as though to drive them away. An Eika soldier leaped, and shoved him off the ramp. They tumbled away down a steep verge with pebbles and small rocks skittering away in ragged trails.

"Fast! Fast! Evil demons come!" As out of nowhere, a Kerayit woman appeared on the road, shouting as she grabbed the reins of the horses out of Breschius' hand. "The holy one must be saved! Fast! Fast!"

She hauled, pulling them forward, yelling in a language whose words were meaningless to Rosvita but which might mean something to Breschius or Sorgatani. Breschius collapsed to his knees, giving way as the foreign woman swung up into the driver's seat. As the wagon passed him, Rosvita reached to grab him. He raised his hand to hers, and she grasped it, but his fingers slipped out of her hand as the newcomer whipped the horses ruthlessly into a run.

"Hei! Hei!" she called in a husky voice. "Make way!"

They left Breschius behind.

Rosvita yelped in fear as the wagon hit the incline. The weight of the wagon pressed it forward into the hindquarters of the beasts. The horses opened into a panicked gallop. A few people stood at the side of the ramp, heads slewing sideways as they stared upward in horror at the wagon careening down. Farther below, horsemen blocked the road, but they reined aside to get out of the way. There was one person in the middle of the road, staggering as though drunk.

The foreigner struggled with the reins, desperately trying to turn them aside from the man fixed in their path, but the horses had opened into a wild gallop and did not—could not—respond.

Rosvita shut her eyes. She whispered a prayer, asking forgiveness for her cowardice, and pitched herself off the side.

When she hit, her breath was knocked out of her as shoulder and hip took the impact. Pain stabbed. She rolled, hit the rim, and tumbled over the verge, coming to rest in a knob of grass grown in among the rocky in-fill.

Ai, God, she hurt as she crawled up the side and lay gasping. Breschius appeared on the ramp far above, calling after them. One moment she saw his familiar face, a good man who had served God faithfully and with joy his whole life long; the blackness devoured him as the galla glided through the space his body inhabited.

She shouted his name, too late, and because she was a coward, she scuttled back from the road as a dozen or more galla flowed down the slope, all fixed on one object.

Below, men scattered. All men but one.

When the wagon out of control and the horses in a blind panic hit the plane where the incline leveled out, the wagon bounced. An axle shattered. A wheel came loose.

The entire assemblage slammed right into the man wearing the dragon helm who stood in the center of the road. His body crumpled beneath hooves. The wagon lurched over him, then overturned and skidded with a grinding roar to one side as the horses screamed and, tangled in their harness, were jerked after it. The driver was thrown free and hit hard, lying still. One horse struggled to rise but fell back on a broken leg. The other did not move at all.

The man's body lay on its back on the ground, helm torn free, black hair fallen over the dark face. There is something about a body that is dead that tells the eye even at a distance. Once the soul is fled, the flesh is nothing but meat.

Never had any held breath lasted as long. It seemed to Rosvita that she had gone utterly deaf, or that all the noises of the world had been smothered.

All but one. A grizzled hand closed on her arm. Pain jarred her shoulder, and she gasped and gritted her teeth.

"Good Lord. Can it be you, Sister Rosvita?"

Her vision was blurred, but she knew that voice. "Wolfhere?"

"Quickly, we must move back. We are not safe here. Crawl this way, out of the galla's path."

"What has happened?" she asked weakly as he dragged her off the ramp.

She was bleeding, scratched, battered, and addled, with a headache building inside her head like the pressure of a storm about to break. But she was too terrified to mind those small inconveniences. The breath of the forge sank into her as the galla passed. Their presence stung her skin like the touch of fire. They sang in their deep bell voices, but in that tune sounded only one word over and over. Yet the tone in their voices had changed. She heard no statement but a question, as a child cries for its lost mother.

Sanglant?

Wolfhere flung himself down beside her and ducked his head to keep out of sight. "It did not play out as I intended," he remarked, not really seeming to speak to her but rather to himself as might a man accustomed to traveling a long road with only his own company to keep him occupied. "I cast a desperate throw, not sure it would work. Yet it seems I have succeeded at long last. He has been well protected by the geas his mother wove into his body."

"What do you mean?" she rasped, staring in horror as the galla swept down toward the body, as soldiers scrambled out of their way. Even those most loyal to their captain and king were too terrified to stand their ground. "What did you intend?"

His voice came to her from a distance, as if muffled by wool, but it was nevertheless astoundingly cool, collected, and at peace.

"Sanglant's death. Just as King Arnulf commanded."

XI

AN UNNATURAL
MEASURE OF LUCK

1

THE irrigation ditch was not more than an elbow deep and
barely shoulders' width. Its bed was slick and slimy, but
Ivar dug in anyway, swallowing water that tasted of dirt
and the foul leavings of night soil. The thunder of hooves,
closing in on his position, shook through the ground.

The two forces hit right above him. The crack of the impact clapped louder than any storm. Hooves pounded
around him as horses were yanked sideways or backward,
as men pressed the enemy. Water slopped over his head. He
scrambled for purchase on the slippery sides, gulping water,
coughing, trying to get out from under. When a broken
spear clattered onto his back, he dragged himself out of the
ditch and scrambled for the line of fruit trees. Cutting zigs
and zags through the seething push and pull of the skirmish,
he got free of it, only to stumble over a dying man. He
wrenched the man's shield off his arm and ducked under it
as he sprinted for the nearest tree. A line of riders broke off
from the melee as a whip uncoils. He flung himself flat as
they galloped over him. A hoof grazed his head, the merest
clip, like the brush of the Lady's Hand. A mercy. A blessing.

He crawled like a worm through the weeds, with the

shield held over his back. One blow in passing shivered it, but it did not shatter. Dirt ground into his elbows. He tasted a coating of weeds as pollen shaken loose by the skirmish dusted his mouth. The line of trees loomed before him, and he stumbled under their cover, such as it was. He huddled against the thickest trunk he could find. A small green apple, early lost from the branches, got under his thigh, digging a painful knot. Scant shelter this proved. The trees were too far apart to provide cover. But it was the only shelter he had against the melee crashing around him. He peeked over the rim of the shield.

Wichman of Saony he recognized at once. No one else fought with such reckless disregard for life and limb. The lord yowled and cackled as if it was the greatest sport in the world as he drove a dozen of his riders in a wide sweep through a field and cut around to try to catch the flank of the guivre's company where the banner of Arconia flew. This path took him right between the trees, his company the weft pushing through the warp of the row of trees. He rode full out, ducking under low hanging branches, bellowing like a madman.

"For the phoenix! For the phoenix!"

Sabella rode with her troops, although she lagged behind to let the front rank meet the charge between ditch and trees. An Arconian captain leaned forward to gain a clean shot at Wichman's head. Lord Wichman's lance caught the man high on the shoulder at the base of the neck and came out through his back with a spray of gore. Their horses collided. Wichman flew over the top of both horses and the other man's slack body, and landed on his back not ten paces from Ivar. His helmet flew off and rolled along the ground. Arconian riders whooped, and pursued him.

Unsteadily, Wichman rose by sliding with his back against the tree as he reached for his sword. But another soldier's lance struck him in the right shoulder, pierced armor and flesh, and pinned him to the tree.

The melee dissolved into chaos, spinning out to all sides as the fighting broke into knots of frantic battering and pressing. Only at this center did a weird lull descend.

Ivar caught his breath—two breaths—as his gaze was

drawn outward over the field of battle; he could see everything, all the way to the walls of Kassel. The fighting was spread across these fields with no purpose or pattern he could discern, a jumble of motion punctuated by the ring of arms, the cries of the wounded, and the obstacles created by the now ruined siege works. Only the huge ramped road that led up the eastern slope into the forest stood clear, an easy landmark to spot from any distance.

Strangely, the only significant motion on that portion of the road was that of a runaway wagon flying down the ramp toward lower ground. A fence of men scattered on the high ridgeline, pouring away from the road. Thunder growled as the solid drumbeat that had shaken the air stuttered into an erratic hammer. Bells tolled. This deep throbbing so frightened him that he pushed up to his feet, meaning to bolt for the western woods. That resonance burned like fire along his skin

Twenty men or more wearing Arconian tabards drew up before the trees. A single rider dismounted and pushed back her helm. Lady Sabella's face was streaked with sweat, and she was clearly straining, red in the cheeks and white with fatigue about the eyes.

"So, Wichman." She hefted a wicked-looking mace as she walked toward the helpless lord. "This will put a stop to your rebellion. You're a pig of a man."

Wichman grinned, although it was more a baring of teeth as he struggled against the lance that had torn through his shoulder. He was pinned tight to that trunk. "That don't mean much, coming from you, Cousin."

She snorted. Her gaze skipped over Ivar, but then she halted, looked a second time, and fixed her gaze on him in a way that made him squirm. "Good God above! I thought I recognized you. You were dead, you faithless liar! It's your fault that I lost my noble prisoners and my pretty cleric. You son of a bitch."

He had not even a knife to defend himself. She raised the mace, and closed on Ivar.

A wild roar of voices lifted off the battlefield as a storm of rage and fear swept the field. Above all this, riding on the wind, a shrill cry rang down from the heavens. A vast shadow scudded over the valley of Kassel. Men staggered to a stop where it passed. Ivar could not move, although he bent his mind on a helpless struggle to get his legs to move. Even Sabella paused in mid-step, her mace lifted above her shoulder, in the act of commencing the blow that would smash Ivar's head in.

All became still. Thunder faded. The rattle of drums fell silent. Men simply ceased moving. Even the horses could only roll their eyes in fear. Moans rose from terrified men as from a choir, but these voices were soft, muffled by this heavy weight that drowned all creatures on the field of battle.

Wichman grunted. His hand twitched. His fingers curled around the hilt of his knife, and he eased it free of its leather sheath. Somehow, where all others stood in a stupor, as if turned to stone, he flicked his hand.

The knife flew, winking.

God knew that Wichman had always possessed an unnatural measure of luck, although only God knew why such an unpleasant man should gain what was denied to others.

The blade buried itself in Sabella's throat.

At first, she hung there as though held up by the same stupifying force that had seized all of them. A single drop of blood pearled from the wound.

That shrill cry raked through the valley a second time. This time Ivar saw the beast fly overhead. Its scaly hide shone with a poisonous glamour that made his eyes ache. Its baleful glare paralyzed all that looked its way, and because it was both beautiful and terrible, all men and women stared to see it fly above them.

"Call me a pig," muttered Wichman. He slumped. His eyes rolled up in his head.

Sabella dropped, with the mace still gripped in her hand and the knife embedded in her throat.

Ivar could not move and he could not hear, not the wind, not any cries of humankind, not the bells. He thought he had gone deaf until the silence was broken by a mundane sound, heard from this distance only because of the uncanny hush.

It was the cheerful barking of a pair of hounds.

2

*EVEN the plans of the canniest leader will sometimes go
astray, because no person can anticipate the twists of fate. It
is always the unexpected blow that brings you down.*

*He holds the standard devised by the old priest. Its haft is
painted wood, and the cross guard is adorned with feathers
and bones, unnameable leathery scraps, the translucent skin
of a snake, yellowing teeth strung on a wire, the hair of
SwiftDaughters spun into chains of gold and silver and
iron and tin, beads of amethyst and crystal dangling by
tough red threads, and bone flutes so cunningly drilled and
hung that the wind moans through them. The haft hums
against his palm as though bees have made their hive inside
the wood.*

*This powerful amulet, woven in and into and of the wood
pole with its cross guard, protects from magic all those he
holds in his hand and under his protection.*

*Yet there are creatures in the world that have a power akin
to magic, woven into their very bones, but which are not
themselves magic wielded by the hand of another.*

This truth he has overlooked.

*When the bell voices throb in the forest, when the pillars
of black smoke glide out of the trees and flense his soldiers,
he knows fear for the first time. His Eika are the bravest of
all soldiers; they do not fear death because they have already
eaten death in order to become men and not remain dogs.*

*What stalks them now is not death but obliteration, and
even so they leap to fight it although they are overwhelmed.
What the creatures of darkness eat is the soul.*

*He is shaken. Standing on the road, surveying what he
knew until this instant was to be his greatest victory, he is too
stunned to move out of the way as the towers of black smoke
cut through his soldiers and loom over him.*

*Last Son slams into him, and they tumble over the side of
the ramped road and roll in a cascade of pebbles and dirt
around and around and around. The standard is ripped to
pieces, shattering. All its parts and pieces spill and spray in
every direction*

*   *   *

Perhaps it was a root that tripped him up, or his own feet, or a hollow in the path they followed. He fell sprawling and smacked into the dirt. The hounds at once swarmed him to lick his face and tug at his clothing. For too long—an instant or an eternity—he lay stunned as a growing wind shook the trees and the guivre chirped restlessly, tail thrashing in the brush.

He was blind to what lay outside him, but in his inner eye a vision of the past bloomed until he could see nothing else.

The Lady of Battles and her white warhorse climbing the Dragonback Ridge.

Brother Gilles stuck through with a spear by a ravening Eika marauder who rips the precious holy book out of the old man's trembling hands.

Aunt Bel standing in the doorway, staring out into the wet night wondering what has become of her foster nephew.

Sparrows eating crumbs off Lackling's hands as the half-wit weeps silently with joy.

Stronghand chained and a prisoner, howling to provoke the hounds.

Lavastine sitting at the count's table, measuring Alain with a keen blue gaze.

Lady Sabella with her hair plaited back and dressed in gold-and-silver ribbons, but left uncovered, like a soldier's.

Brother Agius hand in hand with Biscop Constance as they whisper late in the night, captive both in body to their enemy and in heart to each other—a marriage long ago forbidden and impossible. Beyond them, Biscop Antonia's eyes are open, and she watches as they comfort each other. She is a huge yawning maw sucking in life and air, a gate through which the most unnatural forces can cross. Envy is the shadow of the guivre, the wings of death.

She has called the galla from a far place that is no part of this world, or of the aether that circulates through all things, through the cosmos itself.

"Go," he whispered into the dirt. He shoved himself up. He faced the guivre and caught it with his stare. "Go! As I command you, who spared you once, this favor I am owed in recompense. Go to the field of battle. Fly there until I say otherwise."

On the ground it was an ungainly thing, but when it leaped and caught the high wind, it flew with a grace that makes a man smile with joy to see God's hand in the heavens working such beauty. It cried out once, and then he lost sight of it as it winged away over the trees. He brushed off his forearms and his legs, and pulled a twig out of his hair. Sorrow and Rage sat watching, panting although the wind was brusque enough to make eyes sting when you faced into it. The sky overhead was as dark as pitch, but it was not raining, although it ought to have been. The Lady had called this storm, and it followed no natural course.

"Come." He broke into a steady run. The hounds loped with him, one before and one behind. Yet it was too late. Too late. The battle had already started; he had not prevented it after all.

Except that it is never too late. The world continues on its path despite the accidents and tragedies and joys that unfold in the life of any given individual. You must press forward so long as you have breath. Toil in those fields that God cherish most. You have done as well as any man.

So Lavastine had said. But Alain had lost Tallia, and he had lost Lavastine as well. He had watched the count turn to stone, his own effigy.

Memories chased him as he ran, images rising and falling away in time to the beat of his footsteps pounding on earth.

A dawn battle against the Eika when the Lady of Battles rode at his side.

Henri accusing him of lying in order to gain a count's favor.

Liath weeping by the hearth fire.

The battle at Gent, and the ragged, half-wild prince stumbling away from the victory feast, retching because he was unable to tolerate food after starving for so long.

Tallia on their wedding night. Always there would be a measure of pain, remembering this. Remembering the nail she had used to scar her own hands.

I have been tricked.

He had lost the county of Lavas in the end and marched east as a Lion, where he had killed a man to show mercy and had been himself killed.

Death had taken him to Adica, and death had taken Adica from him—although surely Adica had never belonged to him or he to her in those ancient days, forgotten now by humankind. Only the burial mounds remain, which is memory of a kind, a thing tangible but mute.

He had found peace at Hersford Monastery for a short time, yet peace had a fragile heart and this was soon broken. Falling into the hands of bandits, he had killed the man once known as Brother Willibrod, a creature without a soul who had sucked the life out of others to maintain his rotting shell.

After that, memory scattered. He lost his anchors—Rage and Sorrow—and it seemed to him that his memories of that time toiled around and around in an endless circle until a sharp blow sent him plummeting into the pit. He wandered for a time in darkness and after this in light, and for a time he was caged and after this the tempest rose and the sea swamped him and the dragon broke free of the earth that had imprisoned it for a time beyond memory. Beyond any memory but his own, who because of the intervention of sorcery had witnessed the ancient spell which had set all this in motion.

Who else recalled it?

One: the centaur shaman. But when he sought the breath of her soul in the living world, he could not find it.

Two: the WiseMothers, who were born out of that ancient conflagration and who had spread the nests of their children across the northern lands. But when he sought the spirit of their slow minds in the aether, he could not find them.

It falls to me to do what is right. That is reward enough in the eyes of God.

When he came to the forest's edge high above the fields, the lines of battle had already been drawn and overrun, but soldiers on all sides stood in an uncanny stillness, frozen by the guivre's stare. He stood on the edge of a steep hillside torn by an avalanche. It was loose with debris, too dangerous to cross or descend.

He called. The guivre swept a wide circle and came back to him. He grabbed the hounds by their collars and led them along a tree trunk that had fallen out into the open space to make a precarious ledge. The log slipped sideways under their weight. The hounds yelped in panic. The guivre swooped low as the log gave way and rolled out from under Alain's feet. Its claws fastened on his shoulders, and the startled hounds were silenced as they, too, were yanked upward with the collars biting into their vulnerable throats. Their weight seemed likely to pop his shoulders out of joint, but the guivre plunged with dizzying speed down along the barren slope and over its desolation of splintered and jumbled trunks, snapped and shredded branches, and scraps of vegetation marked by clusters of blooming cowslip and vine-pinks that had taken root since last autumn's tempest.

The lay of the ground—the steep slope dropping precipitously into a hollow backed up into a trio of low hills—had protected the walls of Kassel from destruction. Here the mass of debris had piled up into a fresh berm. The guivre skimmed low along the north and east flanks of the town. Soldiers were fixed at attention along the walls. No one pointed, and if any screamed, all Alain heard was the whistling of wind and a distant mutter as of humankind trying to find a voice.

Made mute and frozen by the guivre's roving gaze, every creature there stood helpless.

Ahead lay the scene of the worst slaughter: a line of siege works overtaken by a charge, men fallen every which way and horses broken down with wounds and shattered limbs. Cavalry had fixed in their tracks along the road—from the height he discerned the paving slabs and graded foundation of the old roadbed, strung so straight and turning at such precise angles that it could easily be seen to be the work of the old Dariyan Empire.

A ramp bridged the bluff that separated the valley from the higher forest to the east. Many soldiers stood paralyzed on the road and within the trees. Along the hills, Eika corpses lay strewn in horrifying numbers, and among them gleamed white bone remains of human soldiers, their bodies consumed by the passing galla.

A score of galla poured down along the ramp. The timbre of their bell voices rang both despair and pain.

He kicked as the guivre dropped low over the high end of the ramp. He and the hounds tumbled to earth, and because he released their collars they bounded away, barking as they found themselves free.

At the base of the ramp lay a wrecked wagon fallen on its side. The bodies of the two horses and the driver were wrapped in the tangle of harness. The cart held a tiny house built over its bed, which remained mostly intact, but the axles had splintered and the wheels shattered into a dozen spars and slivers. A single body sprawled in the middle of the road.

Not one soul moved except the galla. They had crossed into this world through a rent in the fabric of the universe; the guivre's stare could not hold them. They flooded down the ramp and churned in a whirlpool about the wagon and that one isolated figure.

He heard them call: *Sanglant.*

But they could not find Sanglant—they could not find his essence, the substance that caused him to be alive.

Alain approached along the road while, in a mirror of his own movement, a single mounted soldier drew close to face him from the other side of the picket of circling galla. The iron heat that roiled from them forced him to stop well back. That taste of the forge burned his skin and coated his tongue with a sour flavor. But the black pillars—each a void—eddied around the body fallen in the road. They did not approach or retreat; they seemed caught between purpose and confusion.

"He served me well for many long years, dealing death but never suffering death," said the Lady of Battles. "I wondered if any hand could stop him while his mother's curse protected him, but I think that now he is truly gone."

Sanglant had gone under the wheels and been besides pierced through his abdomen by a jagged spoke flung hard away in the wagon's crash. His mangled body was slack.

The strap on his dragon's helm had been severed and the fanciful helmet itself had tumbled an arm's length from the man. A single griffin's feather had come to rest across his body, and possibly it was this guardian that held off the galla.

Possibly Sanglant was still alive.

The cold smile worn by the Lady of Battles goaded him forward. The hounds began to follow him, although they were terrified, so he commanded them to stay well back from the whirlpool of darkness.

He walked, and where he walked the galla swung wide around, avoiding him. His skin prickled where the tide of their passing brushed against him, but their touch did not devour him. As he walked through their ranks, he listened.

They had voices but not precisely words; they spoke, but not with a verbal language in the manner of humankind and her cousins. It sounded at first like the hissing of snakes, but even the hissing of snakes carries meaning. Deep within the tolling he heard what they were trying to communicate.

Pain. Pain. Pain. The breath of this world scalds us. We suffer. Let us go home. This soul called Sanglant is the gateway through which we can cross. Where has it gone?

He knelt beside Sanglant and pressed a hand to the side of that dark neck, but found no pulse. Around him, the galla loomed, more deadly than storm clouds and as black as the Pit. He could see nothing beyond them, only this patch of road and the body of the prince. It was as if the world had vanished, or never existed. Only the Lady of Battles gleamed, a presence without physical substance that yet permeated the world.

In the beginning existed the four pure elements: light, wind, fire, and water. Above these dwelled the Chamber of Light, and below them, in the depths, the Enemy, which is darkness. By chance, as the elements moved and mingled, they transgressed the limits set them, and the darkness took advantage of the momentary chaos to rise out of the pit and corrupt them.

"You will ever be with us," he said to her, "but even so, I will never cease in the struggle against you."

"Stay beside me." Her smile was that of an irresistible temptress or a generous mother. It would be easy to believe that smile a worthy gift, and a worthier reward, but he knew better.

"So I will. You will not escape me."

He picked up the griffin feather. Rising, he stepped in among the galla.

"Go back," he said to them, extending his arm. They swayed into him, crowding as he cut through the black substance of the closest galla. With a snap, and a hiss, and a whiff of the forge, it vanished. The others followed, one by one, until the last agonized voice was drained from the world.

When he turned, hoping he had banished her, the Lady of Battles waited. The griffin feather held no power over her. He placed it on the body.

"The guivre holds these combatants in its thrall," she said, watching him. "It cannot do so forever. Then they will fight. There is nothing you can do to stop it. You have admitted as much yourself. This is the way of the world."

"You are mistaken."

She laughed, turned her horse and, between one breath and the next, vanished into a shower of mist. Rain swept the field and passed swiftly into the west. Thunder boomed. The guivre shrieked, awaiting his command as it circled on an updraft.

He whistled. The hounds loped up to him, butting him with their great heads. He scratched the base of their ears and touched a palm to their cold moist noses. They turned from him and approached the body of the prince with more caution, ears down and tails stiff. Sorrow growled, and Rage nudged the body with her muzzle.

The dead man opened his eyes.

Rage startled back. Sorrow set up such a racket of barking that Alain clapped his hands over his ears. The body jerked in a most unnatural manner. Arms and legs shifted awkwardly as it clambered to its feet in a way no human person had ever moved. The griffin feather fell off its body to the road, and it seemed not even to notice.

"Who are you?" demanded Alain. He felt a little sick, seeing a puppet in what had once been a proud man.

"Where is he?" said Sanglant.

Although his strong tenor with its hoarse scrape sounded the same, Alain knew this was not Sanglant talking. Blood oozed from his belly, smearing the rings of his torn mail. Gray guts pouched from the ragged edges of the wound. One of his hands was smashed, and his leg left should not have been able to hold weight with the foot twisted sideways to the knee and the thigh crushed and shredded until flesh and bone were intermingled.

"Where is the one I love? They told me that I would find him if I came here, but he is not here."

"Whom do you seek?"

"The ones born of earth called him 'Heribert.' I loved him because he favored me who was ugliest among my cousins, for we are born in the sphere of Erekes and many of us have not the beauty of our higher brethren. Yet he spoke kindly to me when others did not. But he walked away by the command of the prince of dogs and even when he returned to me he was not there. Only his shell. Where has he gone?"

"He is dead, I think," said Alain gently.

"What is death?" it asked him.

It used the face of Sanglant to speak, but its grimaces showed neither grief nor anger. It did not comprehend the emotions of humankind and could not imitate them or even know that it might strive to do so. It was a creature of the aether—its substance blazed blue behind the eyes of the prince—and although Alain did not know how it had been coerced out of the spheres and down to Earth, he could see that it had become trapped here because the daimones of the upper air have one thing in common with humankind: they can love.

"Our souls depart this Earth when it is time for them to ascend to the Chamber of Light, a place which lies above the uppermost sphere," he said. "Where is the soul of the body you now inhabit?"

"There is no soul here. It was here when I first came looking, and I pushed it aside while I searched for the one I love. But then a weight struck us and I felt how the threads that weave it to the flesh were severed."

"How can this be? No creature male or female can kill him. You are sure no other soul resides in that body?"

Horribly, it cracked its head sideways, looking up into the sky. Blood leaked from parted lips, although otherwise the face was unmarked, yet the vigor that made Sanglant handsome was extinguished. Here now was merely an assemblage of indifferent features. "I can apprehend its track. It has crossed out of the lower air into the sphere of Erekes."

"Ai, God," whispered Alain. His tears fell as Sorrow whined and Rage gave a hesitant wag to her tail. "He is a good man. Can you not fly after him and bring him back?"

Without anger, without curiosity, without desire, the daimone spoke. "Why should I?"

Alain shrugged helplessly. The hounds nosed his hands, and he stroked them, who loved him and who had stayed with him all this time only because of the affection that binds creatures one to the other. This essence cannot be touched and cannot truly be named, but it exists in the world just as the Lady of Battles does, knit into the bones of the Earth and of every living creature that dwells on Earth or in heaven.

"Because Heribert loved him."

It stared at him as would a man who is amazed to hear you speaking in a language he expects to understand but does not. It blinked, but the movement was as steady as that of a sunning lizard. One shoulder twitched. It lifted a hand and regarded fingers and palm without expression.

Wordless, it staggered, limbs jerking, and turned around in a full circle as if seeking a missing friend. Then the body collapsed onto the ground. Emptied.

He knelt beside it, but Sanglant was dead.

Weeping, he pressed a hand against the dead man's forehead. His voice was no more than a whisper. "God, please heal him."

But the corpse did not breathe, and did not stir. No heart's blood pulsed under the skin.

The guivre's hot breath blew over his back. It hit the road so hard that the shudder passed up through his feet. Its huge beaklike snout lowered until it was at a level with his face. Its breath was hot but not unpleasant; it smelled of calming frankincense.

Its long neck swayed hypnotically, and its eyes whirled until he fell into those depths and saw, within, the field of battle laid below him and all the forestlands and even farther beyond, as the land fell away until all earthly landmarks became tiny scratches on the vast tapestry that is the world. Rivers were threads of blue, and forest swathes of multicolored green. Towns and houses poked ragged holes in brighter colors. Here and there the many creatures crawled within the interstices of the weave as do mice within the church walls and among the meadow flowers. It seemed to him that each living thing appeared as an infinitesimal flare of light and heat against the colder and weightier spans of stone which buttress the architecture of life.

Spread across the lands lie the many stone crowns, a vast loom of magic. Faint passageways link them. Threads strung between crowns and stars grow taut, or loose, as the world shifts its position, ever rolling, and the stars rise and set on their endless round. A bright figure trailing a wispy blue ghost of aetherical wings races along one of those corridors in the company of shadowy companions; their trail leads them to a crown glittering above the solid, familiar compound that he recognizes as Hersford Monastery.

But greater wonders draw his gaze away.

For an instant he believes he can glimpse the span of the heavens and the spheres themselves: the pearl that is the Moon, icy Erekes, rosy Somorhas, the blazing furnace of the Sun, Jedu's angry lair, the hall of Mok, the dazzling light of Aturna. Beyond these and locked around them rests the realm of the fixed stars, with its heavy silver sheet of sky and flashing, molten surface of liquid aether.

And farther yet, beyond all, you may find the pure heart of the universe which is light and darkness, whirling in a silence so vast that it is both something and nothing, substance and void, an infinite span impossible to comprehend but also as finite as a grain of sand resting in the palm of his hand.

This is the Abyss, into which all of humankind falls in the

end. Yet it is also the Chamber of Light, incandescent and encompassing, the rose of compassion whose bloom restores the world.

The guivre nudged him, and he fell flat on his buttocks and found himself back on the road with the hounds whining and his head aching from that guivre's breath blasting right into his face. What calmed others roused in him a nagging discontent. Restlessness stirred in his heart.

Liath was returning to Wendar, but she would come too late to save her beloved.

No matter. Grief and anger will always ride in the world. There was still work to be done.

He stood shakily and raised both hands. "I release you," he said to the guivre. "Go free, friend. You have honored the trust I placed in you."

Its chirp was as high and light as that of a baby bird, incongruous in such a huge and terrifying beast. It opened its wings, spanning the width of the road, bunched its haunches, and sprang heavenward. The draft slapped him back down on the road. The hounds were flattened by it, and men and riders who had until now remained poised like statues were flung aside, tumbling to their knees, horses pushed sideways within the circle of that powerful gust. It gained height, circled once, and arrowed northwest, back toward its old haunts deep in the wild forestlands where few men dared hunt.

He dusted himself off, got to his feet although every muscle twinged, and sought the paralyzed figure of Conrad. The duke of Wayland had been tossed from his horse and was now grimacing, on his knees, struggling to rise and grasp his sword as the influence of the guivre waned. Alain drew the sword, wresting it out of the duke's hand, and heaved it to one side. It rang on the stone paving and tumbled off the roadbed.

Conrad blinked, shook himself, and with a roar of anger staggered to his feet. "What means this?" Then he saw the mangled body and the shattered wagon. "Ai, God!" he cried, stumbling forward to kneel beside the corpse. "What is this? Sanglant! Cousin!"

"Call off your men," said Alain.

Conrad looked up at him in surprise, noted the hounds, and with a shake of his head recognized him.

"Call off your men," repeated Alain. "The battle is over."

Movement stirred along the road, out in the siege works, and up along the ridgeline as soldiers found their legs and crept cautiously to get a view of the field. The silence was oppressive, but it also made men hesitant to strike the first blow at others as bewildered and groggy as themselves.

Alain trotted over to the Wayland's banner bearer, a towheaded lad still rubbing his eyes as he searched for the banner he had dropped which lay folded in the dirt. He wore a horn looped to his belt. Alain tugged it free before the lad had recovered enough strength to protest, and raised it to his own lips.

Four times he blew. The call rang over the field. When it faded, a second horn answered and then a third, one higher voice and one lower. A captain wearing Wendish colors fell to his knees beside Sanglant's body. He lifted a horn to his mouth. It stuttered a weak, weeping cry, and broke off as he folded forward in anguish. Conrad reached to comfort the captain, resting a hand on his shoulder.

To the southeast, a procession—mostly on foot—cut a path toward them, flying the banner of Saony. Of Arconia's banner there was no sign. Individuals rose from the cover they had taken. All converged on the wrecked wagon: a cleric in torn and dusty robes; a dozen soldiers groaning as they saw the wreck of their noble leader; a young Eagle with white hair; a pair of young, dazed-looking noblemen supporting an equally young man who bore the look and dress of the Quman tribes; a straggle of Eika shifting a cautious advance down the ramp while, above them, their brethren eased a pair of wagons onto the slope. Alain saw the one he sought at the head of this company. He was limping as he eased his passage with the broken haft of what had once been his standard. Alain handed the horn back to Conrad's standard-bearer and loped forward with the hounds at his heels.

"Brother!" he called.

The Eika raised a hand in salute.

When only a few paces separated them, Alain halted as Stronghand halted. They stared at each other because they were, in this way and at this moment, scarcely more than strangers although they had dreamed deep into the life of each other for so many years. Stronghand had changed. He had an Eika's posture, bold as predators are bold, accustomed to the kill, but a man's expression.

"I am come." Stronghand scanned the field with a look as weary and filled with pain as that of any human captain who has seen his soldiers scythed down before him. "I am come to find you, as OldMother and the WiseMothers commanded me, their obedient son."

3

SOLDIERS made room as Hanna pushed through the crowd to the body and its attendants. No more than a dozen people had reached the wreckage, but more were coming, shaking free of their stupor to stagger in from all sides. Men wept openly, while others stared in shock, eyes dry. The body had been horribly crushed and mutilated by its impact with the wagon. She could do nothing for the dead man.

But Sorgatani might yet be alive in the overturned wagon.

Turning, she stared into the face of a slender Eika warrior. Like all his kind, he smelled of the scent that rises off rocks baking in the sun. His eyes narrowed.

"I have seen you before." It was startling to hear human words issuing from an inhuman mouth.

She sidestepped without answering, flushed as adrenaline raced. He held no drawn weapon, but he looked as dangerous as any sharp spear and he had besides many ranks of Eika filing down the ramp after him. The front ranks of this silent army halted at a prudent distance rather than descending into the midst of the shaken crowd of Wendish and Varren combatants.

Sorgatani's sorcery could protect her if fighting broke out. It was a coward's instinct, but she was numb to the bone, still reeling from the torpor that had gripped her when the guivre screamed overhead. Her skin burned with a fading memory of the passing of the galla. So close that they might have devoured her, as they had so many others.

All gone, although she did not know what had driven the galla away. Sanglant was dead, but his body was not consumed.

She shuddered, taking a too hasty step away, and tripped over the tangle of harness. A strong hand caught her. She looked up into the face of a young Quman warrior. Swearing, she yanked her arm out of his grasp, and jumped away.

"Hanna! Steady!" A hand braced her.

"Wolfhere! How are you come here?"

"It seems Sanglant is truly dead." The familiar face and his kindly expression soothed her.

"How can it be? I thought his mother laid a geas on him, that no creature could kill him."

He shrugged, surveying the wreckage. "What wagon is this? Not Wendish, by the decorations. What manner of creature bides within? There is sorcery knit into those walls."

Hanna flushed. "A Kerayit shaman, that's all. She can have known nothing of this. It's an accident that her wagon struck the prince—the king—at all. You cannot—you must not—let the blame fall on her."

"So she is a woman," he murmured. "Nothing strange in that."

He looked at the broken form of the driver, who had fallen underneath the still living horse. The beast's hindquarters were crippled, and every time it tried to struggle up, it collapsed again on top of the driver's battered corpse. The other horse was quite dead, neck twisted at an unnatural angle. Flies buzzed around its open eyes, although, strangely, no flies afflicted Sanglant's corpse. "Lord Berthold, here is your healer. I fear she is dead."

A trio of young men pressed forward to surround the body of the Kerayit woman who had been driving the wagon.

"Where did she come from?" asked Hanna. "God Above! Where did all of *you* come from?"

She stepped back as the Quman picked a route past her. He knelt beside the dead woman and pressed his mouth to her mouth in a gesture nothing like a kiss.

Sitting back on his haunches, he spoke to his companions. "Dead in truth, Lord Berthold. No breath lives in her."

"A faithful servant," said the one called Berthold quietly, "if quite the ugliest woman I've ever set eyes on."

The Quman shrugged. "She was one of that kind. I know not your word. In our language, we say they have two spirits."

Hanna happened to be looking toward Wolfhere. Now the Eagle's gaze fixed on the young Quman. His breathing quickened, and he leaned over him to frown at the body. It was true that the Kerayit had a coarse face and big hands; her felt skirts, hiked somewhat up because of the way she had fallen, revealed thickly muscled calves not quite those of even a soldierly woman.

"What do you mean?" The Eagle reached for the skirts to pull them up, but the Quman half drew his sword, a gesture hidden from everyone but the five clustered around the dead Kerayit. The movement was just enough to show that he would allow no desecration of the corpse.

"These, the Kerayit, are enemies of my own people. But we respect those of two spirits. It is ill luck to trouble these who are touched by the gods."

"Odei!" Lord Berthold spoke impatiently, seeing how folk moved around the corpse of the king not a stone's throw from them. "Let us do her honor, who kept faith with us, but let us not stand here talking about nothing. If you have something to say, say it."

"Have you not such kind of people among your tribes? A person born in a girl's body with the spirit of a man. If she can take on a man's life, then who will say she is not a man? This one, also. She holds a woman's spirit, and lives a woman's life, even if she wears a man's body."

"What are you talking about?" cried Berthold.

Wolfhere rose with a grim smile on his face. "So the riddle is solved. And the weapon unlooked for. No creature male *or* female can harm him. It seems I am lucky rather than clever." He touched Hanna on the elbow. "Fare you well, Hanna. Stay strong, for the Eagles will need you."

"What do you mean?" she asked him, but his expression told her nothing and his gaze had already lifted beyond hers to reckon the movement of soldiers and nobles that churned in a massive current drawing them all to the heart of the battle: the fallen king.

"Yes, what *do* you mean, Odei?" demanded Lord Berthold. "Do you mean Berda is really a man? And only dressed as a woman? And we didn't notice *all this time?*"

Odei's jump from crouching to standing grabbed Hanna's attention. Quman soldiers were notorious for being the most phlegmatic of men, immune to hardship, safe from emotion, but he was really angry. "Berda was one person, with two spirits. So it is known among our people, who respect those so favored. We must give her proper burial rites." Seeing the stricken look on the young lord's face, his own expression softened. "You cannot know. You see only with your outer eyes. My uncle is a shaman. He taught his nephews to look with the inner eye."

"Wolfhere," she said, turning back.

The old Eagle had vanished. She turned all the way around, but he was nowhere to be seen among the milling crowd, with more on their way, and the banner of Saony and that of Fesse moving purposefully in their direction. All coming here. All wanting to blame someone.

"Oh, God." The wasp sting burned in her heart.

The axles had cracked. The wheels shattered. The driver's seat had torn free. Worse, the wagon had fallen onto the side with the only door. She slapped the skin of felt stretched taut over the unseen scaffolding that covered the bed of the wagon.

"Sorgatani! Sorgatani! Can you hear me? It's Hanna!"

Did the luck of a Kerayit shaman survive her death? Or was it the other way around? No person can survive without a measure of luck. She remembered the stories she had heard concerning the death of Prince Bayan and his powerful mother.

"Sorgatani!"

A feeble voice reached her. "Hanna. Here I am. But I'm caught beneath. . . ." The rattling cough made Hanna's jaw tighten with fear. "I'm caught. I can't get free."

"Be patient! Try not to move."

She grabbed for the first arm that came within her reach, which happened to be that of Lord Berthold, whoever he was—the name sounded familiar, but she didn't have time to figure it out.

"My lord! A team of men, I pray you, to set this wagon upright." When he hesitated, looking at her in confusion, she added in the tone she had learned from her mother, "Now!"

They were all addled by the cascade of events. He reeled back, beckoned to his companions, and started giving orders. The Quman youth dragged the corpse of the Kerayit woman aside so it could be readied for burial, and the other youth hailed passing soldiers and set them to work.

She trembled, running hot to cold and cold to hot. She had seen Breschius consumed by the galla. Ai, God! Who would serve Sorgatani now? She must find allies quickly if she meant to save the shaman's life.

So many voices crowded her, men wailing, women shouting commands, the tramp of feet, and a chaos of loose horses and dogs. So many smells assailed her, but death's perfume smote her hardest of all.

Tears veiled her sight. Mist spun out of the mountains of storm clouds that surrounded the valley, and the bright blue blaze of the sky overhead was starting to bleed to white as the cloud cover crept back in. The wind shifted west to east, and east to north, and north to south, whipping her braid in gusts that made her eyes tear. Men surrounded the wagon and got their shoulders and boots and hands around it and under where there were cracks and hollows in the roadbed to accommodate such levers as spars of wood and spans of iron.

As they shouted, heaved, and lifted, her gaze was drawn to the top of the ramp, far above. The Eika soldiers gathered at the height formed columns along either side of the road as wagons cleared the line of that foreshortened horizon and began a cautious and controlled descent.

There walked Brother Fortunatus. Safe! She wept to see him, to see others she knew. Behind them flew the proud standard of the Lions.

"Hanna! Hanna!"

But it was not their voices calling her. Their gazes, as all gazes, were pulled to the center of the whirlpool. To the dead man.

She looked west, and saw a figure hobbling at an awkward canter, waving to catch her attention.

He was filthy, as though dragged through the mud, and sopping wet with bits of vegetal matter and slops and drips of slime shaking off him as he ran. But despite the muck, anyone could see the startling flame red of his hair as he lunged up onto the roadbed, grabbed her elbows, and stared at her in disbelief. He had grown taller, his shoulders had gotten broader, and altogether he was a different person in stature and expression, but he was still the same rash, stupid boy she had grown up with.

The one she had always loved.

"Hanna!" He gaped at her as if the sight of her baffled him.

To her surprise—and manifestly to his, for he still looked dazed—he pulled her close and kissed her for a very long time.

"I pray you, excuse me."

They stumbled apart, Ivar blushing and Hanna reeling. The weather had changed, or the world had. She wasn't sure which, but it had gotten hot all of a sudden.

There was a man standing beside them with two huge black hounds, although in truth the hounds were cringing as they gazed at the approaching wagons. One whined, and the other whimpered, tail and hindquarters tucked tight like a dog that fears it is about to receive a whipping. The man knuckled their heads affectionately with one hand, but regarded Hanna and Ivar apologetically as he brushed the back of his other hand along his chin, the gesture a man makes when he feels a little sheepish.

"I pray you, forgive me," he said. "But are you not an Eagle, called Hanna? The one who knows Liathano?"

She blinked. She knew she was gaping. Her lips were warm.

Ivar was still staring at her like a madman, with wide eyes and slack mouth. He appeared not to have heard the question at all. Only he said, without looking at the other man, "You're the one who was named heir to Lavas."

"So I was. I'm called Alain."

"Liath is lost," Hanna cried. "She's missing."

"She lives." He said it so calmly that she believed him. "I have a favor to ask of you, Eagle. Ride west along the path that leads from here to Hersford Monastery."

"I know it," said Ivar.

"Why?" said Hanna. "What of the Eika?"

"An Eika staff will grant you safe passage. Although I think with that hair you'll have no trouble with the Eika, for they will believe you to be kin to them."

"What do you want?" she said.

"Liath is coming to Hersford. It seems likely she will ride this way afterward."

"Ai, God." Hanna looked at the corpse.

The banner of Saony had reached the road, and the crowd parted to let Princess Theophanu pass through. She stopped dead beside her brother's body, gazing at him with such a lack of emotion that all at once Hanna felt grief rip straight into her ribs.

"She hides what she feels," remarked Alain. "But the currents run deep in that one."

"Ai, God," said Ivar. "Liath doesn't know!"

"I'll go." Hanna had thought nothing could be worse than reporting to Sanglant that Liath was missing, but now she knew that wasn't true. There was something much worse. "I'll go," she repeated, because it was better this way, that Liath not ride into Kassel unknowing.

"If you arrive before she leaves Hersford Monastery, convince her to stay there, if you can," Alain added. "I'll see you get horses, and that staff. I pray you, wait off to the side."

"What of Sorgatani?"

"What do you mean?" he asked, turning back.

"The Kerayit shaman. In the wagon. She may be injured."

"I'll see she is cared for."

"Nay, you don't understand! She is bound by a terrible sorcery. To look on her will kill you, or any man or woman. They fear her, those who came with us. But she is no threat to us! She must be cared for. Only I can do it."

He touched the back of his hand to her cheek. He had dark eyes, and an implacable stare that pinned her to the ground. She did not draw breath. "Hanna. Listen to me. I will see she is safe and cared for."

She nodded dumbly, and he moved off, and after a moment she shook herself and walked off to the place where he had told her to wait for horses.

"I'll go with you," said Ivar, following her. He was still red. He was still filthy, shedding muck and fingerling twigs with each step. Some of the mud had rubbed off on her tunic and cloak. But he clasped her hands between his. He bent to kiss her forehead, quite tenderly. "I'll not let you go alone. Never again, Hanna."

Dear Ivar.

She tried to speak, but the sight of him, his look, and his touch, strangled her, and all she could do was cry.

4

SIX carried the litter off the field of battle: Princess Theophanu, Duke Conrad, Duchess Liutgard, Captain Fulk, and two young lords, one chosen from each army to let the battered soldiers see that for now, at least, a truce had been called.

They trudged with their burden through the gate, along Kassel's broad north-south avenue, and up the steep street cut into the hillside that gave access to the fortified palace, home to the dukes of Fesse. Many wept as they passed. Some of the townspeople who flowed out to line the streets whispered to see their duchess with her hair uncovered in grief, and dirt and tears and blood smearing her face. Soldiers with their helmets tucked under their arms stared in shock as their commander and king was carried past. One man holding a bow broke down and had to be supported by his fellows. Even the slinking street dogs kept to the walls, whining with anxious respect.

Rosvita walked directly behind the litter. Behind her came Lord Alain and his hounds, escorting Stronghand, who marched at the head of a hundred loyal warriors. Seeing these creatures enter the town through open gates caused a hush to fall. Some people crept away into their houses, seeking refuge, while others—and many of the soldiers—fingered their weapons thoughtfully. The street dogs did not bark, only faded away into alleys and open spaces grown high with untended grass. Yet among that century of Eika walked a dozen human soldiers, fair Alban men with glossy golden hair and darker-haired men speaking in the Salian tongue. They walked not as slaves but as comrades-in-arms.

There are deep forces at work here, Rosvita thought, and she feared them.

It hurt both her shoulder and hip to toil up that slope to the palace, but Rosvita fixed her jaw and wept a little in order to tolerate the pain. She concentrated on placing one foot ahead of the next. A sharp twinge jabbed through her right hip each time that foot struck earth. Her right shoulder was already tightening into a screaming knot of agony. She was sweating and crying at the same time, too bewildered and stunned to know just what it was she was crying over.

Before they entered the palace through its wide double doors, the litter bearers paused in the forecourt to catch their breath. She halted with a grateful sigh. Turning, she caught in her breath. This vista she had admired before, years ago, when Henry had fought Sabella and defeated her. Then, too, a guivre had stalked the field, but the outcome had proved very different.

How quickly the outlook changes. Kassel town had gained population in the intervening years, much of it recent judging by the fresh look of hovels and houses erected within the shelter of the town walls. There was less open space, and more fields beyond the walls given over to cultivation. Yet half the ground outside—where fields of rye and barley had been sown—was trenched by siege works, while other fields had been trampled. The detritus of battle lay strewn as though a flood tide had swept over the valley floor.

Just outside the town gates, the armies of Wendar and Varre gathered their forces. They were frighteningly few compared to the many dead left lying on the ground beside the pickets or in the earthworks or across the flat fields. What she saw, looking farther afield, were Eika pulling their net in around the valley itself, ranks and ranks of infantry filing out of the forest. That portion of the army marching with Lord Stronghand along the Hellweg had certainly been decimated, but he had brought many more with him, too many to count. Thousands, she estimated. Even at this distance she could identify among his soldiers the human men who had turned their back on humankind to march with the enemy.

The Eika, it seemed, had arrived in time to witness the slaughter of both the Varren and Wendish armies. Lord Stronghand had merely to stand aside and watch them do his work for him.

She found the Eika lord standing directly behind Alain. He had a sharp, intelligent face, and he, too, studied the lay of the ground and the disposition of forces in the valley. What he thought of it she could not read in his expression, only that he measured and calculated and, moving to one side, spoke in a whisper to a pair of his attendant captains, Eika warriors like him although half a head taller.

The procession lurched up the steps. She hurried after, puffing and wheezing and gasping at the pain. The stone lintel that spanned the double doors leading into the feasting hall swam in her sight, a most welcome apparition, and she passed under it and into the hall itself where a flock of palace stewards and servants swarmed to set out benches for the coming assembly. The body was carried up to the dais.

The faithful Eagle, Hathui, came forward to grasp her hands. "Sister Rosvita!" She was weeping.

Ai, God, she was so weary. Too weary to think. Too weary even to wonder or grieve. It was as much as she could do to allow Hathui to lead her forward, in her authority as an honored cleric in the regnant's schola, so that she could stand at the head of the litter as it was placed across three parallel benches.

"He would want you," said Hathui in a choked voice, "to stand guard over his body now that his soul is fled."

"How can it be?" Rosvita asked her. "I thought—we had all come to believe—that somehow his mother's blessing would always protect him."

Hathui shrugged. She could no longer speak. Turning away, she hid her face.

Out of the massing crowd a young nobleman appeared carrying a chair, which he set behind her. "Sister Rosvita," he said, smiling at her. "I pray you, you look tired. Please sit."

She blinked. It seemed apparitions would trouble her today, because this lad looked exactly like young Berthold Villam. "You were lost years ago," she told him, feeling foolish for speaking to a ghost, although in general ghosts could not fetch chairs.

"So I was, Sister, but I am found again. I pray you, Sister. Sit. I will tell you the tale later."

Berthold Villam!

This was a peculiar miracle, one impossible to believe, yet as he walked away to join a pair of young men—one of them foreign and almost certainly a Quman—she saw that he walked like Berthold Villam and he looked like Berthold Villam. Such a good boy, with the charm of his famous father and the sweet vitality of youth. The vision dizzied her. Gratefully, she sank into the seat, although at this level, steadied by the support, she must look on the mangled corpse at close quarters.

His face was undamaged, but his torso and legs were torn and twisted. Without the soul animating him, he was no more than a collection of parts and pieces; the handsome man who charmed effortlessly and led his troops with determination and assurance could not be glimpsed in this empty flesh.

More, and more still, crowded into the hall. Chairs for the great princes were set to either side of the pallet on which he lay, and one by one they took their places: Princess Theophanu, Duchess Liutgard, Duke Conrad. A murmur arose when the Eika commander sat in a chair beside the others, with two human and two Eika standing behind him in close council, often bending to whisper in his ear.

More were coming in. Mother Scholastica strode in with a look of thunderous anger. Although older than Rosvita, she appeared to have no aggravating aches and pains!

"Dead!" she exclaimed, pausing to examine the corpse. "So the report is true!"

"Mother Scholastica," said Rosvita in a low voice, gesturing to get her attention. "I pray you. What of my companions?"

"Among the living," she said curtly. "As are the Lions who protected us. Princess Sapientia was not so fortunate."

"What can you mean?"

"She, too, is dead. Killed by the sorcery of that witch woman you sheltered."

This was too much to take in.

"Yet I suppose God's mercy works in ways beyond our understanding," continued Scholastica. "Both brother and sister were unfit to rule. Now, they are gone, and we may hope for peace with Conrad and Tallia on the throne."

Rosvita tried to speak, to voice a thought, a prayer, an objection, but she could not. This she had wrought, and all for nothing.

Mother Scholastica was already moving away to confront the nobles seated on the dais. Her gaze swept them disdainfully. She gestured toward the Eika without looking at him.

"How comes that creature to sit among you as though he were a great prince of the realm?"

Lord Stronghand had a way of baring his teeth that mimicked a human smile without precisely being one. Jewels winked in his teeth, a barbarian's ornament, but his words were smooth and cool. "Mother Abbess, with all the respect that is due to a WiseMother of your stature and authority, I would suggest that it is the strength of my army that buys me a seat on this council."

Theophanu's mouth quirked. She said, "Aunt, have you not yourself observed that laws are silent in the presence of arms?"

"Let your stewards bring me a chair," said Scholastica, regarding Theophanu with disgust and turning her attention to Liutgard. "If there is to be a council, then I will stand at its head."

"Yes, Mother Scholastica," murmured Liutgard, gesturing for a steward, while Conrad sighed heavily and wiped his forehead with the back of a hand.

Stronghand looked with interest at Theophanu, and she met his gaze, although no emotion could be read behind her careful mask. It was no wonder no one quite trusted her even after all these years of faithful service to her father and his capricious wishes.

Seated in back of the others, behind the pallet, Rosvita had planned to observe without being herself noticed, but after all it took all her effort simply to pay attention. A terrible whisper kept clawing in her mind, saying that Mother Scholastica was right, that it was for the best that Sapientia had died. The poor witless creature could not even obey an injunction to hide her eyes, not to look upon that which would destroy her. She was no wiser than a toddling child. How could it be that she would not fall in the end into the hands of those who wished to put her on the throne and rule her through puppet strings?

That she could even think such thoughts horrified her. The dead man, mercifully, made no comment. No doubt he, also, was not free of sin, for he had abandoned Sapientia in the wilderness. So there they were, the two of them, one living and one dead, who had brought Henry's eldest daughter to an end she did not deserve.

As though the Enemy had heard her thoughts and sent minions to harass her, two huge black hounds padded up to her and sank down on either side. Their tails thumped in a friendly manner, but that did not make her less nervous of those fearsome teeth. A moment later the young man who had once been Count of Lavas came to stand quietly behind her chair. She could not see his face without turning around, but Lord Stronghand nodded at him just as there came a shout of surprise from the doorway.

Conrad leaped to his feet. "Constance!"

Constance, Biscop of Autun and later Duchess of Arconia, was the second youngest of Henry's siblings, about the same age as Liutgard, but she looked older than Scholastica now. She was being carried in a chair tied to poles. Her bearers, astoundingly, were Eika soldiers. With the greatest delicacy, they placed her chair to the left of Lord Stronghand, whom she acknowledged with a nod.

Already benches were being drawn up. Clerics and nobles crowded onto these seats while captains and lords stood behind them. There was Fortunatus! He made a sign with his hand so she could know all was well, and the look of relief on his face assured her that the rest of her precious schola had indeed survived the onslaught unscathed. Farther back she saw Sergeant Ingo of the Lions standing beside the one-handed Captain Thiadbold, now able to walk on his own.

Yet where was Mother Obligatia? What shelter had they found for her? And what of the shaman? What would happen to her?

What sign she made she did not know, but a hand brushed her shoulder, and that brief touch comforted her.

Last, and only with difficulty pushing their way through the crowd, came two litters. One was borne by a quartet of Arconian captains, and the other by stout clerics, four of Scholastica's most martial attendants. Behind them limped a white-faced man whose shoulder was wrapped in linen still stained with oozing red blood. Lord Wichman was so weak from loss of blood that he could not stand unaided but must lean on one of his captains. He reeled up the steps, dropped heavily into a chair behind Conrad, and seemed at once to lose consciousness, eyes closing and head thrown back.

The captains set down the body of Sabella, daughter of Arnulf and Berengaria, beside the corpse of her nephew.

The clerics lowered the litter bearing Princess Sapientia's corpse and placed it beside that of her aunt.

Although the smell of sweaty and bloodstained bodies already permeated the hall, at once the stink of death struck Rosvita hard enough that she flinched from it: the strong sour smell of drying blood, the stench of loosened bowels and voided urine, all these indignities suffered by the dead were eye-wateringly apparent emanating from the two dead women, even though Sabella's body bore only a single wound and Sapientia's no trace of injury at all. No such stink wafted from the corpse of Sanglant, although he ought to smell worse having suffered such gashing wounds.

Mother Scholastica rose. "So are we all come."

The crowd in the hall—and those still pushing into crevices and hand's-width spaces along the back—grew quiet.

"So are we all come. All who are able-bodied and able-minded. For long years we were told that this prince's mother laid a geas on his flesh, that no creature male or female could kill him. But after all, we see that this was merely a tale told by Henry to aggrandize his favorite child. Sanglant's run of luck is over. Now he lies before us, who claimed the throne of Wendar and Varre although he had no right to do so."

"For shame," said Liutgard. "For shame, Mother Scholastica! Those of us who rode at his side out of Aosta and accepted his elevation will not have our decision so easily dismissed. His was the right. Henry named him with his dying breath."

"It's true that my brother Henry showed partiality toward the infant, who was destined for another fate according to the custom of the Wendish people. None among you believe that Henry's decision was made with his dying breath. The day Sanglant was born, Henry confessed his wish to his father, King Arnulf, that he desired to make this bastard child his heir. I recall it!"

She surveyed the gathering with the pride and arrogance that her long years as abbess of the holy and powerful institution of Quedlinhame had granted her.

"I recall it, for I was already invested in the church and soon to become abbess. I was present in the councils of power, and in those councils held more privately with the king. So I tell you: this request went against all of Wendar's customs and traditions! The bastard child must be the king's Dragon, not the king himself. As well, the child was born of a foreign woman, with no maternal kin to support him and besides that an ancient and suspicious tale of old enmity dogging his heels. He could never be trusted."

"Yet he was best among us," said Theophanu in her cool voice.

Her flat statement caused Conrad to begin weeping again, for all his gestures were grand ones that every soul could join with. Many wept in the hall, some louder than others.

"Arnulf knew the child could never be trusted," repeated Scholastica. She swept her hand to include the span of the hall and raised her voice yet more, a strong soprano that carried above the grief and anger of the crowd. "Henry was obsessed with the Aoi woman, but it was obvious to any eye that she did not love him but was at work on some hidden plan. This Arnulf saw. This he strove to prevent.

"So it comes, that my nephew is dead."

Wichman roused from his stupor. "His is not the only death today!" Then he laughed like a man driven mad by pain.

"No, indeed, it is not. Here also died Princess Sapientia, killed by sorcery. And Sabella—my elder sister."

Wichman coughed blood. With the sleeve of his gambeson, Conrad wiped the spume off Wichman's chin, and called servants forward, but the other man waved away these attendants.

"I will hear all of it. I will hear!" he croaked. "Now that Sanglant is gone, there's not one of you left who can best me in combat."

"Let him be," said Scholastica. Her gaze, bent on him, was not kindly. "Let him hear, if he wishes. All these claims are now thrown over. Their souls have ascended to the Chamber of Light. Let us speak a prayer in their memory."

Rosvita wiped her brow, and even that slight movement made her shoulder pinch and smart. She murmured the responses as the abbess intoned the prayer, but her heart was numb and her thoughts strayed.

Where had Constance come from? How came it that she was escorted by Eika soldiers? Had Sorgatani survived?

Rosvita had left the field as soldiers struggled to right the wagon, and when she surveyed the assembly now, she saw no sign of Hanna's white-blonde hair although several times she caught her breath, thinking she had found her, only to realize that the Eika had hair just as bone pale.

Where was Wolfhere? He had spoken puzzling words by the roadside, and she began to think that if she could only recall them exactly that they would answer many questions, but exhaustion muddied her mind. It seemed to her that her eyes watered, that a faint perfume like rosewater drifted off the body of the dead man, a sweet and pleasing smell. She covered her eyes, dizzied.

A hand steadied her. "Patience," he murmured.

The voice soothed her; her thoughts cleared as Mother Scholastica called again for silence.

"Let it be known that a writ of excommunication has reached me, carried by diverse hands. The skopos who reigns in Darre has threatened to lay an anathema on Wendar and Varre if the people are ruled by a bastard half-breed, born to humankind's ancient enemy. Now that threat is lifted."

In the front row of benches, Lord Berthold jumped up. "Let me speak!" he cried. "I have been in Aosta in recent months. Let me tell you the truth about the woman who named herself skopos! She is no Holy Mother. She is the same Antonia, cast out as biscop of Mainni because she soiled her hands with bindings and workings. She knew the secrets of calling the galla. With them, she murdered her enemies without regard to any innocent souls who might be devoured by the galla. She is not Holy Mother! She only called herself by that name, but no college of presbyters elected her. They are all dead!"

"Silence!" cried Mother Scholastica, truly shocked. "What are you saying?"

He roared on. The intensity of voice raised from such a mild-seeming youth was astonishing. "Darre is gone. The holy city is uninhabitable, consumed by the Abyss. It is a place of fire. Pits of steam and poison. What authority can this woman have, who calls herself skopos? With what scepter does she rule?"

"Silence!" demanded Mother Scholastica, turning red. "Who are you?"

"I am Berthold. The son of Helmut Villam, his youngest child."

"Berthold of Villam is lost. Dead."

"I am found. Living. And I am not done speaking! This I have also to report. Blessing, the daughter of Sanglant, lives. She lived also as a prisoner in Novomo for many months, as did I and my companions. She was stolen away by Hugh of Austra, who that same day murdered Elene of Wayland." His voice trembled, but he reined himself in.

"I will not tolerate this disrespect—" began Scholastica.

Conrad rose, and with a curt gesture signaled silence. Although he spoke in a measured tone, his anger had the force of a shout. "Where is the Eagle, Wolfhere? He knows the full tale, and I would like to hear it all now."

"I don't know where he is. I lost track of him after the end of the battle. But as for the manner of Elene's death, there's nothing he can tell you that I cannot answer, for I was there." He choked. Brusquely, he wiped away tears. "That is not all, although to my mind it was the worst. There's this also: Queen Adelheid of Aosta has allied herself with the Arethousan general, Lord Alexandros. He fled a civil war in Arethousa, and now he is married to Aosta's queen. I heard also tales that the city of Arethousa was entirely destroyed in the tempest last autumn. Just as Darre was." He paused, so full of adrenaline that he was panting, flushed, and sweating.

"Is that all?" Conrad asked. Then shook his head, with a kind of grunting laugh that a man might make when he is mired in sorrow but caught nevertheless by life's irony. "To think of Villam's son making this strange journey. Ai, God, my poor Elene."

In answer, Berthold sat down and clasped his hands tightly in his lap.

Scholastica nodded at Conrad, and he smiled mockingly at her, but he sat down.

"So are we answered," she said. "Henry's obsession has been overthrown. Aosta and Arethousa have suffered God's wrath. Yet so have we." She glanced at the Eika lord—the first time by look that she had acknowledged his presence—but did not meet his inquisitive gaze.

The Eika lord listened and watched with a fierce and intelligent concentration that made Rosvita nervous. Despite the trappings—the primitive standard, the gaudy lacework that girdled his hips and thighs, the jewels drilled into his teeth, and the bare chest painted in spirals and cross-hatches—he was not what he seemed. He might appear savage, but far more dangerous currents surged within.

"It is time to acclaim a proper regnant. One who will heal the land, not divide it. So my father Arnulf, of blessed memory, said to me before he died. Better, he said, that if Henry's obsession overtakes all, and my wishes are not followed, the line of Conrad rule rather than half-breeds."

"That would be acceptable to me," said Conrad mildly. "And to my heirs, all descended as I am from the first Henry. The blood of my daughter Berengaria flows also with Arnulf's blood, through her mother, Tallia of Varre."

So it came. The mask cracked. Theophanu rose in clear and blushing fury, a fine figure of anger who in that moment resembled her father in his famous wrath.

"It would not be acceptable to *me*. I love Conrad as my cousin, you may be sure. But in the absence of Sanglant and my elder sister Sapientia, *I* am Henry's rightful heir. I have waited too long. I have been shunted aside too many times. I will not sit quietly and see what is rightfully mine pass to my distant kin."

Such a hush might only be found during the Mass for the remembered dead, when the host of mourners and worshipers reflects upon their own sins. The peace endured a long time, broken at last by Mother Scholastica as she unclenched hands. Rosvita had not seen her curl them into fists, but the rigid line of her figure betrayed the tight control and bitter anger with which she regarded Theophanu.

"Beware Arethousans bearing gifts. You are too much your mother's daughter. None love you."

Theophanu lifted her chin to meet the blow. "Maybe so. But her lineage was of the highest order, a daughter of the empire. It was Arnulf himself who brought her to this country to marry his son."

Wichman stirred, barking out a coarse laugh. "A strange objection, Aunt, since Conrad was also born of a foreign bitch."

With a roar, Conrad jumped up, oversetting his chair, but when he whirled with an arm raised to clout Wichman, he caught himself.

Wichman chortled, then began again coughing up that pinkish spume.

"Carry him out of here," said Conrad with disgust. "He's sorely wounded."

"Nay, nay," rattled Wichman. "I meant what I said. I want to hear. Indeed, I'll risk my life to stay, for I wish to hear my aunt's reply to this puzzling question."

His words had not shaken Scholastica. She regarded him with scorn. "Lady Meriam was unexceptional. She was brought here as a child and embraced the true faith with sincerity and wisdom. I find no fault in her. Sophia, however, was never truly one of us. It is better this way. Conrad will rule, and his daughter by Tallia will be heir to the regnancy."

Theophanu took a step forward, making it easy for her to see each of the great princes in their chairs. To see the bodies of her brother and her aunt and her sister, whose blood she shared.

In Heart's Rest there is a saying: It is the mother's blood that tells.

The princess extended her left hand, palm open, although it wasn't clear whom she meant to include in the gesture. Her expression was clean, her anger strangled. Her voice was clear and strong.

"With Sanglant and Sapientia dead, I am Henry's eldest surviving child. Henry was your regnant. He ruled you well, all of you, before the tide took him. I am not beloved as my brother was, nor will I ever be. But I am wise and canny. I will rule as a prudent steward in troubled times. We must recover what is lost. We must fight against the chaos the tempest has left in its wake. Sanglant knew this. That is why you acclaimed him. That is why I stepped aside in his favor, although my claim was legitimate. Conrad is a fine warrior, but I am a better steward. That is my claim."

Conrad smiled, as though this were all an entertainment put on to make him laugh. "And will you lead us when battle is joined, Theophanu? Or will the armies of Wendar and Varre choose to follow me?"

"What battle? The battle is over. We have lost. Will you fight those who outnumber us tenfold? Will the flower of our armies, the strength of our men, be cut down when we need them most to tend and build and plant? When we need them to protect us from the beasts and renegades who have flourished these past few years? From the threat out of Aosta and Arethousa? From the threat of our ancient enemies, the Cursed Ones?"

Conrad made a hissing, contemptuous sound, indicating the silent Stronghand. "What solution do you propose to combat their army, then? Cousin?"

She smiled, although there was nothing of sweetness in it. "The sensible one."

With the slightest shift of her feet and shoulders, it could be seen that her outstretched hand was offered to the Eika prince, who watched her with a lively amusement, as if he had already guessed her intention.

"Let Lord Stronghand agree to become my husband, and he will rule beside me, consort to my regnant."

The Eika laughed, a shockingly human sound.

The uproar rising from all sides drowned all other words.

5

ALTHOUGH he respected Mother Ursuline and her sisters within the church for their strength, and admired the Hessi merchant women for their quick understanding of the shifting forces that had altered the currents of the northern seas trade, Stronghand had not yet found a woman born of humankind whose intelligence truly reminded him of the deep cunning at work in the mothers who directed the fate of the Eika.

But maybe this one came close.

The attack was so neat and so brutal that he had only seen it coming an instant before it struck. The rest of the assembly was blindsided, taken utterly off guard.

He rose and acknowledged her with a polite nod.

She looked him in the eye, asking a question by the way she lifted her chin slightly. The other great princes were stunned, but even so a few among them were thoughtful rather than outraged.

After a while, because of his silence, and hers, and the absolute silence of his ranks of warriors as they waited for his signal, the crowd's exclamations and muttering died away until he could speak and know he would be heard.

"It is a better bargain than I expected. What terms do you propose?"

"I will never countenance this!" cried Mother Scholastica.

Biscop Constance answered her. "I pray you, Aunt. I would speak."

At the sound of a strong, steady voice issuing from such a crippled body, folk listened respectfully. Even Mother Scholastica waved a hand to show she would not interrupt, and Stronghand had certainly always understood that the mothers of the tribe must be listened to with full attention.

"Let me tell you in short measure my tale. You know that I was made biscop of Autun years ago, and more recently that Henry invested me as duke of Arconia after Sabella's failed rebellion. Later, I was deposed and sent to an isolated monastery called Queen's Grave, for no woman who entered it ever came out again. Queens of old often took refuge there from cruel husbands or rapacious relatives. Be aware that, although I hold no grudge against him, Conrad knew of my imprisonment and acceded to it."

The duke of Wayland stirred uncomfortably in his seat but made neither excuse nor denial.

"This I know," agreed Mother Scholastica. "It is because of your imprisonment that much bad blood arose between Wendar and Varre."

Constance nodded. "Sabella has passed beyond forgiveness or vengeance. Let it be."

"How came you to be released?" asked Duchess Liutgard.

"That is a tale for another day. I took refuge at Lavas Holding with Lord Geoffrey, who stands as regent for the young count, his daughter. Sabella discovered where I was and sent a troop of soldiers to fetch me. I came with the escort rather than risk the lives of innocent children that Sabella was holding hostage. Reaching Autun, we discovered that Sabella had already marched east with an army. On our way here, we were overtaken by the Eika. All of my small company were taken prisoner. So I can tell you something of these Eika and their leader."

"What would you tell us?" asked Theophanu.

Human women were not beautiful. The least of the SwiftDaughters was glorious compared to a body whose flesh was as soft and dull as half-baked dough. But this one had a certain cool presence to her that made her different than her sisters. She was not marked by the constant surge and ebb of emotion that marred their faces. One could look at her and feel restful.

Constance was seated to his left. She lifted a hand—any movement pained her for her body had been racked and ruined in recent years. Such was the weakness of human flesh. Yet a strong light burned within.

"Lord Stronghand spared our lives because we were clerics. He set me in the care of his council, among whom preside human as well as Eika. He spoke to me most respectfully, and over several nights we engaged in a long and fruitful conversation."

"God Above!" said Mother Scholastica. "As well take instruction from a wolf! What can you have talked about?"

Alone of the younger generation, Constance was not one bit intimidated by the older woman, perhaps because her authority sprang from the same source.

"Why, we talked about God, Aunt. And stewardship of land and estate. We talked of trade and trading routes. We discussed the legend of the phoenix, and the tales concerning the spawning of the Eika in ancient days. We spoke of the Cursed Ones, and of the tempest last autumn that swept over the lands. And much more besides. I ask you, Mother Scholastica. Does Wendar suffer? Do folk in Varre starve and die? Since I was freed from Queen's Grave, I have collected stories. I have heard testimony. It seems to me that plague and famine harass us. Villages are raided by outlaws, and by the Cursed Ones wearing the masked faces of beasts. Crops do not grow without the sun. The summer is cold. Certain sea-lanes have changed in the aftermath of the tempest. Creatures prowl abroad that once slept. God enjoins us to build and sow, to reap and to husband. We are meant to be stewards. Now is the time for good stewardship, else many more will die and the land will lie in ruins."

Mother Scholastica had a sharp gaze, which she used now, looking first at Constance and then, with a frown and a crinkling of her brow, at Stronghand. "I consider you beyond corruption, Constance, but perhaps I am mistaken. Has being a prisoner all these years addled your keen mind?"

Constance did not bridle, although the words were meant to offend. Stronghand had come to respect her in the last few days. Although in constant pain, she possessed a mind of greatest clarity.

"Ask yourself this, Aunt. How comes this Eika army to this place, at this time? How did the battle cease, when it was so well begun?"

"The battle ended when those foul creatures—these galla raised by Antonia of Mainni who calls herself skopos—when these creatures of the Enemy swept down and devoured so many. The battle ended when Sanglant was killed. That was shock enough!"

Constance shook her head. With jaw set against pain and a deep crease above her eyes as she braced herself, she made to stand. Stronghand moved to aid her, but her servants were already there on either side, four of them who had traveled this far: two men and two women. The action—for she went white at the effort—brought a horrified hush onto the assembly.

"There is one who walks among us." Her voice rang out into the corners of the hall, even into the rafters. "The emissary of the phoenix, who dies and lives again in the blaze of God's glory. These signs I have seen: Miracles have blossomed in the land. The Rose of Healing flowers. I was mistaken for a brief time, blinded by appearances, and I thought I recognized the holy vessel. But now I comprehend that it is not my part to speak of that which has not yet revealed its presence." The younger of her female attendants—the rabbit-faced girl—had begun to weep silently, her gaze fixed stubbornly on the floor.

"You speak of heresy, with this talk of the phoenix," said Mother Scholastica, but she looked puzzled rather than angry.

Constance shook her head. "I speak truth. That disputation must take place in a different council. A force has entered this assembly and brought a temporary peace upon us. It is up to us to make good—or ill—use of this chance. I would support this marriage if reasonable terms can be agreed upon. Lord Stronghand has shown himself to be an honorable—man—who holds to his agreements. That is all I have to say. Now, I pray you, let me sit."

Theophanu stepped into the breach. She nodded at each of her kinfolk, all those who sat upon the dais, and at various faces staring up at her from the audience, noting them, examining their expressions. Constance's speech had changed the tenor of the assembly. Folk were now willing to consider this change of direction into unknown country.

"Let me address Conrad's objection first. He has brought war into Wendar, and besides countenanced Sabella's assault upon his cousin and my aunt, Biscop Constance. Yet his claim is a strong one. My brother Sanglant would have been first to call Conrad an honorable man." She looked at him, but Conrad was wary, like a dog, not at all cowed by her but unsure whether she meant to toss a bone or a rock in his direction.

"Think you," she asked him, "that Eika and humankind can breed? I do not. Therefore, it is unlikely that any child shall be born of our union. We are stewards, meant to shepherd these lands through the storms to come. So let us, as part of the terms, name our heirs now and see them anointed and crowned. Let there be no question about the succession."

Conrad shrugged. "I'm not greedy for my own sake," he said with an expansive gesture, opening his arms. "But I must look after the rightful claims of my children. On the field of battle I made Sanglant an offer, and I'm willing to stand by it, if you were to name one of my children by Tallia as your heir."

She looked at Stronghand.

He nodded fractionally. "I am still listening. I have agreed to nothing yet. I, too, must ask this same question. What of my children? I control a great deal of land. It is a tricky business holding together an empire."

She did not smile or simper or frown or knot her brow in anxious thought. She had a knack for cutting straight to the bone without preamble or pointless philosophizing and agonizing. "Have you a proposal, to deal with this matter?"

Oh, she was ruthless and single-minded. A rose among thorns, as the church mothers said.

He knew what he had to do. "In truth, I do have a proposal. That this man, called Alain, who stands quietly among us, act as mediator between our parties. I will accept any terms and treaty and alliance that he approves."

Constance nodded. The rabbit-faced girl sobbed out loud, then sucked in her breath noisily as she fought to choke down her crying while one of her companions comforted her.

Stronghand had keen hearing, as did all his kind. He heard the faint sigh made by Alain; it was the kind of grunt made by a person who has just realized that, in fact, he will have to haul those damned logs all the way back up the hill and that there is no use complaining because the master is harsh.

But, after all, he had begun to suspect that the Wise-Mothers had worked a deeper game than even he had ever truly understood. They had ploughed in their slow fashion, where years are as days and the life of their male children and SwiftDaughters flashes past in the blink of one heavy eye. Their spirits had walked in the heavens on the wings of the aether. A mortal could never know how far their vision extended.

The Eika were the children of the cataclysm, born in ancient days, and they, too, had been altered irrevocably by the tempest. The OldMothers would spawn a new generation, which would spawn a generation in its time, in the manner of all life. But the OldMothers would not march up to the fjall to commune with their mothers and grandmothers as they had all these centuries. That thread of immortality had been severed in the tempest last autumn. They, too, would breed and die in the way of mortal kind.

But the Eika were few, and humankind were many. He had no illusions about his empire. The lines of communication and supply would fray, and in the passing of the years the simple toll of numbers would overtake them. The ebb tide had left them tossing on exposed rocks like flopping fish at the mercy of rapacious gulls. There must be a way to save themselves before the feasting gulls swooped down.

One bond remained. Years ago, he and the youth called Alain Henrisson had become brothers, of a kind.

So must it be: *brothers, of a kind.* The road might seem dark now, but that was only because it remained in the shadow of what is not known. No mortal soul can see into the future. Maybe that is a blessing, although any commander would like such a weapon at his disposal.

Theophanu examined Alain with interest and without fear. "Heir to Lavas," she said. "I know what you once were. I wonder what you are now. Very well. I accept."

Alain stepped forward. He was dressed simply, a little trail-worn from his journey. He made no grand gestures. He did not raise his voice. Yet every soul there watched him, and every soul listened when he spoke.

"So be it." His authority was not that of the swordsman or captain; it was not that of the biscop or lord. It came from a deeper place. Even the vicious black hounds loved him, not with submission but only out of love for his pure heart.

"I will do as you ask," he said, "if all are agreed."

He waited. Not even Mother Scholastica gainsaid him.

So he nodded, not arrogantly but as if he were resigned. As if he were accepting his fate. As Theophanu and Stronghand would accept the terms he laid down, because on this day it was necessary.

No mortal soul can see into the future.

These were the words he spoke in the silent hall.

"Quarters will be cleared for the Eika army, but hall and throne will be shared by lady and lord.

"Morning gifts shall be given, each to the other in equal measure.

"Each shall reward among the retinue of the opposing army, gifts according to the honor and status of those companions. In this way bonds of trust and obligation will be formed.

"If one is attacked, the other will come to their aid.

"Among yourselves and in your own lands, you will govern according to the local custom and as you see fit. Such a vast territory will not hold together easily. Or at all. Therefore, as long as this alliance is sealed by the living bodies of each of these two who come to be partner in it, let no spear be cast that is meant to fix blame on another.

"No provocation is allowed among the survivors. All fought honorably. Let no word or deed, no insinuation, give offense.

"What each one brings to the contract will go to their own heirs, as long as they can hold it. To guarantee the peace, let ten beloved children from each lineage be raised in the heart of the other's hall.

"That is all."

He possessed the guivre's stare, whose vehemence had the strength to stop all creatures in their tracks. The easier to gobble them up. Yet after he surveyed the assembly, he simply nodded his head, a modest gesture that released them with his final words.

"Let this contract be sealed. Let the dead be buried. Let the survivors return to their homes."

XII

THE "VITA" OF ST.
RADEGUNDIS

1

LIATH crossed last through the archway woven into the
crown at Novomo. Blue fire tore into hazy shreds. Sparks
winked in a darkening sky as she emerged into a cool twilight breeze. The long slide to night had begun.

She found herself in a broad clearing, surrounded by a
circle of standing stones and grassy mounds like ancient
barrows. Forest stood on all sides. The ground was moist
with recent rains. Drops of water dangled from grasses
bent under that weight.

The ranks of mask warriors had spread out into the
clearing, already on the hunt. A dozen were poking
through the grass just beyond the stone circle.

Sharp Edge beckoned. "Look! There was an Ashioi
camp here recently. One of the war parties came this way."

"Any sign of Hugh?"

They searched in the dusk but except for the unmistakable remains of that small encampment—a fire pit with
charcoal slivers, a pair of white feathers tipped with a glue
that would have held them in an arm guard, a broken,
bloodied fox mask—they found nothing.

Zuangua limped over to her. He still held his left arm

cradled against his chest. "A man and a child could easily have passed through this crown before the rain and left no obvious mark of their passage. Day will bring light to our search."

"We can't let them get so far ahead of us!"

He shook his head, then retreated to the remains of the abandoned camp and sat down. A mask warrior rubbed salve into his wounds and tied a sling around his arm.

Liath stared and hunted until she thought her eyes would burn a hole in the stones, yet even her salamander gaze showed her nothing. In the end, she circled around to the campsite. Despair made her cold, but anger made her burn, and with a thought she called a blaze into the pit. Her companions leaped back as charcoal caught fire, snapping and cracking.

"Can you teach me to do that?" asked Sharp Edge breathlessly.

"Best we rest, Bright One," said Zuangua, who had not moved when the fire flared.

"And then?" she demanded.

The flames lit the mask warriors in such a way that they looked like beasts indeed, less than human but more than animals. While she searched fruitlessly, they had already set up sentry posts and sleeping stations and kindled another five campfires.

"My trackers have other ways of searching, but we must have light. We will not fail. Have you any idea where we are?"

"We are in Wendar, I'm sure of it," said Liath. "That being so, if we find no sign of Hugh or my daughter in the morning, all we can do is try to find Sanglant."

"You may do so. If the search for the Pale Sun Dog is abandoned, we will return to our own country if you will weave us a passage."

Liath looked at Sharp Edge, as did he.

The young Ashioi apprentice grinned defiantly. Like Anna and the four masks sent with Liath by Eldest Uncle, she had not been injured in Hugh's attack. "I don't want to go back," she said.

"She has joined me of her own free will," Liath said. "I have accepted her and put her under my protection."

"So I see. What path she chooses falls on her own head. I will not force her—or any of my people—to return with the rest of us." He shrugged—the movement cost him some pain—and turned away to talk to his fox-masked lieutenant. Now that they had settled down for the night, most of the warriors pushed their masks up on their heads, revealing more ordinary faces.

Liath and Sharp Edge moved away.

"He'll make no trouble," said Sharp Edge in a low voice. "I am free to do what I wish. I want to stay with you."

"Then I am pleased to have you. You are the third."

"The third of what?"

"The third of my nest of phoenix. That is what I will call you, no matter what others say."

"Who are first and second?" Sharp Edge asked with a petulant grimace. "I like to be first!"

"So you do. In this case, you are the first among your people, if we do not count Secha."

"I will not count her!" said Sharp Edge with a laugh. "What others claim a place in front of me?"

"A Kerayit weather witch and her slave, who is a cleric—a holy man—of my own people. Look here." She stared at the crown, counting its stones and studying the burial mounds that rose as hillocks at the edge of the firelight. "I feel I should know this place, yet I do not remember ever being here before. Look how straight and true all the stones stand!"

In their haste to follow Hugh, they had marched without sufficient traveling gear. Even Zuangua's warriors complained at length, but jokingly, about the cold. It was a form of companionship. Everyone complained except Anna, who took her share of the night's waybread and ate alone away from the rest. The mask warriors shared out the watch according to Zuangua's command, but in the end Liath sat all night staring at the blind sky, unable to sleep because when she closed her eyes she remembered the vision she had suffered, the vision of Blessing in the custody of Hugh. Blessing, wed to Hugh. She retched, but her heaving brought up nothing. It was only nerves.

"Bright One, are you sick?" Sharp Edge squatted beside her.

"Sick at heart," she murmured.

Zuangua slept, or pretended to. The others huddled together for warmth. A night breeze moaned among the stones. In its voice she heard the groans of the forgotten dead long buried under earth. They were surrounded by the dead, those buried here in ancient graves and those in the world beyond thrown into new graves, the countless legions who had died in the aftermath of the cataclysm and the armies of the suffering who would die in the months to come.

"How did he call lightning like that? How did he call the storm?" whispered Sharp Edge. "Can you work such sorcery?"

Her jaw was tight, and her voice bitter. "I do not know how."

2

DEATH has a smell and a taste, and it can be heard as a whisper and felt as a touch on the lips when that last breath sighs free of the abandoned flesh. What a man might see, walking through the dusk as it swallows the field of battle, is only a shadow of the full understanding of death. With his hounds, he may kneel beside first one man and then another, and he may wish he had the means to heal them all, but another figure rides beside him and among some of these wounded she has already severed the thread that binds the soul to the body. They are already dead, although those around them do not yet know. Although they themselves may still stare at the sky and at their companions, waiting for aid or water or a comforting word.

In this matter, on this day, the Lady of Battles will defeat him. Her hand has swept the battlefield before he reached it. He can only do so much in the aftermath. This evening as he leaves the council of nobles and walks out of Kassel into the surrounding fields, he knows who will live and who will die.

Here is a young Wendishman with the merest scratch on his leg and a faint and confused smile on his pleasant face, but he has been trampled and badly broken inside. Here is a Varren youth crying, with his shoulder torn open and flesh glistening as a battlefield chirurgeon plies a needle and thread to close it up and her assistant holds a salve of woundwort ready to bind into the injury, and already the lad's humors stabilize.

He hopes this terrible burden will lift soon, that he will wake in the morning restored to blindness, but possibly he will always be so cursed. So be it. He accepts the path God has given him to walk.

The hounds tug at his sleeves and lead him past a row of cooling bodies and a contingent of soldiers digging a long grave under the supervision of a weary cleric reciting psalms. There is a tiny chapel built here atop an old foundation; oak saplings push up around it. A few graves are marked with lichen-covered stones, now unreadable, as though this cemetery was used a century ago and then abandoned. Many will populate it tonight.

The hounds pad past tents marking the Varren encampment and into the entangling siege works that protected the southeastern flank of the Varren camp. They sniff up to a half-finished ditch. Water seeps into the dirt. With the shadows drawing long, it is easy to overlook soldiers fallen where pickets have collapsed. In the ditch, a man lies with his legs pinned by a log and his face inches away from being submerged in the rising muddy seepage.

"Here! Here!" Alain shouts, getting the attention of a trio of filthy soldiers wearing the stallion tabards of Wayland who happen to be walking past.

They do not know who he is, but they respond as soldiers do. When they see the man caught, they scramble down beside him, and with all four of them slipping and sliding and grunting and cursing and the hounds barking, they get the log lifted and the man—he is husky, no lightweight—dragged out of the ditch.

"Tss!" says one man, with the grizzled look of a veteran. "A Saony bastard, all right."

So he is, with a crude representation of Saony's dragon

stitched to his dark tabard. When Alain wipes away the mud crusting his face, he is seen to be young, and the Wayland soldiers mumble and mutter and scratch their heads and finally, with a certain practical fatalism, check him for injuries. He's been cut low, just above the hip, and one foot is broken. The gut injury, especially, is likely to turn black with imbalanced humors, although the youth so far smells no worse than the rest of the dead, dying, and wounded.

He sees her: the Lady of Battles rides across camp, coming into view between a pair of campfires. She is heading in their direction.

"What do we do with him?" asks one of the Wayland soldiers.

The veteran says, "There's the Wendish camp. They can fetch him when their folk make a sweep this way."

"Might not find him till morning," says the youngest of the three. "Because of the dark."

"Best we take him over there now," says Alain. "As you'd wish done if it was one of your men found by the Wendish. He needs care right away."

They look at him. Blood splashes their armor and their exposed skin, mixed with dirt and exhaustion. They don't say what they saw and suffered this day, but after a moment they find a span of canvas—once the awning of a tent—and roll the man onto it. With one holding each corner, they trudge across the encampment and find a cluster of Saony tents under the command of a captain whose right arm is bound up in a blood-streaked sling.

"God be praised!" cries the captain. "That's Johan! I thought we'd lost him. My thanks to you. Here's a sack of ale for your trouble."

The man's gratitude discomfits the Wayland soldiers, but they accept the ale and turn away, and they move back toward the nearest cut of ditches and scramble down to keep looking. Alain lingers as the young soldier is carried off toward the chirurgeon's tent. Campfires flare up in a hundred places, tight rings where companies and militias have grouped themselves within the encampments and along the fields. Farther away, a line of campfires marks the Eika line at the forest edge. The air is strangely quiet, smelling of rain, but no rain falls. The storm threat has faded as a stiff wind pushes the weather away toward the west. The heavens are cloudy once more, and it seems likely to be an unusually chilly night although they are well come into the height of summer, days that should be long and lazy and hot bleeding into sticky warm nights. Men will shiver tonight under a dark sky, with moon and stars shrouded like the dead.

"Brother," says a soft voice out of the darkness.

He turns to see the pair of Eika soldiers who have been shadowing him for the last hour. One is a brawny blond Alban youth with a lurid scar on his cheek; the other is a tall, muscular Eika with the bronze-skinned sheen common especially in Rikin Tribe.

"Need you an escort back to the hall?"

"Has Stronghand set you on me?" he asks them, amused by their earnest and stolid companionship.

"So he has, Brother," says the Eika.

"And charged us to be sure that you return safely to the hall," adds the Alban youth, who is eyeing him with curiosity. "How comes it that you speak the Alban tongue? Not many among your nation do so."

"It's in my blood," says Alain. "What are you called, you two?"

"I'm called Aestan, son of no woman who claimed me," says the Alban youth. "Once slave to the earl of the middle country, but now a free man and a soldier with the rights according to me thereby, under the charter of the new king, Lord Stronghand." He cocks a thumb at his companion. "This is my brother, called Tiderunner, although I just call him Ēagor, which is what we call the flood tide in my country."

"Although his is the tongue that floods," says the Eika with a grin that displays four sparking jewels drilled into his sharp teeth.

Aestan punches him on the arm, and they shadowbox for a moment before recalling where they are and what their mission is.

"Have you lamps?" Alain asks them.

"We do, a pair of them," said Aestan, and adds, "They're not lit yet."

"As if he couldn't see so himself!" retorts his companion.

"Heh! Having you for a companion, I begin to think all men are blind!"

Alain whistles. The hounds stand with heads high and ears pricked up, smelling and tasting the air. "There may be more wounded men lying out here who can be saved if they're found quickly."

They nod obediently.

He marks her in the distance, riding along a flank where men scramble through ruined pickets seeking survivors. The wings of dusk settle over the Lady of Battles until he can no longer see her, but he knows she still stalks the field. Always and ever she will ride. "We are not done yet, you and I," he says to her, knowing she can hear him at any distance. "I challenge you. I challenge you."

He turns to the soldiers. "Light a lamp, I pray you," he says.

Flint snaps. A flame leaps from the wick, and the lamp wakens, spilling light. He leads them out to search the darkening battlefield.

"He is coming," said Stronghand.

Duchess Liutgard and Duke Conrad had long since marched out to the Varren encampment to recover Liutgard's daughter, and returned to their separate quarters in this portion of the new palace. The holy mothers had arranged to meet in the morning for a conclave.

Theophanu and Stronghand sat in chairs on either side of an open window, in the middle chamber of the suite reserved for the regnant. Her servants and stewards and his guardsmen and council members waited in attendance together with a half dozen of the messenger eagles.

All night he and she had sat thus, alone, just talking. She had described the forthcoming conclave at length—and with a subtle humor that repeatedly amused him—in terms that suggested it would be nothing more than a wrestling match argued with words rather than grappling. He had told the story of the Alban conquest. Of Aosta, there was rumor to chew over and discount. Of her father, the king, she spoke affectionately and yet with a kind of bitter reserve that betrayed ambivalent feelings. He told her of what he had seen at Gent in the days when his father, that belligerent warlord, still lived. They touched last on the afternoon's council, when the two of them had come to such an abrupt and instinctive accommodation.

Dawn would come soon.

Flambeaux smoldered in their sconces, trailing smoke and the waxy scent of herbs tucked in to sweeten their burning. A fire burned in twin braziers, because the humans found the night air cold, although the chill made no difference to him.

She wore a shawl draped over her shoulders; her hair was uncovered, twisted back in a single thick braid. She was easy to look on, unusual among humankind for not fidgeting or stretching her mouth into the grimaces called smiling and frowning. Like stone, she had patience and a smooth exterior. She was easy to talk to, and had an exceedingly clever mind, nor did she reveal too much in the manner of a person attempting to ingratiate herself where she feels inferior. He minded the same balance: they must learn enough of each other now to gain a worthy measure of trust, but not too much, lest the arrangement fall through before it is binding.

"If he is not truly the son and heir of Count Lavastine," she said, "then who is he? Who is his mother? Who his father?"

"Does it matter?"

"It matters to you, which tribe you are sprung from. You named your birth tribe and cousin tribes, and those who allied with you early, and those who came late or not at all. You remember their names. Kinship always matters. He is bound to the county of Lavas in some manner. I would like to know how. The count of Lavas controls a great deal of territory along the northeastern coast of Arconia and well inland. The one who rules there would be a welcome ally."

"Against Conrad and the heir to Arconia?"

"Yes. Conrad has multiple claims. His elder surviving daughter will be duke of Wayland after him. His younger daughter by Tallia can claim the duchy of Arconia. The infant son—if the child still lives—also has a claim."

"Do you think it wise to honor the arrangement he claims to have made with Sanglant before the end? That Conrad's infant son, if he lives, marry Sanglant's young daughter, if she lives?"

"We must have heirs."

"My sons in the north and west, your kin here in the south and east."

"One daughter of Wendar to marry one son of the Eika in every generation, to keep the alliance."

"Should it hold," he said, with a flash of teeth.

"That promise lies beyond our power to enforce. We must raise those who will come after us to honor the agreement, and pray that they do."

"It's true that after death our hands clutch nothing but dust. That is fair. You remain suspicious of Conrad, it seems."

"I think it wise to distrust him. He is a likable man. But we hold weapons against him as well. If Lavas supports us, and we enrich Lavas with certain estates and toll routes currently claimed by the duke of Arconia, Lavas will counterweight Conrad's power."

He nodded. "As well, an emporium developed north of Medemelacha—in Osna Sound—would provide another staging ground for a fleet. Supported by the Lavas militia. Their placement along the coast makes them a bridge between the regions of the alliance."

"We'll have Arconia caught in a pincer, and keep her weakened. Cut off her access to trade. Route trade through the north coast, which Lavas can control."

"A good plan. Especially if we institute a census, so we know who has survived and what taxes and tithes and tolls to expect, what regions were hurt most and which harmed least. But we must keep in mind this caution. The shorelines have altered all along the northern sea. It will take years to see how this upheaval has altered the nature and utility of the ports and coastal drainage."

"Yes. When we were in Gent—Sanglant and I—we saw that it may be necessary to abandon Gent's sea trade, although it remains a land crossroads. Much has changed."

So it had.

Hearing the click of nails on the stairs as the hounds padded up to the outer door of the suite, he rose. Now Theophanu also heard voices from the outer chamber as one of her servants admitted the visitors. She stood and went to the window. Resting a hand on the sill, she gazed over a garden made murky by night except where a pair of lamps hung from tripods beside a dry fountain. In that garden stood the battered Kerayit wagon and the dozen silent Eika soldiers who had pulled it all the way up here and now stood guard. The door to the wagon remained shut—in fact it was cracked—because he was no longer sure what would happen to his men were the sorcerer to step forth; his standard had been broken to pieces in the wake of the galla.

The door into the antechamber opened. Papa Otto looked in, and Stronghand nodded at him. The man stepped back and spoke a few words to someone behind him. Then Alain came into the room with the hounds at his heels. The hounds halted on either side of the door, panting. Sorrow lay down and began licking a paw, but Rage was restless and kept shifting to find a more comfortable position.

"Why do we give this sorcerer protection when it seems she could easily kill us all?" Theophanu asked. She shivered in the cold night wind, but no fear or anger stained her voice. She was merely curious, seeking an answer so she could see what use to make of it.

"Compassion alone might make its claim," Alain said, "but if you must have a practical reason, then consider this. She is a weather worker of great power. A tempest brought this change of weather across the land. The heavens remain clouded. You see yourself that the crops do not ripen. That fruit stays green long past its time. Perhaps the skills of a tempestari could aid Wendar in some small way."

"Why should we trust sorcery now," asked Stronghand, "when we have never trusted it before?"

"That it exists and is used is not a matter of trust but a matter of truth. Yet also consider that the Kerayit are the allies of the Horse people. Their children, if you will, adopted into the clan long ago." He faltered. Stronghand watched the way he shuttered his eyes and exhaled a breath. Then shook himself, as if waking up. "The leader of the Horse people, their most powerful shaman, is dead. This woman must return to her people, because it is her obligation to do so. Perhaps she will become their leader. Do you wish her to depart as your ally, or your enemy?"

"She might be dying," said Theophanu. "No one knows how badly she was injured in the crash."

"She will live," said Alain.

"We could kill her," suggested Stronghand. "It would be the most practical measure."

"We could try," said Theophanu. "I suppose we would have to set fire to the wagon to force her to come out, place archers on all sides, but any of them who looked upon her in order to shoot would, on seeing her, die."

"It would be difficult," Stronghand agreed, "but with some careful thought and precise planning it could be done."

She considered him, and after this looked again down at the wagon. Seen at this angle—from the second story of the palace—the lamplight made the painted sigils, already streaked and scraped from the crash, give a kind of wiggle, as though they were alive and moving on the wood. "If she lives, she will always be a threat, no matter how far away."

"Any ally may turn into an enemy," Stronghand replied, "so all alliances must be cultivated in such manner that they will grow and not wither."

"We must decide what she wants, and what will bind her to us. Where is that Eagle? The one called Hanna. I have heard that she can look upon the sorcerer and live. She must act as negotiator." She looked at him, and he at her, and they nodded.

"A reasonable plan," he said.

For a little while she said nothing, regarding him steadily. "It is a rare gift to consider all sides to a question without succumbing to judgment or emotion before the best or most practical answer is reached," she said to him.

She extended a hand. He took a step toward her and placed his hand on hers. She examined it thoughtfully. "I pray you, Lord Stronghand, show me your claws."

He stepped back, lifted his arms square in front of his body, and released the claws that lived within.

She did not flinch. "Thus are we all armed with unseen weapons. Better to see if we can seal a treaty with her, for now. Later, if she returns to her home, as she must, she will be very far away and thereby less of a threat."

"I agree," he said, sheathing his claws. "It is the most practical solution. For now."

"Yet where is the Eagle?" asked Theophanu.

"Riding toward Hersford Monastery," said Alain. "I pray you, Your Highness. Let a procession be made ready to depart as soon as possible for Autun."

"Yes. Mother Scholastica has already claimed the right to bury Sapientia in Quedlinhame. It's best to move Sabella's body to Arconia immediately, so the succession can be set in motion. We must consider where we should first be crowned and anointed. Quedlinhame, or Autun? And what of Sanglant? Where shall we bury him? He has no true home, not really, poor man."

Moisture winked in her eyes, the only real surge of emotion Stronghand had seen in her. In this, at least, her heart was strong: she had loved her brother and been faithful to him. So was he, in his own fashion, true to Alain.

"Let him be carried west as well," said Alain, "with a proper escort. Best if he's carried on a separate track from Lady Sabella and her retinue. There is a more northerly path leading west, that crosses the El River near Hersford Monastery."

He was clear and clean, like an unsheathed sword, beautiful yet filled with a deadly grace and wielded by an unseen hand. It was a mystery that Stronghand did not understand, but no greater a mystery, really, than the day the Eika had come into being long centuries ago, in the aftermath of the first great weaving. There is power in the universe that cannot fully be understood.

Theophanu said, "Who are you, Lord Alain?"

He smiled gently. "My mother is dead, although she was nothing more—and nothing less—than a starving refugee who used what coin she had to feed herself. I do not know who my father is."

"You do not answer my question."

He went to the door. "That I am here is the only answer I know. I pray you, forgive me, but there is one other person here I must meet."

"Before what?" she asked, hearing the unspoken portion of his words.

"I mean to escort Sanglant's body." He nodded at them, as at equals, and walked out. They heard him cross the other room and pad away down the stairs.

Two soldiers looked in. "Continue to guard him," Stronghand said.

"And as you go, send the Eagle called Hathui to me," said Theophanu.

They nodded and left, shutting the door.

"Is Constance right?" Theophanu said. "Is he a messenger sent from God?"

"I am not familiar with such creatures," said Stronghand, "so I cannot be sure what Biscop Constance means."

"You wear the Circle of Unity."

He touched the wooden Circle that hung around his neck, traced its circumference in the remembered way. "So I do. I wear it to remind myself of what once was, and what may be."

She had a way of turning and tilting her head the merest finger's breadth that marked a flash of new thought, an idea to be considered. "The nobles and peoples of Wendar and Varre will not accept you if you are not washed and made clean within the Light, under the authority of the church."

"Very well. I will be washed and made clean, in whatever ceremony is necessary."

She raised one eyebrow. "Do you believe in the Holy Word and in the Light of Unity?"

"Is belief a requirement?"

She laughed, and he smiled, in the human way, and she blushed, a surprising flush of color on her cheeks, quickly controlled as she continued speaking.

"The clerics would say belief is necessary, but I don't know what God would say. Must we know we believe, or is it enough to follow God's precepts and live according to the law?"

He nodded. "The WiseMothers of my people possessed the ability to see beyond the veil which blinds their short-lived children. Perhaps the wise mothers of your kin also have this far-reaching vision."

"Perhaps. Some are wise and honest, but others struggle for power and advancement just like the rest of us. It is ever so. We are imperfect vessels, easily cracked by greed or anger or lust or envy or anguish or fear. Yet some among us are also steadfast and truehearted. Sanglant was such a man. That is why I mourn him, who was best among us."

She wept without sobbing or keening, dignified in her grief.

He could not mourn, who had known this man only as Bloodheart's prisoner, among the dogs. The Eika do not weep.

In truth, it served him well that the captain called Sanglant was dead, because it eliminated a powerful rival, a man who might have outplayed him on the field of blood which is called battle. He was not happy about it; nor was he sad. He used what weapons he could gather.

The invisible tide of fate dragged men to the shore, or into deep waters where they drowned. He and his tribes of Eika had been cast ashore, orphaned on the wings of the same storm that had broken the ancient threads binding the WiseMothers to the aether that was their life. In the fjall of the heavens, the WiseMothers had dreamed of the past and of the future, too steep a climb for mortal legs. No longer would their children benefit from that farsighted vision.

Yet in their passing, they had birthed a new generation of FirstMothers, the dragon kind whose blood had burned fire into stone and flesh to create the Eika long ago. So the tide turns. Who knew what wrack would wash up on the shore out of the fathomless sea?

With an embroidered scrap of linen, Theophanu wiped her cheeks. "Well," she said. "All things die, that walk on Earth. So will we, when God will it." She glanced outside, and gasped. "Look!"

He moved to stand beside her, not touching her, but their shoulders—of a height—so close that her shawl brushed his bare arm as she pointed.

The wind had really picked up, blowing off all but those clouds caught along the horizon. Stars glinted against the veil of night.

"Some say the stars are the souls of the dead." Her hands gripped the sill so tightly that her knuckles were white—or perhaps it was only the cold that paled her skin.

"We call the stars 'the eyes of the most ancient Mothers.' "

She relaxed, shoulders dropping slightly. "Do they watch over you, as kindly mothers do?"

"No. Those whose thoughts have passed into the heavens are indifferent to us, who live here upon the streaming waters and the silent earth. It is cold in the vale of black ice, which we call the fjall of the heavens. The north wind rises there. It is as sharp as a knife, a breath so bitter that it kills. Would we think them as beautiful if they were not so cold and so distant?"

When she did not reply, he turned his head to look at her, who stood so close beside him. A last tear slid down her cheek, one she did not wipe away, and she was looking at him, not at the glorious heavens.

"Perhaps not," she said in that cool, smooth voice that gave away nothing. "Yet we become accustomed to admiring the things we can never quite grasp, and have no hope of truly possessing."

It was obvious she meant more than she said, in the manner of humankind, but he could not quite read into the bones of her words. The span of life is short, and troublesome in large part because there is far more to understand than time to do it in.

He nodded carefully, to acknowledge that he had heard her. "Today we have won a great victory. As for the rest, as we say in my country, we must take it one stone at a time."

3

AT dawn, Zuangua took control.

"We're not to move out of the camp until he gives permission," Liath said to Anna. "He says we've already trampled valuable sign."

Anna obeyed without protest. What else could she do? She was grateful to have been rescued from the country of the Ashioi, but she might as well have been flotsam caught in the current, spinning and tumbling. She stood beside the fire pit, and she watched, because she could do nothing else.

The trackers were one male and one female, maskless and naked except for sandals and a loincloth tied up between their legs so it would not drag on the ground. They made a circuit of the stone crown and slowly widened this spiral to include the grassy mounds. Here, alongside one of the mounds, the female tracker lingered, while the male tracker moved swiftly toward an obvious path breaking out of the trees on the southern side of the clearing.

"Hei!" called the female tracker.

Anna followed Liath and Zuangua, who hurried to the tracker's position. The woman pointed to scuff marks and broken stems of grass beside one of the narrow openings that led under a burial mound. They consulted, then looked around at the mask warriors who had gathered.

"Anna," said Liath. "You're the best fit."

They gave her a torch, lit by a touch from the lady. The way the flame flared made Anna tremble to think of having that kind of power, and she dared not say "no."

In the east, Prince Sanglant had been able to crawl through the passageway to the central chamber of the burial mound in which he had interred Blessing and her six attendants. He would never have fit in this tunnel. Even the Ashioi, none of whom were particularly tall, were a broad-shouldered, stocky people, too wide abeam to fit easily.

Anna got down on hands and knees. Shoving the burning torch before her, she edged forward with elbows leading and feet trailing behind. The smell of earth overwhelmed

her. With each breath she sucked in drifting motes of earth,
the ancient air of the tomb. Stone grazed her head. A bug
scuttled over her hand, and she choked down a shriek. Her
own body blocked much of the light from behind, and in
any case the tunnel was long and the opening small enough
that she was soon swallowed.

What if Blessing had been murdered, and stuffed into
this hole? Her body, decomposing, riddled with worms and
maggots?

But the torch met no resistance. It cleared the lowest
point in the passage, where she had to shinny along the
ground like a snake, and then suddenly the ceiling lofted
away above her. She had come to the heart of the mound.

The flames whispered, echoing off the low vault of cor-
beled stone. Blank eyes stared at her from around the
chamber. Hollow faces leered, mouths agape in white
grins. Skeletons, dressed still in their finery, with wisps of
hair capping their bony heads.

She screamed, slapped her hands over her face.

It was all a vision, a nightmare. Moaning, she tried to
lower her hands, but she could not move, she could not
think, she could not breathe.

They scuffed the dirt. They were moving, scrabbling toward her, reaching out with white fingers to scrape her
flesh from her bones, to make her into one of them . . .

A touch brushed her shoulder.

She sobbed hysterically.

"Anna! Anna! They're dead. They can't hurt you!"

She groaned.

"Here, now, Anna. Just go back, then. I'll look around.
God Above! They're wearing the silver tree, the mark of
Villam! Could these be the companions of Lord Berthold,
who were lost here?"

Shaking, still weeping, Anna lowered her hands.

Liath had crawled in after her, and now, standing but
bent over so her head didn't graze the ceiling, she held a
torch out and examined, each in turn, the remains of seven
dead people. Mostly the flesh had been eaten away, although dried bits adhered in places and they still had much
of their hair. The cloth of their garments had not decom-

posed as quickly. The mark of the silver tree was easily visible on their finely woven tabards. A naked sword lay over the legs of one; rust discolored it.

"These two are dressed differently," said Liath, pausing beside the last two, who lay at an awkward angle to the others, as if they did not belong. "Ai, God!" She held the torch closer, to get a better look.

These wore tabards stitched with the black dragon worn by the retainers sworn to serve Prince Sanglant. One of the tabards was patched in three places easily visible to the eye: a large patch at the dragon's right claw, a smaller mend at the sigil's snout, and a third at the shoulder.

Anna had mended that rip. That was her stitching.

"This is very strange," said Liath. "How came these seven dead men here? I am sure as I heard the tale that these barrows were explored after the disappearance of Lord Berthold, and no remains found. These poor fellows must have crawled in here seeking shelter in recent months, and been lost."

"No," whispered Anna.

Liath turned to look at her. By torchlight, she did not look so very fearsome. The darkness crowding in on all sides made her appear more vulnerable. She was not much older than Anna herself, not truly. She had also traveled a long way, and faced terrible dangers.

"Who do you think they are?"

Anna wiped her cheeks, but the tears kept flowing. She had mended that tabard. She knew her own stitches.

"Those five," she said hoarsely, "they must be as you say. They must be Lord Berthold's retainers, the five he left behind. I told you—" She drew breath, caught her courage, and went on. After all, she had always known the truth in her heart. Now she must accept it. "I told you we had to run. That the caverns were collapsing around us."

"Indeed, you did," said Liath with a slight frown. "Then who are these two others?"

She had not Prince Sanglant's talent for names and faces; he would have known at once; he would not have had to ask. And after all this, Anna could not say their names aloud, although they resonated in her heart.

Thiemo and Matto.

Speechless, she covered her face with her hands.

4

AFTER she had crawled back out of the mound, and wiped off her clothing, Liath waited beside Sharp Edge as the tracker continued her search of the clearing. Poor Anna was huddled on the ground in a stupor, neither crying nor speaking. It was as if she had been struck on the head and gone mute.

"There is some vast labyrinth that connects the whole," she said to Sharp Edge. "Some of it is truly underground, hewn out of the rock, but another part must be the aetherical tributaries, shifting in their channels. We placed Blessing and her companions in a mound far to the east—hoping to save her life, which we did! Lord Berthold and his companions crawled into the mounds above Hersford Monastery. And if Anna's account is correct, and I believe it is, then a group comprised of two from Hersford and five from the east escaped from the cataclysm at Verna, in the Alfar Mountains. How can this be?"

"It must be possible to map these channels," said Sharp Edge. "I'd like to do that!"

Liath shook her head, smiling slightly. Sharp Edge had a strong personality, a little hard to take, but her eagerness was like good wine: it made you want to drink more.

"A map," said Zuangua, "would allow war parties to strike more effectively." He was pale, hurting, but unbowed.

A distant "halloo" drew his attention. The female tracker stood at the northern edge of the clearing beside a narrow track that was, in truth, scarcely more than a parting of branches.

"She's found some scent," said Zuangua. "Liat'dano, go with Tarangi. Take a pair to follow her, but do not confront our enemy without me, if that's where the scent leads you. I'll send a bundle with Calta, on that big path, to see what they find. The rest will remain here with me."

Liath paused beside Anna, but the poor girl was so drawn into herself that she did not even respond to a murmured question. With a shrug, she hurried after the female tracker, already lost among the trees. Buzzard Mask and Falcon Mask stalked behind, eyes wide as they stared around at this alien land. To her surprise, she had not taken more than a hundred steps when she followed Tarangi out of the trees onto a rocky outcrop. A spring leaked from a defile to make a small pool within the rocks. The ridgeline fell away before them in a jumble of cliffs and terraces. Set back against tree and rock, sheltered by the highest thrust of the ridge, a tiny hut stood in isolation. Moss ran riot on the thatched roof. The walls gleamed as though they were freshly whitewashed.

Tarangi had risen to both feet, brushing dirt and bits of grass and leaf from her bare chest.

"Nothing," she said to Liath. "The one we seek did not come here. There is an old magic protecting this place. Can't you smell it? It is powerful, but not angry. It is not against us, but it will reveal no secrets. I will not go in the hut."

"Is it a bad place? Has it a bad heart?"

" 'Bad'? No. It is peaceful but very strong. Like lightning, it is from beyond this Earth. I will not go there." She retreated into the trees and crouched in the shade to wait for them.

"Do we go back?" asked Falcon Mask, all her weight riding on her toes like a dog straining at a leash.

Best to hurry, but Liath herself felt leashed, as if something bound her here. "No. I want to look around first."

Falcon Mask dashed at once to the rock wall rising behind the hut and began to climb. She had a mad grin on her face. Buzzard Mask prowled to the edge of the open space, marking its boundaries. The track itself went no farther. It ended here, where the hill ended, cut off by the precipitous drop in front and the rock wall behind. Forest covered the lands below. In the distance Liath saw a thread of smoke.

She walked over to the hut. Cautiously, she pushed on the door of lashed branches. It resisted for the space of two breaths, and then gave way. She held her breath. She knew where she was, absolutely and without doubt. The discovery of the skeletons beneath the mound had told her what she needed to know. This confirmed it. She knew who had lived long years in confines so small that a man could not lie down in comfort lengthwise. Had they buried his body elsewhere, or did his remains still rest inside?

She stepped over the threshold.

The narrow dirt floor lay empty and unmarked by even the dusty prints of woodland animals, which might be expected to have come scavenging. A wooden bowl and a wooden spoon hung from a wooden hook, strung up by a slender strand of fraying rope so dry that she feared that, if she touched it, it would crack and crumble.

A leather bucket had tipped over in one corner. A faint, sweet aroma drifted from that corner, but the curl of air inside the hut blew it away in an instant. She took another step in, righted the bucket, and found it empty but discolored at the bottom. Beneath, some creature had dug a hole in the ground, like a dog seeking a bone, but it was empty. There was no other sign of the holy man who had bided here for so many years.

This man was supposed to have been the only son and heir of Taillefer and Radegundis; the father of Anne; the husband, however briefly and illicitly, of Mother Obligatia. Once, Liath had believed that Brother Fidelis was her grandfather, but now she knew he was not. All they had in common, if the stories she heard could be believed—and she did believe them—was that he had once sat in the circle of the Seven Sleepers. That he had abandoned their councils, believing them to be corrupt.

He had taken the more difficult path, the life of an ascetic. Some had called him a saint, blessed with that halo of righteousness that the church mothers call the crown of stars.

It was ironic, then, that Brother Fidelis had the right to wear such a crown twice over, once as the heir to Taillefer's empire and once as a holy man who had cut himself off from the court of worldly power in order to pray for the souls of the living and the dead.

Bowl and spoon and bucket were all that remained of him, except his precious book, the *Vita* of St. Radegundis, taken away by Sister Rosvita and still held in her possession.

"Bright One!" Buzzard Mask's voice was breathless, fading into a wheeze of terror.

She stepped sideways out of the hut, and turned. The shock actually made her go rigid. Not six steps from her lay a bold, golden lion, washing its paws with its tongue.

"Bright One!" hissed Falcon Mask from above and to the right. "Step aside. I have an arrow ready."

"Leap back," said Buzzard Mask, to her left. "I'll thrust at its heart."

"Hold."

The lion neither startled nor moved, but kept licking. An arm's length in front of its massive head and fearsome teeth rested a quite ordinary wooden staff.

"If it meant to leap, it would already have done so."

She took one step toward it, and paused. Lowered to a crouch, and paused. She might have been the wind, for all the notice it took of her. Its tongue worked at the pads. She reached, and touched the staff. Its huge slit eyes lifted. It stared at her for an age and an eternity, and she spun into that gaze, falling

a man stands in darkness, holding a newborn. A woman cloaked in robes and shadow faces him, her graceful hands crossed at her chest. He is anxious and troubled. She is as patient and peaceful as death.

"It is a girl," he says with disgust and dismay. "I will not after all these years and all my expectations be superseded by a squalling brat. Yet I dare not. I dare not . . . it would be wrong to kill her."

The cleric answers, softly and persuasively. "I have a use for her. She will vanish. None will ever know, my lord, that she existed. I will be midwife to her transformation. Her twin brother will serve you well enough. No one will ever suspect there was another infant. Your mother is already dead, poor soul. The labor was too much for her."

"Yes, it must be," he said. "It is better so. I am old enough. My people trust me. They expect me to inherit, not to be ruled by an infant only because my mother insisted on the old custom. Better live under a regnant now than suffer a regent for many years and all the instability that portends. Yet what seal will you give me? What pledge, what guarantee, that you will not crawl back here in fifteen years to plague me with her claim?"

Outside, heard through a shuttered window, a hound lifts its voice in a wailing howl, and a dozen similar howls answer. That eerie clamor makes him shudder, but he holds firm.

"Come, my lord. Let me show you the hounds. Then I will take the child, and you and your heirs will be guarded in truth by that which guarantees our bargain."

"It is better so," he repeats, trembling because he does not really believe his own words, but he follows her out through the door into the night.

Falling, Liath tumbled onto her rump as the lion rose and, with a gathering like that of a storm, loomed over her. Its hot, dry breath gusted; it yawned like the gates of the Abyss, displaying sharp white teeth.

"Bright One!"

It leaped and vanished into the rock.

Falcon Mask's arrow skittered over the dirt and clattered out of sight beyond the rocky slopes below. Liath heard the shaft snap, then a patter of smaller falls, and then silence. After a moment, she realized she was holding her breath, and holding the staff.

The two young mask warriors jumped into view, weapons raised and eyes flared with excitement and fear. "Where did it go?"

"It won't be coming back." She got up.

"What is that?" asked Falcon Mask.

The staff was lovingly shaped and smoothed from polished hardwood, oak perhaps, and crowned with a magnificent carving: a pair of miniature dogs' heads remarkably like the heads of the Lavas hounds. A nick had been cut into the haft, as ragged as a sword's blow.

Tarangi sauntered out from the trees, shaking her head.

"I told you. A power as strong as lightning. You are fortunate to be alive."

The raspy call of a tern sounded from the trees. Tarangi did not even look behind her, but the two mask warriors lowered their weapons. Buzzard Mask lifted his mask, put his two little fingers between his lips, and replied with two sharp whistles.

Sharp Edge trotted into view. "Hurry!" she cried, beckoning. "Calta found trace of their passage down the other path!"

She raced away up the path before they could answer. Tarangi and the two mask warriors bolted like arrows loosed.

Liath followed more slowly. As she passed into the shadow of the trees, she heard a deep cough behind her. She paused to look back. In the dusty open space the hut stood alone, but a flash of movement drew her gaze to the top of the outcropping. There the lion prowled, but as she watched, it poured over the rocks in a graceful scramble and vanished from her sight.

A cold shudder passed through her body. The wood of the staff seemed unnaturally warm under her hand.

"Whsst! Bright One!" Ten steps up the path Sharp Edge danced from one foot to the other, waving impatiently at her.

"I have been touched by a strange glory," Liath said.

Sharp Edge looked at her sidelong and hopped a few steps closer. She had blood on her face from a cut over her right eye that was still oozing, as though she'd been slapped by a branch while moving too fast through the trees. "Did your gods give you a vision?"

"Maybe they did."

The clearing lay abandoned except for a single figure curled up on the ground. Buzzard Mask and Falcon Mask and Tarangi trotted past, making for the main path out of the clearing, but Liath halted beside the girl.

"Anna?"

She did not answer or even respond.

"Anna!"

Nothing.

Sharp Edge turned back, nudged the girl none too gently with a foot, and shrugged. "She's useless. She can't even speak."

"Yes, she can."

"She can't speak our tongue. They say she lived several moons among our people but learned nothing. What good is she to you?"

"She looked after my daughter for many years. I won't leave her behind."

Sharp Edge moved away, paused, looked back at Liath. Waited, tapping her foot.

"Anna, we must go." She knelt beside her.

Her eyes were squeezed shut, and her arms curled tight against her body. She had closed in on herself, as might a flower when the cold night air sweeps over it.

"Anna. I need your help. I pray you."

Exasperated, Liath grabbed one of the girl's wrists and tugged her upper arm away from her body. "Here! Here! You need to carry this for me. I can't take it and use my bow, if it comes to that." She unprised the clenched fingers and fixed them around the haft of the dog-headed staff.

Anna gasped. Her eyes opened. She sat up. At first, but briefly, she stared at the object in her hand. Then she looked at Liath.

"They're dead," she said in a voice so soft it was barely audible. "I knew they must be, but I hoped. I hoped maybe they had escaped. But they're dead."

"They served faithfully," said Liath. "Their souls have surely ascended to the Chamber of Light. Anna, we must go. We must find Blessing. We haven't time to dawdle, to hold back, to linger here any longer."

"Yes."

She clambered to her feet, clutching the staff, and began to walk in the stolid manner of a person who knows she has no choice but to move forward. Without joy, but with purpose. Sharp Edge rolled her eyes, then jogged off, too impatient to wait. Liath brought up the rear, and at length, after they had walked some way along the path, through the forest, Anna paused.

"I thank you, lady," she murmured, ducking her head.
"Thank me? For what?"

Her expression, so worn and weary, could break your heart. "For not leaving me behind."

Liath shook her head, too sick at heart to know what to say. "Sanglant would never have left you behind," she said at last, "no more could I, knowing how well you have served my daughter. Now then, let's go on."

They came at last to an overlook where Zuangua had gathered his entire force, five bundles of mask warriors. Together, they gazed over a wide vista. Forest cut away on the hill to either side, bright green with early leaves. A river cut through the valley below, a few farms and hamlets strung along its length. Farther away rose an estate, recognizable as a monastic institution because of its architecture. It was ringed by a livestock palisade, and by stripes of fields and several well tended orchards.

A bird chirruped in the trees. A flight of swifts circled up from the direction of the clearing, as if startled.

"That is Hersford Monastery." She shut her eyes. Pacing through her palace of memory, she climbed through the hierarchy of gates until she came to the circle of the sword of truth. There she made her way into a wooden hall whose floor she had entirely covered with a rimmed basin carpeted with damp sand. Onto this malleable surface she had incised the many tracks and roads on which she had herself ridden while an Eagle and those she had been told of by other Eagles. "Hersford lies a week or two weeks' journey east of Autun, which we must avoid. But it is only a few days' journey southwest, to Kassel. Where Sanglant and Liutgard meant to go."

"What of Hugh of Austra?" asked Zuangua.

She opened her eyes. In the light of day, he looked frightening, his skin on one side of his face blistered and the tip of his curled hand like a claw where it peeped out of the sling. The burns made him appear even more grim and determined.

Sharp Edge and the four masks who had accompanied her looked at Liath, waiting for her to speak, but the rest—even Anna—had fixed on Zuangua, their commander.

"You are a strong man," she said to him, "to keep walking with such injuries."

"Hate makes me strong." He indicated the distant monastery. "What of that place?"

Looking more closely, she saw the inner fields were thronged with a crowd of people, moving among what seemed to be tents and makeshift shelters. "That's where I would go first, if I were Hugh of Austra. He needs provisions, maybe a horse to ride. He's a churchman, too. They'll shelter him for one night."

"After that?"

She shrugged. She burned, thinking of Blessing, so close now. "I don't know how many days ago he reached here, how quickly he crossed through the crowns, how far ahead he is. I must go down. If he's gone, they'll have seen what direction he rode out."

Zuangua nodded toward his trackers, already ranging ahead on the path. "He won't escape us."

5

HE found a court surrounded on three sides by barracks where he could wash his face and hands, and water and feed the hounds. Aestan and Ēagor kept on his tail, although fatigue had deadened Aestan's tongue. At the trough, the two soldiers also scrubbed the night's work from their own hands. Wendish troops eyed them suspiciously but spoke no damning word, holding to the agreement sworn by their leaders the day before. In a neighboring barracks, Eika soldiers lounged at open shutters and doors, but they called no greetings to their brothers, only nodded as Aestan and Ēaagor passed under a portal that led to the vast central courtyard within the oldest portion of Kassel's palace complex.

Servants were up and moving already. Most, he supposed, had not slept on such a night. He and his escort approached the great hall from the east. The hall was a huge timber edifice with thick beams and a massive roof, built in the time of Queen Conradina. The second story of the new palace, where Theophanu and Stronghand had retired, could be seen rising behind the single-storied barracks court that separated the two sections of the palace. A steady wind out of the east beat the pennants and banners flying from the high roof peaks. It was unusually cold.

An honor guard stood at attention in the court, where an empty wagon had been drawn up. These were Sanglant's remaining guardsmen as well as twoscore Lions, some with heads bowed and others with chins lifted. Many had been weeping; some wore clothing stained with blood from yesterday's battle. Seeing Alain, a number of the Lions watched him walk past but said nothing.

The main entrance stood around the corner on the narrow front of the hall where it looked down over the city, hidden from his view here by a wing of the old palace. He followed the stream of servants bearing trays of food and drink toward a side door. As they approached this entrance, the hounds whined and sulked. At the threshold, he had to call them twice, thrice, and then four times, and they crawled forward almost on their bellies because they were so reluctant to enter, ears flat and hindquarters tucked tight. Rage growled in an uneasy undertone; Sorrow yawned repeatedly to show his discomfort.

"Come!" he said sternly to the hounds. His pair of escorts stayed by the door, crossing their arms to stand like glowering statues.

God so loved humankind that They had given them ears to hear with, mouths to argue with, and hands and arms for sweeping gestures that punctuated those statements.

At least twoscore clerics populated the hall. It was a surprisingly contentious gathering given the early hour and the presence of a dead king lying in state—and frankly ignored—in the shadows at the back of the hall where light did not quite reach. The bodies of Sabella and Sapientia had already been taken away to be washed and wrapped, but it seemed no person had yet been detailed to care for Sanglant's corpse.

Most of the conclave clustered on benches at the foot of the dais, although one nervous man paced beside the unlit hearth, pausing to listen carefully only when the conversation got most heated. The rest were grouped in factions, according to the three women seated at the edge of the dais.

The largest group swayed to the words of Mother Scholastica: monks, nuns, noble clerics, and a pair of cowed biscops whom Alain did not recognize. A smaller but equally vociferous number—mostly young and all in monastic or clerical dress—had their sights fixed on Biscop Constance, whose pain-racked face was marked, Alain saw now, with early death. She was not much more than thirty, but he knew she would be dead within the year, and by the vigor of her argument, the fierceness with which she scolded her eminent aunt, he guessed that she knew it, too. Hathumod stood behind her, holding a cup, so intent on Constance that she did not notice Alain.

Seated to the left, speaking least, and least regarded, was Sister Rosvita. She held three books on her lap, guarded by the way her arms crossed over them. She, too, boasted a company of faithful followers, but they were only five in number, watchful rather than talkative. Two men and three young women.

"The writ of excommunication is not a problem, now that Sanglant is dead," said Mother Scholastica.

"It is a problem if there is no skopos willing, or able, to lift it," objected Constance.

"Need we even believe that Antonia of Mainni had the right to elect herself? Or the power to enforce her edicts? I think not."

"Then why insist that the writ mattered at all? You did, so I am told, when Sanglant was still alive."

"Any such writ must be taken seriously! You will cause far more suffering, Constance, with your stubborn insistence in this matter of heresy. Not just excommunication, but war may result. We are weak, and cannot hope to defend ourselves on multiple fronts. I do not approve of Theophanu's alliance, but I admit it spares us from civil war."

"She did what was necessary. I believe we will not be sorry for supporting her. As for the other, we must hold a council. The evidence must be weighed. I have it all written down!"

"Hold a council? Under whose jurisdiction? Whose authority? Are we still at war with Aosta? Will the skopos send a representative? Or is this report true, that Darre is fallen into the pit?"

"I tell you again," said Constance, "we must send a party to Darre to look for ourselves. To report back to us. How else may we determine the truth? How else determine what action to take? Why are you being so stubborn, Aunt? We must act, and act decisively. Send a party to Darre. Call a council, to be held at Quedlinhame, if it pleases you." She turned—even that slight movement caused her face to whiten and her lips to pinch—and held a hand out to Rosvita.

"Sister Rosvita! You walked first among the clerics in King Henry's schola. He trusted you more than any other cleric, so he told me more than once, because of your clear-sighted vision. What do you say?"

"Yes," said Mother Scholastica with an ominous frown. "What do you advise, Sister Rosvita? Be careful what you say, because the words you speak now will always be remembered."

Rosvita had seen Alain and the hounds in the murky shadows under the eaves by the side door, but she drew no attention to him. She waited to speak while Hathumod held the cup to Constance's lips, helped her sip, and patted her lips dry with a cloth. Mother Scholastica glared, an owl impatient for its prey to expose itself.

"We are commanded by God to speak truth," said Rosvita. "I am God's obedient servant, and after that, the regnant's."

"Go on!"

"Belief in the phoenix has spread widely, and into strange nests. I hold in my possession—" her arms tightened over the books, "—a book containing an ancient text written in a forgotten language, but glossed in Arethousan. The words I read there trouble me deeply. They lend credence to those who wish to support the doctrine of the Redemption."

"A forgery! A lie!"

"That is always possible. The Enemy may cast swords among us in the hope that we will grasp their tempting hilts and set to on all sides. But it is also possible that this is the truth."

"Impossible! That battle was fought and won three hundred years ago!"

"By women and men not unlike ourselves. We are imperfect vessels, Mother Scholastica. At times, we can be mistaken."

"No! I will admit no heresy to pollute Wendar. It may be this poison is the cause of all our suffering in these days of tempest and trouble."

"It may be," agreed Rosvita mildly. "That is why I support the recommendations of Biscop Constance. Send a party to Darre, to discover the state of the holy city. We know that Holy Mother Anne is dead. If there are no presbyters living to elect a new skopos, then it is not acceptable that one ambitious woman merely appoint herself. We cannot accept edicts passed by Antonia of Mainni, who has condemned herself twice over by her own malefic actions."

There came a long and grudging silence, while clerics slurped at cups and Alain smelled spilled wine and a finer, more delicate scent of rose water. The hounds did not move; they seemed turned to stone, heads turned toward the bier half hidden by shadows.

"I agree." Scholastica's tone could not have been tighter. "A company must travel south to Aosta to bring our dispute and pleas to the palace of the skopos, and indeed to determine if it—and the presbyter's council—still exists. But as for a council to consider the heresy of the phoenix—I will countenance no such discussion as long as I stand as abbess of Quedlinhame!"

That cowed them.

Or so it seemed, until Sister Rosvita spoke in the most temperate of voices. "What do you fear, Mother Scholastica? It cannot be that you fear the truth."

"These lies are the work of the Enemy."

"Maybe so. None of us are without sin in this matter, I think. You yourself, Mother Scholastica—"

"I?"

"You crowned and anointed Sanglant, but at the same time it appears you were already in league with Duke Conrad and Lady Sabella. Theophanu knows by now that you were ready and willing to pass her over, although hers was the highest claim. Who will trust you, knowing you have shown two faces to those who sought your support?"

The abbess' lips pulled back in a flash of teeth almost like a snarl. "I have remained loyal to Wendar and Varre. That has been my sole concern. Do you believe otherwise, Sister Rosvita? Of what do you accuse me?"

"Of what do you accuse yourself?" Rosvita asked mildly.

Every gaze fixed on the abbess—every gaze, that is, but that of Rosvita. The cleric looked toward the lonely bier. In that moment, the light indoors changed markedly, from a pale filtered glow to a strong yellow glare, as the sun cleared the low-lying clouds. For the first time, Alain saw that the dead man was not, after all, alone and abandoned. The body was flanked by attendants: two nuns and a third figure so bent, doubled over by the head of the corpse, that he could not quite discern what it was. Sorrow whimpered. Rage turned tail and tried to slink away toward the door, but he snapped his fingers and she crawled back.

"Let us see it done quickly, then," said Scholastica hoarsely. "We will hold a council immediately, to begin on the first day of summer, next year. I suppose presbyters, biscops, holy abbesses, and clerics can be called and make their way to Autun in so short a span of time."

Rosvita nodded. "That is acceptable to me."

"Autun?" Constance's hands were trembling and her face was very pale. "Do you still hope for Conrad's backing, Aunt? He remains duke of Wayland. It is Tallia who by right of birth is now duke of Arconia, and you will find her peculiarly sympathetic to the tale of the phoenix."

"I have made my choice," said Scholastica. Her face was white, and she groped for a cup of wine and drained it in one gulp. "Let messengers be sent. Now, I think we are done here."

A tall, hawk-nosed Eagle crossed into the hall through the main doors, walked up to Rosvita, whispered in her ear, and retreated. Rosvita glanced toward Alain, and then raised a hand before Mother Scholastica could, by rising, call a halt to the conclave.

"That leaves only the question of the dead. Both Lady Sabella and Princess Sapientia were taken away last night by stewards and servants to be washed in preparation for their last journey."

The man who had been pacing by the hearth stepped forward. "I am a faithful servant in Lady Sabella's schola. We are only waiting now for the wagon and horses to be brought and her escort to be assembled. Best we leave right away. In summer, the flesh rots quickly. The lady must be buried in Autun, laid to rest beside her mother and her uncle—the last heirs of Varre."

"Sapientia will go to Quedlinhame," said Scholastica, "to be buried by her father's ancestors, as is fitting."

"What of Sanglant?" asked Rosvita.

"None dare touch him," said Scholastica in a cruel voice, "for fear of his mother's curse."

"Many men wait outside who fear no such thing," snapped Constance. Hathumod wiped her brow with a cloth, and after a moment the biscop went on. "But I would ask to hear the testimony of the holy mother who has sat beside his body throughout the last night."

An ancient woman shuffled forward out of the shadows, held upright on either side by two nuns, women so thin they seemed more like cords of strong rope. She was so frail and bent that it was remarkable she could stand; a breath of wind might topple her. Age has its own authority. Even Mother Scholastica gave way before her, rising with every evidence of sincere respect to allow the old woman to sit in her chair.

Just as a child's face hints at the adult visage to come, so the most aged and wrinkled bear in their face a memory of their youth. He saw her full in the light as she settled into the chair, and about the eyes and chin marked the family resemblance.

Heart-struck like a mute beast, his eyes swam with tears. His breath caught as in a cage so that he had to remember to breathe. His hands tingled. For an instant he felt himself weightless, as if his feet were no longer touching earth.

She spoke in a voice strangely powerful, coming from such a fragile, tiny frame. "I have sat vigil this night beside the body, for the sake of my granddaughter, as she would have done herself were she here. These are my observations. When I press a hand to his chest or against his throat, I feel no beat of his heart. No blood pulses from his open wounds. No breath eases from his lips or nostrils. A man cannot live whose heart is silent, and who has no breath. He is surely dead. Yet he does not stiffen or putrefy. He smells of rose water, as though he were but freshly washed. I swear to you that his wounds are healing, knitting and closing in a manner most unnatural."

"Sorcery!" declared Scholastica. "So the curse remains, although his spirit is fled. This is the work of a maleficus, or of daimones out of the upper air. I say he shall be carted to Gent, where he ought to have died but did not. There is a crypt there that might hold him."

Rosvita glanced again toward Alain, but she did not address him or otherwise indicate that she knew he was there and ought to be acknowledged. "Take him west, along the northern path," she said, when he did not speak. "I will escort his body, if you will allow it."

"West?" said Constance. "Why west?"

"What plot is afoot?" demanded Scholastica.

"I will attend the body as well," said the old woman, "as is my right because of my kinship to this man."

"Your *kinship?*" Respect for age was all very well, but Mother Scholastica had clearly swallowed her moment of humility and could endure no more. "Mother Obligatia, I pray you, forgive my bold speaking to a woman of your age and authority. But you are fled from your convent in Aosta and come to take refuge here in Wendar. What kinship do you speak of?" She looked accusingly at Rosvita. "Is there something I have not been told?"

Rosvita opened the topmost book of the three on her lap.

At long last, it was time.

Making ready to step forward, to fulfill his oath, Alain turned to command the hounds to accompany him.

Only to find that after all they had escaped him. He looked around, and saw Sorrow's hindquarters vanish as the hound scuttled out the door. Rage had already fled. Aestan and Ēagor stuck their heads out into the courtyard, staring after the hounds, and then ducked back in again. Aestan was scratching his beard in confusion. Ēagor gestured to Alain, to alert him, and then both soldiers vanished outside.

Alain hurried after them, but the hounds had truly bolted and no one was willing to call them to heel. They had really run this time. He could not keep up with them as they raced down into Kassel town, out the gates, and loped east along the Hellweg.

He followed as well as he could, unwilling to give up their trail. At length an escort of riders caught up with him on the road, with spare horses, and he saw behind them a score of Eika soldiers trotting along at their own tireless jog.

These were powerful reinforcements, but even so, a man must pause to catch breath now and again, eat a slice of bread and cheese when he has not eaten since the day before, and take a drink. Horses must have water. Men muttered that those hounds were demon-get, surely, for how else could their unnatural stamina be explained?

In the end, it took him until midday to catch them, far east along the Hellweg in the midst of forest, but only one sharp word to bring them slinking and shamed to heel.

6

THE stockade surrounding Hersford Monastery had been built to keep wild animals out and livestock in. The gates could not sustain an assault by armed forces, but they were closed nevertheless when Liath limped up the road and halted beyond arrow range. The exertions of the previous day had caused her thigh wound to flare with pain. It was not fully healed. Maybe, with poison scarring the tissue, it would never fully heal.

Anna was her sole attendant. The servant held on to the staff as though it was the only thing that kept her walking.

Folk lined the stockade wall, armed with staves, scythes, sharpened staffs, shovels, and a trio of pitchforks. Beyond the monastic buildings, storm clouds piled up along the eastern horizon but with the wind at her back, she was safe from their rain for now.

"I pray you," she shouted. "I am called Liath, daughter of Bernard. In earlier days I rode as an Eagle at the command of King Henry. I am a loyal servant of Wendar."

To this introduction she got no answer.

"I seek a man named Hugh of Austra. He travels with a girl child, in appearance no more than twelve or fourteen years of age."

In difficult times, strangers are met with distrust, and by their silence she judged her audience suspicious of her. A man dressed in a monastic habit stepped out through the gate and walked toward her, stopping at a distance perfectly balanced to allow him to see the intimate details of her expression but far enough away that he could bolt if she threatened him.

"I am Prior Ratbold. These holy brothers and poor refugees are under my charge. There are others with you, but they hide in the woods. Who are they?"

She did not turn, knowing better, but naturally Anna did, taken by surprise when, after all, they had decided ahead of time to leave the Ashioi in hiding.

The prior smiled crookedly as he glanced at the stockade. When he nodded, shovels and staves and fists were raised and shaken defiantly.

"So we were warned," he said, turning back to face her. "Go on your way. This monastery is a place of refuge. It goes against God's holiest law to abandon one who has begged for Her sanctuary."

The wind shifted, skating in out of the north. Although it was summer, this wind blew chill, and Liath shivered. Far away, thunder growled.

"The girl he holds captive is my daughter, Brother Rat-bold. I *will* come in and fetch her, whatever you say. I would rather do so peaceably."

"That child he saved from the Cursed Ones? Painted like a savage and dressed in scraps? Growling and biting like a dog? He *saved* her from the clutch of the Enemy!"

"So you believe. He has told you lies and woven them to appear as truths. Let me pass. Once I have my daughter, I will leave you in peace."

The prior had the tenacious look of a dog bred to go after vermin, and he had also the broad shoulders of a man once accustomed to wielding a stave or spear in defense of the innocent. He did not back down. "Every person who can bear arms has risen to the defense of this monastery today. All these were driven from their homes by the creatures of the Enemy. Many are dead, many more are missing, and worse still, what crops were sown are left unattended. Famine will stalk us in the seasons to come."

"He could be sneaking out the back right now," muttered Liath to Anna.

The girl shook her head. "Lord Zuangua sent his masks to circle the cloister. We'd have heard their signal by now if there was fighting back there. What will you do, my lady?"

Prior Ratbold had ceased speaking, seeing them talk between themselves. "What will you do?" he asked, in an echo of Anna's soft words.

Liath took one step toward him, and he took one step back. "I am not your enemy. Whatever Hugh of Austra has told you is a lie."

"You are a sorcerer. Is that a lie?"

"So is he."

"You have killed men by burning them alive with fire called from your very hands. Is that a lie?"

"It's true. God help me. Yet he has killed. The trail of death that follows him goes back many years."

"Why should I believe you? You are excommunicated, are you not? Is that a lie?"

Sanglant would have fought this battle of words better than she could. Now that she had Hugh trapped, and knowing he had Blessing in his grasp, she lost hold of what little patience she had mustered. She lifted her left hand, thumb and forefinger raised.

She did not turn. She did not need to. She saw that her allies answered her signal by the expression of fear that fixed itself on Prior Ratbold's face. He backed up slowly, like a man easing away from a rabid dog. Along the stockade, some folk screamed in terror while others shouted in anger; a child bawled; one man cried, "God help us!"

"Hold fast!" called the prior. He reached the gate but, instead of retreating inside, grabbed a stout staff handed out to him by another monk, hefted it in two hands, then twirled it to get his balance and grip. "The Lady will protect us."

The mask warriors loped up to fall in on either side of Liath. All wore masks lowered, presenting a fierce array of animal faces: eagles and ravens, dogs and spotted cats, foxes and vultures and lizards and sharp-tongued ferrets. Zuangua had led a reserve force in a circuit of the stockade. He had given Liath a bone whistle, hanging from a leather cord around her neck, and she put this to her lips and blasted it three times—*shree shree shree*. An answer shrilled out of the eastern edge of the forest.

"They think you are allied with the Enemy," whispered Anna.

Liath ignored her. All this was merely a skirmish distracting from what really mattered. She walked forward, alert to any movement along the stockade that would mark the release of an arrow. Arrows were the only weapon she really feared, beyond the galla. She guessed that one or more men accustomed to hunting in the wild wood stood among this group, and as she neared the stockade, she swept her gaze along the length of the palisade. She looked at every pale face in turn, no longer than it took to blink one's eyes, and they shifted uneasily and betrayed by the cant and leveling of their shoulders what manner of weapon they hid.

There.

She sought with her mind's eye the precise vision that saw into the essence of things and found those substances most thirsty for fire. She had learned over time how these textures and shapes felt from a distance: the cold slumber of iron, the sluggish whisper of stone, the eagerness of wood clasped in a warm embrace of flesh. There, a bow curved, the breath of flame quivering in its layers. With all her concentration fixed to the finest point of control, she called fire in a line along its length.

A shriek. A clatter as a person dropped it. Shouts and consternation broke out about twenty paces to the right of the gate. A man began sobbing hysterically. Someone was slapped.

She reached Prior Ratbold. He did not move, but his eyes were wide. His fear reminded her of Lady Theucinda, only he was a brave man ready to lay down his life to protect those who lay under his charge.

"I do not intend harm to anyone," she said. He stared at her as he would at an adder and—as with an adder—he did not move, fearing perhaps that he might provoke a strike. "I want my daughter, and I mean to get her. If I am touched by any manner of weapon wielded by your people, this place will go up in flames."

"It is wrong to surrender!" he gasped. "We must fight the Enemy. Better to die than to stand aside and do nothing while innocents perish."

"I do not intend to harm any person within these walls, unless Hugh of Austra defies me. Let me retrieve my daughter, and you and all those with you will be left untouched. I promise you, on God's holy Name."

"You walk with the servants of the Enemy," he croaked, letting go of the staff with one hand in order to indicate the line of Ashioi. "There they are! There they are! Begone, foul daimone!"

He curled his thumb around his middle and ring fingers to make the beast's head, raising fore and little fingers as its horns: the sign of the phoenix, the mark of the heretics whose word had spread throughout the realm.

"Don't you see?" she said, with a soft laugh. "I am not a servant of the Enemy. I am the phoenix, who walks living out of fire."

She sought deep in the heart of heaven and Earth. The

aether ran shallow, drained by the cataclysm, but with an effort she found the stream that trickled through the distant stone crown. She gathered as much of it as she could, pulled it to her as carded wool is spun into thread—and her aetherical wings blossomed.

The sound of her wings unfurling cracked like distant thunder. The air sparked, and for an instant those wings blazed so brightly that the prior staggered back, covering his eyes. Folk wept, cried aloud, and prayed. Dogs began barking.

But the breath of aether was too weak to sustain her. The splendor faded as quickly as it had bloomed. Yet that glimpse had been enough. Folk fell back, hiding their eyes. They lowered their crude weapons, and the prior dropped to his knees and braced himself as for a blow.

This was not awe. It was terror.

She pushed open the gate. A wide dirt way led past outbuildings, past the guest compound where a score of faces peeped at her through gaps in the fence, past the beehives, past the stable with a half dozen horses poking their heads out to see what was up, and past a village of tents strung up where sheep would have grazed in more peaceful days. A cold wind chased her, growing in strength. That blast of winter air turned to ice as she broke into a run. Its chill fingers tugged at her. Its chill voice whispered.

Come in now.

The wind fluttered the tent flaps in the refugee camp. A door banged open, caught by a gust. The cold came on so suddenly that it could not have been natural. Memories crowded her, both in mind and in body. Cold ached in her bones. It hit hard, and painfully. Walking hurt, as the cold froze her joints, making each movement into agony. The cold dried her lips until they cracked and bled. The touch of wind on her skin was a slap, stinging and raw.

She did not suffer alone.

Folk huddled, wrapped in the rags of their clothing. Others scattered, seeing her come, while a few monks stood their ground beside the path. They watched her pass, although they made no move to stop her. Each one's accusing gaze stung worse than the wintry wind. She was the monster they feared. Hugh had done his work well.

He had not worked with words alone. Fear of her, of what he had told them of her, could not drive them back, but the harsh weather did. They shuddered in the gale pouring down onto them out of the north. They retreated to porches, where the walls offered meager shelter. But the closer she came to the main compound, the harder it became to fight the winter. Men struggled even to walk. They bent, folded over, as they pushed their way to buildings that might shield them.

The wind howled down. With each breath, with each step, she felt the ice spreading. Where a walkway led between two dormitories, a passageway into the central courtyard, she discovered two novices curled up and sleeping, their lips blue and their fingers white from cold, breath bleeding white clouds into the air.

Cold kills, but she dared not stop to help them.

Her feet rapped on stone as she came out of the covered walkway into the famous unicorn courtyard, with its pillared colonnade, rose garden, and trim hedge of cypresses. Four stone unicorns reared on their hind legs. They gleamed, having been scrubbed clean since she saw them last, and all streaks had been scoured from the mosaic basin. Water spouted from their horns in four arched streams, but as she crossed the empty cloister those slender sprays of water crackled and turned to ice, falling in a patter of shards to earth.

And still the cold wind pressed down from the heavens, until it seemed the air cut as with knives.

The scent of burning—of blessed heat perfumed with lavender—teased her with the sting of magic. Sorcery, like the wind, poured down over her, over all of them. This was Hugh's work. What did he care how many died, as long as he got what he wanted? Always he worked his worst against those helpless to stand against him.

The wind tore away that trace of warmth. She pushed on, hunched over as she fought across the courtyard to reach the chapter house and the side entrance to the church. Her hands were so numb she could scarcely bend them. Her eyes frosted open.

It was so cold.

Cold had defeated her once, when only the pigs had offered her comfort. But the spark of will had never quite died, not even in the depths of that awful winter in Heart's Rest, although she had surrendered in the end in order to save her own life.

Not this time.

All the guilt and grief of those days, which she had carried with her for so long, had burned away. Now the cold, the sorcery, was simply another battle to fight.

A monk sprawled across the doorway into the church, unconscious or asleep. He was shockingly pretty, so perfect in feature that briefly she felt moved to smile, but she could not really move her lips. She knelt beside him and pressed her hands to his cheeks. He had lost so much heat that his skin actually was colder than her chapped and freezing hands. She wasn't sure he was even breathing. Ice rimed his nostrils. With the fine touch of one wielding a needle and not a knife, she carved warmth out of her own core and poured it into his flesh. Although his skin turned red, he rattled and stirred, and a mist of milky breath poured from him as he coughed out a gasp and sucked in air. His eyelids fluttered, but he did not wake. The magic would not let him wake, and save himself.

"Ivar," he murmured.

Startled, she sank back on her haunches and stared at him. Had she seen him before? His was a hard face to forget, and Ivar had spent time in a monastery and might have become acquainted with such a man. Still, Ivar was a common enough name. Her thoughts wound down dreamily, for it really wasn't so much that she was cold but that she was weighed down by an overwhelming crush of exhaustion. It would be so nice to sleep. It would be best to sleep.

"Liath."

The voice roused her. That voice was itself the creep of ice into her body, a hot pain even when it flashes cold. The act of rising bit into her knees and hips, which were by this time so stiff that she wondered if they were freezing into blocks of ice.

Fire is such a fragile thing. Stone and water and earth all smother fire.

"Liath," he said again.

She was not sure whether he meant to wake her, or to lure her into a sleep that would leave her as helpless as the others. Best not to wait to find out.

She stalked through the open door and into the church. Hersford boasted a modest church with fine friezes along the capitals, braided circles enclosing leaves, vines, and birds. She crossed the bema and approached the apse with its dome and piers. Three wide stair steps led up to the altar. A slender form lay athwart these steps, a girl-child dressed in a simple linen shift with her coarse black hair pulled back into a topknot in the manner of the Ashioi, only this girl was Blessing, as limp and lifeless as if she were dead.

She ran, dropped down beside the girl, and pressed her cheek to Blessing's chest and a hand to her throat. The girl's lips were as cold as ice, the lips of a corpse. Liath's own breath ceased, her heart seemed to stop, as she listened, yet after all the child's steady respiration eased in and out as faint as the patter of a mouse's heart.

She was not dead, only sleeping. Freezing to death, like all the others.

A flare of anger burned bright, but she swallowed it. Anger would not help her now. She stood.

Light bled through the rose window, the holy Circle of Unity bounded on all sides by the glorious wisdom of God, who are Lord and Lady and thereby united. That soft light suffused the space around the altar, and here, naturally, Hugh knelt in the perfect repose of a man who is smiled upon by the angels, looking like an angel himself, serene in God's mercy. His palms were pressed together in prayer. His forehead touched his fingers.

"Liath," he said, not looking at her. His voice was as soft and warm as that of a man coaxing a hurt child or wounded dog. "Come in now. Come in."

He stood, turning to face her.

In this way, in the arctic church with the wind whistling in through open doors and with light spilling over him, she stared up at his beautiful face.

God help her. All those years ago he had abused her. For

all the years after he had terrified and tormented her. These memories still had the power to move her, but she was moved with pity and with anger for the helplessness she had endured. She was not the only one who had suffered at his hands, nor was she the only one suffering now. Fumes rose from a brazier burning steadily a few paces away from the altar. The odor of these bindings and workings bled through the monastery to put so many innocents into such a dangerous sleep, as the fierce cold he had called out of the north with his weather working chewed into their sleeping flesh.

Seeing that she watched him, he spoke the words of the psalm in his beautiful voice. " 'You who sit in my garden, my bride, let me hear your voice.' "

"I have a great deal to say to you," she replied. She mounted the last step and halted in front of him. They might as well have been alone in the world. In a way, she had been alone with him for far too long. She had been walking for years now with the memory of what he had done a constant burden, never shaken from her back.

No more. She would bear that burden no longer.

Her voice was clear and strong. "A prince without a retinue is no prince. A lord without a retinue is no lord. You are alone, Hugh. You have cut every tie, severed every bond of kinship. Betrayed every ally. I am come to fetch my daughter. When I leave, you will have nothing."

He did not waver. His grave demeanor gave him an authority that made his words fall with a great weight, like a benediction. "I knew you would come into your power. Now you see what you are. What I always knew you could be."

She shook her head. "I know what you want. But it's not yours and it never will belong to you. This much mercy I have within me. Go now. Go, now, and I'll not kill you. Find what shelter you can—if you can escape the vengeance of the Ashioi. They wait beyond the stockade."

She was cruel enough to enjoy the flash of alarm that widened his eyes and startled the smooth assurance of his heavenly smile. But he recovered swiftly. He always did.

"How can you not see it, my rose? To hurt me would be like hurting yourself. We are alike, you and I."

"So is an adder like a phoenix, for they each have two eyes."

"By denying it, you admit it. We are alike. You fear the truth, knowing it to be the truth."

"It's true we are alike in that we seek knowledge. I do admit it. I've seen it to be true. But the outer seeming does not necessarily reflect the inner heart. We are not alike, because you seek to possess and I seek only to comprehend."

"Is that what you believe? You, who could have anything you wanted? Don't you know the truth about yourself, Liath?"

"That my mother was a fire daimone, and my father born out of the house of Bodfeld. What else is there to know?"

He laughed. "You don't know! You haven't guessed! This is rich irony! Taillefer's great grandchild does not wear the gold torque that is her birthright."

"I am not Taillefer's descendant! Anne was not my mother."

"She was not. Truly, she was not. But who was your father's mother? And who was your father's mother's mother?" He opened his hands in the manner of a supplicant. His voice was pleasing, and his grace and elegance might persuade any woman or man to listen, and to believe. "Have you ever met the hounds of Lavas?"

And here she stood, talking, talking, while the killing cold drowned the monastery and its inhabitants. She found the heart of the fire burning in the brazier, and extinguished it. It snuffed out, wisps of smoke rising with a last, sharp aroma of lavender.

"Enough! Your beauty is undeniable. Your voice is lovely. Your words and your eloquence astound me. But I no longer fear you, I can never trust you, and I will not fall prey to you, in any way or in any manner. Nothing you say can shake me. This is your last warning. Go."

"Can it not?" he asked her. "Nothing I say? I am not done with you, Liath. None will have you, if I cannot. Sanglant is dead."

"Is this the best you can do? Ai, God. You are become pathetic."

She was not fool enough to turn her back on him. She backed up cautiously, felt for the step with a foot, and knelt down to gather Blessing's body into her arms. The girl was all limbs, awkward to hold but not particularly heavy.

He did not move, preferring to remain in the light of the rose window that painted him with its pleasing glow. "I would think, my beautiful Liath, that after all this you would know better than to dismiss my words so lightly. I sent Brother Heribert north because he is infested by a daimone. Heribert is dead. I don't know how he died or how and when the daimone got into his body, although I believe it happened at Verna. But the daimone seeks Heribert, whom it professes to love. I told the daimone to seek Heribert within the body of Sanglant. Once the bastard is possessed—"

She set the girl down.

She rose.

She stepped away from Blessing, for fear of engulfing her in that instant of unbridled rage and fear.

Hugh was ready. A cold howl of wind ripped in through the open doors, so strong that benches tipped over in the nave and slammed into the stone floor. Her clothing writhed around her body, tangling in her legs, and she had to lean backward, overbalancing into the force of that wind, to keep from falling to her knees before him.

Thunder boomed outside. In its wake, shouts and frightened cries split the air and folk shrieked and clamored as Hersford's residents woke from their enchanted sleep to find themselves caught beneath a tempest. The wind screamed over the valley, rumbling along the roof, blasting into the nave like a raging current of water. Hugh's hands were working, in fists and then open, part of the magic of binding and working.

Always, his fingers choked that which he wished to control. Always, he throttled that which did not obey him.

Struggling against the howling wind, she straddled her daughter, a foot fixed on either side of the child's prone body. She fought against sorcery, no longer protected from it by the shield of Da's magic.

How could it be that he knew the secrets of the tempes-

tari and she did not? What would she give for such knowledge? How much would she give up?

They were alike, after all. Ai, God. It was true.

"I am afraid!" she cried in a voice that carried over the
growl of the wind and the cracking shout of the thunder. "I
am afraid of becoming like you. But I never will."

At these words, she saw the truth within him: the twisted
fury that distorted his expression as she defied him.

"It's better you are dead than lost to me!"

"God help me," she rasped. "You dragged off my daughter only to lure me. You threaten my beloved, because you
hope to make me weak, knowing I was weak before. But I
have walked the spheres. I have survived the storm. I am
no longer weak."

"Yet neither am I, my rose. Fear me, as you did once."

Lightning lit the rose window. Its snap sent a shock wave
through the entire stone edifice. Thunder broke as if between them, inside the church itself. The rose window shattered. Its shards rained over them like so many slivers of
ice.

She called fire into the slow glass, and the fragments
poured as shooting stars and peppered the smooth slate
floor of the apse. Hugh staggered back against the altar. He
slapped the burning remnants off his sleeves and his
golden hair. Yet when he looked up, he raised a hand as
against a blinding light shining into his eyes.

"Fear you?" The anger burned at such a blue-white heat
that she could no longer contain it. In her fury, unbidden,
unasked, her wings unfurled with a roar. "I am not the one
you will harm! How many more who are innocent will suffer because of you? God forgive me for thinking I should
let you go unharmed. Because you *will* run, and who will
be able to find you, when you can weave the stars and walk
the crowns?"

He saw her, or saw beyond her, into the heart of her
blazing wings. He saw what she had become and what she
truly was, and his expression changed. In the wreckage of
the rose window he slipped and scrambled.

He fled from what he saw.

A surge of furious triumph scalded her, shameful as it

was, to know that he feared her as she had once feared him. How easy it would be to make him grovel and plead, to make him obey her, to make him crawl.

But she let it go. She had to let it go. Hate makes you blind.

She reached and, with her touch, with the knowledge of the fire that slumbers in all creation, she found the recesses within his eyes where the smallest of messages pass from the world to the mind.

"I beg you." He fell to his knees.

She found the depths within his eyes that formed the passageway of sight, and in this place she sought the slumbering fire. Called fire, with a needle touch, precise and delicate.

Burned him.

Hate makes you blind. And so would he become, who had been blinded by hate and envy for his whole life long.

With a strangled cry, he fell to the floor in spasms as the pain bit deep, but she had already let him go.

Blessing coughed, and came up spitting and growling like a wild creature. Footsteps hammered, and voices shouted outside. The mask warriors poured into the nave, Zuangua in the lead with his obsidian sword held high for the killing stroke.

"Halt!" she cried.

They clattered to a halt and backed away from her, all but Zuangua, who strode boldly up the dais and straddled the wounded man. The Ashioi had a wide, white grin on his face, eerie to look on. Here was a man who enjoyed his revenge.

"I made a pledge—I swore he would live," said Liath. Already she felt the wings furl, die away, because the faint current of aether could not support that blaze.

He looked at her, the unburned side of his face twisted up in a look of disbelief although the other, still red and raw, was pulled tight and unmoving. "You cannot be so stupid."

"The words have been said. I said I would not kill him."

"So you admit it!" He laughed.

"Or let him be killed. The words have been said."

It was clear he did not intend to provoke her by challenging her. "I'm not greedy, Bright One. I see you have crippled him. You've taken his sight. That means he can never weave the looms. He can't threaten us. I'll accept that. I need only proof for my people that we have taken our share, and gained a measure of vengeance for Feather Cloak's death."

He acted so quickly she had no time to react. He bent, tugged Hugh's right arm out straight, and chopped down in a strong stroke, cutting off the hand just above the wrist.

Hugh screamed. He rolled and thrashed.

The Ashioi laughed and howled as they pounded their spears on the paving stones and stamped their feet. She jumped up beside Zuangua, put her hand over the stump pumping bright red blood over the floor, and cauterized it. Hugh gasped—the only noise he could get out—and fainted.

The smell made her sick, and even Zuangua leaped back to get away from that sizzling odor. He retreated down the steps as she rose with blood dripping from her hand and Hugh passed out beside the Hearth.

"Your people have been murdering the Wendish," she said, understanding now the reaction of the monks and villagers. "Packs of them, like roving wolves. That's why they feared me, and hate you. How could you be so foolish as to squander the alliance Sanglant would have offered you?"

Zuangua held up the severed hand. Blood drizzled, although the cut was amazingly neat, sliced by a very sharp edge. The fingers were pale, curled, and there was—she noted—only one simple gold ring on those handsome fingers. Hugh had not been a man greedy for riches. Strange to think he had been spared such a vice.

"I am content," said Zuangua.

But she was not. "Do not offend me and mine, Zuangua. I will keep the peace, if you will."

He shrugged. "Our truce is over."

"That's all you have to say?"

"That's all. Let those of my people who mean to return with me come now."

Sharp Edge stepped out of the crowd. "I'll weave him

through, but I'm staying with you, Bright One. If you'll have me." She said the words with a teasing smile—the kind that men will walk leagues to taste, given the chance. At least one young mask groaned audibly, and a few others muttered and shifted their spears in restless hands.

Liath met her gaze and nodded. "You have a home with me."

"What of the child, my little beast?" asked Zuangua. "I've gotten fond of her."

The girl had seen it all, crouched on the steps. But instead of answering, she lifted her head. Liath, too, heard footsteps. Anna ran into the nave and, with the aid of the staff, shoved her way through the bundle of soldiers, out of breath and crying.

"My lady! Princess Blessing! They're all waking up! And they look so angry!"

The girl looked first at her mother, then at her uncle, and finally at Anna. It was Anna she crawled to, sobbing and coughing between heaves and wheezes.

Zuangua gestured. He and his warriors ran out the door, leaving a stillness behind them, the quiet after a storm. In such stunning calm, one might hear the gentle breath of God.

Liath swayed, rushed by a prickling thrill that ran all along her skin but also made her battle against tears. She could not stop the tremor that afflicted her hands.

"Let us go quickly, Anna. Bring her."

"Where do we go now, my lady?" asked Anna as she gathered Blessing into her arms in an embrace that made Liath want to sob, seeing how the girl clung to Anna so trustingly and yet had not given her own mother a second glance. "Is—he—dead?"

Hugh sprawled on the floor, the stump mercifully hidden under a fold of sleeve. His blood smeared the stone floor. Flecks of soot from the shattered and burned window streaked and spotted his robes and hair. He was still breathing.

"No, but he has been crippled twice over. He'll never weave the crowns again. He'll never read another book. Let us go, immediately. I want no trouble with the poor souls who live here and serve God so faithfully."

Dread already possessed her. Because, after all that, Hugh's last spell had woven into her flesh and her heart to eat at her as one might burn a man from the inside out until he shrieked and howled while his flesh melted away. He was not done yet. She had hurt him, but he had gotten in the last blow.

"Quickly," she repeated. "We must take those horses we saw and ride to Kassel. Ai, God. Sanglant. I fear—I fear—"

She could not say it. The fear choked her, just as Hugh had hoped it would.

XIII
THE ABYSS

1

SHE could no longer ride through deep forest without looking over her shoulder. She could not forget the daimone that had stalked her, or the galla, whose darkness eats souls. She could not forget the elfshot that had killed her mount years ago, although she knew the shades of elves no longer stalked the shadows.

No, indeed, they walked abroad in sunlight, and they were still angry.

She had commandeered nine horses—all that Hersford possessed—but her two Ashioi companions were terrible riders. Again and again she ranged far ahead, only to wait champing, as she did now, for them to catch up together with Anna and Blessing. Usually she heard them coming because of Blessing—the girl had a penetrating voice and seemed determined to comment on everything—but it was getting close to dark and perhaps after all she would have to turn around and ride back.

God, she wanted to leave them behind and move ahead. She could lead her horse all night; her salamander eyes would guide her. But she had to stay with the others. She could not leave Blessing behind again, nor could she expect the two masks to ride into Kassel without her escort. Anyway, there might be bandits on the road, or Zuangua might have changed his mind and followed them. Or worse things might stalk their trail, starving wolves and ravenous guivres, although she could imagine nothing worse than this fear riding as if on her shoulders, claws digging into her neck. Her jaw ached from clenching down tears. She had no reason—no reason—to believe him dead.

Only that Hugh had said so. Only that Hugh could carry out such a plan. He alone might recognize a daimone, might think to push such a complex interlocking set of spheres into motion, hoping that the promised conjunction would fall into place as the spinning orrery came to rest.

It was so quiet here, shaded and peaceful. A bird chirped, giving her heart. It was good to hear the call of birds again. A doe and half-grown twin fawns trotted into view, looked her way, and slipped into the green. She heard no sign of the others.

There.

On the path behind, an aurochs paced out onto the path. It paused, and the wind died, and for an instant there fell a silence that might have extended across the entire world, heavy and profound, woven through all the wild places that have not yet been touched by human hands. Beneath the vault of heaven, a single life is nothing, no more than a catch of breath, a shattering tear, a falling leaf. The tides of the world will ebb and flow regardless. Our lives are less, even, than the wrack upon the shore.

Yet for all that, they are a blessed gift, however small, however brief.

The aurochs bolted, crashing away into the under-growth, swallowed up by the trees.

She heard the slap of hooves coming out of the east. Swinging around, she pulled free her bow and nocked an arrow. Her spare horse tugged sideways, seeking forage along the verge, but the horse she was mounted on held steady, trained and ready for war. As was she.

The rider came clear, emerging around a bend in the path. He was an ordinary figure, covered by a gray cloak trimmed with scarlet and leading a spare mount behind him laden with a pair of saddlebags.

"Wolfhere!"

As he came closer, he said, "I pray you, Liath. Lower that bow."

Startled, she twisted the arrow away and stuck it back in the quiver. "God Above. How come you here, Wolfhere? Where have you been? What news? Oh, God. Oh, God."

Of course, she could not get the words out. He had come from Kassel. Where else? That was where this path led. She feared to ask them, all the heart and breath squeezed out of her.

"Are you alone?" he asked.

She waved toward the west, at her back, and spoke in a voice more squeak than word, "A small group travels with me, but they fell behind."

"Who is with you?"

Only then did she recall how he had come to depart from Sanglant and his army in the Arethousan port of Sordaia. "Where have you been all this time? Is it true you tried to kidnap Blessing?"

He recoiled, raising a hand. "There, now, Liath. I am no threat to you. I am alone."

"What of Anne? You were always her creature, one of the Seven Sleepers!"

He was silent a while. Bunches of bluebells clustered in the shade where the road gave way to underbrush; they nodded as the wind rippled through them. A hawk shrieked far above, unseen beyond the trees. Finally, he shrugged.

"I have spoken of this before. I was raised with Anne. She and I were taught that my service in life was meant for her, for the Seven Sleepers, who continued the work begun by Biscop Tallia and Sister Clothilde. They sought only and always to prevent the return of the Aoi."

"It seems you did not succeed. Anne is dead, the Ashioi are returned, and the Seven Sleepers are scattered or dead. You may be the last one of them who lives." She did not mention Hugh.

"I no longer count myself among their number. I was nothing more than the cauda draconis."

"The tail of the dragon, least among them."

His smile was faint. But there was something about his

smile that she had always trusted, even now, when she knew she ought not to. "As you say. I came to distrust Anne, alas, although I never ceased loving her, as I was taught to do. Some bonds cannot be broken, even when they are betrayed."

She waited, forgiving him nothing and yet wondering what he would say next. An unseen chain bound her to him, since he was the one who had freed her from Hugh. That ought to count for something. But she also waited for the sound of hoofbeats behind her. If he and Blessing must meet again, she would be here to oversee it.

"When she brought that corrupt woman, Antonia of Mainni, into her councils, then I knew I could no longer serve her. That is why I left the Seven Sleepers behind and rode on my own path."

"Then who do you serve, Wolfhere?"

"I am in the service of the king, as I have always been. My first loyalty was always to him, whom I loved best and most faithfully. All I did, in the end, was at his command."

A twig snapped, and she jerked in the saddle. Her mount shied, but after all, it was only a deer in the forest bounding away.

He coaxed his spare mount forward, untied one of the saddlebags, and withdrew a bulky object wrapped in oilcloth to protect it from rain.

"This belongs to you." He held it out, arm trembling at its weight.

Ai, God, it was heavy. She set it across her thighs, settled her reins over her horse's neck, and unfolded the oilcloth. Underneath, a round, spiky shape was tightly bundled in purple silk of the highest quality, so tightly woven she could scarcely perceive the weave.

"What is this?" she asked, knowing the question pointless as she pulled the layers free. Her horse flicked its ears when she gasped. Wolfhere said nothing.

Even in the shady woods, under a cloudy sky, without sunlight to brighten it, the crown gleamed. It was thickset and nothing delicate, a reminder of the burdens of empire that must crush down on the neck of the one who rules. A crown is a form of binding; that she knew. The crown of stars held seven points, each one set with a gem: a shining pearl, rich lapis lazuli, pale sapphire, carnelian, ruby, emerald, and banded orange-brown sardonyx. She almost laughed, seeing the pattern unfold. Even Emperor Taillefer had sought the secrets of the mathematici. His crown mirrored both the stone crowns which in ancient days had forged the great weaving, but also the fabled earthly palace of coils whose winding path echoed the ladder that climbs through the spheres: the Moon, Erekes, Somorhas, the Sun, Jedu, Mok, and Aturna.

"Why do you give it to me?" she said at last. "I am not Taillefer's heir."

"Are you not?"

Her anger sparked. "You know this better than I, since you were there when my mother was called and caged. I am the child of flame. Not Anne's daughter."

"Not Anne's daughter," he agreed, "but who is your father's mother?"

She flashed a smile, meant unkindly, because she was really getting irritated now. Blessing would come, and she desired no conflict, not now, not when she had to get to Kassel to find Sanglant but also had to ride at this agonizingly slow pace in order to protect those she was responsible for.

"I don't trust you, Wolfhere," she said, as if that was his answer. "But in any case, I know who my father's mother is. I have met her. A very aged lady, a holy woman."

"The hand of the Lady has guided you," he said with surprise. "How comes it you have met her?"

"That is a tale I'm not sure I wish to tell you, until you tell me how you are come here this night. And how you came into possession of this crown. And what is happening at Kassel."

He was in a mood to duel. There was a demon in him tonight that made him more oblique and maddening than ever. "What of *her* mother, then? Who was your father's mother's mother?"

"I don't know. Neither does she. She was a foundling, given into the church."

He nodded, as the praeceptor does when the discipla

gives the long awaited, and correct, answer. "Therefore. The crown belongs to you. Your right, to determine who will hold it, who wield it, and who wear it. And if you do not believe me, ask the hounds of Lavas."

Always he had the means to confound her!

A high voice rose in the air, and faded. Liath turned as the sound of approaching riders caught her ear. She had not keen enough hearing to sort out numbers and speed, not as Sanglant could, but she had recognized that voice's timbre immediately. She swung back. Wolfhere's hands had tightened on his reins, and his chin lifted and eyes narrowed as he squinted west along the road.

"If you threaten my daughter," she said in a low voice, "I will kill you. I have come through too much. My patience is all burned away."

He bowed his head without answering; his right hand slid into his left sleeve and he sighed and rested his arm there, as if releasing Taillefer's crown had taken all his strength. She turned her horses all the way around and moved a few paces back the way she had come to get the best vantage of the unwinding path. Wrapping up the crown, she stowed it in one of the saddlebags she had taken from Hersford half-filled with supplies. She refused to mention her encounter with Hugh until Wolfhere confessed the whole, and he seemed just as unwilling to speak.

Silence is a locked chest.

Without speaking, they waited until the company rode into sight with Falcon Mask in the lead, Anna behind leading the string of spare mounts, and Blessing on her own small mare. Buzzard Mask had fallen behind to become rear guard.

"Hai!" called Falcon Mask with a big grin. "We thought you'd outraced us, Bright One!"

"They're too slow!" Blessing had no volume below a petulant shout. "I'm trying to teach them to ride faster. They're so slow! How soon until we reach Papa?" She tilted her head back and sucked in a breath through her nose. "What's that smell? Sharp, like magic."

Anna sneezed.

Buzzard Mask trotted up, clinging to the saddle like a

sack about to slide off. "Ow! Ow! Ow!" he cried as he jerked on the reins, but his horse had already decided to stop, with the others, and he did slide off, starting slow and then falling hard, unable to stop himself. "Ah!" His string of curses was powerful.

Anna dismounted and offered a hand, but he brushed off his legs, tugged with a look of disgust at the short tunic that Liath had insisted he wear over his otherwise naked torso, and offered Anna a grateful smile. He was young, like Falcon Mask, healthy and attractive because of his youth. Anna blushed and backed away. She gripped the dog-headed staff as if it were the only thing holding her upright.

Falcon Mask was rigid in the saddle, fixed at an awkward angle with one hand gripping the cantle behind her and the other holding the reins wrong. "I can't get down!" A wild grin twisted her face; unlike her cousin, she was enjoying this knife edge between triumph and disaster.

"Why are we stopped here?" Blessing brushed dark hair out of her eyes. Bruises purpled her wrists, the marks left by Hugh. Her cheek was split where his ring had gouged her, and she held one leg stiffly. But she challenged Liath with her gaze. Anna, seeing that look, hurried over to grasp Blessing's knee as though her touch might steal the girl's voice. "We're in a hurry. We have to go faster!"

Anna withdrew her hand and ran back to Liath. "I pray you, my lady," she whispered. "Princess Blessing is in pain. That makes her temper short."

"I just want to go!"

"We must rest," said Liath. "Water and feed the horses. It will be dark soon. We'll take a little time to plait torches so we can light our way through the night. Will you ride with us, Wolfhere?"

They all looked at her as if she was a madwoman.

"Wolfhere?" said Anna. "My lady. Are you feeling well? Perhaps we need halt for longer, if you're needing to sleep."

That was when she looked around to see the empty road behind her. Wolfhere was gone. Even the hoofprints of his horses, which ought to have marked the dirt, had vanished.

*   *   *

"And of course," she told Falcon Mask later, "he never answered any of my questions."

They had found a site to rest where a hedge of dense honeysuckle—not in bloom—shielded them from the road. Blessing had fallen asleep soon after choking down a slice of dry bread and pungent cheese; the others had gathered twigs and stems and piled them in a heap. Some of these Liath had kindled into a fire beside which Anna bent studiously to her task, tongue jutting out between teeth as she plaited twigs, both green and dry, into easily-carried torches.

Buzzard Mask took the first watch. His straight silhouette paralleled a slim birch tree growing beside the road; he had a good view in either direction along the road and just enough light to keep watch by. The sky was strangely glamoured this night, the clouds so high and thin that although she could not actually see the moon's disk, she could almost breathe in the misty glimmer of its light seeping through that translucent veil of cloud.

Falcon Mask turned the crown of stars one complete revolution, and shook her head. "Pretty ugly," she said. "I'd take it to the fire workers and let them melt it down for something better. The gems are good, though."

Liath laughed. "Give that back to me!"

Falcon Mask grinned and set the crown on her own head. It stuck on her topknot, and she grimaced. "Too heavy! Eh! This would give you a sore neck. Who wants it?"

"Many people want it. But how and where did Wolfhere get it, and why did he give it to me?"

Buzzard Mask hooted twice, the crude but easy signal they'd agreed on. Two for the east, three for the west, four for the woods. Liath smothered the fire. The flames died, and smoke wisped up in fading trails barely visible to Liath's keen sight. Falcon Mask bundled the crown away and shifted from seat to crouch without a sound, knife drawn. Anna shifted back to kneel beside Blessing while Liath traced a path to a knob of cover they had identified before sunset. Buzzard Mask had retreated here. She crouched beside him.

A pair of lamps, one in front of the other, swayed along the road like will-o'-the-wisps. The walkers came without speaking, but they had horses in their train: one, two, three—probably four. As their shapes got closer, Liath traced the shadows of each creature. There were two men and, indeed, four horses. Travelers meant for reasonable speed, hoping to make better time with a spare mount and a way to travel straight through the night. Just as she hoped to do.

She tapped his arm in a four square pattern; *let them pass*. He returned the tap on her forearm to show he understood. He shifted back as she shifted forward to get a better look. Most likely they were messengers, but it made sense to be cautious until she was sure they were not enemies.

The wind fluttering in the trees and the soft tap of their footfalls covered their words, so it wasn't until they were close enough to toss a stone at that she realized they were speaking in low voices, a murmur as constant as that of a stream. She could not distinguish words, although Sanglant could have, but she could tell that they were arguing. The lamps swayed in their hands; held low to illuminate the road, the swinging lights captured only flashes of a chin or cheek until all at once one of the walkers raised her lamp high and stopped dead. The light shone full on her face.

"What is it?" hissed her companion, stumbling to a halt a step ahead of her as the horses stamped and waited. "I *told* you we shouldn't be walking so fast. We'll hurt ourselves. Or the horses."

"She's here!" said the woman in tones of surprise and dismay.

Liath uncurled with a sharp breath and stepped out onto the path. "Hanna! Ivar!"

Ivar recoiled a step. "God be praised. You're gleaming."

No greeting met her. The message they carried was written on Hanna's face, in the tight line of her mouth and the deep circles under her eyes. "I pray you, Liath, this is not how I wished to find you."

"What is it?" said Liath, her voice gone hoarse.

"Oh, God." Hanna faltered, and could not go on.

So the arrow finds its mark, seeker of hearts, deadly and sure. Pierced there, she went blind, mute, deaf, the dark forest and the night breeze and the dusty path and all the people gathering around her fading to insignificance. There is only the white light of pain blossoming, although it does not yet hurt in the way it will when the blood starts running.

"I don't believe it," she said, because sometimes words are a spell that can alter the fabric of the universe, a weft shuttled through the tight warp of fate. "No creature male or female can harm him."

Hanna's expression, torn by sorrow, was thereby implacable. It is when the ones who truly love you tell you the worst news that you know it cannot be escaped.

"Come," said Hanna gently. "Best we go wait at Hersford Monastery. It will be peaceful there. Have you companions—oh!"

"My friends," said Liath, words emerging by rote. "They are my friends, my allies. And the baby is here. Take us to him. I beg you."

Her companions emerged cautiously from the trees, but what they did or what accommodation they reached with Hanna and Ivar, Liath did not notice, only that Blessing clung to Anna and spoke not one word, as though her voice had broken like her father's long ago in battle, forever altered by an arrow to the throat.

As Liath was herself changed. What she feared most had come to pass. There was no going back. There can never be.

The world had narrowed to a tunnel of shadows down which she must walk.

"Not this way," she said insistently. "Not this way!"

But no one heard her, and she had no power to alter destiny or even the path and direction her feet must take.

Weeping, Hanna took her arm and led her back toward Hersford Monastery, into the darkness.

2

ALAIN caught up with the funeral procession in the late afternoon just before they reached the eastern gate of Hersford Monastery, because a man who walks with two hounds—however unwilling those hounds may be—can move faster than a train of wagons. Theirs was a solemn, formidable procession. In the rear marched two score Lions, led by a one-handed captain with bright red hair. They watched Alain pass them along the side of the road, and although they said nothing they nodded and met his gaze, each one, as a man greets a comrade.

At the end of the line of wagons lurched the closed cart whose scarred walls imprisoned the Kerayit shaman. Her escort came courtesy of Stronghand, two score of Eika and Alban soldiers to match the Lions. These had neither greeting nor words for him, who had never marched to battle at their side.

In the middle of the line rolled the wagon bearing Biscop Constance and her attendants. These, too, remained silent as he overtook them and walked past. Hathumod saw him, but she no longer wept, only marked him; she must tend to the lady as each jolt jarred her; it was a constant struggle to bring the crippled biscop a measure of comfort. One of their number, a stick-thin young man scarcely larger than a child, formed the sign of the phoenix as the hounds passed, before dropping his gaze humbly.

They would believe what gave them comfort. So people always did.

Next in line rode the remaining ranks of Sanglant's personal guard—about thirty men arrayed before and behind the wagon that bore the body carefully tucked in between sacks of grain, cushioned by linen and covered with a silk shroud. These men noted him striding past, but it was the hounds that got their attention and made their horses a trifle skittish.

Loyal men, and truehearted. They would follow until the end.

The vanguard had already reached the gate. Monks and

novices and lay brothers swarmed forward to greet proud
Father Ortulfus, who walked alongside the lead wagon together with Sister Rosvita, her hardy schola, and a dozen
soldiers Alain did not recognize who wore much-mended
tabards sporting the sigil of Austra.

A mob of refugees had gathered behind the stockade, all
amazed and confounded. Churchmen and householders
alike chattered and clamored, wept and cried praises to
God, and drew the sign of the phoenix as thanksgiving until
Prior Ratbold bellowed over their noise.

"Beyond all expectation, you are returned to us, Father
Ortulfus! We came under siege! Yet by the blessing of
God, and with the help of the phoenix, the Cursed Ones
were cast out!"

A miracle!

So they must believe, and perhaps it was even true.

There stood Brother Iso, nervous among the humble lay
brothers. When he saw Alain and the hounds, his eyes grew
wide and he nudged and poked his brethren until they, too,
looked. And said nothing. Father Ortulfus turned, seeing
how the locus of attention shifted, and he stepped away
from the open gate to indicate that Alain should pass
through before him.

But the hounds had a duty and an obligation. They went
reluctantly, ears down, hindquarters in a slow waggle as
dogs will when they mean to show doggish apology. They
crept to the foremost wagon, whining. Even seeing them
display such a frenzy of submission, folk feared those powerful bodies and fierce teeth. Soldiers and clerics sidled
away.

The sight of those huge hounds amused the frail old
woman riding in the foremost wagon. When the hounds
leaped up into the bed, rocking it, clerics shrieked and soldiers shouted, but Mother Obligatia merely extended both
hands and let the cowering hounds lick her fingers.

"Who are these poor, sweet creatures?" she asked, and
looking around saw how far everyone else had retreated.
Shamefaced at abandoning her, the soldiers gritted their
teeth and squared their shoulders and forced themselves to
creep closer, not unlike the hounds.

"You can't think they're *dangerous?*" she added, chuckling as she rubbed their foreheads and scratched over their ears. Seeing that they would be greeted kindly, they flopped down on either side of her, as well as they could on the sacks of grain piled to make her seat, and rolled to expose their bellies and bare their throats.

"What means this?" asked Sister Rosvita. "She was married to the son of Taillefer. She was not a child of Taillefer herself. If these are the hounds descended from those in the emperor's kennel, how come they to bow before her?"

"These are the hounds of Lavas, Sister Rosvita," said Alain quietly. "They know who rules them. *How* they come to her, I know not."

The wagon carrying the old abbess was drawn onto the monastery grounds. The crowd backed away as the mounted guardsmen forced a path for the wagon bearing the body of their dead liege, and some folk even broke and ran when they saw the Eika infantry marching up behind it.

"Clear the way! Clear the way!" cried Father Ortulfus.

Prior Ratbold took up the call as brothers and farmers scattered and took up places on either side of the dirt path that led from the eastern gate to the central compound.

The day was warm despite the haze that whitened the sky. It had thinned until the disk of the sun setting into the west could be discerned as a bright patch beyond the veil. The scene opened with a clarity that astonished Alain: the whitewashed buildings set at neat angles; the covered porch fronting the lay brothers' barracks; the squat, square church tower built of stone; the wide path to the main gate that led past the two-storied guesthouse and the beehives and the smithy and stables and byre; the late flowering orchard overgrown with cloth shelters, sprouted up between the trees like so many unruly weeds, to house the refugees.

A familiar place to one who had lived here many months. Here he had found a measure of peace after losing—forever and irrevocably—the one he loved.

He knew how hard that blow struck.

He saw her emerge with a pair of companions from the guesthouse. The crowd backed away to widen the path by which she might approach them. The sound of her wings unfurling sang as a faint chiming music in his body, the kiss of the aether; they were brilliant to his eyes but lacking true existence, more thought than substance. They blazed, as she did, but with the fire of despair. Maybe, right now, he was the only one who could see them.

Marking the wagon and the riders, she staggered as if hit. The two who stood beside her caught her. They held her, because she could not walk. The wagon's driver brought the conveyance to a stately halt in the middle of a grassy field. She jerked out of their arms and dashed to it, flung herself against the side with a thud, yanked the shroud off the body, and saw his slack face.

Wind raked through the trees and rippled the grass.

What greater cataclysm can there be than this, that which tears the world asunder?

This is the poison that strikes deep, the bee's sting, the nectar of anguish. How can it be that life goes on? What point is there in living? Ai, God. So we fall into the Pit as the black Abyss rips open under our feet.

3

DEAD. Dead. Dead.

All the rest, hands touching her and pressing her this way and that, voices murmuring, faces leering into view and fading away, the roar of the wind and the shuffle of feet and hooves and wheels grinding on dirt and doors shutting and an unexpected laugh heard down the distance and the trickling splash of water and a cough, all this was noise.

She sank into the tide.

"Let me go to her."

Not party to the storm of discussion that followed the ar-

rival of Sanglant's cortege, Hanna stuck close to Liath until
the body was laid on a bier in the nave of Hersford's church.
Lamps were lit along the aisles and blazed beside the Hearth
at the eastern end as dusk fell. Liath clung to his dead hand.
She said no word; she was lost. Father Ortulfus scattered
sprigs of cypress over the body. Mother Obligatia was carried
in, with her attendants and Sister Rosvita at her side. Seeing
that others attended Liath for the time being, Hanna sought
out Sorgatani.

"Is this a good idea?" Ivar dogged her path as she
crunched along the gravel walkway that led along one side
of a dormitory. She wasn't quite sure whether his presence
was gratifying or aggravating. "I heard some awful story
just now, that one look from her eyes and you're a dead
man."

"I'm never a dead *man,* Ivar, and anyway, it's the guivre's
stare that paralyzes you. You must stay outside, though. It's
true that if you looked on her, you would die."

"Well, then, I'm not going to let you look! I'll not risk
you dying, not now!"

"You managed it before!"

"That's not what I meant!"

Before she could turn under the covered walkway that
cut between two dormitories into the famous unicorn
courtyard where, she had heard, they had hauled Sorgatani's wagon, Ivar dragged her to a stop.

"You can't go into the cloister anyway. Only men can—
this is a monastery."

"Shut up, Ivar," she said, and kissed him on the lips,
which shut him up for long enough that she was able to
shake her hand out of his grasp and get five steps ahead of
him.

The unicorn fountain streamed quietly, water burbling
down horns and forelegs. The rose garden was neatly
trimmed, but only a few flowers bloomed, their colors delicate in the deepening light of the dying afternoon. Outside
was brighter than inside; it was still possible to distinguish
bees circling among the flowers.

She was not sure why they had pulled Sorgatani's wagon
all the way in to the fountain courtyard and hidden it be-

side the hedge of cypress, but cypress was said to protect against death. And, in truth, someone had set up a pair of braziers on either side of the wagon and thrust an ever-green bough of cypress into each one. The smell made her nose tickle; she wiped her eyes.

Atop the battered wagon perched a huge owl. She blinked, and it became a thread of smoke winding sky-ward.

The entire roster of Lady Bertha's surviving guardsmen had set up camp in the courtyard, although she wasn't sure who they were guarding from whom. She nodded at Sergeant Aronvald. The wagon creaked under her weight as she set a foot on the step. The wood step gave a high snap and twisted slightly.

"Careful," he said. "That's cracked, there."

The men skittered away behind the hedge as she opened the door, stepped over the threshold, and slid the door closed behind her.

The interior of the wagon was a shambles. The tall chest of drawers had fallen onto its side; two of the drawers were broken; silks and silver bowls and utensils had been shoved into a pile. The boxed-in bed listed, one leg broken off, al-though the bed on the other, empty side of the chamber stood intact and seemingly untouched. On the altar, the golden cup lay on its side, the flask rested against the hand-bell, and a crack sliced through the gleaming surface of the round mirror.

Sorgatani sat on the bed with one arm in a sling and her head back and resting against pillows piled up over the saddle. Seeing Hanna, she rolled to rise, set a foot on the floor, and winced.

"Nay, nay, do not move! God Above! You were badly tumbled."

"But I survived."

"What can I do? How have you eaten and drunk?"

Sorgatani gestured toward the window set into the door. It was shuttered with a square of wood that could be slid open and closed, and screened with strands of beads that formed a concealing curtain. The aroma in the closed wagon was heavy with sweat and mildew. Hanna opened the shutter, and the rising breeze jangled the lengths of beads.

"Help me to go there," said the shaman. "I want to see where I have come."

"Rest a moment," said Hanna. "Let me straighten up. How did you get that sling on your arm?"

"He entered when the wagon was set upright. I feared for him, but, after all, his magic was stronger than mine."

"Who came?"

"I don't know his name. He was attended by a pair of black hounds. He cared for my wounds. My hip is badly bruised. My arm—up at the shoulder—broken. He told me I would heal. He told me that the Holy One—my teacher—Li'at'dano—has passed on beyond this life."

She said the words without tears. They were a statement. A burden.

Smoke coiled around the center pole, which stood straight and true despite the crash. Hanna shivered as cold air winged around her. A sense of being watched prickled along her back. She turned to see the owl perched on the saddle tree. It had not been there a moment before.

"So you see," said Sorgatani. Her headdress was heaped at the other end of the couch, and her hair was tangled. An ivory comb lay on the bed, black strands of hair wrapping the teeth, but she hadn't gotten far in her combing. Maybe it hurt too much. "The owl's coming is a sign that I must return to my people. This is the shaman's messenger. Mine, now."

"Yours?"

"I am the Holy One's heir. The owl came to me last night and led me along the flower trail that leads to the other side. There I met the Holy One. She is dead, as he said she was. I had hoped . . . to stay a while . . . here with those who understand me." She clenched her jaw at a pain, and smiled wanly.

When Hanna sat beside her, Sorgatani grasped Hanna's forearm with her good hand. "I must return to my people. I cannot stay here. Will you come with me, Hanna?"

Tears rose. "I cannot."

She sighed as if this was the answer she expected. "Must

I go alone, then?" She laughed softly, but the sound conveyed only grief. "You were to bring me a pura, Hanna. Breschius served me, and for that I honor him, but he was old. Anyway, a man can only be pura to one woman in his life. Like Liath and her Sanglant."

"He would not take kindly to the comparison," said Hanna with a chuckle that spilled to tears, quickly shed and quickly dried. "I have not done well by you, Sorgatani."

"No. You are my luck. It matters only that you exist."

"Ivar! What are you doing here? Don't you know that wagon is haunted?"

The well-modulated voice, a youthful and melodic tenor, pierced easily the veil of beads. Sorgatani sat up, tugging on Hanna's arm.

"Let me see," she said.

Outside, the two young men fell into a fevered and rather disjointed conversation that seemed mostly to consist of Ivar stammering out the story of his ride to Kassel and the battle while the other one kept interrupting him with questions that never quite made sense.

". . . we ran to get away from the skirmish but were overtaken in the woods by Duke Conrad's men—"

"Why would horsemen be attacking the woods?"

Sorgatani moved slowly but with determination, favoring one leg. She leaned on Hanna and tweaked aside a few strands of beads, allowing her to look out without others looking in upon her. Hanna saw Ivar at once, pulling at his hair as he did when he was nervous and upset and frustrated. An astonishingly pretty young man had hold of Ivar's elbow in a possessive way that forced a slow simmer of jealousy to boil up in her heart. How could anyone be that good-looking? It wasn't right. It wasn't fair. Angels might look so, with their perfect features and their sunlit hair aglow.

"Look there!" murmured Sorgatani huskily, perhaps because standing hurt her. "Now that's a handsome stallion!"

He's mine, she almost blurted, but of course Sorgatani wasn't referring to Ivar. No woman would call Ivar a handsome stallion when he was standing next to that crea-

ture, even though Ivar was the most beautiful man in the
world to her eyes even if she knew very well that he really
wasn't.

She blushed and turned her attention to Baldwin, who
was now gesticulating wildly as he related some tale to
Ivar that Ivar did not, in fact, appear very interested in
hearing. Ivar kept staring at the wagon, shifting his feet,
and tugging on his hair. He was standing off at an angle
and had not noticed the shift in the concealing beads.

Well. It was no surprise that Sorgatani would notice
Lord Baldwin. True enough, he was breathtaking of feature, but it seemed to her as she watched him talking that
there was something a little vacant about that pretty face.

"Is he crippled or injured in some way?" Sorgatani
asked breathlessly. "Has he been wounded? Ah, look! His
hand has been cut off. Just like Breschius! Maybe it's a
sign." Leaning on Hanna, she tightened her fingers as folk
do when they grasp the rope that will save them from
drowning. "What do you think?"

Sorgatani wasn't looking at Baldwin and Ivar. She was
looking beyond them where the fading light poured its
golden aura over a portion of the fountain and the paved
pathway. A pair of sturdy lay brothers was carrying a man
on a litter out of the monks' quarters. They cut along one
of the diagonal paths, bringing them close by the wagon.
They were on their way, perhaps, to the infirmary. They
weren't in any hurry. The presence of the foreign wagon
seemed of no interest to them at all, nor did they show
much interest in their patient. They kept pausing between
strides to look toward the church, although it wasn't clear
what they hoped to see there.

The man lying on his back on the litter was covered from
feet to hips with a thin blanket. Otherwise, he was naked
from the waist up, his left hand resting on a taut belly and
his right arm, slightly elevated on a rolled-up blanket
pressed along his side, ending in a stump at the wrist. He
had good shoulders, and pale, lovely, rose-blushed skin. His
eyes were closed, but in the manner of a person who, although awake, prefers to shut out the truth. His golden hair
had been washed and combed, and it gleamed when they

passed out of the shadow and into that last spill of sunlight lancing through the westward-facing walkway.

"Can I have that one?" Sorgatani said with a ragged laugh.

Ai, God! *Hugh*.

"Is there any man handsomer than you?" Hanna whispered.

"There cannot be," murmured Sorgatani, lips parted, leaning until her face almost brushed the beads as the monks moved past.

"He is dangerous, that one. Unforgiving, unkind, arrogant, vain, proud, obsessed, and cruel. Forget him, Sorgatani."

"But he's so beautiful. I am Kerayit, daughter of the Horse people. I can break the most vicious-tempered stallion that walks Earth. It is in my blood and my breeding and my training. I do not fear him."

The monks passed out of sight. Ivar shook Baldwin's hand free, grabbed his wrist, and tugged him away from the wagon, and it seemed a trick of the air that she could hear Ivar's answers but not Baldwin's questions as they moved away.

"Yes, that's right, they all survived. Yes, Sigfrid, Ermanrich, and Hathumod. They're all here with Biscop Constance. In the guesthouse, I think. Come, I'll take you to them; that's where you belong. No. No. I'm not going to stay in the church. I'm going to become a messenger, just like you, for the phoenix, only not in the church. It's for the best, Baldwin. Trust me."

Sorgatani turned away from the beads to grip Hanna's hands with both of her own, although the gesture caused tears to start up as her lovely face was ripped with desperation and pain. "You are still the King's Eagle, Hanna. And my luck. That is what I ask of you. Let him become my pura, and I can go back to my tribe knowing I will not be alone."

4

GRIEF strikes each body in a different way. For the longest time Liath drifted in a stupor, clutching the cold hand, vainly trying to heat the corpse and ignite the spark of life that no longer burned within. Folk whispered around her, gliding in and out of view, but their motions were meaningless and random. In no way did they move with the sure predictable paces of the stars. Yet the sun and the moon and the canopy of heaven, raised above us, have no liberty to govern themselves. They are subject to the law; they do what they are ordered to do, and nothing else.

How much easier, then, to see the fate that awaits you and brace yourself. Wasn't it better to know the path in advance than to stumble like this?

Ai, God! Ai, God!

The child was screaming. She heard it now, and it occurred to her that these hysterics had been going on for some time.

She had to let go of the hand, and she feared by doing so she would lose him forever, but she had to let go.

There.

She tried to stand, but her legs were all pins and needles. Arms steadied her. She sought and found the child who had thrown herself onto the floor of the nave with a ring of troubled onlookers standing carefully back while she shrieked and shrieked, no matter that she was breaking the sanctuary of the holy church and pounded feet and hands on the floor in the throes of a furious tantrum.

"We were too slow! We didn't get there fast enough!"

"Blessing," she said.

They parted ranks to let her through. Anna knelt just out of range of those flailing hands and feet.

"Careful, my lady," she said in a hoarse voice. She had a purpling bruise on her chin, and she was favoring one arm. "She's gone wild."

"Does the Brother Infirmarian not have some manner of sleeping draught?" Liath asked to the air at large.

There were so many people in the church, crowding and

choking her, that she began to think some were real flesh and others only shadow and light, souls and presences descended from the higher spheres, shifting in and out of existence like a light winking on and off as a hand covers and uncovers its flame.

"Lady? Liathano?" A voice swam past her. A hand brushed her elbow. "I think she is fainting."

Easier to be the sun, who never says, "I will not rise at my regular time." Easier to be the moon, who wanes and waxes according to the law that set it in motion. Easier to be stars, who rise and set as they are commanded, and the winds, who blow, and the mountains, who remain in the place they are set. They are instruments of the power that set them in motion.

"Here, lady. Drink."

She staggered to her feet.

Blessing was still sobbing, lips moist and liquid spattered down her chin. "I shouldn't have stayed with Uncle! I should have gone sooner! Then I would have gotten to him. I would have saved him! I could have! I could have!"

"You must take more, Your Highness." Anna was fixed at the girl's side, holding a cup away and out of arm's reach. "You must."

Captain Fulk stood beside Liath, a hand hovering a finger's breadth from her arm.

"I pray you, my lady," he said in a low voice, "there's something I must speak of immediately." She nodded, because God had given humankind liberty to choose for the good or for ill, for the blessing or the curse. "Princess Theophanu is to become regnant by marrying this Eika lord, called Stronghand. It's agreed that the princess will adopt Blessing as her heir, and that the girl will marry Conrad's infant son, if the little lad lives."

"Become regnant? Blessing?"

The captain was weary, face shadowed, eyes dark, as he considered the girl now dropping off to sleep. "I don't know what to think of this alliance with the Eika. Yet they did have us outnumbered and surrounded. They could have done great damage to the armies of Wendar and Varre, but their lord, this Stronghand, did hold back the killing blow. There's a party of them with us, come to escort the witch woman. To make sure she's not harmed, I suppose, although she's more dangerous to us than we are to her."

Words, like stars, swung on their course overhead and passed on into the night. She knew she ought to concentrate, but it was so difficult.

"What of Sanglant?" she asked. "Hanna, bring me the crown." Then, after all, she remembered he was dead.

"She's all that's left of him." Fulk's face was wet, and he smiled sadly. "The little spitfire. Thinking she could have saved him! Poor mite."

"No, he's not dead," she said, but when she turned around and saw him lying still and silent within the ring of light, she knew he was. "I can't bear it," she whispered.

"Nor can any of us, my lady, but we must. Ai, God! We must."

5

CAPTAIN Fulk carried Princess Blessing to the guesthouse, where a soft bed awaited her. Anna knelt beside her. As the girl slept, Anna undid the awful topknot and combed out Blessing's black hair as well as she could. She could not bear to look at the girl with her hair done up in the manner of savages.

Fulk was speaking at the door in a low voice, arranging for food and drink, water to wash, a guard to be set over the girl. Two lamps were lit, one set on a tripod by the door and one hanging from a hook in the corner, so the girl would not wake to darkness. She would be well guarded. Sanglant's guard would see to that.

She heard them talking: Blessing was to be named as heir to Theophanu. She would marry the son of Conrad and Tallia, now an infant. Someday, God willing, she would be regnant.

Anna caught the attention of one of the guardsmen, Sibold, the man with the torn throat who spoke now in a hoarse croak that would always remind her of Prince Sanglant's injured voice. "Is it true that Princess Theophanu will marry an—an Eika prince?" she whispered.

Sibold had always been a lively, bold man more likely to leap than to look, but his face was pale, he was exhausted, worn right through with grief. "So it is," he said curtly, then shook his head and turned away.

She sat cross-legged beside the girl's pallet, stroking that black hair, too restless to sleep as night came on. With her other hand she traced, over and over, the carved dogs' heads on the staff. Something about the polish and smoothness of the wood comforted her.

From outside, a dog gave a low, whuffing bark, as a man might gently call for attention from a dozing merchant. Voices murmured from the porch. The door opened, and a man walked into the room. She recognized him, although he did not walk with his two massive black hounds in attendance, not in here.

He looked first at Blessing. The princess slept with an arm flung out and her legs tangled in a blanket. He knelt beside her, touched a hand to the girl's cheek, listened, sighed. Then he looked up at Anna. Tipped his head sideways, eyes narrowing.

"I know you," he said softly. "You were at Gent."

Choked, she could only nod. But as her hand tightened over the staff, she found her voice.

"You gave your Holy Circle to an Eika prince," she said.

He smiled, eyes crinkling with surprise. "So I did."

"I–I saw it. Him. He was in the cathedral at Gent. He let Matthias and me escape. He let us go. He could have killed us. Any of the others would have. But he let us go."

The young man's eyes were dark. Like the guivre, his gaze pinned her, as though he would dig all the way down until she had no secrets left. She clutched the staff and, drawn by the movement, he looked beyond her, and saw it.

He gasped. A slap across the face might have struck him, because he recoiled, eyes widened and head thrown back.

Yet the sting, however sharp, was brief.

He coughed, wiped his brow, touched his throat. From outside, a dog barked interrogatively.

"I pray you," he said, voice a bit ragged, "where did you get that staff?"

Must she tell him? He stared at it possessively, and she wrapped both hands around the haft and drew it awkwardly against her body. Words stuck in her throat, but she knew she must speak. She must not remain silent.

"I–I–Lady Liathano gave it to me."

"How came she by it? Do you know?"

"I–I–we didn't have it before. In Ashioi country. She found it up at the crown, the one up here, where we walked through from the south. I heard her telling—as we walked down here—she found it by the hermit's hut. She said—she said—" The words seemed so ridiculous she was afraid to utter them, but he looked at her so steadily that she stumbled on. "She said a—a lion dropped it at her feet." She braced herself for his scorn, for laughter, for anger.

He sat back on his haunches. He let out all his breath, and passed a hand over his hair. "No. No." And then, reluctantly, but as if he could not stop himself from saying it, he said, "It was mine, once."

Almost, she sobbed.

He flicked moisture from beneath an eye. "Might I just—just—" Reaching, he hesitated.

At length, rigid with fear of losing the staff, she released it into his hands. He traced the carved heads, the length of the shaft, the cut where the wood had been hacked. He shut his eyes, and after a moment opened them. Blessing snorted softly in her sleep and turned over, but did not wake.

"Let it be passed on to the one who needs it most," he said, giving it back to her.

She was ashamed at how she grabbed it from him, but he only smiled gently. He rose, took a step away, paused to turn back.

"You are not the only survivor from Gent who walks in royal circles this day, now that I think on it. Lord Stronghand's council includes a man who was once from Gent, called Otto. 'Papa Otto,' I heard the others calling him. He's in Kassel with the rest of Stronghand's army."

Then he left.

She stared at the closed door as the lamps hissed. Papa Otto! If Princess Blessing was to be the heir, and Princess Theophanu and this Lord Stronghand were to rule, and Papa Otto stood in Lord Stronghand's council, then surely she and Papa Otto could be together somehow, sometimes.

Leaping up, she ran after him. He was still on the porch, talking in a low voice to Captain Fulk, whose eyes were red from weeping.

"I'm sorry," she said, grabbing his arm. "Here. Here."

She pushed the staff at him. Reflexively, he took it. He stiffened, holding it, stroking it. He, too, had tears in his eyes.

"I have what I need," she said. "You just gave it to me. Please. This is yours. You must take it."

For a long while he did not move, as if he had been struck dumb. But at length he smiled. He touched her forehead with two fingers.

"For this gift," he said, "I thank you."

Then he was gone.

6

DURING Vespers, Rosvita stayed beside Mother Obligatia, who rested comfortably, propped up on pillows, on a litter set across a pair of benches beside the bier.

"I will remain with my granddaughter," said the old abbess as the service came to a close. Captain Fulk had carried off the sleeping princess, while Liathano remained kneeling by the bier.

Rosvita nodded. "I must pay my respects at the guesthouse, to Biscop Constance."

She left the church and walked alone to the guesthouse.

Although the upper suite was usually given to the highest-ranking guest, Biscop Constance had taken the lower rooms because she could not get up the stairs. She greeted Rosvita from a chair. Now and again she rubbed her hands together as if chafing them against cold. The lamplight softened the lines of pain that creased her forehead and around her eyes and mouth. She even smiled, although the gesture quickly flickered into a wince of pain.

Rosvita kissed the biscop's ring. The young nun who hovered in constant attendance patted pillows and rubbed Constance's shoulders, trying to make her more comfortable.

"I leave in the morning to continue my journey to Autun." Although Constance's body was weak, her will remained strong. "I must return to my seat as biscop. Seal the betrothal between Conrad's son and Sanglant's daughter. Oversee preparations for the crowning and anointing."

"Have we judged wisely, or rashly?" Rosvita asked her.

"We have judged as well as we can. This Eika lord is far more subtle and farseeing than he seems at first glance. In any case, his army would have crushed both Wendar's and Varre's had Theophanu not acted precipitously."

"Had you speech with her beforehand? Did you know what to expect?"

"No. I was as surprised as you. That is not even the greater part of what this cataclysm has brought in its wake. These clerics of my loyal schola will begin preparations for the council to be convened next summer. Best if it is held in Autun, under the shadow of the old emperor and the Council of Narvone."

"When Biscop Tallia was repudiated, the arts of the mathematici and malefici, any sorcery done outside the auspices of the church, were condemned."

Constance reached for and, with an effort, grasped Rosvita's hand, looked searchingly into her eyes. "Will you support me? You understand that I believe in the miracle of the phoenix."

"I will judge fairly. The writings of the church mothers weigh heavily, but I must bow to truth if truth is revealed."

They kissed as sisters.

After checking to make sure the child was settled and her attendant given food and drink and a pallet to rest on, Rosvita walked upstairs where Brother Fortunatus,

Brother Jehan, and the three girls had open the books: the *Vita* of St. Radegundis, their copy of the *Chronicles* from St. Ekatarina, and the *Annals of Autun* salvaged from the library in Darre.

"Fortunatus found a copy of the *Chronicle* of Vitalia in the library here." Heriburg brandished the volume triumphantly. "So it is agreed that Taillefer had four daughters who lived to adulthood. Three entered the church, one of them Biscop Tallia. The fourth, Lady Gundara, married the duc de Rossalia. She had three children by him. The eldest inherited the dukedom, the second entered the church, and the third—a boy named Hugo—married the infant daughter of the count of Lavas, Lavastina."

"So it's true that the only remaining descendants of Taillefer in Wendar and Varre are the line of Lavas," said Ruoda, speaking on top of Heriburg's last sentence. "But we learned this before, in Darre, Sister Rosvita. Why is it of interest now?"

"'The world divides those whom no space parted once.'" Rosvita found that Fortunatus had brought her a chair, and she sank down gratefully. She rubbed her forehead with the heel of a hand, shutting her eyes. "It has all been hidden in plain sight. We know whose child Brother Fidelis was. He was the heir of Taillefer by Queen Radegundis. We are blinded by his piety and his longevity, his good name, his reputation. That is why we never wonder at the girl he briefly wed."

"Why do the hounds of Lavas bow before Mother Obligatia?" asked Gerwita. "We all saw it happen."

Rosvita nodded. "The simplest explanation is usually the correct one."

The room was simply furnished with rope beds, benches, a table, and a chest. The shutters had been taken down from both windows. They had left the door open to help the breeze pass through. Besides their writing implements and the precious books, they traveled with nothing more than a few extra robes and tunics, a pair of combs, brooches and pins for cloaks, blankets, flasks, needles and thread, eating utensils, a maul and muller, a bladder filled with lanolin, a sack of candles, and one iron pot.

They asked for nothing more than this.

She looked at her loyal schola: Fortunatus, who had endured so much and never once complained; the three clever girls; young Jehan, made frail by their journey but hanging on. Sister Amabilia had died long ago, and Brother Constantine had not survived the king's progress. Aurea had died together with Brother Jerome in that first raid, but there would be others, waiting in Theophanu's schola or learning their lessons in some novices' hall, who would join them.

Someone must strike a lamp to flame in the darkness. Someone must care above all things that the truth be illuminated.

"He knows," said Rosvita.

"*Who* knows?" asked Gerwita, but the others were already nodding.

"I saw him," said Heriburg, "as I was coming upstairs. He was in this house, but he left and walked out into the tent camp, among the refugees. Is he a holy man, Sister?"

"He is a mystery, sent by God for us to unravel. He knows the truth. This I must do, as we are commanded by the regnant, whom we serve. Princess Theophanu desires that the rightful heir of the county of Lavas be brought forward. I will see it done. For the sake of King Henry, whom I loved, who loved his bastard son best of all his children, although it was unwise of him to do so."

"Love is not wise," said Fortunatus, whose hand rested on her shoulder. "Love is most unwise of all."

"Yet it sustains us."

7

THE night wind whispers in the trees. Folk huddle under the scant shelter of canvas stretched between limbs, staked down at corners. Some among the children sleep soundly, curled tight in blankets, but one is sobbing with eyes open.

He knelt beside the women tending her. "Is this your child?"

"Nay, not mine. My sister's. She saw her mother murdered, my lord. She has these nightmares. You see." She waved a hand in front of the child's staring eyes, but the little girl did not react. "She is asleep. I always wake her, but when she falls back to sleep, it's the same over again."

He set a hand on the child's dirty brow. The hair was combed back and tightly braided, greasy because unwashed, but otherwise neat. The shift the child wore was smeared with dirt but several tears in the fabric had been precisely repaired with even stitches.

He closed her eyes gently. After a moment her sobs subsided and she sighed and fell into a calm slumber.

"Can you sleep?" he asked her aunt, who was, he saw now, a young woman made old by what she had seen. No older than his foster cousin, Agnes, yet her cheeks were hollows, and her gaze was bleak.

"It's hard to sleep," she admitted.

"You must have a name. What happened?"

"I'm called Leisl. I've six nieces and nephews to tend. Both of my sisters were murdered. And my brother-in-law, hit by a falling branch. The other's husband is gone missing, God help him. I was betrothed to Karl, who lived over by Linde—that's a half day's walk from our village. But I haven't seen him since that day. We've good land where we are, but no man to till and tend the fields. These boys are too young. I can't tend to house and field at the same time. I don't know what we'll do this winter."

She raised her head to stare through the dark night toward the black shadow of the church and its high tower. "They say the phoenix came, that it was a sign from God. But I don't know, my lord. I was frightened. It got so cold, like a winter storm. Maybe it was the Enemy instead. Three demons walk here, with their masks, in the company of the winged one. The same ones that killed my family. How can I think they are beloved of God?"

"These seeds were sown long ago," he said, taking her hand, "but it is our fate to be left with the harvest. Let those who remain here be at peace. God's mercy reaches into many hearts. As for you, Leisl, what needs doing?"

She shrugged, gone beyond sorrow into bitter practicality. "I need a husband. If Karl is dead—and I suppose he must be, since he didn't come here and I heard that Linde was burned right down, all of it—then I must find another man willing. It's a decent household, with good land, and two walnut trees and six fruit trees. We had five sheep and four goats, but they're lost, too. Chickens. Near the river. The house well thatched. Three other families nearby, none of them cousins to us. One family of outlanders up from south of Autun who settled there in my grandmother's time."

"There might be a man among these refugees here, who lost his wife and needs to marry."

She flashed him a look. She had a stark gaze, stripped of illusions. "There is one man I have noticed. He came out of Kien, up in the high country. But he's lost in his mourning, more a mute beast than a man. I don't know if I can carry him out."

"Wounded beasts can be healed by treating them with patience and respect. So may humankind. You are strong."

"What choice have I? I am all that's left. I would not have my family's name die with me, and the good land we farm go to some other, for we've not even any cousins left to us. If I lose the land, the children will have to go out as bondsmen or servants."

He left her and went on, talking to those who were wakeful and smelling out those who were sick. Hamlets and villages and farms all through this region had been laid waste, they told him, crops left unsown, livestock scattered, and many, many folk were dead. It would be a hard winter ahead, but at least they now had the rest of summer to re-build and some measure of peace to build in. At least they now had some hope to hold onto.

Late in the night, he circled back to the main compound. The haze had thinned. The quarter moon faded in and out behind wisps of high cloud. At zenith, the Queen processed in glory with her Sword, Staff, and jeweled Cup. The Dragon had already set.

Lions stood at guard on the porch, and their captain hailed him.

"Lord Alain. You are out late."

"Many sleep restlessly tonight," he remarked. "Now that I think on it, Captain Thiadbold, are there any men among your Lions who are ready to retire from the regnant's service? There's at least one young householder with a grand inheritance who is in desperate need of a partner—a husband—to help her hold her land and title."

"She's too high for me," said the captain with a startled laugh.

Alain was startled in his turn. "I pray you, what do you mean?

"Sister Rosvita has let it be known. The good cleric went inside not long ago, to the mourners."

"Let what be known?"

"About the rightful heir to Lavas County. Who would have guessed it! The holy abbess cannot live long, and so the granddaughter will take the coronet. It's a miracle—don't you think?—for the truth to be known after so long." He paused, seeing that his dozen men on guard had shifted closer to listen. "Still, no triumph, coming in the wake of her grief."

"See there." Sergeant Ingo pointed at the sky over the dormitory roofs. "There's the Phoenix, rising."

Where the haze cleared, the constellation Alain had always known as the Eagle unfurled its great square of wings. No one corrected the other man.

"They're saying it's why you brought the hounds of Lavas, all this way," said the captain. "None dare touch them but the rightful heir to Lavas. That's what they're saying."

"What will you do now, you Lions?" Alain asked.

The lamps lit along the porch illuminated the captain's crooked smile and flame-red hair. "Queen Theophanu herself called me to her chambers before we left. She has asked me to stay on as captain. It's all I'm good for—training new Lions, that is. I'll do it. As for these others, that's up to them. They've served faithfully on a long road."

"There's a young woman named Leisl in the refugee

camp. She's looking for a husband willing to farm the land she inherited, and help her raise her nephews and nieces." He nodded at the gaggle of men. Passing up the steps and under the porch, he crossed into the church.

In silence, the vault of air below the high ceiling of Hersford's church breathes. A pair of monks murmurs prayers, and the lamps lit along the aisles whisper along their wicks, but otherwise the scene looks very like a painted mural.

The bier rests solidly on earth, holding death, which weighs heavily on all mortal kind. The face is uncovered and at peace. The black hair is combed neatly away from the beardless face. He is robed in rich linen, a fitting burial shroud. A glittering crown of stars sits upon the motionless chest. His cold hands hold it, a thing forever beyond his grasp.

Two women crowd close, one kneeling in an attitude of despair and the other standing with hands at rest on those bowed shoulders, but it is youth that has been felled and age that shows resilience. Mother Obligatia has gained remarkably in strength even in the short hours since they entered Hersford Monastery. It may be a tangled skein of sorcery is at work, or perhaps it is simply her joy at being reunited with her granddaughter that invigorates her.

The hounds sit on either side of the old woman. It is they who see him enter. They thump their tails lightly and gaze lovingly at him but do not move. His grip tightens on the staff Kel carved for him so long ago that those days are lost to memory, just as these days will be, in time. Only the daimones of the upper air can see in all directions: north and south, above and below, past and future.

Yet memory prods us. Much of what we are and what we choose and how we act and react come about because of what we remember. Not so long ago he himself knelt beside the bier set in Lavas church; he touched Lavastine's cold right hand and heard the breath of stone.

What seems dead may only be in stasis.

He walked forward. Many had joined the vigil, out of love or respect for the man. Sister Rosvita had brought her schola. A pair of Eagles waited to one side—no, after all, it was only the Eagle called Hanna, with a redheaded companion, a man he had seen before but whose name he did not know. Father Ortulfus prayed by the Hearth together with Prior Ratbold and all the monks and lay brothers. Captain Fulk stood guard over Princess Blessing, who had, it seemed, come back after resting in the guesthouse. The child's eyes were open, and she watched Alain pass. Captain Thiadbold, Sergeant Ingo, and a trio of other Lions moved up behind him, following him in from outside.

Honest witnesses all.

Mother Obligatia turned as he came up behind her. She was frail, tiny, ancient, but nevertheless a woman of immense spiritual power and inner strength. She smiled in the manner of one who has experienced every means and method of betrayal, yet can still find it in her heart to trust humankind, at least one or two of them. Her trust was hard won, but once won, given without reservation.

"Who are you?" she asked him.

The hounds waggled over to greet him. He noticed for the first time how Rage's belly had begun to round. The truth, it seems, is fertile ground. He scratched her under the ear just how she liked it best. Sorrow pressed his big head against Alain's leg.

"Lady," he said, acknowledging her. "Lavrentia, count of Lavas. Great granddaughter of the Emperor Taillefer."

"How can it be?" she asked him. "Although you are not the first to say so." She nodded toward Sister Rosvita.

"There are some links in the chain that I still do not quite understand," said Sister Rosvita. Each member of her schola, clustered around her, clutched a book like a talisman, these keepers of memory. "That the counts of Lavas claim a grandson of Taillefer as their ancestor I can prove through these chronicles. It is the shadow that lies over the succession of the elder Charles that defeats me."

"I know only what I have seen in a vision. Yet this same vision has been woven into a tapestry that hangs in Lavas hall."

As Alain began speaking, Father Ortulfus broke off his prayer and, with the prior, strode to the bier in order to listen.

"Imagine, if you will, a boy born as the only child of a

powerful count. He is raised with every expectation of becoming heir. Then his mother—after eighteen years of barrenness—becomes pregnant late in life. She dies in childbed. She will never know the truth: that she gave birth not to a second son, but to twins, girl and boy. In Varre, according to the old custom, girls take precedence over boys because only through the body of the woman is it sure that the line continues."

Rage whined. Sorrow gave a faint growl that sounded almost like a groan.

"So comes Sister Clothilde, companion and ally to Biscop Tallia, to Lavas Holding. They are in need of a fitting bride for the last heir of the long-dead Taillefer, to set in train a defense against the coming cataclysm they alone perceive. It must not be any girl but one of highest birth. Like this one, descended herself from Taillefer."

"They would be too closely related," protested Sister Rosvita. "The church would never approve."

"None of this was accomplished under the auspices of the church. To the elder Charles—now desperate—they give the hounds as surety for the exchange. He gives them the infant girl. His mother is dead. The midwife's fate I do not know. It is as if the girl never existed, was never born. He becomes count, marries, sires an heir. His younger brother gives birth to children of his own, all unknowing."

"You are saying," said Mother Obligatia, "that I was that infant girl."

The hounds squirmed over to her and licked her hands. They could have knocked her over with a single butt of one of those huge heads, but their touch was as gentle as that of mice.

"And that my granddaughter is therefore my heir. That Liath is heir to the county of Lavas."

Wind gusted through the dark opening where the rose window had once shone. Every lamp flame shuddered. A cold breeze kissed Alain's face, whispering around him. A tickle of cool air slipped in his ears and mouth and nose. For one instant, the essence that is the aether breathed through his limbs and his chest, embracing him, and then it poured away and into a different vessel.

Liath leaped to her feet as Sanglant's eyes snapped open. They shone with sharp blue fire, easy to see in the gloomy light.

She shrieked with rage. "Go! Go! Get out of his body!"

Alain stepped up beside her and stilled her with a hand on her arm.

"You are come back," he said.

"I found what we spoke of," said the daimone through Sanglant's lips, in a voice that was like and yet utterly unlike Sanglant's familiar and well loved voice. "I brought it back."

"Then you have done as he would have done."

The head nodded, an awkward movement learned rather than natural. "I have done as he would have done."

"Go in peace," said Alain.

The flame in those dead eyes wavered. The mouth moved, and after a moment sound came out. "Can I ever find him again?"

Alain touched his cheek to the cool wood of the staff. It was Adica he saw, walking the trail that leads to the land where the meadow flowers bloom. A place far away and long ago, lost to him. He looked up, into the eyes of the daimone.

"Sometimes we are forever separated from the one we love. But, in truth, I do not know what lies beyond the veil."

"Then I will keep looking."

A breath gasped out of those lips.

Liath groaned as the body went slack. She collapsed to the floor.

Now and again, silence is a caught breath, all creation suspended between one heartbeat and the next. No one spoke. No one moved. The lamps burned, but they could not obliterate the shadows.

"He is breathing," said Countess Lavrentia, once known as Mother Obligatia.

Sanglant opened his eyes, dark with the look of his mother's kin. He blinked, as if trying to focus, and he did so finally as Liath staggered to her feet and stared at him incredulously.

"Liath," he said, and he reached for her hand.

XIV

THE CROWN

1

"I PRAY you, Sister. Wake up."

She sighed, wishing for this instant that she might not have to open her eyes and walk into the new day.

Fortunatus chuckled. "You must wake. It is already accomplished three days ago. Fear not. We will stand beside you. But come quickly. Sister Hathumod is asking for you."

She opened her eyes to see his dear face hovering above hers. He had gained weight over the last year. He looked well. The girls—in truth they had earned the right to be called young women, but they would always be girls to her—waited impatiently, all bright smiles and shiny faces, and there was Brother Jehan and the new scribe, shy Baldwin, the frail scholar Brother Sigfrid, genial Brother Ermanrich, and more besides, clerics, presbyters, deacons, fraters, abbesses and abbots, monks and nuns, biscops, and even the humble lay brothers and sisters who worked the holy estates.

Hers, now. All of them.

The chamber was an opulent one, clothed in silks and tapestries. The couch on which she had taken her nap was embroidered in the Salian style with scenes cross-stitched into the fabric, in this case, episodes from the life of the Emperor Taillefer. There he rides with his black hounds

upon the hunt; there he stands with staff and book, one
hand raised, remarking on the stars in the heavens; there
he sits with the crown of stars on his brow while he passes
judgment over the famous dispute between two beekeep-
ers; there he weds for the fourth time, and there he dies,
hand clasping the wrist of his young queen, Radegundis,
who is soon to be known as a saint.

The journey is a long one, and none can know when or
where it will end.

They helped her to rise, and arrayed her in heavy robes,
which she did not like. She thought longingly of her books.
Surely there would be an hour here or there to continue
the *Deeds of the Great Princes* once all the fuss died down.

They escorted her down a wide corridor, down steps to
the lower level, and through a garden heavy with the scent
of roses.

Last summer had remained cool, and the first frosts had
come early. The winter had been hard, and many had died,
and spring had come late again, but the skies had begun to
clear. All summer they had been fortunate in days of lingering heat that caused the flowers to bloom wildly and in
fierce colors.

She heard the swell and murmur of the crowd in the octagonal chapel, constant like the mutter of the sea along
the shore, but Brother Fortunatus steered her to a suite
opening off the rose garden. The shutters were closed because, here at the end, the light hurt the dying woman's
eyes.

Mother Scholastica was leaving. She paused at the door,
and stepped back to let Rosvita pass in before she went
out. She inclined her head, as she must do now, although
Rosvita felt no triumph in it. Indeed, none of this had been
of her doing.

"It is agreed that—with your blessing—Sister Hathumod will become biscop of Autun," said the abbess.

Rosvita nodded. "Are you at peace, Mother Scholastica?
Your voice has been raised many times among those who
argued most forcefully against the final decision made by
the council."

The abbess looked toward the couch placed among the

shadows. Her expression remained disapproving, but her words were firm. "I have spoken last rites over her. At the hour of dying, a person may see the heart of God, and speak true words. So is it written."

She departed, making for the chapel. Rosvita crossed the chamber and knelt beside the couch, but Constance's eyes were closed although a faint rise and fall like the echo of the sea swell stirred her chest.

Sister Hathumod kissed Rosvita's ring. "Holy Mother."

"Has she spoken?"

"Not since three days ago, Holy Mother, when she made conference with the last of them that held out against the truth."

"Does she know that the final vote came last night?"

"I have not told her, Holy Mother."

Rosvita took that limp hand between hers. She felt Fortunatus behind her, a steadfast presence. There were others in the chamber, and it seemed to her that many stood who were living and many who were only there in spirit, waiting to guide Constance's soul up through the spheres to the Chamber of Light.

"I will tell it quickly, Constance. It has come about as you foresaw. The testimony of *The Book of Secrets* has opened its heart to us. The council has spoken. The world has changed. From this day forward the church will follow the path of the Redemption. So be it."

Constance stirred. Her mouth parted. "Who are you?" she whispered.

Rosvita smiled wryly, glancing over her shoulder at Fortunatus and the others. In the room it was too dim to make out any but shadows, figures that might be dream or real, the past or the present or the future.

"I have been elected as Holy Mother, according to the decision of the council and the college of presbyters. Darre lies in ruins. It is uninhabitable, as our agents have seen. Autun will become the seat of the skopos. What is left to tell you? Nothing and everything."

"You are the rose," Constance murmured, in answer to her own question, and Rosvita saw that her vision had, in fact, ascended far past the bounds of mortal Earth. "Yet where have you gone?" Then her eyes opened and her face was transformed as if by light. "Ah! There is your crown!"

The breath left her. She died.

The journey would be a long one, climbing the ladder of the spheres.

Rosvita prayed over the body, and then they must go. Many were waiting.

The day was bright; the sun shone. The octagonal chapel was packed tight, and more spilled into the courtyard, folk from many lands: Wendar and Varre, the Eika north, the marchlands, Karrone, Polenie, Salavii deacons and monks, a handful of renegade Salian clerics split away from the rest of Salia's biscops who had refused even to send an official representative to the council, a straggle of church folk out of Aosta who did not support the unknown skopos appointed by Queen Adelheid, and a party of contentious observers from Arethousa who had nonetheless striven at intervals to strike a note of conciliation. They, too, had suffered. They, too, struggled to recover from the cataclysm. Alba remained stubbornly heathen except where the Eika ruled, and it was rumored that the king would soon set sail to fight a rebellion in the Alban hinterlands.

For now queen and king observed together with other nobles of the land, Prince Ekkehard, the dukes and margraves and nobles and biscops and monastics, any of whom could see the great benefit to Wendar and Varre in having the seat of spiritual power move into the north out of the south. The crown of stars rested in the grasp of Taillefer once again, atop his carved statue, because it had been returned to Autun and laid on his bier in memory of his empire. But after all, it was only an object of gold and jewels. The true crown of stars had no such earthly substance. It could not be grasped or held, fought over or broken, but it could be worn by the one whose heart was pure.

He had vanished after the miracle of Sanglant. That was all anyone knew.

Fortunatus touched her on the elbow. "I pray you. Wake up."

She startled out of her reverie. This was not what she had

expected, nor was it anything she had sought. But it had come to her nevertheless. So be it.

She fixed her courage with a deep breath, and walked forward into the assembly that was waiting for her.

2

HANNA had ridden to Lavas County before, although never with such an escort. All morning the road had pushed through woodland, passing here and there an abandoned or burned-out farmstead or hamlet. For the last three days they had traveled through empty countryside, seeing no one. She remembered the road, and knew they were no more than two or three days out from Lavas Holding.

Near midday, freshly cut fields appeared suddenly along the roadside, ringed by low fences. Ahead, a wide path cut away from the road. In the distance she heard axes ringing against wood. A voice shouted just before the crash of a felled tree resounded. Then the axes started up again.

A wain piled high with hay and a cart loaded with coiled rope were cutting off the main road onto the path. One of the men walking alongside saw their company coming up around the curve, and he broke off from the others and sauntered their way, holding his scythe as if he knew how to make it a weapon.

Hanna pushed forward from the van and rode to meet him. He was a lanky young man with dark hair and a pleasant face.

"Well met," she called out. "I'm an Eagle, riding from Autun."

"A fine company you have to escort you," he said. "I recall when Eagles rode alone on these roads."

"Not that long ago," she retorted, "but you know it isn't safe now. There's some rough country back there, abandoned by honest folk since the tempest."

He grunted, squinting as the company neared, counting them on his fingers: a dozen horsemen and a dozen Eika ambling at that easy stride they could hold for weeks on end, it seemed. Over the course of a day they had to restrain themselves from outpacing the horses.

"Some abandoned their lands," he remarked, looking at the Eika with the usual suspicion. "The others starved or were murdered by savages and outlaws."

"They're our allies."

"So they are, now. But I was at Gent."

She saw no way to answer this, so she changed the subject. "There wasn't so much settlement here last time I passed this way. New fields. What's down that path?"

"Oh, that's Ravnholt Manor, all right. It was cut out of the forest a generation ago, just a small holding, but we've got it building fast, now, quite a few out of Lavas Holding have moved along out this way with the blessing of the count and some have fled to us from farther east, as you saw. We've a stout palisade, and room to grow. We've got our own plough, too!" He grinned, suddenly delighted, raised a hand, and waved frantically. "Ivar! Ivar!"

Ivar broke out of the company—he had been arguing with that impossible chatter-mouth Aestan of Alba about whether the phoenix had two wings or six—and trotted toward them. Ai, God! She bit down on a grin to see his sulky expression break into a broad smile.

"Erkanwulf!"

"What? Are you riding in the regnant's service now, Lord Ivar?"

"I'm an Eagle," he said.

"You can't be. You're noble born. My lord." That last said with a grin.

Ivar pulled up alongside and swung down off his horse. "Maybe so, but my brother Gero is glad to be shed of me. Good God, Erkanwulf! You're looking well!"

Then she must endure greetings and slaps on the back and all manner of hail, fellow and well met cheer, when truly she just wanted to get on to Lavas Holding. At length, it was settled that Ivar would stay overnight in Ravnholt

Manor to catch up on the news and give out his own, and come along afterward.

She rode on with the escort. They were truly in Lavas County now, ripe with summer, trees in full leaf and berries plump and juicy where the sun had sweetened them. Hamlets sprouted at intervals along the road, each ringed by a stockade. Goats grazed, heads deep into brambles. Shepherd children waved at her, then scampered off as the Eika contingent strode into view.

In another day they came to cleared land surrounded by stands of woodland and coppice where flocks of sheep grazed amiably, and after that rode past newly cut fields where men and women were picking out stones so the land could be ploughed for winter wheat. Sooner than she expected, they came over the slope to see the vast spread of striped fields surrounding Lavas Holding. A new stockade had engulfed the old church, which had long stood outside the old earth wall and its four wooden towers. Folk were building a pair of houses along a dirt street struck straight out from the old gate. The company passed a pair of recently planted orchards, still saplings, and a tenting field with fulled cloth strung out taut to dry.

The call came up from the watchtower. She unfurled their banner, and they rode through the outer gate, along the dusty avenue, under the old gate, and into a busy square. Grooms ran up to take their horses and show the soldiers to barracks.

Hanna ran up the steps into the hall, which was empty and peaceful in the late afternoon but with the tables set in place for a feast. The clap of her feet on the plank floor seemed desperately noisy. A steward led her through a tiny courtyard alive with color and fragrant with herbs and flowers, and she almost mistakenly turned through the arch that led into the stable yard beyond but was guided to a door set into the old stone tower, relic of an earlier time. As she climbed the curving staircase that led to the upper chamber, she tried to walk softly.

She paused in the entryway. Two windows set at angles into the walls allowed light into the whitewashed room.

One was a magnificent painted glass scene depicting the martyrdom of St. Lavrentius and the other a simple opening to let in a cooling breeze. Through that window she saw the skeletal rafters of a two-storied wing being added onto the compound, but no one was working there at the moment. A pair of tapestries hung to either side of the door. One depicted the Lavas badge—two black hounds on a silver field—but the murky colors of the other mostly obscured its scene, which seemed to show a procession making its way through a dark forest.

After the steady clop of travel and the hustle of the courtyard, the silence in the chamber weighed heavily, nothing heard or seen except the scritch of a quill on parchment and the press of styluses into wax tablets. This was the count's chamber, with a table, cushioned chair, and a dozen cups and two flasks set along a sideboard, but it appeared more like one of the schoolrooms found in the convent. Yet most of the people hard at work here were not children but adults, both young and old. At intervals, one or another of these glanced up to note her presence before returning to their work. A young woman with the coloring and features of the Ashioi gave Hanna a tartly welcoming smile, and then winked at a good-looking young man, who blushed furiously. It was strange to see one of the enemy dressed in Wendish clothing, although admittedly she wore neither shoes nor leggings under her knee-length tunic.

To one side stood a fine couch on which lay the ancient countess, sleeping while the others worked. Sister Hilaria sat beside her, sewing; she greeted Hanna with a welcoming smile. A pack of yearling hounds stretched out around and under the couch, three plopped on their sides, one rolled onto its back, and the fifth licking a forepaw.

Two fair-haired girls whispered, but so loudly that Hanna could hear them.

"I don't think it's fair, that she got to go out."

"And we had to stay in! But I guess she always gets what she wants."

"She is the heir. She's never said a mean thing to me, Blanche. She's not nearly as mean as you are."

"I am not!"

"You are, too!"

"I just tell the truth. That's not mean!"

"*Blanche*. Lavrentia. Keep to your work, I pray you," said Liath from her writing table, so engrossed in her work that she alone did not look up or even seem to notice that someone had come into the room. From this angle, all Hanna could see was loops and circles and the scratchings that signified letters and numbers.

A horn sounded in the distance. The young hounds leaped into motion, skittered over the floor, streamed past Hanna, and bounded away down the steps. The two girls set their tablets down with a clatter and raced after them before anyone could scold them to a stop.

By now every soul there except the sleeping woman and the oblivious one was looking either at Hanna or toward the window. Finally, the youth got up and stuck his head out the window.

For some reason, this movement drew Liath's attention, and she glanced first at the window and then toward the door.

"Hanna!" She put a hand over her mouth and glanced toward the couch, but her grandmother did not wake.

The youth pulled back in. "Have you a message from the queen? Or my sister?" He was a young man of perhaps eighteen, restless, with a charming smile and ink-stained fingers.

"Afraid it's news of your betrothal, Berthold?" asked one of the other students.

He looked toward the Ashioi woman, who was now deliberately ignoring him, and blushed again.

"Hush," said Liath sternly. "Do not wake my grandmother. Go on. Out with you."

Hanna stepped aside as they filed out of the chamber. Liath sighed, smiled happily at her, and levered herself up out of her chair. The position of the desk had concealed her rounded stomach. She walked over to her grandmother and bent awkwardly to kiss her cheek.

"I'll stay with her," said the nun.

"Thank you, Sister." She hurried over to Hanna.

"You're more than I can embrace," said Hanna with a laugh, kissing her.

"Come," she said to Hanna, taking her arm. "Let me use you as balance going down these steps. I'm afraid I'll topple forward. Ai, God, it is good to see you. What news?"

Hanna waited to answer until they came out into the garden. Bees buzzed, and a fly pestered her until she swatted it away. "The Council of Autun has voted to recognize the Redemption."

Liath caught in her breath, but made no comment.

"I've brought back your Da's book, courtesy of the Holy Mother, who had copies made."

"The Holy Mother?"

"They elected Sister Rosvita. Autun is to be the seat of the skopos. For now. She has lifted the writ of excommunication."

Liath stroked her pregnant belly. "Thank God, for the child's sake as well as my own. If there's more, I pray you, wait until we meet together later, so it can all be said at once. Let my grandmother be awake to hear it."

"Is she well?"

"Very old, and very tired, but her mind remains clear. She could die tomorrow, or five years from now. I just don't know. I pray she stays with us as long as possible." She paused beside a rosebush to touch a blossom whose petals were saturated with crimson. "Oh, look, another bloom."

A commotion blew in from the stable yard, a burst of laughter and bodies flooding through the arched gate and out into the garden, foremost among them the prince.

He marked Hanna instantly, and smiled. "What news for my daughter?" It was a shock to hear him speak. The powerful tenor remained, but that familiar hoarseness was utterly gone.

The young hounds galloped to Liath for pats on the head but immediately returned to circle Sanglant, shoving in to get a rub and a scratch on the head.

After a moment, Hanna remembered herself and spotted the princess lingering under the archway in a patch of shade beside Lord Berthold, who had paused there to talk to Captain Fulk. She was quite a tall girl, well filled out.

"Yes, there is news," said Hanna. "Queen Theophanu sends her affectionate greetings to her dead kinsman. The king is on his way to Alba. He will take Princess Blessing with him on campaign."

"I want Berthold to come with me," said Blessing in that bold way she had. Some things hadn't changed!

Startled, the young man turned around. "To Alba? With the brat?"

"He will be going," said Hanna, "since a betrothal has been arranged for him with one of the surviving daughters of the Alban royal family."

Liath looked at Sanglant. The prince shrugged, lifting one eyebrow. Berthold looked toward the Ashioi woman, who rubbed the back of her neck and preened in the manner of a woman who enjoys teasing men. Blessing sucked in a sharp breath.

After a moment, in which the entire garden and all its inhabitants seemed to hold a collective breath, waiting for the explosion, the girl bit her lip and said nothing. She moved forward to shyly kiss her mother, but like the hounds she swung back to her father's side.

"How soon can we expect Lord Stronghand?" asked Sanglant, resting an arm over his daughter's shoulders affectionately. She leaned against him.

"He will arrive by the Feast of the King."

"Captain Fulk, best take her to the armory and see what needs fitting. We haven't much time."

"Yes, my lord prince."

Sanglant nodded, studied Hanna's state of dress and dust, and called a steward. "See that this Eagle is given whatever she needs, something to drink, and a bath, if she desires it. If you could wait until the count wakes, and give your message then?"

"I'd be glad of it, my lord prince," she said.

"Oh!" said Liath. "You must be thirsty. Come, I'll go with you." She took Hanna's arm, and then turned to the prince. "And your hunt?"

He shook his head. "Escaped us again. There's a score of them, we think, under a cunning leader. I have in mind a trap."

"What is he hunting?" Hanna asked as Liath led her past the barracks to the bathhouse. "Wolves?"

"Outlaws. A pack of them have been preying on the outlying farmsteads to the north. There was so much trouble all last winter along the eastern road that we finally had to bring in the folk who lived there and resettle them in Lavas and Ravnholt. There's been a great deal of stockade building this spring. Wolves, too, coming out of the south. And a raid hit our southwestern border, up out of Salia."

"I saw new fields cleared."

"We've absorbed many new settlers, and we feed a hundred milites as well, courtesy of the queen regnant. You'll have to ask Sanglant about the ploughs. What luck with the Eagle's Council?"

"Sending the Eagles through crowns? Not many favor it. Not more than one or two, I admit. It's too much. They fear it."

"Let it be, for now. The queen and king will come to see its utility, once enough have the skills."

They talked of a hundred things and of nothing as Hanna bathed and Liath sat on a stool beside her. Much later, after she was clean and dry, they returned to the tower.

Count Lavrentia was awake, propped up on pillows, attending to the business of the county with the prince and a chatelaine seated beside her. The count and her grandson-in-law were a good match, and it was well he had an administrator's bent of mind, since Liath was distracted and soon after Hanna's long recital slipped out of the room with a pair of her companions: the Ashioi woman and a man Hanna recognized as an archer who had long fought beside the prince.

At length, disputes were resolved, capitularies sealed, a bull requested for breeding by a nearby manor, a pair of merchants out of Medemelacha interviewed and given the right to set up trading houses at Osna Sound, tithing for St. Thierry's Convent, some question about building, and a report from the Osna shore about five boats that had put in to the ruined monastery and departed again, none knowing who these folk were or where they had come from or what they were looking for. Everyone was anxious about plague, having heard rumors of sickness along the Salian border and in parts of Wayland and Varingia.

"You are weary, Grandmother." Sanglant dismissed the stewards, and bent to kiss the old woman on either cheek. "Rest. I'll go make sure she doesn't fall into a well."

She chuckled, but it was true she was pale and trembling with fatigue, although she had been awake no more than three hours. "Pray the child takes after you, Son," she said to him affectionately.

The hounds whipped their tails hopefully as the prince went to the door, and she released them to seethe after him.

Outside, the afternoon had drawn long shadows over the open courts. The exposed rafters of the new building formed hatch-mark shadows on the dirt. The squat spire of the old church could be seen over the palisade. Hammers rang from the outer town. Nearby, two men were sawing planks out of logs. The kitchens boiled with activity, and the smell of chickens roasting on a spit gave the air a rich savor.

Sanglant had a long stride, but Hanna kept up with him. He whistled a merry tune—actually, now that she recognized it, she recalled its bawdy words. Although he was stopped five times so his opinion might be solicited on some matter or other, he remained fixed to his path with a pleasant determination that soon led them out beyond both old berm and new stockade and onto a path that led up a steep hill. A shout came from behind, and they paused to see a soldier toiling up the slope behind them. Sanglant brushed hair out of his eyes, surveying the wide and open valley that held Lavas Holding. Folk had turned toward home, coming in from the fields and orchards and woodland stretched out on all sides.

"Is it well with you, my lord prince?" she asked quietly, not sure if he would deign to answer.

At first he looked startled. Then he laughed. "God have granted me what I most wished for. How can it not be well?"

"It seemed . . ." He was a generous man, warm spirited

and charming, easy to confide in and trust. He looked and
acted content, but a man might hide his inner heart behind
a mask of outer seeming. "It might be said that you lost a
great deal, my lord prince."

*A crown. A spell woven into the flesh that made you in-
vulnerable.*

She did not say these things out loud.

"I lost nothing that I regret losing." He smiled, looking
not at her but at Lavas Holding. "A grant of land, Liath as
my wife, and peace. You can be sure I'll hold tight to them.
No onion I, Hanna. I am as you see me."

"My lord!" The soldier had the ragged voice of a man
who has had his throat damaged in battle, and never
healed. "They promised me that I could go first, and now
Lewenhardt has gotten the jump on me! Damn him to the
Pit!"

"So he may well fall into the Pit this very night. God
Above! Will you two never be content?" He spoke cheerfully; he was amused.

"I was promised!" said the soldier stubbornly.

"Come, then," he said. "Best if we hurry."

It was a fair long walk curving up along the hill and into
the woods behind, much cut back now, the path beaten into
a broad path where two wagons might roll abreast.

The tree line ended abruptly at the edge of ruins. Beyond an outer wall of stone lay an ancient fort in the style
of the old empire, Dariyan work. The light drew long and
late in summer, and the fallen walls and buildings shone
with an aura of gold where the sun's rays pulled across
them. Most of the building stone was grainy and dark, but
the centermost building—its roof long since fallen in—
had been built in a marbled white stone that had a soft
gleam. The outer walls of this building had been cleared
away to expose its paved, platform of a floor, an ovoid
altar stone, and the six pillars that had once supported the
roof.

Here Liath and her disciplas had gathered, with four
horses tethered nearby. Here, as Hanna and the prince and
the soldier walked up, she heard Liath speak.

"Name the seven spheres and their order."

"The sphere closest to the Earth is that of the Moon!" said Sharp Edge, jumping in before anyone else could utter one word.

They were an unruly lot. Most were young and reckless, although Liath was grateful to have a pair of older and wiser heads among them. It was her own fault, truly. In addition to stamina, strength, courage, and adventurousness, they had to have the patience and wit and desire to learn the art of the mathematici. Sometimes they weren't easy to get along with. She was just like them.

"The second is that of the planet Erekes, and the third planet is Somorhas, the Lady of Light. Fourth is the sphere of the Sun. Fifth is Jedu, Angel of War. Six is Mok. Seventh and last—Aturna."

"The realm of the fixed stars," added Berthold. He was irritated with Sharp Edge, as well he might be. She was a terrible tease, and did herself no favors, but as much as young men hated her for it, they came panting for more. "And beyond all of this, the Chamber of Light, the home of God, and the phoenix."

"And the ladder by which the mage ascends," said Sharp Edge, taunting him. "First to the rose, the touch of healing-"

"Enough!" Liath braced herself, and pushed to her feet. She was getting ungainly, but she felt good, strong, energetic. Not a day's worth of sickness with this pregnancy. "Ah, there's Sibold!"

Lewenhardt groaned.

The other man punched the archer on the shoulder as he swaggered past. "Thought you'd slip past me!"

"Enough!" she repeated, seeing the change in the light as afternoon trickled away into long summer dusk. "Take your places. Shar. Sibold. Get the horses."

Wood burns when touched by threads of starlight, so no crown of wood would serve her, and they had not the leisure in such troubled times to invest a host to raise the huge menhirs as was done in the days of the ancients. But it transpired that the old Dariyans had copied the ladder of the heavens in their architecture. An oval formed by six tall stone pillars could form a gateway as well as any other crown.

A glow still rimmed the western horizon, but she caught the Guivre's Eye as it peered over the northeastern rim of the world and wove its thread into warp. She anchored the gate on the Healer's outstretched arm, rising out of the southeast. Behind her, the disciplas who would learn to do this watched and measured. She had twelve so far, but more would come and more would be born. Eagles were brave souls, and tough messengers, but phoenix could bridge vast distances as long as they had the means and the knowledge to waken the crowns.

A gate flowered over the altar stone.

Her sight had grown keener since the cataclysm, and the current of aether was gaining strength, an upwelling out of the heart of the universe. A road paved with blue fire led straight into the uttermost east, held open briefly by this conjunction of stars. There, as down a long corridor sparkling with light, a veiled Sorgatani waited for the messengers who would come to her.

But there are many roads and many turnings. Sometimes we choose the path we walk on, and sometimes other forces compel our feet onto an unexpected track. Not everything happens according to our will, but neither are we slaves to the law, mere instruments of the mover.

Here we wander in a vast weaving whose twists and turns are like a palace of coils where windows reconnoiter both past and future, a sight denied to mortal kind. Only the daimones who bide above the moon can see in all directions.

We are not the only ones walking the paths.

The goblins hammer in their halls of iron. In the depths, the merfolk excrete a substance that they shape into buildings like pearls, while far above them a slender dragon boat cuts the swells of the Middle Sea. There is Secha, studying an astrolabe!

The path takes a sharp turn. A lion pauses in rocky desert flatlands and looks back, except it is not a lion—it has the torso of a woman—and when it sees her, it spins and pounces, only to vanish in a rush of wings as a pair of golden dragons washes the many threads into ripples of light as they land on a nest cupped into a hollow of hot sand.

So many mysteries to unravel! So much to discover!

Almost, she lost the road, but she pulled it tight again.

"Go. Go," she called to them.

Sharp Edge and Sibold did not hesitate. They were bold and eager. They crossed under the glittering arch and walked into the east, Sharp Edge to teach and learn from the Hidden One and Sibold to guard her and care for the horses and gear.

The threads pulled taut as the stars wheeled on their nightly round. It was time to close the gate, and yet she was caught betwixt and between. Always, the yearning to go, and always, the yearning to stay.

There!

An old man rides alone on a lonely road, his back to her. She cannot see his face, but she knows who he is, the last of his kind. Almost she calls to him, but he has already faded from sight.

She hears the tentative noises of folk beginning to shuffle their feet, yawn, murmur a song. Argue good-naturedly. A stomach growls with hunger. Someone coughs.

Sanglant laughs, a bright sound that lights the world, and, of course, those who are not caught in the weaving as it unravels laugh with him.

A hound yips.

She sees the black hound as it halts to stare back at her through the crown woven out of the stars. Its mate pauses beside it, also looking back. The hounds can see her, because she is heir to Lavas. They gave her a litter of puppies, but they themselves never belonged to her.

Ahead of them on the path, a dark-haired man walks into a meadow. There is still sunlight, shadows falling long but not yet swarming to overtake the grass and bramble vines laced along the edge of the trees. He must be walking farther west where it is still day, or perhaps this is another day, one not yet come. The salamander eyes she took from her mother can discern shapes in what to humankind may seem darkest night.

He pauses where a wild bramble rose has sprouted out of the grass. Its twisting vine boasts only one delicate blood-red bloom, but that is enough to lend the snarl of branches an intense beauty. Because he bends to look more closely, she sees many buds forming within the pale leaves, not yet flowered. It's only that one must be patient, and resolute.

He straightens, calls his hounds, and walks on, into the haze that marks the land beyond. She takes a step, and another, to follow him.

"Liath," Sanglant said, behind her. "Where are you going?"

After all, the gate scattered into a spray of incandescent sparks, and she turned, and came home.

EPILOGUE

ON a hill surrounded on three sides by forest and on the fourth by the ruins of a fortress stood a ring of stones. Some said they were the bones of a castle buried so deeply that only the battlements of the tallest tower rose above the earth. A few claimed that sleeping youths lay drowned in slumber in hidden chambers deep in the ground.

Most simply called them the wings of the phoenix.

On the twelfth day of the month of Setentre, the feast day of St. Ekatarina, the afternoon faded swiftly to twilight as a company of riders splashed across the ford and pushed through the ruins. A pair of watch fires burned on the other side of the river, marking the sentry towers of the prosperous village that lay within sight of the hill crowned by stones.

"Are you sure, my lord prince?" asked the eldest of the riders, a battle-scarred man wearing the black-and-gold surcoat of the elite Dragon guards. "This is the third night, and we've seen nothing . . . Better we rest and make ready. The queen's progress will leave Thersa tomorrow."

The first threads were faint, flowering into brilliance only as the archway snapped fully into existence.

"Hai!" cried the youth, urging his horse forward with his best companion right behind him and the older men trailing after with the kind of looks best known and understood by men who were once as impulsive in days long past.

She came clear in a shower of sparks as the gateway spit and dissolved around her. Her companion was an older man, well armed and well seasoned. He led a string of three horses in the manner of a traveler accustomed to long journeys. Both wore the distinctive black cloak trimmed with gold braid that marked the phoenix messengers and under that a plain wool tunic in the Wendish style, but instead of leggings *she* wore trousers like an easterner, and her black hair was tied back in braids and covered by a lacy waterfall of gold beaded netting that framed her striking dark-skinned face and those astonishing blue eyes.

The most glorious woman in all the world!

He dismounted, dropped his reins, and ran down to meet her. Seeing him, she halted as she came up to the low wall that separated the fort from the crown.

"Fulk! How are you come here?"

He hopped from one foot to the other, wanting to touch her hand, or her face, or her hair, but settled down finally and rubbed his beardless chin sheepishly. "They sent me to court for seasoning."

"Past time! You must be all of—eighteen!"

"As if you're so much older," he retorted, and at once hated himself for the way it sounded.

"A world older!" she said with that laugh that always made him feel a child. "I might as well be your aunt."

"But you're not," he added recklessly, and blushed at his boldness.

The rest of the company guided their horses to level ground, greeted the other messenger and folded him into their ranks, and waited while four men lit torches.

"Well met, Captain," she called.

The captain of Fulk's company lifted a hand in greeting, smiling a little.

What man would not!

As they rode back, she chatted easily with the men she knew among his retinue, soldiers she had spent many years with when she was fostered at Lavas Holding. The new men looked at her askance because she had not the look of his own lineage, which they had become accustomed to, but of something stranger. She was the daughter of the

Hidden One, yet in her the blood of the uttermost east mingled in equal portions with the blood of the west.

"How long have you been back with the queen's progress?" she asked him as they reached the road and she abandoned the soldiers to move up alongside him.

"Two years now."

"You must have come to the progress, then, right after—"

"I don't want to talk about it, I pray you. I was there when it happened."

She shrugged. For a while they rode in silence, serenaded by the steady clop of hooves. Two men walked before them, carrying torches, and two a few ranks behind. The road wound away into the trees, slipping in and out of drifts of rising mist.

The torchlight made the gold-work shimmer around her face. Her expression lapsed into a blank absence, as if she were thinking of a lost lover or some particularly intriguing mathematical problem, but after a moment she shook herself and indicated the young man riding to his right.

"Who is this? We haven't met."

"This is my best companion, Henry."

"Henry?" She seemed about to smile, but did not. "I am named Chabi, although you may call me Judith, after my father's mother, if you wish. My mother was Sorgatani, princess of the Kerayit."

"How could I have guessed, when it is all Fulk has been speaking of this past month?"

"Henry!"

She laughed.

The youth nodded in his quiet way. "Well met."

"You're new to the progress, aren't you?"

"He's been with me for almost three years now," said Fulk. "He came to Lavas just after you left that last time."

But she did not look at him. "Where are you come from?"

"Rikin Fjord," said Henry.

"He's a great grandson of Stronghand," said Fulk.

"Are you so?" she said with renewed interest.

Henry was leaner and shorter than most of the Eika,

with a pure golden color of skin, although he wore
Wendish clothing that mostly covered his body and limbs.
His claws were politely sheathed, and he had such an easy
seat on a horse that Fulk had a difficult time believing that
in the old days all horses had shied from the Eika smell.

"Yes," Henry added. "Some say I resemble him, but of
course I never met him. Originally I was to become a cleric
in the queen's schola."

"A cleric?" She seemed about to sputter, as if she found
the notion of an Eika male praying and kneeling quite
funny, but then caught herself. "But not anymore?"

Henry shrugged. It was a gesture that looked both
strange and familiar in him, but he had been raised as
much among humankind as among his Eika brothers.

"My sister's husband died of the lung fever this past
spring," said Fulk quickly, eager to draw attention. "So now
it seems the queen has remembered the old contract between Queen Theophanu and Lord Stronghand, and she's
talking of marrying Henry to Constance to fulfill the
agreement that an Eika prince be married into the royal
family once in every generation, to renew the alliance."

"It will happen only if the succession is secure," said
Henry calmly.

"Well!" she said. And then, "Well!" She looked keenly at
Fulk. "Is the succession secure?"

He grimaced. He couldn't help himself. "I'm still the
horse kept in reserve. Constance is pregnant—was already,
of course, when Thietmar died—but we've heard nothing
yet. Pray God nothing happens to her! She's near her
time."

"Surely the queen has some alliance in mind for you,
Fulk."

Henry chuckled. Fulk slapped at him, but then the captain called up, "You'll never throw a good blow, my lord, if
it all comes from the arm."

Henry looked away to hide his amusement—he had a
particular way of squaring his shoulders when he was trying not to laugh! Chabi snorted. Fulk found refuge in babbling.

"Now there's talk of marrying me off to some Alban

princess in the western counties, the ones that are pushing into Eika territory. But that's better than the plan they were talking of all summer, sending me to Ashioi country to marry the new Feather Cloak!"

Chabi considered this. Most likely she had ridden recently through those lands, and had a better idea of the troublesome situations there than he did. "Had you a choice, what would it be?"

You! You! You!

He smiled tightly. "I am an obedient son. I do as I'm told."

"I'm sorry to hear that!"

Henry laughed.

She added, "You might become a phoenix, as I am."

Spoken out loud, the words seemed harsh.

"A prince cannot fly," he said bitterly. "Though I would if I could."

"Any person with a willing heart and a stubborn mind can learn to weave sorcery and walk the crowns."

"These are easy words from your mouth! You are a third child and thereby freer than the rest of us. Anyway, your mother was a powerful shaman, and your father—"

"Her pura, nothing better than a slave, and about whom the less is said the better," she said in a tone that cut him.

"We're there," said Henry, lifting a hand to warn him. "And I fear me that your mother the queen is waiting for you, Fulk."

They rode free of the forest to see the walls and sentry fires of Thersa, where Queen Blessing and her progress had rested these past four days. The palisade and palace were old, but the estate had grown and spread in recent years with the shift of population out of the south after the great earthquake. Now, of course, the guesthouse was full and the inner pasture covered with tents and wagons.

The lamps held over the gatehouse revealed a party loitering under the still-open gate: the queen and her Dragon guardsmen. She had not the generous affection that had made her father so beloved, but she was respected. And she was fiercely possessive of all that was hers.

As he was hers. Her only surviving son.

First she had married Benedict, son of Conrad and Tallia, and by him produced her heir, Constance, and two boys. More recently, she had married for a third time, allying herself to the royal family of Karrone because of the incursions out of Aosta.

Born fourth, Fulk had outlasted his two older brothers, and seen a younger half Karronish sister born when he was eight.

But it was because he was the only child of her short-lived second marriage to the man she had loved best—besides her father—that the queen loved him so well. Too well, some said in whispers when they thought he wasn't listening. He should never have been fostered out to his grandfather and grandmother in Lavas, but he had been raised there, and well loved there, and there he had fallen helplessly in love with a young woman not five years older than him who yet seemed so far out of his reach that he might as well have hoped to fly. And it wasn't just calf love, a youth's callow infatuation!

As they rode up, Chabi bent close and murmured one last comment near his ear.

"Your grandmother would never have asked permission. She just would have done it."

He burned. But he said nothing.

"Fulk," said the queen as he dismounted to greet her. She kissed him on either cheek, and turned to the phoenix. "You are come, but I suppose you will wish for drink and food, and perhaps a bath to wash away the dust of your travels."

"So I would, Your Majesty, and be grateful for it, for I've nothing urgent to bring to your attention. I only wondered—" She hesitated, and he saw for the first time that she had a full heart and could not speak.

At last she swallowed and forced out a few words. "I meant to go to Lavas, but now . . . I am not so certain. I've been gone a long time."

The queen nodded. She was scarred, but resilient. "You'll be welcome there, and needed, I am thinking. My younger sister is a strong count, a good steward for her lands, but I fear she does not have the temperament to ad-

vise such an unruly schola. They need a firmer hand to
keep them in line. You were always my mother's best student."

She blanched. "I am accustomed to—a different life,
Your Majesty. I am not accustomed to biding in one place."

The queen nodded. "Yet it is my command, phoenix. I
want you to go to Lavas and become praeceptor at the
schola there. It is what I need from you, right now. Captain,
if you will."

The captain gathered horses and soldiers and directed
them toward the barracks. Henry made his courtesies and
headed for the chapel from which Fulk heard a pair of
handsome voices singing the nightly chain of psalms cele-
brating Mother and Son.

The queen took Fulk's arm and drew him away. Chabi
followed as they crossed the court and entered into the innermost chambers, reserved for the regnant, which looked
out over a garden made invisible by night. The scent of
flowers wafting in on the night breeze teased them. He
yawned, feeling both drowsy and strangely on edge.

As if the tide had already turned, and he was caught in
the rip current, being dragged out to sea.

"Sit down," the queen said to him, but she remained
standing, as did Chabi, and it was to the phoenix that she
addressed her words.

"Let me say this quickly, or I will not say it at all. The boy
is restless. He is much like his father, a quick mind and
eager heart. His father studied for a year at Lavas, that
very first year, and learned much and would have learned
more but he was sent away at the order of Queen Theophanu—of blessed memory—to marry an Alban princess.
It was necessary to preserve alliances and to throw up obstacles in the path of a string of rebellions. I see that now,
naturally. He did as he was told. He was still grieving for
Conrad's daughter. I see that now."

She turned away, hiding her expression in shadow. The
lamps hissed. At the door, a Dragon guard, one of the
Quman youths come in this year's levy from the east,
stepped in with a full pitcher of water and a flagon of wine.

At last, she cleared her throat and turned back to them.

"Even so, when after many years his Alban wife died and he could come home, he asked again to join the schola at Lavas. But it happened that I had been made a widow recently, when Benedict died of the flux, poor man, and the margrave of Villam would see her family raised as high as she could, and naturally my father listened to her second only to my mother, and of course I was all too eager for the match to think of what it might mean to him—"

Again, her voice caught. She touched Fulk on the arm affectionately, but did not smile.

"And then, after all, he died within three years of our betrothal and marriage. I would not have his son be forced onto the path he was commanded to walk. I made no promises at that time, for you know, Berthold died so suddenly."

It was a raw wound still, although Berthold Villam had died almost sixteen years ago.

"Liath always spoke fondly of Lord Berthold," said Chabi.

The queen smiled sadly. "I thank you for saying so."

In Lavas hall the nightly feasting was warm and boisterous. It had always been a lively place, and Fulk noted the contrast with the hushed corridors of Thersa. There had been a feast the first night they had come here, of course, so the locals might greet them and be presented in their turn, but after all the queen preferred a quiet sojourn, her attention fixed on a series of charters and capitularies and disputes brought to her attention from the string of royal estates and monasteries in this part of Wendar.

She sighed. Because he had spent his childhood and youth in Lavas, he did not know his mother well. It was usual to foster a child out in order to cement alliances, but he could not help but wonder how she could claim to love him so well and then send him away so early and for so long—and not even to a distant ally, to foster an alliance, but to the home of her own beloved parents.

"I have had news today, from one of my Eagles. Constance has given birth to a healthy daughter, in Gent. If the infant lives, then she has borne two living children out of her own body, and Fulk takes a second step back from the succession."

"May God bless child and mother both," said Chabi, and Fulk echoed her, although he scarcely knew his older sister and had not spent more than a month altogether in her company in his entire life.

The queen took up a poker as if wielding a sword and stirred the coals on the hearth until they flickered into flame. Two braziers heaped with coals also battled the growing autumn chill.

"I am weary, phoenix," she continued. "I have two husbands dead and the third not at all to my taste despite the importance of the treaty and the child we conceived between us. I do not wish this on my son. I will not put on him the burden that was given onto me. I want him to have what his father could not. If he so chooses."

Suddenly the room was too hot. Fulk was flushed, heart galloping. But the queen's grave expression gave him pause.

He had never seen her weep; one tear, that was all, the day he had arrived at the queen's progress two years ago. The high rafters swallowed all sound and ate at the light. The gloom in the corners was profound. He felt a surge of tenderness for her.

She sent me to the place she loved best.

"I w–would stay with you," he stammered.

She snorted, and a mask twisted her expression so he heard the serpent's tongue and saw the sword's thrust that folk feared. "You would not!"

It had never been turned on him before.

She melted at once. "Ah, poor boy, I don't mean it like that. I mean only that when a lad mopes about the stable yard and rides to every crown he can find, then he is not pining for his mother. However much he loves her. Anyway, it serves my purpose, as my uncle Lord Stronghand was used to say, and these days I suppose I have as little heart as he ever did."

Chabi had remained silent and still all this time, showing neither surprise nor fear. "How does it serve your purpose, Your Majesty?"

"To count a son among my mother's fabled nest of phoenix? To let one among the royal family hold in his hands those secrets, now that my mother is gone? Of course it serves me! The world is a restless place. Night comes quickly."

"Yet the heavens are brilliant in their beauty."

"Maybe for you, phoenix, but I have a habit of stumbling when it is dark. So, Fulk, what do you say?"

He groped for words, but was too stunned to speak, and after a moment she smiled gently, took his hand, and kissed him as if in farewell.

The day her son rode out from the queen's progress, the queen went into the Octagonal Garden to watch him go in something resembling privacy. Decades ago, Queen Sophia had commissioned a garden to be built at Werlida in the Arethousan style. It had eight walls, eight benches, eight neatly tended garden plots that bloomed with brilliant colors in spring and summer but were now brown with autumn's rags. Eight radial pathways spoked in to the center where stood the monumental fountain formed in the shape of a domed tower and surrounded by eight tiers of angels cavorting and blowing trumpets. According to legend, the fountain had ceased flowing on the very day Queen Sophia died, but in fact the mechanism had failed years before because the Arethousan craftsman who had devised the cunning inner workings had died of a lung fever one winter and no one else knew how to repair it.

Or so Queen Theophanu had told Blessing, years and years ago, that winter when the king lay dying. That was the mystery. One night a humble visitor had called on the king in the middle of the night, unseen by everyone except the king himself, who spoke of their long conversation in expansive detail although everyone else was sure he had descended into his final delirium. Yet the fountain had begun running again that very night, and it splashed and gurgled still, many years later. She thought it actually spoke with the last words Stronghand had whispered to her, there at the end: *Be merciful.*

The memory soothed her heart as she stood on the

gravel path and watched Fulk's entourage reach the branching road and his banner turn north.

A magnificent vista opened before her. The land spread out as fields and villages, pastureland and scrub brush and woodland, and farther yet, the distant march of forest. The river vanished into the haze of trees.

From this palace almost fifty years ago her parents had sneaked away in the middle of night, defying King Henry, and at some point on their southerly journey or at Verna, she herself had been conceived. It was a fitting place for her son to ride out on a new path. Fulk was a good boy, but it was really her enduring love for Berthold that had caused her to let him go. Anyway, it was true enough that it served her purpose to have her son educated in the arts of the mathematici. She might gain any number of advantages large and small with this strategy.

Over time, she had discovered she was more Stronghand's heir than her own beloved father's. Impulse must not govern action, Stronghand had taught her; it was a struggle, but she had mastered herself over time.

They had lost part of Alba, regained it, yet were now struggling to keep a foothold there. In the wake of tidal inundations and severe alterations in the ocean currents, the Eika territories were splintering into four petty kingdoms. Ships sailing along the coast had mysteriously vanished, only to drift months later into port with all hands lost. Part of Varingia had been swallowed by Salia, Wayland had for a few years claimed to be an independent queendom with the support of Mathilda of Aosta, while the Villams now styled themselves as dukes, equal to Saony, Fesse, and Avaria. The North Mark had experienced a ten-year drought, followed by floods. In the east, the Polenie had been overrun by a Salavii uprising. All of southern Aosta still lay in ruins, scarred by continual volcanic eruptions, and Karrone had been terribly hard hit in the great earthquake that had driven so many people north as refugees. Meanwhile, her own cousins among the Ashioi pushed their borders northward at a slow but steady pace, causing the Arethousans to send to Wendar increasingly desperate pleas for alliances and treaties of mutual aid.

And so on, and so forth, the unending turn of the wheel.

Still, it could have been worse. Conrad's daughter had changed her mind and cut all ties to Mathilda, who had only a scrap of land near Novomo left to call her queendom. The Ashioi had sent an envoy asking for a marriage alliance. Several trading guilds had established themselves along the Eika shores, and it seemed the Eika liked to trade as much as they liked to fight. Fearsome merfolk swam into ports asking after the health of brothers and sisters and sons and daughters and beloved partners they could certainly never have met or been in any way related to, especially considering that they seemed to have the memories of men who had been lost at sea, and yet in some places strange but lasting bonds were formed between fishermen and merchants and these savage water folk, each helping the others. A Quman muster pushing for an invasion into the marchlands had abruptly dissolved when a pair of griffins had carried away the most belligerent of the war leaders. The civil war in Salia—raging for over three decades—had at last died away, no doubt of exhaustion, and the constant debilitating flow of refugees into Varre had eased in recent years. Just last year, a peculiar party of envoys had arrived at Autun from a stunted, deformed folk calling themselves the Ancient Ones and claiming to be miners and scholars of natural history. Young Henry had come south from Rikin Fjord, and she thought he would be a steadying influence on the volatile Constance.

So, there was also a measure of peace to be found. They had survived the worst, surely. The cataclysm had hammered them forty years ago, and in many ways they were still recovering.

Her Dragon guard spread out along the spokes of the wheel, loitering, enjoying the sun, although the day was cold enough to turn hands white. Her Quman levy, refreshed every five years according to the pledge made by Gyasi forty years ago; her Eika nephews, as she called them, who were really grandsons and great grandsons out of Rikin Fjord; a few pale Albans; and one dark-haired Salavii man who had turned up one day holding a golden phoenix feather in his left hand and who had never left. Once, she had boasted a dozen bold Ashioi mask warriors in their number, but they had been recalled to their own country. Now, the remainder was strong Wendish and Varren soldiers, all wearing the sigil of the black dragon, her father's mark.

The Quman in particular could never get enough of the stern-featured little statues of saints and angels that populated the garden, some freestanding and others half hidden in niches carved into the walls. What piqued their interest she had never understood, but they were at it again. They wandered in pairs to examine each sculpture, often kneeling beside one to point out particularities in its features. Four of them had gathered on the other side of the fountain to stare. She moved, curious to know what they were fascinated by, and found that after all another soul had come to seek peace in the garden. He was seated by himself on a bench, in the sun, with a book and several loose pages of vellum resting on his lap.

Everyone knew the old cleric was her favorite, and that he had been so for years. Despite his age, he retained his remarkable beauty, but what was most curious about him was his lack of vanity considering his exalted station on the queen's progress. Some unkind gossips whispered that in truth he had no great intelligence and had gained his prominent position simply by virtue of his appearance, and wasn't even canny enough to understand the nature of his power, yet even these skeptics had to admit that he wrote with an elegant hand, none better even in the schola of the skopos, where he had come from. He copied charters and diplomas and letters, and in this way had served her for decades until in the end he became one of the last of those who really remembered the year of the cataclysm. Many had been children at that time, as she had been, but a child's memories are malleable and elusive.

She walked over and sat beside him on the bench. "What are you reading, Brother Baldwin?"

He had been studying a dormant rosebush with what was, in truth, a slightly vacant expression, but he smiled amiably and stroked the spine of the book.

"Just looking over what I wrote yesterday, Your Majesty." He indicated the unbound vellum.

After a moment, she said, patiently, "And what was that?"

"What I promised to the Holy Mother—may she rest in peace. To continue the *History of the Deeds of the Great Princes*, and pass on my charge when it comes my time to rise beyond this world and ascend to the Chamber of Light. I fell behind because of the deal of business we got into this last summer."

"Read to me."

He picked up one of the sheets, studied its lovely curling script, frowned, and replaced it with another page. "I'll start here," he said.

"No," she said, curious now, and anyway she had always been goaded by a bit of a nasty temper. "Read that one you were first looking at."

He sighed as he looked at her with those remarkable blue eyes.

"Go on!" She had ruled for many years and was no longer accustomed to being denied. Maybe she had never been so accustomed. Everyone knew she had been a brat as a child.

He hesitated, touched a finger to the first word, and began to read, more haltingly than one might expect given the fluid beauty of his script.

" 'At that time reavers were laying waste to the Osna coast. Although he was full seventy years of age, he took his sword and led his milites to drive off the invaders. No weapon touched him, but the exertion brought him low. He was carried to Lavas Holding, and there after resting a while he rose again, gave alms to the poor, and sat down joyfully to table. Afterward, he became feverish and tired. He bent his head forward as if he were already dead, but he was able to ask for the holy sacrament, the kiss of the phoenix. After this, his breath left his body, and with great tranquillity he released his spirit to ascend to the Chamber of Light. They carried him from that place and laid him in the church beside the bier of Lavastine the Younger. Even though it was then late, they announced his death to all the people.'

"Much praise was spoken of his great deeds, how he had cast the Eika out of Gent, scattered the Quman horde at Osterburg, led the ascent out of Aosta after the cataclysm, and erected churches and established monasteries and convents in the name of the Holy Mother and her Son.

"In the night, with the count still at her vigil within, the church burned down, leaving only the stone bier of the younger Lavastine untouched among the ruins. Those who witnessed the conflagration reported that a phoenix rose out of the flames, but others said it was a dragon, and some said an angel.

"The county passed to Lavrentia the Younger, daughter of Count Liathano and Prince Sanglant. Lavrentia was married to Druthmar, son of Waltharia Villam."

The fountain spilled its angels' tears. Geese flew honking overhead, migrating south for the winter. The Dragons paced, out of boredom or to keep the chill out of their limbs, and she supposed she ought to feel the cold more deeply, but she did not. These days, she was often flushed with warmth.

"There's yet more on the page," she said, prodded by a need to twist the knife. "Read that."

He was the calm beyond the storm. No matter how sharp her tongue, he remained unmoved. Or possibly he just missed all those jabs. He smiled sweetly, the very image of the ornament of wisdom, and continued more easily.

"There is nothing hidden that shall not be revealed, nothing secret that shall not be made known.

"In the year 778, after two years of losing most of their crops and brought close to starvation, the people of Osterburg were visited by a bountiful harvest.

"Refugees fleeing the fighting east of Machteburg, where the Quman vanguard had attacked, arrived safely across the river, losing not one soul to battle or flood. They were attended through the wilderness and across the ford by a pair of black hounds

"A pack of wolves terrorized the king's road in the Bretwald but were driven off by a lone traveler and his dogs.

"The angel of plague rode into the valley of the Alse

River. She carried a sword, and where she knocked upon a door with so many raps, then so many people inside would fall ill and die. But where the road took its turning into the next valley, she was met upon the way by a wanderer, who had blocked the road. Therefore the other valleys were spared, and the angel passed beyond the veil and troubled them no more that season. It is said of the traveler that he walked into the valley of the Alse River to bring aid to the afflicted, and was not seen again."

"What are these you write of?" she asked.

"This is a change wrought by the hand of the Highest," he read. "I keep a record, as I was commanded to do by Biscop Constance, of blessed memory."

He leaned forward so suddenly that she, trained for battle, shifted her feet under her for the leap, and every Dragon within sight changed stance and came to the alert, the movement rippling out through the ranks. She caught herself as he probed among the thorns and the last, withered leaves of the rosebush.

"Look, here." A pale bud pushed up out of last year's growth.

She lifted a hand, and the Dragons relaxed.

"Here's another," he said, tracing it with a scribe's precise and practiced touch. "And here. Can roses bloom in winter?"

She thought of Fulk, and bowed her head.

Looked on the parchment. She could read, of course. Her mother had insisted that she learn. There was more written on the page in his clear and lovely script.

There was always more. One life may end but another begins.

The branches of the rosebush trembled in the wind. A horn rang, far off, that might be a greeting or a fare-thee-well. Or a pack of young riders out on autumn's hunt, eager to try their skills, heedless of the ebb and flow around them.

A child's memory is malleable and elusive, and she had only seen him that one time, really, in the dark church at Hersford when her father had woken out of the Abyss into which he had fallen, although most people call it death.

We are all changed by the tempest, each in our own way.

Impulse must not govern action.

Be merciful.

Then you have done as he would have done. Go in peace.

Some say he died in that distant valley and lies in an unmarked grave. Some say he was translated up to the Chamber of Light by the hand of God our Mother, because of his great holiness. Some say he took a vow of silence and retired to an isolated monastery to pray and to teach by his example of humility and good works. But there remains a story— among the common folk from whom he sprang—that he walks abroad still. That he walks unseen to the sight of mortal women and men, except to those in hunger, those who suffer, those in need. That as he walks among the common people he touches a few, and at his touch the rose of compassion blooms in their hearts.

The Golden Key

Melanie Rawn
Jennifer Roberson
Kate Elliott

In the duchy of Tira Verte fine art is prized above
all things. But not even the Grand Duke knows
just how powerful the art of the Grijalva family is.
For thanks to a genetic fluke certain males of their
bloodline are born with a frightening talent: the
ability to use their paintings to cast magical spells
which alter things in the real world. Their secret
magic formula, known as the Golden Key, per-
mits Gifted sons to vastly improve the fortunes of
their family. Still, the Grijalvas are fairly circum-
spect until two talents come into their powers:
Sario, a boy who will learn to use his Gift to make
himself virtually immortal; and Saavedra, a girl
who may be the first woman ever to have the Gift.
Sario's personal ambitions and thwarted love for
his cousin will lead to a generations-spanning
plot to seize control of the duchy.

0-88677-899-9

To Order Call: 1-800-788-6262